PENGUIN BOOKS

WOLF TOTEM

'A serious, thoughtful, intense and melancholy read filled with culture clashes, animal hunting and bloodshed'
Sunday Herald

'Powerful, striking, harsh and beautiful' *Times Literary Supplement*

'A rich, densely written novel that will make you fear to read *Little Red Riding Hood* to small children ever again'
Independent on Sunday

'A multi-layered epic: part mystical tale; part history lesson; part ecological plea; but above all a celebration of freedom'
Metro

'Compelling, moving . . . a lament for the end of peasant life'
Spectator

'A stirring tale of a boy's struggle for individuality . . . offers a piercing insight into how China views itself' *Sunday Telegraph*

'A fascinating tale of Mongolian nomads'
Harper's Bazaar

'A remarkable documentary record of a vanished civilization'
Esquire

'A moving novel of nomads and settlers and their relation with wolves on the Mongolian steppes' *Independent*

ABOUT THE AUTHOR

Jiang Rong was born in Jiangsu in 1946. His father's job saw the family move to Beijing in 1957, and Jiang entered the Central Academy of Fine Art in 1966.

His education cut short by events in China, the twenty-one-year-old Jiang volunteered to work in Inner Mongolia's East Ujimqin Banner in 1967, where he lived and laboured with the native nomads until the age of thirty-three. He took with him two cases filled with Chinese translations of Western literary classics, and spent eleven years immersed in personal studies of Mongolian history, culture and tradition. In particular, he developed a fascination for the mythologies surrounding the wolves of the grasslands, spending much of his leisure time learning the stories and raising an orphaned wolf cub.

In 1978 he returned to Beijing, continuing his education at the Chinese Academy of Social Sciences one year later. Jiang worked as an academic until his retirement in 2006.

Wolf Totem is a fictional account of life in the 1970s that draws on Jiang's personal experience of the grasslands of China's border region.

Wolf Totem

A Novel

Jiang Rong

Translated by Howard Goldblatt

PENGUIN BOOKS

PENGUIN BOOKS

Published by the Penguin Group
Penguin Books Ltd, 80 Strand, London WC2R 0RL, England
Penguin Group (USA) Inc., 375 Hudson Street, New York, New York 10014, USA
Penguin Group (Canada), 90 Eglinton Avenue East, Suite 700, Toronto, Ontario, Canada M4P 2Y3
(a division of Pearson Penguin Canada Inc.)
Penguin Ireland, 25 St Stephen's Green, Dublin 2, Ireland (a division of Penguin Books Ltd)
Penguin Group (Australia), 250 Camberwell Road, Camberwell, Victoria 3124, Australia
(a division of Pearson Australia Group Pty Ltd)
Penguin Books India Pvt Ltd, 11 Community Centre, Panchsheel Park, New Delhi – 110 017, India
Penguin Group (NZ), 67 Apollo Drive, Rosedale, North Shore 0632, New Zealand
(a division of Pearson New Zealand Ltd)
Penguin Books (South Africa) (Pty) Ltd, 24 Sturdee Avenue, Rosebank, Johannesburg 2196, South Africa

Penguin Books Ltd, Registered Offices: 80 Strand, London WC2R 0RL, England

www.penguin.com

First published in Great Britain by Hamish Hamilton 2008
Published in Penguin Books 2009
1

Originally published in Chinese as *Lang Tuteng*
by Changjiang Literature and Arts Publishing House, 2004

ISBN: 978-0-141-04065-3

www.greenpenguin.co.uk

Penguin Books is committed to a sustainable future for our business, our readers and our planet. The book in your hands is made from paper certified by the Forest Stewardship Council.

Translator's Note

In 1969, a young Chinese intellectual from Beijing answered Chairman Mao's call for city dwellers to go "up to the mountains and down to the countryside," joining as many as a hundred like-minded youngsters in traveling to one of China's most remote, most "primitive" spots: north-central Inner Mongolia. While most of the fifteen to twenty million young urbanites who were sent out of the cities to be "rusticated" dreamed constantly of going home and, insofar as possible, shunned close attachments to their rural hosts, Jiang Rong did in fact learn from and befriend the herdsmen with whom he lived and worked. In all, he spent more than a decade as a shepherd on the sparsely populated Olonbulag, a fictional setting in the Ujimchin Banner, a hardscrabble existence in a place where life is unimaginably hard on all its inhabitants, man and beast.

Despite its remote location and hostile environment, Inner Mongolia was not spared the excesses of the disastrous Cultural Revolution (1966–1976), when the nation was on war footing, arrayed against domestic enemies of the state and international enemies of the nation, real and imagined. The "four olds" (old thought, old culture, old customs, and old practices) were under attack, targeting, in particular, ideologically "backward" members of superstitious and conservative rural societies.

When they weren't working to bring down important political, military, and cultural figures, Red Guard factions spent their time tormenting ordinary citizens. Military organizational schemes replaced traditional tribal order, military terminology was in vogue, and military commanders, competent or not, were placed in charge of production activities. In Mongolia, it was an onerous time for people whose lives were centered on respecting the ways and superstitions of their ancestors. They took great pride in the military conquests of those ancestors—the great Mongol hordes of the twelfth and thirteenth centuries—and were unmoved by the ideologies of Mao and his followers, whose Han ancestors had been no match for the mounted warriors of Genghis Khan. The key to the success of the khans, according to Mongol legend, as the author discovered during his years on the grassland, was the wolf, the only significant land-bound predator that was able to thrive for thousands of years.

Wolves have captured the imagination of peoples everywhere, but seldom have they been venerated to the extent that they are by nomads of the Mongolian grassland. Their paradoxical role in the people's lives—as predator and prey, as defilers of herds (the "little lives") and protectors of the grassland's ecology (the "big" life), and as animals to be feared and at the same time revered—forms both the actual and the metaphorical core of this magnificent novel. Wolves, courageous and ferocious, loyal to the pack, and respectful of their environment, are posited as an antidote for what ails Chinese society—a society the quasi-autobiographical protagonist compares to the sheep he tends and which he must protect against the clever, almost supernaturally shrewd wolves he so admires. The symbiotic relationship between the herdsmen and the wolves, participants in a delicate ecological balancing act of keeping at bay the Gobi to the west and the Han Chinese to the south, is threatened by encroachments by both. *Wolf Totem,* which sold in the millions in China—in both authorized and pirated editions—ushered in heated debates on the Chinese "character." It is a work that compellingly blends the passion of a novelist who lived the story he tells and the intelligent ethnological observations of a sympathetic outsider.

In 1979, when Chinese society was trying to rid itself of the effects of the Cultural Revolution, Jiang Rong was admitted into the Chinese Academy of Social Sciences as a graduate student. In 1988, Jiang Rong, who had become a political scientist attached to Beijing University, began writing this novel, obsessed with a story that had stayed with him for nearly twenty years; six years later it was finished and instantly became a runaway bestseller.

In the translation of *Wolf Totem,* I have been aided by several people. First and foremost, the author and his wife graciously and enthusiastically responded to all my inquiries concerning both textual and cultural matters. Mongolian spellings were supplied by Chigchin, a graduate student in English at the Inner Mongolia University. At Penguin, both the novel and the translator were aided by Jo Lusby in Beijing and Liza Darnton in New York, and, most significantly, by the skillful and imaginative editing of Beena Kamlani. Sandy Dijkstra was instrumental in getting the project started. Finally, Sylvia Lin read and commented on the entire translation, as she always does. To all, my heartfelt thanks.

Union of Soviet Socialist Republics

People's Republic

Nepal

Bhutan

India

Burma

Laos

Thailand

0 Miles 250 500

0 Kilometers 500

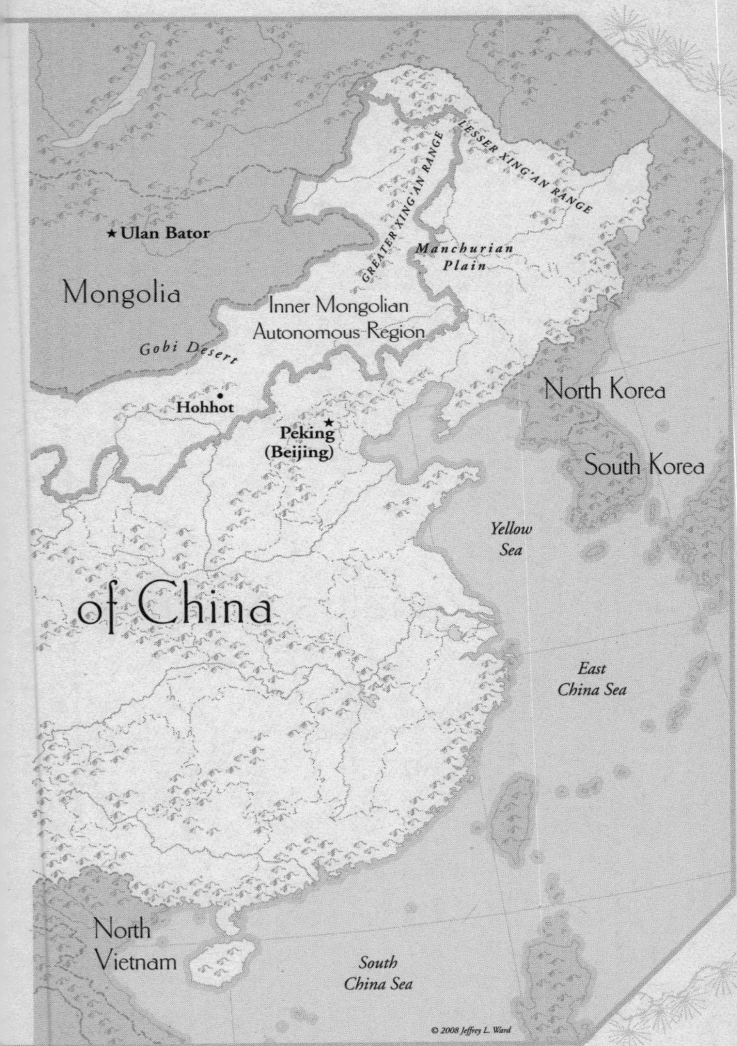

Ulan Bator
Mongolia
GREATER XING'AN RANGE
LESSER XING'AN RANGE
Manchurian Plain
Inner Mongolian Autonomous Region
Gobi Desert
Hohhot
Peking (Beijing)
North Korea
South Korea
Yellow Sea
of China
East China Sea
North Vietnam
South China Sea
© 2008 Jeffrey L. Ward

Wolf Totem

I

As Chen Zhen looked through the telescope from his hiding place in the snow cave, he saw the steely gaze of a Mongolian grassland wolf. The fine hairs on his body rose up like porcupine quills, virtually pulling his shirt away from his skin. Old Man Bilgee was there beside him. This time Chen did not feel as if his soul had been driven out of his body, but sweat oozed from his pores. He had been on the grassland two years but still had not lost his fear of Mongolian wolves, especially in packs. Now he was face to face with a large pack deep in the mountains, far from camp, his misty breath quivering in the air. Neither he nor Bilgee was armed—no rifles, no knives, no lasso poles, not even something as simple as a pair of metal stirrups. All they had were two herding clubs, and if the wolves picked up their scent, their sky burial would come early.

Chen exhaled nervously as he turned to look at the old man, who was watching the wolf encirclement through the other telescope. "You're going to need more courage than that," Bilgee said softly. "You're like a sheep. A fear of wolves is in your Chinese bones. That's the only explanation for why you people have never won a fight out here." Getting no response, he leaned over and whispered, "Get a grip on yourself. If they spot any movement from us, we'll be in real trouble." Chen nodded and scooped up a handful of snow, which he squeezed into a ball of ice.

The herd of Mongolian gazelles was grazing on a nearby slope, unaware of the wolf pack, which was tightening the noose, drawing closer to the men's snow cave. Not daring to move, Chen felt frozen in place, like an ice sculpture. This was Chen's second encounter with a wolf pack since coming to the grassland. A palpitating fear from his first encounter coursed through his veins.

Two years earlier, in late November, he had arrived in the border-region pasture as a production team member from Beijing; snow covered the land as far as the eye could see. The Olonbulag is located southwest of the Great Xing'an mountain range, directly north of Beijing; it shares a border with Outer Mongolia. Historically, it was the southern passage between Manchuria and the Mongolian steppes, and, as such, the site of battles between a host of peoples and nomadic tribes, as well as a territory in which the potential struggles for dominance by nomads and farmers was ever present.

Yurts had not yet been assigned to the Beijing students, the so-called educated youth, so Chen had been sent to live with Old Man Bilgee and his family, and given duties as a shepherd. One day slightly more than a month after his arrival, he and the old man were sent to headquarters, some eighty *li,* to fetch study materials and purchase daily necessities. Just before they were to head back, the old man was summoned to a meeting of the revolutionary committee. Since headquarters had said the study materials had to be delivered without delay, Chen was told to return alone.

As he was about to leave, the old man swapped horses with him, lending him his big, dark mount, a fast horse that knew the way. Bilgee warned Chen not to take a shortcut, but to follow the wagon road back; since there were yurts every twenty or thirty *li,* he ought to be able to make the trip without incident.

As soon as he was in the saddle and on his way, Chen sensed the power of his Mongol horse and felt the urge to gallop at full speed. When they reached a ridge from which he could see the peak of Chaganuul Mountain, where the brigade was quartered, he forgot the old man's warning and left the road—which curved around the mountain, adding twenty *li* to the trip—to take a shortcut that led straight to camp.

The temperature began to fall, and when he was about halfway home, the sun shivered from the deepening cold before retreating to the horizon and slipping from view. Frigid air from the snowy ground rose up, turning Chen's leather duster hard and brittle. The hide of his mount was covered with a layer of sweat-frost. Their pace slowed as the snow deepened and little hillocks rose in their path. They were deep in the wilds, far from all signs of habitation. The horse trotted on, straight and smooth, so Chen relaxed the pressure on the bit to let the horse determine the pace and direction, as well as how hard it wanted to work. For no obvious reason, Chen suddenly tensed; he shuddered, becoming fearful that the horse might lose its way, fearful that the weather would turn ugly, fearful of being caught in a snowstorm, and fearful of freezing to death on the glacial grassland. The only thing he forgot to fear was the wolves.

Just before they reached a ravine, the horse stopped, pointing toward a spot down the ravine. It tossed its head and snorted, its pace no longer steady. Chen Zhen, who had never before ridden alone deep into the snowy grassland, had no inkling of the danger ahead. But the agitated horse, its nostrils flaring, its eyes wide, turned to head away from what lay in front of them. Its intuition was lost on Chen, who pulled the reins taut to turn the animal's head and keep it moving forward at a trot. Its gait grew increasingly jerky, an erratic combination of walking, trotting, and jolting, as if the animal might bolt at any moment. Chen pulled back hard on the reins.

As if frustrated that its warning signals were not being heeded, the horse turned and nipped at its rider's felt boot, and at that moment Chen recognized the danger facing them by the fear in the horse's eyes. But it was too late, for the horse had carried him into the flared opening of a gloomy ravine on trembling legs.

Chen turned to look down the ravine and was so terrified he nearly fell off the horse. There on a snow-covered slope not less than fifty yards away was a pack of golden-hued, murderous-looking Mongolian wolves, all watching him straight on or out of the corners of their eyes, their gazes boring into him like needles. The closest wolves were the biggest, easily the size of leopards and at least twice the size of the wolves he'd seen in the Beijing Zoo, half again as tall and as long, nose to tail. All dozen or so of the larger wolves had been sitting on the snowy ground, but they immediately stood up, their tails stretched out straight, like swords about to be unsheathed, or arrows on a taut bowstring. They were poised to pounce. The alpha male, surrounded by the others, was a gray wolf whose nearly white neck, chest, and abdomen shone like white gold. The pack consisted of thirty or forty animals.

Afterward, when Chen and Bilgee were rehashing the circumstances of the encounter, the old man wiped his sweaty brow with his finger and said, "They must have been holding a council. The alpha male was likely passing out assignments for an attack on a herd of horses on the other side of the hill. You'd have realized your luck had you known that when their coats shine, they aren't hungry."

In fact, Chen's mind was wiped clean the moment he spotted them, and the last thing he recalled was a muted but terrifying sound rising up to the top of his head, not unlike the thin whistle you get by blowing on the edge of a coin. It must have been the *ping* his soul made as it tore through his crown on its way out. He felt that his life had stopped for a minute or more.

Long afterward, whenever he recalled his encounter with the wolf pack, he silently thanked Papa Bilgee and his dark horse. The only reason he hadn't fallen off was that the animal had lived its entire life in wolf territory, a battle-tested horse perfectly suited to the hunt. At the critical moment, as their lives hung in the balance, the horse grew extraordinarily calm. Acting as if it didn't even see the pack or that it had any intention of interrupting their council, it continued on at a leisurely, just-passing-through pace. With all the courage it possessed, and in full control of its hooves, it neither struggled to keep moving nor broke into a panicky gallop, but carried its rider at a steady pace that allowed Chen to sit up straight.

Maybe it was the horse's extraordinary courage that summoned back Chen's departed soul, but when that spirit, which had hovered in the frigid air for a moment, returned to his body, he felt reborn and was extraordinarily tranquil.

He forced himself to sit firmly in the saddle. Taking his cue from the horse, he pretended not to have seen the pack, though nervously keeping them in sight. He knew all about the speed of wolves on the Mongolian grassland. It would take but seconds to close the gap. And he knew how important it was not to show fear. That was the only way to avoid an attack by these grassland killers.

He sensed that the alpha male was gazing at the hill behind them; all the other members of the pack turned their pointed ears in the same direction, like radar locking on to a target. They silently awaited orders as the unarmed man and his horse pranced boldly past them; the alpha male and his followers were not sure what to make of this.

The sunset slowly faded away as man and horse drew ever nearer. The next couple of dozen steps comprised the longest journey of Chen Zhen's life. A few steps into that journey, he sensed that one of the wolves had run up to the snow-covered slope behind him, and he knew intuitively that it was a scout sent by the alpha male to see if other troops lay in wait. Chen felt his soul straining to leave again.

The horse's gait faltered slightly; Chen's legs and the horse's flanks were trembling. The horse turned its ears to the rear, nervously monitoring the scout wolf's movements. Chen imagined himself passing through an enormous wolf's maw, with rows of razor-sharp teeth above and below; once he was in the middle, the mouth would snap shut. The horse began to gather its strength in its rear legs, preparing for a mortal engagement. But the burden on its back put it at a terrible disadvantage.

Suddenly, Chen Zhen, like the shepherd he was supposed to be, appealed to Tengger, Mongol heaven, in a moment of peril: Wise and powerful heaven, Tengger, reach out and give me your hand. Next he summoned Papa Bilgee under his breath. In the Mongol language,

Bilgee means "Wise One." If only the old man would find a way to transmit his knowledge of the grassland directly into his brain. No echoes anywhere disturbed the stillness of the Olonbulag. Gripped by despair, Chen raised his eyes, wanting the last thing he saw to be the ice blue beauty of the heavens.

Then something Papa had said dropped from the sky and struck his eardrum like a thunderclap: Wolves are afraid of rifles, lasso poles, and anything made of metal. He had no rifle and no lasso pole, but did he have anything made of metal? His foot felt warm. Yes! There under his feet were two large metal stirrups. His legs twitched excitedly.

Papa Bilgee had lent him his horse, but the saddle was Chen's. No wonder the old man had picked out the largest stirrups he could find for him at the beginning; it was as if he knew that someday they would come to Chen's rescue. Back then, when he was learning to ride, the old man had said that not only did small stirrups make staying in the saddle difficult, but if the horse bucked you off, your foot could get caught and you could be dragged along, which could lead to serious injury or death. These stirrups, with their large openings and rounded bottoms, were twice the size of the more common small-mouthed, flat-bottomed ones, and double the weight.

The pack was waiting for the scout's report; horse and rider were now directly opposite them. Chen quickly removed his feet from the stirrups, reached down, and pulled them up by their leather straps. Holding one in each hand, and calling upon all his strength, he spun the horse around, roared in the direction of the wolf pack, raised the heavy stirrups chest-high, and banged them together.

Clang clang...

A crisp, ear-splitting clang, like a hammer on an anvil, tore through the silent air of the grassland and straight into the ears and the seats of courage of every wolf in the pack, like a sword. Nonnatural metallic noises frighten wolves more than any thunderstorm; they produce a sound that has a greater and more devastating impact on them than the snap of a hunter's trap.

The wolves trembled when the first clangs from Chen's stirrups resonated in the air. The next burst sent them turning away; led by the alpha wolf, they fled into the mountains like a yellow storm, their ears pinned against their heads and their necks pulled into their shoulders. Even the scout abandoned its mission and followed the other members of the pack in flight.

Chen Zhen could hardly believe his eyes as he watched the wolves frightened off by a pair of metal stirrups. As his courage made its belated return, he banged the stirrups together wildly, then windmilled his arms like a shepherd and shouted, "Hurry! Hurry! There are wolves everywhere!"

For all he knew, the wolves understood Mongol and knew the meaning of human gestures; perhaps they'd been frightened into dispersal by what they'd assumed was a trap laid by hunters.

But they dispersed in orderly fashion, maintaining the ancient organizational unity and group formation characteristic of grassland wolves: The most ferocious members serve as a vanguard, with the alpha male out in front, the pack's larger wolves behind it. There is never any of the confusion commonly seen among fleeing birds and other wild animals. Chen was overwhelmed by the sight.

In a moment, the pack had vanished without a trace,

and all that remained in the ravine were a white mist and swirling flakes of snow.

By then night had fallen. Before Chen could step fully into the stirrups again, his horse took off like a shot, racing toward the nearest camp. Frigid air seeped into Chen's collar and sleeves; the cold sweat on his body had turned to ice.

Having escaped from the wolf's maw, he became an immediate convert to the devotion paid to Tengger, just like his Mongol hosts. He also developed a complex attitude of fear, reverence, and infatuation toward the Mongolian wolf. It had touched his soul. How could it possess such a powerful attraction?

Chen did not catch sight of another wolf pack over the next two years. During the day he tended his sheep, occasionally spotting a lone wolf, maybe two, off in the distance. Even when he was far from camp, he never saw more than four or five at one time. Often, however, he came across the remains of sheep or cattle or horses that had been killed by wolves, individually or in packs. There might be one or two dead sheep, two or three cows, and maybe three or four horses; but sometimes carcasses would be strewn over a wide area. When he was out making calls on people, he regularly saw wolf pelts hanging on tall poles, like flags waving in the wind.

Now Bilgee lay flat in the snow cave, not moving a muscle, his eyes glued to the gazelles grazing on the slope and the wolf pack that was inching nearer. "Stay calm," he whispered to Chen. "The first thing you need to learn as a hunter is patience."

Having Bilgee beside him was comforting. Chen

rubbed his eyes to clear away the mist and blinked calmly at Bilgee, then raised his telescope again to watch the gazelles and the wolves. The pack still had not given itself away.

Since his earlier encounter with the wolves, he had come to understand that the inhabitants of the grassland, the nomads, were never far from being surrounded by wolves. Nearly every night he spotted ghostly wolf outlines, especially during the frigid winter; two or three, perhaps five or six, and as many as a dozen pairs of glittering green lights moving around the perimeter of the grazing land, as far as a hundred *li* or more distant. One night he and Bilgee's daughter-in-law Gasmai, aided by flashlights, counted twenty-five of them.

Like guerrilla fighters, nomads strive for simplicity. During the winter, sheep pens are semicircles formed by wagons and mobile fencing, with large felt rugs that serve as a windbreak but cannot keep out the wolves. The wide southern openings are guarded by packs of dogs and women on watch shifts. From time to time, wolves break into the pens and fight the dogs. Bodies often thud into yurt walls, waking the people sleeping on the other side; twice that had happened to Chen Zhen, and all that had kept a wolf from landing in bed beside him was that wall. Frequently nomads are separated from wolves by no more than a couple of felt rugs.

At night, when the wolves came out to hunt, Chen would sleep lightly. He had told Gasmai to call him if a wolf ever broke into the pen when she was on guard duty, assuring her that he would help drive the animal away, fight it head-on if necessary. Bilgee would stroke his goatee, smile, and say he'd never seen a Chinese so fixated on wolves. He seemed pleased with the unusual degree of interest displayed by the student from Beijing.

Late one snowy night during his first winter, Chen, flashlight in hand, witnessed at close quarters a battle between a wolf, a dog, and a woman.

"Chenchen! Chenchen!"

Chen was awakened by Gasmai's frantic cries and the wild barking of dogs. After pulling on his felt boots and buttoning up his Mongol robe, his deel, he ran out of the yurt on shaky legs, flashlight and herding club in hand. The beam of light sliced through the snow to reveal Gasmai holding on to the tail of a wolf, trying to pull it away from the densely packed sheep. The wolf tried desperately to turn its fangs on her. Meanwhile, the stupid, fat sheep, petrified by the wolf and nearly frozen by the wind, huddled together and kept backing up against the windbreak, packed so tightly the snowflakes between their bodies turned to steam. The front half of the wolf was immobilized; it could only paw at the ground and snap at the sheep in front of it, all the while engaged in a tug-of-war with Gasmai. Chen staggered over to help but didn't know what to do. Gasmai's two dogs were hemmed in by the huddled sheep. Unable to get to the big wolf, they were reduced to wild, impotent barking. At the same time, Bilgee's five or six hunting dogs, together with their neighbors' dogs, were fighting other wolves east of the pen. The barks, the howls, and the agonizing cries of dogs shook heaven and earth. Chen wanted to help Gasmai, but his legs were so rubbery he could barely move. His desire to touch a living wolf had vanished, replaced by paralyzing fear.

Gasmai cried out anxiously, "Stay where you are! Don't come near us! The wolf will bite you. Get the sheep to move! Let the dogs in!"

Gasmai was tugging so hard on the wolf's tail she was nearly falling backward, her forehead bathed in sweat. Her grip on the tail caused the wolf so much pain that it had to suck cold air through its bloody mouth. Desperate to turn and claw its tormentor and seeing it was futile to press forward, the wolf abruptly backed up, spun around, and came at Gasmai, fangs bared. With a loud ripping noise, the lower half of her fur deel was torn off. A panther-like glare flashed in her Mongol eyes, and she refused to let go of the tail. She jumped backward, straightening the animal out once more, and began dragging it over to the dogs.

Thrown into a panic, Chen raised his flashlight and shone it on Gasmai and the wolf to help her see better and avoid getting bitten; then he brought his herding club down on the head of the sheep next to him. That threw the flock into chaos. Frightened of the wolf in the dark, they fought to huddle against the light shining in their midst; Chen had failed to get them moving. Even worse, he saw that Gasmai was losing the tug-of-war with the wolf, which was dragging her forward.

"Mother! Mother!" The fearful screams of a child tore through the air.

Gasmai's nine-year-old son, Bayar, burst out of the yurt. The moment he saw what was happening, there was a change in his screams. He ran straight to his mother and, as if mounting a pommel horse, flew over the sheep and landed next to her, where he grabbed hold of the wolf's tail.

"Grab its leg!" she shouted.

Bayar let go of the tail and grabbed one of the hind legs, pulling it backward and slowing the animal's forward progress until the two of them managed to stop it altogether. Mother and son staunchly held their ground, making sure the large wolf in their grasp was unable to drive any sheep out through the felt-topped windbreak.

By then Bilgee had reached the flock, pushing the sheep out of the way as he called to his dog: "Bar! Bar!" In Mongol *bar* means "tiger"; Bilgee's was the biggest, most ferocious wolfhound in the camp. It was not as long from nose to tail as one of the large wolves, but it was taller and broader in the chest, thanks to its partial Tibetan lineage. At the first call of its name, it withdrew from the battle outside and rushed to its master's side, where it stopped, its mouth reeking of wolf blood. Bilgee took the flashlight from Chen Zhen and turned its light onto the wolf, which was still imbedded in the flock of sheep. Bar bounded over the backs of the sheep, stepping on heads along the way, rolling and scrambling as it charged the wolf.

"Drive the sheep toward the wolf," Bilgee shouted. "We'll pen it in so it can't get away!" He took Chen Zhen's hand, and the two of them herded the sheep toward the wolf and Gasmai.

Finally, Bar, his breath fouled, blood spurting from his nose, was standing beside Gasmai, but the wolf was still wedged in tightly among the sheep. Mongolian hunting dogs are trained not to bite wolves on the back or other spots on the torso, so as to preserve the pelt. Bar was going crazy trying to find a spot to sink his teeth into. Seeing Bar there beside her, Gasmai turned sideways, lifted one leg, and grabbed the wolf's tail with both hands, laying it across her own leg. Then with a shout, she cracked the tail over her knee. With an agonizing howl, the wolf loosened its claws in the dirt, allowing mother and son to jerk it free of the sheep. The big animal, its body convulsing with pain, turned to look at its wounded tail, which gave Bar an opening to go for its throat. Letting the wolf claw at will, Bar pressed down with his front legs on the animal's head and chest, and as he bit down, two streams of blood spurted from the wolf's carotid arteries. It struggled madly for a minute or two before going limp, its long, bloody tongue slipping out through its teeth. Gasmai wiped the wolf's blood from her face and panted. To Chen Zhen, her face, red from the bitter cold, looked as if rouge made of wolf's blood had been smeared over it. She struck him as the picture of prehistoric woman—brave, strong, and beautiful.

The rank smell of blood rose into the air from the dead wolf, and the growls from dogs off to the east ceased abruptly as the other wolves fled, vanishing in the dark of night. Moments later, from the marshland in the northwest came the mournful bays of wolves venting their grief over the loss of one of their own.

"I'm worse than useless," Chen said with a sigh, deeply ashamed. "Gutless as the sheep. A dog is worth more than me, not to mention a woman. Even a nine-year-old boy showed me up."

With a smile, Gasmai shook her head. "No," she said. "If you hadn't come out to help, the wolves would have gotten our sheep."

Bilgee smiled too. "This is the first time I've seen a Chinese student help get sheep moving and light the area up with his flashlight."

Chen Zhen bent over and felt the still-warm body of the dead wolf. He hated himself for not having the courage to help Gasmai pull on the animal's tail while it was alive, and for passing up a once-in-a-lifetime opportunity for a Chinese student to know what it's like to fight a wolf with his bare hands. The wolf was as intimidating dead as it had been alive. Chen rubbed Bar's big head, then found the courage to squat down and, with his thumb and first finger, measure the dead wolf, from its nose to the tip of its tail. It was longer than he was tall. He sucked in a breath of frigid air.

Old Man Bilgee checked out the flock of sheep with the flashlight. The thick tails of three or four of them had been bitten off and eaten by the wolf, leaving a bloody mess that had already frozen. "Trading a few sheep tails for a wolf this big counts as a good deal," Bilgee said as he and Chen dragged the carcass into the yurt to keep greedy neighboring dogs from venting their anger and ruining the hide.

The wolf's paws were much bigger than a dog's; measuring one against his palm, Chen saw that they were about the same size. No wonder wolves run so effortlessly through snow and across rocky hills.

"Tomorrow," Bilgee said, "I'll teach you how to skin a wolf."

Gasmai carried a big pot of meat outside to reward Bar and the other dogs. As Chen Zhen followed her out, he rubbed Bar's big head and stroked his back, which was the size of a small table. The dog wagged his tail gratefully. "Were you scared back there?" Chen asked.

"Sure," Gasmai said with a little laugh. "Of course I was. I was scared the wolf would drive the sheep out of the pen. I'd lose all my work points. I'm the head of a production team, and you can imagine what a humiliation it would be if I lost my sheep." She bent down to pat the big dog's head and said, *"Sain Bar"* (Good Bar), over and over. Bar dropped the bone he was chewing and raised his head to nudge his mistress's hand, then stuck his nose up her sleeve, happily wagging his tail and sending out little eddies of air. "Chenchen, I'll give you a puppy after New Year's," Gasmai said. "There are all sorts of ways to raise a dog. Do a good job, and it'll grow up to be like Bar."

He thanked her repeatedly.

Back in the yurt, Chen admitted that he'd been scared to death. Old Man Bilgee laughed. "I could tell when I grabbed your hand. You were shaking like a leaf. Do you think you could hold a knife in a fight like that? If you plan to stay on the grassland, you'll have to learn to be tougher than the wolves. One day I'll take you out to hunt them. Back when Genghis Khan formed his army, he always picked the best wolf hunters."

Chen nodded. "I believe that," he said. "I really do. If Gasmai rode into battle, she'd be more fearful than the female general Hua Mulan."

"You Chinese don't have many Hua Mulans, but there are lots of Mongol women like Gasmai. At least one in every family." The old man laughed again like an alpha wolf.

After that incident, Chen Zhen wanted to get as near to the wolves as possible so that he could study them. He sensed that only by gaining an understanding of the wolves would he be able to comprehend the Mongolian grassland and the people who lived there. He even entertained the idea of stealing a cub from its den and raising it one day.

Although Bilgee was the most renowned hunter on the Olonbulag, he seldom went out hunting, and when he did, it was for foxes, not wolves. People had gotten so caught up in the Cultural Revolution over the past couple of years that the traditional life of the grassland—a mixture of tending sheep and hunting wild animals—had been turned upside down, like a flock of sheep scattered in a blizzard. Then, in the winter of that year, herds of Mongolian gazelle migrated across the border into the Olonbulag, and the old man decided it was time to fulfill his promise to Chen to take him to see the wolves at close range so as to boost the young man's courage and increase his knowledge.

Chen Zhen felt the old man nudge him with his elbow and saw him point to the snow-covered slope. Chen trained his telescope on the spot. The gazelles were still grazing nervously. He watched as one of the wolves left the pack and ran off to the mountain west of them. Chen's heart sank. "I guess they aren't going to attack," he whispered. "Apparently, we've let ourselves freeze for nothing."

"The pack won't pass up an opportunity like this," Bilgee said. "The leader must have felt there are too many gazelles, so he sent a runner to bring more troops. An opportunity like this comes maybe once every five or six years, and it seems they've got quite an appetite. They're getting ready for a major battle. You'll see that this was worth the wait. As I said, patience is the key to a good hunt."

2

Six or seven new wolves quietly joined the encirclement, its three sides formed and ready. Chen Zhen covered his mouth with the horseshoe-shaped sleeve of his heavy fur deel and said softly, "Are they going to close the circle now?"

"Not quite yet," Bilgee replied softly. "The alpha male is waiting for the right moment. Wolves are more meticulous about their encirclement formations than we are. See if you can figure out what he's waiting for." Each time the old man's bushy white eyebrows twitched, shards of frost fell to the ground. A frost-covered fox-fur cap with flaps that fell to his shoulders covered his forehead and much of his face, but not his light brown eyes, which gave off a heavy sheen, like pieces of amber.

They had been hiding in their snow cave for some time already, and now they turned their attention to the gazelles grazing on the slope. The herd numbered as many as a thousand, of which several large males, with long black horns, kept watch as they sniffed the air. The others were grazing the land under the snow.

The area was a winter reserve pastureland for the Second Production Brigade, a defense line against natural disasters. Measuring roughly twenty square miles, it was a large mountain pastureland where, protected from the wind and relatively free of snow, fine grass grew tall and thick.

"Watch carefully, and you'll understand," the old man whispered. "This is an ideal spot, open to the northwestern winds that keep the snow from piling up. When I was eight years old, the Olonbulag was hit by the largest snowstorm in centuries, a true white scourge. The snow covered our yurts. Fortunately, under the leadership of some old-timers, most of the people and animals managed to get out. When the snow was still only up to our knees, our several thousand horses were brought out to trample a path in the snow. Then several dozen oxen tamped it down more, opening up a trough through which our sheep and carts could travel. It took three days and nights to reach this pastureland in safety. Here the snow was only a foot or two deep, allowing the tips of the long grass to push through. Cows and sheep and horses, all half dead from the cold and hunger, made a dash for it as soon as it came into view. As for the people, they threw themselves down onto the snow and wept, then banged their heads on the ground in thanks to Tengger, until their faces were covered with snow. The sheep and the horses knew how to move the snow out of the way to get to the grass, while the more passive cows simply followed along behind them to forage. It was enough to sustain the greater half of the animals until the snow melted in the spring. People who hadn't moved their animals in time lost them. They themselves made it to safety, but their animals were buried in the blizzard. If not for this stretch of pastureland, every inhabitant of the Olonbulag, human and animal, would have died. We stopped being afraid of white scourges after that; we knew that if one came along, we could move to this pastureland and take refuge here."

The old man sighed. "This spot is a gift to the Olonbulag people and animals from Tengger, our sustenance. In the past, herdsmen made an annual trek to the top of that mountain to worship Tengger and the Mountain God. But with the current political situation, no one has dared go up for a couple of years. But we still worship in our hearts. This is our sacred mountain. Even if there's a drought and no grass to forage, the mountain is off-limits to herdsmen from spring to autumn. Preserving it is particularly hard on people who tend horses. The wolves also preserve the mountain, and once every five or six years they go on a killing spree of gazelles, their sacrifice to the Mountain God and Tengger. The mountain doesn't only save people and their animals; it also saves the wolves, who are cleverer than both. In the past the wolves arrived ahead of the people and their animals, and during the day they hid among the rocks on the mountaintop or behind the mountain, where the snow had turned to ice. They came down at night to dig up cows and sheep that had frozen to death. Wolves won't bother people and their animals as long as they have food to eat."

Patchy clouds floated above. The old man gazed up into the icy blue of Tengger, a look of devotion on his face.

The snows had come early this year and had stuck, covering the bottom half of the grass before it turned yellow; now the grasses were like greens trapped by ice. The subtle fragrance of tasty grass emerged from the hollow stalks and the cracks in the snow. The smell of grass drew starving gazelles across the border from the blizzard-ravaged neighbor to the north; to them the spot was a wintry oasis—they ate until their rounded bellies looked like drums, making running all but impossible.

Only the alpha male and Bilgee knew that the gazelles had made a tragic mistake.

It was not a particularly large herd. During his first year on the grassland, Chen had often seen herds of ten thousand or more. A cadre at brigade headquarters had said that during the three difficult years in the 1960s, soldiers from northern military regions had come in vehicles and mowed down vast numbers of gazelles with machine guns to supply food to their troops; as a result, they drove the surviving gazelles out of the area. But in recent years, given the tense military situation in the border regions, large-scale hunts had ceased, and the Olonbulag had witnessed the return of gazelles in spectacular numbers. Chen frequently encountered large herds when he tended his flock, a vast sea of yellow close to the ground, passing by his sheep, relaxed and carefree, but causing his animals to huddle together in fear, watching bug-eyed with a mixture of alarm and envy as their wild cousins raced past, free as the wind.

Mongolian gazelles ignore unarmed humans. On one occasion, Chen Zhen had ridden down the middle of a dense herd with the idea of roping one to get a taste of gazelle meat. He failed. The fastest four-legged animal on the grassland, the gazelle can outrun hunting dogs, even wolves. Chen whipped his horse and charged the herd, but they kept passing on both sides, no more than ten or twelve yards away, then flowed back together ahead of him and continued on their way. He could only watch in awe.

The gazelles they were observing now may have comprised no more than a medium-sized herd, but Chen was sure it was too big for a pack of wolves numbering in the dozens. People had told him there is no animal more determined than a wolf, and he was eager to see not only how great the wolves' appetite and determination might be but also what kind of hunters they were.

For the wolves, this was too great an opportunity to miss. Their movements were slight and slow. When the male gazelles looked up, the wolves flattened out and did not move; even the steam in their breath was light and gentle.

The herd continued its desperate grazing, and the human observers settled in to see what was going to happen.

"Gazelles are a scourge on the grassland," the old man whispered. "They run like the wind and eat all the time. Just look how much good forage they've already gone through. The brigade has done everything it can to keep this pastureland in good shape, but the gazelles will have destroyed nearly half of it in days. A few more herds like this, and the grass will be gone. The snows have been heavy this year, and a blizzard is always a possibility. Without this pastureland in reserve, we'd probably not survive—neither us nor our animals. Luckily, there's the wolf pack. Within days this herd will be driven off, those that aren't killed, that is."

Surprised by this comment, Chen looked at the old man and said, "No wonder you don't hunt wolves."

"Oh, I hunt them," the old man replied. "But not often. If we killed them off, the grassland would perish, and then how would we survive? This is something you Chinese cannot understand."

"It's starting to make sense to me," Chen said. He was getting excited, without quite knowing why. The vague image of a wolf totem formed in his head. Before leaving Beijing two years earlier, he'd read and collected books on the inhabitants of the grassland, and had learned that they revere a wolf totem, but only now did he have an inkling of why they treated the wolf, a beastly ancestor, an animal despised by the Chinese and by all people who tilled the land, as their totem.

The old man looked at Chen; his broad smile turned his eyes to narrow slits. "You Beijing students threw up your yurt more than a year ago," he said, "but you don't have enough felt padding around it. We'll take a few extra gazelles back with us this time and trade them at the purchasing center for some felt. That way the four of you will be a bit warmer this winter."

"That's wonderful," Chen said. "We've only got two layers of felt now, and even our ink bottles freeze inside the yurt."

The old man smiled again. "Well, take a good look, because this pack of wolves is going to hand you a nice gift."

On the Olonbulag at the time, a full-grown frozen gazelle, meat and hide, sold for twenty yuan, equivalent to a herder's wages for two weeks. Considered choice material, its hide was used to make pilots' jackets. But China's pilots could not get them, since the gazelle hides produced in Inner Mongolia were for export only, a commodity of exchange with the Soviet Union and Eastern European countries for steel, automobiles, and munitions. The choice meat cuts were canned and exported. The remaining meat and the bones were targeted for domestic consumption but only occasionally appeared in butcher shops in the Mongolian banner territories, where ration coupons were required.

In the winter of that year, great quantities of gazelles had streamed across the border, creating excitement among leaders of the various Mongolian banners. Purchasing stations made space in their storerooms for the carcasses. Officials, hunters, and herdsmen were like fishermen who had been told the fish were schooling. Nearly all the hunters and herders had saddled up the fastest horses and were heading out with hunting dogs and rifles to kill as many gazelles as possible. That did not include Chen Zhen, who had his hands full with his sheep and, of course, had no rifle and no ammunition. Besides, a shepherd was given only four horses, while the horse herders had seven or eight, and as many as a dozen for their exclusive use. So the students could only look on enviously as the hunters went out.

A couple of nights before, Chen had visited the yurt of the hunter Lamjav. The gazelles had only been in the region for a few days, yet he had already bagged eleven, once bringing down two with a single shot. For a few days of hunting he had earned nearly as much as a horse herder made in three months. Proudly he told Chen that he'd already taken in enough to supply himself with liquor and cigarettes for a year. After a few more days out on the grassland, he planned to buy a Red Lantern transistor radio, leaving the new one at home and taking the old one to the herders' mobile yurt. That night, for the first time in his life, Chen had a true taste of the wild grassland. There is no fat on gazelles, and the leanness of their meat, which tastes like venison, can be attributed to their perennial battle with wolves.

Once the gazelles had migrated onto the Olonbulag, the Beijing students were demoted to second-class citizens. In their two years on the grassland, they had learned to tend cows and sheep by themselves, but they were incompetent hunters, and in the nomadic existence of people in eastern Inner Mongolia, hunting ranks higher than tending livestock. The Mongols' ancestors were hunters in the forests surrounding the upper reaches of the Heilong River who slowly migrated onto the grassland, where they lived as hunter-herdsmen. Hunting was a significant and often a major source of income. On the Olonbulag, horse herders held the highest status among the herdsmen, and most of the hunters came from their ranks. Hardly any of the Beijing students managed to rise to that level, and for those few who did, the best they could hope for was an apprenticeship to a full-fledged herder. And so, on the eve of the big hunt, the students, who had begun to consider themselves a new breed of herdsmen, were left out completely.

After finishing his meal, Chen took the gazelle leg Lamjav had given him and, somewhat dispirited, ran over to Bilgee's yurt.

Even though the students now had their own yurt, Chen often went to visit Bilgee, whose yurt was larger, nicer, and much warmer. The walls were hung with Mongol-Tibetan religious tapestries, and the floor was covered with a rug that had a white deer design; the tray and silver bowls on the squat table and the bronze bowls and aluminum teapot in the cupboard were polished to a shine. In this remote area, where "heaven is high and the emperor far away," the Red Guards' fervent desire to destroy the Four Olds—old ideas, culture, customs, and habits—had not yet claimed Bilgee's tapestries or rug.

The four students in Chen's yurt had been classmates at a Beijing high school; three of them were sons of "black-gang capitalist roaders" or "reactionary academic authorities." They shared similar circumstances, ideology, and disgust for the radical and ignorant Red Guards; and so, in the early winter of 1967, they said good-bye to the clamor of Beijing and traveled to the grassland in search of a peaceful life, where they maintained their friendship.

For Chen, Old Man Bilgee's yurt was like a tribal chief's headquarters where he benefited from his host's guidance and concern; it was a safe and intimate refuge. There he was treated as a member of the family; the two cartons of books he'd brought from Beijing, especially those dealing with Mongol history, in Chinese and in English, had established a close bond between him, a Han Chinese, and his Mongol host, who often entertained guests. Among those guests had been musical performers whose songs were replete with Mongolian history and legends. As soon as he saw Chen's books, in particular those with maps and illustrations, Bilgee became interested in Mongol histories written by Chinese, Russian, Persian, and other scholars. With his limited Chinese, he took every opportunity to teach Mongol to Chen, wanting to have everything in the books explained to him; he reciprocated by telling Mongol stories to Chen. Over the two years, these conversations in Mongol and Chinese between the two men—one old, the other young—had progressed smoothly.

Chen did not want to leave Bilgee's yurt, but the quantity of livestock kept growing on the lush pastureland. The number of sheep in his flock, after the birthing of the latest batch of lambs, exceeded three thousand, far more than any one shepherd could tend. So they were divided into smaller flocks, requiring Chen to leave his patron's yurt and follow his sheep. He and his three classmates set up a yurt and began living on their own. Fortunately, the two camps were close enough that the bleating of sheep and the barking of dogs in one camp could be heard in the other, so they met on their way out in the mornings and back at night.

A man could reach his neighbor's place before his saddle was warm. Chen often visited the old man's yurt to continue their conversations, but now he wanted to talk about gazelles, and wolves.

Chen parted the door curtains, thick felt sewn into auspicious patterns with camel hair, and joined Bilgee in a cup of butter tea.

"Don't envy people just because they've bagged gazelles. Tomorrow I'll take you out and you can get a wagonload of your own. I've been up in the mountains the past few days, and I know where to find them. This will be the perfect opportunity to get firsthand knowledge of a wolf pack. That's what you've been wanting, isn't it? You Chinese have the courage of sheep, who survive by foraging grass. We Mongols are meat-eating wolves, and you could use a bit of wolf courage."

Early the next morning, they traveled to a southwestern mountain slope, hiding themselves to watch. The old man had brought neither a rifle nor a dog along, only his telescopes. Chen had hunted with Bilgee before, but only for fox, and this was the first time he'd gone out empty-handed. "We're not going to try to bring down a gazelle with a telescope, are we?"

The old man smiled and said nothing. He was always happy when his apprentices came loaded with curiosity and doubts.

Finally, when Chen spotted the wolf encirclement through his telescope, the old man's hunting plan became clear, and Chen was delighted. Bilgee flashed a crafty smile. Chen forgot the cold the moment he spotted the wolves; blood seemed to race through his veins, and the terror he'd experienced the first time he saw the big wolves vanished.

* * *

There wasn't a breath of wind deep in the mountains; the air was cold and dry, and Chen Zhen's feet were nearly frozen. The blasts of cold air were getting stronger. If only he had a wolf pelt to lie on! He turned to the old man and whispered something that had been bothering him: "Everyone says that wolf pelts make the warmest bedding you can find anywhere, and the people around here, hunters and herdsmen, kill plenty of wolves. But I've never seen them in a herdsman's home. Why is that? The only pelts I've seen are a wolf-skin mat in the home of Dorji and a pair of chaps his father wears over his sheepskin pants, with fur on the outside."

The old man replied, "Dorji is a northeastern Mongol. They're farmers who own a few cows and sheep, but they've been around Chinese so long they've begun following Han customs. People who come here from the outside have forgotten the Mongol gods and their own origins. When someone in their family dies, they put him in a box and bury him in the ground, instead of feeding him to the wolves, so of course they don't see anything wrong with using wolf pelts as chaps. Here on the grassland, wolf pelts are the thickest and the densest, so there's nothing better for keeping out the cold. Two sheepskins put together won't keep you as warm as a single wolf pelt. But we don't use them as bedding. We respect the wolves too much. Any Mongol who doesn't isn't a true Mongol. Out here, a Mongol would freeze to death before he slept on a wolf pelt, since doing so would offend the Mongol gods, and their souls would never go to Tengger. Why do you think Tengger bestows its favors on wolves?"

"Didn't you say that wolves are the protective spirits of the grassland?" Chen Zhen asked.

"Right," the old man said, his wide smile slitting his eyes. "That's it exactly. Tengger is the father, the grassland is the mother, and the wolves kill only animals that harm the grassland. How could Tengger not bestow its favors on wolves?"

There was movement in the wolf pack, and the two men trained their telescopes on a pair of wolves that had looked up. The animals quickly lowered their heads. Chen searched through the tall grass but saw no more movement by the wolves.

The old man handed his glass to Chen so that he could observe the situation with a full pair of binoculars. The original double-tube glass was Soviet military issue. Bilgee had found it on the Olonbulag twenty years earlier, on an old battlefield from the Soviet-Japanese war. During World War II, a major battle between the Russians and the Japanese had occurred nearby to the north. Toward the end of the war, the Olonbulag had been the primary military artery for the Russo-Mongolian army into Manchuria. Even now there were deep ruts left by tanks, as well as the hulks of Russian and Japanese tanks and armored vehicles.

Nearly all the old herders owned Russian or Japanese bayonets, canteens, spades, helmets, binoculars, and other military equipment. The long chain Gasmai used to tether calves came from a Russian army truck. But of all the military equipment left behind by the Russians and the Japanese, binoculars were the herders' favorite and had become an important tool for production.

The herdsmen, who treasured things they could not produce themselves, usually took the binoculars apart to make a pair of "telescopes," for the reduced size made them easy to carry and doubled their usage. "These have helped us in hunting," Bilgee said, "and have made it easier to find lost horses. But the wolves' eyesight seems to have improved, and if you observe a wolf through one of these things, sometimes you'll see that the he's looking right back at you."

One day after Chen had been living in the old man's yurt for six months, Bilgee took a telescope out of the wagon box and handed it to him.

The Russian telescope was old and the copper non-skid surface had been worn smooth in places, but the powerful lens was of the highest quality. Chen treasured the gift, which he wrapped in red silk, using it only when he was helping cowherds run down strays or horse herders find lost horses, or when he went hunting with Bilgee.

Chen surveyed the area through his telescope; his latent hunting instincts were awakened as he looked through his "hunter's eye." These hunting instincts had awakened too late in his life, he felt, and he was saddened to have been born into a line of farmers. Farmers had become as timid as sheep after dozens, even hundreds, of generations of being raised on grains and greens, the products of farming communities; they had lost the virility of their nomadic ancestors, going back to the legendary Yellow Emperor. No longer hunters, they had become the hunted.

The wolf pack still showed no signs of attacking, and Chen was beginning to lose patience over their extraordinary ability to hold back. "Are they going to complete the encirclement today?" he asked. "Are they waiting until it gets dark to attack?"

"War demands patience," the old man replied softly.

"Opportunities present themselves only to the patient, man and beast, and only they take advantage of those opportunities. How do you think Gen-ghis Khan was able to defeat the great armies of the Jin with so few mounted warriors? And all the nations that fell to him? Displaying only the power of wolves isn't enough. You must also display patience. Even the largest and mightiest armies can stumble. If a mighty horse stumbles, it is at the mercy of even a small wolf. Without patience, you are not a wolf, you are not a hunter, and you are not Genghis Khan. You are always saying you want to get an understanding of wolves and of Genghis Khan. Well, then, lie there and be patient."

There was an angry edge to the old man's comment. So Chen tried to cultivate a bit of patience. He trained his telescope on a wolf he'd observed several times already. It lay there as if dead. After a few moments, the old man softened his tone and said, "After lying here all this time, have you figured out what the wolves are waiting for?"

Chen shook his head.

"They're waiting for the gazelles to eat their fill and doze off," Bilgee said.

"Are they really that smart?" Chen asked in amazement.

"You Chinese don't know a thing about wolves. People aren't as clever as they are. Here, I'll test you. Do you think a single wolf, even a large one, can bring down a gazelle?"

Chen thought a moment before answering: "No, you'd need three, two to chase it and the third lying in ambush. No wolf could do it alone."

The old man shook his head. "Would you believe that one ferocious wolf can bring down a gazelle all by itself?"

"Really?" Chen said, finding it hard to believe. "I can't imagine how."

"Wolves have developed a special skill. In the daylight, a wolf will concentrate on a single gazelle but do nothing until nightfall, when the gazelle will look for a place with tall grass out of the wind to lie down and sleep. That still isn't the time to strike, because even though the gazelle is asleep, its nose and ears remain alert. At the first sign of danger, it will leap up and run off, and the wolf won't be able to catch it. So the wolf waits, all through the night, lying nearby. At sunrise the gazelle gets up with a full bladder, and now the wolf is ready to pounce. A gazelle can't urinate while it's running, so before it's gone far, its bladder bursts, its rear legs cramp up, and it stops. You see, a gazelle can run like the wind, but not all the time, and wise old wolves know that's when they can bring one down alone. Only the cleverest gazelles are wise enough to forsake the warmth of sleep to get up to relieve themselves at night. They never have to worry about a wolf running them down. Olonbulag hunters get up early in the morning to claim gazelles taken down by wolves, and when they open up their bellies, there's urine everywhere."

Chen Zhen laughed softly. "I couldn't have come up with that strategy under the threat of death. That's remarkable. But Mongol hunters are crafty too!"

The old man laughed. "We're the wolves' apprentices, so we have to be."

Finally, most of the gazelles looked up. Their "drums" were tauter than ever, more than a night with a full bladder. Some were so full their legs were splayed in four directions. The old man looked through his telescope and said, "They're so full they can't run. Watch closely. It's time for the wolves to strike."

Chen tensed. The pack was slowly tightening the semicircle; there were now wolves to the east, north, and west of the gazelles. A line of mountains lay to the south. Chen assumed that wolves on the other side of the mountain were waiting for the main body to drive the gazelles toward where they lay in wait, and the slaughter would begin. Herdsmen had said that wolves often employ this tactic. "Papa," he said, "how many wolves are there behind the mountains? Enough to close the circle on all these gazelles?"

"There are no wolves behind the mountain," the old man replied with a sly smile. "The alpha male wouldn't send any over there."

"Then how will they close the circle?" Chen asked doubtfully.

"At this time, in this place, they can get more with a three-sided encirclement than a full circle."

"Then I don't understand what they're doing."

"One of the biggest and best-known snowbanks on the Olonbulag is on the other side of that mountain. The grazing land here is a windward slope, and during a blizzard the snow is blown to the other side of the mountain, turning it into a basin with snow from a depth of waist-high to higher than a flagpole. Pretty soon the wolves will drive the herd to the other side of the mountain. As they press forward, they'll tighten the circle. What do you think it will look like?"

Everything turned dark for Chen, as if he'd fallen into a snowdrift that kept out all light. If he'd been a Han soldier in ancient times, he was thinking, he could not have seen through this strategy, this trap. Now he began to understand why the great Ming general Xu Da, who had driven the Mongols back onto the grasslands, had won every battle he fought south of the Great

Wall but had seen his armies annihilated on the grassland. He also understood why the other great Ming general, Qiu Fu, with his hundred thousand soldiers, had driven the Mongol hordes to the Kerulen River in Outer Mongolia, only to be ambushed. When he was killed, his army's morale plummeted, and all the Han soldiers were taken prisoner.

"In war," the old man said, "wolves are smarter than men. We Mongols learned from them how to hunt, how to encircle, even how to fight a war. There are no wolf packs where you Chinese live, so you haven't learned how to fight. You can't win a war just because you have lots of land and people. No, it depends on whether you're a wolf or a sheep."

The attack was launched. The wolf with the gray neck and chest led two large wolves on the western flank in a lightning assault on a hilly protuberance near the gazelle herd. This, obviously, was the final gap in the three-sided encirclement. By occupying this hill, the wolves completed the encirclement. This sudden action was like sounding the bugle for all three sides to charge. The wolves, which had patiently lain in wait for so long, rose up out of the grass and charged the gazelles from the east, west, and north. Never had Chen Zhen witnessed such a terrifying attack. When men charge the enemy, they shout "Charge!" or "Kill!" Dog attacks are accompanied by frenzied barking to intimidate and instill fear. But when wolves attack, they do so in silence—no shouts, no wolfish howls. Warrior wolves!

The wolves flew out of the tall grass like torpedoes armed with the sharpest, most fearsome teeth and menacing glares, heading straight for the herd.

Stuffed from overeating, the gazelles were thrown into a panic. Denied their primary weapon—speed—

they were now little more than sheep, nothing but meat on the hoof. Chen imagined their great terror. Souls had probably already fled from most of them and were on their way up to Tengger. Many merely stood where they were and quaked; others crumpled to the ground as if kneeling, their tongues out, their short tails twitching.

Chen was witness to the wolves' intelligence and patience, their organization and discipline. Faced with a combat opportunity that came around only once every few years, they were still able to wait patiently, keeping their hunger and their appetite in check, then disarm the enemy—the herd of gazelles—with ease.

Now he understood how the great, unlettered military genius Genghis Khan, as well as the illiterate or semiliterate military leaders of peoples such as the Quanrong, the Huns, the Tungus, the Turks, the Mongols, and the Jurchens, were able to bring the Chinese (whose great military sage Sun-tzu had produced his universally acclaimed treatise *The Art of War*) to their knees, to run roughshod over their territory, and to interrupt their dynastic cycles. They had the greatest of all teachers in military strategy; they had an excellent and remarkably clear model of actual combat; and they had a long history of struggle with crack lupine troops. To Chen, these hours of exemplary combat tactics had proven more enlightening than years of reading Sun-tzu or Clausewitz. He had been smitten by the study of history at a very young age, obsessed over solving one of the great mysteries of world history: Where had the tiny race of people who had swept across Asia and Europe and created the Great Mongol Empire, the largest land-holding in the history of the world, learned their military secrets? He had asked that question of Bilgee more than once, and this old man, whose educational level was low but whose erudition was broad, had gradually answered all his questions by enlightening him on the combat methods of wolves. Chen felt a sense of deep veneration for the grassland wolves and for the people who worshipped the wolf totem.

The battle and the observation continued.

The moment had finally arrived when the herd of gazelles began to stir. Only those older members with previous battlefield experience and the herd leaders had been able to resist the seduction of fragrant, mid-winter grass and had not eaten a quantity that would impede their speed; they immediately took off running toward the mountains, at the same time urging the rest of the herd to run for their lives. But they didn't have a chance, given their full bellies, the deep snow, and the angle of the slope. It was a bloodbath, a punishment by the wise on the stupid and careless. In Bilgee's view, this was a sacred cleansing of the grassland, a good and benevolent deed.

Ignoring those fallen gazelles who had eaten so much they could not run, the wolves went straight for the standing clusters of animals. The larger wolves quickly brought down victims and bit through their throats, sending crimson streams gushing into the air and staining the snow. The frigid air suddenly filled with the heavy stink of blood. The gazelles, with their keen sight and smell, were so terrified by this strategy—killing the chickens to frighten the monkeys—they broke for the mountain. Several large bucks led families of gazelles up to the top of the slope, where they stopped and ran around in circles, unwilling to go down the other side. Obviously, the lead animals had discovered the danger in the white snowdrift, where not a single stalk of grass was visible; the older animals, who were familiar with the landscape, had seen through the wolves' strategy.

All of a sudden, the closely packed group of gazelles turned and came back down, like a landslide, as a dozen or so large males weighed the dangers they faced. They decided on the least risky choice by turning to break through the encirclement.

The bucks knew that their fate hung in the balance. In groups of four or five, shoulder to shoulder, they lowered their heads to create a phalanx of deadly horns and charged the wolves. Other gazelles that could still run fell in behind them.

Chen knew the damage those horns could do. On the grassland, herdsmen used them as leatherworking needles; so sharp they could penetrate cowhide, wolf skin would be no problem. The counterattack worked as they tore a hole in the encirclement, through which a yellow flood poured. Chen Zhen tensed, afraid that this rent in the line would ruin the wolf pack's plans.

But then he discovered the pack leader standing near the break in the line, looking untroubled, like a man opening the dam to release floodwaters. As soon as the gazelles that had maintained their running speed and kept their horns out in front had passed through the open dam, he led his troops in closing the breach. Now the encirclement contained only gazelles that could not run fast, had no weapons, and were not very smart. A ragtag pack of them, now that their leaders and more powerful males were outside the circle, terrified to face the charging wolves, ran up the slope and then down into the deep snowdrifts. Chen knew at once how the pursued animals—with their pointed hooves, thick legs, and bellies filled with grass—would end up.

Both gazelles and wolves disappeared where the mountain met the horizon. As a thousand gazelles ran for their lives, the blood-soaked encirclement area went quiet. Seven or eight carcasses lay on the grassy slope; other injured members of the herd struggled weakly. No more than ten minutes had passed from the moment the attack was launched until the battle was over. It seemed to Chen that he had held his breath the whole time; his heart was racing.

The old man stood up and stretched, then sat cross-legged in the tall grass on the edge of the snow cave, where he took a pipe with a jade mouthpiece out of his felt boot. He filled it with tobacco, lit it, and, covering the opening with a lid made of an old silver coin, inhaled a mouthful of smoke.

Chen knew that as a young man, Bilgee had given a Han Chinese trader from Zhangjiakou twenty fox pelts for this pipe; the students considered it a bad deal, but the pipe was one of the old man's prized possessions, and he had sympathized with the trader, who'd had to travel all the way to Mongolia to do business, risking death at the hands of highwaymen along the way.

The old man kept smoking. "We can head back after this pipe," he said.

But Chen was still on a hunting high. "Aren't we going to take a look on the other side?" he asked anxiously. "I'd like to see how many gazelles the wolves trapped."

"That's too dangerous. Anyway, I know without looking. There will be hundreds of them. Outside of the young animals, plus the thin ones and the lucky ones that can somehow make it out of the snowdrift, the rest are all fated to go to Tengger. You needn't worry. This pack of wolves won't be able to eat all their kills, and even after our group goes out and brings back all we can, there'll still be plenty left out there."

"The young animals, and the thin ones, how do they manage to get away?"

The old man's eyes crinkled in a smile as he said, "Young animals are thin, which makes their bodies light, so they don't go deep into the snow. They can usually find a way out, and the wolves won't go after them." He beamed. "My boy, today you've witnessed the virtues of wolves. Not only do they watch and preserve the grassland, but they've delivered New Year's gifts to us. Thanks to them, it's going to be a good year. There's a grassland rule here that the spoils of a hunt belong to whoever sees them first. Since you and I are the witnesses, we'll make sure your yurt gets a bit extra. We Mongols place much importance on repaying debts of gratitude. In the future, don't waste your time talking about the wolf hunt with other Chinese or outsiders."

Chen Zhen could barely contain his excitement; he was impatient to fill a wagon with gazelle carcasses and take them back to the yurt. "In the two years I've been here," he said, "the wolves have caused me nothing but trouble. I never expected that one day I'd benefit from their efforts."

"We Mongols benefit from their efforts all the time," the old man said. He raised his herding club and pointed to a mountain range behind them. "There's another range of mountains behind that one. It's not part of our pastureland, but it's famous around here. The old people say that Genghis Khan's great general Muqali fought a battle there. He drove several thousand mounted Jurchen warriors of the great Jin dynasty into a snowdrift, and the following spring he sent men back to collect the spoils of war. There were mountains of swords and spears and bows and arrows, plus helmets and armor, and saddles and lanterns. Where else could he have learned that but from wolves? If you add up all the major battles involving Mongols, more than half were fought with skills learned from the wolves."

The two men walked back to the ravine behind them, and when the dark horse saw its master, it jerked its head up and down excitedly. Every time Chen saw this horse, which had once saved his life, he patted it on the head to once more show his gratitude. The horse accepted his thanks by nudging him on the shoulder. This time, however, Chen felt a powerful impulse to somehow pat a wolf on the head.

They removed the cowhide fetters from the horses' hooves, mounted up, and rode off at an easy canter toward home.

The old man looked up at the sky, "Tengger is protecting us," he said. "The weather will hold tomorrow. If a blizzard came tonight, we wouldn't wind up with a single gazelle."

3

Fine weather greeted them the following morning. Kitchen smoke rose from the yurts like slim white birches, the tips of their highest branches boring into the heavens, into Tengger. The cows and sheep were ruminating leisurely; the sun had driven off the cold night air, and frost on the animals' hides was just then turning to dew, to eventually rise from their bodies as mist.

Chen Zhen asked his neighbor Gombu to tend his sheep that day. As a onetime herd owner, Gombu was kept under surveillance, and his right to tend sheep had been taken from him; but the four Beijing students asked him to watch their animals whenever they could, for which Gasmai would let him earn the appropriate work points. Chen and one of the other herders, Yang Ke, yoked up a light cart and headed to Bilgee's yurt.

Yang, a classmate who lived in Chen Zhen's yurt, was the son of a famous professor at one of Beijing's most prestigious universities. They had as many books at home as a small library. In high school, Chen and he had often traded books. They'd exchange views when they finished, and were best friends. In Beijing, Yang had been a shy, mild-mannered boy who blushed whenever he met a stranger. No one could have predicted that after two years of eating lamb and beefsteaks and cheese, after baking in the strong rays of the Mongolian sun season after season, he would be transformed into a brawny son of the grassland, with a face as sunburned as the native herdsmen and none of the bookish manners he'd brought with him.

Yang was more excited than Chen, and as he whipped the back of the ox he said, "I didn't sleep at all last night. The next time Bilgee takes you hunting, be sure to let me go along, even if I have to lie there for two whole days. This is the first time I've heard of wolves performing good deeds for people, and I won't believe it until I personally drag one of the gazelle carcasses out of the snow. Can we really take a cartload of them back with us?"

"Would I lie to you?" Chen smiled. "Papa said that no matter how hard it is to dig them out, we're guaranteed a cartful, which we can swap for other things, like New Year's items and some large pieces of felt for our yurt."

Yang was so pleased he whipped the back of the ox until it glared angrily. "It looks like your two-year fascination with wolves is beginning to pay off," he said. "I'll have to start studying their hunting techniques myself. Who knows, it might come in handy in a real fight one day... What you said could be a pattern. Living on the grassland over the long haul as a nomad, it makes no difference which ethnic group you belong to, since sooner or later you'll start worshipping wolves and treating them as mentors. That's what happened with the Huns, the Wusun, the Turks, the Mongols, and other nationalities. Or so it says in books. But the Chinese are an exception. I guarantee you, we Chinese could live out here for generations without worshipping a wolf totem."

"Maybe, maybe not," Chen said as he reined in his horse. "Take me, for instance. The wolves have won me over in a little more than two years."

"But the vast majority of Chinese are peasants," Yang countered, "or were born to peasants. The Han have a peasant mentality that's impossible to break down, and if they were transported out here, I'd be surprised if they didn't skin every last wolf on the grassland. We're a farming race, and a fear and hatred of wolves is in our bones. How could we venerate a wolf totem? We Han worship the Dragon King, the one in charge of our agrarian lifeline—our dragon totem, the one we pay homage to, the one to whom we meekly submit. How can you expect people like that to learn from wolves, to protect them, to worship and yet kill them, like the Mongols? Only a people's totem can truly rouse their ethnic spirit and character, whether it's a dragon or a wolf. The differences between farming and nomadic peoples are simply too great. In the past, when we were immersed in the vast Han Chinese ocean, we had no sense of those differences, but coming out here has made the inherent weaknesses of our farming background obvious. Sure, my father is a renowned professor, but his grandfather and my mother's grandmother were peasants."

"In ancient times," Chen said, picking up the thread, "the impact of Mongols on the world was far greater than that of the Han, who outnumbered them a hundred to one. Even now, people in the West call us members of a Mongol race, and we accept that. But back when the Qin and Han dynasties unified China, the word *Mongol* didn't exist. I tell you, I feel sorry for the Han Chinese. We built the Great Wall and crowed about what an achievement it was, considering ourselves to be the center of the world, the central kingdom. But in the eyes of early Western people, China was only a 'silk country,' a 'ceramic country,' a 'tea country.' The Russians even thought that the little Khitan tribe was China, and to this day, they still call China, Khidai."

"It looks like your fascination with wolves was worth it," Yang said. "It's contagious. Now when I read history, I keep looking to the barbarian tribes of the four corners and am tempted to look for their connections to wolves."

"Look at you," Chen said. "You're damned near a Mongol yourself. All you need is an infusion of wolf blood. Hybrids are always superior creatures."

"I can't tell you how happy I am that you urged me to come to the grassland. Do you know what it was you said that touched that special spot in me? You've forgotten, haven't you? This is it: you said, 'The grassland contains the most extensive primitivism and freedom anywhere.' "

Chen loosened his horse's bit and said, "I think you're putting words in my mouth."

They laughed happily. Snow flew from the wheels of the cart as it sped along.

Humans, dogs, and carts formed a scene on the snow like a Gypsy carnival. Every member of Gasmai's group—four *hots* (two adjacent yurts comprised a *hot*), altogether eight yurts—sent men and carts. The eight carts were loaded with felt, ropes, hoes, kindling, and wooden-handled hooks. Everyone was wearing grimy old clothing for the dirty, tiring work ahead—so grimy it shone, so old it was black, and dotted with sheepskin patches. But the people and the dogs were as cheerful as the tribes that had followed the ancient Mongol hordes in sweeping up battlefields to claim the spoils of war. A large felt-wrapped flask of liquor was passed from the head of the procession all the way to the rear, and from the hands of women to the mouths of men. Music filled the air: Mongol folk songs, songs of praise, war chants, drinking songs, and love songs—the dam had broken. The forty or fifty furry Mongol dogs were acting like children, giddily showing off on this rare and happy occasion, running around the carts, rolling in the dirt, play-fighting, and flirting.

Chen Zhen and two horse herders, Batu and Lamjav, plus five or six cowherds and shepherds, clustered around Bilgee, like bodyguards for a tribal chief. Lamjav, a man with a broad face, straight nose, and Turkish eyes, said to Bilgee, "I could be the best marksman anywhere and I still wouldn't be your equal. Without firing a shot, you've made it possible for every family in the team to enjoy a bountiful New Year's holiday. Even with an apprentice like our Han friend Chen Zhen, you haven't forgotten your old Mongol apprentices. I'd never have predicted that the wolves would launch their attack out here yesterday."

The old man glared at him. "In the future, when you have a successful hunt, don't you forget the old folks and the Beijing students in the team. I've never seen you deliver meat to anybody. You only gave Chen Zhen a gazelle leg because he visited your yurt. Is that how we treat our guests? When we were young, the first gazelle or snow otter of the year always went to the old folks and to guests. Young people today have forgotten customs handed down from the great khans. Let me ask you, how many wolves do you have to kill to catch up with Buhe, the great hunter of the Bayan Gobi Commune? You want to see your name in the newspaper, hear it on the radio, win a prize, don't you? If you hunt the wolves to extinction, where do you think your soul will go after you die? Don't tell me you want to be like the Han, buried in a hole in the ground, where you can feed the worms and other insects! If you do, your soul will never make it to Tengger."

"Batu is your son," Lamjav said as he touched the back flap of his fox-fur cap. "You may not believe me, but you ought to believe him. Ask him if I have any interest in becoming a great hunter. A journalist from the Mongol League came to the horse unit to see me the other day. Batu was there; you can ask him if I didn't cut the number in half."

"Is that true?" the old man turned and asked his son.

"Yes," Batu replied, "but the man didn't believe him. He asked people at the purchasing station how many wolf pelts Lamjav had sold them. You know that after they check the quality of the pelts to determine the price, they give the seller twenty bullets. And they keep records. After the journalist returned to the league, he said over the air that Lamjav had nearly caught up with Buhe, which so frightened Lamjav that he asked others to sell his pelts for him."

The old man frowned. "You two hunt wolves too often. You get more kills than anyone on the pasture."

Batu defended himself: "The grazing land for our herd of horses is the closest to the border with Outer Mongolia, and that's where most of the wolves are. If we don't hunt them, they'll cross the border in even greater numbers. Most of the foals that year did not survive."

"Why are both of you here? Did you leave the herd in the care of Zhang Jiyuan?"

"The wolves come at night," Batu said, "so we relieve

him then. He's never taken gazelles during the day, so we came instead. We can work faster."

The winter sun lay low in the sky, appearing to settle close to the land. The blue sky turned white, as did the dry grass; the surface of the snow began to melt, forming a glittery mirror. Humans, dogs, and carts had a spectral quality. The men put on their sunglasses, while the women and children covered their eyes with their flapped sleeves. A few of the cowherds, who suffered from sun-blindness, shut their eyes, but not in time to stanch the flow of tears. The big dogs, on the other hand, were either watching wide-eyed at bounding hares or sniffing the side of the road, where foxes had recently left tracks in the snow.

As they neared the site of the encirclement, the dogs discovered something new on the slope and raced over, leaving frenzied barks in their wakes. Those that were still hungry tore into gazelle carcasses the wolves had left behind. But Bilgee's Bar and a few of the team's better hunting dogs, their hackles raised, ran over to where the wolves had left droppings in the snow, searching the area to determine how many wolves there had been, how powerful a force, and which alpha male they had followed. "Bar recognizes the scent of most of the Olonbulag wolves," Bilgee said, "and they recognize his. The way the fur on his neck is standing up is a sure sign that it was a large pack."

As the riders entered the hunting ground, they sized the scene up by keeping their eyes to the ground. All that remained of most gazelles on the slope were heads and a scattering of bones. Bilgee pointed to the tracks in the snow and said, "Some of them came back last night." Then he pointed to tufts of grayish-yellow wolf fur and said, "A couple of wolf packs had a fight here.

It was probably a pack from the other side of the border that followed the scent of the gazelle herd. The shortage of food there makes them more ferocious than ever."

The horse team finally made it up to the ridge, where they reacted as if they'd discovered a cornucopia, whooping it up like mad. They waved their hats to the carts behind them. Gasmai jumped down off her wagon and grabbed the bridle of the lead ox to get it to trot. So did the other women. They gathered speed, since the oxen were fast and the carts light.

When Lamjav saw the sight below, his eyes nearly popped out of his head. "Yow!" he exclaimed. "It took an amazing pack of wolves to herd in that many gazelles. Last year it took more than twenty of us herders to pen thirty, and we nearly ran our horses into the ground doing it."

Bilgee reined in his horse and took out his telescope to pan the snow-drift and the surrounding mountains. Everyone else reined in their horses too and looked around, waiting to hear what he had to say.

Chen viewed the slope through his telescope. Countless gazelles were buried in the snowdrift, which could also have been the burial site of ancient warriors. The center of the drift was relatively smooth, like a mountain lake sealed by snow and ice. A dozen or so gazelle carcasses dotted the sloping area around the lake, but the shocking sight was seven or eight yellow dots on the lake, some still moving. Chen realized it was a cluster of gazelles that had been driven into the lake but had not been swallowed up by the snow. The surrounding area was pitted with hollows, some large, some small, off into the distance, the only visible traces of gazelles that had drowned in an ocean of snow. Unlike lakes of water, snow lakes indicate where the drowning victims have fallen in.

Bilgee said to Batu, "You and some of the others start shoveling snow to let the carts come up closer." Then he led Chen Zhen and Lamjav up to the edge of the lake. "Make sure you check for gazelle and wolf tracks before you take a step, and avoid spots with no grass."

They rode their horses carefully down the slope. The snow kept getting deeper, the grass less visible. They moved down a little more. The surface was peppered with holes about the thickness of a chopstick tip. A dry yellow stalk of grass stood rigidly in the middle of each hole. Bilgee said, "Tengger gave those air holes to the wolves. Without them, how could they detect the smell of their dead victims in snow this deep?"

Chen Zhen smiled and nodded. The holes and grass stalks were safety signs. A few paces farther down the slope they disappeared, but there were still gazelle and wolf tracks. The powerful Mongol horses' hooves broke through three inches of crusty snow and settled into deep drifts as they moved closer to the snow lake, heading toward the nearest dead gazelles.

Finally, the horses could go no farther. The men dismounted, broke through the crusty surface, and sank into deep snow. They struggled to stomp out a platform on which they could turn around. A half-eaten gazelle lay at an angle in the crushed snow beside Chen Zhen's foot. All around it was frozen grass from the gazelle's stomach. The remains of thirty or forty gazelles that had been caught and eaten lay in the immediate area. That was as far as the wolves had gone.

Chen Zhen gazed out at the most tragic scene he'd ever encountered. Eight or nine little gazelles stood trembling on the lake a hundred yards or so from him, surrounded by holes in the snow, where other gazelles were now buried. These surviving animals were too frightened to move, but the tiny spot of hard snow on which they stood could crumble at any moment. There were others whose thin legs were buried in the snow but whose bodies remained supported by a crusty layer. They were still alive but immobilized. These fleet-footed free spirits of the grassland were hungry and cold, unable to move, suffering one last torment from Death itself.

But the most heartbreaking sight was a series of gazelle heads poking up out of the snow, their bodies completely submerged. They might have been standing on a little hillock or perhaps on the corpses of their companions. By using his telescope, Chen thought he could see the animals' mouths move, as if crying for help, although no sound emerged.

The crusty surface sparkled like ice, beautiful yet treacherous and cruel, another gift from Tengger to the wolves and humans, a deadly hidden weapon safeguarding the grassland. The crusty layer is a product of winter blizzards and the sun. The winds that sweep across the land are like winnowing machines, removing the powdery snow and leaving a dense carpet of pellets that make up the snowy landscape. In the windless mornings, all the way up to midday, under intense rays of sunlight, the snow begins to melt, but cold afternoon winds freeze it again. After several blizzards have blown across the landscape, a three-inch crust, a mixture of ice and snow that is harder than snow alone but more brittle than ice, remains; smooth and slippery, it is uneven in its depth. At its thickest, it can support a man, but there are few places that can withstand the sharp hooves of the Mongolian gazelles.

The scene made Chen tremble with dread. Wolves had dragged all the gazelles they could out of the snow, creating long troughs crisscrossing the edges of the deep snow as they hauled their victims away. The far ends of the troughs were the abattoirs and picnic areas. Only the innards and the choicest flesh were eaten; the rest was left as waste. The wolves had obviously heard the approach of the people and dogs, and had left in a hurry, for the snow pellets were still shifting on the surface, and spots where the wolves had defecated had not completely frozen over.

Mongolian wolves are brilliant fighters on a snowy field, fully cognizant of the limits of battle. They will ignore gazelles out in the deeper snow, those lying on top and those sunken beneath the surface. There wasn't a single track from a probe outside the safe zone. The animals dragged out of the snow could have fed several large wolf packs; the ignored frozen carcasses were the wolf pack's guaranteed fresh food, for they would keep till the spring thaw, when the wolves would return for more tasty meals. This enormous snowdrift and snow lake was a wolf pack's natural cold storage. Old Bilgee said, "There's ice and snow storage for wolves all over Olonbulag. This is just the biggest one. The wolves often store their kills in places like this to keep from starving the following year. The meat of these frozen gazelles is life-saving food for wolves that grow lean in the spring and have a lot more stored-up fat than the live, and very thin, gazelles." The old man pointed to one of the holes and said with a laugh, "Wolves out here really know how to live. We're no match. As winter sets in each year, herdsmen slaughter their cows and sheep before they start losing their autumn fat and then they store the meat, which will take them through the winter. They learned that from wolves."

When Bar and the other dogs spotted live gazelles, their hunting instincts kicked in and they ran toward them. But when they reached the spot where the wolves' paw prints ended, they stopped. Denied the kill, they stretched out their necks and barked madly in the direction of the gazelles. Some of the targets were so frightened that they broke for the snow lake. But before they'd gotten far, the crust gave way and they sank into the quicksand-like snow, struggling briefly before disappearing from sight. The snow above them shifted like sand in an hourglass, until it formed a funnel. One of the animals broke through the crust, thrusting out its front legs and supporting the front half of its body while the rear half sank into the snow. Half a life was saved—for the moment.

The team dug a path to allow the carts down off the ridge, and when the lead cart reached a point where it could go no farther, a line of carts stretched out behind it. The men got out and shoveled away the snow around them so that they could unload the carts.

The men walked up to Bilgee. "All of you, see how the snow off to the west has frozen solid?" he said. "There aren't many holes there, but there are a lot of gazelle droppings and tracks, and that means that many got away."

The sheepherder Sanjai said with a laugh, "I can see that wolves miscalculate sometimes too. If the alpha male had sent four or five wolves over here to close off this route, those gazelles wouldn't have gotten away so easily."

"If you were the alpha male," Bilgee snorted, "you'd starve to death. If you kill off all the gazelles at one time, what will you eat the following year? Wolves aren't greedy like humans. They know how to figure things out, big things!"

"There are too many gazelles this year," Sanjai said. "You could kill a thousand more and still have plenty left. I want to get my hands on enough money to build a new yurt and get married."

The old man glared at him. "When your sons and grandsons get married and the gazelles are gone, then what? You young people are getting more like those outsiders all the time."

Seeing that the women had unloaded the carts and dug paths to the deep snow by clearing out troughs the wolves had made when dragging the gazelle carcasses through the snow, and that they'd also built up a snowbank, Bilgee looked skyward and chanted something. Chen Zhen guessed that he was asking Tengger for permission to go out in the snow and bring up the dead gazelles.

The old man closed his eyes briefly, then opened them again and said, "There are plenty of frozen gazelles at the bottom of the snow, so don't get greedy. When you're out there, first free the surviving animals, all of them, before coming back to dig out the frozen ones. Tengger didn't want those animals to die, so we must save them." He lowered his head and said to Chen Zhen and Yang Ke, "When Genghis Khan finished an encirclement hunt, he let a small number of animals go. The Mongols have fought like that for centuries, and the reason we can have these hunts year after year is that, like the wolves, we don't kill off all the prey."

Bilgee assigned gazelle collection sectors to each

family, then let them go off and work on their own. Everyone followed hunting custom by leaving the nearest and most plentiful holes for the students and for Bilgee, who led Chen and Yang over to his cart, where they unloaded two large rolls of felt, each about two yards wide and four yards long. They appeared to have been sprayed with water beforehand, for they were frozen stiff. Chen and Yang each dragged one along the cleared path, while Bilgee carried a long birch club, tipped with a metal hook. Batu and Gasmai also carried large rolls of felt to the deep snow; little Bayar walked behind his parents with a hook over his shoulder.

After they reached the edge of the deep snow, Bilgee had Chen and Yang spread one of the rolls of felt over the crusty snow, then asked Yang, the heavier of the two, to see if it could sustain his weight. It was like a gigantic skateboard. Yang stepped onto the felt, drawing crunching sounds from the snow under it, but no signs of danger. He jumped up and down. The felt sank beneath his feet slightly but not perilously. The old man quickly made him stop. "Don't do that when we're out on the deep snow. If you break through the felt, you'll become a frozen gazelle yourself, and that's no joke. Now then, Chen Zhen is lighter than you, so I'll go dig out a couple of gazelles with him. After that, you two can go out on your own."

Yang jumped off and helped the old man onto the felt. Chen followed. The felt easily withstood the weight of the two men and looked as if it would hold up under the added weight of a couple of gazelles. Once they were steady, they dragged up the second roll of felt and laid it out in front of the one they were standing on. They squared the two pieces and then stepped onto the second piece. After laying down the hooked pole, they repeated the process, moving the first piece out in front of the second. This they did over and over, as if piloting a pair of felt boats, gliding toward a living gazelle.

At last, Chen Zhen was aboard one of those marvelous creations, which grassland inhabitants had devised to transport themselves across the snow and avoid calamitous blizzards. Countless Mongol herdsmen had ridden these boats over the millennia, escaping the snowy abyss and rescuing vast numbers of sheep and dogs. It had also allowed them to drag out victims of hunts by wolves and humans and to claim spoils of war abandoned on snow lakes. Rather than keeping this Mongol secret from an outsider, Bilgee was teaching the Beijing student how to use it. Chen Zhen thus had the good fortune to be the first Han Chinese to actually navigate one of those ancient, primitive boats.

From time to time, as the felt boat picked up speed, the crusty snow beneath them cracked and crunched, and Chen felt as if he were riding on a magic carpet, gliding across the snowy whiteness below, trembling with fear, excited by a sense of danger, floating like an immortal, and immensely grateful to the wolves and human inhabitants of the grassland for introducing him to an almost mythical sort of primitive life. Eight felt boats, sixteen flying carpets, converged on the snow lake as if chasing one another, raising clouds of powdery snow and sprays of ice. Dogs barked, people shouted, Tengger smiled. Suddenly a heavy cloud passed overhead, sending the temperature plummeting. Snow that had begun to melt was immediately transformed into brittle ice, which hardened the crusty surface and tripled the degree of safety in retrieving gazelles, with no need to change tactics. The men took off their sunglasses, opened their eyes wide, and looked up into the sky. "Tengger!" they shouted joyfully. "Tengger!" Now the boats picked up speed, their pilots emboldened, and at that moment Chen actually sensed the existence of the Mongols' eternal Tengger, which once more caressed his soul.

Then, without warning, shouts of joy from Yang Ke and Bayar erupted behind them. Chen turned to look. "We got one!" Yang and Bayar shouted together. "We got one!" Chen trained his telescope on them and saw that somehow, under Bayar's direction, Yang had dug a large gazelle out of the snow. They were dragging it by its leg back to the cart, while others were running up with shovels over their shoulders.

The felt boat had traveled far from the safety of the shore and was getting closer to one of the gazelles, a pregnant female with a look of fear and hopelessness in her eyes, an almost prayerful look. Surrounded by holes in the snow, she was standing on a crusty spot no bigger than a small table, which could give way at any moment. "Slide the hook over slowly," the old man said. "Don't frighten her. We're dealing with two lives here. Life on the grassland is hard for us all, and it's sometimes important to spare lives."

Chen nodded, lay down on his belly, and lightly moved the felt in front past the holes until it was up next to the female gazelle's feet. The crust was holding. Maybe the animal had been rescued before, or maybe she recognized a slim chance of survival for the fetus she was carrying, but she leaped onto the felt and immediately fell to her knees, quaking all over. She seemed paralyzed with exhaustion, nearly frozen, and frightened out of her wits.

Chen breathed a sigh of relief as the two men stepped lightly onto the front sheet of felt and carefully dragged the rear sheet around the holes in the snow, pushing it to the west, where the snow was harder. After repeating the maneuver a dozen or so times, they reached a gentle slope where holes in the snow were replaced by gazelle droppings and tracks. "All right," the old man said, "let her go. If she falls in now, it will be because Tengger wanted her to."

Chen approached the gazelle slowly and looked into her eyes. He didn't see a gazelle; he saw a docile deer about to become a mother. She possessed motherly beauty in her big, tender eyes. He rubbed the top of her head; she opened her eyes wide, now seeming to beg for mercy. Chen stroked the helpless, feeble creature kneeling at his feet, and felt his heart shudder. Why did he not strive to protect these warm, beautiful, peace-loving herbivores instead of gradually moving closer to the wolves, whose nature was to kill? Having grown up hearing tales that demonize wolves, he said without thinking, "These gazelles are such pitiful creatures. Wolves are evil, killing the innocent, oblivious to the value of a life. They deserve to be caught and skinned."

Old Man Bilgee's expression changed abruptly, and Chen nervously swallowed the rest of what he was about to say. He knew he'd offended the old man's deities and the grassland inhabitants' revered totem. But the words were out of his mouth, and there was nothing he could do about that now.

Glaring at Chen, the old man said angrily, "Does that mean that the grass doesn't constitute a life? That the grassland isn't a life? Out here, the grass and the grassland are *the* life, the big life. All else is little life that depends on the big life for survival. Even wolves and humans are little life. Creatures that eat grass are worse than creatures that eat meat. To you, the gazelle is to be pitied. So the grass isn't to be pitied, is that it? The gazelles have four fast-moving legs, and most of the time wolves spit up blood from exhaustion trying to catch them. When the gazelles are thirsty, they run to the river to drink, and when they're cold, they run to a warm spot on the mountain to soak up some sun. But the grass? Grass is the big life, yet it is the most fragile, the most miserable life. Its roots are shallow, the soil is thin, and though it lives on the ground, it cannot run away. Anyone can step on it, eat it, chew it, crush it. A urinating horse can burn a large spot in it. And if the grass grows in sand or in the cracks between rocks, it is even shorter, because it cannot grow flowers, which means it cannot spread its seeds. For us Mongols, there's nothing more deserving of pity than the grass. If you want to talk about killing, then the gazelles kill more grass than any mowing machine could. When they graze the land, isn't that killing? Isn't that taking the big life of the grassland? When you kill off the big life of the grassland, all the little lives are doomed. The damage done by the gazelles far outstrips any done by the wolves. The yellow gazelles are the deadliest, for they can end the lives of the people here." The old man's wispy goatee quivered, worse than the gazelle at their feet.

Chen Zhen was deeply moved by the old man's monologue; it beat on his heart like a war drum, persistent and painful. The inhabitants of the grassland were far ahead of any race of farmers not only in terms of battle strategies and strength of character but in their modes of thought as well. This ancient logic went to the core of why, over millennia, there has been constant and violent conflict between the carnivores and the herbivores. The old man had delivered his monologue as if he were standing on the Mongol plateau and looking down on the plains of Northern China: commanding, wolf fangs bared, forceful and resonant, pointed and convincing. Chen, who had been a skilled debater, could say nothing. Much of his worldview, based on the Han agrarian culture, crumbled in the face of the logic and the culture of the grassland. The nomadic inhabitants safeguarded the "big life"—the survival of the grassland and of nature were more precious than the survival of people. Tillers of the land, on the other hand, safeguarded "little lives"—the most precious of which were people, their survival the most important. But, as Bilgee had said, without the big life, the little lives were doomed. Chen repeated this over and over, and it pained him somewhat. But then he was reminded of the large-scale slaughter of tillers of the land by nomads throughout history, and the actions they took to return croplands to pastureland, and the doubts returned. He'd always considered these actions to be backward, regressive, and barbaric. But he was forced to reconsider his position after being scolded by the old man, who had employed the yardstick of big and little life. Both Easterners and Westerners all refer to the land as the mother of humanity. How then can anyone who does injury to Mother Earth be considered civilized?

Timidly, he asked, "Then why is it so important for you to free this gazelle?"

"Gazelles attract wolves," the old man said. "Wolves hunt the gazelles, and that makes for fewer losses of cows, sheep, and horses. The gazelles also provide extra income for the herdsmen. In fact, many Mongols rely on what they earn from hunting gazelles to build their yurts, get married, and have children. Half of a Mongol is hunter. If we could not hunt, our lives would be like meat with no salt, tasteless. We Mongols go crazy if we can't hunt, partly because that safeguards the big life of the grassland. We hunt animals that eat our grass many times more than we hunt animals that eat meat." He sighed. "There are so many things you Chinese don't understand. You read books, but what you find in them is false reasoning. Chinese write their books to advocate Chinese causes. The Mongols suffer because they can't write books. If you could turn into a Mongol and write books for us, that would be wonderful."

Chen nodded as he thought back to all the fairy tales he'd read as a child. The "gray wolves" were stupid creatures, greedy and cruel, while foxes were clever and likable. Not until coming to the grassland did he realize that in nature there is no wild animal that has evolved more highly or more perfectly than the gray wolf. Books, and especially fairy tales, he saw, often misled people.

The old man helped the gazelle to her feet and nudged her out onto the snow, in a spot where the tips of a few weeds poked through the surface. The hungry pregnant gazelle bent down and gobbled them up. Chen hurriedly pulled up the felt. The gazelle took a few wobbly steps, spotted the tracks of other gazelles, and ran off toward the ridge without looking back; she quickly vanished in the mountains.

Batu and Gasmai also brought up a live animal, a half-grown gazelle. Gasmai muttered, *"Huolehei, huolehei"* (Mercy, mercy), as she picked it up in her arms, set it down on the snowy ground, and sent it off running toward the ridge with a pat on its rump.

Chen gave Gasmai a thumbs-up. She laughed and said, "Its mother fell into a hole in the snow, and it just kept running around, not wanting to leave. We had a terrible time trying to catch it, until we managed to hold it down with our poles."

The other snow boats drew near, and the surviving gazelles on the snow lake eventually formed a small cluster that went over the mountain ridge and disappeared. The old man said, "Those animals have learned something here. In the future, the wolves won't be able to bring them down."

4

Finally, the people were able to claim their well-deserved New Year's provisions. The freezing air over the snow lake was becoming heavier, the snow on the surface harder. The old man said to the hunters, "Tengger is urging us to move quickly." So the men ran to their spots, and the hunting ground once again steamed with exuberance. Bilgee led Chen Zhen to an average-sized depression in the snow, where they stopped. "Don't look for the largest depressions," he said, "because they usually contain seven or eight suffocated gazelles, and all that heat keeps them from freezing right away. As the heat builds up overnight, the animals get bloated, their legs turn rigid, and the skin over their abdomens turns purple. As much as half the meat on them is bad by the time they finally freeze. So what you get is a frozen gazelle with half its meat inedible. At the purchasing station, you'll get less than half the price of a whole gazelle, money for the hide only, not a cent for the meat. But rotting meat is the wolves' favorite, and the gazelles buried here will be on their mind all winter. So we'll leave the choice wolf food for the wolves."

The old man lay down on the felt and thrust his hooked pole into the depression, which was at least six feet deep. He probed and probed until he abruptly jerked the pole upward. "I've hooked one," he said to Chen. "Help me pull it up." They began raising the animal, dropping it back a little between pulls to let the displaced snow fill the gap beneath it. They stood on the felt, bending over to pull the pole up; before long, the snow-covered head of a dead gazelle broke the surface. The hook had caught the animal in the throat, which preserved the integrity of the hide. Chen bent over, grabbed the gazelle (which weighed fifty or sixty kilos) by the head, and pulled it onto the felt. It was completely frozen, its abdomen neither distended nor purple; it had died and frozen quickly. "A perfect specimen," the old man said. "It'll bring the highest price."

"There are more down there," he said, taking a deep breath. "You try to snag one. It's like hooking a bucket at the bottom of a well. When you've found the right spot, pull with all your might. Don't hook it where you'll spoil the pelt and lower the price." Chen agreed eagerly, took the pole, thrust it into the depression, and began to probe. He could feel two or more gazelles down there but kept moving the pole around to outline the shape of one of them. When he felt the throat, he jerked the pole upward until it felt well snagged. At long last, Chen had caught a "big fish" in a snow lake on the Mongolian grassland. It too weighed in at fifty or sixty kilos, a quarry that could outrun even the fastest horse. Filled with excitement, he shouted to Yang Ke, who was still on the lakeshore, "Look, I caught one, a great big one! It was quite a fight!"

"Come back here, would you?" Yang Ke replied, fit to be tied. "Come back and let me have a shot at it! And let Papa get some rest."

Excited shouts rose on the lake and on the slope as large gazelles with plenty of meat and unbroken hides were brought to the surface and, one after the other, snow rafts sped to the shore. Some of the fastest workers were already out on their second voyage. The raft manned by Batu, Gasmai, and Lamjav was the most efficient. They snagged the largest gazelles unerringly and with amazing speed. When they pulled up medium or small-sized animals, or full-grown ones with distended or purple abdomens, those that would not bring in good prices, they tossed them back down into the empty depression. A rich harvest, normally only seen in the springtime, when baby lambs are born, spread across the barren, snowy plateau. Even predators sometimes turn into prey, Chen thought with grim satisfaction.

Chen and the old man sailed their raft, now weighted down with two large gazelles, back to shore, where Yang Ke and Bayar helped Bilgee step off. Chen pushed the two gazelles off the raft, and the four men dragged them over to their carts. There Chen discovered that the two carts were already piled high with large gazelles, and asked why that was. Yang Ke said, "Bayar and I bagged one of them. The rest are gifts from some of the other families. An Olonbulag custom, they said." He laughed. "Hanging around Papa has brought dividends."

Bilgee joined in the laughter. "You're citizens of the grassland too," he said. "So learn our customs and stick to them." The old man, clearly tired, sat cross-legged alongside the cart to smoke his pipe. "You two go out," he said, "but be careful. If you happen to fall in, spread your legs and stick out your arms immediately, and hold your breath. That way you won't be in too deep. Whoever's on the raft, stick in the pole, but be careful not to hook the person in the face. That will ruin your marriage prospects." He choked on his laughter. Then he told Bayar to find some kindling for a cook fire.

Bursting with excitement, Chen and Yang walked over to the felt raft, and as they neared the deep snow by the shore, Chen spotted a hole that looked like a tunnel to the depths of the snow lake. Yang Ke said with a laugh, "I didn't want to say anything a moment ago, because Papa was there beside us, but this hole in the snow, Bayar and I dug it, it's where we found that big gazelle. I tell you, that Bayar may be small, but he's got guts. When he saw you out there, he opened his fur coat and, because he weighs so little, crawled out on the snow without falling in. He found a depression before he'd gone more than five or six yards, so he crawled back and we dug a tunnel in the snow. We didn't have to dig far to reach the gazelle, so he went down and tied a rope around one of its legs. When he came back, I pulled the animal out of the snow. He was fearless, but the whole time he was down there I was worried the snow might cave in and bury him."

"That doesn't surprise me," Chen said. "Anyone who isn't afraid to grab hold of a wolf with his bare hands isn't going to be scared by a hole in the snow. Now you know what a Mongol kid is capable of doing. Just think what he'll be like when he grows up!"

"When I told him not to go down into the snow," Yang said, "he said that when he was seven, he crawled into a wolf's den and stole a litter of cubs, so a snow cave is nothing! You've talked about wanting a wolf cub, haven't you? Well, take Bayar along and get one."

"Not me," Chen replied. "These Mongols, all I can do is stand back and admire them."

As the two students rode their Mongolian snow raft, Yang's face was joyfully wrinkled. "I can't believe how great it is to hunt on the grassland. Shepherding is so boring. As soon as wolves entered the picture, our lives got a lot more interesting and a lot more exciting."

"This is a vast, sparsely populated territory," Chen said. "Sometimes there isn't a yurt within miles. Without the wolves and the hunt, life out here would be stultifying. I've gotten hooked on reading lately and it appears that these people have revered the wolf totem for thousands of years."

Having eaten braised venison with their tea that morning, they had an abundance of energy, so, with clouds of white steam bursting from their mouths, their arms and legs churning like dragon-boat racers, they skimmed the snowy surface, the two halves of their felt raft rapidly changing positions. Eventually, Yang also managed to hook a gazelle and was so excited he nearly tipped the raft over, causing Chen to break out in a cold sweat as he rushed to calm his friend down. With a smack of his hand against the frozen animal, Yang shouted, "I thought I was dreaming when I saw people hook these things and bring them up, but now I know I wasn't. This is terrific! And all thanks to you, wolves. Wolves! Wolves!"

Yang refused to turn the hooking pole over to Chen, who was too concerned with their safety to wrangle over it, and content to be his friend's muscle. All in all, Yang hooked three gazelles and got so addicted to what he was doing that he didn't want to head back to shore. With a wicked smile, he said, "Let's drag some more out and take them back all at once. More efficient that way." Without a second thought, he laid the frozen carcasses flat on top of the hardened snow.

Back on the shore, Bilgee had finished a pipeful of tobacco and was telling people to clear a wide space, where women from each family piled up broken boards, wooden axles, and the like as kindling. Then old felt was spread around and piled high with insulated bottles of milk tea and liquor, wooden utensils, and salt cellars. Sanjai and one of the boys slaughtered a pair of half-dead gazelles, both with broken legs. People on the Olonbulag only eat meat from freshly slaughtered animals, so these would serve as the hunters' noonday meal. The dogs, who had stuffed themselves with kills left behind by the wolves, gazed on the two skinned, gutted, steaming gazelles with indifference. Bilgee and the women and children speared chunks of fresh, still-twitching meat onto metal and wooden skewers, added salt, and held them over the blazing bonfire. Then they sat back to eat the meat and drink tea; its seductive fragrance, along with that of the liquor and the meat, spread across the lake and drew the hunters back to eat and rest.

By midday, all the rafts had made two or three trips to shore to unload their quarry, and each family's cart was piled high with six or seven frozen gazelles. It was time for the men to turn the work over to the well-fed women and children, who climbed aboard the felt rafts and went out onto the snow lake to bring up more animals.

Freshly roasted gazelle is a delicacy of the Mongolian grassland, especially after a hunt, when the meat is roasted and eaten on the spot. Historically, it was a favorite of the khans and royalty, and an essential component of gatherings of ordinary hunters. As newly acknowledged hunters, Chen Zhen and Yang Ke were invited to participate in the feast. The thrill of the hunt, along with sheer exhaustion, had given Chen such an appetite that he felt he appreciated the event more than any Mongol khan ever could; it was an outdoor feast for humans following an outdoor feast by a pack of wild wolves. Chen and Yang, who at that moment felt as free and powerful as any Mongol, impulsively grabbed flasks from the hands of fellow hunters who were drinking and eating and singing with fervor and passion, and gulped down great mouthfuls of liquor.

With a burst of laughter, Bilgee said, "I'd be afraid to go see your parents in Beijing a year from now, since by then I'll have turned you into Mongol savages."

"We Han could use a heavy dose of Mongol spirit," Yang Ke said, the smell of liquor strong on his breath.

At the top of his lungs, Chen Zhen shouted "Papa" three times, raised the flask in his hand above his head, and toasted the "Venerable Tribal Leader." The old man took three drinks from his flask and responded, *"Minihu, minihu, minisaihu"* (My child, my child, my good child).

Batu, giddily drunk, slapped Chen on the back and said, "You . . . you are only half a Mongol, wh . . . when you, you marry a Mongol girl . . . a woman, father a . . . a Mongol brat, then you'll be a true Mongol. You, you're on the weak side, no good, not good, not good enough. Mongol women under . . . under the bedcovers, make you work, worse than wolf . . . wolves. Mongol men, most of us, are scared of them, like sheep."

"At night," Sanjai piped in, "men are sheep, women are wolves. Especially Gasmai."

The hunters all roared with laughter.

Lamjav was in such high spirits that he flipped Yang Ke heavily onto a snowdrift. "When . . . when you can do that to me," he stammered, "that's when you . . . the day you're a Mongol." Yang grabbed hold of Lamjav and tried to wrestle him to the ground, only to be flipped head over heels three more times. Lamjav laughed. "You . . . you Han Chinese are grass-eaters, like sheep. We Mongols are meat-eaters, like wolves."

As he brushed the snow from his clothes, Yang said, "Just you wait. Next year I'm going to buy a full-grown ox and eat every bite of it myself. I plan to keep growing till I'm a head taller than you, and then you'll be like a sheep."

"Yes!" the other hunters shouted approvingly. "Good comeback!"

Grassland Mongols are known more for their capacity for liquor than for their appetite for meat. After a few rounds, all seven or eight flasks were empty. Seeing that there was no more liquor, Yang boldly proclaimed to Lamjav, "You can outwrestle me, but let's see who can outdrink who."

"Playing the fox, are you?" Lamjav retorted. "Well, out here, wolves are cleverer than foxes. Wait here. I've got more liquor." He ran over to where his horse was standing and took a bottle of clear liquor out of his felt saddlebag, that and two cups. Waving the bottle in front of Yang, he said, "I was saving this for . . . for guests, but now I'm going to use it to punish you."

"Punish!" the hunters shouted. "Punish him! Give him what he deserves!"

With an embarrassed smile, Yang Ke said, "It looks like this fox is no match for a wolf. I'll take my punishment."

"Listen . . . listen closely," Lamjav said. "To follow our custom, you . . . you must drink as many cups as I say. I misspoke myself once and was outdrunk by a journalist who knew both Mongol and Han customs. This time I'm going to make sure you taste defeat." He poured a cup and, in halfway decent Chinese, intoned, "Meadowlarks fly in pairs, two cups from a single wing."

Yang Ke blanched. "Four wings times two cups, ah! That's eight cups! How about one cup from each wing?"

"If you don't play by the rules," Lamjav replied, "I'll make it three, I mean...three cups from a single wing."

The crowd of hunters, Chen Zhen included, shouted in unison, "Drink! You must drink!"

Seeing no way out, Yang belted down eight cups, one after the other. The old man laughed. "Trying to trick a friend out here gets you into trouble every time," he said.

Chen and Yang took skewers of cooked meat from the old man and, with bloody grease dripping down their chins, ate with gusto.

"Papa," Chen said, "this is the first time I've eaten wolf food, and it's the best thing I've eaten in my life, the best meat I've ever tasted. Now I know why so many emperors and their sons were avid hunters. Taizong of the Tang, China's greatest emperor, loved to hunt. His son, his heir, used to come to the grassland with his Turkish bodyguards to ride and hunt. He even set up a grassland-style tent in the palace courtyard, where, like you, he slaughtered sheep and ate, slicing the meat off the bones with his own knife. For him, life on the grassland was better than being emperor. All he wanted was to hunt with his Turkish bodyguards under his own Turkish wolf flag, to live like a Turk on the grassland. Eventually, he lost his claim to the throne and his father picked his brother as heir. Life out here can even win over an emperor."

The old man listened wide-eyed. "You never told me that," he said. "It's a good story. It would be wonderful if all you Han could appreciate the grassland like that prince did, but it would have been better if he hadn't lost the throne. The Qing emperors often came out here to hunt and to find Mongol girls to marry. And they didn't allow their Han subjects to open the grassland to raising crops. Back then, there was no fighting between the Mongols and the Chinese; we were at peace."

Bilgee loved listening to Chen's historical tales, and repaid the debt with tales of Mongolia. "Anyone who doesn't eat wolves' food is not a true grassland Mongol. There would probably be no Mongols without it. In days past, when Mongols were driven to the brink of destruction, they survived by eating wolves' food. One of Genghis Khan's ancestors, who was driven deep into the mountains, was on the verge of starvation, like a common savage. He was reduced to following the path of wolves; whenever they had a kill, he would wait until they'd eaten their fill and moved on, then he'd eat what they left. He lived like that, alone in the mountains, for years, until his brother found him and took him home. Wolves are the Mongols' benefactors, sometimes their saviors. Without them there would have been no Genghis Khan, and no Mongols. Wolf food is delicious. See what the wolves have given us for our New Year's celebration . . . though it doesn't come that easily most of the time. That's something you'll learn someday."

The two gazelles were picked clean and the bonfire began to sputter. Bilgee had the people smother the fire with snow.

The cloud cover thickened, and blowing snow began to reach them from the mountaintops, creating a gauzy veil. The brawniest hunters boarded their snow rafts again and headed out to the snow lake. It was essential to fill the carts before the blowing snow filled in the depressions. Each gazelle hooked and brought up meant six or seven bricks of Sichuan tea or a dozen or so cartons of Haihe cigarettes from Tianjin, or fifteen or sixteen bottles of Mongolian clear liquor. Under Bilgee's command, all the rafts were maneuvered by the hunters from the deepest section of the lake to shallower spots, where it was easier to hook the frozen gazelles. The old man also divided the people into teams, the most adept users of the poles concentrating on hooking animals, and those better at manipulating the rafts focusing on transporting the animals back. As the rafts neared the shore, ropes were put to use, with several men standing at the edge of the lake flinging them like mooring lines to the carcass-laden rafts, where hunters tied one end to the raft and flung the other end back so that the men there could pull them back to shore. The process was repeated over and over.

By the time all human shadows on the snow lake had been swallowed up by mountain shadows, the carts were piled high, but there were a few men who wanted to hunt into the night by lamplight, piling the surplus gazelles on the lakeshore, with armed guards, to be picked up the following morning. Bilgee stopped them. "Tengger has given us a good day," he chastised them. "Tengger is fair. Since wolves have eaten our sheep and horses, these are the reparations. Now Tengger has started the winds blowing, telling us to leave the remaining gazelles for the wolves. Which of you is willing to disobey Tengger? Which of you is willing to stay behind in this snowdrift? If the wolves came out with a blizzard tonight, I wonder who among you would still be around tomorrow morning."

His comments were met with silence. He gave the command to head back. The exhausted but happy people pushed the heavy, overloaded carts to help the drivers navigate the hills and ridges, then mounted their horses or climbed aboard the carts and headed back to camp.

Chen Zhen felt the sweat on his body chilling. He could not stop shivering. Everywhere—on the lake and off, on the ridges and the paths through the snow—the humans had left their imprint: bonfire ashes, cigarette butts, and liquor bottles, plus tire ruts all the way back to camp. Chen kneed his horse to ride up to Bilgee. "Papa, this time the wolves lost. Will they seek revenge? You're always saying they have long memories. They remember their food and their fights—how about their enemies?"

"We dug out a lot of gazelles, but left more than half the number for the wolves. Next spring the wolves will feast on frozen gazelle and won't stick around to trouble us. Besides, they did us a favor, so we should leave them something. Don't worry, the wolf leader knows what to do."

A blizzard swept the area that night, and the students' yurt sweltered. Chen Zhen put away his copy of *The Secret History of the Mongols* and said to Yang Ke, "The man Bilgee mentioned, the one who picked over the food left by the wolves was Budoncher, Genghis Khan's great-great-grandfather's great-great-grandfather. Genghis Khan's family was part of the Borjigin tribe, whose historical founder was Budoncher. Subsequent generations would witness monumental changes."

"That must mean that if there'd been no wolves, those great war counselors and leaders, there'd have been no Genghis Khan, no golden tribe, and of course no wise and brave Mongol fighting horsemen," Yang said. "Wolves have certainly played a prominent role in the history of the Mongol people."

"Why stop there? They've played a prominent role in the lives of the Chinese, in the lives of all the world's people. The arrival of Genghis Khan and his Mongol horsemen on the scene led to a rewriting of the history of China, from the Jin and Southern Song on. So too the histories of Central Asia, Persia, Russia, and India. Gunpowder, invented in China, was introduced to the West by Mongol hordes as they cut their murderous swath through Europe and Asia, bringing down the castle of feudalism in the West and sweeping away all obstacles to the emerging system of capitalism. Gunpowder then made its way back to the East, where it blew open the door to China and, ultimately, ended the reign of the Mongol horsemen and turned the whole world upside down. But the historical impact of wolves has been written off by historians. If Tengger had recorded events, wolves on the Mongolian grasslands would have had their place in the annals of history."

Gao Jianzhong, the cowherd, could not contain his excitement over the arrival of the largesse. "What are you two doing, dredging up the ancient past? Our first priority ought to be to dig all the gazelles out of the snowbank and get rich."

Chen Zhen said, "Heaven keeps its eye out for the wolves, and we should be grateful for this cartload of gazelles. The blizzard will blow for three days at least, adding a couple of feet or more to the snowbank and filling in the depressions. Looking for gazelles in that would be like searching for a needle in a haystack."

Gao walked out of the yurt and looked up at the sky. "It's really going to blow for three days," he said when he was back inside. "I should have been there today. Damned if I wouldn't have planted poles in the largest depressions." He sighed. "I guess I'll have to wait till spring. But then I'll go out, fill up a cart, and personally take it to the purchasing station at the Bayan Gobi Commune. If you two say nothing, no one else need know."

The livestock made it through the latter half of winter without incident. The Olon wolf pack followed the gazelles far away, where it dispersed. The great blizzard did not come.

Over the lonely winter, when Chen Zhen was neither tending the sheep nor on night watch, he made his rounds of the grassland, searching out tales of wolves, spending most of his time on the legend of the "flying wolves." Known throughout the Olonbulag, it had recent origins and, as it turned out, was set in the area of Chen's production brigade. He was determined to get to the bottom of the legend and satisfy his curiosity as to how wolves were able to "fly" on the Olonbulag.

Soon after their arrival, the students had been told by herdsmen that Tengger had sent the wolves down to Earth, which meant they could fly. Over the centuries, when a herdsman died, his body was taken into the wilds and laid out in open view for the wolves to dispose of. The "sky burial" was completed once the wolves had eaten every morsel of human remains. It was called a sky burial owing to the belief that the wolves could fly to Tengger, taking the human soul back with them, just like the magic eagles of Tibet. But when the students labeled this as superstition, one of the "four olds" attacked during the Cultural Revolution, the herdsmen insisted that wolves could fly. As recently as the third year of the Cultural Revolution, they said, a pack of wolves flew into Second Brigade Cherendorji's stone enclosure, where they ate a dozen sheep and killed more than two hundred. After satisfying their appetite, they flew away. The stone wall was six or seven feet high, too high for a person to climb over, so how did the wolves get in there if they didn't fly?

Director Uljii had taken all the leaders over to see, including even the head of the police station, Harbar. After taking pictures and measurements, they agreed that the wall was too high for the wolves to jump over, and noted that there were no breaches through which they could have gotten in. Several days of investigation turned up no explanation for how the wolves had gotten in and out. But the herdsmen knew.

The tale had stuck in Chen's mind for a long time; now, as his fascination with wolves grew, it resurfaced. So he saddled up and rode out to see the wall with his own eyes. After examining it carefully, he was no closer to an explanation than anyone else, so he went to talk to the old-timer Cherendorji.

"I still don't know which of my idiot sons offended Tengger," the old man said, "but my family is cursed even today."

The old man's son, who had attended middle school, said, "The affair can be blamed on stupid pasture regulations. There were no such walls on the Olonbulag before, but headquarters decided to build stone enclosures in the birthing meadow, both to protect the sheep and to cut back on expenses by reducing the work points given out for night watches. The wolves can't climb the walls, they said, so there'll be no need for night watchmen, and everyone can sleep easy at night. So we closed the gate and stayed inside our yurt. That night I heard the dogs bark and I knew something was wrong, as if a pack of wolves was in the vicinity. But since headquarters had said there was no need to go on watch, we didn't even go out to check. Unfortunately, when we opened the gate in the morning, we were struck dumb by the sight of all those dead and dying sheep. There was blood all over the ground, as thick as two fingers in places, and more on the stone wall. The marks of four fangs stood out on the necks of the dead animals, whose blood had even flowed outside the wall. There were also several piles of wolf dung... Later on, headquarters changed the regulations, requiring people who lived near one of the enclosures to recommence night watches, for which work points would be given. More and more stone and rammed-earth enclosures have been built on the birthing meadows in recent years and, since there are night watchmen again, there have been no more stories of wolves flying into an enclosure and eating our sheep."

But that wasn't enough for Chen Zhen, who went around asking other herders. All of them—men and women, young and old—told him that wolves could fly. They also said that when a wolf dies, its soul flies up to Tengger.

Eventually, Police Chief Harbar was released from confinement in the banner interrogation unit and sent back to assume his position again. Taking a pack of Beijing cigarettes with him, Chen went to call on the chief to get an explanation as to how the wolves had "flown" in and out of the enclosure.

Chief Harbar, a graduate of the Inner Mongolian Police Academy and fluent in Chinese, said, "The case is closed. Unfortunately, the scientific explanation has no standing on the grassland, and most of the herders don't believe it. All but a few educated and experienced hunters, who accepted the results of the investigation, were convinced that the wolves could fly. If we respect the beliefs and customs of the local population" he laughed—"then the wolves flew into the enclosure. There's a bit of truth to that, since wolves do sail through the air a long ways.

"The herders were in a state of anxiety that day," he went on, "believing that Tengger was angry enough to send down a scourge. They left their herds up on the mountain and rushed back to see what was happening. Women and old men went down on their knees to Tengger. Children were so frightened they didn't cry even when grown-ups slapped them. Worried that the commotion would adversely affect production, Director Uljii gave me two days to solve the case. I called the cadres together to safeguard the site, but it had already been corrupted. All the clues on the ground outside the enclosure had been trampled on by people and sheep, and I had to examine every inch of the stone wall with a magnifying glass. Finally, on the outside of the northeast corner of the wall, I found two faint, bloody wolf-paw prints. That solved the case. Can you guess how the wolves got in?"

Chen shook his head.

"I determined," Chief Harbar said, "that one large wolf had leaned its front paws against the wall, rear legs on the ground, and made its body available as a springboard. The other wolves ran full speed, jumped on its back and shoulders, and sailed into the enclosure. From inside, wouldn't it look like they flew in?"

Amazed by what he was hearing, Chen said, "Those Olonbulag wolves are incredibly smart. Almost as soon as the stone enclosures went up on the grassland, they figured out how to deal with them. It's like they're bewitched... The herders aren't that far off when they say that the wolves can fly. And when they fell out of the sky in the midst of the sheep, the flock must have been scared half to death. The rest was easy. After a killing frenzy, they ate their fill, all but the poor wolf springboard on the other side of the wall. It got nothing. It must have been a special animal, devoted to the pack, obviously an alpha male."

Chief Harbar laughed heartily. "Wrong," he said. "The way I see it, that wolf flew in and ate just as much as the others. You should know that these wolves have a strong collective spirit; they stick together. It's not in their nature to abandon one of their own. A wolf on the inside acted as a springboard for another one, which had eaten its fill, to leap back across the wall. Then it acted as a springboard for the hungry wolf to fly into the enclosure and eat its fill. Those two bloody paw prints were left by the second wolf. How else would they have been bloody? The first wolf hadn't made a kill when it was the springboard, so its paws were clean, no blood. Right? Think about it. They played a neat trick on the people. The pack was inside the enclosure, where it killed at will. The people built the wall to keep the wolves out, but wound up keeping the sheepdogs out instead. I guarantee you that Cherendorji's dogs' anger pushed their noses out of joint. They weren't smart enough to follow the wolves' example; nor would they if they could have, because once they flew inside, they'd have been no match for the smarter wolves."

"They're smarter than me too," Chen said. "But one problem remains. How did the last member of the pack get out safely? Where was its springboard?"

The question delighted Chief Harbar. "People really are stupider than wolves," he said. "That's what puzzled everybody back then too. That is, until Director Uljii went into the enclosure, sloshing through all the blood. He discovered a pile of six or seven sheep carcasses up against the northeast wall, and everyone assumed that the last wolf was one of the smartest and most powerful pack leaders. All by itself, it had made a springboard out of a pile of sheep carcasses and flown out of the enclosure. There were those who didn't think one wolf could have managed it alone, and that several of them had done the piling, then jumped out. When it was all over, Director Uljii summoned the team leaders to the site and described to them how the wolves had leaped into the enclosure, and back out. That brought a sense of calm to the pasture. Cherendorji was not punished, but Director Uljii made a self-criticism, acknowledging that he'd underestimated the wolves, that he'd taken them too lightly."

Chen Zhen's hair stood on end. Although he accepted the chief's conclusion, from that day on fantastic images of flying wolves frequently visited his dreams, and he often woke up drenched in cold sweat. No longer did he treat grassland legends simply as entertainment.

Several days passed, and Chen decided to get a close look at the brigade's two open-air sky-burial sites. One was on the northern slope of Mount Chagantolgai, the other on the northeastern slope of Black Rock Mountain. At first glance the two burial sites looked pretty much like other hillside grazing land. But up close, there were distinct differences. Both were far from the ancient nomadic trails, in a bleak location north of the grasslands' sacred mountains, close to wolf territory and to Tengger, thereby shortening the distance that souls had to travel to reach heaven. In addition, the ground was rocky and uneven, bumpy enough for the carts.

For centuries on the Olonbulag, when a herder died, people stripped him naked and tied his body up in a roll of felt, although sometimes they left the corpse clothed so they could forego the felt. Then they loaded the corpse onto a cart on which a long board had been laid across the shafts and made secure. In the predawn hours, two senior male members of the family, each holding one end of the board, drove the cart to the sky-burial site, where they whipped their horses into a gallop. Inevitably, the deceased bounced out of the cart, and that was the spot where the soul would return to Tengger. The two relatives dismounted and, if the corpse was naked, unrolled the felt and lay the deceased out on the grass, facing the sky, exactly the way he (or she) came into the world, naked and innocent. At that moment, the deceased belonged to the wolves, and to the gods. Whether or not the soul of the deceased would enter Tengger depended on the virtues, or their lack, of the life lived. Generally speaking, that would be known within three days. If, by then, nothing but bones was left of the corpse, the soul of the deceased had entered Tengger. But if the deceased remained more or less whole, the family was thrown into a panic. There were, however, many wolves on the Olonbulag, and Chen had never heard of a single person whose soul had not entered Tengger.

He had known of Tibetan sky burials, but not until arriving on the grassland had he discovered that it was also a Mongol practice, with wolves replacing eagles as the burial agents. Since all herdsmen of the Olonbulag would one day wind up in the bellies of wolves via the sky burial, they had, for millennia, been at peace with the idea of death.

Chen's sense of dread was overcome by his curiosity. After learning the precise locations of the burial sites from the proprietor of wagons who delivered production materials, he secretly went out twice to observe burials. Each time, unfortunately, the sites were covered by snow and he missed what he'd hoped to see. But then one day, as winter was about to give way to spring, he spotted the tracks of horses and cart ruts in the snow leading in the direction of one of the burial sites. He followed the tracks until he came upon the corpse of an old man who had died a natural death and had, it seemed, been there a short time. The snow was disturbed by fresh animal and human tracks in addition to the wheel ruts; not even the powdery snow had been blown away. The old man lay there looking peaceful and innocent, supine, his body blanketed by a thin layer of powder, a look of devotion on his smooth, seemingly veiled face.

The anxiety and the dread Chen had experienced on the way over were gradually supplanted by a sense of the sacred. The dead man exhibited no sign of someone meeting death, but of someone attending a feast in Tengger, a second baptism, a rebirth. At that moment, Chen shared the reverence in which the grassland Mongol people held the wolf totem. At the end of a life, the body was served up as an unadorned sacrificial offering, providing a clean and absolute liberation; now Chen understood the deep reverence of the Mongols for Tengger, the wolves, and the souls they entrusted to them. He had no heart to loiter at that sacred place, fearful of agitating the soul of the deceased and of desecrating the sacred beliefs of the grassland people; so, with a respectful bow to the old man, he led his horse away from the burial site.

Three days later, the family of the deceased had nothing to worry about, which greatly relieved Chen Zhen. The family, following local custom, had gone to verify the burial and must have seen the traces of an outsider among the tracks of men and horses; but none came to Chen Zhen with accusations. That would not have been so had the soul not gone up to Tengger. Chen, realizing that his curiosity and interests had begun to clash with his hosts' totems and taboos, took care to concentrate on tending his sheep and working hard, even as he sought to move closer to the mysterious people about whom he was so curious and whom he so deeply respected.

Spring came strangely early that year, more than a month earlier than usual. Warm winds turned the Olonbulag a golden yellow. Autumn grass, pressed down by the snow for an entire winter, burst onto the surface, and on some of the slopes that faced the sun a smattering of green buds appeared. Dry winds and warm days came hard on the heels of these changes, and when the teams went to their birthing meadows, the people were kept busy with wildfire prevention and antidrought measures to safeguard newborn animals.

Gao Jianzhong was too late. Laborers and members of the floating population who had streamed into the city to work in transportation and construction teams had, earlier in the year, viewed with envy the lively scene that occurred when Gasmai's team had brought cartloads of gazelles to the purchasing station. They had crowded around the hunters, trying to learn the whereabouts of the hunt. After being told that all the frozen gazelles had been retrieved, they had approached Bayar with candy from the Northeast, but he had directed them to an empty mountain valley. Finally, these men, mostly Mongol outsiders from Manchurian farms, had found the grassland Mongols' weakness—liquor. They had gotten the shepherd Sanjai drunk and learned the location of the gazelles. Moving quickly, they had beat the wolf pack and Gao Jianzhong by arriving just as the gazelles were breaking through the surface of the snow. They had pitched a camp nearby and, within a single day, retrieved every last animal, big and small, good and bad. They had then loaded them onto carts and transported them overnight to the purchasing station at the Bayan Gobi Commune.

Over the next several nights, the horse herders heard the plaintive, angry howls of hungry wolves echo up and down the valley. They grew tense, keeping close watch over their horses, never letting them stray from their sight. The lovers they'd left behind in yurts, knowing that there would be a high price to pay for the wolves' hunger, beat their livestock out of anger and sang sad songs, bitter melodies of frustration.

Soon after, a formal notice arrived from headquarters reinstating the once annual tradition of stealing wolf cubs. The rewards were to be higher than in previous years, thanks to the personal intervention of Bao Shungui, the military representative. Word had it that the wolf-cub pelts would bring in a better price than ever. Those pelts, soft and shiny, rare and expensive, were used for women's leather jackets, and were cherished items of the wives of northern officials; they also provided hard currency for lower-ranking officials willing to do business out the back door.

Bilgee was silent, smoking one pipeful after another. Chen overheard him mutter, "The wolves will soon have their revenge."

5

Dense dark clouds raced over from the northern horizon, tumbling and roiling their way through the blue sky, ferocious as dense smoke or a black fire. In a matter of seconds, clouds swallowed up many miles of mountain ranges, like a colossal black hand pressing down on the pastureland. Off to the west, the orange-colored sun was not yet consumed, as a northern wind carrying powdery snow swept quickly across the vast Olonbulag. Swirling flakes sparkled in the slanting rays of sunlight like hungry locusts.

A Mongol proverb: Wolves follow the wind. For decades, the Olonbulag pack, which had fought guerrilla wars on both sides of the border, took advantage of the rare early spring to come south, leap across fire breaks, and force its way past guarded public roads to return to the grassland. The wolves had suffered the bitter cold and, since there was little grass, scant prey, which had left them desperately hungry. But the cache of frozen gazelles in their home territory had been pillaged, while beyond their territory famine raged, making it impossible to catch the light-footed gazelles. Great numbers of starving wolves had formed a pack on the frontier, eyes burning red as they entered the territory; their appetites were gargantuan, their killing methods ruthless, their behavior unmindful of consequences. Alpha males, filled with murderous thoughts of revenge, and ready to die for food, led the pack ever nearer, at a time when the people were so caught up in raids on wolf dens that they were oblivious to the scourge bearing down on them.

During the latter half of the 1960s, if rain was predicted, a drought occurred; if a clear, bright day was on tap, the sun never made an appearance. "Those weather reports are a joke," Director Uljii commented. Except for Bilgee and some of the other old-timers, who worried that the pasture leadership had taken too many people away from their jobs to raid wolf dens, no one had anticipated the early spring or the wolf scourge. The men at the frontier station, who had always shown concern for the herders and the livestock production, failed to warn of what was on its way. In the past, when they discovered tracks of a wolf pack during their rounds, they notified headquarters and the herdsmen. Low hills occupied the frontier grazing land, offering neither cover nor barriers, and arctic currents produced blizzards known locally as white-hair winds. Wolves, unmatched at climatological warfare, often launched lightning strikes during blizzard conditions.

A new herd of horses had recently been guided to a patch of fine grazing land on the Olonbulag, seventy or eighty of the finest horses among the dozens of herds belonging to a certain regiment of the Mongolian mounted militia. They had been sent there to await the results of a medical examination. If none of the horses was found to be suffering from glanders, they could be on the road. Given the tensions of war preparedness, the herdsmen were saddled with great responsibility. The military representative and revolutionary committee had specifically selected four dependable, vigilant, and courageous herdsmen, who were also excellent horsemen, divided them into two teams, and assigned them the task of watching over the horses twenty-four hours a day. The two teams were led by Batu, who was a company commander in the Second Militia Group. In order to keep the horses from running back to their own herds, he ordered all the other herds moved to a distance of several miles. The breezes were light, the spring air warm, the water clear, the grass lush; the year's first buds had appeared, setting the scene for a contented herd of warhorses that happily stayed together. The four herdsmen took their task seriously, and all was well for several days.

Suddenly the gentle breezes were replaced by sweeping gale-force winds. Lake water poured onto the grassland, and livestock began breaking out of their pens. Yurts set up along wind tunnels were blown upside down, turned into huge bowls that tumbled briefly before falling to pieces. Carts heading into the wind lost their felt canopies, which flew off into the sky. The blowing snow was so dense that anyone riding a horse could see neither the head nor the tail of his mount. The snow stung like buckshot, whistling through the air as it tore millions of white scars across the sky. Old Man Bilgee said that in ancient times there had been a shaman who exclaimed, "Blizzard, blizzard, the madness of a white goblin with unkempt hair!" The shaman's words had survived into modern times. Everywhere between heaven and earth on the grassland, the mere mention of a blizzard struck fear into man and beast. People screamed, horses neighed, dogs barked, and sheep bleated—a cacophony that came together in a single sound: the crazed howls of the monstrous white-hair blizzard.

People preparing to continue their nightly foraging

for wolf dens were stranded in the mountains, with no way in or out. Hunters heading home lost their way. Laborers, the old and the sick, women, and children who stayed behind to tend livestock were kept busy chasing down and penning up stray animals. On the grassland, the ability to hold on to savings accumulated over years of labor was often tested in the space of a single day or night.

The primary target of an organized attack by the wolf pack that had crossed the border was the thriving herd of warhorses. Bilgee, who assumed that the horses had already been sent off as ordered, secretly rejoiced when the blizzard rose up. He later learned that the herd's departure had been delayed by one day, pending the medical report, and that the person who was to deliver the report had chosen instead to follow the military representative up the mountain to look for wolf cubs. A larger number had been found that year than usual, more than a hundred from at least a dozen dens, and grieving mothers whose cubs had been taken joined the pack, turning it especially frenzied and cruel.

Bilgee said, "Tengger has presented the wolf leader with this opportunity. There's no doubt that the white wolf king, so familiar with the Olonbulag, has chosen this path to vengeance."

At the first sound of wind, Batu had burst out of the small yurt for the temporary herders. After several night watches in a row, this was supposed to be his day of rest. He was exhausted, as was his horse, but he could not sleep and hadn't closed his eyes all day. Having grown up around horses, he had suffered through many blizzards and had often been victimized by wolves. But now a number of uneventful days had put him on edge, and his nerves were as taut as the string of a Mongolian lute.

The slightest breeze, the mere swaying of grass made his ears buzz. All the seasoned herders had committed to memory a grassland maxim, written in blood: On the Mongolian grassland, peace does not follow peace, but danger always follows danger.

The moment he stepped out of the yurt, he could smell the coming blizzard, and when he saw the direction of the wind, his broad ruddy face turned a grayish purple and his amber eyes glowed with fear. He rushed back into the yurt and nudged his sleeping comrade, Laasurung. Then, in rapid order, he picked up his flashlight, loaded his rifle, looped his herding club over his wrist, put on his fur deel, doused the fire in the stove, and picked up fur jackets for the two men watching the horses. He and his comrade, rifles slung over their backs and carrying long flashlights, mounted up and galloped north to where the herd was grazing.

As soon as the sun set behind the mountains, the grassland was cloaked in darkness. The two riders had no sooner reached the bottom of a slope than they were met head-on by the blizzard, like a tidal wave or an avalanche. It swallowed them up. The men choked on the wind until their faces turned purple; the pounding snow pellets forced them to shut their eyes. The horses too succumbed to fear, throwing their heads up in a desperate attempt to turn and flee from the wind. The men had started out shoulder to shoulder, but Batu, who could not see his hand in front of his face, shouted frantically; there was no response from Laasurung. Wind and snow consumed everything in a raging howl. Batu reined in his horse, wiped the frost from his forehead, and tried to calm himself. Then he tucked the flashlight under his arm and turned it on. Usually, it would light up the area like a searchlight, sending out a beam that could illuminate a horse at a hundred yards or more. Now he could see no more than a few yards ahead; dense horizontal strands of white hair filled his sight. Suddenly, a snowman and snowhorse entered the beam and, at the same time, sent a weak light his way. The two men made circles in the air with their flashlights as they strained to control their panic-stricken mounts. Finally, they were side-by-side again.

Batu grabbed Laasurung, raised one of his earflaps, and shouted into his ear. "Stay here, don't move. This is where we need to stop the herd. Then we'll drive it east. We have to avoid the small lake at Jiazi Mountain at all costs. All is lost if we don't."

Laasurung shouted back, "My horse is spooked, the way it gets when there are wolves around. If there are, how will the four of us manage?"

"As if our lives depended on it," Batu shouted.

They aimed their flashlights to the north and waved them back and forth as a signal to their two comrades.

A gray horse appeared in the two beams of light; it slowed and stopped next to Batu, as if it had found its savior. The gray was snorting anxiously. It had been bitten below the neck, and blood leaking from the steaming wound formed lines of red ice. The sight of blood spooked Laasurung's mount, who trampled the ground in a frenzy, then lowered its head, thrust out its neck, and single-mindedly galloped off with the wind. Batu spun around and raced after his comrade; the gray ran into the blinding snow.

By the time Batu managed to catch up to Laasurung and grab the reins of his horse, the herd was right next to them. All the horses he could see with the aid of his flashlight were as spooked as the big gray. They whinnied into the wind, their shuddering hooves madly kicking up waves of snow that obscured the ferocious, turbulent whirlwind down below their flanks. When Batu and Laasurung fearfully shone their lights down there, the sight so unnerved Laasurung that he fell forward and wrapped his arms around his horse's neck, all that kept him from falling off. The beams of light were not so dim that the two sharp-eyed herders could not make out the outlines of wolves, one or more of whom was sinking its fangs into every horse the men could see. The fur of the pack leader was inlaid with snow driven there by the wind, turning it a spectral white. The wolves' bodies appeared larger than usual, terrifyingly large, and so white it made the men's skin crawl. A white wolf pack, a ghostly wolf pack, an evil wolf pack that frightened the herders half to death. Wolves that normally turned and ran in fear from flashlights were so set on revenge that they were uncommonly ferocious and fearless, led by the alpha male and the mother wolves.

When Batu and Laasurung realized that the other two herdsmen were nowhere to be seen, they assumed they were half frozen by the blizzard, or had been taken away by their terrified mounts. Since they had been on a day watch, they were unarmed and had no flashlights; nor were they protected by fur jackets. Batu was forced to make a painful decision. "Forget about them," he said. "Saving the horses is more important!"

The herd was still running in the beam from Batu's flashlight, seventy or eighty Ujimchin warhorses, the treasure of a dozen herds and dozens of horse herders; of noble bloodlines, famous as warhorses throughout Mongol history, they were known historically as Turks. Fine-looking steeds, they were able to endure hard, taxing work; they feared neither hunger nor thirst; and they held up well in boiling heat and bitter cold. Able to run long distances at great speeds, they were normally ridden only by their herders and headquarters leaders. If they wound up as food for the wolves or drowned in the lake while fleeing, the other herders would, just like the wolves, tear Batu and his comrades to shreds.

Seeing that Laasurung was holding back, Batu dug his knees into his horse, rode over, and smacked his comrade on the head, then nudged Laasurung's horse toward the herd. He aimed his flashlight at the other man's face and shouted, "If you run away, I'll kill you myself!"

"I'm not afraid," Laasurung shouted back, "but this horse is." He jerked the reins to bring the horse under control, then flicked on his flashlight and, waving the herding club over his head, charged toward the herd. He and Batu led the horses with their lights, beat the recalcitrant animals with their clubs, and got them to follow the rest of the herd to the east instead of running with the wind. Batu reckoned that they were nearing the small lake, no more than three or four miles away. The big, broad-chested geldings had none of the burdens of ordinary horses—pregnant mares, young horses, or old ones. They were so fleet-footed that in less than half an hour the entire herd could be stuck in the muddy lake. The biggest problem the men faced was that the lake was narrow from north to south and wide from east to west, which meant that it spread horizontally directly ahead of them, difficult to skirt unless the direction of the wind changed. In Batu's mind, it was the gaping mouth of a gargantuan demon, waiting for a feast of fat horses, delivered by the wind devil and wolf god.

The direction of the blizzard—due south—did not vary, and the wind raised a steady howl. Even in the dark, Batu could get a feel for the topography by changes in the way his horse trampled the grass. He could tell where he was and where he was going by the alignment of the earth's veins and the spongy quality of the ground. He was beyond restless, feeling that the female wolves whose dens had been plundered were more frenzied even than the alpha male. He disregarded the fact that he was surrounded by wolves, ignored the possibility that they could bring down his mount at any moment, and ignored the prospect of his horse losing its footing and sending him down into the midst of a starving, vengeful, enraged pack of wolves. He ignored it all as he screamed and shouted and struck out madly with his herding club. He had but one thought on his mind, and that was to stabilize the horses and keep the herd together as he drove them eastward, around the lake, and from there to the yurts, where men and dogs could fight off the wolves.

Led by flashlights and beaten by two herders who refused to leave them, the horses gradually regained their poise. A white horse took the lead, raising its head and whinnying loudly as a sign that it was assuming leadership of the herd. Batu and Laasurung immediately shone their lights on this new leader, whose presence provided a stimulus for the others to quickly reestablish the disciplined unity of Mongolian warhorses, as they organized themselves in the traditional battle array necessary to fight this enemy. The lead horse sounded the battle cry, drawing the herd around it and forming a seemingly impregnable rampart of horses. Hundreds of hooves struck with great force, stomping, crushing, kicking. Caught by surprise, the savage wolves suddenly lost their tactical advantage. The few that had been caught in the circle could not get out from under the horses' bellies; their legs were broken, their spines smashed, their heads crushed. The shrill, demonic, agonizing wails were more hideous than the sound of the blizzard. Batu began to breathe a little easier, knowing that no fewer than three of the wolves had been killed or injured by the horse hooves. He committed the spot to memory, for when the wind died out and the sky was clear again, he'd return to skin the fallen predators. With these kills behind them, the horses closed ranks, with more timid members of the herd protected by an outer rank of stronger horses. Using explosive force, they formed a line of defense against a pack of wolves that resembled a chain of iron fists.

The lake was drawing nearer, and Batu was satisfied with the formation of the herd, which made giving commands easy; so long as he could control the lead horse, safely reaching the eastern edge of the lake was certainly possible. But remnants of fear remained stuck in his heart, for this was no ordinary pack. Striking out at a crazed wolf only increased its savagery and led to even more frenzied killing. Everyone who lived on the grassland feared the vindictiveness of a crazed wolf. The entire pack surely heard the agonizing wails of its injured brethren, and danger lurked on all sides. Batu saw that many of the horses had sustained injuries. But these were fine warhorses, steeled in battles with wolves, and so, wounded or not, they still ran in formation, refusing to give an opening for further attacks.

That said, the herd had a fatal flaw. Made up exclusively of geldings, it lacked a "son horse," a powerful uncastrated animal that could be counted on to carry the fight to the wolves. On the Mongolian grassland, herds of horses were made up of a dozen or more families, large and small, and each family was led by what was known as a "son horse." These horses, whose flowing manes reached their knees, sometimes even touching the ground, were a head taller than the other horses in the family, valiant males that were true leaders and fearless killers. Whenever they encountered wolves, the son horses formed the herd into a circle, with females and young horses on the inside, males on the outside, while they remained on the margins to fight the enemy head-on, manes flying, flared nostrils snorting, rearing up on their hind legs, a flesh-and-blood mountain suspended above the wolves. When such a horse came thundering down, it crushed the wolves' heads and torsos with its enormous hooves. And if a wolf turned tail and ran, the horse lowered its head and gave chase, fiercely kicking out and nipping at its flanks. The largest and most ferocious of these horses had been known to pick up wolves with their teeth and fling them into the air, waiting for them to hit the ground before stomping them to death. Even the most savage wolves were no match for son horses, which kept vigil over their herds, day and night. They protected their families not only against wolf packs but also against lightning strikes and wildfires, minimizing injuries to mates, offspring, and the very old and always leading them to safety.

Batu wished he had a son horse at that moment, but the white horse that took the lead was a gelding, like all the others; while it was clearly powerful, it lacked aggressiveness, which meant a less potent tendency to attack. Batu grumbled inwardly. It had been years since the military had come to the grassland to recruit horses, and people had neglected the consequences of not having a son horse in a herd of warhorses. Even if they'd pondered the matter, they'd figured that the horses would be taken away within days anyway, at which time the pastureland would play no further role. There'd been only a slim chance of something going wrong, and yet the wolves had found an opening. Batu was forced to admire the vision of the leader, which had likely known that this was a herd without a son horse.

Batu rushed to the front and whipped the lead horse as hard as he could to get it moving to the east, at the same time switching hands to grip his semiautomatic rifle and release the safety; he'd fire only when it was absolutely necessary, for these were novice warhorses and gunfire would likely scatter them. Like Batu, Laasurung prepared for what was coming. The blizzard had increased in intensity, and the two horsemen were so exhausted they could barely wave their herding clubs. But the lake drew nearer. Under normal conditions, by this time they could have smelled the alkali.

Batu, his eyes red from the tension, decided to fight fire with fire. He sat up in the saddle, thumped the lead horse on the head, and let loose with a shrill watering whistle. All the horses appeared to understand their herder's warning: the lake where they were taken to drink once every two days was due south. The spring season had been characterized by drought, and the lake had nearly dried up. It was surrounded by muddy land, and only in two spots, where watered animals had tamped down the dirt, was there a measure of safety; everywhere else was a death trap. Since the beginning of spring, a number of domestic animals had suffocated in the mud or starved when they could not free themselves from it. Each time the horses went to drink, they were led nervously down safe paths to the water by whistles from their herders. They would never have rushed toward the lake at this speed on their own, even during the daytime.

But Batu's whistling did the trick. The horses, so familiar with the grassland, understood that danger awaited them to the south. They whinnied forlornly, shaking all over; they stopped, changed direction, and, with the intense wind now coming at them from the side, galloped to the southeast for all they were worth. Due south lay a trap of sticky mud; due north was where the wind and vicious wolves waited, leaving only the southeast as a possible road to safety. Panic filled their wide eyes as they ran madly, heads lowered. Sounds of labored breathing replaced the whinnies as the herd raced against death under a cloud of tension and terror.

The shift in direction changed the face of battle. As the formation headed to the southeast, the poorest fighters, those with the weakest defenses, were suddenly exposed to the wind and the wolves, while those whose rear hooves were most capable of dispensing death and injury were out of position. The gale-force winds slowed the pace of the herd and weakened its ability to ward off the wolf-enemy's weapons. The wind lent the wolves wings. Under normal circumstances, wolves can outrun horses, with the wind or against it. But with the wind, even though they are faster, they would not dare to try to bring horses down from the rear, afraid of meeting up with a clever horse that might suddenly dart ahead, causing the wolf, aiming for the back of its prey, to land on its hooves; injury or death would be inevitable. To be successful, they would have to attack obliquely. But that would affect the speed of attack. Even if they somehow managed to leap onto the horse's back, sinking claws or fangs into the animal would be all but impossible; at most they would leave a few gouges as the attack failed. But this change in direction gave the pack an ideal chance to make a kill. With the wind behind them, and a slowing herd of horses, there was no need to attack obliquely. They needed only to leap from the side, the wind propelling them onto the horses' backs or necks, where they could dig in their claws and clamp down on the horses' vital spots with their razor-sharp fangs, then jump to the ground. If a horse tried to dislodge the wolf by rolling on the ground, one wolf would be taken care of, but the rest of the pack would make the kill in short order.

Desperate cries rose from the herd as the wolves tore into one horse after another—sides and chests spurted blood, the stench of which drove the crazed predators to commit acts of frenzied cruelty. The raw meat in their mouths meant nothing to the wolves; only the murderous tearing of horseflesh mattered. More and more horses suffered grievous injuries as wave after wave of wolves attacked. The wolves that led each charge and those that followed were absolutely wild; they leaped onto the backs of horses, gathered their strength, clamped down with their feet, and bounced around like taut springs as they tore off chunks of hide, hair, and flesh with their razor-sharp teeth. After spitting out what they held in their mouths, they leaped to the ground, did a somersault, regained their feet, ran a few steps, and pounced on another horse. The entire pack followed the example of its lead males. Every wolf was giving full and vivid play to the killing instincts passed down by its ancestors.

The herd was being decimated; blood stained the snow on the ground. The merciless grassland was once again a backdrop to ruthlessness, as it had been for thousands of years. Wolf packs had gobbled up countless fresh souls and, generation after generation, left their bloody imprint on the thin grassy slopes.

In the pale, murky light of their flashlights, the two herdsmen were witness to the slaughter. Although it seemed like an annual ritual, it was harder to accept this time, because these celebrated horses, representing the glory of the Olonbulag, were to be handed over to the military, and had, until now, managed to escape all the wolf massacres; they were the pride of the herdsmen who had desperately and anxiously brought them to maturity. Seeing the horses being butchered had Batu and Laasurung beyond tears. They were choked with anger and anxiety, but they knew they had to brave it out, suppress their emotions, remain calm, and do everything in their power to protect the horses that were still alive. Batu's worries mounted. Years of experience told him that this was no ordinary wolf pack. It was led by astute animals who knew the Olonbulag well, and included male wolves crazed by hatred over having their food plundered, and even more by crazed females who had lost their litters. But the alpha wolf was anything but crazed. His scheme became clear by the way the pack had driven the horses south. The alpha wolf was intent on driving the herd to the lake at all costs. That was a common wolf strategy. Batu's sense of dread grew. He'd seen wolves trap gazelles in mud, and he'd occasionally seen them drive cows and horses into muddy ground. From old-timers he'd heard of wolves trapping horses in pools, and he wondered if this was the night he was fated to have encountered one of those packs. Could they possibly swallow up an entire herd of horses? He forced himself to stop thinking those thoughts.

After signaling Laasurung with his flashlight to follow, Batu raced desperately from behind the herd all the way around to the east to block its passage; both men waved madly, struck madly, and harassed the wolves with their herding clubs and flashlights. Wolves are afraid of bright light; it hurts their eyes. By racing up and back, flashing the beams of their flashlights, the riders managed to hold the line east of the horses, whose terror seemed to lessen a bit. They quickly straightened out their stride and raced toward the east edge of the lake; this would be their last chance. The herd knew it had only to skirt the lake, then it could race with the wind all the way to the birthing basin, where there were many yurts and many people who could shout and shine blinding lights, and where their good friends—mean, snarling dogs who would fight the wolves until stopped by their masters—waited.

But wolves are demonic fighters with incredible patience in locating and waiting for opportunities. And when those opportunities arrive, they squeeze them until there is nothing left but pulp. Now that they had set the stage and found the opportunity, they had to make it theirs, do whatever it took to not let a single horse slip through the net.

Man, horse, and wolf ran in tandem. The wolf pack briefly called off the attack. Batu's hands were sweating from clutching the stock of his rifle. Ten years of tending horses told him that the wolves were massing for a final surge; the opportunity to mount a successful attack would be lost otherwise, and this pack was in no mood to abandon its chance for revenge.

But before he could control his shaking enough to fire, terrified whinnies erupted from the herd and his own mount seemed to stumble. He rubbed his burning, teary eyes and shone his light in front, illuminating several large wolves loping ahead of his horse. Turning to look behind him, Batu saw that Laasurung was in the same predicament. Struggling to ease his horse's fears at the very moment the wolves began to attack, he flashed a signal for Laasurung to catch up, but Laasurung's mount was too terrified to do anything but kick and buck. The wolves were taking turns pouncing on it, tearing flesh from its body. Eventually, the hem of Laasurung's deel was ripped off, causing such panic he barely knew where he was. He threw away his herding club, which was too long to be of any use, and employed the thick handle of his flashlight as a weapon, battering the heads of the leaping wolves. The light went out, the handle was crushed, the heads of wolves were split open, but the alternating attack continued. Finally, one of the largest wolves took a bite out of the horse's shoulder, driving the animal crazy with pain. Abandoning its rider's flirtation with danger, the horse chomped down on the bit, lowered its head, and took off toward the southwest, fleeing for its life. Laasurung was powerless to hold it back, no matter how hard he pulled on the reins. Seeing they'd driven a troublesome combatant from the field of battle, the wolves broke off the chase, turned, and headed back to the herd.

Batu, now alone, was surrounded. Acting out of desperation, he transformed himself from a herdsman into a Mongol warrior. He and the wolves were in a fight to the death, and for the first time in a long time, he prepared to use the wolf-fighting skills and devious tactics that had come down to him through the centuries. His club was as long as a cavalry sword, a weapon given to him by Bilgee, the kind that his ancestors had used to fight and kill wolves. The tip of the sturdy club, which was as thick as a shovel handle, had rows of iron coils, the spaces between stained with the dried blood of generations of wolves. Several of the large wolves took turns pouncing on his horse from both sides, which gave him the necessary angle to use his club, his best chance that night to kill wolves. Everything depended on his nerve and his aim.

He was ready. Taking a deep breath, he turned his light to the right and raised the club over his head. Seeing an opening, he twirled his arm and brought the club down as hard as he could on the hardest yet most vulnerable spot on a wolf's head—its fangs. The airborne wolf, claws bared, had all four of its fangs smashed by the force, a mortal blow.

The wolf fell to the snowy ground, where it licked mouthfuls of blood and raised its head to the skies to howl, the sound of grief more chilling than a death cry. On the grassland a wolf's fangs have always sustained its life. Without them, the wolf is lost. No longer can it hunt its favorite prey, large domestic animals; no longer can it defend itself against hunting dogs or rival wolves; no longer can it rip and tear, feast on chunks of meat and mouthfuls of blood; no longer can it adequately replenish its energy on the unforgiving grassland.

Caught up in the stink of death, as one horse after another was killed, Batu was bent on killing wolves and giving the pack a taste of a grasslander's ferocity. Before the other wolves could regroup, he saw another opening and swung hard. But though his aim was off, he managed to strike the animal on its snout, ripping the flesh from the bone. The animal fell to the snowy ground, where it curled up into a writhing ball of fur. With two large members of the pack howling in pain, the other wolves seemed temporarily cowed into submission by Batu's skills and might. Abruptly shaken from their fury, they stopped leaping and pouncing; yet they remained in the space between Batu and his herd.

Now that he had beaten off the attack, Batu looked

over at the herd, sensing that time was running out for them but at the same time aware that the wolves behind them had suffered a setback. They set up a quivering buzz like wind whistling past electric wires, a sound filled with deathly terror and agitation.

Under the command of its leader, the pack launched yet another offensive, employing the cruelest, bloodiest, most inconceivably suicidal methods in the arsenal of Mongolian wolves. One after the other, especially females that had lost their cubs, they leaped onto horses, sinking their fangs into the tender spot below the shoulder, then hung there heavily, willing to sacrifice their own bodies. This tactic was dangerous to both horse and wolf. As the horse ran, the lower half of the wolf's body became wedged between its rear legs, where, as the panicky victim tried to throw its tormenter off, its powerful hooves could shatter the attacker's bones and tear her hide, even disembowel her. Only the largest and strongest wolves could hang on with no leverage, eventually ripping the horse's abdomen with their fangs and then dropping to the ground in safety. If the horse failed to kick the wolf from its body, the predator's weight would slow it down, until it was set upon by the pack and killed. If it managed to kick the wolf, the added force could well accelerate the mortal injury to its abdomen.

The horses attacked in this way, as well as the suicidal attackers, all shuddered as if in tragic despair.

Most of the wolves who brought down horses at the cost of their own lives were female. They were lighter than the males, making it more difficult for them to rip open the horses' abdomens simply by hanging on, so they had to rely on the might of the horse itself. They offered up their lives, obsessed with vengeance, staring death calmly in the face, devoted to the cause, merging blood and milk. They faced the danger of fatal wounds to belly, chest, organs, and teats with a willingness to die alongside the horses they killed.

Horses whose bellies had been ripped open by wolves had just filled their stomachs with the first grass shoots of the year, mixed with some that remained from the previous autumn, and their abdomens were taut and low-slung; when the thin hide covers were torn away by wolf fangs, the stomachs and supple intestines spilled out onto the snow.

The final maniacal assault by the wolves crushed the herd's resistance. The grassland was transformed into an abattoir. Horse after horse, gutted by its own hooves, lay writhing in the snow, wracked by spasms. In seconds, chests in which hot blood had flowed only moments before were now filled with ice. Surging horse blood stained the swirling snow.

The wolves' suicidal war of vengeance paralyzed Batu with fear; cold sweat froze on his body. He knew that all was lost. His only wish now was to salvage a few of the horses. After pulling back hard on the bit to slow his horse momentarily, he abruptly dug his heels into its sides, released his hold on the bit, and flew past the line of wolves between him and the remnants of the herd, heading for the horse leader. The herd had already been scattered by the wolf attack, an army in full flight, running with the wind, so panic-stricken the horses had forgotten that the lake lay straight ahead to the south.

A downhill slope that led to the lake increased their speed, and the blizzard, with its mounting force, pushed them even faster, until their hooves barely touched the ground, their momentum like an avalanche crashing down a mountainside and into a morass. The thin layer of ice shattered under their hooves, and the viscous mud flew; the bog was about to claim the remaining horses, whinnying forlornly and struggling to keep moving, their fear and loathing of the wolf pack at its peak. Now hopelessly mired in the bog, they hesitated briefly before mustering the strength to plow into the deepest part, choosing self-inflicted death and burial in the bog over letting the wolves feed on their flesh and prevail in their quest for vengeance. These horses, castrated by humans, their virility lost to a knife, would end their lives with one final act of resistance: they would respond to the wolves' attack by committing suicide en masse. At this moment they represented the most intrepid life force on the ancient grassland.

But the cruel grassland scorns the weak, refusing to bestow on them even the slightest measure of pity. As night fell, the plummeting temperature turned the muddy surface into a thin layer of brown ice. The edges of the lake were frozen solid, but the ice over the boggy center was not thick enough to withstand the weight of the horses; their hooves cracked the ice as they moved into deeper water and into thicker mud, made stickier than usual by the swirling snow and bitter cold air. They were trapped, though they kept struggling, each torturous step bringing more snow and cold air into the spaces that opened up between hoof and mud. Their struggles turned the bog into a frozen morass. Finally, inevitably, their strength ran out and they could no longer move. Denied the quick death they had sought, the herd voiced their desperate agony; their breaths created a mist of steam, and their hides were coated in hoarfrost. Every member knew that salvation was impossible, that nothing and no one could prevent the coming butchery.

Batu carefully reined in his horse at the edge of the lake, yet the moment the big black's hooves touched the water, it snorted fearfully, lowered its head, and nervously eyed the muddy scene ahead, not daring to approach any closer. Batu shone his light on the surface of the lake and saw the hazy outlines of trapped horses where the flying snow of the blizzard weakened here and there. The heads of a few swayed weakly, a plea for help to the man responsible for their survival. He dug the heels of his boots into the sides of his horse to get it to move closer. But before it had gone more than five or six steps, its hooves broke through the ice and sank into mud, an alarm that sent it back to solid ground. This time Batu hit his mount on the flank with his herding club, but it refused to move. He thought of getting down, crawling out onto the ice, and standing guard over his horses with his rifle. But he knew that once he was off his horse and in the midst of the wolf pack, he would lose the commanding position from which he could use his club and the iron shoes of his horse as weapons; as soon as the wolves no longer feared him, man and horse would be torn apart. Besides, he only had ten bullets, and even with perfect marksmanship, killing a wolf with each shot would leave many standing. Icy tears covered his cheeks as he looked to the east, turning his head to the sky. Tengger, Tengger, eternal Tengger, give me the wisdom and power to save this herd! To which Tengger responded by puffing out its cheeks and blowing harder, dissolving the sound of Batu's voice in the roar of the white-hair blizzard.

Batu wiped the tears from his cheeks with the sleeve of his deel, looped the herding club around his wrist again, armed his rifle, and cradled it and his flashlight in his left hand to await the arrival of the wolves. A single thought ran through his mind: Kill as many as possible.

Time passed, and Batu sat nearly frozen in his saddle. Without warning, the wolves slipped by him, low and quiet as a spectral wind, and moved out onto the ice. They stopped at the eastern edge, where they were hidden by a snowy fog bank. A moment later, a thin wolf emerged from the fog and approached his horse, one cautious step after another, testing the ice. Batu held his fire. The wolf was too small. After a dozen or more steps, it raised its head and ran toward the trapped horses. But it had barely started when a white whirlwind rose on the edge of the lake and sped in the direction of the herd; when it reached the horses, it swirled around them, raising clouds of snow and mist, blotting out heaven and earth.

Batu, blinded by the snow, shivered from the immobilizing cold. His horse, with its keen sense of smell, was wrapped in swirling snow, shuddering from the cold; lowering its head, it voiced its torment. In the heavy darkness of night, the boundless white-hair blizzard once more covered a slaughterhouse, where flowing blood froze on the ice.

Batu, nearly frozen stiff, listlessly turned off his flashlight so that he could vanish in the darkness. He lowered his head, aimed his rifle in the direction of the lake, but then abruptly raised the barrel skyward and fired slowly—once, twice, three times . . .

6

Sunlight shone weakly through the thin dark clouds, and drifting snow powder fell on the vast Olonbulag. After the two murderous days and nights of the white-hair blizzard, the sky had lost its power to send any more snow; no pellets, no flakes. A pair of eagles glided leisurely below the clouds. Warm early-spring air floated above the landscape, turning to mist carried off by the wind. A covey of red and brown sand grouse flew out of a copse of bushes that resembled white coral, rustling the branches, shaking off velvety snow like dandelion down, and exposing the deep red color of the grassland willows. To the observer, it was like red coral in a bed of white—colorful, eye-catching. The mountain range to the north pierced a clear sky, where blue clouds rose and fell atop the dazzling white of the snowcaps. Peace had returned to the ancient Olonbulag.

Laasurung and Chen Zhen treated Batu's frostbite and stayed with him all day. But it was hard for them to believe his fearful grassland tale as they sat beneath a clear, beautiful sky. Everyone who worked a pasture, of course, had struggled against the blizzard for two days and nights, but Chen was unconvinced by what Batu was telling them.

Breathing in the cold spring air helped, for the heavy snowfall meant that the spring drought would come to an end. Every day it had been dry winds, dry dust, dry grass, and dry manure, until Chen's eyes stung and felt crusty; now that was over. Following the storm, the melting snow brought clear water to the rivers and lakes, filled the plains with green grass and beautiful flowers, and was a sign that the livestock would grow plump in the spring. Old Man Bilgee was fond of saying that springtime was the best of the three periods for livestock to accumulate fat. If they failed to plump up in the spring, they wouldn't be able to catch up in the summer, with what they call water fat, and would have no chance to add oily fat in the fall. If they hadn't accumulated a three-finger layer of fat in the fall, before the grass turned yellow, they likely would not survive the seven-month-long winter. Those sheep would have to be sold cheaply in China before winter arrived. In bad years, it was necessary to sell off half a herd, sometimes even more, before winter set in. Spring was the critical season on the grassland, and everyone hoped that the spring snows would make up for some of the previous losses.

Chen Zhen and the other students, both from his and other units, went to the site of the slaughter along with the disaster inspection team sent by headquarters and the production brigade. On the way over, somber looks filled the faces of leaders of the revolutionary committee—Bao Shungui, the military representative, and Uljii, the pasture director—the herdsmen Batu and Laasurung, and all the other representatives of mass organizations; even brawny young herdsmen had been brought along to clean up the site. Chen's heart sank when he reflected on the anger expressed by the military and local leaders at the knowledge that an entire herd of horses had been lost before they could join military service. Batu was on a new mount, his big black horse being treated by the veterinarian after sustaining debilitating injuries. The ointment covering his face could not conceal the disfigurement that was almost too terrible to look at. The skin on his nose and cheeks was black from frostbite and scarred with wrinkles from which pus oozed. Pink new skin forced to the surface created a startling contrast on his brown face. A big wooden shovel handle was stuck through his belt across his back as he rode along listlessly beside Bao Shungui.

Laasurung had found Batu behind an abandoned animal pen on the southern tip of the big lake after the blizzard had blown all night and half the next day. His horse, severely injured, could not move, and Batu was frozen half to death. Laasurung managed to get horse and rider back home. In order to describe to the investigation team exactly what had happened, Batu had to mount up and lead the way back to the site, however much pain it caused. The other two herdsmen, also badly frostbitten, had already been interrogated separately.

Chen Zhen rode along with Bilgee behind the main body. "Papa," he said softly, "how will they punish Batu?"

The old man wiped the dew from his wispy goatee with his sleeve, a look of sympathy deep in his eyes. Without turning his head, he stared off at the distant mountains and said slowly, "Do you students think he should be punished?" He turned and added, "Headquarters and the military representative are interested in your opinions. That's why they invited you along."

"Batu is a good man. He nearly gave his life for those warhorses. He just ran out of luck. Personally, I think he's a hero whether he succeeded in saving them or not. I lived in your house for a year, and everyone knows I consider Batu my big brother. But I can appreciate Bao Shungui's stance, so my opinion probably doesn't count. Besides, we students don't agree among ourselves. So I think that you, as a representative of the poor herdsmen, a member of the revolutionary committee, and someone everyone listens to, ought to have the last word."

"What do the other students say?" the old man asked, clearly concerned.

"Most of the ones in our unit have only good things to say about Batu. What happened this time, with a killer snow, a killer wind, and a killer wolf attack, could not have been averted by anyone, and they don't think Batu should be punished for it. But there are some who say that the herdsmen may have used a natural disaster for evil purposes, an antimilitary, counterrevolutionary act, and that the backgrounds of all four need to be closely examined."

Bilgee looked grim. He said nothing more.

After skirting the eastern edge of the lake, the party reached the spot where Batu had fired his rifle. Chen Zhen held his breath, preparing himself emotionally for what he was about to see.

There wasn't a drop of blood anywhere; a foot of new snow had covered the bloody scene following that night of butchery. There were no horse heads poking up out of the lake, nothing but undulating snowbanks, between which the snow was especially deep. The snowdrifts spread out, carved by a nighttime of winds to cover the corpses of horses that ought to have been in full view. The people looked on silently, seated in their saddles, unwilling to pull back this blanket of snow. Everyone was trying to conjure up an image of what had occurred at that spot.

Bilgee broke the silence. "What a shame." Pointing to the eastern edge of the lake with his herding club, he said, "See there, that's how close they were to making it. It was no easy matter for Batu to drive his herd from the grassland to the north over to this spot, given the terrible winds and all those wolves. Even if he wasn't afraid, the horse he was riding was. He stuck with his herd from start to finish, fighting the wolves all the way. He did what he was supposed to do."

The old man found it easy to argue his son's case.

Chen edged up next to Bao Shungui. "Batu fought the wolves all night to safeguard communal property," he said, "and nearly died in the process. He should be commended to the authorities as a hero—"

Bao glared at Chen. "Hero, you say?" he roared. "A hero would have saved the herd." He turned to Batu. "Why was the herd north of the lake that day? With all your experience tending horses, how could you not have known that the wind would drive them right into the lake? That's what led to what happened here."

Batu could not look Bao in the face. "It's my fault," he said, "all of it. If I'd driven the herd to the eastern pastureland before nightfall, none of this would have happened."

Laasurung spurred his horse up to disagree. "Headquarters told us to graze the horses there, saying that's the only place where there was plenty of autumn grass, and where new spring grass was already sprouting. We were told to make sure the militiamen who came to claim the horses were happy with their mounts. I recall that Batu stood up at the 'grasp revolution, promote production' meeting and said that grazing the horses at the northern tip of the lake was unsafe. And now that his prediction has come true, how can you pin the blame on him?"

Headquarters leaders looked on quietly, until Uljii cleared his throat and said, "What Laasurung says is right. That's how it happened. Everyone wanted the horses to get big and strong so they could travel great distances and contribute more to strategic plans. Who could have predicted a white-hair blizzard? One from the north, mind you. And, of course, the wolf pack. If not for them, Batu would have driven the herd to safety, guaranteed. A killer wind, a killer snow, a killer wolf attack, a once-in-a-century chain of events, if that! I'm responsible for production, so if anyone is to blame, it's me."

Bao Shungui pointed his whip at Laasurung's nose. "You're not blameless in this," he said. "Bilgee was right when he said they were close to reaching safety. If you three hadn't fled the field of battle and had instead stayed with Batu to keep the herd moving, none of this would have happened. The only reason I haven't sent you to be interrogated is that you rode out and saved Batu's life."

Bilgee reached out and lowered Bao's whip with his herding club. "Representative Bao," he said with a stern look, "as a Mongol from a farming region, you should at least be aware of our customs out here. You do not point a whip at people's noses when you talk to them. That was a prerogative reserved to kings and pasture lords."

Bao lowered his whip and shifted it to his left hand. He pointed first to Laasurung, then to Batu with his right index finger. "You!" he barked. "And you! Why aren't you down there shoveling and sweeping snow? I want to see those remains. I want to see how big a wolf pack we're talking about. Don't try to pin the blame for what happened on the wolves. Chairman Mao tells us that man is the primary element!"

The men climbed down off their horses; picked up their spades, shovels, and brooms; and began clearing the graveyard. Bao Shungui rode around taking pictures with a Seagull brand camera as evidence and giving commands: "Sweep it clean, absolutely clean! Inspection teams from the prefecture and the banner will be here in a few days."

Along with Uljii, Bilgee, Batu, and Laasurung, Chen Zhen walked toward several snowbanks in the middle of the lake, where the ice was hard and the snow crunched beneath their feet. "To determine how ferocious a pack it was, all we need to know is whether the horses buried out there were killed by the wolves," Bilgee said.

"How come?" Chen asked.

"Think about it this way," Uljii said. "The farther out you go, the greater the danger. The mud out there would be the last to freeze, and no wolf would risk the possibility of drowning. So if those horses were killed by wolves, that'll tell us how ferocious a pack we're dealing with."

The old man turned to Batu. "Didn't it help to fire your rifle?"

"No," Batu said with a sad face. "I only had ten bullets, and they were gone in no time. The wind swallowed up the sound. But even if I'd scared them off, they'd have returned when I was out of ammunition. It was pitch-black, and my flashlight was dimming. I couldn't see a thing.

"But I wasn't thinking about that at the time." Batu reached up and touched the frostbitten skin on his face. "The snow kept falling. I was afraid I'd shoot the horses. I was hoping the wind would die down and the lake wouldn't freeze so that the wolves would stay back. That way some of the horses could have lived. I recall raising the angle of my rifle a foot or so."

Bilgee and Uljii sighed heavily.

When they were standing in the middle of the lake, Batu hesitated before clearing the snow near the horses' heads. The men sucked in their breath. Half of the exposed neck of a great white horse had been chewed off and the head had been pulled around until it was lying on the animal's back. Its bulging eyes, frozen into nearly transparent black-ice eggs, were stamped with the despair and fear of the horse's last moments, a terrifying sight. The snow beneath the head was stained red by frozen blood, so hard that the men's tools couldn't crack it. Without a word, the men shoveled and swept the snow away, exposing half of the carcass. To Chen it looked as if the horse's abdomen had been torn open by an explosion, not by wolf fangs.

They stood around gaping at the sight. Chen's hands and feet were cold as ice, the chill seeping deep into his bones.

Holding a spade in his hands, Bilgee looked thoughtful. "This may be the second or third largest wolf pack I've ever encountered," he said. "I don't have to see any more, since the innermost horse has been torn apart like this. Not a single horse escaped the carnage."

Uljii, his face a study in dejection, sighed. "I rode this horse for two years," he said. "Together we caught three wolves. It was one of our fastest horses. I never rode a better one, not even when I was suppressing bandits as company commander of a mounted unit. No horse thief could have devised the strategy or tactics this wolf pack employed. They took advantage of the wind and the lake, which makes you wonder just how smart we are. If I'd been a bit smarter, this horse would still be alive, and I have to accept some of the blame for what happened here. If only I'd been more forceful in my comments to old Bao that day."

The greater half of the carnage site had been cleared. Carcasses lay all over the frozen lake, with its bloodred ice. Broken limbs were strewn everywhere, as on a battlefield after heavy bombardment. The two horse herders sat on their heels on the ice, cleaning the heads of their favorite horses with fur-lined sleeves and the hems of their deels, weeping nonstop. Every man in the party was stunned by the miserable scene. Chen Zhen and other students who had never witnessed the bloody results of battle or the aftermath of a wolf attack stared at each other, their faces turned ashen by visceral fright.

The old man's displeasure was obvious. "You Chinese are poor horsemen. When the riding gets rough, you can't even stay in the saddle."

Not used to being reproached by Bilgee, Chen understood the implication in the old man's comment. The wolf totem occupied a more unshakable place in his soul than a skillful rider on a Mongol horse. After thousands of years, during which unknown numbers of minor races had died out or were violently displaced, the grasslanders would never question their predatory totem, which would remain their sole icon even after killing seventy or eighty fine horses. Chen was reminded of the sayings "The Yellow River causes a hundred calamities but enriches all it touches"; "When the Yellow River overflows its banks, the people become fish and turtles"; "The Yellow River—our Mother River";

and "The Yellow River—cradle of the Chinese race." The Chinese would never deny that the Yellow River was the cradle of the Chinese race or that it was crucial to the survival and development of their race even if it sometimes overflows its banks and swallows up acres of cropland and thousands of lives. The grasslanders' wolf totem deserved to be revered in the same manner.

Bao Shungui, who had stopped shouting commands, rode around to get a fuller picture of the carnage. As Bao took photographs of the scene, Chen Zhen noticed his hands trembling violently; he was having trouble keeping his camera steady.

Bilgee and Uljii were shoveling snow in an area where several rendered carcasses lay, digging here and poking there, as if looking for evidence. Chen Zhen hurried over to give them a hand. "What are you looking for, Papa?" he asked.

"The path the wolves took," the old man replied. "We need to proceed carefully."

Chen bent over and, stepping carefully, helped them look. It didn't take long. There on the ground they spotted a path where the snow was tightly packed atop the frozen mud. After it was swept clean of the powdery snow that had settled on it, they saw wolf prints as large as an ox hoof and as small as a large dog's paw print. There were traces of blood in some of the heel marks.

Uljii and Bilgee called the others over to help clear the snow from the wolf path; according to Bilgee, what they learned from the path would bring them closer to the size of the pack. As the path was gradually revealed, they saw it was curved, not straight, and farther along they noted that it became a semicircle. It took more than an hour to clear away the entire length of the path, and to learn that it ran in a complete circle, a circle of ice and blood, of red-stained snow that was as thick as a fist; the black and red frozen mud and red ice was a terrifying sight, like a sort of demonic writing. Shocked to their core, the men shuddered as they discussed what they'd found.

"I've lived a long time, but I've never seen this many wolf prints in one place."

"This wasn't a wolf pack; it was a gang of fiends."

"The numbers are scary."

"Forty or fifty at least."

"Batu, you've got guts, going up against this pack. If it'd been me, I'd have been scared off my horse and straight into the bellies of those wolves."

"It was dark that night, and snow was falling; I couldn't see a thing. How was I to know how big the pack was?" Batu said.

"This will make things tough on our pastureland from now on."

"The women won't dare go out walking at night."

"Damn those idiots at headquarters for pillaging the food the wolves had put away for the lean days of spring. That's why they were on the trail of revenge. I'd have done the same thing if I'd been their alpha male. But I'd have gone after their pigs and chickens."

"Headquarters can do something right for a change by organizing a wolf hunt. If we don't kill them now, we're next on their menu."

"I vote for fewer meetings and more wolf hunts."

"The way they gorged themselves this time, it looks

like we might not have enough animals to satisfy their appetites."

"People from farmlands have been shipped in as leaders of our pastureland, and everything they do is wrong. Tengger sent the wolves as a lesson to us."

"Watch what you're saying, or the next criticism session will be for you."

Bao Shungui examined the path with Bilgee and Uljii, stopping to talk with the two local men as he took pictures. His face gradually relaxed, and Chen Zhen suspected that Bilgee had said some things to undermine his concept of "man as the primary element." Was man able to successfully resist this killer wolf attack, this natural disaster? You can send all the inspection teams you want, but one look at the carnage here is enough to convince you that man was powerless to keep this from happening, especially when you factor in the blizzard. Chen's concern for Uljii and Batu gradually lessened.

He turned to a closer scrutiny of the wolf path. The strange circular shape made his hair stand on end; it wrapped itself around his heart, as if a pack of wolf sprites were racing inside his chest, until he could hardly breathe. Why a circle? What were they trying to do? What was their goal? Grassland wolves were impossible to figure out. Every clue to their behavior presented a new puzzle.

Was it to keep out the cold? Did running somehow warm them?

Or was it to aid their digestion? Burning off excess energy might have increased their need for horseflesh. That too was possible. Unlike other grassland creatures, such as ground squirrels and golden prairie dogs, wolves do not store up food. What they can't eat from a kill, they leave, so in order to get the most out of their kills, they gorge themselves until they can eat no more. Then they run to facilitate digestion and store up as much nutrition as possible, emptying their stomachs to go back and eat more.

Or was it a dress parade for future battles? Even that was possible. The tracks made it clear that the wolves were organized and highly disciplined. From end to end the path was a little more than a yard in width, and there were hardly any tracks outside it. If that wasn't a march of troops in review, what was it? Chen was thinking. Wolves often fight alone, though they also hunt in small packs of three to five or do their plundering in families of eight to ten. What occurred here, with a small army of wolves, was rare. They had decided to organize themselves into a field army for mobile warfare. During the war years in China, the Eighth Route and New Fourth Armies underwent a large-scale makeover, a Herculean task. Did this sort of reorganization come naturally to wolves?

Then again, was it a victory celebration? Or signs of wild ecstasy preceding a grand feast? That was even more likely. In this murderous attack, they'd butchered every horse. Not one got away. Revenge. Slaking hatred. Total victory. An unburdening. How could they not celebrate the killing of so many horses? The level of excitement must have been fanatical as they surrounded the large cluster of trapped horses and performed their death dance.

Chen discovered that by considering wolves' behavior from a human perspective, some of the puzzling behaviors could be reasoned out logically. Dogs display human characteristics, men display wolf characteristics, or vice versa. Heaven, earth, and man are a unity; it's impossible to categorically separate men, dogs, and wolves. Otherwise, how does one explain the fact that there were so many overlapping latent human traces found at the site of this horrible carnage? When confronting one another, all humans turn into wolves as an article of faith.

As the line of men and horses followed Batu north away from the scene of the incident, Chen drew up next to Bilgee. "Papa," he asked, "why did the wolves make that path?"

The old man looked around and reined in his horse so they could fall back behind the other members of the party. "I've lived more than sixty years on the Olonbulag," he said softly, "and I've seen wolf circles like that a few times before. I asked that same question of my father once. He told me that Tengger sent wolves down to the grassland as protectors of the Bayan Uul sacred mountain and the Olonbulag. Tengger and the sacred mountain are angered anytime the grassland is endangered, and wolves are sent to kill and consume the offenders. Every time they receive this gift, they joyfully run circles around it until they've tramped out a path as round as the sun and the moon. That circular path is their acknowledgment to Tengger, a sort of thank-you note. Once the acknowledgment has been received, the feast begins. Wolves are known for baying at the moon, which is their call to Tengger. If a halo appears around the moon, a wind will blow that night and the wolves will be on the move. They are better climatologists than we are. They make circles to mirror those in the sky. In other words, they are in perfect sync with the heavens."

Chen Zhen, a fan of popular legends, was delighted. "Fascinating," he said, "utterly fascinating. The sun can be ringed by a halo, so can the moon, and when herdsmen signal to someone far off they make a circle in the air with their arm. The circle does seem to be a spiritual sign. What you're telling me makes my hair stand on end. That the wolves out here are so mystical they make circles as signs to Tengger is downright creepy."

"They are supernatural," the old man said. "I've dealt with them all my life and I've always come out second best. But even I never anticipated something like this. Wolves appear when and where you least expect them, and often in overwhelming numbers. How can anyone think they could be so potent without the help of Tengger?"

The men up ahead stopped; some dismounted and began digging in the snow. Chen and Bilgee spurred their horses to catch up. There were more carcasses, but scattered helter-skelter in fours and fives. Suddenly, someone shouted, "Wolf! There's a dead wolf here!"

"According to Batu, this must have been where the wolves made their suicidal attack on the horses' bellies," Chen surmised, "and where the tide of battle turned, the beginning of the end for the horses." His heart began racing, faster and faster.

Bao Shungui waved his whip in the air and shouted from the saddle, "Don't go running off. Come back here, all of you. Dig up a couple of these horses. Horses first, wolves last."

They all gathered around and began digging.

As the animals came into view, it was obvious they'd trampled and ripped their own internal organs with their hind legs, spreading them over a great distance. It was also clear that the wolves had left them alone after they'd died. By then they'd probably joined the slaughter on the lake. These latest horses had been given a reprieve of sorts. But to Chen Zhen, who dug along with the others, these horses had died more tragically than those on the lake, their deaths an affront to all. The agony and fear frozen in their dead eyes was more conspicuous than in those of the lake dead.

"These wolves were crueler even than the Japanese devils," Bao Shungui shouted in anger. "They knew that all they had to do was rip open the bellies and let the horses die under their own hooves. I've never seen anything more sinister, more savage in my life. Those wolves embody the spirit of Japanese samurai. Suicidal attacks don't faze them, and that makes Mongol wolves more fearful than any others. I won't rest till I kill every last one of them!"

"If a man or a race lacks the death-before-surrender spirit, a willingness to die along with the enemy, then slavery is the inevitable result," Chen said. "Whoever takes the suicidal spirit of wolves as a model is destined for heroism, and will be eulogized with songs and tears. Learning the wrong lesson leads to samurai fascism, but anyone who lacks the death-before-surrender spirit will always succumb to samurai fascism."

Bao Shungui held his breath for a moment. "You've got a point," he said.

Uljii, looking grave, said to Bao, "How could Batu and the others have beaten off a diabolical, suicidal attack like this? He fought them from the grazing land up north all the way here. I don't know how he did it. He survived thanks to the protection of Tengger. Have the inspection teams see this, and I'm sure they'll reach the right conclusion."

Bao Shungui nodded his agreement. He turned to Batu. "Weren't you afraid the wolves would do this to your horse?" he asked in a conciliatory tone.

"I was so fixated on trying to get the herd past the lake, I didn't have time to think about anything else," he replied naively. "We came so close."

"Didn't the wolves come at you?" Bao asked.

Batu lifted up his herding club, with its iron rings, and showed it to Bao. "I knocked out the fangs of one wolf with this," he said, "and broke the nose of another. They'd both have gotten me if I hadn't. Since they didn't have one of these, Laasurung and the others had no way to protect themselves. They didn't desert me."

Bao took the herding club from him and felt its heft. "A good club!" he exclaimed. "A very good club! It takes real ferocity to knock out a wolf's fangs with this. Good! The fiercer the better, where wolves are concerned. Batu, you've got guts, and you know how to fight. When they send the inspection team, I want you to tell them how you fought the wolves, tell them the whole story."

Bao handed back the herding club and turned to Uljii. "These wolves of yours are supernatural," he said. "Smarter than humans. I see how they did it. They had a clear goal in mind, to drive the horses into the lake at any cost. Look..." He began counting on his fingers. "Here's some of what the wolves knew: weather, topography, opportunity, their and their enemy's strengths, military strategy and tactics, close fighting, night fighting, guerrilla fighting, mobile fighting, long-range raids, ambushes, lightning raids, and concentrating their strength to annihilate the enemy. They made plans, they set goals, and they undertook a measured campaign of total annihilation. It was a textbook battle plan. You and I are military men, and in my view, except for positional and trench warfare, they were as conversant with guerrilla tactics as our Eighth Route Army. I used to think that wolves were foolhardy fighters that went after an occasional sheep or chicken. Obviously, I was wrong."

"I haven't felt far from a battlefield since the first day I was sent to work here," Uljii said. "I fight wolves year-round. I take my rifle with me wherever I go, and I've become a better marksman than when I was a soldier. You're right, the wolves know military strategy and tactics, at least the most important elements. After fighting them for more than a decade, I've learned a lot. If I was ordered out on another bandit annihilation campaign, I'd be one of the best."

"Are you saying that men have learned how to wage war from wolves?" Chen Zhen asked, his interest growing.

Uljii's eyes lit up. "Yes. Much of what we know about waging war we learned from wolves. In ancient days here on the grassland, the herdsmen fought farming people from down south using tactics they'd learned from wolves. You Chinese learned more from nomadic peoples than how to dress in short clothing, or how to use a bow and arrow on horseback, what you call 'barbarian attire and horse archery.' You also learned a lot about warfare. When I was studying livestock farming in Hohhot, I read books on warfare, and in my view there's little difference between the arts of warfare described by Sun-tzu and those employed by wolves."

"But there's no mention of the grassland people or wolves in Chinese books on war," Chen Zhen said. "That isn't fair."

"We Mongols suffer from cultural backwardness," Uljii replied. "The only book of any value we've introduced to the world is *The Secret History of the Mongols.*"

"Apparently," Bao said to Uljii, "when you're engaged in livestock farming out here you need to study wolves and how to wage war. If you don't, you suffer. It's getting late. What do you say we go take a look at that dead wolf? I need some more pictures."

After the two leaders rode off, Chen Zhen leaned on his shovel and stared into space. The battle-site investigation had increased his fascination with the people of the grassland and the military miracles performed by Genghis Khan. How could he and his progeny have swept across Asia and Europe with fewer than a hundred thousand fighters? They exterminated hordes of Western Xia's armored cavalry, a million troops of the Great Jin, a million waterborne and mounted forces of the Southern Song, the Russian Kipchaks, and the Teutons of Rome. They occupied Central Asia, Hungary, Poland, and all of Russia; they attacked such large civilized nations as Persia, Iran, China, and India. Beyond that, borrowing the Chinese policy of marrying their daughters to minority nationalities, they forced the emperor of Eastern Rome to give the hand of Princess Maria to the great-grandson of Genghis Khan. The Mongols founded the largest empire in the history of the world. How could a nomadic, uncivilized, backward race of people with no writing system, one that used arrows tipped with bone, not steel, be in possession of such advanced military capabilities and wisdom? That was one of the great unanswered questions of history.

Chen's experience with wolves during his two years on the grassland and the countless tales he'd collected, plus the brilliant annihilation of the gazelle herd he'd witnessed and the classic example of warfare against the herd of horses, had pretty much convinced him that the answer to the military marvels of Genghis Khan lay with the wolves.

On the grassland there are no tigers or leopards or jackals or bears or lions or elephants, Chen Zhen was thinking. They could not survive the brutal climate; but even if they could, they could not adapt to the cruel wars of survival, and would not be able to withstand assaults by grassland wolves and grassland humans, finalists in the heated competition for grassland primacy. Wolves are the only match for humans in the struggle for survival. Although there are wolves nearly everywhere on earth, they are concentrated on the Mongolian grassland, where there are no moats or ramparts, common to advanced agrarian societies, or great walls and ancient fortresses; it is the spot on earth where the longest-lasting struggle between wise and brave combatants—men and wolves—has taken place.

Chen felt himself to be standing at the mouth of a tunnel to five thousand years of Chinese history. Every day and every night, he thought, men have fought wolves on the Mongolian plateau, a minor skirmish here, a pitched battle there. The frequency of these clashes has even surpassed the frequency of battles among all the nomadic peoples of the West outside of wolf and man, plus the cruel, protracted wars between nomadic tribes, conflicts between nationalities, and wars of aggression; it is that frequency that has strengthened and advanced the mastery of the combatants in these battles. The grassland people are better and more knowledgeable fighters than any farming race of people or nomadic tribe in the world. In the history of China—from the Zhou dynasty, through the Warring States, and on to the Qin, Han, Tang, and Song dynasties—all those great agrarian societies, with their large populations and superior strength, were often crushed in combat with minor nomadic tribes, suffering catastrophic and humiliating defeat. At the end of the Song dynasty, the Mongol hordes of Genghis Khan invaded the Central Plains and remained in power for nearly a century. China's last feudal dynasty, the Qing, was itself founded by nomads. The Han race, with its ties to the land, has gone without the superior military teachings of a wolf drillmaster and has been deprived of constant rigorous training exercises. The ancient Chinese had their Sun-tzu and his military treatise, but that was on paper. Besides, even they were based in part on the lupine arts of war.

Millions of Chinese died at the hands of invasions by peoples of the North over thousands of years, and Chen felt as if he'd found the source of that sad history. Relationships among the creatures on earth have dictated the course of history and of fate, he thought. The military talents of a people in protecting their homes and their nation are essential to their founding and their survival. If there had been no wolves on the Mongolian grassland, would China and the world be different than they are today?

Suddenly, everyone was running and shouting, startling Chen out of his thoughts. He jumped into the saddle and followed the crowd.

Two dead wolves had been excavated, part of the cost of driving the horses onto the lake. Chen went up near one of them as Batu and Laasurung swept snow off one of the carcasses and described the suicidal belly-ripping battle. The wolf was slimmer than most, a female. The rear half of her body had been battered bloody by horse hooves, but her teats were still visible.

"What a shame," Bilgee said. "Her cubs were stolen from their den, that's for sure. She and the other mothers who had lost their offspring called this pack together to get their revenge. For her, there was no reason to go on living. On the grassland it's not a good idea to overdo anything. A cornered rabbit will try to bite a wolf, so how could a frantic female wolf not fight to the death?"

Chen turned to some of the students. "History books tell us that wolves have strong maternal instincts," he said. "There are recorded instances of wolves raising human children. The ancestors of the Huns, the Gaoju, and the Turks were wolf children, all raised by wolf mothers."

"What's all this nonsense about wolf children?" Bao Shungui interrupted. "Wolves kill and eat humans; they don't raise them as their own. For people and wolves, it's a life-or-death relationship—you or me. I'm the one who ordered people out to snatch the wolf cubs. In years past, it was an annual hunt that kept tragic encounters with wolves at a minimum, a fine tradition. But keeping them at a minimum isn't enough; we need to wipe them off the face of the earth! Let them get their revenge? We'll see how they do after I've killed them all! I'm not going to rescind my order. Once this business is cleared up, I'm sending the people out again. Every two families will be responsible for one wolf-cub pelt, and if they can't manage that, they can substitute an adult pelt. Otherwise I'll deduct work points!"

Bao took a picture of the dead wolf, then had the carcass loaded onto a cart.

The men then moved to the second wolf. In his two years on the grassland, Chen had seen lots of wolves, alive and dead, and plenty of wolf pelts, but nothing like the animal that lay at his feet. Its head was nearly as big as a leopard's, its chest even broader. Once the snow had been swept away and its grayish yellow fur fully exposed, Chen noticed countless thick, black, needle-like hairs poking up through the yellow fur on the neck and down its back. The rear half of the torso had been kicked bloody by horse hooves, leaving a puddle of red ice on the ground.

Batu pushed the frozen animal, but did not succeed in moving it. "This one wasn't as smart as the others," he said as he wiped the sweat from his forehead. "It didn't get a good bite on its target. If it had, big as this head is, it would easily have ripped open a horse's belly and then tumbled to the ground and gotten away without injury. It might have inadvertently clamped onto a bone. Served it right!"

Bilgee squatted down and studied the animal, pulling back the fur on its neck to reveal a pair of bloody holes as thick as two fingers. The students were astounded. They'd seen holes like that before, on the necks of the sheep taken down by wolves, two on each side, the marks of four wolf fangs across the carotid arteries.

"This wolf didn't die from being kicked by a horse," Bilgee said. "Mortally wounded, maybe, but it was killed by another wolf after it had eaten its fill of horseflesh."

"Wolves are worse than outlaws!" Bao Shungui cursed. "They even kill their own wounded!"

Bilgee glared at Bao. "Dead outlaws don't go up to heaven. Dead wolves do. This wolf was mortally wounded by a horse. It didn't die right away, but it had no chance of living. What's better, hanging on and suffering, or dying? A live wolf suffers from seeing one of its own like this, so it puts it out of its misery, releasing its soul to Tengger. That's an act of mercy, not cruelty, and a means of keeping the dying animal out of human hands and certain humiliating treatment. Wolves are unyielding creatures. They'd rather die than suffer humiliation. And an alpha male won't let that happen to a member of his pack. You come from a farming community. How many of you would choose death over indignity? Old-timers out here tear up when they ponder this aspect of the wolf's nature."

Seeing a look of displeasure on Bao's face, Uljii said, "Have you ever wondered why these wolves are such excellent fighters? One important factor is that the alpha male won't hesitate to kill one of his wounded comrades, lightening the burden on the pack and ensuring the continued effectiveness of all the troops. If you understand this trait, you'll do a better job of evaluating the situation in a fight with wolves."

Bao nodded. "You may be right," he said. "Wounded troops require stretcher bearers, medics, guards, nurses, and doctors. And you need ambulances and aid stations. I was a rear echelon soldier for many years, and we calculated that a single wounded soldier required the services of at least a dozen people. During wartime, this support staff affects combat effectiveness. Seen in that light, wolves are more flexible. But many wounded soldiers are courageous fighters, and when their wounds have healed, they're often the backbone of their unit. Won't killing your wounded hurt your combat effectiveness?"

Uljii sighed. "Of course there are explanations for this behavior. To begin with, wolves have a high birthrate. A female wolf can produce seven or eight, sometimes a dozen or more, cubs in one litter. And the survival rate is high. One autumn I saw a female with eleven youngsters, born that spring. They were nearly as big as their mother and could run as fast. The females among them would begin having their own young in a couple of years. Cows are born at the rate of five every three years. How many female wolves do you think are born in that same period? A whole squad of them. And wolves are combat ready when they're a year old. By the second spring, they're mature, fully competent animals. A dog at one year can hunt rabbits, a wolf at that age can hunt sheep, and a one-year-old child is still in diapers. Humans are outmatched. With all those troops at their disposal, of course they kill their wounded. As I see it, wolves kill their own because it's a natural form of population control. Culling troops ensures that the pack will include only crack fighters. That, in essence, is how they've maintained their grassland dominance for centuries."

Bao Shungui's knitted brow relaxed. "Thanks to this inspection tour," he said, "I can see that the wolves are formidable opponents. Weather predictions help us withstand the ravages of weather, but predictions are useless where wolves are concerned. Those of us who come from farming communities have no idea what they're capable of. This incident was indeed beyond human control. The inspection teams will understand."

"To get a clear picture, they'll need to know everything," Uljii said.

"But that doesn't alter the fact that we're going to have wolf hunts. If not, our pasture will quickly become their canteen. I'll request a supply of ammunition from headquarters."

Off to the side, some of the students were having a heated discussion. A Team Three middle school student, a minor Red Guard leader of the Beijing Dongjiu faction named *Li* Hongwei, said emotionally, "Wolves are the true class enemies. Reactionaries throughout the world are all ambitious wolves. Wolves are cruel. Putting aside their slaughter of people's property—our horses, cows, and sheep—they even slaughter their own. We need to organize the masses to hunt them down and apply the proletarian dictatorship against all wolves. We must resolutely and thoroughly wipe them off the face of the earth! We must also subject all old ideas, customs, and habits—such as sympathy for wolves, appeasement of wolves, and feeding wolves with the corpses of our dead—to severe criticism."

Certain that the fellow was about to point the finger of accusation at Bilgee, Chen cut in before he could finish: "That's taking things a bit far, isn't it? Class distinctions apply to two-legged animals. If you insist on bringing wolves into the class system, then what are you, man or wolf? Aren't you afraid of including our great proletarian leaders in the same category as wolves? When men kill other men, isn't that slaughtering your own kind? Men kill other men far more often than wolves kill other wolves. World War I, World War II, the dead numbering in the tens of millions. The habit of creatures killing their own kind began with Peking Man. Viewed from the perspective of natural instincts, man is crueler than the wolf. I advise you to catch up with your reading."

The Red Guard angrily pointed his whip at Chen and said, "You think you're so clever just because you finished high school! Those books you read, filled with capitalist, feudal, revisionist garbage. Nothing but poisonous weeds! You're like that dog-father of yours. At school you kept to yourself, a member of the leisure class, but out here in the most primitive, backward spot in the world, you're like a fish in water. You fit right in with the stinking Four Olds!"

Feeling the blood rush to his head, Chen wanted to run over and, like a wolf, sink his teeth into the Red Guard and drag him down off his horse. But, reminded of the wolves' unswerving patience, he merely glared at the man, slapped the sides of his boots loudly, turned, and rode off.

Dusk was setting in, and the students, who had grown accustomed to meat and tea in the morning and a full meal in the evening, were half starved and shivering in the cold. The leaders of the headquarters inspection team and most of the militiamen and students had fallen in behind the cart with the dead wolves to head back to camp. Chen Zhen, Batu, and Laasurung went searching for Batu's treasured lasso pole, at the same time looking for more wolves that had been killed or wounded by flying horse hooves.

7

Most wolf hunts on the Mongolian grassland take place in early winter. By then, the marmots have begun their hibernation. Fatter and more nutritious than rabbits, marmots are among the wolves' favorite foods. But once the marmots go down their holes, the wolves turn their attention to domestic livestock, forcing the pasture residents to launch counterattacks. At this time of year the wolves have new winter coats, supple, unmarked, bright, and thick. Pelts from this season command the highest prices. Early-winter wolf hunts were the primary source of income, outside of work points, for livestock herders, and an excellent opportunity for young hunters to display military skills and courage; they honed their scouting abilities, choosing the right place and time to fight. In the past, early-winter wolf hunts were used by tribal heads, barbarian leaders, khans, and Great Khans to train and drill their people. This tradition, passed down over the millennia, has been followed in modern times. Preparations for the hunt were completed after the first big snow of the year, when the tracks of wolves in the snow were the clearest. Even with their long legs, wolves cannot run particularly fast in fresh, wet snow, which gives the advantage to horses, whose legs are so much longer. Early winter, with its new snow, is the season of death for wolves, and the herders use it to repay the wolves for their arrogance and allow the people to take revenge for a year of hardships.

The customs of the grassland are understood by people, and by wolves. As this hunt would make clear, the wolves had gotten smarter in recent years, for as soon as the first snow settled on the ground, and the grassland turned from yellow to white, the wolves either crossed the northern border, went deep into the mountains to hunt gazelles and wild rabbits, or remained in the wild country once the snows had sealed up the mountains. They endured despite their hunger, getting through the days by gnawing on animal bones or the dried, rotting skins of earlier kills. Then, once the ground hardened, they became fast runners again and, sensing that the people had lost their fighting spirit, returned to plunder and loot.

At the headquarters meeting Uljii said, "In early-winter hunts over the past few years, we've brought back mainly half-grown and small animals, few big ones. So from now on, we need to be more like the wolves and abandon conventional tactics. We hunt when and where we feel like it and take them by surprise, stopping for a while, then hunting some more, winning the fight by being random and unpredictable. That way the wolves won't be able to spot patterns and cannot guard against us. We don't normally hunt in the spring, so I suggest we break with tradition and have a spring hunt, mounting a surprise attack. The pelts might not be as fine as those in early winter, but it'll be a month before they begin to molt, and even if we don't get the highest prices, we'll be rewarded with an additional supply of ammunition."

It was decided at the meeting that, in order to lessen

the terrible impression left by the wholesale slaughter of horses, and to carry out orders from above to eradicate the evil Olonbulag wolves, all able-bodied headquarters personnel would be mobilized for a major antiwolf campaign. “Since it’s springtime, I understand that you’re all busy with the birthing of livestock, and that it won’t be easy to take you away from your work,” Bao Shungui said, “but if we do not take the offensive against the wolves, we’ll have failed to carry out our responsibilities.”

“It’s been our experience,” Uljii said, “that after a major battle, the main body of the pack leaves the area, since they know we’ll retaliate. I’m guessing they’re in the border region somewhere, and as soon as they think something’s up here, they’ll rush across the border. We need to wait awhile, at least until the horseflesh they gorged themselves on is only a memory, and they start thinking about all the frozen meat they left behind. The marmots and field mice haven’t come out of their holes yet, so there’s nothing else for the wolves to eat. They’ll risk a confrontation to return for more horsemeat, I’m sure of it.”

Bilgee nodded his agreement. “I’ll set some traps around the dead horses as a decoy,” he said. “The alpha male will spot the traps and assume we don’t plan to attack. When headquarters organized hunts in the past, they always took a pack of dogs along when they set the traps. This time we’ll set the traps before the attack, which will confuse even the smartest alpha male. If we catch a few of the wolves in the traps, the rest of the pack won’t know what to do. They’ll stare at the horsemeat from a distance, not daring to approach but unwilling to leave. That’s when we surround them. We’ll have them right where we want them, most of them anyway, and this time we’ll bag several alpha males.”

Bao Shungui turned to Bilgee. "I hear the wolves out here avoid places where there are traps or poison, and that older animals or pack leaders will leave tooth marks on poisoned meat to ensure that the females and the young eat only around the poisoned area. I've even heard there are alpha males that can drive a hunter crazy by removing his traps as if they were land mines. Is that true?"

"Not quite," Bilgee replied. "The poison sold at the co-op has a strong odor, and if dogs can smell it, you know the wolves can. I don't use poison, since there's always the chance I'd kill the dogs. I prefer traps. I've got a special way of laying them so that hardly any wolf can sniff them out."

Bao sensed that assigning Uljii, the commander of a cavalry company, to the grassland had been the right decision. Sending Bao as military representative had also been the right thing to do. He tapped his mug with his pen and announced, "Then that's how we'll do it!"

The order was given that no one was to hunt wolves north of the grazing land without headquarters permission, especially with rifles, which would frighten them off. Everyone was told to be ready to set out on a wolf extermination campaign at a moment's notice.

People began choosing their horses, feeding their dogs, repairing lasso poles, sharpening knives, cleaning rifles, and readying ammunition. Everything progressed with a quiet rhythm, as if they were preparing to tend to birthing stock around the Qingming Festival, or to shear sheep in midsummer, or to bale straw at midautumn, or to slaughter animals in early winter.

Early morning. Clouds darkened the sky and pressed down on the distant mountains, shaving off the peaks. The Olonbulag seemed flatter than ever, and gloomier. Snow swirled lightly; the wind barely blew. Metal chimneys poking through the tops of yurts were like asthma victims struggling to breathe, releasing an occasional cough and sending puffs of smoke to settle on the ground around the snow-covered barracks that was dotted by animal droppings, patches of hair, and tufts of dying grass. The late-spring cold front was hanging on, giving no sign that it was ready to yield to warmth. Fortunately, the livestock still had a layer of fat sufficient to keep them warm until the snow melted and the grass sprouted with the coming of spring. New buds were close enough to the surface that sheep could get to them by kicking the snow away.

The sheep lay quietly in their pens, lazily chewing their cud, content to stay where they were. Three cold and very hungry guard dogs that had barked through the night huddled together and shivered in the doorway of the yurt. When Chen Zhen opened the door, the dog named Yellow stood up and rested his paws on Chen's shoulders as he licked his chin and wagged his tail ferociously, begging to be fed. Chen laid down a big platter of bones. The dogs grabbed them and lay down, stood the bones on end, and began to chew and gnaw. Crunching sounds accompanied the gradual disappearance of the bones, marrow and all.

Chen also brought out some lamb from inside the yurt for the bitch Yir, a dog with a shiny black coat. Like Yellow, she was a hunting dog from the Great Xing'an Mountains, with a large head, a long body, long legs, a narrow waist, and short fur. Both were born hunters, fast, agile animals that could do considerable damage with their teeth. They were excellent foxhunters, especially Yellow, a well-bred, quick-learning dog with unique skills. He was never fooled by how a fox swished its bushy tail, but caught it in his mouth, then put on the brakes and let the fox strain to keep moving. By abruptly opening his mouth, he sent the fox tumbling in a somersault, its neck and abdomen facing up. Yellow had only to trot up and sink his teeth in the fox's neck, and the hunter was presented with a flawless fox pelt. If they encountered a wolf, Yellow and Yir alertly, nimbly, and fearlessly engaged it, snapping and grappling, but always managing to avoid being bitten, buying time for the hunter and other dogs to catch up.

Yellow had been given to Chen by Bilgee and Gasmai. Yir had been brought over by Yang Ke from his landlord's place. The Olonbulag residents always gave the students the best things they owned, and when these two dogs grew to adulthood, they outstripped their canine brothers and sisters in every respect. Batu often invited Chen and Yang to go hunting, mainly because of the two dogs. Just since the previous winter, Yellow and Yir had caught five large foxes. The fur caps Chen and Yang wore in the winter were gifts from their two favorite dogs.

Yir had a litter of six pups soon after the Spring Festival. Three were immediately spirited away by Bilgee, Lamjav, and one of the students. That left one female and two male pups, a black and two yellows. They were roly-poly animals, like little piglets but more appealing.

Yang Ke, cautious by nature, fawned over his dog and her pups. He prepared a meaty broth of millet and shredded lamb for Yir nearly every day, using up half the yurt's monthly ration of grain, which was based on a Beijing standard—thirty *jin* a month per person: three of "fried rice" (cooked corn millet), ten of flour, and the remaining seventeen in millet. Most of the millet went to feed Yir, so the students had to model themselves after the Mongols by making meat the foundation of each meal. The herdsmen were given only nineteen *jin* of grain a month, all of it millet. Gasmai had taught Yang and Chen how to prepare food for a bitch with new pups. As a result, Yir had an abundance of milk, which made her pups hardier than those raised by the Mongol herdsmen.

The third guard dog was a husky black five- or six-year-old Mongol breed with a broad snout and wide mouth, a burly chest, and a long body, a male who roared like a tiger and was absolutely ferocious. He was covered with battle scars: black, hairless gouges on his head, chest, and back, all of which made him both ugly and fearsome. At one time there'd been a pair of yellow eyebrows above his eyes, but one of them was missing, lost perhaps to a wolf. Now it almost looked as if the dog had three eyes, and Chen called him Demon Erlang, after a fictional character in classical literature.

On his way back from a neighboring co-op one day, Chen had felt a chill on his back, something that made the ox up front jittery. He turned to look, and nearly fell off the wagon when he found himself face-to-face with an ugly, fiendish-looking dog the size of a wolf, his tongue lolling out of the side of its mouth. He tried to scare him off with his cow-herding pole, but that didn't work, and the dog followed him all the way home. Several of the horse herders recognized the dog. They said he was a mean animal with a bad habit of attacking sheep. He'd been driven out by his owner. The herdsmen advised him to drive the dog away, but Chen felt sorry for him, and the fact that he could live with wolves and survive the brutal winters piqued his curiosity. There had to be something special about the animal. Then too, since moving out of Bilgee's yurt and losing contact with the impressive Bar, Chen felt as if he were missing his right arm. "The dogs belonging to the students," he said to the herdsmen, "are hunters, fast but young, and they lack the ferocity of a big dog like this, with experience guarding a livestock pen. I think I'll keep him around and see how he does. If he kills another sheep, he'll pay with his life."

Two months passed, and Demon Erlang still hadn't gone after another sheep. Chen could tell that the dog was fighting the urge by staying clear of the pens. "In recent years," Bilgee said to Chen one day, "there's been an influx of short-term laborers, and they've just about killed off the grassland population of wild dogs, which wasn't all that big to begin with. They lure them into adobe houses, where they hang them up and drown them by pouring water down their throats. Then they skin and eat them. This dog looks like it barely escaped the same fate; it stopped its roaming and kept its wildness in check. Wild dogs aren't afraid of wolves that eat sheep, but they are afraid of men who eat dogs."

Demon Erlang guarded the sheep and drove off would-be attackers with his vicious barking, and he never shied away from a good fight; there were often traces of wolf blood on his snout when morning came. Winter passed, and few of Chen's or Yang's sheep had been taken off or killed by wolves.

There were times when Chen felt that Demon Erlang was more wolf than dog. The wolf is the ancestor of the dog. One of the earliest inhabitants of the northwest grassland—the Quanrong race—considered a pair of white dogs to be their original ancestors. The dog was their totem. Chen often wondered why the inhabitants of the grassland would venerate a domesticated animal—the dog—and he concluded that grassland dogs had been savage animals many centuries before, wild beasts whose wolfish nature had not receded, or wolves that possessed some of the characteristics of dogs. The dogs venerated by the Quanrong people might well have been a pair of white wolves. Was this ferocious animal he'd brought home one of those dogs with strong wolfish instincts? Or might it be a wolf with dog instincts?

Intent on getting close to the dog, Chen often squatted down to rub and scratch him, but there was hardly ever a reaction. To Chen the animal was an enigma, but that did not stop him from treating him well and learning more about him as he went along. Wanting to become his friend, he stopped calling him Demon.

As he waited for Yang and Gao to get up, Chen stayed outside to feed the dogs, play with the pups, and pat the expressionless Erlang.

The four Beijing classmates—one horse herder, one cowherd, and two shepherds— had shared a yurt for more than a year.

The horse herder, the perfectionist Zhang Jiyuan, tended a herd of nearly five hundred horses with Batu and Lamjav. Because their appetites were so large, the horses were taken into the mountains so that there would be no competition with the cows or sheep over grazing land. It was wolf country. The herders lived in a tiny felt yurt that slept two at a time; in their makeshift kitchens, they cooked on a small stove fueled by dried horse dung. It was a primitive, dangerous, and exhausting life with heavy responsibilities, which is why their status among the herdsmen was so high. It was the proudest occupation among people who spent so much time on horseback.

Lassoing horses is a graceful, skilled art that lends

itself superbly to the martial art of catching and killing wolves. In order to change horses, for themselves or for others, or to cut their manes or medicate them, or to geld or examine or break them in, horse herders have to lasso horses nearly every day. Since ancient times, grassland horsemen have been experts in the use of the lasso pole; they thrust the long pole out ahead of them as they race along on horseback, then loop a rope at the far end around the neck of the horse they're chasing. An accomplished horseman will hardly ever miss. When the target is a wolf, as long as the horse is fast enough to keep up, sometimes aided by hunting dogs, the success rate is about the same. The noose is tightened around the wolf's neck; then the rider drags the animal behind it, either choking it to death or letting the dogs kill it. Wolves are rightly terrified of the lasso pole, and if they spot a rider carrying one in the daytime, they flee or hide in the grass. Perhaps that was why the wolves only fought at night.

The Olonbulag lasso poles were the most efficient of their kind Chen had ever seen. They were longer, more finely made, and more functional than the poles from other banners he'd seen in magazine photographs back home; the Olonbulag horsemen were justifiably proud of their poles. The northern part of the Majuzi River region is where a breed of fine warhorses, the Ujimchin, have been bred throughout Mongolian history. For Mongols, horses are not just companions, but comrades-in-arms; survival has demanded it. In this sort of existence lasso poles are essential. The Olonbulag poles are unusually long, very straight, and polished to a sheen. The poles—anywhere from ten to twenty feet—are made of two lengths of birch glued end to end. Chen had seen one that was nearly twenty-five feet long; naturally, the longer the pole, the easier it is to lasso a horse or a wolf. They are as straight as a bamboo pole with no joints. To make them that way, the horseman must plane away the knots and other natural imperfections. Then the pole is heated over burning cow dung; once the wood is pliable, it is pulled straight with a special tool. A thin rod about five feet in length is fastened to the tip of the long pole, with braided horse mane on the end. A virtually unbreakable noose is then added to the braid. Woven not of cowhide strips, but of sheep intestine, it is the only part of the lasso pole the horsemen do not make themselves, given the skill involved in its construction. They buy them at a special counter at the co-op. Once fresh sheep droppings have been rubbed into the pole with sheep's wool until it turns from white to the color of manure, it is dried and polished with a cloth until it shines like old bronze.

When a horseman rides with his lasso pole out in front, the weight of the noose causes the end to sag slightly; it sways with the motion of the pole, rising and falling gracefully, snakelike, with the movement of the rider. Wolves have all seen their brethren throttled by one of those lasso poles, which they likely assume to be some sort of magical and fearful snake. During daylight hours, a lone rider out in the wilds or up in the mountains—man, woman, old, or young—can travel undisturbed if he holds a lasso pole, almost as if it were a safe-passage tally given by Tengger.

Experienced horse herders were allocated eight or nine fast horses apiece, not counting the wild animals that belonged to no one in particular, all of which they were free to ride. They rarely rode one horse more than a day and often changed mounts more than once a day. The last thing they worried about was tiring their horses; they proudly galloped everywhere. Whenever one of them visited a yurt, out came the requests for favors: to swap horses, to deliver letters or bring things back, to send for a doctor, or to pass on the latest gossip. They always received the most smiles from the girls, which drove other men, those with only four or five horses, mad with envy. For all that, herding horses was the hardest and most dangerous work on the grassland, and the production team chose only the hardiest, bravest, smartest, most resourceful and alert individuals to be horse herders, men who were not afraid to go hungry or thirsty, men who could withstand extreme cold and heat, men who had the constitution of a wolf or a warrior. Only one out of four had the good fortune of being chosen as a horse herder; the grazing land they patrolled was the front line of the war with wolf packs. Many of the wolf tales Chen Zhen collected had come from Zhang Jiyuan. Whenever Zhang returned from the grazing land, Chen brought him food and drink and treated him like a favored guest; then they would sit up talking about wolves half the night, occasionally arguing heatedly. Before heading back to his herd, Zhang usually borrowed some books.

Gao Jianzhong was a cowherd in charge of 140 animals. It was the least taxing of all the jobs on the grassland, and people were fond of saying that a cowherd would not trade jobs even with a county chief. The cows, which went out early and came back late, knew where the grazing land was and how to get home. The calves were tied by braided horse mane in front of the yurts, waiting for their mothers to return and feed them. Bulls, on the other hand, were a handful. They headed straight for the best grazing spots and were never eager to return home. The hardest job the cowherds had was rounding up stray animals. Stubborn creatures, if they didn't feel like moving, the cowherd could beat as much as he wanted, and they would just straighten their necks, flutter their eyelids, and remain standing where they were. But the cowherds enjoyed more leisure time, so whenever one of the shepherds needed help, that was who they turned to. No yurt could get by without cows. They pulled wagons and moved belongings; the people drank and cooked with their milk, burned their dung, skinned them for their hides, and ate their flesh. All domestic matters were tied to cows. People who spent so much of their lives on horseback needed cows for the family. Cowherds, shepherds, horse herders, they all had their duties and were all linked together, each indispensable to the others.

Chen Zhen and Yang Ke tended a herd of more than seventeen hundred sheep, nearly all of them the Olonbulag bushy-tailed variety, famous throughout China. Their tails were as big as a small basin, the tail fat nearly transparent, plump and crisp but not greasy, the meat fresh and aromatic without having a strong muttony smell. According to Uljii, Olonbulag grass was the finest anywhere in the league, which made their sheep the best. In ancient days, they were given as tribute to the emperor, a favorite of Kublai Khan after he entered Beijing. Even now it is on the menu when national leaders hold banquets for Arab Muslim dignitaries at the Great Hall of the People, and, it is said, the leaders of these countries are more interested in the origin of the lamb than in national affairs. Chen Zhen wondered if the reason the Olonbulag wolves had such large heads and so easily outsmarted humans was that they often dined on Olonbulag mutton. A second variety in the flock was an improved sheep from Xinjiang, a hybrid created from breeding local sheep with the fine-haired sheep of Xinjiang. They produced great quantities of excellent wool, which commanded a price three or four times higher than wool from local sheep. The meat, however, was loose and gamey, and the herdsmen would not eat it.

Then there were the goats, not more than 4 or 5 percent of the entire flock. They did most of the damage to the grassland, the way they grazed, but the cashmere they produced brought a high price. On top of that, castrated animals were fearless. With them in the herd, lone foxes and wolves usually steered clear, not wanting to taste the sharp horns of the goats. For that reason, the role of lead animals went to the eighty or ninety goats in Chen's herd. They knew where the grazing lands were, knew how to return home at night, and were choosy. When led out to lush grounds, they planted their feet and began grazing; if the grass was scarce, they quickly moved off. The goats were superior to the sheep in one additional respect: at the first sign of a wolf attack, they bleated, raising the alarm for the shepherds. The sheep, cowardly and stupid, would not make a sound even when the wolves were ripping open their bellies, and would passively accept the slaughter. Chen Zhen concluded that the herdsmen were experts at striking a balance, weighing the pros and cons of each animal, and accommodating them in the calibration so that the least harm and greatest benefits were achieved. The herders were superb at utilizing the strong points of every animal in the grassland.

Both shepherds worked together: one grazed the flock; the other kept watch at night. Ten work points were given for grazing the flock, eight for night watch. They alternated shifts and schedules. If one of them needed to be away, the other one could take both the day and night shifts, sometimes two days in a row. If the pen was in good shape, with good dogs guarding it, it was all right to sleep during the night shift, at least in the spring. But during the other three seasons, when they were on the move, away from the walled pens used for birthing, the sheep were kept within a semicircle constructed of wagons and large pieces of felt as a windbreak, but useless for keeping predators away. When wolves were on the prowl, the night shift made for hard, exhausting work, with no sleep, and constant rounds with a flashlight and a pack of dogs, shouting the whole time. The main goal of the night watch was to protect against wolves, Uljii said. Work points for night watchmen totaled roughly a third of all the points given out during the year. A major expense, thanks to the wolves.

Night watches were an important job for women on the Mongolian grassland. They stayed up all night watching the flock, then took care of their domestic chores during the day, which meant they seldom enjoyed a good night's sleep. The people worked during the day; the wolves came out at night. The people were tired and sleepy, the wolves energetic and well rested. The wolves turned the people's days upside down, beating down the women in one family after another, generation after generation. That was why the women in many yurts were often sick and died young, although the system also produced strong women who were not easily beaten down. Wolves multiplied quickly, while the number of grasslanders increased only slightly, which was why throughout history there had never been a large-scale land reclamation for the purpose of feeding the people. The wolves controlled the gradual development of the human population.

Sheep were the foundation of livestock farming in the

grassland. They supplied meat for food, hides for clothing, dung for cook fires, and two sets of work points. They ensured a continuation of the nomadic lifestyle. But tending sheep was boring, wearisome work that tied people down. From morning to night, out on the green or snow-blanketed wilds, a man had only a flock of sheep to keep him company. If he climbed to a high spot and looked around, he would not see another person for miles in any direction. The weedy land attached itself to the lonely man like a disease. Chen Zhen felt old, very, very old. The grassland had not changed from time immemorial, nor had the nomadic lifestyle of its inhabitants; they continued to compete with the wolves for food, a merciless fight with no clear winner. The Olonbulag existed in a frozen time where the grassland had taken on an eternal ancient patina. Could the wolves have caused it?

For Chen Zhen there was one distinct advantage in tending sheep. Being alone gave him time to let his thoughts roam. The two cartons of books he'd brought from Beijing, plus the histories Yang Ke had brought, were just what he needed to mull over, like sheep chewing their cud, slowing digesting their contents. Every night he consumed the classics, old and new, under lamplight; in the daytime, he chewed on some of the finest examples of writing, domestic and foreign, as he watched over his flock. The aging paper of the book he was reading became as fresh and wholesome as the green grass. There were times when he would quickly read a few pages, but only after assuring himself there were no wolves in the area. People are out in the light; wolves stay back in the dark. The baying of wolves can usually only be heard from a distance. An idea that was never far from Chen's thoughts had grown stronger in recent days: he was determined to find a wolf cub and raise it in his yurt, watching it day and night as it matured, hoping that familiarity would lead to greater understanding.

Chen Zhen was thinking about the female wolf that had taken one of his lambs a few days before and of the cubs that must be hidden in a den somewhere nearby.

He had just returned from checking the flock, and everything seemed normal. He lay down in the grass and stared fixedly at soaring vultures in the blue sky. Suddenly, he heard a disturbance among the sheep and jumped to his feet, just in time to see a large wolf holding a lamb by the neck. With a flick of her head, she flung her prey onto her back, held it there in her mouth, and ran along a stream up into Black Rock Mountain, where she disappeared. Normally, lambs will bleat in a crisp, shrill voice, and the bleats of one will get an immediate reaction from hundreds of others and their mothers, filling the sky with noise. But by sinking her fangs into the lamb's neck, the wolf stifled the cry and was able to get away without disturbing the tranquillity of the flock. Hardly any of the sheep knew what had just happened, and maybe even the lamb's own mother was unaware of what she had just lost. If not for Chen's keen hearing and his alertness, he wouldn't have known one was missing until he counted them that evening. As it was, he was as shocked as if he'd been the victim of a master pickpocket.

Once his breathing was back to normal, he rode

over to where the lamb had been taken. There he discovered a depression in the ground. The flattened grass was all he needed to see to know that the wolf had not just come down out of the mountains; if she had, he might have spotted her earlier. No, she had lain in the depression, waiting for the flock to draw near before making her move. Chen looked up to see where the sun was in the sky. He calculated that the wolf had lain hidden for more than three hours. During that season, only female wolves would take a lamb in broad daylight, as a hunting lesson for her young cubs. Lamb was also the most tender, most easily digested meat for cubs that had not yet opened their eyes and were still suckling.

Seething with anger, Chen also felt lucky. In recent days, he and Yang Ke had lost a lamb every few days, and they wondered if eagles or vultures had carried them away. Thieves from the sky struck quickly, often catching the herders off guard long enough for them to fly off with one of the lambs. But an eagle swooping down out of the sky sent fright waves through the flock, which reacted with bleats that would not escape the shepherd's attention. It was a mystery he and Yang had not been able to solve. Now that he had seen the wolf run off with a lamb and had discovered the depression in the ground, the mystery was solved. No more lambs would be lost to that trick.

No matter how guarded he was, Chen could not guarantee there would be no incidents. The wolves used tactics to fit a situation. While they lacked the wings of vultures, they were the true flying burglars on the grassland. Time after time they found ways to surprise people, always resulting in increased vigilance and the wisdom of hindsight.

Chen scratched Erlang lightly behind the ear, for which he received no sign of gratitude.

Snowflakes were swirling in the air when he stepped into the yurt and, together with Yang Ke and Gao Jianzhong, warmed himself by the stove, where dried dung burned. They drank tea and ate fatty meat and some curds that Gasmai had brought over. Since they had idle hours ahead, Chen tried to get them to go looking for a wolf cub. His reasoning, he believed, was convincing: Fights with wolves are inevitable, so by raising one of our own, we can get a better understanding of what makes them tick. Then we'll know the enemy the way we know ourselves.

Gao Jianzhong, who was cooking meat, had a pained look. "Stealing a wolf cub isn't child's play," he said. "The other day, Lamjav and some of the others smoked a female wolf out of a den when they were trying to steal a cub, and she nearly tore his arm off before three horse herders, one cowherd, and seven or eight dogs managed to kill her. The den was so deep it took them two days, working as teams, to get at the cubs. Even a sheep will defend her young. With a wolf, it's a fight to the death. We don't have a rifle. Do you expect us to take on a wolf with spades and herding clubs? Besides, digging up a wolf's den is exhausting work. The last time I went out with Sanjai, we dug for two whole days and still didn't reach the end. Finally we lit a fire and sealed the opening, figuring we'd suffocate the cubs inside. Sanjai said the mother wolf would know how to block off the smoke, and that there'd be a secret exit somewhere. By now you should know how wolves can trick us. The herdsmen say, 'Wolf den, wolf den, empty nine times out of ten.' The wolves move their dens all the time. If it's that hard for the locals, what makes you think we're up to it?"

Yang Ke, on the other hand, thought it was a great idea. "I'll go with you," he said. "I've got a pointed rod, sort of like a bayonet. I don't believe the two of us can't handle one female wolf. We'll also take a chopper and some double-kick firecrackers. By hacking with the chopper and setting off the crackers, there isn't a wolf alive we can't scare off. And if we manage to kill one in the process, everyone will be talking about us."

"Dream on," Gao said sarcastically. "You need to be careful a wolf doesn't turn you into a one-eyed dragon or give you rabies. That'd put an end to your scrawny life."

Yang wagged his head. "Back at school, during the Red Guard faction fights, four out of the five members of our group were wounded. I came through without a scratch. So I know I've got luck on my side. Lamjav likes to say I'm a grass-eating sheep and he's a meat-eating wolf. But if we go out and come back with a wolf cub, he won't be able to say that anymore. I'd do it even if it cost me an eye."

"Great!" Chen said. "You're in? Don't back out later."

Yang banged his mug down on the table. "When do we go? The sooner the better. After this, maybe they'll let us join their wolf-encirclement hunt, something I've dreamed of doing."

Chen stood up. "How about as soon as we finish eating? We need to do some scouting first."

After wiping his mouth, Gao said, "Gombu will have to watch the flock for you, and that means our yurt will lose a day's work points."

Yang replied snidely, "You're so damned petty. What about that time Chen returned with a wagonload of gazelles—how many work points was that worth? You're pathetic!"

Chen and Yang were saddling their horses when Bayar rode up on a big yellow horse. He told Chen that his grandfather, Papa Bilgee, wanted to see him. "It must be important if Papa sent for me," Chen said.

"Maybe it's about the hunt," Yang said. "Go on. While you're there you can get some hints on what we need to do to get one of those cubs."

Chen jumped into the saddle. Since Bayar was too short to remount his horse on his own, Yang offered to give him a boost. Bayar said no. He led the horse over to the wagon, stood on one of the shafts, and climbed into the saddle. The two horses sped off.

8

Before Chen had dismounted, he smelled the meat cooking inside the old man's yurt. Strangely, it didn't smell like mutton, so he rushed inside. "Not so fast," Bilgee barked. Chen stopped and immediately noticed that three sides of the floor covering were rolled up, and a new horsehide was spread out in the middle, on top of which lay seven or eight wolf traps. Steam rising from the pot filled the yurt with a rank odor; inside a black, oily liquid bubbled. Gasmai was on her knees next to the stove, her face covered with grimy sweat as she stoked the fire with dried dung. Her five-year-old daughter, Checheg, was playing with sheep bones, sixty or seventy of them. Batu, who was still recuperating at home, his face a patchwork of new skin, was polishing traps with Bilgee's wife, Eeji. Chen sat down beside the old man.

"What are you cooking? Wolf traps?" Chen asked jokingly. "You must have strong teeth."

Bilgee's eyes narrowed when he laughed. "You're half right. I am cooking traps, but my teeth are no good. If it's good teeth you want, look at the traps. Good ones, wouldn't you say?"

"But why are you cooking them?" Chen asked.

"To catch wolves," Bilgee answered. "Let me test your sense of smell. What kind of meat is that?" Bilgee pointed to a bowl beside the stove. Chen shook his head.

"It's horsemeat. I brought it back from the frozen lake. First I cooked a pot of horsemeat in water, and then cooked the traps in the soup. Know why? It's how I get rid of the rusty smell."

"I see!" Chen grew excited. "So that's how you get the wolves to step into your traps. I guess we're smarter than wolves, after all."

The old man stroked his gray beard. "Not if you think like that. They have a keener sense of smell than dogs, and if there's so much as a trace of rust or human odor, you've wasted your time. Once I cleaned my traps until there wasn't a spot of rust anywhere. No wolves. Eventually, I figured out why. After setting the traps, I coughed up a bit of phlegm, and if I'd scooped it and all the snow around it up, that would have been fine. But I stepped on it, covering it with snow, and figured that would do it. The wolves smelled it out."

"That's incredible!" Chen said admiringly.

"Wolves are intelligent, they're looked after by the gods, and they get help from all sorts of demons. That makes them a formidable enemy."

Chen was about to ask about the gods and demons when the old man rose up on his knees to take a trap out of the pot. After Chen helped him fish it out, they laid it on a greasy gunnysack and put another one into the pot. The traps were so big and so heavy that he could only cook one at a time. "I had everyone in the family clean traps yesterday," he said. "I've already cooked them once; this is the second time. And this won't be the end of it. Pretty soon I'm going to brush on intestinal oil from a horse with hairs from its mane, then repeat the process. That's when they'll be ready to use.

I'll wear gloves and add dry horse dung when I set the traps. Fighting the wolves is like waging war. If you're not careful, you're lost. You need to be more meticulous than a woman, even more meticulous than Gasmai," he added with a chuckle.

Gasmai looked up and pointed to a bowl on the rack. "I know how much you like my butter tea," she said. "My hands are dirty, so help yourself." Chen, who did not like stir-fried millet, was especially fond of Gasmai's curds. He put four or five pieces in a bowl, took down a warm teapot, and poured a bowl of butter tea. "Papa was going to take Batu with him to lay traps, but Batu can't go outside with his face like that, so Papa's taking his favorite Han Chinese with him."

Chen laughed. "Whenever wolves are involved, Papa can't help thinking about me. Right, Papa?"

"Young fellow," Bilgee said, "I think the wolves have got you in their clutches. I'm an old man, so I'm passing what knowledge I have on to you. Learn it well, and you'll get your wolves one day. But don't forget what I told you, that wolves are sent by Tengger to safeguard the grassland. Without them, the grassland would vanish. And without wolves, we Mongols will never be able to enter heaven."

"Papa, since wolves are the divine protectors of the grassland," Chen asked, "why kill them? I understand you agreed to the hunt at the headquarters meeting."

"If there are too many of them, they lose their divine power and turn evil. It's all right for people to kill evil creatures. If they killed all the cows and sheep, we could not go on living, and the grassland would be lost. We Mongols were also sent by Tengger to protect the grassland. Without it, there'd be no Mongols, and without Mongols, there'd be no grassland."

"Are you saying that wolves and the Mongols protect the grassland together?" Chen asked, moved by what the old man said.

A guarded look came into the old man's eyes. "That's right," he said, "but I'm afraid it's something you . . . you Chinese cannot understand."

"Papa, you know I'm opposed to Han chauvinism and that I oppose the policy of sending people here to open up farmland."

The old man's furrowed brow smoothed out and, as he rubbed the wolf trap with horse's mane, he said, "Protecting the grassland is hard on us. If we don't kill wolves, there'll be fewer of us. But if we kill too many of them, there'll be even fewer."

An almost mystical truth seemed hidden in the old man's words, one not easily grasped. Chen swallowed the rest of his questions, feeling a sense of uncertainty.

Once the traps were ready, the old man turned to Chen. "Come with me to set these," he said. "Watch closely how I do it." Bilgee put on a pair of canvas gloves and handed a second pair to Chen. Then he picked up one of the traps and took it outside where a light wagon was waiting. The bed was covered with a tattered piece of felt that had been soaked in the intestinal grease of a horse. Chen and Bayar followed with more traps; as soon as they were outside, the grease froze into a thin, oily coat, making the metal invisible. Once they were all loaded, the old man went to the side of the yurt and returned with a sack of dried horse dung, which he also loaded onto the wagon. Now that everything was ready, the three of them saddled up. But before they started, Gasmai ran out and shouted, "Chenchen, be careful with those. They can easily break your arm." He assumed she was actually saying that for the benefit of her son.

As soon as Bar and some of the other big dogs spotted the traps, their hunting instincts kicked in, and they were about to run after them when Batu grabbed Bar by the neck and Gasmai wrapped her arms around one of the other dogs. Bilgee told them to stay. Then the three men and four horses trotted off toward the lake ahead of the loaded cart.

Clouds were pressing down on the mountaintops; a light snow was falling, velvety and dry. The old man leaned back to let the snow land on his face, where it quickly melted. Taking off a glove, he caught a bit more snow and rubbed it all over his face. "I've been so busy these past few days," he said, "I forgot to wash my face. Snow does a decent job, and it feels good. My face gets smoky when I sit by the stove for a long time. The snow gets rid of the smell and makes the job easier."

Chen washed his face with snow too, and then sniffed his sleeve. He detected the faint odor of sheep dung. "Will this smoky odor make a difference?" he asked.

"Not really. It'll be gone by the time we get to where we're going. Just remember, don't let your coat or leather pants touch the frozen horsemeat and you'll be okay."

"Fighting wolves is tiring business," Chen said. "The dogs kept exchanging howls with the wolves last night, angry howls, and I didn't sleep a wink."

"At home you Chinese get a good night's sleep every night. But this is a battlefield, and we Mongols are warriors who are born to fight. People who need peace and quiet to sleep make poor soldiers. You must learn how to fall asleep as soon as your head hits the pillow and wake up the minute you hear a dog bark. Wolves sleep with their ears pricked, and at the first sign of danger, they're up and away. You have to be like that too if you're going to fight them. Me, I'm an old wolf." He laughed. "I eat, I fight, I sleep, and I know how to cat-nap. Olonbulag wolves hate everything about me, and when I die they'll chew me up, bones and all. I'll get to Tengger faster than anybody. Ha ha . . . "

Chen yawned and said, "Students out here are beginning to suffer from nervous breakdowns. One girl's already been sent back to Beijing. At this rate it won't take many years before the wolves have sent at least half of us back down south. I'm not going to feed the wolves when I die. I want to be cremated."

The old man was still laughing. "You Han are wasteful, and a whole lot of trouble. A man dies and requires a coffin, wasting wood that could be used to make a wagon."

"I won't need a coffin," Chen said. "Just toss me onto a fire."

"But a fire requires wood too," the old man said. "Wasteful, really wasteful. We Mongols are frugal revolutionaries. Lay us out on a cart when we die, head south, and where the body bounces out is where the wolves get their next meal."

"Are you saying that besides letting the wolves eat the body so that the soul can go to Tengger, it's also to save trees? There are no trees out here."

"Even more than saving trees, it's important to turn meat-eaters into eaten meat."

"Meat-eaters into eaten meat?" That was a new phrase for Chen, and thoughts of sleep vanished. "What exactly does that mean?"

"We grasslanders eat meat all our lives, for which we

kill many creatures. After we die, we donate our meat back to the grassland. To us, it only seems fair, and it's good for our souls when we go up to Tengger."

"You're right," Chen said. "It is fair. If the wolves fail to drive me back to Beijing one day, I might just say okay to letting them eat me when I die. With a whole pack sharing one body, it has to be a quick meal, probably faster than cremation."

This pleased the old man, but a worried look soon darkened his face. "In the past not many Chinese ever came to the Olonbulag. The seven or eight hundred inhabitants of the one hundred and thirty or forty yurts were all Mongols. Then came the Cultural Revolution, and a hundred of you students arrived from Beijing. You've been followed by soldiers and big wagons, with drivers, and now they're putting up buildings. They hate wolves, except for the pelts, which they love, and sooner or later their guns will put an end to them. Then you won't be able to feed the wolves even if you want to."

"Don't worry," Chen said spiritedly. "When the big war comes one of these days, the atomic bomb will get us all, people and wolves, and no one will be feeding anyone."

The old man made a circle in the air with his hand. "Atom . . . atomic bomb, what's that?"

Chen Zhen did what he could, including gestures, to explain, but it was no use: the old man couldn't comprehend it.

They'd nearly reached the northern edge of the frozen lake, where the horses had died. Bilgee reined in his horse and told Bayar to stop the cart and wait there. With two of the traps and a small spade, along with the bag of dried horse dung, he and Chen rode over to where the dead horses had lain. Stopping from time to time, he checked out the area. The dead horses, of course, had all been touched, and it was possible to see under the light blanket of snow where animals had sunk their teeth, that and the paw prints in the snow. "Have the wolves been back?" Chen asked.

The old man examined a few of the carcasses. "Not the big pack," he replied. "Uljii was right when he said it was probably up north past the public road. They are masters at waiting patiently."

"Then what about these tracks?" Chen said as he pointed to the ground.

"Mostly fox, plus the tracks of one female wolf. There must be several females up here who are staying with their cubs, all operating independently. He thought for a moment, then added, "I was hoping to catch the alpha males and some of the larger males in the pack, but with all these foxes around, that won't be easy."

"Have we wasted our time?"

"Not really. Our most important job is to trick the wolf pack, make them think that since we're laying traps, we won't bother to launch an encirclement attack against them. That way they'll be back to finish off these horses. We'll surprise them."

"Any chance we could get a wolf in one of these traps, Papa?"

"You bet there is. Let's set them for big animals, wolves not foxes."

The old man circled the area twice before choosing a spot next to one of the carcasses. Chen dismounted and started digging in the snow, while Bilgee crouched down and scraped out a circle about a foot and a half across and a couple of inches deep with his little spade. He then gouged out a depression in the middle. After putting on the gloves smeared with horse grease, he laid his trap on the ice and stepped down on both sides to set the springs, like a pair of oversized tweezers, pulling the sides, with their pointed teeth, down flat on the ground. Then he laid a cloth pad, shaped like an embroidery frame, over the depression, but beneath the metal base of the trap. Finally he hooked a metal rod onto the pad.

With his heart in his throat, Chen watched the old man complete the dangerous, difficult job, setting a trap that could crush a man's arm. Bilgee was breathing hard and drenched in sweat. He carefully wiped the sweat off with his sleeve, not wanting it to drip onto the dead horse. Now that Chen was on his first trap-laying trip with the old man, he was able to see how it worked. When a wolf stepped on the cloth pad, the weight would push down and release the metal rod from the hook. The springs would snap and close the serrated ends around the animal's leg, breaking the bone and tearing the tendons. No wonder the wolves were afraid of the traps. If they hadn't been frightened by the metallic sound of snapping traps, Chen would have died for sure during his earlier encounter with the wolf pack.

All that remained was to cover and disguise the trap. This too had to be done with extreme care. After catching his breath, Bilgee said, "You can't cover this with snow, it's too heavy, it'll push the pad down. Also, if the sun comes out, the snow will melt, the metal parts will freeze, and the trap won't snap shut. Hand me the horse dung."

Bilgee took the sack, grabbed a handful of dried dung, rolled it into little balls, and spread it on top of the cloth. The airy dung gradually filled in all the gaps, and the pad stayed suspended above the trap; also there was no fear of melting snow. The last thing the old man did was hook the chain connected to the trap to one of the horse bones and told Chen he could cover that with snow. After he'd instructed him on how to cover all the exposed parts, he sprinkled a little snow over the dung and smoothed out the surface with a sheepskin until it appeared undisturbed.

A light snow continued to fall, quickly erasing all traces of activity. "How will the trap catch wolves but not foxes?" Chen asked. "I set the rod deeper than usual," Bilgee replied. "A fox will be too light to spring the trap. But not a wolf."

The old man surveyed the area again and paced off a few steps. "You do it this time," he said after choosing the second spot. "I'll supervise."

"Why so close together?"

"A wolf can be merciless with its own body. If one of its legs is caught in a trap, it'll chew it off and escape on three legs. By setting two traps, if I get a leg in the first one, the pain will have the animal running around in circles, pulling on the chain, and its rear leg could trip the second trap, which I'm setting at the far reach of the chain. If a front and a back leg are caught, even if it chewed them both off, it couldn't get away."

Chen felt his heart clutch and his hair stand on end as he tried to come to grips with the ruthlessness of the war between man and wolf. Both sides used cruelty to attack cruelty and cunning to thwart cunning. However much Chen hated the ferocity of the wolves, when he contemplated the sinister use of the cruel trap he was setting, his hands shook. The trap would be perfectly concealed alongside the irresistible temptation of a meaty horse carcass, where only the smell of horsemeat, horse grease, and horse dung hung in the air—no human or metal odors. In Chen's mind, even the most cunning wolf would take the bait, suffer a broken leg, and wind up being skinned, its bloody, hideless carcass thrown to the wild. He was reminded of all the Han armies, from the Zhou through the Qin, the Han, the Tang, the Song, and the Ming, that had been drawn deep into the grassland, thanks to beautifully executed traps, and annihilated. Mounted warriors in olden days had not relied on overwhelming numbers to sweep away advanced civilizations. The true defenders of the grassland had employed military prowess and wisdom learned from the wolves to protect their territory against the fire and steel, the hoes and plows lined up behind attacking Han armies. The old man spoke the truth, but Chen could not keep his hands from shaking.

Bilgee laughed spiritedly. "A little soft in the heart, I take it. Have you forgotten that the grassland is a battlefield, and that no one who's afraid of blood can call himself a warrior? Doesn't it bother you that those wolves wiped out an entire herd of horses? If we don't use violent means, how will we ever beat them?"

Acknowledging the truth of the old man's words, Chen breathed deeply and, despite his mixed feelings, scraped out a spot in the snow and ice. But as he was placing the trap in the indentation, his hands shook again; this time it was from fear over what could happen if he wasn't careful with this, his first attempt. As the old man stood beside him giving instructions, he stuck his herding club into the trap's gaping mouth; if it accidentally snapped shut, the club would keep Chen's hand from getting caught. He felt a warm current throughout his body; with the old man standing by to help, he managed to stop his hands from shaking and laid his first trap without incident. As he was mopping his brow, he discovered that Bilgee was sweating more than he was.

"Young man," Bilgee said after exhaling his relief, "you do the next one all by yourself. I think you're ready."

Chen nodded and walked back to the cart to get two more traps. Picking a spot by a second horse carcass, he carefully laid the third trap; then they each took two of the final four traps and set them separately, the old man telling Bayar to assist Chen.

The sky remained overcast as dusk settled in. After examining Chen's work, the old man smiled and said, "You've concealed them well. If I were a wolf, you'd get me for sure. But it's getting late. What do we do now?"

"Well, I'd say we use a broom to remove our footprints and count our tools to make sure we don't leave anything behind."

"You've learned a bit of cunning," the old man said approvingly.

They began sweeping, from where they'd started all the way back to the wagon, inspecting their work as they went along. "How many wolves do you think we'll catch with these traps?" Chen asked as he was putting away the tools.

"Don't ask about numbers when you're hunting. You won't catch anything if you do. After the people do their job, they leave the rest to Tengger."

They mounted up and, pulling the wagon behind them, rode off.

"Will we come back tomorrow morning to see how we've done?" Chen asked.

"We can't go back, whether we get any or not. If we catch one, we need to give the pack plenty of time to see what's happening. They'll get suspicious when no one comes to claim their prey, and they'll surround the dead horse site to figure out what to do next. The job we've been given isn't to trap a few wolves, but to draw the pack out. No need for you to come here tomorrow. I'll check things out from a distance."

They made their way home in a good mood. Chen was thinking about a litter of wolf cubs and was planning to ask Bilgee how he should go about getting one, knowing it was a dangerous, difficult type of hunting that required exceptional skill, but was also one of the most important means of controlling the rampant growth of wolf packs. Wiping out one den of cubs meant one less wolf pack to worry about. But wolves call upon their highest powers of intellect and most ferocious skills in order to keep their young safe. Chen had heard tales of gripping adventure and lucky escapes regarding the theft of wolf cubs, and he was mentally prepared to take on the challenge. Two spring seasons had passed since the hundred or more students had come to the grassland, and none of them had single-handedly stolen a litter of cubs. Chen knew there was no guarantee that he'd be the first, yet he'd planned to accompany Bilgee as often as necessary to learn how it was done. But after the killing of the horse herd, the old man had no time for cubs, and all Chen could do was ask him to pass on his experience.

"Papa," he said, "while I was tending sheep the other day, a female wolf took one of my lambs right under my eyes and carried it up to Black Rock Mountain. She must have a den up there, and I'm thinking of going back tomorrow. I was going to ask you to go with me..."

"I can't tomorrow," Bilgee said. "There's too much

to do around here. You say she went up to Black Rock Mountain?"

"Yes."

The old man stroked his beard. "Did you follow her?"

"No. She was too fast for me. There was no time."

"That's good. If you had, she'd have led you on a wild-goose chase. They won't return to their dens if they're being chased." The old man paused a moment. "She's a clever wolf," he said. "Last spring the production teams found three dens with cubs up there, so this year no one's going back. I'm amazed that a wolf would go there to have her cubs. You can go tomorrow, but take others with you, and plenty of dogs. Make sure you take brave and experienced herdsmen. I don't want you and Yang to try it alone; it's far too dangerous."

"What's the hardest challenge?" Chen asked.

"There are plenty of things to worry about," the old man replied, "but finding the den is the hardest. I'll tell you how to do it. Get up before dawn and find a spot high up in the mountains. Lie there until just before sunup, then scan the area with binoculars. After hunting all night, the wolf will be coming back to feed her cubs. If you see where she goes, that'll be where her den is. Start a circular search with some good dogs, and you should be able to locate it. But then you're faced with the difficult task of actually getting the litter, and that means dealing with an angry mother wolf. Be very careful." His eyes became veiled. "If not for the loss of those horses," he said, "I wouldn't let you do this. Stealing wolf cubs is normally something old people on the Olonbulag are reluctant to do."

Chen didn't dare ask any more questions. Bilgee

had been incensed over the decision to launch a large-scale raid on wolf dens, and Chen was afraid he'd stop him from going if he pressed the issue. And yet stealing wolf cubs required knowledge; since his goal was to raise a cub, not kill it, he'd have to move quickly, not waiting until the cubs were weaned and had opened their eyes. He planned to check with Batu, the best wolf hunter in the brigade. Still incensed over the loss of the horses, he would definitely share his experience with Chen.

Night had fallen by the time they made it back to the old man's yurt. Inside, the rug had been restored to its original state; three lanterns in which sheep's oil burned lit up the spacious yurt, and the squat table in the center was laid out with platters of fresh-from-the-pot blood sausage, sheep's stomach and intestines, and fatty meat, all emitting fragrant steam. The stomachs of the three hardworking men growled. Chen took off his deel and sat at the table; Gasmai laid the platter of sheep gut in front of him, since that was his favorite, then picked up a platter of the old man's favorite, sheep breast, and placed it in front of him. She then handed Chen a little bowl of sauce made of Beijing soy paste and grassland mushrooms; it was what he liked to dip the fatty lamb in. The condiment had become a staple in both yurts. Chen cut off a slice of meat, dipped it in the sauce, and put it in his mouth; it was so delicious he all but forgot about the wolf cub. What they called fatty sheep intestine, the finest meat available in the grassland, wasn't fatty at all. About a foot in length, it was stuffed with strips of greaseless sheep stomach, small intestines, and strips of diaphragm. In short, while it was made of sheep parts that were normally discarded, it was a vital part of any Mongol banquet, crisp and chewy, fleshy but not greasy.

"You Mongols aren't wasteful when it comes to consuming a sheep. Instead of throwing away the diaphragm, you turn it into a delicious dish."

"When hungry wolves eat sheep," the old man said with a nod, "they finish it off—fur, hooves, everything. When natural disasters hit the grassland, finding food isn't easy, not for people and not for wolves, which is why every part of a sheep is consumed."

"Then you must have learned how to eat sheep from the wolves," Chen said.

They laughed. "Yes, that's about it," they agreed. Chen ate three more lengths of sheep intestine.

Gasmai laughed happily, and Chen recalled her telling him that she preferred guests who wolfed their food down. But knowing just how wolfish he must have seemed embarrassed him, and he dared not eat more. He knew how much Bilgee and his family liked this particular delicacy, and he'd already finished half of it. Gasmai cut off a piece of blood sausage and picked up another length of intestine with the tip of her knife. "I knew you wouldn't be in a hurry to leave," she said with a smile, "so I cooked two lengths of intestine. One's for you, all of it, and I expect you to be like a wolf, no leftovers." Everyone around the table laughed as Bayar reached up and took the second link from Gasmai. In the two years he'd been there, Chen had still not figured out what sort of relationship he should have with Gasmai. Elder sister-in-law seemed most appropriate, but sometimes he felt she was more like his own big sister, while at other times she was like a kindly old aunt or a perky younger one. Her happy nature was like the grassland itself—bighearted and innocent.

Chen finished off an entire length of intestine, which he washed down with half a bowlful of butter tea. "Bayar isn't afraid of grabbing a wolf's tail or crawling into a wolf's den or riding a wild horse," he said. "Aren't you afraid that something will happen to him?"

"That's how we Mongols are," Gasmai said with a smile. "When he was young, Batu had more courage than Bayar. There was no adult wolf in the den Bayar crawled into, and since cubs don't bite, clearing out the den was nothing to brag about. But when Batu crawled into a den, the mother was still inside. And he had the courage to drag her out."

Amazed by this bit of news, Chen asked Batu, "How come you never told me? I want to hear it now, in detail."

The laughter during the meal had lightened Batu's spirits a bit, so he took a big swig of the liquor in his glass and said, "I was thirteen. Papa and some other men had just found a den after a long search. It was so big, so deep, there was no way to dig in far enough, so Papa decided to see if there was a mother wolf inside by smoking her out. But even after all the smoke had cleared, no wolf emerged, and we assumed the den was empty. So I took some matches and a gunnysack and crawled in to get the cubs. I was barely inside when I saw the wolf's eyes, no more than two feet from me, and I nearly peed my pants. I lit a match and I saw that that scared her, her tail between her legs like a frightened dog. I lay there, not daring to move, but as soon as the match went out, she charged. I didn't have time to back out, and I figured that was it for me. Imagine my surprise when I realized she wasn't coming at me, but was going to jump over me to get out of the den. Well, I knew they weren't expecting that outside, and I didn't want the wolf to get to Papa, so I found the nerve somehow to straighten up and block her way. My head rammed into her throat, so I pushed up and drove her head against the ceiling. Now she couldn't get out and she couldn't get away. She clawed madly, ripping my clothes, but it was me or her, so I sat up straight, pinning her throat and head against the ceiling to keep her from biting, then reached out and managed to grab her front legs. Now she couldn't get her teeth *or* her claws in me. But I was stuck too. I couldn't move, and my strength was running out."

Batu related his experience dispassionately, as if it had happened to someone else. "Meanwhile, the people outside wondered what was keeping me. Sensing that something was wrong, Papa crawled in and lit a match. There I was, pinning a wolf to the ceiling with my head. He told me to hold on and not move as he wrapped his arms around my waist and began slowly edging toward the opening, with me pushing up with my head and holding on to the wolf's legs as it moved with us. Papa yelled for the people outside to grab hold of his legs and pull; they had no idea why until his body was halfway out the opening. They stood there with their knives and clubs, and as soon as we got the wolf to the entrance, someone jabbed a knife into her mouth and stuck her to the top, while the others ran up and beat her to death. Once I recovered my strength, I crawled back into the tunnel, which kept getting narrower, until it was barely big enough for a child. But then it opened onto a room where a litter of cubs was curled up on a chewed sheepskin with clumps of fur everywhere, nine altogether, all alive. To protect her litter, the mother had nearly shut the entrance to the room where they slept with dirt and kept guard outside. The smoke hadn't killed her because she'd made small openings here and there to the outside. All I had to do was move the dirt out of the way, reach in and grab the cubs, throw them into my sack, and back out . . ."

Chen could hardly breathe as he listened. Apparently, the family hadn't heard the story in a long time, for they too were tense. Batu's story was different from others Chen had heard about taking cubs from a den. "People say a wolf will fight to the death to protect her cubs," he said. "But not this one. Why?"

"Actually," the old man said, "wolves are afraid of people, since we're their only predators. This wolf had nearly been smoked out, and when she saw someone holding a lit match as he worked his way into her den, how could she not be afraid? She was a mature wolf, but I could see she was no more than two years old, and that this was her first litter. It was sad. It's something no one would have brought up if you hadn't asked."

There was no smile on Gasmai's face. Her eyes glistened from a layer of tears.

"Chen Zhen's going up to the mountains tomorrow to get a cub," Bayar said, "and I want to go along. He and the others are too big to crawl inside. I'll stay in their yurt tonight and head out with them first thing in the morning."

"All right," Gasmai said, "go ahead. But be careful."

"No!" Chen said, waving his hands. "Something might happen. He's your only son."

"This spring our group raided one den," Gasmai said, "and we still owe them three. If we don't deliver at least one more litter, Bao Shungui will punish us."

"I don't care," Chen insisted. "I'd rather not go than take him with me."

The old man pulled his grandson over. "You stay home, Bayar. I'm going to catch a big wolf or two, and instead of cubs, I'll give them the pelts to meet our quota."

9

By half past three in the morning, Chen Zhen and Yang Ke, along with two big dogs, were perched on a hill in the vicinity of Black Rock Mountain. Their horses, cowhide fetters in place, were hidden behind the hill. Erlang and Yellow had strong hunting instincts, and getting up so early could only mean one thing: a hunt. They were sprawled atop the snow, not making a sound and alertly looking all around. Clouds blotted out the moon and the stars, turning the gloomy grassland extraordinarily cold and terrifying. Chen and Yang were the only two people within miles, at a time when the wolf pack was on the prowl, when an attack was most likely. Close up, Black Rock Mountain was like a sculpture of enormous beasts, its sinister presence bearing down on the two men and raising chills on Chen's back. He was worrying about the horses and beginning to panic over this dangerous exploit.

Suddenly the baying of a wolf off to the northwest tore through the silence and echoed in the valleys around them, the fading strains sounding like a flute or a reed pipe, drawn out and cheerless. The sound died away and was followed by the distant barking of a dog. Neither sound stirred the two dogs beside Chen. They were familiar with hunting protocols: guarding the pens at night required constant barking; hunting in the mountains demanded strict silence. Chen stuck one of his hands down into the fur between Erlang's front legs to warm it and wrapped his other arm around the dog's neck. Yang had fed both dogs about half full before setting out; on a hunt a dog must not be too full or overly hungry. Too much food deadens the dog's fighting spirit; too little saps its strength. The food they'd been given was already doing its job; Chen's hand warmed up quickly, and he used it in turn to warm the dog's icy nose. Erlang wagged his tail lightly. Having the dog beside him steadied Chen's nerves.

After several rough nights, Chen was as tired as he'd ever been. Two nights earlier, Yang had invited a few herdsmen friends to come along for some cub hunting, though he didn't believe there could be any active dens on Black Rock Mountain and no one was willing to get out of bed so early. The herdsmen tried to talk Chen and Yang out of going. Instead, feeling rebuffed, the two friends decided to go on their own, which is why their only companions on the mountain were the two loyal dogs.

Yang held Yellow tightly in his arms and whispered to Chen, "Look, even Yellow's kind of spooked out here. He can't stop trembling. I wonder if he smells a wolf nearby..."

Chen patted the dog on the head. "Don't be afraid," he whispered. "There's nothing to be scared of. The sun will be up soon, and wolves are afraid of people in the daytime. Besides, we brought a lasso pole along." Chen felt his hand tremble slightly as it rested on Yellow's body. "You and I are like secret agents," he said, in part to calm himself, "late at night behind enemy lines, yanking a wolf's fangs. You know, I'm not sleepy."

Yang Ke also puffed himself up. "Fighting wolves

is like fighting a war: strength against strength, spirit against spirit, wisdom and courage against wisdom and courage. All the thirty-six stratagems, except for using the wiles of a beautiful woman, are in play."

"Let's not get complacent. I'm not sure thirty-six stratagems will be enough when wolves are the enemy."

"Good point," Yang said. "So which one do we use? Follow the mother wolf when she goes back to feed her young and find the entrance that way? That's not one of the thirty-six. Papa's the sly one. This is actually pretty cruel."

"Who told the wolves to kill all those horses?" Chen said. "They forced his hand. When we were laying traps, he said he hasn't done that for years. He's never been in favor of the wholesale killing of wolves."

As the sky lightened up in the east, Black Rock Mountain shed its sculptural image and became a mountain again. The first rays of sunlight filtered through the thin cloud cover, expanding the men's field of vision as they and their dogs lay sprawled on the snowy ground. Chen Zhen swept the mountainside with his telescope; there was nothing but scenery in his lens, since fog hugged the ground. He was worried that the wolf might have made it back to her den under the cover of fog, which would mean that he and Yang and the dogs had frozen up there half the night for nothing. But then, happily, the fog lifted and turned into a thin, transparent mist hovering above the ground, and any animal passing by would penetrate the mist and reveal itself.

All of a sudden, Yellow turned his head to the west, his hackles standing up, his body tense. Erlang turned his head in the same direction, and Chen, sensing that something was up, turned his telescope to see what had caught the dogs' attention. A stretch of dry yellow reeds in a marshy spot that followed the curve of the mountain was a favorite place for the wolves, with its hiding places and the wind at their backs; as the spot where they preferred to launch their guerrilla attacks on humans, it had gained the nickname Green Curtain. Bilgee was fond of saying that in winter and in spring this was where the wolves moved around, hid themselves, and slept; it was also a battlefield for wolf-hunting humans. Yellow and Erlang may have heard a wolf's footsteps crushing the dry reeds. It was the right time of day and the right direction, and Chen knew it had to be the female returning to her den. He scanned the area, waiting for her to appear. The old man had said there was shallow water in the reedy patch, runoff from melting snow, so the wolves would never make their den there. Mostly they chose higher ground, above spots where water would accumulate, and Chen was sure that if she appeared, her den was somewhere nearby.

The dogs fixed their gaze on a spot in the reeds, and Chen hastily swung his telescope to it. His heart lurched as a large wolf poked its head and upper body out from the reeds and looked around. The dogs immediately lowered their heads, until their chins were buried in the snow. The men flattened out on the ground, keeping as low as humanly possible. After scouring the mountainside, the wolf emerged from the reeds and ran toward a ravine. Chen followed her progress with his telescope; she resembled the wolf he'd seen the last time. She loped along with effort, probably having taken a sheep that night and eaten her fill. If this was the only wolf around, Chen saw no reason to be afraid. Two men and a pair of dogs, especially when Erlang was one of them, were easily a match for one female wolf.

The wolf climbed up the slope. All I need to see is which direction she takes, Chen was thinking, and I'll have a pretty good idea where her den is. But at that moment, she stopped abruptly, turned, and looked first to one side, then the other, and finally toward the spot where the men and their dogs lay unmoving on a hill-top. The men didn't dare breathe; she was now higher up than when she'd emerged from the reeds, and things she couldn't have seen then she could easily see now. Chen regretted his lack of experience; a moment earlier, when she was running toward the ravine, he and his companions should have backed off a few yards down the hill. The wolf's suspicions had taken him by surprise. She stretched her body taut, adding height to her stance, and checked again to see if there were dangers in the area. She made two complete circles, hesitated a moment, then spun around and darted onto a gentle slope to the east, where she headed for a cavelike hole and disappeared inside it.

"Great! There's the door! Now we've got them, the mother and her litter," Yang blurted out with a clap of his hands.

Chen stood up, bursting with excitement. "Come on, let's go get the horses."

The dogs were jumping around, panting excitedly and waiting for a command from their masters, which Chen had forgotten in his excitement. "Go!" he said, and the dogs tore down the hill, heading straight for the den entrance. The men ran to the rear of the hill, removed their horses' fetters, mounted up, and galloped off toward the den, where the dogs were waiting for them, barking loudly at the entrance. Erlang, fangs bared, was going crazy, storming the entrance, then backing out, not venturing in too far. Yellow remained at the entrance, adding his voice to the vocal assault and pawing the ground, sending snow and dirt flying. The riders jumped down off their horses and quickly sized up the situation. What they saw stopped them in their tracks: Just inside an oval opening some two or three feet across, the wolf was guarding her den and its contents with her life, sending Erlang back outside with her fangs after each feint, then emerging halfway to snap and snarl at both dogs.

Chen threw down his lasso pole, picked up his spade, and swung it at the wolf's head. She was too quick, and the spade hit nothing but air. Then she burst out of the entrance a second time, fangs bared; Yang swung with his club, and he too missed. Again she retreated, and again she attacked, round after round, until Chen was finally able to connect with her head, and Yang also made contact. That only made her angrier, more crazed than ever. This time, she retreated a yard or so, followed by Erlang. He was immediately bitten on the chest and scurried back outside, blood oozing from the wound, his eyes rage red. With an angry roar, he exploded back inside, until only his tail, swishing back and forth, was visible.

At that moment, Chen was reminded of his lasso pole, which he picked up off the ground. One look, and Yang knew what Chen had in mind. "That's it," he said. "We'll get a rope around her." Chen loosened the noose at the end of the pole so that he could hang it in the entrance to the den. When she poked her head out the next time, he'd jerk the pole up and tighten the noose around her neck, then drag her out. Once that was done, Yang Ke's club and the two dogs would finish her off in short order. Chen was so nervous he could hardly breathe. But he'd no sooner set his trap than Erlang was driven out of the den again, his rear legs knocking the noose askew. Seconds later, the wolf, her head bloodied from fighting the dog, emerged again, but she stepped down on the noose, and when she saw the lasso pole, she fled back inside as if hit by a jolt of electricity.

Chen stuck his head in the hole, seeing a steep downslope, thirty-five degrees or so, for the first couple of yards, then a turn, making the remainder of the den a mystery. Yang screamed at the entrance in anger, the sound quickly swallowed up by the tunnel, while Chen sat down, disheartened. "I'm an idiot," he said. "If I'd thought of the lasso pole first, that wolf would be dead by now. You have to be on your toes when you're fighting a wolf," he added. "And make no mistakes."

Yang Ke, even more disheartened, jammed the end of his club into the ground and said, "Shit, the wolf won because we didn't have a rifle. If I'd brought one along, I'd have blown off the top of her head."

"Headquarters says we're in a heightened state of battle preparedness, and no one is permitted to fire a weapon. A rifle wouldn't have done us any good."

"At this rate," Yang said, "we're going nowhere. What do you say we light off some double-kick firecrackers?"

"What's the difference between that and a rifle?" By this time Chen had calmed down. "If we frighten off the wolves up north, the hunt plans will be ruined, and you and I will be in hot water. Besides, you can't kill a wolf with firecrackers."

"So?" Yang said, apparently disgruntled. "We can scare the hell out of her, smoke her out. We're a good ten miles from the frontier, so the wolf pack won't hear a thing. But if you're still worried, how's this? I'll take off my deel, and after I throw some crackers inside, I'll hold the deel over the entrance to muffle the sound. You won't hear a thing."

"What if the wolf doesn't come out?"

"She will, trust me," Yang said as he untied his belt. "A herdsman told me that wolves are terrified of gunfire and the smell of gunpowder. I'll throw in three double-kicks, six explosions, and the sound reverberating in that enclosed space will be much louder than outside. It'll scare the hell out of her. And since the entrance is so narrow, she'll choke on the thick smoke. I'm betting that three is all it will take to drive her right into your arms. And I wouldn't be surprised if the whole litter of cubs followed her out. A windfall."

"Okay," Chen said, "go ahead. But let's be prepared for anything. I'll look around for more holes in the area. Even rabbits make three escape routes, so she must have more than one entrance. Wolves are crafty, and no matter how clever we are, we could still come up short."

Chen climbed into the saddle and circled the area several times with the dogs, assuming that dark holes would be easy to spot in the snow. They found nothing within a hundred-yard radius, so he dismounted, led the horses off a ways, and fettered them. Then he walked back to the entrance and laid out the lasso pole, the spade, and the club. Erlang was trying to stanch the flow of blood from his chest with his tongue; the wolf had torn off a chunk of flesh the size of two fingers, and the flesh was still twitching. In obvious pain, he didn't make a sound. The men had not brought along any ointment or gauze, so all they could do was watch Erlang employ the dog's traditional healing method of sterilizing the wound, stopping the bleeding, and lessening the pain with his own saliva. They'd take care of it when they were back at camp. The other scars on Erlang's body looked to have been caused by wolf bites, which was why his eyes turned fiery red at the mere sight of a wolf.

Yang was ready. His deel draped over his shoulders, he held three double-kick firecrackers as thick as tubular hand grenades; a lit cigarette dangled from his lips, a sight that drew laughter from Chen. "You look more like a Japanese tunnel rat than a hunter," he said.

"Just going local," Yang replied, "dressed like a barbarian. I'm betting this wolf is ill-prepared for a gas attack."

"Okay," Chen said. "Throw them in. We'll see what happens."

Yang lit one of the fuses, watched it sizzle for a moment, and then flung it as far inside the tunnel as he could. He did the same with the second cracker. After throwing in the third one, he watched briefly as all three rolled down the steep slope of the tunnel before covering the entrance with his deel, just in time to hear a series of six muffled explosions that made the ground shake. Inside the tunnel, the sound must have been earsplitting, the concussion powerful, the smoke suffocating. No grassland wolf den had likely ever witnessed explosions of that magnitude. Unfortunately, the men did not hear agonizing howls from the wolf deep down in her tunnel, and that was not good news.

Yang hugged himself to keep from freezing. "So, when do we open it up?"

"Let's give it some time. We'll open a little hole and wait till some smoke comes out, then we can open it all the way."

Chen peeled back a corner of Yang's deel but replaced it when he saw only a wisp of smoke. Seeing how cold Yang was, he offered to wrap his deel around them both. But Yang waved him off. "Stay focused. The wolf will be coming out any minute! Loosening your belt will restrict your movements. Don't worry about me, I'll be okay."

They were still talking when Yellow and Erlang jumped to their feet and looked off to the northwest. Soft whines marked their tension. Chen and Yang quickly turned to see pale blue smoke emerge from the ground some twenty yards away. "Uh-oh," Chen blurted out. "There's another hole over there. Stay here; I'll go take a look." He picked up his spade and ran over, followed by the dogs. Smoke burst from the hole; so did a very big wolf, like a guided missile, bounding off toward the reedy area at the foot of the mountain. She was out of sight before Chen could react. Erlang followed her into the reeds, the rustling moving northward. Stunned, Chen shouted, "Come back here!" Erlang ignored the command. Yellow ran over to the edge of the reeds but lacked the nerve to go in. After a symbolic bark or two, back he came.

Wrapping his deel around himself, Yang walked up to the second hole, where Chen was standing. It was, they were surprised to see, newly dug, a hidden emergency exit.

Yang was so enraged that the tendons in his neck stood out. "That damned wolf has made a fool of us!"

Chen sighed. "No matter how many escape routes a rabbit has, they're fairly easy to find. But there's no way to tell how many escape tunnels this crafty wolf has. This one's perfectly planned. See, there's a steep falloff beyond the opening, and from there straight to the reeds. The wolf can reach them in no time. This one hole is more useful than eight or ten rabbit escapes. Bao Shungui says that wolves are skilled in close fighting, night fighting, long-range raids, guerrilla fighting, mobile fighting, all sorts of things. The next time I see him, I'm going to have to tell him they're not bad at tunnel warfare and camouflage either, and can even combine the two. Soldiering is the art of deception, and wolves are the world's finest soldiers."

But Yang's anger lingered. "Movies go on and on about tunnel warfare and camouflage in North China, like that's where they were invented. Well, here's some news: wolves were the inventors, about ten thousand years ago."

They walked back to the opening, where emerging wisps of smoke were thick with the smell of gunpowder.

Yang stuck his head in and looked around. "The cubs ought to be crawling out after an explosion like that. Do you think the smoke killed them?"

"I've been wondering that myself. If the cubs are dead, where does that leave us?"

Yang could only sigh. "If Bayar were here, he could crawl in."

Chen echoed the sigh. "I couldn't take the chance of bringing him along. Can anyone guarantee there aren't more adult wolves in there? These things are never easy for the Mongols. Gasmai only has the one son, and still she didn't stop him from grabbing a wolf's tail or crawling into a den. The old Chinese saying 'Don't fight wolves if you're unwilling to sacrifice your son' must have come from the grassland. Don't forget, the Mongols ruled China for nearly a century. I used to think it meant using your son as wolf bait, believe it or not. Now I realize it means letting your son risk crawling into a wolf's den to get the cubs. Only a youngster could handle a tunnel this deep and this narrow. If Mongol women doted on their children the way Han women do, their race probably would have died out long ago. But they don't, so Mongol youngsters grow up strong and fearless."

Chen went to his horse, took down the canvas bag, and brought it back to the opening. Yellow spotted the bag and ran over, wagging his tail and panting greedily. It was the bag in which Chen had put food for the dogs. He opened it, took out the smaller of two pieces of meat, and gave it to Yellow. The other piece was for Erlang. But he hadn't returned, and Chen was worried. In the winter and spring, reeds are the wolves' domain, and if this wolf had enticed Erlang into the middle of the pack, that probably spelled trouble. He was the mainstay where keeping the sheep safe was concerned. Things had not gone well on this outing, and losing their canine general would be the worse thing he could imagine.

Yellow's tail wagged feverishly as he ate. He was a clever animal, bold and fearless around rabbits, foxes, and gazelles. But with wolves he took care to size up the situation. If there were more dogs than wolves, he attacked. But without strong backup, he had no interest in showing off his fighting skills. Moments earlier, he'd stopped short of coming to Erlang's aid when the fight was at hand, afraid of running into the pack in the reeds. He was good at protecting number one, which was how he survived. Chen was fond of Yellow, who seemed quite human, and didn't blame him for his lack of loyalty. But since the onset of spring, he'd grown increasingly fond of Erlang, whose brutish nature was intense and who didn't seem human at all. He stood up and trained his telescope on the reeds in the northwest, hoping to get a glimpse of the dog.

But there was no sign of him. Chen reached inside his coat and took out a little sheepskin bag. It was a waterproof, oil-resistant food pouch Gasmai had given him. Under his coat it had stayed warm and hadn't soiled his clothes. He took out some flat bread, some fatty meat, and two chunks of curds. He handed half the food to Yang, and as they ate, they tried to devise a new plan.

Tearing off a piece of the flat bread and putting it in his mouth, Yang said, "This den is full of tricks and dodges, a real maze. They always keep their cubs in places we'd never think of. We went to a lot of trouble finding this one, and I'm not ready to quit, not yet. Since we didn't smoke them out, let's see how we do with water. If we brought up nine or ten water wagons, we could drown every last one of those little bastards."

"In this sandy soil?" Chen replied with a sneer. "You could bring an entire reservoir up here, and it'd all seep into the ground."

"Got it!" Yang exclaimed after a moment. "The adult wolf is gone, so why not send Yellow in there and have him bring the cubs out in his mouth, one at a time?"

This time Chen had to laugh. "That dog has already developed human traits and lost half its wolfishness. He's got such a keen sense of smell he can sniff out any wolf that's nearby. If a dog could bring cubs out like you say, then all we'd ever have to do is wait for the mother to leave the den and send in the dogs. That, of course, would spell the end of the wolves on the grassland. What kind of morons do you take the herdsmen for?"

"We could try," Yang said defiantly. "What would it cost us?" He called Yellow over to the entrance, where the smell of gunpowder was nearly gone. He pointed to the tunnel and called out, "Go get 'em!" Yellow knew exactly what Yang wanted, and backed off in fear. Yang straddled the dog and closed his knees around his middle, grabbing his front legs and dragging him back to the entrance. Yellow tucked his tail between his legs and whined as he struggled to break free, casting a pleading look at Chen Zhen, begging him to rescind the command.

"See what I mean?" Chen said. "You're wasting your time. Progress is hard; regression is harder. Dogs have regressed far from their wolfish origins. These days dogs are weak, or lazy, or stupid. Just like people."

Yang let Yellow go and said, "Too bad Erlang's not here. He'd go in."

"Of course, but he'd kill every cub he found. I want a live one."

"I know what you mean. That dog wants to kill every wolf he sees."

After finishing the meat he'd been given, Yellow walked off to check things out. He sniffed around and lifted his leg to leave his mark on the ground, drifting farther and farther away. Erlang, meanwhile, had still not returned, and Chen and Yang sat by the entrance waiting and watching, not knowing what else to do. No signs of life in the tunnel, yet the cubs couldn't all have died. At least one or two would have survived the smoke, and they should be trying to get out. But another half hour passed, and none emerged. Either they were dead, the two men surmised, or there hadn't been any in there to begin with.

While they were getting ready to head back to camp, they suddenly heard Yellow barking—now loud, now soft—somewhere behind the hill to the north, sounding like a hunting dog that had found its prey. They jumped onto their horses and rode as fast as they could up to the top of the hill; they couldn't see Yellow but could still hear him, so they followed the sound until the rocky ground made it too hard for their horses to run and they were forced to rein them in. Crisscrossing gullies stretched out in front on the weedy, rock-strewn ground. The snowy surface was covered by the tracks of animals—rabbits, foxes, corsacs, and wolves—all of which had passed by the spot at one time or another. A profusion of waist-high cogon grass, brambles, and other underbrush filled the spaces between splintered rocks, all dried-out and withered, presenting a scene of desolation to match an abandoned Chinese graveyard. The riders kept a tight grip on the reins as the horses slipped and stumbled on the dangerously uneven ground. No cow, sheep, or horse ever grazed there; neither Chen nor Yang had ever been there.

Yellow's barks were getting closer, but there was still no sight of him. "With all the tracks around here," Chen said, "I wouldn't be surprised if he's caught a fox. Let's speed up a little. At least the trip won't be a total waste."

Finally, after skirting the brambles, they reached the bottom of a ravine, where, as soon as they turned the corner, they spotted Yellow and were stunned by what they saw. Yellow, his tail sticking up in the air, was haranguing the entrance to an even larger, and much darker, den. The ravine was gloomy, the presence of wolves palpable. As a cold wind blew past, Chen felt his skin crawl. He wondered if they had stumbled into a wolf-pack ambush, with lupine eyes burning holes in him from their hiding places, and his hair stood on end.

The men dismounted, fettered their horses, and ran to the entrance, weapons in hand. The opening, which faced south, was at least three feet high and a couple of feet wide. Chen had never seen one bigger, not even one of the wartime tunnels he'd seen as a high school farm laborer in Hebei Province. It was so well hidden in a tiny gully, and so protected by needle grass above and rocky ground below, that it was visible only close-up. Delighted to see them, Yellow jumped and ran around Chen, as if wanting to be rewarded for his discovery. "I think we've found what we were looking for," Chen said. "The way Yellow's strutting around, he might actually have seen some cubs here."

"I think you're right. This looks like a real wolf's den, gloomy as hell."

"And there's a strong wolf smell," Chen said. "They're in there, I know it!"

Chen bent down to examine the berm in front of the opening, typical of dens, built by moving rocks during the digging process; the bigger the hole, the bigger the berm. This one was the size of two school desks placed side by side. There was no snow on it, but plenty of wolf prints and bone fragments. Chen's heart was thumping; this was what he'd been looking for. He called Yellow over and had him stand guard. Then he and Yang knelt down to examine the berm. By then Yellow had stepped all over the animal tracks, but the men could distinguish the prints of two or three adult wolves and five or six young ones. The cubs' prints were like plum blossoms, small, delicate, quite lovely. They were so well defined that the cubs might have been playing there only moments before, running inside only when they heard the barking dog; the berm itself looked as if the mother wolf had built it as a sort of playground. There were shards of lambs' bones and bits of hide here and there, with traces of nibbling on the tender bones by the cubs. Little piles of cub droppings were visible alongside the berm, thin as chopsticks and oily black, like little honeyed Chinese medicine pills.

Chen slapped himself on the knee. "The cub I've been looking for is in there," he said. "That mother wolf made suckers out of us."

Yang also realized what she'd done, and he pounded the berm. "You're right. This is where she'd been running to, and when she spotted us on the mountain, she made a detour and tricked us into searching an empty tunnel, then made us believe it was the real thing, drawing the dog into a fight, like any mother protecting her young. You damned wolf, you got us that time."

Chen thought back and said, "I had my suspicions when she changed directions, but she quickly made a believer out of me. That's a wolf that knows how to adapt. If you hadn't tossed those three firecrackers in there, she'd have gone around and around with us till nightfall, and we'd have been the ones who got screwed."

"We're lucky we had good dogs with us. If not for them, we'd have had to slink back to camp empty-handed."

"We're not in much better shape now," Chen said. "This wolf has kept us busy most of the day and got us to waste three bombs. This den goes down into the belly of the hill, deeper than the first one, with more twists and turns."

"We haven't got much time," Yang said as he stared at the opening, "and we don't have any more bombs. I think we're done for the day. Maybe we should check the area to see if there are any more openings, and seal up any we find. Then tomorrow we ask some herdsmen what we should do now, especially Papa, whose ideas are always the best."

Chen Zhen, not happy with how things had turned out, said, "There's one thing we can try. This is a big opening, probably the size of that Hebei tunnel, which we were able to crawl into. Why can't we do the same here? After all, Erlang's out dealing with the mother wolf, and there shouldn't be another adult wolf in there. If you tie your sash around my foot and lower me in, who knows, we might find our cubs. And even if we don't, I can get an idea of how the den is laid out."

Yang Ke shook his head. "That's suicide. What if there *is* another wolf in there? I've been tricked by wolves enough for one day. How confident are you that this is her den? What if it belongs to another wolf?"

The desire Chen had suppressed for more than two years suddenly burst to the surface and drowned out his fears. Clenching his teeth, he said, "If a Mongol boy has the guts to crawl into a wolf's den, and we don't, what does that make us? I'm going in, and that's that. I just need you to give me a hand. I'll take my flashlight and spade with me, in case there's an adult down there."

"If you're intent on going in, let me go first. I'm stronger, and you're too skinny."

"Being skinny gives me an advantage. If the tunnel narrows, you could get stuck. So no more arguments. The fat guy stays behind."

After Chen took off his deel, Yang reluctantly handed him the flashlight, the spade, and his bag. He tied Chen's Mongol sash, which was several feet long, around Chen's foot, then tied his own sash to Chen's. Just before he went in, Chen announced, "If I'm afraid to enter the wolf's den, I don't deserve a wolf cub!"

"If there's an adult in there," Yang reminded him, "don't forget to shout and give a hard tug on the sash." Chen turned on the light, got down on his hands and knees, and slid down the forty-degree slope into the passage. The smell of wolf was heavy in his nostrils, nearly suffocating him. Not daring to breathe deeply, he moved slowly past slippery walls with an occasional tuft of hair stuck to a protruding rock, on ground that was covered with tiny wolf tracks. I could be getting my hands on the cubs within a few feet, he was thinking happily, once he was completely inside the tunnel; Yang was feeding him the tether little by little, constantly asking if Chen wanted to come back out, to which he responded by telling Yang to keep going as he inched along on his forearms.

The first gradual turn in the passage came when he was five or six feet inside the den, where light from outside did not reach. Chen could now see only that much of the tunnel illuminated by his flashlight, and as he negotiated the turn, the tunnel gradually leveled out, though the walls abruptly narrowed and the ceiling lowered. He could move forward only by keeping his head down and holding his arms close into his body. As he crawled along, he studied the walls, which were slicker than the ones just inside the opening, and firmer, as if a spade had been used on them. Hardly any dirt fell when his shoulder brushed against the walls or when he scraped his spade against the ceiling, which eased his fears of a cave-in. He doubted that a single wolf could dig out such hard-packed dirt with her claws, certainly not this deep. All the sharp edges had been rubbed smooth, like cobblestones, so this must have served countless wolves—male, female, adult, and newborn—for a century or more. He had entered the world of wolves, and its smell was overpowering.

The farther in he crawled, the greater his sense of terror. On the floor beneath him, the tracks of adult wolves lay beneath those of cubs; would his spade be enough to allow him to survive if he encountered a mature animal? The tunnel was so narrow that it might be difficult for a wolf to use her fangs to full effect, but her claws would easily make up for that. She could probably rip him to shreds. Why hadn't he considered that? He began to sweat. Hesitation. All he had to do was jerk his leg, and Yang Ke would drag him out of there. But thoughts of the eight or nine cubs, or more, waiting up ahead convinced him that he couldn't stop now, so he clenched his teeth, relaxed the leg tethered to the outside, and continued crawling tenaciously. By now the walls were hugging him tightly, and he felt less like a hunter than a grave robber. The air thinned out, the smell of wolf got stronger, and the thought that he could die of suffocation came to him. Archaeological digs often turn up the remains of grave robbers trapped in just such narrow passages.

An opening loomed up ahead. Big enough for an adult wolf to squeeze through, but too small for him, it clearly was the wolf's defense against her sole predator on the grassland. Chen knew she'd built it to protect her litter against water and smoke; it also succeeded in stopping him. But there was no surrender in him. He tried to breach a wall with his spade, but it didn't take long to see how cleverly she'd chosen this site: the walls were constructed of large rocks with abundant gaps, making them sturdy yet dangerous. He was beginning to have trouble breathing, and his strength was ebbing. Even if he'd been able to keep hacking away, a cave-in was a possibility and he'd succumb to the wolf's trap.

Chen breathed in a mouthful of air with more wolf

smell than oxygen, and he knew he'd been defeated, that there would be no cub for him today. But he wasn't ready to head back quite yet; he wanted to get a closer look at the construction of the opening, hoping to at least catch a glimpse of a cub or two. He put what little remained of his strength in the service of this last desire: sticking his head and right arm through the narrow opening, he shone his flashlight inside. What he saw was demoralizing: just beyond the opening, the passage continued on upward and out of sight. Up there somewhere was a drier, cozier spot for the wolf to raise her litter and protect them against flooding. She'd put a great deal of thought into creating a complex den for her offspring and, he was amazed to see, a roadblock for him.

He cocked his head to see if he could hear anything. No sound; either the cubs were asleep or they'd already developed the ability to hide from danger, keeping absolutely still in reaction to unfamiliar sounds. Suddenly feeling dizzy, he summoned up the strength to jerk his tethered leg. Worried and excited at the same time, Yang pulled with all his might and managed to drag Chen back out of the hole. His face covered with dirt, Chen sat weakly in the opening sucking in big gulps of air. "No way," he said to Yang. "It's a fiendish cave that goes on forever." With a look of disappointment, Yang draped Chen's deel around his shoulders.

After Chen had rested, they scoured the area within a couple of hundred yards for half an hour, and found only one large exit, which they stopped up with rocks. Once they'd sealed up both openings, they stuffed dirt into the cracks and packed it in tight. Just before returning to camp, Chen, still fuming over his failure, stuck the business end of his spade in the dirt around the main entrance as a sign to the female: They'd bring more people back the next day, and more effective methods.

The sun was going down, and Erlang still hadn't returned. The dog's courage and ferocity might not have been sufficient to deal with a wolf so sinister and so cunning, and the two men were anxious and concerned. But they couldn't wait, and would have to head back with Yellow. Just before they reached camp, when the sky was pitch-black, Chen handed his tools to Yang, telling him to take Yellow home and let Gao Jianzhong know that everything was okay. Then he reined his horse to the side and rode off to Bilgee's yurt.

IO

The old man smoked his pipe and said nothing as he listened to Chen Zhen relate their adventure. Then he reproached him angrily, mainly over their use of the firecrackers, unaware of how powerful and effective they were. After tapping the cover of his pipe bowl, he stroked his beard and said, "That was cruel, unforgivably cruel. You drove her out of her den. You Chinese, with your powerful firecrackers, didn't even give her time to stop up the entrance with dirt. Mongolian wolves fear gunpowder more than anything. If you'd used those things in a den with a litter of cubs, they'd have tried to escape, and you'd have caught them all, and at that rate it wouldn't take long for all the wolves on the grassland to vanish. We kill wolves, but not like that. If we did, Tengger would be angry, and that would be the end of the grassland. Don't ever do that again, and don't tell the horse herders or anybody else what you did. I don't want them learning such terrible things from you."

Unprepared for the tongue-lashing, Chen realized the possible consequences of their action. With widespread use, the concussion waves and smoke from the explosions would overwhelm even the impregnable den fortifications. "We don't celebrate holidays with fireworks out here," Bilgee continued. "The migrants and you students brought them with you. We have strict controls over ammunition, but we were unprepared for an influx of firecrackers, for which there are no restrictions. A large-scale introduction of firecrackers, gunpowder, pepper powder, and tear gas could threaten the survival of the wolves, which have dominated the grassland for thousands of years. Out here, where nomadic existence is the norm, there's nothing more destructive than gunpowder. And once a people's totem is demolished, their spirit dies. The grassland, on which we rely for our very existence, could easily perish."

Chen wiped his sweaty brow, alarmed by what he was hearing. "Don't be angry, Papa. I swear to Tengger that we'll never again use explosives in a wolf's den, and I promise we won't teach anyone else how to do it. On the grassland, a man's word counts for everything."

The muscles in the old man's face relaxed. "I know you fight the wolves to protect your flock and the horses," he said to Chen, "but protecting the grassland is more important than protecting livestock. Youngsters and horse herders seem to be having a contest to see who can kill the most wolves. They don't understand what they're doing. All you hear on the radio is how heroic the wolf killers are. Things are only going to get worse for us from here on out."

Gasmai handed Chen a bowl of lamb noodles and made a special point of placing some pickled leek buds in front of him. She knelt by the stove and handed the old man a bowl of noodles. "People these days pretty much turn a deaf ear to what Papa has to say," she said. "He tells them not to kill wolves, but then does it himself, and that keeps them from putting stock in what he says."

The old man smiled bitterly and took the bowl from

his daughter-in-law. "How about you?" he asked Chen. "Do you put stock in what I say?"

"I do, I honestly do. Without the wolves, the grassland dies. There's a country far, far off to the southeast, called Australia. They have grassland there too, and there never used to be any wolves or rabbits. But then someone introduced rabbits into the country, and since there were no wolves, the rabbits reproduced like mad, littering the countryside with their burrows, holes all over the place; eating up most of the vegetation; and creating enormous losses for the livestock farmers. The government tried everything they could think of to fix the problem, but nothing worked. Finally they began covering the ground with steel-wire netting that allowed the grass to grow but kept the rabbits from digging out, hoping to starve the rabbit population in their underground burrows. This plan also failed. The grassland was too vast, and the government couldn't lay out enough netting to cover it all. I used to think that the Mongolian grasslands were so lush that there must be vast numbers of rabbits. But then I came to the Olonbulag and saw that the rabbit population was actually quite small. A major contribution by the wolves, I take it. When I'm tending my flock, I often see them catch rabbits, and when there are two working together, they never miss."

The old man seemed caught up in his own thoughts, but his eyes grew gentle as he murmured, "Australia, Australia, Australia. Bring a map with you tomorrow. I want to see this place for myself. Then the next time someone says they want to wipe out our wolf population, I'll tell them about Australia. Rabbits are a scourge. They have many litters a year, far more than wolves. When winter comes, marmots and field mice close up their burrows and hibernate, but rabbits never stop looking for food. Still, they feed the wolves during the winter and thereby keep the wolves from killing our sheep. Wolves can't eat all the rabbits, but they eat enough so that we're not stepping in a rabbit hole every three paces."

"I'll bring a world map tomorrow," Chen assured him. "You can study it all you want."

"All right. You've worn yourself out the past few days, so go home and get some rest." When he saw that Chen was hesitant about leaving, he said, "You want to ask how to get to that litter of cubs, is that it?"

Chen hesitated, then nodded. "It's my first time, Papa, so you have to tell me how to do it."

"I don't mind telling you," Bilgee said, "but it's not something I want you to do often."

"Of course," Chen promised.

The old man took a drink of tea and smiled mysteriously. "If you hadn't come to me, you'd never get your hands on that litter of cubs. First of all, give the mother wolf a reprieve. Don't pass the point of no return in matters like this."

"Are you telling me I'll never get my hands on them?" Chen asked anxiously.

The smile left the old man's face. "Well, you tossed explosives into the first tunnel and crawled into the second. You left your smell inside and sealed up both holes. She'll move tonight, that's for sure. She'll dig another hole and tunnel her way in. Then she'll bring out her cubs, one at a time, and deposit them for safety in a temporary den. In a few days she'll find a new permanent den, someplace humans will never find."

Chen's heart was beating wildly. "Is this temporary den somewhere that can be found?" he asked.

"Not by people, but maybe by dogs. That yellow dog and a couple of the black ones ought to do it. By the look of things, you're not going to be talked out of it."

"Papa," Chen said, "why don't you go with me tomorrow? Yang Ke says that the wolf has tricked him enough already."

"I have to go up north to check the traps," the old man said with a little laugh. "We caught a wolf last night, but I haven't touched it. The wolves up north have returned. They're hungry, so I might remove all the traps tomorrow. I think you should rest up the next couple of days to get ready for the hunt. We can take care of this other matter after the hunt."

Chen blanched, and the old man noticed.

"Or," he said more agreeably, "you and Yang Ke go check things out tomorrow. The wolf smells will be strong, so let the dogs sniff around, and I'm sure you'll find it. New dens aren't very deep. If she moved her litter to another old tunnel, they'll be out of reach. Luck plays a role in stealing wolf cubs. If you can't get to them, I'll go take a look. I won't let Bayar crawl into a den unless I'm there."

Bayar, exuding confidence, said, "I could wriggle through the hole you found. If you'd taken me with you today, you'd have your cubs by now."

Yang Ke was waiting for Chen when he arrived back at the yurt. Chen reported Bilgee's conclusions and recommendations, but that did little to ease Yang's concerns.

A burst of intense barks woke Chen in the middle of the night, and he knew that somehow Erlang had made it back home, that no wolf pack had gotten him. He could hear his powerful footfalls outside the yurt as he took up his guard duties. He should have fed him and tended to his injuries, but he was so tired he rolled over and, as soon as Erlang stopped barking, fell back to sleep.

When Chen awoke the next morning, Yang Ke, Gao Jianzhong, and Dorji were sitting around the stove drinking tea and eating slices of meat as they discussed the theft of the cubs. Dorji, a cowherd with Team Three, was a clever and experienced man of twenty-four or twenty-five who had come back to herd cattle after graduating from middle school. He doubled as the brigade's bookkeeper and was a hunter of renown. Yang Ke had invited him over out of concern that they would once again fail or would run into danger. Dorji would be their adviser and bodyguard. He was a cautious hunter, one who never loosed his hawk until he saw a rabbit, and his presence greatly enhanced the chance of getting the cubs.

Chen rolled out of bed, got dressed, and greeted Dorji. "I hear you wormed your way into a wolf's den," Dorji said with a smile. "Be extra careful from now on. Now that she's picked up your smell, she'll come after you no matter where you go."

That came as such a surprise that Chen got all tangled up in his down coat. "Does that mean I'll have to kill her, so she won't kill me one day?"

"I was just teasing. Wolves are afraid of humans. Even if she picks up your scent, she won't dare get too close. If they were that good, I'd have been eaten long ago. I went into a tunnel once when I was thirteen or fourteen and brought out a litter of cubs. And I'm still around, aren't I?"

Chen relaxed. "You must have killed a lot of wolves over the years."

"Sixty or seventy, I guess, not counting cubs. With them you'd have to add seven or eight litters."

"Seven or eight—that makes fifty or sixty cubs, so altogether a hundred and twenty or thirty wolves. Haven't they ever tried to square accounts with you?"

"Of course they have. Over the past ten years, wolves have killed seven or eight of our dogs, and too many sheep to count."

"If you kill off all the wolves, what will you do with your dead?"

"We Yimeng Mongols are like you: we don't feed our dead to the wolves; we bury them in coffins. The Mongols here are backward.'

"The Tibetans feed their dead to eagles. Here it's wolves. If you kill off all the wolves, won't the locals hate you?"

"You can't kill off all the Olonbulag wolves. The government tells us to hunt them, saying that each wolf killed saves a hundred sheep and each litter of cubs taken saves ten flocks. If you think I've killed a lot of wolves, you should see the champion wolf hunter of the Bayan Gobi Commune. One spring a couple of years ago, he brought out five litters of cubs, almost as many as I've managed over a decade. Lots of people from outside live in Bayan Gobi, including Mongols from Manchuria, and many of us hunt wolves. That's why there are fewer wolves there than here."

"How's their livestock production?" Chen asked.

"Not as good as here. Their grazing land is inferior, because there are so many rabbits and field mice."

Chen finished putting on his coat and went outside

to look at Erlang, who was eating a skinned lamb. In the springtime a lamb died from injury or sickness or the cold every few days, and they were fed to the dogs, which wouldn't eat them before they were skinned. Chen saw that he kept looking over at the lambs as they frolicked in the pen while he ate. Chen called him, but instead of looking up, he remained sprawled on the ground, his tail waving slightly. Yellow and Yir, on the other hand, came running over and laid their paws on his shoulders. Yang and the others had already treated Erlang's injuries, but he kept trying to remove the bandages with his teeth so that he could lick his wounds himself. Going back up the mountain was not going to be a problem with this spirited animal.

After breakfast, Chen went to the neighboring yurt to ask Gombu to watch the flock for him. Seeing that Chen and Yang were determined to lay their hands on a litter of cubs, Gao Jianzhong also appeared to get the itch, so he asked Gombu's son to watch his flock for the day. On the Olonbulag, stealing a litter of wolf cubs brought glory to anyone who could manage it.

The four men set out for Black Rock Mountain with their tools and weapons, a day's provisions, and two dogs. A cold front came at them like an avalanche, but left like silk from a cocoon. Four or five days had passed without the sun breaking through the thick cloud cover; on the gloomy grassland, herders' faces gradually gave up their wintry purple hue in the spring and turned ruddy red. New grass beneath the snow turned yellow, slowly, like hotbed chives under a blanket, showing no trace of green. Not even the sheep would eat it. Dorji's face creased in a smile as he looked up at the puffy clouds and said, "The frozen ground has kept food out of the wolves' bellies for some time. Last night the barracks dogs were barking ferociously, and it's a sure bet that the pack has returned."

After following the tracks Chen and Yang had made the day before for more than two hours, they arrived at the bramble-infested ravine. The spade was still stuck where Chen had left it, but there were fresh adult tracks on the berm. The rocks and dirt with which Chen and Yang had sealed up the entrance had not been disturbed; apparently the spade had frightened the female off. The dogs grew agitated as soon as they neared the sealed-up entrance, and began sniffing around; Erlang was restless, his eyes glowing with vengeance. Chen pointed to the nearby slope and called out, "Go." The two dogs turned and followed the scents up the hill, each taking a different path, as the men went up to the second opening, where they found more fresh tracks. The seal there was also undisturbed. Dorji sent the others off to look for more openings, but before they'd made two turns around the area, Erlang and Yellow began barking off to the north. Abandoning their search, they turned and rode up the hill, Chen taking his spade with him.

When they reached the top of the hill, they spotted the dogs down below. Erlang was pawing at the ground and barking wildly; Yellow was helping. Dirt flew. "They've found the litter!" Dorji shouted as the four men rode down the slope, their horses nearly losing their footing on the loose rocks, until they were alongside the dogs, where they slid down out of their saddles. Instead of making way for their masters, the dogs kept digging; Erlang stopped every few moments to stick his muzzle in the hole, impatient to drag out whatever was in there. Chen walked up, wrapped his arms around the dog, and dragged him away. He was discouraged by what he saw: a hole no wider than a few inches had been opened in the ground, a far cry from the large dens he'd seen up to then. There was no berm, just some loose dirt covering the snowy surface, which the dogs had already trampled.

With a sneer, Gao Jianzhong said, "You call this a wolf's den? A rabbit burrow is more like it, or home to some field mice."

"Look closer," Dorji said calmly. "This is a new hole. The dirt has been dug recently, and I'll bet this is where she moved her cubs."

Chen was not so sure. "Even a new hole would be bigger than this, wouldn't it? How could an adult wolf squeeze through that?"

"It's only temporary," Dorji said. "Female wolves are thin enough that she could make it through. She'll have left her cubs here and will have a new, permanent den somewhere else in a few days."

"I don't care if it's a wolf or a rabbit," Yang said, holding out the spade, "as long as it's alive. We're not going back empty-handed. Stand clear, I'll start digging."

Dorji went up and stopped him. "First let me see how deep it is, and whether or not there's anything in it." He picked up his lasso pole, turned it front to back, stuck the thick end into the hole, and moved it around. When it reached three feet or so he smiled. "There's something down there," he said, "something soft. Here, you try it."

Chen took the pole and poked around. He too felt something soft and springy, and could barely contain his excitement. "There *is* something down there! There definitely is. Let's hope it's cubs."

Yang and Gao each took turns and came to the same conclusion—there was something down there and it was alive. But none of them was quite willing to believe it was a litter of wolf cubs.

Dorji stuck the pole in as far as it would go, put his hand on it at the opening, and slowly pulled it out; he laid it on the ground following the direction of the tunnel below to determine the location of what they'd felt down there. He stood up, paced off the distance, and announced, "Dig here, but be careful; we don't want to injure the cubs."

Chen grabbed the spade away from Yang and asked, "How deep?"

"A couple of feet. The warmth from a litter of cubs is enough to soften the frozen earth, so don't push too hard."

After scraping away the snow above the spot, Chen placed the tip of the spade on the ground and gently stepped down, slowly increasing the pressure. The dirt caved in, and the dogs made a mad dash for the sunken tunnel, barking wildly. Chen felt the blood rush to his head, which began to throb. To him, this was more exciting than digging up a Han Dynasty tomb site, and brought a greater sense of accomplishment. In the midst of the fallen dirt, a litter of baby wolves, with gray coats and patches of black wolf hairs, came into view. "Wolf cubs! Wolf cubs!" all three students shouted after a moment of disbelief. Chen and Yang stood there immobilized.

"Why do I think I'm dreaming?" Yang said. "We really, actually got ourselves a litter of cubs."

"Who'd have thought you two Beijing blind cats could stumble on a litter of Mongolian wolf cubs?" Gao smiled wickedly. "I wasted days preparing for a fight."

Chen squatted down, carefully brushed the dirt

off the cubs, and took a count. There were seven, each barely bigger than his palm, seven tiny heads snuggled up in a bunch, like a single, unmoving organism. Their eyes were partially open, covered with thin membranes, blue and moist, with little black dots in the center. "I've been looking for you for a very long time," he said silently, "and now here you are."

"These were born about three weeks ago," Dorji said. "Their eyes are just about open."

"Are they asleep?" Chen asked. "Why aren't they moving?"

"Wolves are born sneaks," Dorji replied. "All that barking and shouting a moment ago woke them up for sure. They're playing dead. Pick one up if you don't believe me."

For the first time in his life, Chen was about to hold a living wolf in his hands, and he wavered. Picking one up by the ear, he held it between his thumb and forefinger. It didn't move, its legs hung limply—no wolf-like reaction, no resistance, more like a dead kitten than a live wolf. Chen held it up so that they could all get a close look. He'd seen puppies that close before, and was immediately aware of differences between wild and domesticated canines. A puppy was born with a neat, glossy coat. But not a wolf cub. Granted, it had a coat of fine, soft gray fur, but mixed in were long, bristly, black wolf hairs. The cub's head was black and shiny, as if coated with tar. Its eyes were only partially open, but its tiny fangs were fully formed, sticking out ferociously between the lips. Having been dug out of the ground, it carried the smells of dirt and wolf. No puppy ever smelled like that. But in the eyes of Chen Zhen, this was the noblest, the most treasured, the most beautiful little creature anywhere.

All the time he was holding the cub by the ear, it played dead, not moving a muscle, not making a sound. But when he touched its chest, he could feel the tiny heartbeat, frighteningly fast. "Put it down on the ground," Dorji said, "and see what it does." As soon as it touched the ground, the cub sprang to life and crawled as fast as it could away from the humans and the dogs. It moved like a windup car. Yellow was on top of it in two or three strides and was about to sink his teeth into it when all four men shouted for him to stop. Chen ran over, scooped up the cub, and stuffed it into his canvas schoolbag. Yellow glared angrily at Chen, a look that said he wanted to kill the thing to vent some of his loathing. Erlang, on the other hand, as Chen discovered, had just stared at the cub and wagged his tail.

Chen opened his bag, and the other men leaped into action, like boys out in the Beijing suburbs stealing birds' eggs. Reaching and grabbing, they emptied the den of cubs, one at a time, holding them by the ears and dumping them into Chen's canvas bag. After tying off the opening, Chen hung the bag from his saddle and prepared to head back.

Dorji looked around. "The mother is around here somewhere, so let's take the long way around. Otherwise, she'll follow us all the way to camp."

The three students were suddenly aware that danger lurked nearby and that there were tiny wolves in Chen's canvas bag, the very animals that caused such fear in the hearts of Han Chinese.

II

The three students mounted up and followed Dorji as he headed west through the reedy land, then turned south, skirting alkali dunes, intentionally choosing land too hard to leave hoofprints as they sped home. They were unavoidably nervous, feeling not in the least victorious, and overcome by guilt and trepidation.

Chen felt better when he thought about the wolf running off with one of his lambs. As a shepherd, he'd avenged a slaughtered member of his flock. Removing a litter of cubs, difficult as it might be, was easier than killing the same number of adult wolves. But the question remained: Why, if the Mongols had stumbled on this lethal means of keeping down the wolf population, did the wolf scourge persist? Chen decided to ask Dorji.

"The wolves are too clever," Dorji replied. "They choose the perfect time to bear their litters. Everyone says that dogs and wolves were the same family back in antiquity, while in fact wolves have always been stealthier than dogs. Dogs have their litters about half a month after Lunar New Year's. Wolves, on the other hand, have theirs at the very beginning of spring, when the snow has melted and sheep are having their young. That's the busiest time of the year for us, the most exhausting and the most urgent. Once the lambs have been born and the people can relax a bit, the cubs have grown out of their dens. The only time wolves live in dens is when the females bear their litters. The cubs open their eyes at about a month, and a month or so after that, they're out romping with their mother. There's another advantage to having their cubs in early spring. The mothers can hunt newborn lambs to feed their offspring and teach them how to hunt. Tender lamb is a wonderful diet for the cubs."

As Yang yawned over and over, Chen suddenly felt so tired he could barely stay on his mount. The prospect of sleep sounded good. But he couldn't get the wolves out of his mind. He asked Dorji, "How come the herdsmen out here aren't enthusiastic about looking for wolf cubs?"

"The local herdsmen are Lamaists," Dorji replied. "In the past, nearly every family had to send one member out to become a lama. Lamaists believe in doing good deeds, so they forbid random killing. Killing lots of wolf cubs, they believe, will shorten their own lives. Since I'm not a Lamaist, I'm not afraid of shortening my life. Manchurian Mongols don't feed their dead to the wolves, and I wouldn't shed a tear if every last wolf was killed. Once we learned how to plant crops, we began following the Han custom of burying our dead in the ground."

Chen felt as if an ill wind were following him, stirring up a deep-seated fear in his soul. After having had no contact with wolves in the city, he now was the master of seven cubs whose mother was unimaginably fie[illegible]ce and cunning. Who could say that the litter in hi[illegible] had not been sired by the leader of the pack? Or t[illegible] est of the breed? If not for his obsession, the t[illegible] tures would surely not have fallen into human hands; they would have grown to adulthood and become intrepid fighters. But his arrival changed their fate, and he would forever be linked to all the wolves on the grassland, their eternal enemy. Wolf families on the Olonbulag, led by the implacable mother wolf, would come to him in the dark of night to demand retribution, forever nipping at the edges of his soul. He suddenly sensed that he may have committed a terrible sin.

By afternoon they were back in the yurt; Chen hung his bag on the wall, and the four men sat around the stove drinking hot tea, eating roasted meat, and discussing what to do with the seven cubs.

"What's there to talk about?" Dorji said. "After we're finished here, watch me. It won't take two minutes."

Chen was now facing the dilemma he had anticipated—the raising of a wolf cub. From the moment the thought had first occurred to him, he knew there would be resistance from the herdsmen, party officials, and fellow students. Raising a wolf cub was something only someone with an ulterior motive would consider. It not only flew in the face of politics, faith, religion, and ethnic relations but also adversely affected production, safety, and their state of mind. During the early years of the Cultural Revolution, the Beijing Zoo attendants had kept an orphaned tiger cub and a canine surrogate mother in the same cage, and that had turned into a serious political incident, viewed as extolling the virtues of the reactionary theory of class harmony, for which the attendants were subjected to strident criticism. Wouldn't raising a wolf around flocks of sheep, herds of cattle, and packs of dogs be a public disavowal of separating friend and foe? Would he be seen as advocating the idea of considering one's enemy a friend? Since wolves were the enemies of herdsmen, as well as their revered divinities, their totem (especially in the minds of the elders), their bridge to heaven, and as such, creatures to whom homage was paid, how could they be raised as pets, like domestic dogs? From the perspectives of religion, production, and safety, one need only consider the saying "Raising a tiger invites peril; raising a wolf brings disaster." For Chen, the greatest concern was whether Bilgee would still consider him as a second son if he decided to raise the wolf cub.

Chen was not motivated by a desire to blaspheme the Mongols' divinity, nor did he wish to defile their religious beliefs. Quite the opposite: He felt an increasing sense of urgency to raise a cub owing to his deep-seated respect for the Mongol people's totem and his obsessive interest in the profound mysteries surrounding wolves, the way they came and went like shadows. But to avoid creating enmity with the herdsmen, especially with the old man, it was important to come up with reasons they could accept, however reluctantly.

Even before finding the litter, after racking his brain for days, Chen had finally found an argument he thought they might find reasonable: raising a wolf would be a scientific experiment to create a new breed of wolfhound. Wolfhounds enjoyed an excellent reputation on the grassland. Guards at the frontier station had five or six of the large, ferocious, and speedy animals. When they hunted wolves or foxes, they were fast, ruthless, and successful nine times out of ten. Commander Zhao of the frontier station had once gone out with two soldiers and a pair of wolfhounds to inspect the work of the militias in livestock regions. Along the way, his dogs had caught four large foxes. The commander had moved from place to place on his inspection tour, skinning foxes along the way, to the amazement of all the hunters who saw him. Not surprisingly, the herdsmen all wanted one of those wolfhounds; unfortunately, they were a rare breed at the time, and were considered army materiel. The herdsmen had no chance of ever getting a wolfhound cub, even if they were on good terms with the military. What were wolfhounds but the spawn of a male wolf and a female dog? Chen reasoned. So all he had to do was raise a male wolf to maturity and mate it with a bitch to produce a wolfhound, which he would donate to the herdsmen. Since Mongolian wolves were considered the finest in the world, if his experiment was a success, he might well produce a breed superior to German and Soviet army dogs, and might even be responsible for developing a new form of livestock farming.

Chen set down his tea and said to Dorji, "You can dispose of six of the cubs, but leave the most robust male for me. I want to raise it."

Speechless at first, Dorji stared at Chen for a good ten seconds. "You want to raise a wolf?" he said finally.

"That's right. When it reaches maturity, I'll breed it with dogs, and we'll wind up with cubs like the wolfhounds at the frontier station. When they start coming, every Mongol family will want one."

Dorji's eyes lit up, like a hunting dog spotting its prey. He nearly gasped. "What a great idea! It might just work. If we all had wolfhounds, catching foxes and wolves would be like child's play. Selling wolfhound pups might even make us rich someday."

"What if the brigade won't let me do it?"

"Say you're raising a wolf to fight wolves," Dorji said.

"To safeguard collective property. Anyone who opposes you will be out of luck when the pups start coming."

"You're not thinking of raising one too, are you?" Yang Ke asked with a laugh.

"If you're going to do it," Dorji said, "then I will too."

Chen smacked his fist into his hand. "Great!" he said. "With two yurts involved, we'll double our chances of success." He paused. "But there's no guarantee that a male wolf will mate with a bitch."

"Don't worry about that," Dorji said. "That I can take care of. Three years ago, I managed to get a terrific bitch, which I wanted to mate with my fastest, meanest male dog. But we had ten dogs altogether, eight males, good and bad, and if the bitch had decided to mate with one of the bad ones, what a waste that would've been. So here's what I did. When she was in heat, I found a well that had been dug halfway, about the size of a yurt and twice the depth of a man's height. I put her and one of my good male dogs inside, added a dead sheep, and made sure they were fed and watered for twenty days. When I took them out, the bitch was pregnant. She had a litter of fine cubs just before Lunar New Year's, eight in all. I killed the four females and kept the four males. Among all our dogs, more than a dozen, they're the biggest, the fastest, and the most powerful. Every year they get credit for more than half the wolves and foxes we take. If we do that here, we'll get our wolfhound pups. But don't forget, you need to raise your wolf cub with a female pup."

Chen Zhen and Yang Ke whooped in delight.

There was movement in the canvas bag. The cubs were probably uncomfortable and hungry, so it was time for them to stop playing dead and start struggling to find a way out of the bag. They were seven noble lives, the sort that Chen Zhen valued and admired, and five were about to be killed. His heart was heavy, and a picture of the sculpted wall at the main gate of the Beijing Zoo flew into his mind. Wouldn't it be wonderful, he was thinking, if I could send them there, members of the purest possible wolf breed, from the heart of the Mongolian grassland? At that moment he sensed how rapacious and vain humans can be. There would have been nothing wrong with picking the biggest and strongest of the seven cubs. So why had they brought the entire litter home? He should never have taken Dorji and Gao Jianzhong along. But would he have only brought one cub back with him if they hadn't been there? Probably not. Bringing back the whole litter represented conquest, courage, reward, and glory; it won him the respect of others. Compared to that, those seven lives were like grains of sand.

Chen's heart ached, for he had developed a fondness for wolf cubs almost from the beginning. They'd been on his mind for more than two years, until he was nearly spellbound, and now he wished he could keep them all. But that was out of the question. Seven cubs—how much food would it take to raise them to adulthood? Then an idea came to him. Why not get on his horse and return the remaining five cubs to their den? But other than Yang Ke, no one would have gone with him, and he certainly wouldn't go on his own, a four-hour trip there and back, more than he or his horse had the stamina for. At that moment the mother wolf must have been wailing grievously alongside her ruined den, howling madly, so going back would be suicidal.

Chen took the bag off the hook and walked slowly

out of the yurt. "Wait a few days before you take care of them, all right? I'd like to study them awhile."

"What do you plan to feed them?" Dorji asked. "Cold as it is, they'll all die if they go a day without being fed."

"I'll feed them cow's milk," Chen said.

"No you won't," Gao Jianzhong said, obviously displeased. "I tend those cows, and their milk is meant for humans. Wolves eat cows, so feeding them cow's milk would be an affront to the heavens, and the herdsmen wouldn't let me tend the cows anymore."

Yang Ke stepped in to smooth things over. "Go ahead and let Dorji take care of them now. Gasmai is worried about not meeting her quota. If we give her five cub pelts, she'll be able to squeak by, and we can raise one on the sly. Otherwise, the whole brigade will come over to see the litter of live cubs and you won't be able to hold one back. So let Dorji dispose of them. I couldn't do it, and I know you couldn't. We're lucky to have him here to do it for us."

Chen's eyes stung as he sighed and said, "I guess we have no choice."

He went inside and dragged out the box in which they stored dried dung for the stove. After dumping out the dung, he emptied the contents of the canvas bag into the box. The cubs immediately scrambled this way and that, but when they reached a corner they stopped and played dead, anything to escape a cruel end. They were trembling, the rigid black wolf hairs oscillating as if electrified.

Dorji moved them around with his fingers, and looked up at Chen. "Four males and three females," he said. "You can have this one, the biggest and brawniest. This other one's mine." Then he picked up the rest, put them back into the bag, and carried it over to an open space in front of the yurt, where he picked out one, turned it upside down, and announced, "This one's a female. Let her be the first to go to Tengger."

Kneeling on one knee, he windmilled his right arm and flung the plump little cub as high into the air as possible, the way herdsmen disposed of excess baby dogs in the spring: What goes up to heaven is its soul; what falls to the ground are its mortal remains. Chen and Yang had seen this ancient ritual many times in the past, and they'd heard it was how herdsmen disposed of wolf cubs. But this was the first time they'd witnessed it performed on stolen cubs, and their faces were drained of color, like the dirty snow alongside the yurt.

The female cub, apparently unwilling to go to Tengger so early, had played dead in order to stay alive. Now that she was up in the air and knew where she was headed, she spread her tiny legs and performed a strange dance, as if wanting to grab hold of her mother or dig her claws into her father's neck. She opened her mouth as she reached the apex of her arc and began to fall.

The cub hit the hard snow-swept ground in front of the barracks with a thud, like a melon, and stopped moving. Trickles of pink blood seeped out through her mouth, her nose, and her eyes, a milky color mixed in. Chen's heart slipped back into his chest from his throat, the pain moving beyond consciousness. The three dogs ran toward the corpse but were stopped by a shout from Dorji, who kept them from reaching the dead animal and destroying its valuable pelt. To his astonishment, Chen saw that Erlang had rushed over, not to join his companions, but to stop them from getting their teeth into the dead cub. With his commanding presence, he was not an animal to tear into a carcass; maybe he too had developed a fondness for the wolf cubs.

Dorji took a second cub out of the bag. This one, it seemed, could smell the milky blood of its sister, and as soon as she lay in Dorji's palm, she stopped playing dead and fought to free herself, scratching the back of his hand with her tiny claws. He was about to fling her skyward when he stopped and said to Chen, "Here, you can kill this one, see what you're made of. No grassland shepherd can go through life without killing wolves."

Chen took a step backward. "No, you go ahead."

"You Han Chinese have no guts," Dorji said with a laugh. "You hate wolves, but you can't even bring yourself to kill a cub. How do you expect to fight a war? No wonder you put all that time and energy into building a wall all the way across your northern border. Watch me..." His words still hung in the air as the second cub flew skyward, and before she hit the ground, the third one was on its way up. The killing excited Dorji, who murmured, "Up to Tengger you go; there you'll enjoy a happy life!"

Five pitiful little cubs had flown through the air; five bloody corpses now lay on the ground. Chen scooped them into a dustpan and stared up into the sky, hoping that Tengger had accepted their souls.

Dorji seemed exhilarated by what he'd done. He bent down and wiped his hands on the toes of his boots and said, "You don't get many chances to kill five wolves in one day. They're better at this than we are. Given the chance, a wolf will kill a hundred, even two hundred sheep at a time. I only killed five, big deal! It's getting late. I have to go round up my cattle." He walked over to pick up his wolf cub.

"Don't go yet," Chen said. "Help us skin these."

"No problem," Dorji said. "It'll only take a minute."

Standing guard over the dead cubs, Erlang snarled at Dorji and tensed. Chen wrapped his arms around the dog's neck to give Dorji a chance to skin the cubs, which he did as if he were skinning a lamb. They were so small he didn't need to skin the legs. After the five cubs were skinned, he spread their pelts over the rounded top of the yurt and pulled them taut. "These are fine pelts," he said. "If you had forty of them, you could make a wonderful coat—light, warm, good-looking. You couldn't buy one for any amount of money."

Dorji cleaned his hands with snow and walked over to the wagon to get a spade. "You guys are useless," he said. "I have to do everything. Dogs won't eat a wolf, so we have to bury these right away, and deep, to keep the mother from picking up their scent. That would be the end of your flocks and herds." They picked a spot west of the yurt and dug a four-foot hole. After tossing in the five skinned cubs, they filled in the hole and tamped down the surface. Then they spread medicinal stomach powder over the grave to cover the smell of the corpses below.

"Should we make some sort of den for our cub?" Yang Ke asked Dorji.

"No, dig a hole for it." So Chen and Yang dug a hole a dozen or so paces southwest of the yurt. It was a foot or so deep and a couple of feet across. They covered the bottom with well-worn sheepskins, leaving a spot of muddy ground uncovered, and put the little male cub inside.

It came to life the moment it touched the muddy ground, surveying its surroundings with its nose and its eyes, as if it thought it might be back home. It calmed down slowly and curled up on a sheepskin in the corner, still sniffing and looking around, as if trying to find its brothers and sisters. Chen was about to put the second cub in the hole to keep the first one company, when Dorji scooped it up and held it close; he jumped onto his horse and galloped off. Gao Jianzhong cast a cold look down at the cub in the hole, then climbed onto his horse and rode off to round up his cattle.

Chen Zhen and Yang Ke, weighed down with anxieties, crouched beside their new wolf den and stared at the cub. "I don't know if we're going to be able to do this," Chen said. "There are troubles ahead."

"With him on our hands," Yang said, "the good can't get out the door; the bad goes on forever. You just wait. The whole country's singing 'We won't stop fighting until all the jackals are dead,' and here we are, raising a wolf, treating an enemy like a friend."

"Out here," Chen said, "heaven is high and the emperor is far away. Who will know what we're doing? What worries me is that Bilgee won't let us do it."

"The cows are back," Yang said. "I'll go get some milk. This guy must be starving."

Chen waved him off. "Dog's milk is better," he said. "We'll give him Yir's milk. If a tiger cub can live off dog's milk, a wolf cub is a sure bet." Chen picked the cub up out of the hole and held it in both hands. Its belly had caved in with hunger and its paws were cold, like little icy stones. It was trembling. Chen quickly held it close, under his coat, to warm it up.

As dusk was falling, the time for Yir to return to her pups, Chen and Yang went over to the dog pen, dug a hole, and lined it with a thick layer of old sheepskins. A stiff, untanned horsehide curtain kept the den warm for Yir and her three puppies. After Yang fed her a soupy mixture of meat and millet, Yir ran back to the den, muzzled aside the horsehide curtain, and lay down gently against the wall. Her pups found her nipples and sucked greedily.

Chen approached Yir warily, crouched down, and rubbed her head to block the view down below. Happy as always when someone rubbed her head, Yir licked Chen's hand while Yang pushed one of the pups away and squeezed some milk into his palm. When he saw there was enough, Chen took the wolf cub out from under his coat and Yang smeared milk on its head, back, and paws, the way herdsmen tricked ewes into feeding orphaned lambs. But dogs are smarter than sheep, their sense of smell keener. If Yir's pups had died or been taken from her, she might have accepted the wolf cub. But with three of her own, that would not happen. As soon as she detected the presence of the wolf in her den, she tried to raise her head to make sure she could see her own pups. Using force and guile, Chen and Yang kept her down.

When the cold, hungry little wolf was laid down next to one of Yir's teats and could smell the milk, he stopped playing dead and, as if detecting the scent of blood, opened his mouth and bared his fangs, instinctively displaying an attitude of "If there's milk, she's my mother." Born a month later than the dog pups, the cub had a tinier head and was smaller overall. But he was already stronger than the little dogs, and his skill at latching on to the closest teat was superior to theirs. There were two rows of teats, some larger than others, so the supply of milk varied. Chen and Yang watched with amazement as the little wolf seemed less interested in drinking than in finding the largest teat, in pursuit of which he nudged the puppies out of the way. An intruder, a thug, a brigand had been introduced into a peaceful den. His wild nature was revealed as he sent the puppies reeling on his search for the largest teat. He sampled one, spit it out, and tried the next, over and over until he settled on the largest, fullest nipple right in the middle, and began sucking greedily. As he drank, he spread his paws over neighboring teats, as if eating out of a bowl and guarding the pot, hoarding the best for himself. The three docile puppies were kept away.

The two friends could not believe their eyes. "Wolves are scary," Yang remarked. "This little bastard's eyes aren't even open and he's already a tyrant. Now we see what it means to be the pick of the litter. I'll bet he'd have acted the same around his brothers and sisters."

Chen, mesmerized by the sight, was deep in thought. "We'll have to study him closely," he said finally. "There's a lot we can learn from this. Our dog pen is a microcosm of world history. I'm reminded of something Lu Xun once wrote. He said that Westerners are brutish, while we Chinese are domesticated."

Chen pointed to the cub. "There's your brute." Then he pointed to the pups. "And there's your domestication. For the most part, Westerners are descendants of barbarian, nomadic tribes such as the Teutons and the Anglo-Saxons. They burst out of the primeval forest like wild animals after a couple of thousand years of Greek and Roman civilization, and sacked ancient Rome. They eat steak, cheese, and butter with knives and forks, which is how they've retained more primitive wildness than the traditional farming races. Over the past hundred years, domesticated China has been bullied by the brutish West. It's not surprising that for thousands of years the Chinese colossus has been spectacularly pummeled by tiny nomadic peoples."

Chen rubbed the cub's head and continued. "Temperament not only determines the fate of a man but also determines the fate of an entire race. Farming people are domesticated, and faintheartedness has sealed their fate. The world's four great civilizations were agrarian nations, and three of them died out. The fourth, China, escaped that fate only because two of the greatest rivers—the Yellow and the Yangtze—run through her territory. She also boasts the world's largest population, making it hard for other nations to nibble away at her or absorb her, but maybe also because of the contributions of the nomadic peoples of the grassland . . . I haven't satisfactorily thought out this relationship, but the more time I spend on the grassland—and it's already been two years—the more complex I think it is."

Yang nodded. "I think raising this wolf will be good for more than just studying wolves. We can also study human nature, wolf nature, and domestication. It's a condition you can't find in the city or in farming areas, other than people perhaps and their pets."

"But if you don't study them in tandem with wolf nature, you'll never come up with anything worthwhile."

"You're right," Yang agreed happily. "Our first day has already produced rewards."

The commotion in the dog pen, and the whining protestation of the bullied pups increased Yir's suspicions and vigilance. She fought to break free of Chen's grip and see what was happening down there. Worried she might spot the cub and kill it, he held her head down and softly called her name, rubbing and stroking her to keep her calm until the cub's belly was full. She managed to turn her head enough to see that there was an extra puppy in her den, and sniffed out the wolf. Maybe because the wolf had some of her milk on its body, she hesitated briefly, then nudged it away with her nose and struggled to get to her feet and step out of the den, where the light was better, to see what was going on.

But Chen pushed her down again; it was important for her to learn what he needed, and he was counting on her to accept this new reality, to obey, not resist. She began to whimper, appearing to comprehend that her master had brought a wolf cub back from the mountains and put it into her den with the idea of having her nurture one of her mortal enemies. Several times she tried to stand and pull her nipple out of the wolf's mouth, but Chen kept pushing her back down. She was angry, agitated, uncomfortable, and disgusted, but she didn't dare disobey her master and was forced to lie down indignantly and not move.

Calm gradually returned to the den. Yir was the first bitch Yang and Chen had raised, and they had lavished attention on her during her pregnancy, when the litter was born, and throughout the nursing period, with good food, good drink, and whatever else she needed. She had plenty of milk; in fact, after several of her litter had been taken away, she had more than she needed. The additional mouth, the wolf cub, had no effect on her supply, and even though her own three puppies had been pushed over to thinner teats, they slowly ate their fill, then crawled up onto their mother's back and neck, where they began playfully nipping at one another's tails and ears. The wolf cub was still suckling.

Chen looked on, and did not like what he was seeing. The cub's belly was already more bloated than those of the puppies, so he reached down and touched it. It was taut as a drum and thin as paper. He worried that it might actually pop at that rate, so he pulled it back gently by the neck. But the cub refused to let go, stretching the nipple two inches and drawing yelps of pain from Yir. Yang anxiously reached down and pinched the sides of the cub's mouth, finally breaking the connection. He breathed a cold sigh of relief. "Herdsmen say that wolves' stomachs are made of rubber. I believe it."

Chen was visibly pleased. "What an appetite!" he said. "He's full of life; raising this one shouldn't be hard. From now on, we'll let him eat as much as he wants."

Night had fallen, so Chen returned the cub to his den and put one of the female pups in with him so he'd feel comfortable around her even before the membranes fell from his eyes. He wanted them to become friends. They sniffed each other, Yir's milk closing the distance between them; then they curled up together and slept. Chen spotted Erlang standing nearby, watching the cub and observing his master's every move, wagging his tail, the sweep a little broader than before, as if to show his approval to his master for taking in a baby wolf. Just to be safe, Chen covered the little den with a wooden plank and held it down with a large rock.

Honest, sincere Gombu, so easy to get along with, had already penned the sheep, and when he heard that Chen and the others had stolen a litter of wolf cubs, he ran over with his flashlight to take a look. He spotted the five little pelts on top of the yurt and was shocked. "Here on the Olonbulag, no Han Chinese has ever taken a litter of wolves. Never. That's the truth."

As the three students sat around the metal stove eating lamb noodles, the sounds of barking dogs and running horses entered from the outside. A moment later, Zhang Jiyuan parted the felt curtain and opened the door. Squatting in the doorway, holding the reins of two horses, which were stamping their hooves, he said, "Headquarters says the big wolf pack has drifted back in smaller groups, and they've ordered all three production brigades to begin the encirclement hunt tomorrow. The northwest sector is our responsibility, with the help of some hunters from other brigades, and under the overall command of Bilgee. The brigade leaders want you to assemble at Bilgee's yurt at one in the morning. Everyone but most of the old people and children, who will tend the cows and sheep, is expected to be part of the hunt. The horse herders will make sure everyone has a horse, and they'll arrive at the ambush sites ahead of the rest of us. Get some sleep. I'm going now. Make sure, make absolutely sure, that you don't oversleep."

Zhang shut the door, jumped into the saddle, and rode off.

Gao Jianzhong put down his bowl, pulled a long face, and said, "We just got our little wolf, and now the big ones are here. These wolves are going to be the death of me."

"A few more years out here on the grassland, and we might become wolves ourselves," Yang Ke said.

They began making preparations for the hunt. Gao ran out to the pasture to bring their horses back to the hay enclosure, leaving them just outside while he ran in, picked up a pitchfork, and carried out three piles of hay. Yang fed the dogs some sheep bones and some lamb he took from a willow basket and checked the saddles, belly straps, and lasso poles. Then he helped Chen Zhen find a couple of leather dog collars. They had participated in small-scale hunts before and knew the importance of dog collars and leashes. Chen fastened one of the collars around Erlang's neck and threaded a leash through the metal ring, then held both ends in his hand. He led the dog a few steps; then he pointed to the northern edge of the sheep pen, shouted "Go!" and released one end of the leash. Erlang ran over, turning the two lengths of rope into one, which came out of the ring. He ran into the dark night wearing only the collar, the long leash still in Chen Zhen's hand. Handling dogs this way during a hunt meant the dogs were always under the hunter's control, which kept them from going off on their own and throwing the hunt into confusion. At the same time, many dogs could be used without tangling them up in the leashes and slowing them down.

Yang Ke did the same to Yellow, threading the leash and practicing once. Both dogs obeyed commands, and the men's actions were flawless, keeping the dogs from running off with the leashes.

12

The men and horses of the production brigade, along with a pack of hunting dogs, raced through the inky blackness behind Bilgee, heading northwest on the open grassland. Every man had at least one dog; some had two. Winds from the northwest hit them full in the face, neither softly nor with excessive force. A dense cloud cover pressed down on the land, blotting out all light from the moon and stars. Unrelieved darkness surrounded them; even the snow on the ground was invisible. Chen Zhen was tempted to strike a match to see if his eyes were still functioning.

Using sound alone, he moved closer to Bilgee. "Papa," he said softly, "can I turn my flashlight on inside my sleeve? I'm not sure I still have eyes."

"Don't even think that!" The old man chastened him in a low voice that betrayed a prebattle case of nerves and a measure of concern.

Chen didn't reply but continued on blindly, accompanied by the clip-clop of his horse's hooves.

The hunting party moved quietly through the night. Wolves are superb night fighters, but grasslanders are also adept at surprise night attacks. Chen sensed that they were up against an uncommon pack of wolves; even with hunger gnawing at them, they had waited for a pitch-black night to emerge in full force. The looming battle was unfolding in accordance with Bilgee's unusual prediction and in ways for which the old man had planned. Knowing he was about to participate in a contest acted out on the primitive grassland between a pair of wolf kings, Chen was exhilarated.

After negotiating a gentle downslope, the hunting party began riding up a much steeper one. Bilgee rode up next to Chen Zhen, covered his mouth with his sleeve, and said in a more relaxed voice, "You need to train your ears if you want to become a decent hunter. Wolves' hearing is even keener than their vision."

Chen also covered his mouth with his sleeve and asked, "Aren't you afraid the wolves will hear us now?"

The old man whispered, "We're on a mountain slope, and the sound can't travel to the other side. There's also a headwind, so we're safe if we keep our voices down."

"Papa," Chen asked, "can you really lead us to the appointed spot by hearing alone?"

"No," the old man replied. "Memory is the other factor. I listen to my horses' hooves to see what kind of ground we're on, if it's sandy or rocky under the snow, and I can tell where we are. And to keep from losing my way, I feel how the wind is hitting my face. I also smell things. In other words, I travel with the wind and the smells. The wind carries smells of snow, grass, sand, saltpeter, alkali, wolves, foxes, horse dung, and the camp. Sometimes there are no odors at all, and then I have to rely on my ears and my memory. Your Papa could find the way if the night turned even darker."

Chen sighed. "How long will it take me to learn how to do all that, Papa?" he asked.

They crossed the peak and moved down onto a flat, vast grazing area, where Bilgee picked up the pace; the others followed, quickly and quietly. The riders felt like a well-trained cavalry unit on a mission, while in fact they were a ragtag group brought together at a moment's notice, one that included some of the old, the weak, women, and children.

The tension increased as they neared their appointed spot. It had not been long since the wolf pack had taken the first round with its stunning annihilation of the herd of warhorses; now, as the Olonbulag grasslanders were about to throw everything they had against the enemy, whether or not they would even the score was still in doubt. Chen began to worry that launching a surprise attack and an encirclement array against the wolves, with their superior sense of smell, and at night—their favorite time to fight—was like an apprentice showing off before his master. In the past, large-scale hunts had been organized yearly, and had always ended with no more than partial success, half the encirclements coming up empty. The head of the transport section had said sarcastically, "Encirclement hunt, encirclement hunt, a donkey with one ball, always wide of the mark."

Given the disastrous slaughter of the warhorses, if the hunt fell short this time, the pasture leadership would likely be replaced. Headquarters personnel had said that their superiors were preparing to transfer officials from communes that had enjoyed success in killing off wolves to reinforce the Olonbulag leadership. That was why Uljii, Bilgee, and the horse herders were determined to crush the arrogance of the Olonbulag wolf pack. At the mobilization meeting, Bilgee had said, "This time we'd better be prepared to deliver at least a dozen pelts of big wolves. If we don't, we might as well bring in hunters from other communes to run things here."

The night was getting darker, and colder. The

oppressive frigid air and encompassing darkness nearly took their breath away. Yang Ke rode up to Chen Zhen and whispered in his ear, "When we spread out, the gaps between us will be so big that we won't be able to see the wolves when they slip past our horses' hooves. I wonder what Bilgee has up his sleeve." Yang stuck his head up his wide sleeve to check the time on his luminescent wristwatch. "We've been on the road for more than two hours," he said. "About time to split up, don't you think?"

Chen leaned over and stuck his face up Yang's sleeve until he could read the dial on the old Swiss watch. He rubbed his eyes as his fears grew.

Suddenly, a chilled fragrance wafted over on the wind. It was the sweet medicinal smell of artemisia, a strong, cold, refreshing smell. As soon as the horses stepped on the thick artemisia, Bilgee reined in his horse. So did the others. The old man and the heads of the production teams behind him, as well as the hunters in the party, exchanged whispered comments, and the line began to spread out in both directions. A column of more than a hundred riders was quickly transformed into a straight rank of evenly spaced fighters. The sound of horse hooves stretched far and eventually died out. Chen Zhen stayed close to the old man.

All of a sudden, Chen was blinded by a light. A beam from Bilgee's flashlight tore through the darkness and was answered by lights from both directions. The old man swung his light three times, and the distant lights forwarded the signal up and down the line.

Then the old man's dry, shrill voice broke the silence: "Wu—hu—"

The sound echoed and splintered, and within

seconds was answered: "Wu—hu—" "Yi—hu—" "Ah—hu—"

Male voices, female voices, old voices, youthful voices, all merging together. The calls from the nearest group, Gasmai's Mongolian women's unit, were loud and crisp, ranged from high to low, and hung in the air a long time. Her calls were especially resonant as all the women and all the men in the brigade shouted as if they were on night watch in order to frighten and trick the wolves; the sound rumbled through the night, wave after wave pressing toward the northwest.

At the same time, more than a hundred dogs strained at their leashes and filled the air with frenzied barking, thundering through the sky.

In the wake of the sound war, the opening salvos of a light war commenced, with beams from all sorts of flashlights sweeping the northwestern darkness. The inky-black, snow-covered ground suddenly reflected countless beams of cold light, creating a scene more awesome and more fearsome than a flash of swords slicing through the frigid air.

Waves of sound and beams of light filled the gaps between the people and the dogs. The humans, the horses, the dogs, the sounds, and the lights formed a loose but effective, powerful, and dynamic net spreading over the wolf pack.

Chen Zhen, Yang Ke, and all the other Beijing students were so excited by the extraordinary scene that they whooped and hollered and gestured wildly. The people's morale soared, their voices rocked the heavens. Chen was now able to see where he was. It was a spot just south of the site of the horse massacre. Bilgee had unerringly led the party to the northeastern edge of the great lake, where they had then fanned out to form a net. Before he knew it, men, horses, and dogs had all skirted the lake and, with amazing speed, set up an encirclement on its northern edge.

Bilgee whipped his horse as he galloped down the line of hunters, anxiously searching the ground with his light for tracks in the snow as he inspected the formation, moving people when necessary. Chen followed close behind him. The old man reined in his horse. "The pack passed by here not long ago. A lot of them. See those tracks? They're fresh. It looks like we'll get them this time, and all these people won't have frozen out here for nothing."

"Why not just encircle the wolves here at the lake?" Chen asked.

"That wouldn't work," the old man replied. "The pack feeds on frozen horsemeat in the early-morning hours and slips away before the sun is up. If we surrounded them while it was still dark, how would we be able to trap them? The dogs couldn't see them, and the wolves could run in all directions. We'd come up empty. The party had to set out after midnight and have the encirclement in place before daybreak."

Flashlight signals continued from left and right. Bilgee stood up in his stirrups, holding on to the horn, and sent a stream of light commands in both directions, some long, others quite short, with crosses and circles, all part of a complicated set of signals. The semicircle of hunters moved ahead nervously but in orderly fashion, with human shouts, horse whinnies, and dog barks advancing in waves. Beams crisscrossed on the snowy ground and in the air, creating fans of light. Humans, horses, and dogs shrieked and snorted and yelped when they spotted wolf tracks in the snow, a sure sign of excitement as the battle loomed.

"What are you signaling?" Chen asked.

Without a break in his signals, the old man said, "I'm telling the people to the west to slow down and the ones to the east to hurry a little to link up with the people coming down the mountain. And I need for the people in the middle to hold the line and not get overanxious. Moving too soon is as bad as starting too late."

Chen looked up into the sky, which no longer resembled a steel curtain; he could make out the shapes of clouds that were drifting to the southeast and a bit of gray on the edges.

The big dogs had already picked up the scent of wolves, and their barks took on greater ferocity and irritability. Erlang was biting his leash, fighting it, struggling to burst ahead. Holding him back with all his strength, Chen reached out and tapped the dog on the head with his lasso pole to get him to obey.

While most of the wolf tracks pointed northwest, some went in other directions. Bilgee never stopped inspecting the tracks or flashing signals.

"How did people manage before there were flashlights?" Chen asked.

"With torches, wood wrapped with butter-soaked felt. They were as bright as these, and the wolves were scared to death of them. If one came at you, you could burn its fur."

As the sky lightened, Chen could make out the sights of the grassland; it was where he had grazed his sheep for several months. Off to the northwest, in his mind's eye he could see a broad basin ringed by mountains on three sides, with a gentle slope on one. That was likely where Bilgee planned to tighten the noose. The horse herders were lying in ambush behind the mountains, so as soon as the wolves were driven into the basin, the men, horses, and dogs behind them would close the door, and the war of annihilation would begin. But Chen could not even guess how many wolves might be caught. If the pack was really big, the cornered wolves would fight back, and the hunters would have to engage them in close combat. Chen removed his herding club from the saddle and looped it around his wrist, ready to try Batu's special wolf-killing skill but still feeling jittery.

The wind was getting stronger, the clouds moving more rapidly; the sun's rays seeped in between the clouds to bring some hazy light to the grassland. Cries of surprise erupted from the men when they reached the mouth of the basin. In the faint morning light, they saw two dozen big wolves pacing and stopping, looking all around, but not daring to move into the basin. Near the opening to the pass, another pack moved in and out of sight; they too appeared concerned about the lay of the land. For all he knew, they may have already gotten a whiff of the danger ahead.

Chen gasped in admiration over Bilgee's precise calculations and his guidance in the formation of the encirclement line. By the time the wolf pack realized where they had been driven and saw the array of hunters around them, the noose had been tightened; as soon as the flashlights lost their power to intimidate, the hunters' lasso poles were in sight. The wolves were, in fact, trapped as the two ends of the semicircle neared the outer limits of the basin.

* * *

After several of the leading wolves assessed the situation, they turned and, without a moment's hesitation, led the pack back to where it had come from. They had just eaten their fill of horseflesh and were incredibly spirited. They ran with power and awesome ferocity. A terrifying layer of wolf mist rose from the snow as they streamed past; nothing, it seemed, could stop them. Shouts erupted from the herdsmen as they brandished their lasso poles and rode out to meet the charging wolves. The riders on the two ends moved quickly to seal the gaps that had opened up.

The wolf pack offensive remained strong but slightly altered the direction of its main attack as it stormed the group of women, who wore the most colorful clothing and had the fewest lasso poles. None of the women, including Gasmai, blanched in the face of the attack. Standing up in the stirrups, they flailed their arms and shouted at the top of their lungs, as if prepared to block the way with their arms alone. But since the women had few lasso poles, the wolves saw this as the weak link in the chain and hoped to break through with a concentration of might and determination. Chen's heart nearly stopped as the likelihood of a breakdown loomed.

At that moment, Bilgee stood up in the saddle, raised his arm high, and brought it down sharply. "Release the dogs!" he shouted. From up and down the line, whistles and commands arose, as the handlers let go of the leashes and more than a hundred snarling dogs with harnessed power and red eyes exploded in the direction of the wolves from the east, the south, and the west. Bar, Erlang, and several other of the biggest, bravest, and fiercest assassin-dogs of the brigade headed for the leaders of the pack. The other dogs followed, anxious to show their mettle in the presence of their masters, barking madly as each tried to outcharge the others.

Meanwhile, horsemen sped to strengthen the array, those with lasso poles spurring their horses on to join the charge by the dogs. Snow and dirt flew from the pounding hooves; the intrepid Mongol warriors filled the air with bursts of murderous shouts once feared the world over—Hah! Hah! Hah!—accompanied by the rhythmic tattoo of galloping horses.

The daunting offensive rocked the wolves, whose leaders skidded to a stop, turned, and led the pack in a race to the mountain pass, their only means of retreat and a chance to link up with the wolves just beyond. They split up, heading toward three separate slopes to break out of the encirclement and take the high ground, either to reach the mountain peaks and negotiate a circular route or to charge downhill.

The formation of hunters stretched out into a straight line and sealed the mountain pass. Bilgee had the wolves just where he wanted them.

On the other side of the mountain, the director Uljii and the military representative Bao Shungui stayed hidden in tall grass, nervously observing the situation on the battlefield before their eyes. Bao excitedly hit the snowy ground with his fist. "Who said that Bilgee always takes the wolves' side?" he exclaimed. "You see, he trapped this pack exactly when and where he was supposed to. He's amazing. I've never seen so many wolves. You have to hand it to the old man. I'll see he's rewarded for his service."

Uljii too breathed a sigh of relief. There were, as he

could see, forty or fifty wolves caught in the trap. In years past, a pack of ten or twenty was the best they could hope for. But Bilgee was the Olonbulag alpha male. At each year's encirclement hunt, if he wasn't in charge, hunters did not feel like participating. But the slaughter of the horses had enraged him. Uljii turned and said to Batu, "Pass the word: no one is to fire his weapon, not even into the air. There are too many people out here today, and we can't take the chance of a stray bullet hitting someone."

"I've told them several times already," Batu said.

Behind the mountain, the horse herders and hunters were in the saddle, waiting for a signal. They were the best the pasture had to offer, expert riders with superb lasso-pole and herding-club skills. For this hunt, they had chosen their fastest, most spirited mounts, horses they normally pampered, for they were still filled with anger over the loss of the horse herd, anger they planned to purge on this day. The horses, hearing the frenzied barking of dogs, were in the grip of prebattle tension. Their heads lowered as they tugged on the reins, they pawed at the snowy ground, chest and leg muscles pulled taut. Their hind legs were like springs in a trap, and the moment their riders relaxed the reins, they would burst forward. The leashed hunting dogs had also been chosen for their ferocity, alertness, and extensive training. They too had heard the sounds of impending battle, but they remained silent, mouths open, eyes glued to their masters, well-disciplined and battle-tested veterans.

Uljii and Batu slowly arched their bodies, ready to give the signal.

The main force of the wolf pack seemed focused on breaking through the encirclement at the highest point off to the northwest. Neither men, horses, nor dogs are a match for wolves in gaining high ground. With their powerful physiques, unparalleled stamina, and enviable lung capacity, they are used to leaving their enemies behind as they race to the tops of mountains. Even the few hunting dogs and lasso horses, which can outrun wolves on level ground, quickly drop behind once the wolves begin running uphill. When they reach the mountaintop, they stop to catch their breaths, search for the surest way to elude their enemy—the steepest slope, a hidden valley, a ravine—and move like lightning. Often, by the time horse and rider are at the top, the wolves have vanished without a trace; if they happen to be in sight, they will already be far out of rifle range.

The wolves ran for the mountain at full speed, their pursuers lagging behind. The fastest wolves were at the head of the force, the alpha male and several large wolves off to the side. Uljii pointed to one of them, a wolf with mixed gray-and-white fur on its neck and chest, and said to Batu, "That's the leader! He's the one who led the pack in the horse massacre. He's yours. Let's go!"

The pack was several hundred feet away. Batu stepped back, grabbed his lasso pole, and jumped into the saddle. Uljii climbed onto his horse and yelled, "Attack!"

Batu thrust his pole high into the air, like a battle flag, as the horse herders cried out "Go! Go!" Dozens of hunting dogs and horses were on the mountaintop almost at once. The dogs zeroed in on their targets like torpedoes. Two-thirds of the horse herders rode out in front and formed a semicircle nearly halfway down the slope, where they linked up with the hunters under the command of Bilgee. The remaining third rode straight at the wolves with their long poles.

When the ambush was sprung on the wolves, their

ranks were thrown into chaos. They were caught in the sort of trap they themselves used with such skill and familiarity. With that knowledge, they were more panic-stricken than the gazelles they had once trapped, and they were furious. As their sense of disgrace gave way to rage, they turned and headed back downhill, giving up the higher ground to engage in a decisive battle with the men and dogs. With reckless disregard for their own lives, they tore into the line of charging dogs, sending many of them tumbling. The snowy slope was turned into a site of terrible tangled warfare, with fangs—wolf and dog—ripping and tearing, sending snow and animal fur flying. Dogs whined, wolves howled, dog blood and wolf blood spurted from necks and heads. The horrified students, who had never seen such bloody warfare, were speechless.

At that moment, Batu was staring down at the gray-coated wolf king from high up on the hill. Brandishing his lasso pole, he charged. But the leader did not dash downhill with his pack, choosing instead to turn and run due west. Four or five big wolves surrounded him in an attempt to break through the encirclement. Batu, along with three hunters and five dogs, took after the leader and his escort. But the wolf king, with his intimate knowledge of the area, had his eye on an alternative, but dangerous, escape route. The ground beneath the snow was covered with small but slick rocks, and as soon as the wolves landed on them, the rocks began to roll downhill. But with their large, thickly padded paws, they were able to race across the slippery rocks without sliding downhill themselves, leaving behind a roaring avalanche. The dogs, with their smaller paws, were able to stumble along and keep the chase alive, but the horses were not. The three hunters had barely reached the stony slope when one of the horses lost its footing, sending it and its rider tumbling down, his lasso pole snapping into three pieces. The other two frightened hunters reined in their horses, jumped out of their saddles, and ran to rescue their comrade.

Batu, obsessed with vengeful thoughts, dismounted, stood his lasso pole straight up to use as a walking stick, the narrow tip threading the spaces between rocks, and continued the chase on foot, leading the horse behind him. "Catch him!" he shouted. "Catch him!" As he crossed a ridge, he heard the pitiful yelps of dogs, so he vaulted back into the saddle and rode quickly to where the sound was coming from. A moment later he saw one of the dogs lying on the ground, half dead, and another with a missing ear and a bloody face. The other three dogs were backing up in terror, their hackles raised. As soon as they saw the lasso pole, the wolves turned and ran into a reedy valley, followed by Batu, one of the hunters, and the three uninjured dogs.

After Uljii saw Batu ride over the ridge, he led Bao Shungui to the best vantage spot in the encirclement, where he could observe the battlefield and effectively deploy his troops, slowly tightening the noose to trap the pack. All the battle-tested Mongol hunters had an instinctive grasp of the situation and a perfect understanding of their responsibilities; no one fought to gain personal glory. Any wolf that broke through the encirclement was immediately set upon by one or two of these "outside" hunters and either caught by a lasso or driven back inside the circle. Even the spaces that opened up when these hunters were on the move were quickly filled by others to maintain the integrity of the formation.

The center of the circle was a mass of men, horses,

dogs, and wolves. A few dogs and wolves lay on the ground without moving, blood and steam rising from their mortal wounds. Forty or more wolves had been surrounded by as many as 170 dogs. They stood shoulder-to-shoulder, back-to-back, tails touching, fangs bared, facing death with a unified defense. The chests and shoulders of many wolves and dogs were torn and bleeding. Behind the front line of dogs, several dozen riders swung their lasso poles at the innermost wolves. The wolves and dogs fought viciously, biting and clawing; it was virtually impossible to tell where the wolves ended and the dogs began, making it difficult for the hunters to reach out with their lassos, since none wanted to snare a dog by mistake or catch one of each in the same noose. Nor did they dare launch an attack, since there were too many wolves with too much fighting spirit; not many had been taken out of the battle, and an inadvisable attack could initiate a coordinated attempt by the wolves to break through the ranks of dogs and men in the confusion, and from there put pressure on the loose net of riders beyond.

A few of the more experienced hunters swung their lasso poles out over the heads of the wolves, waiting for one to separate itself from the pack; when that happened, they dropped the noose—not caring if it settled around the neck, the body, or a leg—pulled it tight, and dragged the animal far enough for the assassin dogs to pounce on it and tear out its throat.

The students and the women and children were deployed outside the encirclement. Bilgee had sent Chen Zhen and Yang Ke halfway up the mountain, where they had an unobstructed view of everything happening down below.

Inevitably, one after another, the wolves were lassoed, dragged away, and taken down by dogs. Husky howls burst from the throats of trapped wolves, who immediately changed tactics: instead of leaping up and going after the dogs' necks, they lowered their heads to fight, making it impossible to lasso them from above.

Chen observed the battle through his telescope and saw that even though the wolves had no chance of escape, they kept their wits about them. Not content to take down one enemy or to be overjoyed to take down two, they were driven to kill as many of the hunting dogs—the main force surrounding them—as possible. They fought in threes and fours, coming to one another's aid, using their deadly fangs and tasting blood with every bite.

Bilgee, who was directing the campaign from behind the ring of hunters, abruptly shouted, "Charge, Bar, charge!" Then he gave the sign to retreat.

Chen and Yang knew what the old man had in mind. "Erlang, charge!" they shouted. "Erlang, charge! Charge! Charge!"

The two savage, red-eyed dogs understood both the shouts and the hand signals; they backed up several steps and changed tactics. With loud roars, they made a mad dash for the biggest wolf in the pack, the leader. Erlang, the quickest, hit the wolf first, knocking him back some three or four yards; but he stayed on his feet, just in time for the fierce, heavier Bar to hit him like a sledgehammer and send him tumbling. Then, before he could get to his feet, Erlang charged and, without waiting for support, sank his teeth into the leader's throat, sending four streams of blood skyward and onto the snowy ground; Erlang's red-stained face threw a fright into the pack. The dying leader, fangs bared, clawed wildly with what strength remained, leaving bloody tracks across Erlang's chest and belly; but the dog's wildness was greater, and nothing was going to make him let go of his victim's throat until the wolf was dead. The pack knew this savage dog; they had encountered his fighting skills before. They backed off, wanting to stay clear of their leader's killer.

The other big dogs learned from the tactic, it seemed, since they began butting the wolves and sending them flying. Erlang and Bar, the assassins, went on a murderous rampage, opening a hole in the wolves' defenses and letting the hunters in. Lasso poles rained down on the pack, disrupting their formation and driving many of them into the nooses or the teeth of waiting dogs.

Seeing that the battle was lost, the pack split up and, relying on the might and courage of each individual wolf, ran to break through the encirclement in all directions, throwing the battle plan into confusion; it was their last chance to escape with their lives. But each wolf was immediately surrounded by several dogs and a hunter or two; escape was impossible. With a chorus of shouts, the outer ring of hunters—men and women, young and old—charged with their lasso poles.

In the inner circle, Lamjav, who invariably compared himself to a wolf, saw a pair of dogs grappling with a wolf; he rode over, bent down in the saddle, and held his lasso pole low enough to let the wolf pass over it, then jerked it up and caught the animal's hind legs in the noose. Before the wolf could turn and attack the pole, Lamjav spun around and dragged it away like a gunnysack. Scraping its front claws on the ground in a desperate attempt to get away, it left furrows in the snow as Lamjav called for the dogs.

Lassoing a wolf on the grassland is hard, killing one even harder. Wolves' necks are so short and thick that they can easily slip a noose. It is like roping a log, and pulling it tight often makes it slip off. Experienced hunters therefore prefer to snag a wolf around the hips, the thinnest part of its body; if successful, this hold is escape-proof. But then comes the tricky business of killing the wolf. Dragging one by the neck usually ends in strangulation, but when the noose is down around its hips, and if only one hunter is involved, the difficulties mount, for when the hunter climbs down off his horse, the wolf will charge back toward the pole, often snapping it in two, and then either attack the hunter or run off. Only the most courageous and skillful hunter will not wait for the wolf to get to its feet, but will drag it up close and kill it with his herding club or a knife. Most do not dare take on a wolf single-handed, and will sacrifice the pelt, forced to drag the animal over to another hunter or to the dogs.

Lamjav dragged his wolf to a spot where the snow was deeper and searched for an assassin dog. Several dogs surrounded the wolf, filling the air with their barks and nipping here and there before falling back, unwilling to go in for the kill. Seeing that Erlang had just brought down one wolf by its throat, Lamjav dragged his wolf toward Erlang and shouted, "Kill! Kill!"

Erlang abandoned the mortally wounded wolf, turned, and went after the one snagged by Lamjav, held its head and chest down with his front paws, and sank his teeth into his throat. Even with its carotid arteries severed, the wolf tried to fight Erlang off with its claws; it failed.

Lamjav jumped down out of the saddle and shouted to other hunters, "Drag them over here. They're no match for this dog!"

Nearby, Bar was killing a wolf caught in a noose. Several hunters who had trapped wolves with their lasso poles dragged their victims over to Erlang and Bar to dispatch.

But they were not the only dogs involved in the frenzy of killing. Several huskies were also showing their mettle. Renowned wolf killers owned by Dorji, each was a trained assassin, and there were eight of them, perfectly suited to work in concert with the others: the fast ones ran down the wolves; the slow ones butted them to the ground and held them down for their more ferocious comrades, who went for the throats. They fought as a unit, never alone. That is how they were working now: a team of eight dogs killing one wolf after another, quickly, efficiently, already three and counting.

The hunters too were working in groups of three or four. As soon as one bagged a wolf, the others jumped down, grabbed it by the tail and hind legs, and crushed its head with their clubs. Wild shouts erupted in the northwest, where five or six hunters were chasing a pair of large wolves.

The two animals, driven dizzyingly from one hunter to the next, had nowhere to go. After being knocked to the ground several times, one of them could no longer run. So Laasurung threw down his lasso pole, took his feet out of the stirrups, and jumped up until he was crouching on the saddle, from where he leaped onto the wolf's back. Before it could react, he was sitting astride it. Grabbing it by the ears, he thudded its head to the ground; blood seeped from its mouth and nose. Other hunters rode up and threw themselves onto the wolf, until it could barely breathe. Finally, Laasurung drew his knife and killed the beast. The other wolf was harassed by three young horse herders who took turns kicking it, until one of them ended the game by killing it.

Chen Zhen, Yang Ke, and the other students let their lasso poles droop to the ground. Their role in the hunt had been as observers. What disappointed them most was that the only one of their number who had been sent into battle, the horse herder Zhang Jiyuan, had failed to lasso a wolf.

Seeing that all was well in hand, Bilgee rode up to Chen and Yang. "You students did a fine job," he said. "You held your positions. With you here, I was able to send more hunters into the battle with their lasso poles." Noting the disappointment on their faces, he laughed and said, "That dog of yours made a heroic contribution. I counted for you: by himself he killed two wolves, and he helped hunters kill two more. So each of you has a pelt coming. Custom dictates that the other two go to the men who lassoed the wolves." He turned and led them down the slope.

The hunt was over. Except for half a dozen especially fast or skillful or just plain lucky members of the pack who had used speed or cunning or a shattered pole to break out of the encirclement, all the wolves had been killed.

The hunters in the outer ring came charging downhill, shouting the whole way, to get a close look at the spoils of the battle. Bilgee had already told people to drag two carcasses to where Chen and Yang were standing, then rolled up his sleeves and helped skin them. Gasmai had people bring over the two wolves Bar had killed and two others that Sanjai's dogs had killed. Sanjai and Gombu came to help her skin them.

Chen had learned from Bilgee how to skin a wolf;

now it was his turn to teach Yang. He began by cutting the skin away from the jawbone, then tugged it back over the head. After having Yang anchor the teeth with a leather strip, he pulled the skin back to the neck. From there he kept pulling backward, cutting skin from flesh, like removing a set of leotards, and ending by cutting away the legs and the tail. At this point, the pelt was turned inside out, so the two men reversed it, as if it were a length of intestine, to expose a perfect pelt.

"Good job," Bilgee complimented them. "Not much grease. When you get home, fill it up with dry grass and hang it on a tall pole. That way, the people of the Olonbulag will acknowledge you as true hunters."

Erlang and Yellow sat on their haunches beside their masters looking on; Erlang licked the blood from his injured chest and front legs the whole time. He appeared to be enjoying it. Yellow, who was uninjured, licked the injuries on the top of Erlang's head, like a pampered pet. Still, many of the hunters were praising him, telling how he had wrestled several wolves to the ground and taken bites out of their rear legs. If not for Yellow, Lamjav would have been unable to get his noose on the wolves.

That made Yang happy. "Lamjav is like me, after all," he said, to even a score, "standing brave behind his dog."

Chen took some hard candies out of his pocket and gave them to the canine generals, three for Erlang, two for Yellow. He'd had a premonition that Erlang and Yellow would make him proud that day. The dogs laid the candy on the ground and peeled the paper away with their teeth, then picked each piece up with their tongues and, heads held high, crunched them loudly. All the other dogs could only look on and slobber, or lick the paper on the ground. The students' arrival had taught the dogs that there were more good things to eat in the world than they were used to, and eating candy in front of all those dogs brought Erlang and Yellow canine glory.

Grinning, Gasmai walked over and said to Chen, "I guess you've forgotten your old dog since moving out of our place." She reached into his pocket, retrieved some candy, and gave it to Bar. Chen hurriedly took out all the remaining candy and handed it to Gasmai. She smiled, peeled the paper from one piece, and popped it into her mouth.

A layer of heat had settled over the hunting ground; steam rose from the wolf carcasses, the horses' bodies, the dogs' mouths, and the people's foreheads as they separated into family units and skinned the dead animals. Tradition was followed in dividing up the spoils of battle. There were no arguments. The herdsmen always knew which dog or hunter had killed which wolf. A few words might pass between two men who had both gotten their nooses around a single animal, but Bilgee settled the matter with a single comment: Sell the pelt, buy a crock of liquor, and split it. Hunters and herdsmen who had killed no wolves watched enthusiastically as the others skinned their kills, even offering positive comments on the pelts and the people's dogs. With good dogs, the pelts were flawless; with bad dogs, the pelts were chewed up. Those who wound up with the most pelts loudly invited everyone to their yurt for a drinking celebration. On the grassland, everyone benefited from an encirclement hunt.

People rested on the now quiet site of the hunt.

Women had the most unpleasant work—

patching up the injured dogs. Men used dogs during a hunt, but women relied on them for watching the livestock at night. And it was they who raised them, almost as if they were their children. When dogs were hurt, or when they died, it was the women who grieved. A few of the dogs lay dead on the ground. Where they lay was where their souls had flown up to Tengger; what had sent them on their way was their mortal enemy—the wolf. "The dogs should thank the wolves," Bilgee said, "for without them, the herdsmen would have no need to keep so much meat on hand, and their pups would be off to Tengger soon after they came into the world."

The dead dogs lay undisturbed, for no grassland Mongol would give a second thought to the lush, beautiful coats. Dogs were their comrades-in-arms, their best friends, their brothers. Grasslanders survived in two enterprises: hunting and tending livestock. For both, dogs were indispensable. As production instruments and livestock guards, they were more important to them than oxen were to farmers on the Central Plains. And their relationship to the humans was closer; they helped to dispel the loneliness of the wildwood.

The Mongolian grassland—vast, underpopulated, and dangerous—was a place where dogs kept people safe. Gasmai told Chen and Yang that she could not forget how Bar had saved her one autumn when she was out dumping stove ashes and hadn't noticed a still-smoldering piece of dried sheep dung. A strong wind ignited a fire that quickly spread to the dry grass in front of her yurt. She was alone that day with old Eeji and her child, doing needlework, unaware of what was happening outside. Suddenly she heard Bar barking violently and ramming the door. She ran outside, where a fire was threatening haystacks belonging to other production brigades; they were tall, densely packed, and oily, and if they caught fire, there would be no saving them. Animals that were not killed or injured in the fire would starve without that year's hay, and she would be punished. Bar's warning had given her time that was more valuable than life itself. She ran out with a large piece of wet felt straight into the flames, wrapped herself in it, and rolled on the ground, managing to crush the fire before it reached the hay. She often said that without Bar she'd have been lost.

"Our men are such big drinkers," she said to Chen and Yang, "that sometimes they fall off their horses and freeze to death. Those who don't die can thank their dogs, who run home, grab their mistresses' clothing with their teeth, and lead the women to their husbands, where they dig them out of the snow and bring them home. Every yurt has someone whose life has been saved by the family dog."

And so eating dog meat, skinning a dog, or sleeping under a dog skin were considered acts of unforgivable betrayal. This was one of the reasons why herdsmen had come to hate inhabitants of farming regions and Han Chinese.

Bilgee said that in olden days, Han armies would come to the grassland and start killing and eating dogs, infuriating the herdsmen and inciting armed resistance. Even now, shepherds' dogs were often stolen by outsiders, who killed and ate them. Their coats were secretly sent to the Northeast and to China proper. The pelts of Mongolian dogs—large, with lush fur—were favorites for making hats and bedcovers. The old man commented angrily, "But you'll never find that mentioned in books written by Chinese!"

Bilgee and his family often asked Chen: "If you Chinese hate dogs, curse them, even kill them, why do you eat them?"

Embarrassed by the question, Chen had to think long and hard to give them a satisfactory explanation.

One evening he said to the family as they sat around the fire, "There are no nomads among the Han, and few hunters. Just about every wild animal that can be killed and eaten has been. So we Han don't know the value of dogs. With our dense population, it's hard for Chinese to be lonely, so we don't need dogs to keep us company. We have dozens of curses based on dogs: 'rapacious as a wolf and savage as a dog'; 'A dog in a sedan chair does not appreciate kindness'; 'You can't get ivory from a dog's mouth'; 'Only busybody dogs catch rats'; 'Throw a meaty bun at a dog, and it won't come back'...And some have entered politics. Everyone in the country is shouting slogans like 'Smash in Liu Shaoqi's dog head' and 'Down with Liu the dog.'

"Why do we hate and curse dogs? Mainly because dogs don't follow Chinese rules. You know all about our ancient sage Confucius, right? Well, even emperors throughout our dynastic history have bowed down before him. He established a series of rules to live by, and over the centuries we've followed those rules. Every literate person had his own 'quotations,' like today's little red book of quotations by Chairman Mao, and anyone who didn't follow the rules was considered a barbarian; death awaited the worst cases. The biggest problem with dogs is that they don't follow the Confucian rules of behavior. They bark at strangers, violating our rules of hospitality; they are incestuous; and they eat human feces. But the main reason we hate dogs, why we kill and eat them, is that we're a farming people, not nomads, and we seek to impose our habits and customs on other people."

Bilgee and Batu heard Chen out in silence, and did not appear to be offended. "Young man," Bilgee said after a while, "it would be a good thing if more people, Han and Mongol, were as reasonable about such things as you."

Gasmai sighed and remarked indignantly, "The worst thing that ever happened to dogs was being introduced into Chinese society. What they do best they can't do there, and their shortcomings are all you see. If I were a dog, I'd stay as far away from there as possible. I'd much prefer to stay here, even if a wolf got to me."

"Not until I came here," Chen said, "did I realize that dogs and humans are so much alike, that dogs are truly man's best friend. It's only the impoverished, backward farming peoples who will eat anything, including dogs. One day, maybe, when all Chinese are well off, when there's enough food for everyone, they'll make friends with their dogs and stop hating and eating them. I've grown to love dogs. A day without dogs is a wasted day for me. If someone were to kill the dogs at our yurt, Yang Ke and I would beat the hell out of him." Chen's emotions got the better of him, to his own amazement. Having grown up with the concept that a gentleman argues but does not fight, he now found himself articulating feelings more wolfish than human.

"When you return to Beijing one day," Gasmai said, "will you raise dogs?"

"I'll love dogs for the rest of my life," Chen replied with a smile. "Love them as much as you do. Just so you'll know, I haven't eaten all the fine hard candies my family sent me from Beijing. I haven't even given many to you or Bayar. I've saved them for my dogs."

Batu slapped Chen on the back. "You're at least half Mongol now."

More than six months had passed since that conversation about dogs, but Chen would never forget the promises he'd made that day.

Quiet had settled over the site of the hunt. The exhausted and injured dogs were grieving over the loss of their comrades, sniffing their bodies nervously, fearfully, and circling them over and over, a rite of farewell perhaps. A young boy lay prone on the ground, his arms wrapped tightly around the body of his dog. Adults tried to get him to leave, but he wailed mournfully, his tears falling on the lifeless body of his beloved dog. His wails hung in the air for a very long time, and all Chen Zhen could see was a blur.

13

After Bao Shungui and Uljii led a party of pasture officials to view the spoils at the site of the hunt, they rode up to Bilgee. Bao dismounted and said excitedly to the old man, "A marvelous victory! Truly wonderful! And we have you to thank for that. A signal accomplishment, as my report to my superiors will state."

He reached out to shake hands with Bilgee, who responded by spreading out his bloody fingers. "Too dirty," he said.

But Bao grabbed the old man's hands. "Some of your good luck might rub off on me with a little of that wolf blood, and some of your glory."

The old man's face darkened. "Please don't talk about such things as glory. The greater the glory, the deeper my sins. This cannot happen again. If there are any more hunts like this, the wolves will disappear, and the gazelles, the ground squirrels, the rabbits, and the marmots will rise up. That will be the end of the grassland, and will infuriate Tengger. We and our livestock will pay dearly." He raised his bloody hands to Tengger in fear and trepidation.

With an embarrassed laugh, Bao turned to look at Erlang, covered with blood. "Is that the wild dog I've heard about?" he asked emotionally. "He's so big it's scary. I watched him fight from up on the slope. A real tiger. He was first to charge the wolf pack. He killed one of its leaders and scared off most of the others. How many wolves did he kill altogether?"

"Four," Chen replied.

"A hell of a dog!" Bao remarked. "I'd heard you had a big, wild, sheep-killer of a dog. People complained that you were making a mockery of grassland rules and wanted me to have the dog killed. Well, I'm in charge here, and I say keep that dog and make sure it's well fed and well taken care of. If he kills any more sheep in the future, I'll spare him. But the skins of sheep he kills will belong to the commune and you'll have to pay for the meat."

Chen and Yang happily agreed to the conditions. "We students didn't kill a single wolf, which means we're not the equal of dogs, and certainly not this one." Everyone laughed, even the other students.

"That doesn't sound like something a Chinese would say," Uljii said with a laugh.

Bilgee was visibly pleased. "This youngster respects the grassland; he'll be one of us someday."

The battlefield was strewn with pale wolf carcasses and stained with their blood. Patches of fur above their paws were all that remained of their coats. Bao had the hunters gather them up and stack them to form the character *jing*, 井, for a well. When they were finished, the three dozen or so dead wolves were stacked nearly head high. Bao brought out his camera and took pictures from four or five angles. Then he had the successful hunters raise their trophies and stand on both sides of the stacked carcasses. More than thirty hunters held their pelts high, tails hanging to the ground, with the badly injured, blood-covered assassin dogs crouching in front of their masters, steam rising from their bodies. Bao asked Chen to take a picture with him in the center, holding up the biggest pelt of all. Bilgee stood there, a pelt draped over his right arm, his head lowered, and a sad smile on his face. Chen snapped two pictures.

Bao stepped forward and turned to the hunters in front of him. "As representative of the Banner Revolutionary Committee," he said, "and commander of the military district, I thank you all! You are heroes of the wolf hunt, and your pictures will be in the papers in a few days. I want all people to see with their own eyes the wolf scourge of the Olonbulag, to see how many wolves were killed in a single hunt, wolves that came mainly from Outer Mongolia and were the perpetrators of the warhorse massacre. I also want to tell them that the Olonbulag officials, herdsmen, and Chinese students did not bow down before those wolves and that, thanks to steely determination and careful organization, they counterattacked with a vengeance. This extermination campaign has just begun, and we are confident it will continue until every Olonbulag wolf is dead."

Bao ended his speech by thrusting his hand in the air and proclaiming, "We won't stop fighting until all the jackals are dead!"

There was no reaction from anyone except for Dorji's family and a few of the students. Bao disbanded the hunting party. The people sat down to rest and wait for Batu.

As he sat cross-legged on the ground, Bao said to Uljii, "The border situation is very tense, and my superiors are pressing me to organize a militia and begin training. It was an unexpected stroke of good luck that this hunt produced some hand-to-hand combat."

"Grassland Mongols are born fighters," Uljii said. "Give them a weapon and they'll join the fight. This hunt has provided you with a double victory: the killing of wolves and the training of troops. I say write up two summary reports, and that will satisfy your superiors."

The Chinese students crowded around Chen Zhen and Yang Ke to look at their pelts and touch them enviously. A student named Wang Junli said, "If you two hadn't taken in this dog, we students would have no face at all. We'd be nothing but a bunch of retainers to the Mongol cavalry."

Chen said, "We Chinese have never had the fighting skills or courage of nomads, and when others are your betters, you do well to learn from them. We've been given the rare opportunity to serve as retainers to the herdsmen when they fight wolves."

With a superior tone of voice, Wang said, "Sure, nomads have made many incursions into the Central Plain. But both times they ruled the nation they eventually surrendered to the advanced culture of the Chinese, didn't they? The grasslanders have had their moments of grandeur, but in the end they haven't moved beyond the talent of shooting birds out of the sky with bows and arrows, and can display only military might."

"You might be right," Chen countered. "But be careful when you place the civil over the military. Without military might, the most glorious culture ever will eventually be reduced to rubble. The civil control of the Han and Tang dynasties was founded on military might. Just think how many great civilizations throughout the world have come to ruin at the hands of backward but militarily strong races. Even their written and spoken languages were lost as a result. You're wrong when you say the Han civilization destroyed the backward grassland people, for they've retained their language, their totemic faith, and their traditional customs. Khrushchev tried to supplant the Kazakhstan nomadic culture with Russian agriculture and industry. And what happened? One of the world's great grasslands is now a desert."

Seeing that the combative male students were on the verge of another argument, the student Sun Wenjuan spoke up. "Okay," she said, "that's enough. We hardly ever get to see each other, since our flocks are so far apart. Let's not ruin this reunion by fighting. You guys turn into wolves as soon as you come to the grassland, nipping at each other nonstop!"

Erlang, clearly uncomfortable with people putting their hands all over his pelt, walked up slowly. Assuming no dog taken in by students would bite any of them, Sun took two chunks of curd out of her pocket to reward him. "Good boy, Erlang."

Without wagging his tail or making a sound, Erlang glared venomously as he approached the student group, frightening Sun, who backed up. "Come here!" Chen yelled, but not in time to keep the dog from growling and threatening to attack the students. In her fright, Sun stumbled and sat down hard.

"You son of a bitch!" Yang shouted as he raised his herding club threateningly. But Erlang tightened his neck and showed he'd rather be hit than retreat. He was, after all, a once feral dog that had just killed four wolves, and Yang was afraid of arousing his still-smoldering wolfish nature. Knowing it would be foolish to use his club, he let it drop.

"No one will dare visit you two in your yurt after this," Wang Junli said. "If he hadn't killed all those wolves, I'd be ready to skin and eat him."

"He's a strange dog," Chen said apologetically, "a lot like a wolf, and he doesn't take easily to humans. Come by more often and he'll get used to you."

The students drifted away. Chen patted Erlang on the head. "See what you've done," he said. "You've offended my friends."

Erlang took a few steps toward the pile of carcasses and stared blankly at their pale bodies. Dozens of other dogs standing off at a distance, respectful and somewhat afraid, wagged their tails in his direction. But only Bar, head held high, came up to him; Erlang, neither overbearing nor servile, brushed noses with him. Now that he'd gained the approval of the pasture leaders and the herdsmen, he was being welcomed into the ranks of Second Brigade hunting dogs.

But Chen Zhen detected a look of loss in Erlang's eyes. He wrapped his arms around the dog's neck, wishing he knew of a way to console him.

Bao Shungui invited Bilgee over to where most of the hunters had gathered. The old man sat in the center and spread out an array of sheep and horse droppings to describe the battle in detail. His audience listened raptly, with Bao asking a few questions and every once in a while shouting his approval. "This battle," he said, "should be entered into a military textbook. It was more brilliant than the plan the wolves engineered in massacring the warhorses. You, sir, are a military genius."

"In the days of Genghis Khan," Chen volunteered, "Bilgee would have been one of his great generals, as great as Muhuali, Jebe, and Sabutai."

The old man waved off the compliment. "Don't compare me with those Mongol sages, or Tengger will be angry. If not for them, the grassland would have been tamed long ago. I'm just an old slave who mustn't be mentioned in the same breath with them."

It was nearly noon, and Batu still hadn't returned, but it was time to head back to camp. Then a horse raced up with a sense of urgency. Buhe jumped down and reported breathlessly to Uljii and Bao Shungui, "Batu says come at once. The wolves you fought this morning were only half the pack. The other half slipped away before daybreak and made its way to the reedy valley at the base of the mountains."

Bilgee glared at him. "You must be wrong."

"Batu and I rode into the valley," Buhe replied, "where we saw fresh wolf tracks in the snow. Batu says there are at least twenty of them, and he thinks that includes the old gray wolf, the alpha male that led the attack on the horses. He says that's one wolf we have to catch."

Uljii turned to Bao. "All of us, horses included, have gone without food all night and half the day. And there are many injured dogs. I know that valley, it's huge, thousands of acres, much too big for us to encircle. I say forget it."

Bao stared suspiciously at Bilgee. "The nonnatives and the Chinese students tell me you usually take the wolves' side. You didn't plan this, did you? Your men and dogs should have been able to surround an additional twenty wolves so that we could wipe them out."

"No," Uljii said. "Today we trapped many wolves, like stuffing a big dumpling. If there'd been more of them, we'd have been stretched too thin, and the dumpling skin would have broken."

Bao turned back to Bilgee. "I think you let them escape on purpose."

Bilgee stared back at him. "Trapping wolves isn't the same as scooping noodles out of a bowl! It was pitch-black and there were gaps between the riders. Of course some of the wolves got away. If you'd led the hunt, I'm willing to bet you wouldn't have gotten a single one."

Bao's face colored as his anger grew. Smacking his whip into the palm of his hand, he bellowed, "There may not be enough men and horses, or dogs, but we haven't used our rifles yet. Now that we've located more wolves in the reeds, I'm not letting them go. I'm taking charge of this campaign!"

Bao rode partway up the slope, turned, and said, "Comrades, another pack has been discovered in the reedy valley. There are many among you who still have no pelts, right? Especially you students. Weren't you complaining that you were kept away from the front line? Well, this time that's exactly where you'll be. Comrades, we must prove that we can overcome exhaustion and keep our fighting spirit alive as we annihilate this wolf pack!"

Several of the students and some of the hunters were itching to give it a try.

"Here's my plan," Bao announced loudly, "one that will take a relatively small expenditure of energy. We'll surround the valley and burn them out. Then we can pick them off with our rifles, using as much ammunition as necessary."

The herdsmen and hunters were shocked. For them grassfires were taboo.

"A grassfire violates heavenly laws," Bilgee said. "It blackens the face of Tengger, and you know what that will mean for us. The rivers will turn black, and the water gods will give us nothing to drink. Shamanism and Lamaism do not permit fires out here. In the past, the Great Khans would kill the entire family of anyone who lit a fire on the grassland. Even the current government forbids them."

Gasmai was so enraged her face was red. "Fire is the grassland's greatest scourge. If we catch a child playing with fire, we spank him till his rear end swells up. If you set one now, when children play with fire after this, they'll say they learned that from Representative Bao."

Lamjav's thick neck bulged. "In ancient times," he said angrily, "the Han armies burned our grasslands. It was the cruelest thing they could think of doing. They don't dare do that anymore. How could a Mongol set fire to his own ancient grassland? Are you a Mongol, Representative Bao, or aren't you?"

"There's snow on the ground," Sanjai said, "which means we're not into the fire season yet. But if we set a fire now, prevention will be harder in the future. And it will singe the wolves' coats and ruin their pelts."

Laasurung said, "Burning the wolves is mean and cruel. But let's say you burn them all up—then who pays when the fire kills our livestock? The stench would fill the air and could cause an epidemic. Not only that, kill off all the wolves, and the field mice and rabbits will bring the Gobi desert over."

Zhang Jiyuan said, "We horse herders came out this time to fight the wolves. We've been away from our herds for a day and a night, and if we don't get back now, the wolves will outflank us. We have to get back to our horses. I won't be responsible for anything that happens."

"Quiet down!" Bao Shungui shouted. "Quiet down all of you! Nobody's going anywhere. We're killing the wolves to eliminate a destructive force and protect national property. The best defense is a good offense. The only way to keep the wolves from outflanking us is to wipe them out. We don't do it for the pelts. A dead wolf with a burned coat constitutes a victory. I want to see another stack of dead wolves, take some more pictures, and let our superiors look upon our great achievement. I'll arrange a criticism session for anyone who doesn't obey me! Now, let's go, everyone!"

A murderous glare emanated from Lamjav's wolfish eyes. "Arrange what you want," he bellowed. "I'm not going! My horses need me."

Several of the other herders turned their horses' heads. "We're going back!" they said.

Snapping his whip in the air, Bao roared, "I'll take away the job of anyone who deserts on the eve of this battle. That goes for your backers as well."

Bilgee glanced at Uljii, then waved his hands helplessly and said, "No more of this quarreling. I led this hunt, so I'll have the last word. One horse herder will head back to each of the herds, all the others will go with Representative Bao. End of discussion."

Lamjav said to Zhang Jiyuan, "I'll tend the herd. When this is over, you go home and rest for a couple of days." He turned and rode off with eight or nine horse herders.

The hunting party crossed three mountain ridges to arrive at a vast expanse of reeds spread out below like white gold, surrounded by snow. Wang Junli and half a dozen other students escorted Bao Shungui, assuring him that it was an ideal spot to burn the wolves out.

Batu emerged from the reeds and rode up to Bao Shungui and Uljii. "I didn't alert the wolves," he said. "It's a big pack, and they're still in there."

Pointing to the reeds with his whip, Bao said, "Listen up, section leaders. Section One take the east, Section Two the west, and Section Three the north. Section Four, you circle around to the south and light fires between there and the eastern section. First seal off all escape routes, then move upwind out of the way. When you men in the other three sections see smoke in the south, light your fires. Then everyone, dogs included, wait at the outer rim. Loose the dogs as soon as the wolves appear, and start shooting."

The students of the Fourth Section took off at a gallop, followed by the herdsmen. The other sections turned and headed to their assigned sectors.

Chen Zhen followed Bilgee into the reedy area to check it out. Undisturbed by natural fires for several years, the reeds had grown to twice the men's height; the ground was covered by a blanket of dead, dry reeds at least two feet thick. Dry as a bone, the reeds—living and dead—could not have been more flammable.

"The wolves know we're out here," the old man said, "but they're not afraid. The reeds are so dense that dogs are no threat, and the lasso poles are useless. The sound of horse hooves on the undergrowth in the dark tells the wolves exactly where we are. There are many paths in here, paths that will take them behind any horses, men, or dogs that come in. This is their territory in the winter and spring, their refuge. Olonbulag wolves have seen their share of natural fires, but fires set by humans are alien to them. Nothing like this has ever happened before. You outsiders have all sorts of ideas, but this one is especially cruel. This pack of wolves is doomed."

"Light the fires!" someone shouted, breaking the silence. "Light the fires!"

Chen grabbed Bilgee's horse's halter and raced out

of the reeds. Black smoke billowed above the southeastern edge. Then flames leaped skyward in the eastern, western, and northern sectors. Bao Shungui ordered the hunters to use reeds as torches to start the fire spreading deep into the reeds with the wind. The densely packed, dry, oily reeds nearly exploded when the fires touched them, sending flames and thick smoke high into the sky. Acres of dry reeds were turned into a sea of fire, with black leaves and stalks dancing in the air currents above, like a cloud of bats. High up on a slope looking down, Bao Shungui liked what he saw.

On the western edge of the billowing smoke, Bilgee dismounted and fell to his knees, facing east, tears wetting his face. He was murmuring prayerfully. Chen Zhen couldn't hear clearly, but he knew what the old man was saying.

Suddenly the wind turned, sending the choking black smoke and flames in the old man's direction. Chen and Yang quickly lifted him off the ground and ran with him up the snow-covered hillside. The old man's face was sooty black; so were his tears. Chen gazed at him, suddenly feeling the creation of a silent spiritual resonance between them; at the same time, he could imagine a fearful yet revered wolf totem rising up to take the Mongol people's tenacious souls away with it. Their survivors—sons and daughters, grandsons and granddaughters—would continue to live on the Mongolian grassland, taking the bitter with the sweet, bringing pride and glory to their race.

Waves of fire carried by the wind incinerated the old reeds and sent hot cinders into the sky and onto the snow-covered pastureland. The fire raged for much of the afternoon, leaving in its wake a torched wasteland. Finally, inevitably, the fires died out above a vast blackened landscape and acres of black snow. But the dogs and the rifles remained silent.

After the winds swept the smoke away, the cold settled in. Bao Shungui ordered everyone to form a single line and comb the battlefield to get a count of dead wolves. One man estimated they'd find twenty or more; another predicted a count to exceed that of the morning hunt.

"I don't care how many there are," Bao said. "Just find them, no matter what shape they're in, even if they're unrecognizable. I want to photograph them so that no one can accuse me of sending up false reports. I want all the banners in the entire league to know that this is what is meant by 'Kill a wolf and remove a scourge,' and that this has not been done for the sake of a few wolf pelts."

On the far end of the line, Chen Zhen said softly to Bilgee, "How many animals do you think were burned up, Papa?"

"This scorched-earth tactic was the brainchild of a Han Chinese," Bilgee said. "We Mongols fear nothing more than fire, so how am I supposed to know how many wolves it claimed? What concerns me is this: now that Bao has burned off the reeds, he'll start thinking about opening up the area to farming."

They followed the easy pace of the line as they searched through the ashes. Whenever they came across a higher pile, they nervously poked it with their lasso poles and stirred it up a little. When nothing turned up, the old man sighed in relief.

The winds had died down, but the ashes loosened by horse hooves still brought tears to people's eyes and made the horses and the dogs cough. The dogs yelped in pain whenever they stepped on smoldering cinders.

Nothing had been found by the time the sweep had passed the halfway mark, and Bao Shungui's nerves were on edge. "Slow down!" he shouted. "Not so fast! Don't overlook a single ash pile."

The worried look on Bilgee's face was fading.

"Do you think the wolves got away?" Chen asked.

"They must have, or we'd have found at least one by now," the old man replied hopefully. "Maybe Tengger came to their aid."

A distant shout interrupted their conversation. "There's a dead wolf here!"

The old man's face fell as he and Chen rode over to see. They were joined by the others, with Bao Shungui in the center. He was excitedly motioning for Bilgee to come up and identify the carcass.

It was curled up on the ground, burned beyond recognition, a greasy stench rising from its body. Everyone was talking at once. "The burn was a success, it worked!" a keyed-up Wang Junli said. "We've found one, so the rest have to be here somewhere."

Then Laasurung spoke up. "That's not a wolf—it's too small."

"It shrank in the fire," Bao said. "Of course it's small."

Wang nodded. "Probably a young wolf."

Bilgee dismounted and turned the carcass over with his herding club. Every hair had been burned off, and it was obvious that whatever it was had burned on a pile of reeds. "It's no wolf, not even a young one."

Bao stared doubtfully at the old man. "How can you tell?" he asked.

"Look at its mouth," Bilgee said. "A wolf's fangs are longer than a dog's, and sharper. If you don't believe me, take a picture and see what your superiors say. Anyone who knows a thing about wolves will realize you've sent up a false report, calling a dog a wolf."

Displaying sudden anxiety, Bao said, "Put a marker here. If we find some more, we'll know if this was a wolf or a dog."

The old man gazed down sadly. "This old dog knew it was finished, so it came here to die," he said. "The wind was behind it, and there were wolves everywhere. Too bad the wolves didn't find it first."

"Spread out and keep searching!" Bao demanded. "Straight line. Comb the area." So they spread out and continued examining each ash pile, but found nothing. Several of the students were starting to feel uneasy. The hunters, experienced in everything but fire tactics, wondered if Batu could have given a false report.

"I swear to Chairman Mao," he said under the pressure of questioning, and to Tengger. "Buhe and I saw them. The rest of you saw their tracks, didn't you?"

"This is odd," Bao said. "I know they couldn't have sprouted wings and flown away."

Bilgee smiled. "I thought you knew that wolves could fly. They're marvelous animals that don't even need wings to do it."

Bao replied angrily, "Then how did we manage to kill so many of them this morning?"

"That was payback for the horse massacre. Tengger won't let you kill any more; it wouldn't be fair."

Bao cut him off. "That's enough talk about Tengger this and Tengger that. That's one of the Four Olds." He turned. "Spread out and finish the job," he ordered.

Almost immediately, two horse herders shouted, "Bad news—there are a couple of incinerated stud bulls here!"

The party rode over to see. Both the herdsmen and the hunters grew tense.

Stud bulls, called *buhe,* are the freest, most carefree, and most respected male steers on the grassland. Selected by experienced cowherds as breeding animals, once they reach maturity, except for the summer months, when they travel from place to place to mate, they spend their time away from the herd, wandering the grassland freely, requiring no one to tend or feed them. They are big, brawny animals with thick necks and great strength; their faces are covered by beautiful curly hair below a pair of short, thick, and very sharp horns, perfect weapons for close fighting. The powerful marauders of the grassland—the wolves—stay clear of these bulls, even when they travel in packs. Their fangs are useless against the thick hide, and they haven't the strength to overwhelm the animals.

Stud bulls therefore have no natural enemies. They normally travel in pairs, grazing together on the best grass during the day and sleeping tail-to-tail at night. They emit a sacred air, symbols of strength, power, virility, courage, freedom, and good fortune. The grasslanders have long viewed them as supernatural; their health is a sign of the prosperity of cattle herds and sheep flocks. A sickly bull foretells disaster. Since there are scant few of these bulls, no more than one for several herds of cattle, the news that two of them had died in the conflagration produced panic among the herdsmen, as if they'd learned of the death of a loved one.

The herdsmen climbed down off their horses and stood quietly around the huge carcasses, the animals' legs spread out stiffly on the scorched earth, their thick hides a mass of black bubbles with yellow grease oozing from the cracks. Their eyes were like black lightbulbs, their tongues stuck out as far as they would go, and black liquid seeped from their mouths and noses. The cowherds and women recognized the two animals by their horns, and rising anger swept over the crowd.

"This is unforgivable!" Gasmai exclaimed. "These were the best stud bulls in our production brigade. Half our herd came from these two, and you've burned them up! You're well on your way to destroying our grassland!"

"Those were the finest breed of Mongol bulls we have, what we call red bulls," Bilgee said. "Cows that mate with them produce the most milk; their offspring have the most meat, and the best. I'm reporting this incident to the banner authorities, demanding an investigation. I'll bring them to this spot so they can see for themselves. The human destruction far outweighs any losses from wolves!"

"A few years back," Uljii said, "the Mongol League's Livestock Bureau wanted these two, but we wouldn't part with them and gave them instead a pair of young bulls these two had sired. This is a tremendous loss!"

"The reeds kept the wind out," Laasurung said, "so the bulls came here to sleep. And wound up burning to death. They were too slow to have any chance of escaping, even if they hadn't suffocated in the thick, oily smoke. This is the first time in our history that someone has incinerated cattle on the grassland. Anyone who disobeys Tengger is bound to suffer the consequences."

The charred hides of the animals were still splitting, producing terrifying cracks like ominous spirit writing and mystical curses. Frightened women covered their faces with their wide lambskin sleeves and ran outside the circle of onlookers. Everyone shunned Bao Shungui, who stood there, alone, alongside the bull carcasses, his face and clothes soot-covered. Suddenly he blurted out, "The wolves will pay for the deaths of these two bulls! I don't care what any of you say—I won't rest until I've killed every last wolf on the Olonbulag!"

The sunset had disappeared and the early-winter cold had settled over the land like a net when the horses, the people, and the dogs—hungry, tired, and cold—returned sadly to camp, heads down, like a defeated ragtag army. No one knew how the gray wolf king had managed to lead his pack out of the fire and through the encirclement. There was plenty of talk, with competing views, but all were convinced the wolves had flown to safety. "There was a fatal flaw in this encirclement," Uljii said. "The people and dogs made too much noise before we were in place. The gray wolf led his pack out before the fires were even set."

The horse herders raced anxiously to their herds. Chen Zhen and Yang Ke, who had been worried about their wolf cub, signaled Zhang Jiyuan and Gao Jianzhong to leave the hunting party with them and take a shortcut back to camp as fast as they could get there. As they rode along, Yang muttered, "Before we left, I gave the cub a couple of pieces of overcooked lamb, but I don't know if he's ready to eat meat yet. Dorji says he won't be weaned for another month or more."

"Don't sweat it," Chen said. "Last night he ate so much I thought his belly would pop. He won't starve even if he doesn't eat the meat. What worries me is that we've been away all day, leaving the place unguarded. If the mother found him, you know what that means."

It was midnight by the time they made it back to camp. Erlang and Yellow were waiting for their food in front of the empty dog trough. Chen rolled out of his saddle and gave the dogs some meaty bones, while Zhang and Gao went into the yurt to wash up, boil some water for tea, and get some sleep after they ate. Chen and Yang ran out to the wolf burrow, where they removed the boards over the top and trained flashlights into the hole. The little wolf was curled up in a corner, fast asleep. The little bitch, on the other hand, was whining from hunger and trying to claw her way up the walls to find her mother's teat. Yir was anxiously pacing the area, so Chen reached down, brought the pup up, and handed her over to Yir, who picked her up with her teeth and carried her away.

Chen and Yang examined the burrow carefully. The two pieces of lamb were gone; the cub's belly bulged in both directions and spots of grease dotted his nose and mouth. As he slept, his mouth curled up at the corners, like he was enjoying a wonderful dream. Yang was thrilled. "The little bastard gobbled up all that meat," he sighed. "Apparently, his mother is busy elsewhere."

14

Rays of long-absent sunlight streamed into the yurt through the wood-framed opening at the top. Chen Zhen opened his eyes and looked up into the blue sky of a cold spring morning. He jumped out of bed, dressed hurriedly, and ran outside, straight to the cub's burrow, squinting from the sting of bright sunlight.

Gombu had already led the lambs out of their pen; they made their slow way over to the hillside grazing land. Another cluster of sheep, those that had recently lambed, were grazing nearby. All but a few of the ewes had lambed by now; the flock moved at a glacial pace. Chen saw that Yang Ke hadn't gone out and that he and Zhang Jiyuan were learning from Gombu how to stuff wolf pelts, two of which were draped over the empty oxcarts. Chen walked over to watch. The elderly Gombu had carried an armful of hay from a nearby stack and was now stuffing it gently into the pelts, which slowly took the form of the wolves. "This is how you keep it from shrinking and prevent the inside surfaces from sticking together," he said. "That lowers their value." Once he'd finished stuffing the pelts, he bored a hole through the nostrils and strung a thin rope through it.

Then he asked Zhang Jiyuan if he had a spare birch rod for use as a lasso pole. Zhang said he did and led the old man over to an oxcart, where Gombu picked out the longest and straightest of the four or five birch poles, one that measured some twenty feet in length. He then tied the rope he'd strung through the nose of the pelt to the tip of the pole, dug a hole several feet deep in front of the yurt, and planted the pole securely in it. When he had finished, two stuffed wolf pelts waved in the wind high above the ground like signal flags.

"That's how you dry them," Gombu said, "and at the same time announce to passersby that successful hunters live in this yurt. In olden days, pelts like those would keep robbers and bandits away." Chen, Yang, and Zhang stared at the wolf flags put in motion by the wind, which flattened out the fluffy fur and turned the pelts into the image of a pair of live wolves charging into battle.

Yang sighed. "The wolves are dead, but not their form or their souls. They're up there in full attack, spirited as always. It gives me the creeps."

Chen too felt his emotions rise. "Seeing those pelts up there reminds me of the Turkish flags gilded with wolf heads that ancient horsemen carried into battle, galloping across the grassland, wolf blood coursing through their veins, filled with the courage, ferocity, and wisdom they'd learned from those very wolves, to become conquerors of the world."

"You know," Zhang said, "I now share your view that the wolf is a very complex subject, one that touches on many important issues. No wonder you're so fascinated by them."

"The way I see it," Yang Ke said, "the three of us should forget about studying university courses on our own and concentrate on the far more interesting wolfology."

The wind billowed the wolf pelts and combed the fur until it was soft and shiny, the dark wolf hairs emitting a lustrous glow in the sunlight, like banquet attire. The pair of wolves frolicked in the blueness of Tengger, embracing one another and tumbling over and over, the relaxed behavior of a freed creature. To Chen, the wolves were stuffed not with straw but with the passion of life and a joyful fighting spirit. Swathed in the white smoke of the yurt's chimney, they appeared to be dancing in the clouds or breaking through the mist. They were flying up to Tengger, up to Sirius, up to a Paradise they had revered all their lives, taking the souls of grasslanders with them.

Chen realized that what he was doing, standing and gazing skyward, was itself a sort of ritual; without being aware of it, he was standing at the foot of a totem, in a place where respect and admiration reigned. The spirit and faith of the grassland envelops you like the air, and to sense them you need only possess the anxieties and yearnings of the soul...

Chen said to Zhang, "Come with me to look in on the cub."

They walked over to the new burrow, where Chen removed the rock and slid back the wooden cover. The little female pup was sleeping lazily in a corner, with no thoughts of a morning meal. The wolf cub, on the other hand, sat in the middle of the burrow, looking up hungrily, impatiently. As soon as the bright sunlight lit up the burrow, he stood on his hind legs, energized, and began clawing at the wall. He climbed no more than a couple of inches before tumbling back down, then scrambled to his feet and tried again, digging his claws into the dirt and pulling himself up with all his strength, like a little lizard. When the dirt gave way, he landed like a fur ball and began growling at his own shadow on the wall, angry at it for not helping him out of the hole.

Zhang, who'd never seen a live wolf cub before, felt like reaching down to pick him up and study him closely.

"Hold on a minute," Chen said. "Let's see if he can get out on his own. If he can, I'll have to make the burrow deeper."

After falling back twice more, the cub gave up on that part of the wall and began moving around the burrow, sniffing here and there, as if trying to devise a new escape plan. All of a sudden, he discovered the presence of the little bitch and, without wasting a second, clambered onto her back and from there onto her head. He started climbing again, sending loose dirt raining down on the pup; awakened from her sleep, she stood up, whimpering, and shook the dirt from her back as the cub fell yet again. Now in full anger, he wrinkled his nose at the pup, bared his fangs, and howled. "The little bastard has plenty of wolf in him already!" Zhang exclaimed with a laugh. "He looks pretty smart to me."

Chen saw that in two short days, the membranes covering the cub's eyes had become much thinner; still quite watery, the eyes looked almost diseased. Nevertheless, the cub appeared able to make out some hazy shapes and react to hand gestures. When Chen opened his hand and held it out, the wolf followed it with his eyes. So as to begin conditioning the cub's reflexes, Chen said slowly, "Little... Wolf... Little Wolf... food... food." The wolf cocked his head, pricked up his catlike ears, and listened with a mixture of fear and curiosity.

"I'd like to see if he has any memory of his original den," Zhang said as he cupped his hands over his mouth and made wolf sounds. The cub moved nervously, then leaped back onto the dog's body and clawed madly at the wall, falling back once, twice, until he curled up in a corner as if seeking the safety of his mother. The men knew they'd done something cruel by letting the cub hear sounds from the realm of wolves.

"Raising this one isn't going to be easy," Zhang said. "This isn't the Beijing Zoo, where he could be taken out of his natural habitat and gradually shed some of his wildness. Out here in these primitive surroundings, when night falls, we're surrounded by baying wolves, and I don't know how he's going to change under those conditions. He'll hurt someone once he's fully grown. Be very careful."

"It's never been my intention to rid him of his wildness," Chen said. "What would be the point? I just want to be in contact with a living wolf, to stroke him and hold him, to get closer to him each day, and see if I can figure him out. You can't know wolves without going into their den. Which means you can't be afraid of getting bitten. My only concern is that the herdsmen won't let me raise him."

The cub was still trying to get out of his burrow, so Chen reached down, grabbed him by the scruff of his neck, and lifted him out. Zhang cupped the little animal in his hands and studied him closely as he rubbed his coat. He tried to smooth it down, but when he lifted his hand, the wolf hairs stood up wildly. "I'm embarrassed to admit that here I am, a horse herder who has to come to a sheep's pen to touch a living wolf. Lamjav and I went out looking for litters twice but came back empty-handed. I'll bet not one in a hundred thousand Chinese has ever actually touched a living grassland wolf. We hate them, which means we hate whatever they're good at. Just about the only people who have learned from wolves are the nomads."

"In world history," Chen continued the thought, "nomads have been the only Easterners capable of taking the fight to the Europeans, and the three peoples that really shook the West to its foundations were the Huns, the Turks, and the Mongols. The Westerners who fought their way back to the East were all descendants of nomads. The builders of ancient Rome were a pair of brothers raised by a wolf. Images of the wolf and her two wolf-children appear on the city's emblem even today. The later Teutons, Germans, and Anglo-Saxons grew increasingly powerful, and the blood of wolves ran in their veins. The Chinese, with their weak dispositions, are in desperate need of a transfusion of that vigorous, unrestrained blood. Had there been no wolves, the history of the world would have been written much differently. If you don't know wolves, you can't understand the spirit and character of the nomads, and you'll certainly never be able to appreciate the differences between nomads and farmers or the inherent qualities of each."

"Don't worry," Zhang said. "I understand why you want to raise this wolf, and I'll talk to the herdsmen for you."

Chen held the cub under his coat and walked over to the dog pen. When Yir saw that a wolf was feeding on her milk, the moment Chen let down his guard, she stood up and turned to bite it. But the cub held on to the nipple and wouldn't let go, hanging from her belly like a leech, like an empty milk bottle. Yir turned around and around, swinging the wolf with her, trying but failing to bite him. To Chen and Zhang it was comical yet maddening. Chen reached down and pried open the cub's mouth to make him let go of the teat. "A real bloodsucker," Zhang said with a laugh.

Chen held Yir down and stroked her gently to get her to let the little wolf drink. When the cub was full, Chen stood up and said, "I think we should let the youngsters play together." So they carried the puppies over to dry grass, where Chen set the wolf down among them. The instant his paws touched the ground, he took off as fast as he could, away from the puppies and the men. With his belly rubbing the ground and his bowlegs churning, he looked more like a hairy tortoise than a wolf. One of the male puppies tried to run with him, but the wolf showed his fangs and snarled.

Chen was surprised. "When he's hungry," he said, "anyone with milk is his mother, but when he's had his fill, there's no such thing as mother. His eyes aren't fully open, but his nose is working fine. It's a wolf's best weapon."

Zhang said, "I can see he already knows this isn't his real home, that the bitch isn't his real mother, and that those pups aren't his brothers and sisters."

"When we found him out there," Chen said, "he already knew how to play dead."

They stayed four or five paces behind the cub, following to see what he would do. He crawled several yards over ground covered with patches of snow and dry grass before stopping to sniff the area. He smelled horse dung, cow patties, cow and sheep bones, and whatever else happened to be there—territory-marking dog piss, maybe. His nose led the way, and it wasn't until they'd followed him several hundred feet that they realized he wasn't wandering aimlessly, but had a clear objective in mind: he was running away from the yurts, the camp, the pens, and the aura of humans, dogs, smoke, and livestock.

The cub had a natural stubborn streak, Chen realized. He possessed a nature that was more fearsome and more worthy of respect than other animals. Chen had always held sparrows in high regard, for they were impossible to domesticate. As a child, he'd caught many of them and brought them home as pets. But as soon as they were in captivity, they stopped eating and drinking, refusing to adapt to their new surroundings. Their answer to the loss of freedom was death every time. He never once succeeded in keeping a captured sparrow alive. Wolves were different, he realized. They cherished their freedom, but they cherished life as well. A captured wolf ate and slept as always. Instead of fasting, it gorged itself and slept as much as possible to store up energy. Then it escaped at the first opportunity in a quest for renewed freedom and a new life. Chen felt he was witnessing the rare character and human qualities one saw in gladiators. A people who adopted the wolf's temperament and made it their totem—beastly ancestor, god of war, and sage—would always be a victorious people.

Chen was grateful to the cub, whose sturdy little body had the power of transporting him all the way to the heart of a mystery.

Gombu rode up and told Chen to come with him to pair up the newborn lambs with their mothers. It took the two men no more than an hour to match all the ewes and their lambs, which nursed twice a day, morning and afternoon. Lambs that could not find their mothers would quickly starve. Pairing also gave the shepherds the opportunity to count their flock. To avoid the blistering sunlight, newborn lambs often curled up in marmot burrows, and shepherds could easily lose them if not for the pairings. Chen once went looking for missing lambs after a count and found three of them in marmot burrows.

Gombu was satisfied with the flock. "We have good grass and water here on the Olonbulag," he said, "so the sheep have plenty of milk and they know their own lambs. That makes things easy for us. If the grass and water quality were poor, the sheep wouldn't have enough milk and they'd reject even their own lambs. We're lucky we have good leaders who understand the grassland and understand wolves. They don't focus their effort on the flocks, but on the grass and on the pastureland. When people take care of the important business, the lambs pretty much tend themselves. Shepherding is carefree work on the Olonbulag. In a few days, I'll be able to pair the sheep and lambs by myself."

Gombu wasn't one to go around boasting, but he knew the grassland like the back of his hand.

15

Warm, moist spring winds caressed the Olonbulag; massive, blindingly white clouds hung low in the sky. The somnolent grassland sprang to life, transformed into an alternating bright and dark, yellow and white slide show. When the clouds blotted out the sun, Zhang Jiyuan felt as if a cold wind had penetrated his deel. But when the clouds moved on, powerful sunbeams made him feel as if he were baking, sweat oozing from the pores in his face and on his hands, until even his deel felt sun-baked. But then, as soon as he started unbuttoning it to let in some air, another cloud would move in and transport him back to a cold spring day.

The ice was softening, the snow melting, revealing vast stretches of yellowed grass. Early buds that had appeared before the latest snowfall had turned yellow, with a tinge of green. The air was suffused with the heavy odor of rotting vegetation; spring runoff once again flowed in the streams, down from the mountains to saturate the marshes and create pools in which white clouds were reflected. The Olonbulag seemed to dance in the air.

Zhang and Batu had been hidden in the tall circle grass for more than an hour, waiting for wolves. The horse massacre, followed by the "false report" in the reedy valley, had made it impossible for Batu to hold his head up among the herdsmen, and the anger building inside him was directed at the wolves. As for Zhang, since he'd had no success in the encirclement hunt, only a wolf kill would reestablish his reputation. So following several days of rest, they returned to the hillside near the big lake with their semiautomatic rifles. Batu was sure that surviving wolves hated the thought of letting all the remaining horse carcasses sink into the lake. The snow was melting and the water was rising, but there was still some meat on the lake's edge, where the wolves could get to it, though not for long.

The pools of water on the mountain, bright one moment and dark the next, made the men's eyes tear up as they searched the hillside with their telescopes, noting every suspicious spot—black, gray, or yellow. Batu suddenly lowered his head and whispered, "Take a look to the left." Zhang gently shifted his telescope, holding his breath but unable to keep his heart from racing as he watched a pair of wolves emerge slowly from behind the hill, first their heads, then their necks and chests.

The hunters' eyes were glued on their prey. The wolves stopped when the front half of their bodies were out in the open and cautiously surveyed their surroundings. Instead of moving farther out of the tall circle grass, they lay down and kept out of sight, as if they were the hunters, not the hunted. Two men and two wolves lay hidden in the grass, waiting for their chance. The wolves were in no hurry. They were content to see what tricks the humans had up their sleeves, and patient enough to wait till dark.

Circle grass was the name the Beijing students had given this variety of meadow grass. Commonly seen on the Mongolian grassland, it was prettier but stranger than most grasses. Level stretches of grass on the pastureland or hillsides were notable for occasional patches of waist-high grass, straight and even, like densely packed rice plants or clumps of squat reeds.

Circle grass wasn't just attractive; it was also a strange plant that grew in discrete patches. Circle grass, circle grass, a circle of grass, from the outside densely packed, like a curtain of reeds, but empty on the inside, as if nothing grew there. It grew in a true circle, as if laid out carefully with a compass. The size varied, from a couple of hand-spreads to a radius of a few feet. Herdsmen out with their sheep or horses rested on its springy stalks. It didn't take the students long to appreciate the circle grass, which some of them called sofa grass or armchair grass.

With its unique shape and construction, it was a natural hiding spot for humans and for wolves, a place either to rest or to set an ambush. Wolves had ruled the grassland much earlier than humans and were the first to discover and utilize circle grass. Batu said they preferred to hide behind patches of the grass, from which they could surprise passing herds of gazelle or flocks of sheep. Zhang Jiyuan had found wolf droppings in the center of patches, proving to him how much they liked such places, and Bilgee said they were hiding places Tengger had given to the wolves.

Now both humans and wolves were well hidden; the wolves could not see the men, who had no clear shot at the wolves, though they had seen them briefly. Batu was hesitant and Zhang was getting worried. Might the wolves have seen the men earlier, when they'd first moved into the circle grass? One military notion they had taught the Mongol fighters was that on the grassland anything is possible.

Batu considered the situation and decided against any action. With his eyes on the hill across the way, he told Zhang to commit the features of the other hillside to memory as they quietly backtracked to where they'd left the horses, removed the fetters, and led them down the slope, then turned and headed southwest on foot. Not until they were downwind and far enough from the wolves did they mount up and circle around toward the wolves' hiding spot. Their horses made no sound on the damp ground, aided by the soughing of the wind.

Batu carefully charted the hills as they went, and within half an hour they were on the far side of the slope nearest to the wolves. Batu slowly led his horse up the slope. Just before they reached the top, he stopped, but instead of fettering his horse, he wrapped the reins around its front legs and tied a slipknot. Zhang did the same.

After releasing the safeties on their rifles, they walked ahead, bent at the waist. Once they'd reached the peak, they crawled on their bellies until they spotted the tails and hindquarters of the wolves in the circle grass, no more than a hundred yards away. Their vital spots—heads, chests, bellies—were hidden by the grass.

Apparently, they were still focused on the spot where Batu and Zhang had come from, since they were looking that way through gaps in the grass, their ears pricked up and turned in the same direction. They were attentive to the rest of their surroundings as well, sniffing the air from time to time to detect signs of danger.

Batu signaled Zhang to aim at the closest wolf, the one to the left. He'd take the other one. The wind continued to blow, bending the circle grass in a low arch, brushing the stalks against one another, and keeping the wolves well hidden. Zhang closed one eye, and could no longer see the wolf.

They waited for the wind to let up. Batu told Zhang that when he heard Batu's gun fire, he was to pull the trigger. Zhang knew that even if he missed, Batu could easily get off another shot. He was, after all, one of the brigade's finest marksmen; within a range of two hundred yards, his aim was deadly. Many of the hunters said that wolves aren't worried about a hunter with a rifle at five hundred yards, or even four hundred. But when the distance closes to three hundred or less, they run off. This behavior, they said, came about because of Batu. Less than two hundred yards separated them from the two wolves in the grass, so Zhang calmly took aim on his unmoving target.

The stalks straightened up in a sudden lull in the wind, but just as the animals' bodies were exposed, a slender wolf burst out of a patch of circle grass off to the right and ran downhill, in front of the two hidden wolves, which leaped up as if snakebit, pulled in their necks, lowered their heads, and followed the third wolf down the slope. The slender wolf had obviously been standing guard for the other two and spotted the hunters at the moment they had the wolves in their sights. The largest of the three animals, the one being guarded, was no ordinary member of the pack, but one of its leaders. All three ran for the steepest hillside in the area.

Batu jumped to his feet and cried out, "To the horses!" They ran around to the rear of the hill, pulled the reins loose, and jumped into their saddles. The chase was on. But when they reached the top and looked down the dangerously steep slope, Zhang felt as if he were staring into an abyss, and reined in his horse.

"Grab the saddle horn and ride!" Batu shouted, showing no fear. With typical daredevil, death-defying

Mongol spirit, he turned his horse's head to one side and raced downhill.

A thought crossed Zhang's mind: Courage and cowardice are decided at moments like this. He clenched his teeth and loosened his reins as he raced downhill, normally a taboo among horsemen, especially on unfamiliar territory, where a marmot burrow or a rabbit or field mouse hole could trip up a horse and send it and its rider down to certain injury or death.

Zhang's horse tore down the hillside so fast that it felt as if they were in a free fall. The angle was so steep that he could not stay in the saddle without grabbing the horn and leaning until his back was touching the horse's rump and the stirrups were touching the animal's ears. He was virtually lying on his mount. He fought to keep his legs close to the horse, a survival trick all horsemen knew. If he lost his courage at that moment, all his desires would go straight to Tengger. Several days later, when he learned that there had been at least half a dozen marmot burrows and mouse holes on that slope, he broke out in a cold sweat. But Batu told him that Tengger favors people of courage and had moved the dangers out of his way.

When he reached the bottom of the hill, Zhang had nearly overtaken Batu, who looked back, surprised, and smiled. For Zhang, the smile was more radiant than a gold medal.

Roundup horses on the Olonbulag all experience the same emotional response to a mission such as this—impatience when things are going well and dejection when they're not. When Zhang and Batu's horses saw they had shortened the distance between them and the wolf by a third, their excitement became a stimulant, and at that moment they could have outrun a gazelle.

The gap shrank even more before the wolves reached the next hilltop. Batu sized up the terrain and the location of the wolves. "They're about to split up," he said. "Forget about the small one and focus on those two big ones. Watch and see which one I shoot, then fire at the rocks in front of them, starting with the one on the right." They raised their rifles. The horses' steady gait made it easy for their riders to take aim and fire straight. By this time the wolves knew the strength of their enemy and were running as fast as they could to the hill ahead. Neither the horses nor the wolves could keep up their frenetic pace for long, and Batu was waiting for one of the wolves to peel off in a new direction, which would reduce its chances for survival. If they all took different directions, the one that went to the right was the one he'd take down.

Seeing they were unable to outdistance their pursuers, the wolves were about to split up, a guarantee that at least one would get away. When the distance had shrunk to about three hundred yards, the ones flanking the head wolf peeled off and ran in opposite directions. Batu fired at the one on the right. He missed. Zhang took aim and pulled off two shots at a spot in front of the wolf; one hit the ground, the other a rock, sending sparks and shards of stone flying. The terrified wolf stumbled, and it no sooner was running again than Batu's rifle rang out. It crashed to the ground, hit on its right side. Zhang cried out happily, but Batu did not share his delight. "No good," he said. "The pelt is ruined."

Both riders turned to take out after the lead wolf. "Let's not use our rifles on this one," Batu told Zhang. "I know another way to bring him down." Energized when they saw that their riders had dispatched one wolf, the horses ran up the hill with amazing speed, at the cost of considerable stamina; within a few dozen yards, they were gasping and snorting, their speed in rapid decline. The lead wolf, on the other hand, displayed greater talent for climbing by increasing the length of its stride and putting on a burst of speed that not only opened up the distance but also lent it new confidence in its ability to get away. Batu and Zhang whipped their horses and dug their heels into their sides. Unused to being whipped, the horses ran like the breeze, their slobber catching on the wind. But the wolf was running with greater ease by now, without slowing. Zhang looked down at the wolf's tracks and could tell that its strides were longer than those of the horses, and when he looked up, he saw that it had nearly reached the hilltop; once it crossed the peak, the hunters would not see it again.

Suddenly Zhang heard Batu shout, "Get off your horse!" and saw him rein his horse to a stop in a sort of maneuver that roundup horses do better than any other. It is what they are trained to do for catching wild horses, a skill that served the hunters well at this moment. Both horses skidded to a stop so sudden that their riders were thrown out of the saddles and over their heads. Batu executed a perfect somersault as he landed; he then sprawled on the ground, held his breath, and took careful aim at a spot on the hilltop. Zhang sprawled beside him, rifle at the ready.

The wolf, no longer hearing hoofbeats, alertly stopped running. Grassland wolves have such short necks that to look behind them, they must turn around completely to see the location of their pursuers and the direction they're headed. When this one turned, the outline of its figure stood out against the sky on the hilltop, appearing three times the size it had been when running in a straight line, like a firing-range target. While this can give the hunter a clear shot, most of the time the wolf will still manage to get away. But by bringing his horse to a sudden stop, Batu had made the wolf suspicious, forcing it to stop and look back to see what he was up to.

The wolf had taken the bait, and Batu's rifle rang out. The animal fell forward, and its outline disappeared above the hilltop. "He was too far away," Batu said. "I didn't hit a vital spot. But he won't get away now. Let's go!" They remounted and spurred their horses up to the crest of the hill, where they spotted a pool of blood on the grass and rocks, but no wolf, not even when they swept the area with their spyglass. That meant they'd have to follow the trail of blood.

"Too bad we didn't bring dogs along," Zhang remarked with a sigh.

They rode slowly and in silence for a while, until Batu said, "My bullet broke one of its front legs. See how there are only three paw prints? This one won't get away."

Zhang replied, "No three-legged wolf can outrun a four-legged horse."

Batu looked at his watch. "Don't be so sure," he said. "This is a pack leader. What if he finds a deep den? We'll never get him then. Let's speed it up."

They followed the sporadic trail of blood another hour or more, until they came to a grassy knoll, where they were amazed by what they saw: there on the ground was the wolf's front leg, with tooth marks on the coat, the tendons, and the bone. "See there," Batu said, "the wolf knew that his leg was slowing him down, dragging along on the ground, so he chewed it off."

Zhang felt his stomach lurch. "I've heard people say

that a warrior will cut off his arm if it's been hit by a poisoned arrow, though you couldn't prove it by me. But this makes the third time I've seen a wolf chew off its own leg."

"People differ from one another," Batu said, "but wolves are all alike."

They continued on, noting that the trail of blood was lessening, while the strides were getting longer. What worried them most was that the wolf seemed to be looking for a shortcut to the border, just north of an off-limits military area. "That's one remarkable pack leader," Batu said. "We can't let it lead us wherever it wants us to go." They sped up and took a shortcut to the border.

The farther north they traveled, the higher the grass grew, a gray vastness like an enormous wolf pelt. It was going to be harder to find their wolf than to dig up a lamb in a mountain of newly shorn wool. Heaven and man do not easily come together, but a wolf and the grassland merge like water and milk. For all they knew as they rode along, the crippled animal could be right under their noses. Zhang was once again made keenly aware of the close relationship between wolf and the grassland, and between wolves and Tengger. When it's a matter of life or death, the grassland provides an avenue of escape; when they're in peril, the grassland supplies wings for them to fly away like birds. It keeps them under its wing. The vast expanse of Mongolian grassland favors and protects its wolves. They are like an old couple, devoted to one another for life. Even Mongols, who are loyal and steadfast to the grassland, cannot reach the exalted position the wolves occupy.

The horses, after stopping from time to time, had regained their strength and were able to increase the pace. The mountain range to the north drew closer; that was where the grassland ended. According to the herdsmen, the mountains, with their barren and cold deep valleys, are the wolves' last base on the Olonbulag, a place where they have no enemies. But even if the crippled wolf somehow reached that refuge, how would it live? That thought no sooner occurred to Zhang than he realized he was measuring the wolf by his own standards. In the end, man has the capacity to kill a wolf, but not its spirit.

Finally, the horses stepped onto the public highway, which was actually a dirt or, at best, gravel road used for military patrols. The wheels of all-terrain vehicles and transport trucks had created a wide hollow nearly three feet deep, until the road, from one end to another, was a winding trough, like a sandy dragon, rising and falling. The fragility of the grassland, the terrifying reality of the land beneath the thin grassy surface, was exposed by this road. The top layer of grass was moist, but the sandy roadway had been blown bone-dry by winds from the west, creating a dragon hundreds of miles long. The hooves of passing horses raised a storm of sand that flew into the faces of the riders and their mounts, choking them and burning their eyes.

The two hunters headed east; there were no wolf tracks to follow. But when they crossed a gentle rise in the road, a wolf appeared out of nowhere some thirty yards ahead, struggling to climb out of the rut in the middle of the road, something a healthy animal could have done easily; but it was the final barrier for this wolf. It fell back, causing excruciating pain when the wounded stump hit the ground.

"Dismount," Batu said as he stepped down. Zhang followed, nervously watching to see what Batu was going to do and reaching out for the herding club hanging from his saddle. But instead of reaching for his club or approaching the wolf, Batu let his horse move over to a grassy spot to graze, after which he sat down on the ridge of the road, took out a pack of cigarettes, lit one, and quietly smoked. Through the haze of smoke, Zhang saw a complex set of emotions in the man's eyes. Freeing his horse to graze, he sat down next to Batu and bummed a cigarette.

The wolf struggled to its feet and sat down, listing to one side, yellow sand stuck to its bloody chest. Defiantly, it stared at its enemies, not for a minute forgetting its dignity. It vigorously shook the sand and grass from its body as if tidying its battle attire. But all its attempts to stop the stump of its missing leg from shaking failed. A look of savage righteousness emerged from its eyes; it breathed deeply, reaching down for whatever strength was left in its body. Zhang Jiyuan lacked the courage to look into the wolf's eyes; standing on the ancient grassland, that is, looking from the standpoint of the grassland, the wolf had wrenched justice and righteousness from the humans.

Batu held the cigarette in his fingers, gazed thoughtfully at the struggling wolf, the look in his eyes was one of a student who has just beaten his teacher and has begun to feel remorse and a growing sense of unease. Seeing that its enemies had not made a move for a long time, the wolf turned and began to claw at the dirt with its remaining front paw. The black topsoil on the exposed section of ground beside the road was no more than an inch or two thick. Below that was a layer of sand and tiny pebbles. The digging eventually opened up a gap, releasing sand that crumbled on the floor of the rut and made it possible for the crippled wolf to jump and crawl out onto the grass. Then it hopped on three legs in the direction of the distant firebreak and boundary marker.

The firebreak was a wide tractor-leveled lane parallel with the border, a hundred or more yards across. Replowed once every year, it was nothing but sand, without a blade of grass anywhere, and was intended to stop the spread of wildfires from the other side of the border and small fires from this side. It was the only plowed land on the Olonbulag tolerated by the herdsmen. Old-timers said it constituted the only benefit farming brought to their land.

The wolf ran until it had to stop and rest, then ran again, eventually disappearing in the tall grass. There would be no more obstacles.

Batu stood up to look but said nothing. Then he bent down, picked up the cigarette butt Zhang had left on the ground, and spit on it. He dug a small hole in the moist grassy surface with his fingers and buried the two cigarette butts. "Get used to doing that," he said. "The grassland cannot tolerate carelessness." He stood up. "Let's go," he said. "We'll go back for the wolf we killed."

They mounted their horses and rode off toward the hillside with the circle grass. The snow on the ground was clean, the horses' hooves light. They didn't talk.

16

A heavy, unpleasant odor rose from the hillside near the birthing camp, warmed by the sun after a spring rain. The rotting remains of weak animals that had frozen to death over the long winter, along with those of livestock killed by wolves, were exposed on the grass, which was stained with dark blood. Yellow and black fouled water oozed from decaying autumn vegetation. Liquefying animal dung discolored the grassland.

The stenches of an early-spring day did nothing to dampen Chen Zhen's spirits. Foul water was necessary on the grassland. "Inspection teams and poets from the cities like the smell of spring flowers on the grassland," said Uljii, "but I prefer the spring stench. One sheep expels fifteen hundred catties of dung and urine each year. Do you know how much grass that feeds? Cow manure is cold, horse manure is hot, but sheep manure equals two years of manual labor. If you control the quantity of livestock, not only will they not deplete the grassland, but they'll actually enrich it. The best tribal leaders of the past were able to turn sandy soil into rich grassland."

In the spring the water on the Olonbulag was rich with nutrients, and the grass grew in front of people's eyes. After a couple of weeks of sunny days, the new green grass completely covered the decaying grass of the previous year. The hillside grazing areas were green, all green. Plants and flowers bore up through the fertile ground, making the topsoil denser and tougher, and keeping the desert at bay. Chen was on Old Man Bilgee's big yellow horse, trotting across the land and joyfully taking in the green rebirth. To him, the vast grassland, the stage on which men and wolves held their cruel battles, was transformed into a place where Mother Earth received loving tribute.

The ewes' teats swelled, the lambs' coats whitened, the cows lowed loudly, and the horses' heavy coats fell away; the livestock had made it through another year with the return of fresh green grass. It was going to be a fine year on the Olonbulag. Even though the spring cold spell had killed many lambs, the brigade's birthing rate, buoyed by a high percentage of twin births, had increased dramatically.

Still, the shepherds were filled with foreboding. With the spectacular increase in the sheep population, the Olonbulag was in danger of being overgrazed. If the shepherds sold a large quantity of newborn lambs, they would later fail to meet their production quota. So the brigade held a series of meetings. Uljii could see only one solution, which was to open up a new grazing land.

Chen Zhen accompanied Uljii and Bilgee to inspect the chosen site. Bilgee had lent him a good horse, fast, with exceptional stamina. Uljii carried a semiautomatic rifle, Bilgee brought Bar along with him, and Chen brought Erlang, leaving Yellow back at the yurt to watch over things. The two dogs, avid hunters, were on the lookout for anything to chase along the way. Like Chen, they were in high spirits. "You shepherds and sheepdogs have been bottled up for more than a month," Bilgee said with a laugh.

"Thanks for bringing me along, Papa. I needed a break."

The old man replied, "I've been worried you might ruin your eyesight reading all those books."

At the northeast corner of the brigade territory stood some forty square miles of barren, hilly land. According to Uljii, no one had ever lived there, so it was especially fertile, with several streams and some lakes of various sizes. The grass grew three feet tall or more, with a ground accumulation at least a foot thick. Given the abundance of water and the dense grass, the mosquito population was immense. In the summer and autumn, these insects could collectively kill a cow. When the men stepped on the thick ground cover, swarms of mosquitoes rose into the air; it was like stepping on land mines. Both people and their animals feared the mountainous terrain and refused to go there. With the ground cover so thick, the grass had to grow tall in order to get any sun; the livestock didn't like it, and it was no good for fattening them up.

Uljii, the head of the pastureland, had anticipated that under the policy of quantity over quality, sooner or later the Olonbulag would be overgrazed. For years he'd had his eye on this unused tract of virgin land, looking forward to an autumn wildfire that would burn off the ground cover. Over the following spring, he could then drive large herds of the production brigade's horses and cows to trample down the loose earth and eat the new grass, which would control its growth. The land would become harder, the soil enriched, and the short grass would deter the mosquito population. Within a few years, an unusable tract of wild land would become an excellent summer field for grazing, providing a new seasonal pasture. Finally, they would turn the original summer pasture into a spring pasture. That way the brigade could double its quantity of livestock and none of its land would be overgrazed. But then the herdsmen, who feared the mosquitoes, opposed his plans. So he sought out Bilgee's help, asking him to inspect the area with him. If Bilgee gave the nod, Uljii could set up a new grazing land with two brigades.

As they passed through a neighboring brigade's winter grazing land, Chen saw that the grass was still thick, and a full four fingers high. "You keep saying there isn't enough grazing land," he said to Uljii, "but look, sheep and horses have been grazing here all winter, and there's still all this left."

Uljii looked down. "That's stubble grass," he said. "It's too hard; the animals have trouble biting it off, so they wind up pulling it out by its roots. And the poor quality of the grass stubble can't fatten them up. The grazing has to stop when it gets like this; if not, the grassland will begin to deteriorate. There are too many of you Chinese, and not enough meat to feed you, so the country depends on the lamb and beef from Inner Mongolia. But to produce one ton of beef and lamb requires seventy or eighty tons of grass. When you people come demanding our meat, what you're really asking us for is our grass, and if you keep it up, you'll kill off the grassland. The pressure from government quotas has nearly turned several banners in the southeast into desert."

"Raising livestock seems a lot harder than planting crops," Chen Zhen said.

Bilgee nodded in agreement: "The grassland is a big life, but it's thinner than people's eyelids. If you rupture its grassy surface, you blind it, and dust storms are more lethal than the white-hair blizzards. If the grassland dies, so will the cows and sheep and horses, as well as the wolves and the people, all the little lives. Then not even the Great Wall, not even Beijing will be protected."

"I used to attend meetings in Hohhot once every few years," Uljii said emotionally. "The pastureland there is in even worse shape than ours. Several hundred miles of the western portion of the Great Wall have already been swallowed up by sand. If the government continues increasing our supply quotas, the eastern portion of the wall will be in danger of suffering the same fate. I hear some foreign governments have passed laws to protect their grasslands, that restrictions on types of livestock permitted to graze are in place, and that even the number of animals per acre is regulated and enforced, with stiff monetary penalties for overgrazing. That can only keep existing grassland from further decline. Once it's gone, it's gone forever. If our people wait to gain an understanding of the grassland until it's been claimed by the desert, it'll be too late to do anything."

"People are just too greedy," Bilgee said, "and too many are ignorant. You can give these fools a hundred reasons to do the right thing, but you're just wasting your time. Tengger understands that the only way to deal with those greedy fools is with wolves. Let the wolves control the livestock population, and the grassland will survive."

Uljii shook his head. "The old Tengger ways don't work," he said. "China has tested an atomic bomb. Eradicating a bunch of wolves couldn't be easier."

Chen Zhen felt as if his heart had filled with sand. "I haven't heard the wolves or the dogs for several nights. We've driven them away, Papa, haven't we? If they don't come back, we're sunk."

"Thirty or so wolves, the equivalent of four or five litters, is a tiny fraction of the Olonbulag wolf population. They haven't shown up, not because we scared them off, but because they have other things to do this time of year."

"What are they up to?" Chen asked, growing excited again.

The old man pointed to some nearby mountains. "Come with me, I'll show you." He smacked the rump of Chen's horse with his whip. "Let him run. Horses need to sweat in the spring. It helps them shed their winter coats. It also helps fatten them up."

Like a trio of racehorses, their mounts galloped off toward the mountains, sending grass and dirt flying behind them, the fresh green grass staining their hooves. Luckily, there would be no other horses in that area for several months. Chen, who was bringing up the rear, was beginning to understand the true implications of the saying "Horse herds are the grassland's enemy."

The horses reached a hillside, where they were greeted by the high-pitched yelps of marmots, burrowing animals found all over the grassland. Nearly half the hills on the Olonbulag were home to Mongolian marmots. Every autumn Chen saw marmots the old man had shot and was treated to their fatty, delicious meat. Like bears, they hibernate during the winter and survive on stored-up fat. The distinctive meat has a layer of fat, like pork, and, since it has no gamey taste, it is among the Mongols' favorite foods; they prefer it over beef and lamb. A grown marmot provides enough meat for a meal for a whole family.

Chen was amazed by the array of marmots in front of him: no fewer than sixty or seventy of the animals, big and small, stood on the slopes and peaks of a string of hills, looking like tree stumps after the loggers have left. Large brown males in front of large isolated burrows, the slightly smaller females with fur as yellow as wolf coats in front of burrow clusters. Babies, sometimes as many as seven or eight of them, their heads like little rabbits, stood around their mothers. The arrival of humans did not send them scurrying into their burrows; instead, they rose up on their hind legs, front legs in front of their chests, like little fists, and barked, each bark accompanied by an upward jerk of their bottlebrush tails, as if to warn the intruders away.

"People call this place Marmot Hill," Bilgee said. "It's crawling with them. Up north there's another spot with even more than here. This place was once the salvation of the grassland's poorest residents. In the fall, when the marmots were big and plump, they'd come here to catch them, eating the meat and selling the pelts and oil for money or for lamb. You Chinese are crazy about marmot overcoats, so each fall, the fur traders from Zhangjiakou come here to pick mushrooms and buy marmot skins, which are three times as expensive as lambskin. These little animals have saved more people than you know, including Genghis Khan's family when they were living in hard times."

"Marmots are tasty because of the fat," Uljii said. "Other burrowing animals, such as ground squirrels and field voles, store up food for the winter months. But marmots get through the winter thanks to their fat."

"After making it through the winter," Bilgee said, "they have lost nearly all their fat, but there's plenty of meat on their bones. See how big they are? Well, thanks to the abundance of grass this year, they'll fatten up in no time."

"No wonder the wolves haven't been harassing us lately," Chen said. "They like a change of diet too. But how do they catch them, since marmots never stray far from their deep burrows?"

"They're expert marmot hunters," Bilgee said with a laugh. "The big ones dig into the burrow entrance, sending the occupants scurrying out escape holes, where other wolves are waiting to kill and eat them. Sometimes smaller wolves actually dig their way deep into the burrow to catch and drag them out. Desert foxes also burrow in to get at them. When I come out to shoot marmots, I trap six or seven foxes every year, and once I trapped a small wolf. We learned to let our children crawl into wolf dens to get at the cubs from the wolves and the desert foxes. If their burrows are too shallow, the marmots will freeze, so they dig very deep—ten, maybe twenty feet. Can you tell me why wolf dens are so deep, since wolves don't hibernate in the winter?" the old man asked Chen.

Chen shook his head.

"Because they often take over marmot burrows. A wolf will clear out one of these burrows and have her cubs inside."

"That's amazing," Chen remarked. "Killing and eating a family of marmots isn't enough for them. They have to take over their home as well."

Uljii smiled with admiration. "That's how they keep the marmots in check. They perform a great service, since the rodents are no good at all for the grassland. See what they've done to this hillside, burrows everywhere. They produce litters of six or seven every year. If their burrows stay small, there isn't enough room for them all, so they dig bigger ones, destroying the grazing land for miles around. The four destructive pests of the grassland are field mice, wild rabbits, marmots, and gazelles, in that order. Marmots are relatively slow animals, and ought to be easy to catch. So why do we need to trap them? Because their burrows are interconnected.

At the first sign of danger, they disappear in the web of tunnels. They forage voraciously, and in the fall they feed on seeds. One of those plump little bodies requires several acres of grass and seeds each year. There's nothing worse for horses than a marmot colony. Every year we lose several horses that break their legs when they step in one of these burrows and throw their riders.

"Actually," Uljii continued, "the burrows cause even more trouble than that. During the winter, they're home to mosquitoes. The mosquitoes of Eastern Mongolia are world renowned. Mosquitoes in the Manchurian forests can eat a man alive. Ours can eat a cow. You'd think that out here, where the temperature plunges to thirty or forty below in the winter, cold enough to turn a sick cow into an ice sculpture, that it ought to freeze the mosquitoes. How do they make it through the winters? Marmot burrows. When winter closes in, they follow the marmots into the deep burrows, which are sealed up to keep the snow and ice out and the warmth in. The marmots sleep, going without food and water. But the mosquitoes have plenty of food and water, all from their hosts, making for a comfortable winter. Then when spring arrives, and the marmots leave their burrows, the mosquitoes follow them out and, given all the little lakes on the grassland, fly off to breed the next generation on the water. Come summertime, the grassland is mosquito heaven. See what I mean? Wolves are the prime marmot killers out here. We have a saying that goes, 'When marmots leave their burrows, the wolves go up the mountain.' Once the marmots are out in the open, the livestock can rest easy for a spell."

Chen had been severely bitten for two summers, and the sound of mosquitoes was enough to make his hair stand on end. His skin felt as if it were being cracked and split; the Chinese students feared mosquitoes more than they did wolves. Eventually, he got his family to send mosquito netting from Beijing, and he began sleeping through the night. The herdsmen thought the netting was a wonderful thing, and it quickly became an essential part of the Mongol yurts. They called the nets "mosquito houses."

"I've never seen in any book a word about the relationship between mosquitoes and marmots, or how the burrows are the mosquitoes' bandit hideouts, or how wolves are their mortal enemies," a skeptical Chen said to Uljii.

"The grassland is a complex place," Uljii said. "Everything is linked, and the wolves are the major link, tied to all the others. If that link is removed, livestock raising will disappear out here. You can't count all the benefits the wolves bring, far greater than the damage they cause."

With a laugh, Bilgee said, "But don't think that the marmots don't benefit us at all. Their fur, their meat, and their oil are extremely valuable. Marmot skins are an important source of income for the herdsmen. The government trades them for automobiles and artillery. The wolves are smart, they don't kill off all the marmots, so there'll always be a supply for the next year. That's true for the herdsmen as well. We take only the adults, not the young animals."

As the horses sped through the mountains, the fearless marmots kept up the chorus of barks. Hawks attacked out of the sky, but failed most of the time. The farther northwest the men traveled, the fewer people they saw, and the fewer signs of habitation, until finally there weren't even horse droppings anywhere.

* * *

When the three riders reached the top of a steep slope, spread out before them were hills so green they seemed unreal. As they crossed the hill, they saw yellow mixed in with the green, the color of last year's grass, but the green on the mountains ahead was like a dyed stage curtain, or a fairyland in an animated movie. Uljii pointed with his whip. "If you'd come here last fall, you'd have seen only black mountains. It looks like they've been dressed in green felt, doesn't it?" The horses picked up speed when they spotted the green mountains. Uljii led the way across gently rising land.

After crossing a pair of ridges, the party reached a green slope. It was covered with barley; not a single blade of yellow grass in sight, nor a trace of any unpleasant scent. The fragrance grew stronger, and Bilgee sensed that something was different. He looked down. The dogs also picked up a scent and checked out the area, nose to the ground. The old man bent down to get a closer look at the tall grass around the horses' hooves. When he looked up, he said, "What do you smell?" Chen breathed in deeply, and could smell the fragrance of the tender new grass. It was like sitting on a horse-drawn mower in the fall, when the smell of cut grass floods the nose. "No one was out here cutting this, were they?" he asked. "Who could it be?"

The old man got off his horse and poked at the grass with his herding club, looking for something. Before long, he found something green and yellow. He pinched it, then smelled it. "This is gazelle dung," he said. "They passed through here not long ago."

Uljii and Chen also got down off their horses and

examined the gazelle dung the old man was holding. Gazelle dung is wet in the summer, tightly packed, not pellets. Uljii and Chen were surprised by the find. They walked a few steps and spotted patches of grass that looked as if they had been attacked with scythes, but unevenly.

"I thought I saw gazelles out by the birthing pens this spring. So this is where they came to graze. They cut through the grass more savagely than mowers."

Uljii loaded his rifle and flicked off the safety. "Every spring they migrate to the birthing pens, where they compete for grazing land with ewes that have just given birth. But not this year, and that's because this is better grass. They think like me."

Bilgee's eyes turned into slits as he laughed. "They're experts at finding good grazing land," he said to Uljii. "It'd be a shame if they chose the best land and we and our livestock stayed away. You were certainly right this time."

"Not so fast," Uljii counseled. "Wait till you see the source of water."

"But the lambs are still too young," Chen said. "They can't walk all the way out here. It'll be at least another month before they'll be able to walk long distances, and by then this grass will all be in the bellies of gazelles."

"Don't worry," Bilgee said. "Wolves are smarter than people. Sooner or later they'll be here too. The birthing season for gazelles hasn't ended yet, and neither the adults nor the young can run fast. This is the time of the year when the wolves can feast on gazelle. It won't take many days for them to drive the entire herd out of here."

"No wonder the survival rate among newborn sheep was so high this year," Uljii said. "With the growth of this grass, the gazelles and the wolves all came out here. There was no fighting over grazing land."

Hearing that there might be wolves around, Chen anxiously urged the two men to get back onto their horses. As they crossed another ridge, Uljii reminded them to be alert, since just beyond the next ridge lay a vast grazing land, and that, he guessed, was where they'd find both gazelles and wolves.

They dismounted when they reached the top of the ridge; bending low and stepping quietly, they led the horses with one hand and held the dogs with the other as they made their way to a spot among several large boulders. The two big dogs could smell a hunt and crawled along, sticking close to their masters. Just before they reached the rocks, the men wrapped their reins around their horses' front legs. Then they sprawled on the ground behind the boulders to survey the area through telescopes.

At last Chen laid eyes on virgin grassland, possibly the last of its kind in all of China, and breathtakingly beautiful. Spread out before him was a dark green basin, dozens of square miles, with layers of mountain peaks to the east, all the way north to the Great Xing'an range. Mountains of many colors—dark and light green, brown, deep red, purple—rose in waves as far as one could see, to merge with an ocean of pink clouds. The basin was surrounded by gentle sloping hills on three sides. The basin itself looked like a green carpet manicured by Tengger; patterns of blue, white, yellow, and pink mountain flowers formed a seamless patchwork of color.

A stream flowed down from a mountain valley to the southeast, twisting and turning as soon as it entered the basin, each horseshoe twist like a silver band, the many bands lengthening and curving until the stream drained into a blue lake in the center of the basin. Puffy white clouds floated atop the clear water.

That centerpiece was a swan lake, which Chen Zhen never dreamed of seeing. Through the lens of his telescope he saw a dozen white swans floating gracefully on water ringed by dense green reeds. The swans were surrounded by hundreds, perhaps thousands of wild geese, wild ducks, and other nameless waterbirds. Five or six large swans flew up into the air, accompanied by a flurry of waterbirds. They circled the lake and the stream, crying out like a welcoming orchestra. The lake was quiet, white feathers dancing on its surface, an otherworldly haven of peace.

A natural outlet opened to the northwest, diverting the lake's water to thousands of acres of marshland.

This was likely the last spot in the northern grassland that still retained its primitive beauty. Chen Zhen was mesmerized by the sight. But even as he marveled, anxiety entered his heart. Once men and horses come, he was thinking, the primitive beauty of the place will quickly be lost, and no Chinese will lay his eyes on such natural, pristine beauty ever again.

Uljii and Bilgee kept their telescopes trained on spots below. The old man nudged Chen's leg with the tip of his boot and directed his attention to the third bend in the stream, off to the right. There on the bank at one of the horseshoe bends he saw a pair of gazelles in the water, straining to climb onto dry land, their upper bodies safely aground, their rear legs apparently stuck in the mud. They lacked the strength to pull themselves out. Not far away, in the grass, lay the bodies of a dozen more, their abdomens torn open...Chen swung his telescope slowly toward the tall lakeshore grass. His heart lurched. Several large wolves were sprawled near their kills, fast asleep. The grass was too tall for him to get an accurate count.

Uljii and Bilgee continued scanning the area, stopping on a slope off to the southeast, where the dispersed members of the gazelle herd were grazing in small clusters, the newborns staying close to their mothers. Chen watched as one of the gazelles cleaned her newborn calf with her tongue, looking up anxiously every few seconds. The calf was struggling to get to its feet; once a gazelle calf is standing, it can run so fast not even a dog can catch it. The minutes during which it tries to stand will determine whether it lives or dies. Chen didn't know what to do. At this distance, they had to make a decision: Go for the wolves or for the gazelles?

Bilgee said, "Look at those wolves, sleeping out in the open. They know there's nothing anyone can do to them. We're too far for our rifles to be of any use, and if we show ourselves, they and the gazelles will be gone before we know it."

"But those stuck in the lake are ours," Uljii pointed out. "Lunch."

They mounted up and rode off toward the lake; the minute they, their horses, and their dogs were out in the open, the wolves fled toward the mountains, spread out, and headed south. They were immediately swallowed up by patches of reeds. The gazelles reacted the same way, and just as quickly, leaving behind the ones stuck in the mud and the mothers licking their calves.

The riders approached a bend in the stream that surrounded an acre of land. A dozen or more gazelles, adult and young, lay in the grass, their innards gone, their legs chewed down to the bone. One was stuck in the mud, unable to move an inch; the others were still making feeble attempts to pull themselves out, the wounds in their necks still bleeding.

By now Chen was familiar with the wolves' tactics, but this was the first time he'd seen how they could use the bend in a stream to do the work. He rode around examining the tactics of the attack.

"See what geniuses they are?" Uljii said. "They hid in the grass the night before and waited until the gazelles came to drink. Then they quickly sealed off all avenues of escape, and trapped the gazelles with the help of the stream. As easy as that. The stream was their sack, and all they had to do was tighten the drawstring around the meat they needed."

The dogs, smelling the wild meat all around, were in no hurry to eat, and they ignored the gazelles the wolves had eaten from. Bar charged a gazelle that was barely alive, and grabbed it by the throat. He glanced over at Bilgee; the old man nodded. "Go ahead, eat." The dog lowered his head and bit down hard, and the gazelle was dead. He then ripped a chunk of meat off the animal's thigh and began to eat. The sight of the bloody kill sent the hair on Erlang's back straight up, like a wolf, and stirred his killer instinct. Seeing a live calf near a bend in the stream not far off, he jumped into the water and swam across. Bilgee stopped Chen from calling him back. "That dog has a wild streak. If you don't let him kill wild animals," he said, "he'll turn on our sheep again."

They rode up to the stream, where Bilgee took a leather rope from his saddle and tied it into a loop. Chen removed his boots, rolled up his pant legs, and waded into the water, where he looped the rope around the neck of a gazelle. Bilgee and Uljii dragged the animal up onto the bank, where they placed it on the ground and hogtied it. Then they dragged the second gazelle out of the bloody stream, laid it out on a clean patch of grass, and selected a site for their cookout. "We'll eat one and take the other back with us," Bilgee said. While Uljii was slaughtering one of the gazelles, Bilgee took Chen up into the mountains to the northwest to look for firewood.

They reached a ravine with a copse of wild apricot trees, only a few of which had died. But there were plenty of burned branches on the three-foot-tall trunks. The scent of apricot blossoms that had recently fallen to the now colorful ground permeated the ravine, the floor of which was buried under a layer of rotten apricots. They tied up two bundles of firewood and dragged them back to the cookout site, where Uljii had already skinned the gazelle and sliced off hunks of raw meat; he'd also picked wild onions and leeks, as thick as chopsticks, that grew by the stream.

The men removed their horses' bits and saddles. After shaking off the effects of their burdens, the horses sought out a gentle grazing slope, then walked up to the stream, where they eagerly drank their fill. Bilgee was feeling good about everything. "There's good water here," he said, "very good water. That's the first thing you look for in summer grazing land." The horses drank until their bellies were taut, then went up the slope and began to graze, snorting happily.

The cook fire blazed, sending the fragrance of gazelle meat into the air above the swan lake for the first time ever, along with oily smoke redolent of leeks and peppers. They sat close to the lake. The meat, speared on thin branches, was so fresh it seemed to still twitch.

Having set out that day before dawn, the men were famished. One after another, Chen polished off strips of meat with peppers and leeks, washing them down with gulps of liquor from the old man's flask. "This is the second time I've been fed by wolves," he said, "and I've never tasted anything better, especially eating it at the site of the hunt."

Bilgee and Uljii were searing gazelle legs over the fire, slicing off layers as they got cooked, then making several cuts and adding salt they'd brought with them, onions, and a few peppers to cook some more. The old man ate heartily, finishing off layer after layer. After drinking from his flask, he said, "I'm glad we've got the wolf pack to watch over this new pasture. In another twenty days, when the lambs are strong enough to make the trip, we'll move the production team out here."

Uljii wrapped a strip of meat around a wild onion and bit into it. "Do you think the whole team will come?" he asked.

"The wolves are here," Bilgee replied, "and so are the gazelles. Why wouldn't they? If the grass were no good, would the gazelles be here? If there were few gazelles, would the wolves come? I'll take that gazelle back with us and call a meeting at my place tomorrow. There will be gazelle-stuffed buns for everyone. Once they know how good the water is, they'll fight to come. For a summer pasture, good grass isn't enough; you need good water too. There's nothing worse in summer than having stagnant, dirty water. It makes the animals sick."

Uljii said, "If anyone objects, I'll bring them out to see for themselves."

The old man laughed heartily. "No need for that," he said. "I'm the alpha wolf. If I come, the other wolves will follow. You can never be hurt by following the alpha wolf." He turned to Chen Zhen. "All the time you've been following me, has it ever hurt you?"

Chen laughed. "By following the wolf king, I eat good food and drink strong liquor. Yang Ke and the others would love to travel with Papa."

"Then it's settled," Uljii said. "When we get back, I'll call a meeting to announce the move. The quotas we've been given over the past few years have got me to where I can hardly breathe. Opening this new pasture will bring four or five years of relief."

"And after that?" Chen asked. "Is there any more land out there somewhere?"

"No," Uljii said, his mood darkening. "There's the border to the north and other communes west and south. As for the northeast, the mountains are too steep and too rocky. I've been there twice. There's no more available pastureland."

"So what will you do?"

"We'll have to control the size of the herds and improve the quality. For instance, we can raise Xinjiang improved sheep," Uljii said. "They produce twice the amount of wool, and it's better stuff. Our wool sells for a little over one yuan a pound, but better-quality wool goes for more than four. Wool is our greatest single source of income." Chen had to agree that this was a good plan. But then Uljii sighed. "China has so many people that I figure our pastureland will fall behind in production in a few years. After people of my generation retire, I don't know what you youngsters are going to do."

Bilgee stared at Uljii. "You're going to have to talk to the people in charge. Tell them to ease the pressure on the livestock units. If they keep it up, the sky will turn yellow, the earth will rebel, and the sand will bury us all."

Uljii shook his head. "Who's going to listen to us? Farming officials run the show these days. They're more cultured than us, and they speak Chinese. Besides, officials in the pasture areas are obsessed with hunting wolves. By competing over the quantity of livestock, those who know nothing about the land actually get promoted faster."

The horses had eaten their fill and were resting, heads down, eyes closed.

Uljii led his companions on a tour of the rest of the basin, discussing with Bilgee where to have the four companies set up camp. Chen was greedily soaking up the incredible scenery, wondering if he'd landed in a Garden of Eden in the midst of the grassland. Or a grassland in the midst of a Garden of Eden. Whatever it was, he didn't want to leave—ever.

After returning to the site of the cookout, they slaughtered and skinned the second gazelle, and as Chen looked out at the carcasses strewn around the horseshoe bend, he felt empty and suddenly gloomy. The smell of blood had driven out the peaceful, romantic feelings he'd experienced when he first stepped foot on the grazing land. After a thoughtful moment, he reluctantly said to the old man, "When wolves kill gazelles in the winter it's to keep them on ice for the spring. But why do they kill so many in the summer? There are probably more in some of the other bends. They'll begin to stink in a couple of days and won't be edible. Maybe the wolves just love killing."

"They don't kill all those gazelles for the fun of it," Bilgee said, "or to display their power. They do it so that the old, sick, and wounded wolves will have something to eat. Do you know why tigers and such can't survive out here? And why wolves dominate the grassland? It's because of their pack mentality. Tigers make a kill for themselves, not for other tigers, not even for their mates or offspring. But wolves kill for themselves and for the rest of the pack, even those that can't be in on the kill—the old, the crippled, the nearly blind, the young, the sick, and the nursing females. All you see now are the carcasses, but when the alpha male howls tonight, half the wolves in the Olonbulag and any others that can claim some kinship with this pack will show up, and there won't be anything left by morning. A wolf takes care of the pack, and the pack takes care of each wolf. They stick together, which is what makes them such formidable foes. Sometimes the howl of the alpha male will draw a hundred wolves into a battle. Old-timers tell us there used to be tigers out here, but they were all driven off by wolves. Wolves are more family-oriented than people, and much more united."

The old man sighed. "Back in the time of Genghis Khan, that's when the Mongols really learned from wolves. Every tribe came together, like spokes on a wheel, or a quiver of arrows. Their numbers were small, but they had considerable power, and every one of them would have gladly given up his life for their mother, the grassland. How else were they able to conquer half the world? Our downfall came when we lost that sense of unity. Now it's tribe against tribe, individual arrows fired in anger, but easily deflected and broken. Wolves have it all over people. We can learn from their tactics in battle, but the way they stick together seems to elude us. For hundreds of years we've tried, but we still haven't mastered it. But that's enough—just talking about it is painful."

* * *

Chen looked out over the breathtakingly beautiful swan lake and was lost in thought.

The old man wrapped the meat from the gazelle in its skin and stuffed it into a pair of gunnysacks. After Chen got the horses saddled, the two older men each threw one of the bags over the rump of his horse and secured it behind the saddle.

The three horses galloped off toward brigade headquarters.

17

The final disposition of the case involving the war-horse massacre came down from higher authorities. A major administrative demerit was recorded for Uljii, who was responsible for all production; he was dismissed from the three-in-one leadership body and was to be sent down to a grassroots unit to toughen himself up through manual labor. Similar demerits were also recorded for the herders—Batu, Laasurung, and the two others—and Batu was replaced as militia company commander. In addition, Bao Shungui, who had by then returned to civilian life, was made head of the leadership body and would be in charge of all revolutionary activities and production.

Bao Shungui and Zhang Jiyuan accompanied Uljii to the livestock brigade. Prior to the Cultural Revolution, Uljii had made his office in the livestock brigade or the livestock section. He kept his all-season deel and boots at the livestock brigade, where they were cleaned and tended by women who lived in yurts there. He was used to spending time at the grass roots whether he was sent there or not, doing whatever had to be done, whether it was his job to do or not, his prestige and influence unaffected by this development. But the journey this time proceeded at half the normal speed. He rode an aging white horse suffering from the late-spring cold and, since it was still shedding its coat, it looked like an old man wearing a padded jacket at the beginning of summer.

Zhang wanted to give Uljii his fast horse, but Uljii refused to take it and urged Zhang to let his horse run instead of wasting time plodding alongside him. Zhang had come to the brigade headquarters for batteries to take back to the horse herders, and when he met the two leaders, one current, one former, he decided to see Uljii on the road. He felt better when he heard that Uljii would be staying in Bilgee's yurt.

Bao Shungui was riding Uljii's special horse, a yellow skewbald with a velvety, high-gloss coat. Bao was frequently forced to rein it in to stay close to Uljii; it chomped at the bit, unused to its new rider, who kept burying his heels in its sides. From time to time it slowed down to nudge its former owner's knee with its nose and whinny sadly.

"I did the best I could, Uljii," Bao said, "to keep you in the leadership group. I don't know anything about raising livestock. I've spent my life in farming villages. But my superiors have assigned me the responsibility over this big pasture, though I'm not sure I'm up to the job."

Uljii's forehead was beaded with sweat over the need to constantly spur his horse to keep moving. Riding an old horse is hard on the rider and on the horse; Zhang used his whip on Uljii's horse to help out, but Uljii reached out and stroked the animal's head to keep it calm. "They were fair," Uljii said, "calling it a production issue and not a political problem. The incident had a wide-ranging impact, and if they hadn't punished me, there'd have been hell to pay in other quarters."

"I've been out here almost a year," Bao said, "and I

can say that the pasture is a lot harder to manage than a farming community. Another major incident or two, and I won't be running the show for long... Some people wanted you to be sent to the Capital Construction Brigade, but I insisted that you be sent to the Second Production Brigade. With your knowledge of raising livestock, I'll breathe easier knowing you're staying with Bilgee. That way, if anything I can't handle comes up, I'll look to you for answers."

Uljii's face brightened. "Has the revolutionary committee approved the move of the Second Brigade to the new grazing land?"

"Yes, and brigade headquarters has ordered me to see that it's done, with Bilgee in charge of the move itself. He'll decide when to move, how to set up the headquarters, and assign sectors. There were objections: too far, too many wolves, too many mosquitoes, no facilities; if something goes wrong, I'll be responsible. Which is why I've decided to go there with you. I have to take a capital construction unit along to build a medicinal pool, a storage facility for the wool, a temporary headquarters and clinic, and to lay some roads through the mountains."

Uljii had a glazed look, as if his thoughts were elsewhere.

"You'll get the credit for this," Bao said. "For your vision. There isn't enough beef or pork for the needs of the country, so the government has increased our quota. All the brigades are complaining they're short of grazing land, and no one will be able to fill the new quotas without opening up new land."

"The lambs are still too young," Uljii said. "They won't be ready to move to the new grazing land for a while. What are your plans for the next few days?"

"I'm going to select the best hunters for a wolf team," he said candidly, "and start sharpshooting training. I've already requested an increased supply of ammunition. I won't rest until I've relieved the Olonbulag of the wolf scourge. I recently read a report of pasture losses over the past decade. Over half were attributed to wolves, more than blizzards, drought, or disease combined. Increasing the livestock population requires two conditions: eliminate the wolves and open new grazing land."

"You're making a mistake," Uljii said. "Yes, the wolves are responsible for losses, but if you wipe them out, the absence of those losses will prove catastrophic."

Bao looked up at the sky. "I've heard people say that you and Bilgee and some of the older herdsmen always take the side of the wolves. Go ahead, say what you want to say, you needn't worry . . . "

Uljii cleared his throat. "Worry? I worry about the grassland. I can't be the one to see the land our ancestors passed down to us destroyed. I've been telling people about the wolves for many years, and I'm not going to stop now . . . I took on the responsibility for the grassland more than a decade ago, and I've seen the livestock population more than double. We supply twice as many cows and sheep as other pastures. Our most important responsibility has been to protect the grassland, since it's the foundation of livestock raising. It's a difficult task that requires keeping the population of grazing animals in check, especially the horses. Cows and sheep are ruminants, so they don't graze at night. But horses never stop eating—they have to eat in order to stay fat and healthy—which means they never stop shitting either. It takes twenty acres to feed a sheep for one year, but two hundred for a horse. And their hooves are murder on the grassland. A herd can be in one place for a couple of weeks and leave it in ruins, nothing but sand. It rains a lot in the summer, so the grass grows fast, but for the rest of the year we have to move the livestock every month or so to keep the animals from eating every blade of grass in sight. Cows are also hard on the grassland. The biggest problem with them is that they come home every night, and not when they feel like it individually, but always together. Their weight and their heavy hooves tear up the ground, and if you don't move often, the area around the yurts for a mile or more winds up as nothing but sandy ruts. Add sheep to the mix, and you have to move your base every couple of months or nothing will grow within a mile of the base camp. We live as nomads in order to give the land a chance to breathe. Heavy hooves and overpopulation are its greatest enemies."

Seeing that Bao was paying close attention, Uljii continued, "The key to protecting the grassland is limiting the number of wolves we kill. There are many destructive animals on the grassland, but ground squirrels, rabbits, marmots, and gazelles wreak the greatest damage. If there were no wolves, squirrels and rabbits alone would lay waste to the grassland within a few years. Wolves are their natural enemy; they keep them in check. Protecting the grazing land increases our ability to ward off natural disasters. Take blizzards, for example. We experience them more often than most other areas. When a blizzard hits the grazing lands at other communes, they can lose up to half their herds. Our losses are never that great. Why? Because our land flourishes. Every autumn we cut down enough grass for emergencies, and now that we have grass cutters, we can mow the entire pasture and store up all we need against the possibility of a natural disaster. And because the grass flourishes here, it grows so tall that most snowfalls aren't heavy enough to cover it completely. With a healthy grassland, erosion is avoided and the wells don't dry up, so even during a drought, the animals have water to drink. With good grass, the animals thrive. No diseases have spread through our herds in recent years. Our production is up, so we've been able to buy machinery that helps us dig wells and build pens, which increases our resistance to natural disasters."

Bao nodded and said, "What you say makes sense. Protecting the grazing land is what makes raising livestock possible. I won't forget that. I'll take officials down to the brigades as often as possible and make sure the herdsmen move on when they're supposed to, and I'll see that the horse herders stay with their herds twenty-four hours a day to keep them on the move and not let them stay in one spot too long. I'll inspect every team's grazing land once a month, and if there's overgrazing, I'll deduct work points. I'll reward those teams that take pains to protect the land, labeling them model units. As long as I employ military management methods, I'm confident the Olonbulag will continue to be well managed . . . But I still don't see how you protect the grazing land by relying on wolves. Are they really that effective?"

Seeing that Bao was still listening, Uljii smiled and said, "You'll be surprised to learn that a nest of ground squirrels will eat more grass in a year than a gazelle, and they store up food for the winter. I've dug up their nests and found bales of the stuff down there, and it's all the finest grass and grass seeds. They have four or five litters a year, ten or more young each time, and by the end of the year, one nest has become ten. You can figure how much grass that many squirrels can eat in a year.

Rabbits are the same, with several huge litters every year. And you've seen the marmots, how they dot the mountainsides with their burrows. Figuring roughly, all those creatures eat several times more grass in any given year than all hundred thousand head of livestock in our pasture, which is the size of one of your counties down south. But there are only about a thousand people living here, and if not for the students from Beijing, there wouldn't even be that many. With those numbers, what do you think the chances are that we could eradicate all those pests?"

"I haven't seen many rabbits over the past year or so," Bao said. "I admit there are a lot of ground squirrels near headquarters, but I haven't seen them anywhere else. I've seen plenty of marmots and their burrows. But it's the number of gazelles I've really noticed. I've seen herds of ten thousand more than once. I've even shot a bunch of them. They're a true scourge, the way they graze like locusts."

"Our pastureland is good," Uljii said, "with tall, dense grass that hides the squirrels and rabbits. You have to look carefully to see them, but they're there. You'll see them in the fall. All those piles of cut grass are laid out to dry by the squirrels before they take it into their nests. The gazelles are nowhere near as destructive, because while they eat the grass, they don't burrow into the ground. Ground squirrels, rabbits, and marmots not only eat and dig burrows but also reproduce wildly. Without the wolves, those pests would eat all the grass on the Olonbulag and have holes everywhere in a few years. The desert wouldn't be far behind. If you insist on annihilating the wolves, you won't have a job three or four years from now."

With a snicker, Bao said, "I know that cats and raptors and snakes catch rodents, but I never heard that wolves catch them too. Even a dog won't waste the energy to go after a rodent. Are you saying that wolves do? They eat sheep, and they eat horses. There isn't enough meat on those rodents to stick between their teeth. Sorry, I don't believe that rodents are on their menu."

Uljii sighed. "That's a mistake all you farming people make. I grew up on the Olonbulag, so I understand wolves. They prefer to eat big animals, like cows, sheep, horses, and gazelles. But the first three are tended by humans, which makes them difficult prey, and the wolves have to eat to survive. Gazelles are so fleet-footed, they're hard to catch. Ground squirrels, on the other hand, are there for the taking. In olden days, poor people survived the lean years by catching and eating the squirrels. I was a slave as a boy, and anytime I didn't get enough to eat, I caught squirrels. They're big, plump rodents, from a few ounces to a full pound, and three or four of them will tide you over. For the ones you don't eat right away, you skin them and dry the meat, a tasty meal for the next time. If you don't believe me, I'll catch a few one day and roast them for you. You'll find the meat quite tender. Even Genghis Khan ate squirrel."

Zhang Jiyuan, caught up in the discussion, felt a need to add his views. "I've been tending horses for two years now, and I've watched wolves catch squirrels, sending dirt flying. They're better at it than dogs. Ground squirrels are the favorites of female wolves and their cubs. Before the young ones are weaned, their mothers teach them how to hunt, beginning with ground squirrels. When a female's litter is still young, they seldom join the other wolves in a hunt. Their cubs learn to fear humans when they've grown to about a foot in length and have just begun to run. When a hunter spots a female wolf and her cubs out in the open, if he shoots the adult, the cubs are all his. All he has to do is scoop them up as if they were baby lambs, which is why the female will take her young as far from human habitation as possible, where they're safe. But since there's no livestock in those places, what do they eat? Well, except for the occasional meat and bones the older wolves bring them after a successful hunt, they survive on ground squirrels and marmots."

"And there's more." Uljii seemed somewhat stressed. "If there were no wolves, we and our livestock would be in big trouble during a natural disaster. When the grassland is hit by a hundred-year or two-hundred-year blizzard, the toll on our livestock is enormous. Then, when the snow melts, the ground is cluttered with the carcasses of dead cows and sheep that quickly begin to stink. If they aren't buried, an epidemic could kill off half the people and animals of an entire banner. But wolves will dispose of the dead animals in no time. Plagues aren't a problem as long as there are wolves around. We've never had one on the Olonbulag. In the old days, when wars were fought out here, the battlefields would be strewn with thousands of dead men and animals. Who disposed of them? Wolves. Old-timers tell us that if there'd been no wolves, a plague would have wiped out the human population of the grassland long ago. We can thank the wolves for keeping the Olonbulag a place with fresh water and lush grass. Without them, we wouldn't have such flourishing herds. The communes down south have killed off their wolves, and their grazing land is dying. They'll never raise livestock there again."

Bao had been listening without saying a word as the

three horses rode up a slope, with its fragrant green grass and the sweet fermenting smell of rotting grass from the year before. Meadowlarks singing in the air above them plunged down into the tall grass, while those on the ground soared up into the blue sky, where they hovered above the party and sang their own tunes.

Uljii sucked in his breath. "Isn't that a gorgeous sight?" he exclaimed. "As unspoiled as it was thousands of years ago. This is the most beautiful grassland in China. Men and wolves have fought battles to seal this place off and keep it unspoiled over the centuries, and we simply must not let it come to grief in our hands."

"You need to hold a study session for us students," Zhang Jiyuan said, "to teach us what we need to know about the grassland and its wolves."

Uljii's face darkened. "I'm a deposed official. I don't have the authority to hold anything. You need to learn from older herdsmen. They know more than I do anyway."

After they crossed another ridge, Bao finally spoke up: "Uljii, no one will deny the depth of your feelings for the grassland or what you've accomplished. It's your politics that get you into trouble. You talk about things that happened in the past, but this is a new age, an atomic age for China. Using primitive forms of thinking to deal with current needs is a big problem. I've thought long and hard since coming to the pasture. In terms of size, it is, as you say, the equivalent of a whole county down south, and a population of a thousand people is less than one of our villages. That's incredibly wasteful. In order to create the greatest wealth for the party and the nation, we must bring an end to this backward, primitive nomadic way of life. I did a little exploring a few days ago. There's quite a bit of land with black soil south of us, each section thousands of acres in size. I dug with a hoe and found that the topsoil was two feet thick. It seems a shame to devote good soil like that to graze sheep. At a league headquarters meeting, I asked an agricultural expert from an autonomous area about the land, and he said it was ideal for wheat. If we don't attempt a large-scale reclamation project, only a few hundred acres, maybe a thousand or two, there's no danger of desertification."

Uljii said nothing, so Bao continued. "I looked into the water situation too. It's easy to get to. We dig a trough and bring the river over. We have plenty of cow and sheep manure, which makes ideal fertilizer. If we plant wheat there, I'll bet that in the first year we'll produce more per acre than they do in the Yellow River region. If we keep at it, in a few years agricultural production could outstrip livestock. When that happens, not only will we supply all our own food and animal feed, but we'll assist the rest of the nation, where grain is in short supply. In my hometown the people don't have enough to eat; on average they come up short by three months' supply every year. Now, when I see all that good black soil left fallow and turned over to sheep to graze on for more than a month, it pains me. I'm going to plant an experimental plot, and if it's successful, we'll go all out. I hear that some communes down south are running out of grazing land and may have to stop raising livestock. They've decided to set aside land for crops, and I think that's where Inner Mongolia's future lies."

Uljii's face fell. "I knew this day was coming," he said with a sigh. "You people never give a thought to livestock capacity. You keep forcing us to increase the numbers, and now you've gone on a wolf-killing spree, just waiting for the day when the grass is gone and you can cover the land with your crops. Your homeland was pasture a few decades back and was converted to cropland only a decade or so ago, but there isn't enough grain to go around. This is already the frontier, so after you turn this fine pastureland into what you've got down there, where will you go next? The Xinjiang Desert takes up more space than any province in the country, and no people live in the Gobi. Would you call that a waste of land?"

"You needn't worry," Bao said. "I've learned the lesson of my hometown, and will make a distinction between land that's arable and land that's not. Going only one way—crops or pasture—is wrong. Half and half is the way to do it. I'll do everything I can to safeguard the good pastureland and keep raising fine livestock. Without it we won't have fertilizer. Where's the grain production going to come from without manure?"

"When the farmers come out here," Uljii said angrily, "and see this land, you won't be able to control them. And even if your generation somehow manages, how will you control the next generation?"

"Each generation controls its own affairs," Bao said. "The next generation is not my concern."

"Do you still plan to hunt down the wolves?"

"Not supporting the hunt is what got you into trouble, and I won't take that path. If the wolves wound up massacring another herd of horses, I'd be in the same fix as you."

They saw chimney smoke above the base camp off in the distance. "By giving you an old horse, those upstarts at pasture headquarters have really slowed us down." He turned to Zhang Jiyuan. "When you get back to the herd, pick out a good horse for Uljii. Tell Batu I said so."

"When we get to the brigade," Zhang replied, "no one will let Uljii ride a nag."

"I have things to do," Bao said, "so I'll go on ahead. I'll wait for you at Bilgee's. Take your time." He loosened the reins and rode off at a gallop.

Zhang rode up alongside the plodding old horse and said to Uljii, "Old Bao treats you well enough. At headquarters they say he tried to get them to keep you in the leadership group. But he's ex-military and has his share of warlord habits, so don't be angry."

"Old Bao charges ahead on everything he does," Uljii said vigorously and resolutely, "and he's usually up there on the front line. There'd be no one better in a farming area. But out here he's a danger to the grassland."

"If this had happened when I first arrived," Zhang said, "I'd probably have taken his side. Lots of people are starving in farming villages down south, while there's all this land lying fallow. A lot of the students support his view. But I don't see things the same way anymore. Yours is the visionary view. Numbers of grazing animals mean nothing to farming people, nor do those people understand the effects of human population. As for big lives and little lives, they don't have a clue. Chen Zhen said there's a simple grassland logic that's been in place for a thousand years or more, one that's in accord with objective laws of development. He thinks that the Manchu rulers had a brilliant policy during the first two hundred years of the Qing dynasty; they prohibited a large-scale migration of people from farming areas, believing that would have led to grievous consequences."

Uljii was intrigued by the term *grassland logic.* He repeated it a couple of times to commit it to memory. "But during the later years of the Qing," he said, "they couldn't stop the flow from China, so the grassland shrank northward, and then westward, until it was right up against the Gobi. If desertification occurs north of the Great Wall, what will happen to Beijing? That's something even the Mongols dread, because Beijing was once their capital—they called it Dadu—and it's now an international city."

Zhang saw his horses drinking at a well. Time to pick out a good horse for Uljii.

18

Chen Zhen stirred the milk and meat porridge. The rising steam smelled so good that all the dogs were lined up at his door whining hungrily. The porridge was for the wolf cub.

Gasmai had taught him the secret of feeding puppies. "They need to be fed milk and meat porridge as soon as they're weaned," she said. "It's a sure-fire way to get them to grow big and strong. What they eat the first three or four months after being weaned determines their growth patterns, especially their bones. If you miss that window, you won't have big, strong dogs, no matter what you feed them after that. Well-fed pups can grow to be twice the size of poorly fed pups, which will never be decent wolf fighters."

Once, when their team was hauling rocks to build a wall, Gasmai pointed to someone else's squat, skinny dog with ratty fur and whispered to Chen, "That dog is from the same litter as Bar. Quite a difference, wouldn't you say?" Chen found it hard to believe that two dogs from the same litter could be so different. "On the grassland, it's not enough to have dogs of good breeding; you also have to feed them aggressively." Chen took that to heart, attending carefully to what went into his cub's stomach. He followed Gasmai's puppy recipe to the letter.

Gasmai had added, "After puppies are weaned, a contest develops between women and wolf mothers. The wolves hunt ground squirrels, marmots, and lambs to feed their young and teach them how to hunt. They're good mothers. No stoves, no fires, no pots, so they can't make meaty porridge for their young. But their mouths are better than the pots we use. They turn the squirrels and marmots into a soft, warm meaty mix with their teeth, their saliva, and their stomachs, just what their cubs need and like. They grow like weeds.

"Women on the grassland earn work points by taking the night watch with their dogs, which is why they must be even more conscientious, more hardworking than the wolf mothers. Lazy women raise mongrel dogs; good women raise big dogs. Look at a dog and you'll know what sort of woman lives in that yurt."

Chen had changed many of his habits once he'd taken on the responsibility of raising a wolf cub, and Zhang Jiyuan teased him by wondering when he'd become so industrious, so motherly. In fact, Chen felt that he took more care than either a wolf mother or Gasmai. By increasing the number of daily chores he did, he was given the go-ahead by Gao Jianzhong to take some cow's milk, which he supplemented with a meat pulp. Milk was clearly inadequate for developing strong bones; additional calcium was essential, which he supplied by including shavings of soft bone in the meat. He'd even gone to the medical clinic at the pasture headquarters to get some calcium tablets, which he ground up and mixed into the meat, something that neither the wolf mother nor Gasmai could have thought of. Even the meaty porridge seemed insufficient to Chen, who added butter and salt, making it so fragrant that he himself was tempted to try a bowlful. But since there were also the three dogs, he swallowed hard and decided against it.

The cub was filling out, its belly tight as a drum after each meal, like the fat, squinty-eyed laughing Buddha. He was growing faster than an autumn mushroom, and was already half a snout longer than the puppies he was with.

The first time Chen fed the mixture to the cub, he was concerned the animal might turn his nose up at the millet in the mixture, since in the wild wolves fed only on meat. He was pleasantly surprised when the cub buried his nose in the bowl and gobbled up the fragrant, warm contents, snorting and rumbling until he licked the bowl clean and, finally, raised his head. Chen later discovered that the cub would only eat millet when there was plenty of meat and milk mixed in with it.

The porridge had cooled off, so Chen placed the bowl on a rack just inside the door, opened it a crack, slipped out, and quickly shut it behind him. All the dogs in the area, except for Erlang, rushed up. Yellow and Yir stood and laid their paws on Chen's chest; Yellow licked his chin to show his affection. The three puppies nibbled at his pant cuffs. But the cub stormed the door, buried his nose in the crack, and greedily sniffed the porridge inside the yurt. He clawed at the door frame, trying to get in.

The last thing Chen wanted was to put any of the animals ahead of the others. The cub was his favorite, but he was fond of the puppies as well, his puppies, and he couldn't stand the thought of any of them being neglected. He wouldn't feed the wolf until he'd pacified the dogs.

Chen wrapped his arms around Yellow and then Yir, and twirled them in the air, rewarding them in the most intimate expression he knew. They responded happily by slobbering all over his chin. Then he picked up each of the puppies and lifted them high in the air. Once they were back down on the ground, he rubbed their heads, patted them on the back, and stroked their fur. All these were things he'd begun doing after taking in the wolf cub; prior to that, only when he felt like it would he show that sort of attention. Now, however, if he didn't treat all the dogs the same, and they one day felt a sense of envy toward the cub, they might well turn on him and kill him. Chen had been surprised to learn that raising a wolf in a nomadic environment was like sitting on a powder keg, and that each day presented a challenge. At the time, everyone was busy with the birthing of new lambs, so there was little socializing among the herdsmen. Few knew that Chen had a wolf cub, and even those who had heard rumors did not come by to see for themselves. What would happen when the word got out? Riding a tiger was bad enough; getting off was worse. That went double for a wolf.

As the temperature rose, frozen winter meat was cut into strips and dried in the sun and wind. The bones, with shreds of meat that were covered with mildew and emitted a strange smell, were fine for late-spring dog food. Chen had a following of dogs as he headed toward the meat-basket wagon, Erlang out in front. He wrapped his arms around the dog's massive head. Having grown more familiar with human behavior, Erlang knew this meant he was going to be fed, and he nudged Chen under the arm as a sign of thanks. Chen took a basket of bones down from the wagon, divided the contents in accord with the dogs' appetites, and then ran back to his yurt.

The cub was still trying to open the door with his

fangs. By this time, a month after his arrival, he was over a foot in length, and his legs were nice and straight; more and more, he was beginning to look like a wolf, especially now that the blue membranes had disappeared to reveal gray-yellow eyes, with pinpoint black dots in the center. His snout was longer and his ears were no longer catlike, having developed into triangles that stood erect above his head. He spent much of each day playing with the pups; but when no one was around and during the night, he was put back into his enclosure to keep him from running off. Even Yellow and Yir tolerated the presence of the wild addition, though they kept their distance. Whenever he went up to Yir and tried to find a teat, she flicked him away with her nose. Only Erlang was friendly toward him; nothing the little wolf did bothered him. He could crawl on the dog's belly, he could jump all over his back and head, he could bite his coat and nibble at his ears, and he could relieve himself wherever he wanted. Erlang often licked the little cub, sometimes rolling him over on his back with his snout to clean his belly with his tongue, as if he were his own offspring. The little wolf had come to accept his surroundings and was happy to frolic with his puppy friends, even though his nose told him that this wasn't his real home.

Chen picked up the cub, but no further intimacy was advisable when the little wolf was eager to eat. Chen opened the door and stepped inside, where he set the cub down in front of the stove in the light from the opening above, which he'd gotten used to. He turned to stare at the aluminum pan on the rack. Chen tested the porridge with his finger to see if it was too hot. It had cooled to room temperature, just the way the cub liked it. Wolves cannot handle food that's too hot. The one time he'd been given hot food, he'd reacted by curling his tail between his legs, shuddering, and running outside to lap up the snow. It was only after Chen replaced the old pan with a new aluminum one that the cub would draw near to eat again.

Chen worked on the wolf's conditioned reflexes by calling out, "Little Wolf, Little Wolf, food, food," before each meal. The cub immediately leaped into the air, his reaction to the word *food* already stronger than the dogs' reactions to commands. Chen quickly laid the pan down on the ground, squatted a couple of paces away, and pressed down on the edge of the pan with his spatula to keep the wolf from stepping on it and turning it over as he buried his snout in the food and gobbled it up.

Humans display that kind of gusto only during famines. This cub, though every meal was guaranteed, ate like a starving animal, as if the sky would fall if he didn't bolt down every bite. Wolves eat without a thought for anyone else, and this one, true to form, did not display a hint of gratitude toward Chen Zhen, who patiently tended to his every need. To the contrary, at that moment he saw Chen as a mortal enemy intent on taking his food from him.

In the space of a month, Chen had drawn closer to the young wolf in a number of ways: He could rub him, hold him, kiss him, pinch him, carry him, and scratch him. He could carry him on his head, lay him across his shoulders, rub noses with him, and even stick his fingers in his mouth. But when the cub was eating, Chen didn't dare touch him and could only crouch a safe distance away and watch. If he so much as moved, the cub would snarl, his black wolf hairs would stand up, and he would tense his hind legs, ready to pounce if necessary, quite prepared to kill. In order to change this behavior, Chen once reached over with a broom to stroke the cub lightly; before he knew it, the wolf had pounced on the broom, sunk his teeth into the sorghum stalks, and yanked it out of Chen's hands. Chen backed up, shocked and more than a little frightened, while the cub, as if attacking a lamb, shook his head violently, tearing several stalks from the handle. Refusing to be deterred by a single incident, Chen tried the same thing several times more, with no change in the result; it was as if the cub saw the broom as its enemy, now a ruined enemy. Gao Jianzhong, who had recently bought the broom, was so angry that he knocked the cub over with the handle. In the end, Chen had to abandon his desire to touch the cub while he was eating.

Chen had prepared twice the usual amount of porridge this time, hoping there'd be some left over so that he could add a bit of milk and a little more meat, and feed it to the puppies. But when he saw how the wolf attacked the food, he knew that wasn't going to happen.

Chen was given an opportunity to see how hard it was for wolves to survive on the grassland. In spite of their fertility, probably only one in ten cubs lived to adulthood. Bilgee said that Tengger sometimes punished the wolves mercilessly. A sudden storm that drops several feet of snow in a short period can kill off vast numbers of wolves, from cold or from hunger. A wildfire that blots out the sky can also wipe out vast numbers, burned or suffocated. Packs of starving wolves fleeing famine or natural disasters can slaughter half the local wolves. Few can survive the spring thefts of newborn cubs from their dens, autumn trapping, early-winter encirclement hunts, and the deep-winter hunts. The old man said that the grassland wolves are the descendants of hungry wolves. The original animals, which lived lives devoid of want, were subdued by hungry wolves fleeing from famine. The grassland had always been a battlefield, and those that survived were the strongest and wisest, the ones best suited to eating and fighting, animals who could eat their fill yet never forget what it was like to be hungry.

Chen discovered over time that grassland wolves held many sacred articles of faith where survival was concerned, of which the fight for food and independence were among the most fundamental. When he was feeding the cub, he never felt as if he were giving it life, as he did with the dogs. The wolf showed no gratitude, for he did not consider himself as being raised by a human and was incapable of reacting slavishly just because he saw his master coming with his food. The word *raise* was absent in the relationship between Chen and the cub. The wolf was his prisoner for the time being, not his ward. A unique spirit of obstinacy underlay his territorial nature; this knowledge sent chills up Chen's spine, for he was no longer confident that he could successfully keep the cub and see him to adulthood.

In the end, Chen abandoned the desire to pet the wolf while he was eating and respected his noble natural instincts. He continued to crouch down a few paces away and observe the cub quietly, grateful for the lessons in wolf behavior.

The cub gradually slowed down, but even though his belly seemed about to burst, he kept his head buried in the bowl and continued eating. Chen saw that when the cub's basic appetite was satisfied, he began picking and choosing, starting with the strips of meat and ending with the last little bits, his tongue like tweezers, picking up every little piece until all that remained of a once meaty porridge was a bowl of light yellow millet—no more meat, no more bone, no more fat, just grain. And still he didn't look up. He was concentrating on the milk at the bottom, since that too was a favorite food. When he finally looked up, only dry kernels of tasteless, odorless millet remained. Chen laughed out loud. When it came to food, the little wolf was very shrewd.

Chen had no choice but to add a little meat, the remaining milk, and a bit of warm water, stir it into a soupy mix, and take it outside, where he poured it into the dog bowls. The dogs rushed up hungrily but immediately whined their disappointment, and Chen was made pointedly aware of the obligations of livestock raising, of which caring for dogs is an essential component.

The cub, so stuffed he could barely move, sprawled on the floor and gazed outside, where the dogs were finishing off his leftovers. Chen went up and called out to him: "Little Wolf, Little Wolf." He just rolled over, legs held in close, belly sticking up, and head on the ground, where he looked at Chen, a mischievous glint in his eyes. Chen picked him up and lifted him high in the air, five or six times, frightening and delighting him simultaneously. His mouth was open, but his hind legs pressed against his tail and trembled. By now the cub seemed to be getting used to this game, recognizing it as a friendly gesture. Chen laid the cub on top of his head, then on his shoulder, where the still-frightened cub dug his claws into Chen's collar.

After bringing the cub back down, Chen sat cross-legged and laid him belly-up to give him a good rubbing, the way both dog and wolf mothers do to their young to help them digest their food. Chen enjoyed gently rubbing the little wolf's belly and listening to him moan contentedly, burp occasionally, and pass a bit of gas. The wild animal at his food had become a well-behaved pet, grabbing Chen's finger with his paws and licking it, even biting it playfully. The look in his eyes was gentle and at times—when the rubbing was most pleasurable—tinged with laughter, almost as if Chen were a surrogate mother.

The wolf was a handful, but an enjoyable one. Chen imagined a scene from antiquity or from some current distant spot in which a loving wolf mother licked the belly of her "wolf boy" after his feeding, and the cub grabbed his toes and giggled. A wolf pack surrounded the scene peacefully, even bringing meat to feed the little one. Throughout time, how many wolf mothers had raised infant children and how many humans had raised wolf pups? Chen found himself living out some of the marvelous tales of wolves he had heard over the years, and he was able to both sense and actually touch the warm, gentle side of wolf nature. Deeply moved, he wished he could repay the respect the world of humans felt for these wolf boys, be they Hun, Gaoju, Turk, Roman, Indian, or Soviet. He bent down to touch the cub's wet nose with his own; like a dog, the wolf licked his chin, which pleased and excited him. It was the first time the cub had shown any trust in him. They were growing closer emotionally, and he wanted to savor everything this pure, innocent friendship offered. He fantasized that his own life had begun to stretch back into antiquity, and he felt unimaginably old.

The one thing that nagged at him was that the wolf had not been orphaned or abandoned; raising an animal under those conditions constituted a natural, primitive love. He, on the other hand, had stolen his cub from its den, an entirely selfish act intended to satisfy a desire for novelty and for study. His story was not a patch on the stirring tales of humans and wolves that had been passed down through the ages. The thought that the mother would one day come to seek revenge was never far from his mind. His impulses had not been noble; rather, he had acted in the name of scientific and cultural progress. He hoped Tengger would understand this callousness and new savagery—for what he wanted was to enter the wolf totem realm of the grassland people.

After eating his portion of the food, Erlang walked slowly over to Chen. Every time he saw Chen stroking the wolf cub, he came up to watch inquisitively, and sometimes he licked the cub's bulging belly. Chen rubbed Erlang's head; the dog smiled at his master. Ever since Chen had taken in the wolf cub, the distance between him and Erlang had shrunk dramatically. Was there a bit of the wolf in him too, something Erlang had sniffed out? He suddenly saw how intriguing his situation had become—for here were a man with wolfish characteristics, a dog with a wolfish nature, and a genuine wolf all living together on the grassland. His life had suddenly become more exceptional than the stories of wolf boys.

Since becoming bewitched by the grassland wolves, Chen felt that his already listless, weary blood had weakened further and that what seemed to be alien wolf blood had begun to flow in his veins. His view of life had altered—he treasured it even as it became more vigorous and fulfilling. He now understood why Jack London's story "Love of Life" was tied up with a dying wolf, why when Lenin was critically ill, he had asked his wife to reread it aloud to him. The Russian dictator had died peacefully, listening to the struggle between man and wolf. His soul may well have been taken to see that of

Marx by a wolf totem that belonged to a different race. If even the truly great, with their astonishing vitality, come to the grassland—the land of the wild wolf, and its life force—then why not an ordinary man like him?

The cub began to squirm in Chen Zhen's lap, a sign that he had to relieve himself. He also spotted Erlang and wanted to play with the big dog. So Chen let go, and the wolf bounded up and onto the ground, where it created a puddle of urine, then flew at Erlang, who happily sprawled on the ground to let all the pups climb him like a mountain. The wolf was first onto Erlang's back, and then proceeded to knock away all the puppies that tried to follow, howling to any that would challenge him as king of the mountain. Two male puppies fought back, biting the wolf cub's ears and tail, until all three tumbled off their mountain, with the puppies landing on top; they began biting the cub all over. He fought back angrily, legs flailing, sending dust flying. A moment later, Chen heard one of the puppies yelp in pain and saw blood on its paw. Obviously, the wolf was no longer just playing.

Chen picked the cub up by the scruff of his neck and carried him to the puppy, where he held the wolf's nose up against the injured paw and rubbed it in the blood. It had no effect on the cub, who bared his fangs and showed his claws, sending the puppies scurrying in fright over to Yir, who first licked the bloody paw, then bounded over to the wolf and roared at it, ready to bite. Chen quickly scooped him up in his arms and turned his back to Yir, his heart pounding, dreading the possibility that someday one of the big dogs would kill his wolf cub. Raising a little tyrant like this with no cage or pen worried him. But first he needed to calm Yir down, which he did by rubbing her head. When he set the wolf cub on the ground again, Yir ignored him and led her puppies off to play by themselves. The wolf clambered again onto the back of Erlang, a fierce animal that was both tolerant and fond of the cub.

After he'd fed the animals, Chen cleaned out the wagon to move to the new pastureland. When he looked up, he saw Bilgee coming toward him on a wagon filled with wood. He jumped down, scooped up the wolf cub, and put him back in his burrow, quickly covering it with the wooden plank and setting the rock down on top. His heart was racing.

Yellow and Yir, tails wagging, rushed out with the puppies to greet the old man. Chen followed to unload Bilgee's cart, take care of the ox, and lift down the old man's heavy carpenter's kit. Prior to every move to new grazing land, Bilgee came over to make repairs to the students' wagon. "Papa," Chen said nervously, "I can manage; you don't need to come do that for us."

"Manage isn't good enough," the old man said. "This is going to be a long trip, and there are no roads. It'll take two or three days to get there. One wagon breaking down along the way will slow the entire brigade."

"Well, at least you can go inside for some tea while I unload our wagon."

"Your tea is too black for me." Then, without warning, he walked over to the burrow. "Let me see your wolf cub," he said darkly.

Flustered by this unexpected development, Chen tried to stop the old man. "There's nothing to see," he said. "Why not have some tea?"

"It's been almost a month," Bilgee said, his rheumy eyes glaring, "and still you won't let me see it!"

"Papa," Chen said somewhat desperately, "I'm raising it to breed a litter of wolfhounds . . . "

The old man's face showed how angry he was. "Nonsense!" he roared. "This is absolute nonsense. You might be able to get a wolfhound with wolves from somewhere else, but not Mongolian wolves. What makes you think a Mongolian wolf would mate with a dog? He'd just as soon kill and eat her." As his anger grew, his goatee quivered. "I don't know what's gotten into you people lately. I've lived on the grassland for over sixty years, and this is the first time I've even heard someone suggest what you're doing. Do you really think you can raise one of these? Alongside a litter of dogs? How can you speak of wolves and dogs in the same breath? Dogs eat people's shit; wolves eat people. By eating shit, dogs are nothing but slaves to humans. But wolves eat human corpses to send the souls into the bosom of Tengger. Wolves and dogs, as different as heaven and earth, and you plan to raise them together? And if that wasn't enough, you're actually hoping to mate this one with dogs! If we Mongols wanted to mate your Dragon King to a sow, what would you Chinese think about that? You'd call it blasphemy! Well, what you're doing is an affront to our ancestors. And to Tengger! You'll pay one day, and so will this old man..."

Chen had never seen Bilgee so furious. The powder keg had finally exploded, blowing Chen's heart to pieces. The old man was like an angry wolf, and Chen was afraid he might kick the rock and hurt himself or, worse, pick it up and crush the wolf cub with it. And he was getting angrier by the minute. "When I first heard that you were raising a wolf cub, I wrote that off as an example of how you Chinese students really don't understand grassland customs, that you are ignorant of our taboos, and were just trying something new that you'd give up after a few days. But then I heard that

Dorji was raising one too and that you planned to breed wolfhounds. You can't do that! I want you to dispose of that cub right now, in front of me . . ."

Chen knew he'd really stepped over the line this time. No one had raised a wolf on the grassland for all these thousands of years. You can kill a warrior; you cannot humiliate him. You can kill a wolf; you cannot raise it. Now here was a young Chinese deep in the heart of the grassland, on Mongol ancestral land, where the inhabitants worshipped Tengger, a sacred place where they paid homage to their wild forebear, their master of wisdom, their war god, and the protector of the grassland, the wolf totem, and he was raising a wolf as he would a dog, a true outrage. If this had occurred in ancient times, he would be labeled a sinner, a pagan, and would surely have been drawn and quartered, his corpse thrown to the dogs. Even now, what he was doing ran counter to the national policy on ethnic minorities, an act that unavoidably incensed the grassland inhabitants. But what disturbed Chen the most was what this was doing to Bilgee, the elderly Mongol who had brought him into the mysterious realm of the wolf totem, and whose careful instructions had made it possible to steal the cub in the first place. He could hold out no longer, could not keep defending his actions. "Papa," he said, his voice quaking.

The old man waved him off. "Don't call me that!"

"I was wrong, Papa," Chen said, pleading with the old man, "and you're right, I don't understand grassland customs, and I've offended you . . . Tell me, how do you want me to dispose of this poor little wolf?" Tears virtually gushed from Chen's eyes, spilling onto the grassy ground where the cub had been playing happily only a short while before.

The old man, caught by surprise, could only stare at Chen, suddenly not sure what to do now. He knew that no matter what Chen said, the young man had been bewitched by grassland wolves. He was, after all, a sort of adopted half-Mongol son, and his fascination with the wolves far exceeded that of most Mongol youths. But now he'd done something the old man found intolerable. He'd never encountered anything like this before, and didn't know what to do about it.

Bilgee looked up at Tengger and sighed. "I know you Chinese aren't religious and that the soul means nothing to you. You've really taken to our wolves over the past couple of years, I know that, but you don't know what's in my heart. I'm old and getting frailer by the day. The grassland is a hard, cold place to live in, and we Mongols spend our whole lives here doing battle, like savages. Sickness takes its toll, and we don't live long lives. I'll be going to Tengger in a few years. How can you think of keeping a wolf that might one day take my soul up to Tengger and raise it with a bunch of dogs? That would mean that I'd committed a sin and Tengger might not accept my soul, but send it down to the dark, suffocating hell under the Gobi. If everyone out here treated wolves like slaves, the way you do, the souls of Mongols would be lost."

"Papa," Chen said quietly, defending himself, "I'm not treating this wolf cub like a slave. If anything, I've become its slave. I wait on it like I would a Mongol king or a prince. I milk a cow to feed it, I mix porridge for it, I cook meat. I worry about it being cold, or sick, or bitten by dogs or hit by people, or carried away by an eagle or by its mother. I haven't been sleeping well lately, and Gao Jianzhong has begun calling me the wolf's slave. You know I revere wolves more than any of the other

Chinese. Tengger sees everything, Tengger is fair, Tengger won't blame you for anything."

This stopped the old man. He knew that Chen was being earnest with him. If Chen waited on the little wolf the way he would a deity or a king, then was that offending the gods or revering them? Bilgee wasn't sure. Even though Chen Zhen's methods ran counter to traditional Mongol customs, he had a good heart, and there was nothing the grassland Mongols valued more. The old man's gaze softened; he was no longer an angry wolf. Chen hoped that with his wisdom and farsightedness, the old man would be willing to break precedent for a young Chinese man who truly valued the wolf totem and would spare the life of the month-old wolf cub.

Chen saw a glimmer of hope. He dried his eyes and took a deep breath. Forcing himself not to panic and to stay calm, he said, "Papa, the only reason I want to raise this wolf is to understand what they're really like and how they behave. I want to figure out why they're so formidable, so smart, and why the people revere them. You can't imagine how much the Chinese hate wolves. We call the most malicious people wolves; we call sex fiends wolves; we say the greediest people have the appetite of a wolf; the American imperialists are referred to as ambitious wolves; and anytime an adult wants to frighten a child, he cries out 'Wolf!' "

Chen could see that Bilgee's attitude had softened, so he mustered up the courage to soldier on: "In the eyes of Chinese, wolves are the worst, the most vicious, the cruelest things alive, but you Mongols revere them as if they were gods. You learn from them in life and feed them in death. But still, watching and studying wolves from a distance doesn't tell me what I need to know. I figured the best way to do that was to raise a cub on my own, to observe it close up, to be with it every day. I've only been at it a little more than a month so far, and already I've seen incredible things I never saw before. These animals are truly worthy of reverence. But most of the students out here still haven't changed their opinion. If they don't understand wolves, just think of all the millions of Chinese who've never been out here. More and more of them will be coming, and if they really do manage to wipe out the wolves, what will happen to the grassland? It'll be disastrous for the Mongols, but in the long run even worse for the Chinese. I tell you, I'm worried. I couldn't stand to see the destruction of this beautiful grassland."

The old man sat on the rock over the cub's burrow and took out his pipe. Chen hurriedly lit it for him. "It's my fault," Bilgee said after taking a puff. "I've been a bad influence on you... But now what? I know you weren't thinking of me when you decided to raise that wolf, but you have to think of Uljii and of the brigade. He lost his official position, and demerits were recorded against four horse herders. You know why, don't you? They say it was because he came down on the side of the wolves, that he held off organizing a wolf hunt for too long. They also said that I'm an old wolf, the head wolf in the brigade, and that our Second Brigade is a wolf's den. And now, at a critical moment like this, the brigade has a student who's raising a wolf cub. Why aren't students in other brigades doing that? Doesn't that prove that you've been badly taught by someone in the Second Brigade. Wouldn't you say you've handed them the 'weapon' they need?"

The look of melancholy in the old man's eyes came to Chen in waves; the dejection in his voice increased.

"The mother of your cub will come one day," he said.

"That's for sure. And she won't come alone. Olonbulag wolf mothers protect their young like no others. They have an amazing sense of smell, and I predict that this one will find her cub one day. When she does, she'll take her revenge on this camp. There's nothing Olonbulag wolves won't do, however evil, and this brigade doesn't need another incident. If something terrible happens, Uljii and the other brigade officials will be down for good. If a wolf pack came after your sheep and killed great numbers of them, the cost of raising this wolf cub would be a huge loss of communal property, and there'd be no excuse. You could count on jail time..."

A chill gripped Chen's heart, which had barely begun to warm up. Raising a wolf in minority territory violated ethnic policy; doing it around a flock of sheep was just inviting the wolves to come, and that would be an indication that he had intentionally sabotaged production. If that somehow was tied to his father's problem as a "capitalist roader," which would definitely be in accordance with policy, that would implicate lots of other people. Chen's hands began to shake; it was looking more and more as if he'd be sending the wolf cub to Tengger that day.

The old man softened his tone even more: "Bao Shungui is in charge now. He's a Mongol who forgot his roots a long time ago. He hates wolves more than you Chinese do, and he won't keep his job if he doesn't hunt them down. Do you think he'll let you raise this cub?"

Chen felt he had little hope, but he had to try: "Can you talk to him, tell him I'm raising it to get a better handle on how to deal with wolves? A scientific experiment."

"You talk to him. He's staying with me tonight, so come over tomorrow." The old man stood up, turned for a last look at the rock, and said, "Aren't you afraid that when the wolf grows to adulthood it'll attack your sheep? Or you? Or somebody else? Wolf bites are toxic; a man can die from one. I'm not going to look at it today after all; that'd just upset me. Come on, let's work on the wagon."

The old man didn't say a word while he was repairing the wagon. Chen Zhen still hadn't prepared himself emotionally for the possibility of having to kill the wolf cub, but he knew he mustn't make things any more difficult for Bilgee and Uljii.

Chen and the old man finished repairs on two wagons and were starting on the third when the dogs began barking. Bao Shungui and Uljii rode up, Bao leading the way. Chen quieted the dogs. "Your wife said I'd find you here," Bao said, "and this gives me an opportunity to see Chen's wolf cub. The pasture revolutionary committee has decided to let Uljii stay with you. At first they wanted to send him to perform manual labor with the Capital Construction Brigade."

Chen's heart was racing. Word traveled across the grassland faster than a horse.

"Yes," the old man said. "You did well for him on that."

"The league leadership was excited to learn that you were opening up new grazing land. They view it as extremely important, and want it to be as successful as previous years. With that much added grazing land we can double the number of livestock, and that's good news. You two took the lead on this, so I made a point of letting Uljii stay with you. That will make it easier for you to discuss things."

"Uljii's the one who took the lead. His heart is never away from the grassland."

"That goes without saying," Bao said. "I've already reported that to the leadership, and they hope Comrade Uljii will find a way to make amends for his errors."

Uljii smiled weakly. "Let's forget amends," he said, "and talk specifics. The new grazing land is a long way from here, and moving is going to present lots of problems. The pastureland truck and two tractors with rubber tires should be assigned to the Second Brigade to help out. And we'll need extra hands to clear a road."

"I sent someone to call a meeting of brigade officials tonight. We'll see what happens." Bao turned to Chen. "Those two wolf pelts you sent up, I gave them to the tanner and had them delivered to my old boss. He was impressed that a student from Beijing could bring down such big wolves. He sends his thanks."

"How could you tell him I killed them? The dogs did it. I can't take credit for what they did."

Bao patted him on the shoulder. "If they were your dogs, then you killed them. Authorities always get credit for their subordinates' contributions. That's one of the great traditions in our armed forces. Well now, let's have a look at that cub of yours."

Chen glanced at Bilgee, who held his tongue. "I've decided not to raise it after all," Chen replied quickly. "It's against the customs of the herdsmen, and dangerous to boot. Being responsible for a wolf attack would be too much for me." While he was talking, he removed the rock and slid the plank away.

Down below, the cub was trying to climb up the side, but when the dark human silhouettes loomed above, it huddled in the farthest corner, wrinkling its nose and baring its fangs, even though it was quaking.

Light shone in Bao's eyes. "Hey!" he exclaimed. "He's big! It's only been a month, but he's twice the size of the pelts from the other pups. If I'd known they were going to grow like that, I'd have let you raise the whole litter. When they reached adulthood we could have killed them and supplied enough pelts to make a fine leather jacket. Would you look at the coat on this one! It's much fuller than a cub that's still suckling."

Chen frowned. "I can't keep feeding it; it eats too much. A huge bowl of meaty porridge every day, and a bowl of cow's milk."

"Swapping a little millet for a fine pelt is a bargain. Next year, when the brigades are out looking for newborn litters, we won't kill any of them, not until they've doubled or tripled in size."

The old man sneered. "It's not as easy as you make it sound," he said. "This one was fed by a bitch at first. Where are you going to find enough bitches to feed all the cubs you plan to raise?"

Bao pondered that for a moment. "Good point," he said.

Chen picked the cub up by the scruff of his neck. He struggled, kicking and clawing the air. As he set him on the ground, Bao reached down and stroked his back. "I've never touched a live wolf before. Nice and plump. Very interesting."

"Chen Zhen," Uljii said, "you've devoted a lot of care to this cub over the past month or so, that's obvious. Wolves don't grow that fast in the wild. You're a better mother than its real mother. I've known for some time about your fascination with wolves, how you ask everyone to tell you what they know about them, but I never thought you'd actually raise one in captivity. I wonder if you might be going a bit too far with this."

Bilgee stared at the wolf cub. He put out his pipe and fanned the last of the smoke with his hand. "I've lived a long time," he said, "and this is the first wolf in captivity I've seen. I have to admit it looks like it's in good shape. Chen Zhen is devoted to what he's doing. But raising a wolf around a flock of sheep doesn't seem right. If you ask the herdsmen, they'll be against it, down to the last man. Now that you two are here, let's hear what you have to say about this youngster's plan to perform a scientific experiment."

Bao Shungui seemed taken by the idea. "It'd be a shame to kill it now," he said. "Its pelt isn't big enough to be of any use. It's taken a lot to raise an unweaned cub this long, so here's what I think. We let him continue for the time being, as a scientific experiment. Chairman Mao said, 'We study the enemy in order to defeat the enemy.' I'd like to learn more about wolves myself, so I'll come by regularly to see how he's doing. They say you're planning on breeding a strain of wolfhounds."

Chen nodded. "I thought about it, but Papa says it can't be done."

Bao turned to Uljii. "Has anyone on the grassland ever tried it?"

"The herdsmen venerate wolves," he replied. "They don't use them to breed hybrids."

"It's worth a try," Bao said. "That would be a true scientific experiment. If you can come up with a breed of Mongolian wolfhounds, you'd have something that would make Siberian wolfhounds puny by comparison. Mongolian wolves are the world's biggest and fiercest, so any mixed animals they sire will be the best. The army would be interested in something like that. If this works, we won't have to go abroad to buy dogs for them. And if the herdsmen had Mongolian wolfhounds to watch over the sheep, wolves would probably stay away. So if any of the herdsmen complain, just tell them it's a scientific experiment. But don't forget, safety first."

"If Bao says you can raise the cub, then go ahead," Uljii said. "But I'm warning you, if something goes wrong, it's on your head. Don't make things hard on Bao. I think this is risky, and you're going to have to keep it on a chain for the safety of people and sheep."

"That's right," Bao said. "Don't let it harm anyone. If he does, I'll kill him on the spot."

Chen was so nervous his heart nearly leaped out of his chest. "Absolutely!" he said. "But I have one request. I know the herdsmen won't approve, so please help me out with them."

"They'll listen to Bilgee more than they will to me," Uljii said.

"Ah," the old man sighed. "I'm afraid I've led this youngster astray. I'll have to do something, since it's my fault."

The old man left his carpenter tools with Chen Zhen, harnessed the ox to his wagon, and headed home, followed on horseback by Bao Shungui and Uljii.

Like someone who has just won a reprieve, Chen was excited and exhausted. He sat down weakly beside the wolf pen and held the cub in his arms, squeezing him so hard he wrinkled his nose and bared his fangs. Chen quickly rubbed him behind the ears to relax him. Shutting one eye, the cub closed his mouth halfway, his tongue lolling from the side, and pushed up against Chen's hand. Then he lay out straight and moaned contentedly.

19

Bao Shungui led Batu, Laasurung, and three other hunters, along with Yang Ke and seven or eight big dogs, to the new grazing land. A pair of horse-pulled carts piled high with tents, ammunition, and kitchen items followed.

When they reached a mountain peak west of the new land, Bao and the hunters surveyed the basin and the surrounding ravines, the river's bends and branches, and the grassland through binoculars; there were no wolves and no gazelles. Nothing but ducks, wild geese, and a dozen or so swans on the lake.

Most of the hunters had little interest in hunting wolves on that early summer day; they were mesmerized by the vast emerald grassland arrayed before them. Yang Ke felt as if the sight had turned his eyes green, and when he looked at the others, he saw the same color in theirs, like the beautiful yet terrifying eyes of a wolf on a winter night. As they made their way down the green mountain slope, their nostrils were filled with the scent of new grass carried on the clean, fresh air. The horses' hooves and the carts' wheels were stained green, as were the ends of the lasso poles that scraped along the ground. The horses strained at the bit to start grazing. The one thing Yang Ke would have liked to see was the blanket of flowers Chen Zhen had described for him. It had withered and fallen, leaving a monochromatic green panorama.

Bao Shungui looked like a man who had found a gold mine. "This is a perfect site!" he shouted. "A jade cornucopia. We should have let the military brass drive over here for a few days' vacation, hunt some swans and ducks, and have a barbecue."

Yang Ke didn't like the sound of that, as the image of the "Black-winged Demon" in the ballet *Swan Lake* flashed before his eyes.

The horses ran down the mountainside and crossed a gentle slope. "Look to your left," Bao Shungui said, keeping his voice low. "There's a flock of swans over there. They're busy eating. Let's go get one." He signaled a couple of hunters to follow him before Yang Ke could stop them. So he fell in behind them, rubbing his eyes as he ran. Suddenly the hunters reined in their horses and lowered their rifles. They shouted something. Bao Shungui also brought his horse to a stop and took out his binoculars. Yang Ke quickly did the same. He could hardly believe his eyes. The expanse of white that filled his eyes turned out to be a vast array of white herbaceous peonies. The previous summer he'd seen peonies on the old grazing land, in patches here and there, but never in such tight profusion. He fantasized that he was looking at a field of transformed swans.

Bao Shungui was not upset by what he saw; rather, he was happy. "My god!" he exclaimed. "I've never seen such gorgeous peonies. They're so much nicer than the ones in Beijing parks. Come over here and look at them!" Several horse riders rode up.

When he reached the flowers, Yang Ke nearly fainted. Thirty or forty patches of flowers were blooming in wild profusion in the rich soil. The bushes stood three feet tall. He went up for a closer look. The pistils were in clusters, the petals sprinkled with water, delicate and more handsome than ordinary peonies, more sumptuous and graceful than Chinese roses. Never before had the natural world presented him with such unspoiled beauty.

Bao Shungui was also spellbound. "This is a true rarity!" he exclaimed. "How much do you think these would sell for in town? I'm going to send some of these bushes to the military brass, let them share in this wonder. The older officials have no interest in money, but they love celebrated flowers. They'll take these to their heart. Yang Ke, I'll bet you don't have peonies like this in your Beijing guesthouses."

"Guesthouses? You won't find flowers like these in royal gardens."

Bao turned happily to the hunters. "Did you hear that? These flowers are a real treasure. Make sure you take special care of them. When we get back, cut down some apricot branches to make a fence."

"What happens if we move away? Someone else will come out and dig them up."

Bao Shungui thought a moment. "I've got a plan, don't worry."

Yang looked troubled. "Don't try to transplant them; you'll only kill them."

The horses and wagons arrived at a bend in the river, where the hunters quickly spotted places where wolves had surrounded groups of gazelles. Only skeletons, horns, hooves, and patches of hide remained; even the skulls had been picked clean. "There's been more than one attack here," Batu announced. "And plenty of wolves. By the amount of droppings, I'd say that even old and lame wolves participated in these hunts."

"Where do you think they are now?" Bao asked.

"My guess is they followed the gazelles into the mountains, or maybe they're off hunting marmots. Or they could have followed gazelles up to the border. At this time of year, the young gazelles run as fast as the adults, which means the wolves have trouble catching them. That's why they picked the bones clean."

"Now you see the positive side of wolves," Batu said to Bao. "If not for them, this virgin land would have been destroyed by gazelles, not just by grazing, but by what they left behind. When our sheep come out here, if they smell gazelle urine, they won't eat the grass, not a bite. This is a perfect spot. Even the horses want to stay. Let's find a spot to pitch our tents so the horses and dogs can rest. We'll go into the mountains tomorrow."

Bao gave the order to cross the river, so Batu chose a spot where the water was shallow and the riverbed sandy. Then, after he and some of the hunters had fashioned ramps on both banks with their hoes, he led one of the wagons across the river. Meanwhile, the other hunters set up a tent on the eastern slope. Batu told them to erect a stove and make some tea, then said to Bao, "I'll go check out the ravine to the south. I might find an injured gazelle. People haven't come all the way out here just to eat the dried meat we brought along."

Bao agreed enthusiastically. So Batu and a couple of hunters rode off to the mountain, taking the big dogs with them. Bar and Erlang, who had hunted gazelles in that area, raced ahead, driven by their hunting instincts.

Yang Ke was so fascinated by the swans out on the lake that he reluctantly, even painfully, passed up the chance to go hunting with Batu so that he could sit on a slope and gaze down at his swan lake. In order to keep watching the swans, he'd pestered Bao Shungui and Bilgee for two days to let him come ahead of the brigade—all the people, the horses, and the livestock. He wanted to take full advantage of the opportunity to drink in the beauty of the swan lake scenery, which easily eclipsed Chen Zhen's descriptions. He sat on the ground, took out his telescope, and watched breathlessly. Sitting all alone, he was immersed in tranquil thoughts when he heard a horse ride up behind him.

"Hey!" It was Bao Shungui. "I see you're studying the swans too. Let's go, just you and me—we'll bag one and get something good to eat. The herdsmen won't eat fowl, not even chicken. I tried to get them to go with me, but they said no. They won't eat it, but we will."

Yang turned to see Bao holding up his semiautomatic rifle and nearly wet himself. Waving his arms, he stammered, "Swans . . . precious, rare creatures . . . can't kill them! Please, I beg you. I've loved *Swan Lake* since I was a kid. During the three difficult years I cut school one day and went hungry so I could stand in line late at night just to buy a ticket to watch a performance by a joint troupe of young Soviet and Chinese dancers. It's truly beautiful. Educated people and great men everywhere love swans, so how could we come to a true swan lake just to kill and eat them? If you need to kill something, kill me."

Bao was shocked that anyone could be that ungrateful. He glared at Yang, his enthusiasm dampened. "*Swan Lake*—what the hell is that all about? Capitalist hogwash. You're a high school graduate, and you think that makes you better than me? We can't stage *The Red Detachment of Women* till we drive *Swan Lake* off the stage."

When Laasurung saw Bao heading toward the lake

with a rifle, he galloped over to stop him. "Swans are a sacred bird, given to us by Mongol shamans. You can't shoot them, you can't. Besides, Chairman Bao, it's wolves you want to kill, isn't it? Well, when the wolves up in the mountains hear gunfire, they'll take off, and we'll have come for nothing."

That stopped Bao. He reined his horse in, turned to Laasurung, and said, "It's a good thing you alerted me to that, or I might have done something stupid." He handed his rifle to Laasurung, and then turned back to Yang Ke. "Come with me," he said. "We'll scout the area around the lake."

Yang listlessly saddled his horse and followed Bao. As they drew up to the lake, flocks of ducks, wild geese, and a variety of waterbirds soared into the air and dropped water on their heads as they flew over. Bao grabbed the horn of his saddle and stood up in the stirrups to look over the reeds as a pair of swans stretched their wings, thrust out their necks, and skimmed the tops of the reeds, frightening him by passing no more than ten feet above his head. He sat down hard in the saddle, startling his horse, which burst forward and nearly threw its rider. The swans, apparently unafraid of people, soared lazily above the basin, circled the lake, and disappeared behind the reeds.

Bao got his horse back under control and adjusted the saddle. He laughed. "This must be the easiest place anywhere to hunt swans. All you need is a slingshot. They're the emperors of birds. One bite of their flesh makes life worth living. But we'll wait till we've finished off the wolves; then we'll come back for these."

Yang Ke said tentatively, "When you saw those peonies a while ago, you said they were a treasure and needed to be protected at all costs. Those swans are national treasures, international treasures, so why won't you protect them?"

"I'm a farmer," Bao replied, "and I look at the practical side of things. Treasures are things people can get their hands on. If you can't, they're not. Peonies have no legs, so they're not going anywhere. But swans have wings, and when the people and the livestock arrive, they'll fly north and wind up as pan-fried treasures for the Soviet or Mongolian revisionists."

"The Soviets will treat them as treasures; they won't kill and eat them."

"If I'd known how unenlightened you are," Bao said testily, "I wouldn't have brought you along. You wait and see. I'm going to turn your swan lake into a watering hole for horses and cows."

Yang swallowed his response. He'd have loved to pick up a rifle, fire into the air, and send the startled swans flying out of the grassland, out of the country, and all the way to the nation that produced the ballet *Swan Lake*. That's where you find people who love swans, he thought. How could this nation, where even sparrows have been eaten nearly to extinction, where the only things left are toads, be a place for swans?

Laasurung signaled for the two of them to return, so they rushed back to camp, where Sanjai, who had come from the southeastern mountains, was harnessing up his wagon. Batu and his party had shot wild boars up in the mountains and sent him for a cart to haul the carcasses to camp. They told him to bring Chairman Bao back with the cart. Bao could barely contain his delight. He slapped himself on the leg. "Are you telling me there are edible wild boars here on the grassland? That's a surprise. They're better eating than domestic pigs. Let's go." Yang had heard of hunters bagging wild boars, but he hadn't seen one since coming to the grassland. So he and Bao rode off in the direction Sanjai pointed out for them.

They saw where the wild boars had rooted the ground even before they reached Batu. Acres of rich soil by a stream, at the foot of the mountain, and in the ravine, looked as if they'd been plowed by an out-of-control ox. The fat, big-leafed stalks of tall grass had been eaten, leaving the area around them strewn with dry leaves and stalks; much of the foliage was buried in the rich soil. Fine grazing land now looked like a potato patch in which pigs had been let loose. The sight infuriated Bao Shungui. "Those damned boars are a menace! If we plant crops here one day, they could be very destructive."

The horses slowed down, shying away from the sight as they approached Batu, who was sitting at the foot of the mountain smoking his pipe. The two new arrivals dismounted and saw a pair of untouched carcasses next to Batu; another pair was being torn apart by the dogs, who were sprawled on the ground, eating voraciously. Erlang and Bar were each feasting on a leg. The boars beside Batu were smaller than full-grown domestic pigs, no more than three feet long, and sparsely covered with spiky bristles. Their snouts were twice as long as domestic pigs'. They were fat, and with teeth of average length, they didn't look particularly intimidating. There were fang marks on both their necks.

Batu pointed to the ravine. "The dogs picked up the scent of wolves and chased the boars all the way over to that ravine, where the ground was full of holes and bumps. We saw the carcasses of three or four boars that had been killed and eaten by wolves, and the dogs stopped there, not wanting to go after the wolves.

Instead they followed the scent of the boars down the ravine, flushing out a group of piglets. Big boars have tusks and run like the wind. The dogs wouldn't go after them, and I didn't dare fire at them, since I didn't want to alarm the wolves. The dogs eventually killed these piglets, so I let them have the two that were the most chewed up. The other two are for us."

Bao Shungui rested his foot on one of the dead boars. "Good job," he said with a smile. "The meat on this young one will be nice and tender, and delicious. I'll treat you all to some good liquor tonight. Apparently, there are wolves around here, and it would be a good idea if you men go out tomorrow and bag a few."

"These boars came from a forest hundreds of miles from here," said Batu, "where there are lots of them. They followed the river to get here. If not for the wolves, they'd have destroyed this grassland a long time ago."

Sanjai's wagon pulled up and they loaded the carcasses. Batu signaled the men to let the dogs keep eating their kill while the hunters returned with the wagon. Since the bonfire was ready by the time they made it back to camp, they immediately gutted, skinned, and filleted the larger of the two boars. Before long, the fragrance of barbecued meat filled the air. Taking Bao's lead, Yang Ke wrapped some lean meat in fatty lining, which produced loud sizzles as it cooked, and an aroma that beat anything they could get from domestic pigs. While the others were preparing the animal for cooking, Yang had picked wild onions and garlic and leeks; he'd learned the primitive method of barbecuing meat on the grassland, spicing it up with wild herbs, and was feeling quite proud of himself. Having seen the swans and the herbaceous peonies before Chen Zhen had a chance, and having learned how to barbecue boar out on the grassland, he could, when they got back to the yurt in camp, boast a bit about his rare sightings and the mouthwatering food.

As for Bao Shungui, while he was treating the hunters to good liquor, he regaled them with tales of imperial feasts where swan was served. They shook their heads, and he soon lost interest. The hunters ate only ground creatures, since they revered anything that could fly up to Tengger.

The hunting dogs returned to camp to patrol the area. The men, having eaten and drunk their fill, stood up and put the remains of the boar into a metal wash basin. Except for the heart and liver, they tossed the organs and the head onto the grassy ground for the dogs' next meal.

Just before nightfall, Yang Ke went alone to a spot where he could observe what was happening on his swan lake. He sat down, elbows on his knees, and, through his telescope, drank in a sight that could well disappear before long.

Ripples appeared on the lake surface, those in the west mirroring the cold blueness of the night sky, while those in the east reflected the warm colors of sunset. The ripples spread slowly, concentric circles of agate red, emerald green, translucent yellow; then came crystal purple, sapphire blue, and pearl white, alternating cool and warm, the tones of noble quality. The view that spread out before him seemed to augur the sad yet enchanting death of the swans. Tengger had sent down the precious lights as a prelude to the parting of its beloved swans from the clear waters.

The ripples continued their slow march, like the overture to a tragic drama in which the audience can hardly bear to watch the lead actor. Yang wished that the ballet about to unfold would have a natural background and that the lead actor would never appear. But from amid the inky green reeds, one swan after another glided out onto the lake, its multicolored surface and the canopy of sky above creating an enormous stage. The swans had changed into blue evening wear, which turned the yellow spot on the crowns of their heads a cold purple. Their graceful, curved necks looked like bright question marks, questioning heaven, questioning earth, questioning the water, questioning people, questioning all living creatures on earth. They moved silently, then waited for answers. But none were forthcoming. The reflecting ripples on the surface shimmered slightly, transformed into their own question marks, until a breeze splintered them amid the light of tiny wavelets.

Yang thought he and Chen were undeniably the luckiest Han Chinese alive. If the brute force and wisdom of the wolves somehow grew even greater, perhaps they could further delay the expansion and encroachment of men and their livestock on the grassland. The driving force behind that expansion was a society of Chinese farmers whose population was out of control. Yang was deeply moved and deeply saddened. He was also deeply grateful to the wolves. Their imminent defeat would be the first sign of the grassland's defeat, and the defeat of man's concept of beauty. Tears blurred the lens of his telescope. The pristine swan lake faded slowly into the distance...

The next day the hunters went up into the mountain and searched one ravine after another, but came up empty. The day after that they went deeper; by afternoon, men and horses were exhausted. Then Bao Shungui, Batu, and Yang Ke heard a gunshot ring out not far away. They turned as one in the direction of the noise and spotted a pair of wolves on a ridge to the east. The animals were running and stumbling up the mountain, and when they discovered that there were men here as well, they turned and ran around a promontory. Batu trained his binoculars on the spot. "The main pack is long gone," he said. "Those two lagged behind, too old to keep up."

"Who cares?" Bao said excitedly. "Young or old, two pelts mean victory however you look at it."

As he took off after the wolves, Batu mumbled, "How could he miss the fact that they haven't shed the old coat on their back half? What a shame."

Hunters and dogs ran up the mountain from two directions. One of the wolves was large, the other smaller. The front left leg of the larger wolf could not stretch out straight when it ran, which probably meant a torn tendon from a dog bite during a previous battle. The second wolf was an aging female, bony and old-age gray. When Bar, Erlang, and the other hunting dogs saw how old and crippled they were, they slowed down. All but one young adult male, that is; wanting to get the jump on the others, he took off at full speed, ignorant of what could happen.

The wolves ran into an area where the weathered surface created a complex terrain of outcroppings and loose, shifting layers of rock. Every step sent crumbling rock noisily down the mountainside. The going was too hard for the horses, so the hunters dismounted, rifles and poles in hand, and closed in from three directions.

The male wolf dashed over to a precipice about the

size of a couple of tables, three sides of which were walls of stone; the only escape was a steep slope down the mountain. So it backed up against one of the walls, a shrewd and ruthless glare emanating from its rheumy eyes, took a deep breath, and readied itself to fight for its life. The dogs formed a semicircle, growling and barking, but holding back, fearful of losing their footing and falling over the side. Then the hunters arrived. Bao was delighted with what he saw. "Don't anybody move," he said. "Watch me!" He took the bayonet off of his rifle, rammed a bullet into the chamber, and went up to get a clear shot.

But no sooner had he reached the line of dogs than the wolf sprang from the precipice onto a slope with loose rocks, digging in with its claws and flattening out against the rocky ground to slide down the mountain, carried by the flow of rocks. As the rocks pressed into its body, a cloud of gray sand quickly swallowed the wolf up, all but buried it.

The men walked gingerly up to the edge of the precipice and looked down. When the dust settled, the wolf was nowhere to be seen. "What just happened?" Bao asked Batu. "Was it killed or did it get away?"

"What difference does it make?" Batu said glumly. "Either way it's one pelt you'll never get."

Bao stood there speechless. Then loud, persistent barks from the dogs guarding the cave opening reinvigorated him. "There's still one more," he said. "Let's get back there! One way or the other, we're getting a wolf today."

The hunting party reached the cave, which had been formed by erosion and was a refuge for all sorts of grassland animals. Petrified eagle droppings were visible on many of the rocks. Bao Shungui scratched his head as he sized up the cave. "Damn!" he said. "If we try to dig it out, there'll probably be a cave-in, and we can't smoke it out, because there are too many places where the smoke will dissipate. Any ideas, Batu?"

Batu probed the cave with his lasso pole. The sound of shifting rocks emerged. He shook his head. "There's nothing we can do. The only thing that moving the rocks will do is bring them down on us and the dogs."

"How deep is the cave?" Bao asked him.

"Not deep," Batu replied.

"Then I say we smoke it out," Bao said. "You fellows gather some sod. After we light it, we stop up any holes where smoke comes out. I brought some pepper along. That'll drive it out. Go on, now, all of you! Yang Ke and I will keep watch here. If a hunting party with the best hunters can't bag a single wolf after three days of trying, we'll be a laughingstock."

The hunters split up and went looking for kindling and dry sod, leaving Bao and Yang at the cave entrance. "This wolf is old and she's sick, skinny as a rail. She hasn't got long to live, that's for sure. Besides, a summer coat has soft fur, and the purchasing station won't be interested. I say let her go," Yang said.

Bao's face darkened. "I tell you the truth: people are no match for a wolf. I've led soldiers into battle, and there's never been any guarantee against desertion or rebellion in the ranks. But why would a wolf rather die than come out of that cave? I'm not afraid to admit that the Olonbulag wolves are fine soldiers, that even the wounded, the old, and the females can strike fear into a man. But you're telling me that no one wants a summer pelt, which proves there are things you don't know. Back where I come from, no one uses a pelt with thick fur as a blanket, because you can get a bloody nose from overheating while you sleep. A light coat is everyone's favorite. Don't go soft on me now. In war it's them or us. You need to back your enemy into a corner and then kill him, giving no quarter."

Batu and some of the others walked up with bundles of dry branches; Laasurung and his party came up grasping the hems of their deels, which held sod. Bao piled the kindling up at the mouth of the cave and lit it, while the hunters knelt beside the fire and fanned the smoke into the opening with the hems of their deels. Thick smoke poured into the cave and seeped out between gaps in the rocks. The hunters began plugging up the holes with sod. It was a scene of frantic activity amid the sound of coughing, as smoke emerged from fewer and fewer gaps.

Bao Shungui threw a handful of half-dried peppers onto the fire, sending clouds of acrid smoke into the cave; the men and their dogs stood upwind. The cave was like the grate opening of a gigantic stove, and pepper smoke soon engulfed it. The hunters had left two small gaps unplugged to release wisps of smoke. When coughs from the old wolf emerged from inside, the hunters gripped their clubs, ready to strike; the dogs were prepared to pounce. The coughs grew more pronounced. But no sign of the wolf. Yang Ke was coughing so hard that tears were running down his face. "I can't believe her capacity to endure," he said. "Even the threat of death couldn't keep a human being in there."

Suddenly, the rocks slipped three feet or more, opening up gaps through which the smoke poured out, and before long smoke was emerging from all around. Several boulders broke loose and crashed down the mountain, barely missing the hunters who were fanning the flames. "The cave is collapsing," Bao cried out. "Get out of the way!"

The coughing sounds inside the cave stopped and there was no movement. Peppery smoke billowed skyward instead of entering the cave. "It looks like you lost again," Batu said to Bao. "You were up against a suicidal wolf. She loosened the rocks around her and buried herself. She wouldn't even give you her coat."

"Start moving rocks!" Bao barked angrily. "I'm going to dig that wolf out of there if it's the last thing I do."

Having worked hard for several days, the hunters stayed seated. Batu took out a pack of cigarettes and passed them around. As he handed one to Bao, he said, "Everyone knows you're not hunting wolves for their pelts, but to eradicate what you consider to be a scourge. She's dead, so you got what you came for, right? There are only a few of us here, and we could dig till tomorrow and still not get to her. We're witnesses to the fact that you led a hunting party against a pack of wolves, killing two big ones, sending one over a cliff and suffocating the other in a cave. And don't forget, summer pelts are pretty much worthless." He paused, looked around, and said, "Are you all okay with that?"

They said yes. Bao, who was as tired as everyone, took a drag on his cigarette and said, "All right, we'll rest awhile, then get out of here."

Yang Ke stood stunned in front of the pile of rocks, as if a falling rock had driven his soul out of his body. He seemed about to kneel down and pay his respects to the Mongol warrior inside, but he just stood there stiffly. Finally he turned and asked Batu for a cigarette. After taking a few drags, he raised the cigarette over his head with both hands and bowed deeply toward the rock pile, then reverently wedged the cigarette between a couple of rocks, part of an apparent grave mound. Wispy smoke rose into the air, taking the old wolf's soul skyward, up into the blue, to Tengger.

The hunters stood up but did not add their incense to the monument. Mongols considered smoked cigarettes to be fouled; they could not be used to pay respect to the gods. But they were not offended by Yang Ke's well-intentioned, if unclean, act. After stubbing out their cigarettes, they stood straight and looked up to Tengger; though they said nothing, the purity of their gazes sped the old wolf's soul to its glory more quickly than Yang's cigarette had done. Even Bao refrained from smoking more of his cigarette, which burned down to his fingers.

"Today you've seen something new," Batu said to Bao Shungui. "Genghis Khan's warriors were like those two wolves, choosing to die in ways that kill their enemy's spirit. You're a descendant of our Mongol ancestors, your roots are here on the grassland, and you should be paying your respects to our Mongol gods."

Yang Ke sighed with quiet emotion. "Dying can be a show of might," he said. "The wolf totem has nurtured a willingness to sacrifice one's life in countless Mongol warriors. Did the spirit of the people wither because of the extermination of the ferocious, magnificent wolf teacher?"

The hunting party had nearly reached the tent when Bao Shungui said to Batu, "You go on ahead. Boil some water. I'll go get a swan and treat you to some good food and liquor."

"Director Bao," Yang pleaded, "don't kill any of those swans."

"I have to," Bao said without looking back. "That's

the only way to purge the bad luck of these past few days."

Yang Ke followed him to try to talk him out of it, but Bao's horse was too fast. Waterbirds, wild geese, and ducks were circling low over the water, unconcerned about the man riding up with his rifle. Seven or eight large swans rose into the air, like a squadron of aircraft taking off in formation, but with wings that fanned the air gracefully; they cast oversized shadows down on the head of Bao Shungui, who had fired three times before Yang rode up. A large white bird fell to the ground in front of Yang, startling his horse, which reared up and threw him into the damp grass on the lakeshore.

The swan struggled, bleeding profusely. Yang had watched the death scene at the end of the ballet many times, but there was no grace, no beauty in the death throes of the bird he was looking at now. Its feet, like those of a common goose whose neck has been snapped, jerked spastically, and its wings flailed awkwardly as it tried vainly to right itself; the will to live remained strong, even as its life was slipping away. Blood spurted from the bullet wound in its snow white breast. Yang ran to catch it, but it jerked out of his reach time after time...

Finally, Yang was able to wrap his arms around the swan. Its soft abdomen was still warm, but the lovely neck had lost its power to form a question mark; now it was like a snake hanging limply across his wrist. He gently raised the swan's head. A blue-black sky was frozen in its open eyes, as if it were glaring angrily at Tengger. Tears blurred Yang's vision—a noble, pure, free soaring creature had ended up like a common chicken, killed by man.

Yang could barely control his grief. The thought of

diving in and swimming over to the reeds to sound the alarm for the other swans actually occurred to him.

That night, as the last hues of sunset faded, Bao Shungui was accompanied only by a pot of boiled swan; no one spoke to him. The hunters ate roasted wild boar; Yang Ke trembled the whole time he picked at the meat with his knife.

In the sky above the lake, the sad plaints of swans carried on throughout the night.

Yang was awakened in the middle of the night by the wolf like howls of the dogs. Then they stopped and Yang heard faint, distant, intermittent sounds of mourning—desolate, weathered, and stifling. The bleak chill of the sorrowful howls tore through him. The old wolf that had gone over the precipice hadn't died after all; after crawling half the night, severely injured, it made it over the mountain and was, no doubt, wailing in front of the burial spot of its mate, heartbroken, soul-stirred, devastated. He surely lacked the strength to move the rocks in order to see his mate one last time. A swan's lamentation over the death of its mate and the heartbreaking cries of the old wolf came together in pulsating waves of mourning.

Yang Ke wept until daybreak.

Several days later, Laasurung returned from headquarters to report that Bao Shungui had taken half a cartload of herbaceous peony roots into town.

20

On the highlands, the early-summer sun lit up an archipelago of floating clouds above the basin, so bright the people below could barely open their eyes. The air was filled with the smell of mountain onions and wild garlic as sheep and their lambs grazed the land, heavy and acrid. The people had to blink to moisten their burning eyes. Chen Zhen closely observed the new grassland and the camp, still fearful that the mother wolf would come looking for her cub and take her revenge on his sheep.

More than thirty yurts belonging to Second Brigade had been thrown up at the base of a gentle mountain slope on the northwestern edge of the basin, the two-yurt *hots* separated from one another by less than a thousand feet. The camp occupied a small fraction of the area, on the orders of Bilgee and Uljii, as a precaution against attacks by wolves, both from the new camp and the old, even, perhaps, a combined attack. There was no way, Chen felt, that an Olonbulag wolf pack could penetrate the line of defense. If they tried, dogs from all corners would launch a counterattack. That thought lessened his worries, and he squinted a bit to take in the beauty of the grazing land.

Herds of cattle and horses and flocks of sheep and goats were already making their way onto the new grazing land; what had been virgin land only the day before was now a pasture on which sounds of singing, whinnying, bleating, and lowing were carried on the wind; joy was in the air, emanating from the people, the horses, the sheep and goats, and the cows.

Chen and Yang's flock, exhausted after their long trek, was grazing on a slope not far from the men's yurt. With an emotional sigh, Chen said, "This new summer land and the old one are as different as night and day. I feel a sense of pride, as if we were reclaiming new land somewhere, the rewards far outweighing the losses. Sometimes I think it's all a dream and that we've taken our flock to the Garden of Eden."

"That's how I feel," Yang said. "This is an almost otherworldly place, a grassland of swans. All that keeps it from being perfect is the presence of Bao Shungui, the Chinese students, and the other outsiders. The Olonbulag shepherds would have no trouble living in peace and harmony with the swans. Just think how romantic it would be to tend our flock as swans glided across a blue sky. In a few years, marrying a Mongol girl brave enough to grab a wolf by the tail, and fathering some half-breed kids who wouldn't shy away from crawling into a wolf den is all I'd need in life." He breathed in the smell of fragrant grass.

"If even a Tang prince wished he could be a grassland Turk," he said, "why not me? Out here dogs are needed and are loved, unlike places like Beijing, where all you hear is people talking about 'smashing someone's dog head.' For a 'reactionary academic authority' like me, a 'damned cur,' there's no place better to put down roots and start a family than the grassland."

"You say it'd be better without the Chinese students, but you're one, aren't you?"

"Ever since I prostrated myself at the feet of the wolf totem," Yang said, "I've been a Mongol. These people place the big life of the grassland above their own lives. I can't help seeing people who come from farming districts as evil. No wonder the nomadic shepherds have fought farmers for thousands of years."

Chen said, "Farmers and shepherds have been doing that throughout history, stopping only long enough to intermarry and live together peacefully for a while. Truth is, we're all descendants of unions between people on the Central Plain and those on the grassland. Uljii said that this new grazing land will serve the people and their livestock for four or five years. He should be reinstated as a reward for what he's done here. What worries me is whether he and Bilgee have the power to overcome the forces that want to make the grassland theirs."

"You're a dyed-in-the-wool Utopian!" Yang exclaimed. "My father told me once that China's future lies in reducing its peasant population to under five hundred million. But I'm afraid the population explosion among peasants can't be brought under control, not by the Mongols' Tengger and not by our Old Man in Heaven. Over the past two decades, vast numbers of peasants have gone to work in factories, moved into cities, and started school, and then they've done all they can to drive the intellectuals into the countryside to become second-class peasants. They forced millions of students like us out of the cities. What power do a couple of Mongols like Uljii and Bilgee have? It's the mantis trying to stop a wagon."

Chen glared at him. "Apparently, you don't see the wolf as a real totem after all. Do you really know what it is? It's the spiritual power of one to ten, or a hundred, a thousand, ten thousand. It's what protects the big life of the grassland. Heaven has always seen that the big life manages the little life, that the heavenly life manages the human life. Without heavenly or earthly lives, what kind of tiny life would there be for people? If you truly revere the wolf totem, then you need to stand by heaven and earth, by nature, by the big life of the grassland, and you must struggle as long as a single wolf exists. Trust in the concept that fortunes change. Tengger will protect the grassland. By standing on the side of the big life, the worst that can happen is you'll die along with the force trying to destroy the big life, and your soul will ascend to Tengger. That is a worthy death. Most grassland wolves die in battle!"

Yang Ke was silent for a long spell.

Chen leashed the cub on orders from Uljii. The leash was fastened to a leather collar around the cub's neck on one end and a metal ring placed loosely around a three-foot mountain elm post that was buried two feet in the ground. A metal cap atop the pole, strong enough to hold an ox, kept the ring from sliding off the post; the cub could run around without shortening the leash or being choked.

And so a week before the move, the cub lost his freedom, became a prisoner restrained by a five-foot-long metal chain. It pained Chen to watch the little wolf turn his anger on the leash, which he did all that week, his slobber dripping from half its length. Try as he might, he could neither bite through the leash nor uproot the post, and he was forced to pass the days in an open-air circular prison, ten or twelve feet in diameter. Chen kept increasing the amount of time he spent walking the cub to make up for torturing him with a leash. The cub was happiest when a puppy was let into the pen to play with him, though he inevitably wound up sending his playmate scurrying off with a series of yelps and painful bites, and was once again all alone. Erlang was the only adult dog who occasionally wandered into the wolf pen, sometimes to rest for a while and let the cub jump on top of him or nibble at his ears or tail.

The cub's most important daily activity was staring at his food dish, which rested beside the yurt, waiting impatiently until it was filled and carried over to him. Chen could not tell if the cub knew why he had become a prisoner, but the hateful glare in his eyes was unmistakable, as if he were saying, "The puppies get to run free; why can't I?" He took his anger out on the dogs, occasionally drawing blood. Given the primitive, nomadic conditions, raising a wolf near dogs, sheep, and men required inhumane treatment. If Chen let his guard down for even a moment, the wolf was likely to attack the sheep or the men, and that would seal his doom. He whispered this to the cub many times, but of course that had no effect. Chen and Yang began to worry that this sort of treatment might adversely affect the young wolf's development. Depriving him of his freedom by tethering him to a chain removed both the conditions and opportunity for his personality to develop naturally. Would a wolf raised under such conditions still be a real wolf? Chen and Yang felt, however dimly, that they had, as the saying goes, mounted the wolf and didn't know how to get off. Maybe the seeds of failure had been sown in their experiment from its inception. Yang was inclined to give up, but Chen would have none of it. In truth, Yang too was growing increasingly attached to the cub.

It was time for the cattle to mate. One of the bulls

came frighteningly close to the wolf cub, sending him cowering into a clump of tall grass. Then when the frenzied bull mounted one of the cows, the cub was so frightened he burst out of the grass, trying to get away, but was jerked to a halt by the taut chain, which nearly strangled him; his tongue shot from his mouth, his eyes rolled back. Not until the bull took off chasing another cow did he calm down.

By this time the cub had more or less gotten used to his prison site and had begun to romp and tumble in his pen. The ground was covered by grass that grew a foot or more, making the pen much more comfortable than his first pen, with its dry, sandy ground. Here he could lie on his back, looking up into the sky, or lazily chew the grass; he could play for half an hour all by himself. So full of vitality, he had found a spot and a sport that would let him come alive, and so he began a regimen of running in the pen several times a day, hugging the outer wall and running around and around, seemingly never tiring.

First he'd make a complete turn in one direction, screech to a halt, and then reverse direction. When he finally wore himself out, he'd sprawl in the grass, mouth open, tongue lolling to the side, panting and slobbering. Chen discovered that the cub was spending more time and making more revolutions every day, and he realized that the little wolf was making his body work harder in order to shed his old coat for the new one coming in. The first time a wolf sheds its coat, Bilgee had said, comes later in the year than mature animals.

Zhang Jiyuan galloped up on his horse, his forehead bandaged in white. Chen and Yang, surprised by the unexpected visit, ran out to greet him. "No!" Zhang cried out. "Stand clear!" The horse he was riding, spooked by the movement, was bucking and kicking, keeping everyone at bay. Obviously, the horse had only recently been broken, so they kept their distance to let Zhang get down as best he could.

Mongol horses are fiery animals, especially the high-strung Ujimchin. They cannot be broken until the spring of their third year. Though they're thin at that time of the year, they're big enough to accommodate a rider. If this moment is lost, the horse will never take a saddle or bit. It will remain a wild horse.

Each spring, the horse herders chose three-year-olds that were relatively tame and gave them to the cowherds and shepherds to break. Those who were successful could ride that horse for a year. If, after a year, the rider determined that the horse was inferior to his other horses, he could return it to the herd, at which time it was given a name. Traditionally, each horse was named after the person who tamed it, with a color added. Bilgee Red, Batu White, Lamjav Black, Laasurung Gray, Sanjai Green, Dorji Yellow, Zhang Jiyuan Chestnut, Yang Ke Yellow Flower, and Chen Zhen Green Flower were notable examples of names those horses would carry throughout their lives. Having several horses with the same name on the Olonbulag was a rarity.

Horses were the lifeblood of grasslanders. Lacking good horses or a sufficient number of them made it hard for people to escape the ravages of snowstorms, wildfires, and enemy attacks; to make timely deliveries of medical personnel and medicine; to sound the alarm in time to ward off military or natural disasters; to catch a wolf; or to catch up to panicky herds of horses and cattle or flocks of sheep during a white-hair blizzard. Bilgee once said that a grasslander without a horse was like a two-legged wolf.

As Zhang Jiyuan rubbed his horse's neck, he gently slid one foot out of the stirrup and, with the horse's attention diverted, jumped to the ground. The startled animal bucked several times, nearly throwing its saddle, so Zhang quickly grabbed the reins and jerked the horse's head toward him to keep from getting kicked. It was a struggle, but somehow he managed to lead the horse over to a wagon, where he hitched it to the axle. The animal fought to break loose, making the wagon rock and creak.

Chen and Yang breathed a sigh of relief. "You're courting disaster," Yang said. "Do you really think you can subdue a horse that wild?"

Zhang rubbed his forehead and said, "It threw me this morning and I took a hit on the head from one of its hooves. It knocked me out, but thankfully Batu was there with me. Lucky for me it's still young, and its hooves haven't rounded out yet, so I got off without a broken nose. If it had been an older horse, I probably wouldn't be here now. But it's one hell of a horse, and in a few years it'll have quite a reputation. Out here you have to put your life on the line if you want a truly fine horse. It's the only way."

"You know, you're starting to make us worry about you. The day you can get control of a fine horse without bandages all over you is the day you've finally arrived."

"Give me two more years," Zhang said. "This spring I broke six young geldings, all good horses. In the future, when you go hunting, if you're short of horses, look me up. My plan is to swap all your present horses for good ones."

* * *

The new grazing land offered plenty of fresh grass and water, all for a single brigade's livestock, so they decided to let the horses graze in the proximity of cattle and sheep, at least for a while. With no one to move them along, the horses lowered their heads and began grazing.

Chen and Yang were captivated by the sight of all those big, powerful young stallions with shiny new coats. With each movement, the muscles under the satiny coats rippled, as if carp were swimming beneath the skin.

The most notable difference between Mongolian stallions and other horses is their long mane, which covers their eyes, necks, chests, and upper legs. The hair grows longest around their necks and on their shoulders, some of it reaching their knees, their hooves, even the ground. The mane flows when they lower their heads to eat, covering half of their bodies and turning them into headless, faceless, hairy demons. When they run, heads held high, that mane billows and flows in the wind, like a Mongol battle flag in all its fullness, the sight of which can throw an enemy into headlong, panicky retreat. Given their violent, mercurial nature, they are horses no one dares try to tame, or rope, or ride. They have two functions on the grassland: stand at stud, and defend the herd. Possessing a strong sense of family responsibility, they never shy from danger; they are mean and tenacious. Stud bulls are idlers that move on after mating, but stallions are the great heads of grassland households.

It didn't take long for a fight to break out among the horses. Once each year, the fillies were driven out of the herds in anticipation of a mating war, and this time it occurred right below where the three men were standing.

They sat on the ground by the wolf pen to watch the battle unfold, joined by the cub, crouched at the end of his chain to watch the action, shuddering like a starving wolf in a snowbank but not otherwise moving. He instinctively feared the powerful stallions yet watched them in utter fascination.

The herd, which numbered in excess of five hundred horses, was made up of more than a dozen families, each led by a stallion. The largest families had seventy or eighty members, the smallest as few as ten. The families comprised the sons and daughters of the stallions and their wives and concubines. Mating conditions among the ancient horse herds had evolved to a level of civilization greater even than that for humans. The horse herds were able to survive in the cruel grassland environment, surrounded by wolves that could attack at any time, by ruthlessly eradicating the possibility of inbreeding, which prevented a deterioration of the breed and a lessening of fighting ability.

At the onset of summer, three-year-old females approach sexual maturity, and the stallions abandon their fatherly airs by ruthlessly driving their daughters out of the family, refusing to allow them to remain by their mothers' sides. Angry, nearly maniacal long-maned fathers drive their complaining daughters away, biting at their flanks as if they were chasing wolves, creating chaos in the herd. For those that find their way back to their mothers' side, their fathers run up to them, fuming with anger, before the young females can catch their breath. They kick them, nip at them, do whatever it takes to ward off any resistance, until the young horses have no choice but to leave the family herd. They whinny pitifully, begging their fathers for leniency. But the stallions glare, snort, and paw the ground threateningly, refusing to allow them to remain with their mothers, who also suffer the rage of their mates when they try to protect their daughters. In the end, the mothers take a neutral stance, having come to understand what lies behind their mates' actions.

Once the daughter banishment wars have run their course, the real battles, the cruel combat over mate selection is launched; it is a true volcanic eruption of male unruliness. The young females who have just been driven away from their families and have nowhere to turn quickly become the objects of contention among stallions of other families; as the males rear up on their hind legs and engage in mortal combat, they tower above the rest of the herd. Their powerful hooves are their weapons, which they wield like hammers, like fists, like axes. Amid the thudding of hooves and clashing of teeth, weaker horses flee in defeat, but well-matched combatants fight on and on. If hooves don't win the day, they use their teeth, and if that doesn't do it, they turn and kick with their hind legs, weapons that can crush the skull of a careless wolf. Some of the horses fight on even with their heads split open, or their chests bruised and swollen, or their legs badly injured.

If the young females take advantage of the chaos to return to their mothers, they now face the wrath of their fathers as well as stallions who would have them as mates, now comrades-in-arms, who chase them back to where they belong.

One beautiful, robust young female attracted the attention of two of the most ferocious stallions. The filly's snow white coat shimmered; she had big, beautiful, deerlike eyes. She was tall and slender, and had the light gait of a deer when she ran. Yang Ke was completely taken by her. "What a beauty," he said. "If I were one of those stallions I'd fight for her."

The stallions fought like lions in the Colosseum, caught up in mortal combat. Zhang Jiyuan unconsciously stamped his foot and wrung his hands. "Those two have been fighting over her for days. She's such a beauty I call her Princess Snow White. But she's a little princess you have to feel sorry for. One day she's forced to stay with the family of one stallion, the next day she's taken away by another. Then those two males fight over her, and who knows where she'll wind up the next day. When the first two have worn themselves out, a third comes up to take them on. And our princess goes to another home. Now she's nothing but chattel to be taken at will, first by one stallion, then by another, not even given time to graze on the fresh grass. Look at her—she's skin and bones. It's like this every spring. When some of the fillies learn they can't stay with their own family, they go straight to the family with the most powerful stallion for protection, which keeps them above the fray and provides less wear and tear on their bodies. They've seen what wolves can do to a horse, and are smart enough to realize that without a family, without the protection of a powerful father or mate, they're in danger of becoming the next meal for a pack of wolves. In the end, it's no exaggeration to say that wolves are behind the wild, ferocious nature of Mongol stallions.

"Stallions are grassland despots," Zhang continued. "They worry that a wolf pack might attack their mates and offspring, but other than that, they fear nothing, not wolves, and certainly not humans. We used to talk about working like an ox or a horse, but that has nothing to do with these stallions. There isn't much difference between a Mongol herd of horses and a wild herd, except, of course, for the geldings. I've spent a lot of time with horses, but I still can't imagine how primitive people went about domesticating them. How did they figure out that they could ride a horse by gelding it?"

Chen and Yang exchanged looks and merely shook their heads. Pleased by the silent response, Zhang continued, "I've thought about that for a long time, and here's what I think. The early inhabitants of the grassland found ways to catch wild stallions that had been wounded by wolves. After nursing them back to health, they couldn't ride them, even if they had some modest success with horses that were still small. So they kept trying, one wounded horse after another, generation after generation, until one day the horse they caught had had its testicles bitten off, a new two-year-old. This one they were able to ride after it grew to maturity... That led them to the obvious conclusion. However it happened, it was complex and it must have taken a very long time. And a lot of early grasslanders must have died trying. That's one of the great advances in the history of man, much more significant than China's four great inventions of paper, printing, the compass, and gunpowder. Without horses, life in ancient times would have been unimaginable, far worse than getting by without automobiles, trains, and tanks in modern society. And that's why the contributions to mankind by ancient nomads are incalculable."

Chen Zhen broke in excitedly: "I agree a hundred percent. It was a lot harder for the grasslanders to first break wild horses than for ancient farmers to domesticate wild rice. Rice, at least, can't run away, it can't buck and rear up, and it can't kill or injure you with its hooves or drag you to your death. Domesticating crops is peaceful labor, but domesticating wild horses and oxen is a battle bathed in blood and sweat. Farming people are still enjoying the fruits of the nomad people's magnificent battles."

Chen sighed. "The way I see it, the most advanced people today are descendants of nomadic races. They drink milk, eat cheese and steak, weave clothing from wool, lay sod, raise dogs, fight bulls, race horses, and compete in athletics. They cherish freedom and popular elections, and they have respect for their women, all traditions and habits passed down by their nomadic ancestors. Not only did they inherit their courage, their militancy, their tenacity, and their need to forge ahead from their nomadic forebears, but they continue to improve on those characteristics. People say you can tell what a person will grow up to be at the age of three and what he'll look like in old age at seven. The same holds true for a race of people. In the West, primitive nomadic life was their childhood, and if we look at primitive nomads now, we are given access to Westerners at three and at seven, their childhood, and if we take this further, we get a clear understanding of why they occupy a high position. Learning their progressive skills isn't hard. China launched its own satellite, didn't it? What's hard to learn are the militancy and aggressiveness, the courage and willingness to take risks that flow in nomadic veins."

"Since I've been herding horses," Zhang said, "I've felt the differences in temperament between the Chinese and the Mongols. Back in school I was at the top in just about everything, but out here I'm weak as a kitten. I did everything I could think of to make myself strong, and now I find that there's something lacking in us . . ."

Chen sighed again. "That's it exactly!" he said. "China's small-scale peasant economy cannot tolerate competitive peaceful labor. Our Confucian guiding principle is emperor to minister, father to son, a top-down philosophy, stressing seniority, unconditional obedience, eradicating competition through autocratic power, all in the name of preserving imperial authority and peaceful agriculture. In both an existential and an awareness sense, China's small-scale peasant economy and Confucian culture have weakened the people's nature, and even though the Chinese created a brilliant ancient civilization, it came about at the cost of the race's character and has led to the sacrifice of our ability to develop. When world history moved beyond the rudimentary stage of agrarian civilization, China was fated to fall behind. But we're lucky, we've been given the opportunity to witness the last stages of nomadic existence on the Mongolian grassland, and, who knows, we might even discover the secret that has led to the rise in prominence of Western races."

Out on the grassy field, as the horses fought on, with no end in sight, the lovely Princess Snow White was taken by an opportunistic stallion into its family herd. But there was no surrender in the losers, which raced over and kicked the princess to the ground. Not knowing where to turn for rescue, she lay there emitting long, sad whinnies. Her anxious mother made as if to go to her, but was sent back into the herd by the flying hooves of her almost demonic mate.

Yang had seen enough. He nudged Zhang Jiyuan. "You're a horse herder—why don't you do something?"

"Do what?" Zhang asked. "Go over there, and they'll stop fighting. Leave, and they're back at it. Herders play no role in the herd's battles for survival. They've been doing this for centuries. If the stallions don't drive their daughters out of the herd in the summer and fight to diversify the herds, these fights will go on forever. The most powerful stallions emerge from these summer wars, ensuring a successive generation of fast, smart, ferocious horses. The battles produce fine horses, year after year, increasing the stallions' courage and fighting skills, and their families flourish. This is where the stallions hone their skills for fighting and killing wolves. Without these drills, the herds of Mongol horses could not survive on the grassland."

"It seems to me," Chen said, "that the Mongol warhorses that shocked and amazed the world must have been a product of their battles with wolves."

"You said it," Zhang agreed. "Wolves out here do more than just foster Mongol warriors; they also foster Mongol warhorses. Ancient China's regimes had massive mounted armies, but their horses were, for the most part, raised and trained in ranchlike surroundings. We've been sent out to labor in the countryside, so we know how they raise horses in farming villages. They're let out into a pen, where they're watered and fed and given extra hay at night. Those horses have never seen a wolf and they've never engaged in horse wars. During the mating season, there's no mortal combat, since there's always someone around to take care of matters. They tether the female to a post, then lead a stud horse up to her. When the coupling is over, the female doesn't even know what her mate looks like. What kind of nature and fighting spirit can a horse from this mating have?"

Yang Ke laughed. "Whatever comes from arranged marriages is bound to be stupid! We're lucky we didn't come from arranged marriages, so there's still hope for us. Arranged marriages in farming villages are still common, but what comes out of them is at least better than plow horses, and the young ladies at least know what the men look like.

"In China we call that progress," Chen said.

"Horses belonging to the Chinese," Zhang said, "are animal coolies. They work all day and sleep at night, just like the peasants. So in this regard the Chinese are laboring peasants and their horses laboring horses, which is why they're no match for Mongol fighters and Mongol warhorses."

With a sigh, Yang said, "There's no way a stupid horse can win on the field of battle. But the main reason the horses are stupid is stupid people."

Smiles of resignation all around.

Zhang Jiyuan continued, "A fighting spirit is more important than a peaceful laboring spirit. The world's greatest engineering feat, in terms of labor output, our Great Wall, could not keep out the mounted warriors of one of the smallest races in the world. If you can work but you can't fight, what are you? You're like a gelding, you work for people, you take abuse from them, and you give them rides. And when you meet up with a wolf, you turn tail and run. Compare that with one of those stallions that uses its teeth and its hooves as weapons."

Yang Ke was in total agreement. "Ai, the work on the Great Wall was dead labor, while those battles on the grassland were full of life."

Gao Jianzhong rode up on an oxcart. "We've struck it rich!" he shouted excitedly. "I stole a bucketful of wild duck eggs!" His three comrades ran over and took down a water bucket filled with seventy or eighty duck eggs, yellow liquid seeping out through the cracks of the broken ones.

"You've just wiped out a flock of wild ducks," Yang Ke said.

"I wasn't alone. Wang Junli and a bunch of the others were doing the same thing. Near the southwestern lake, in the grass by a little stream, you couldn't walk more than ten steps without coming upon a nest of a dozen or so duck eggs. The first people there stole buckets of them. Actually, they saved them from horses that were trampling the grass on their way to the water. The area is littered with eggshells and yolks. What a waste."

"Are there any left?" Chen asked. "We can go get more and salt the ones we don't eat now."

"No more around here," Gao said. "How many do you think were left after four herds of horses had passed by? But there might be some on the eastern shore."

"Come on, all of you," Gao ordered. "Separate the broken eggs from the unbroken ones. I haven't eaten a fried egg in a couple of years at least. Let's put away as many as we can. Fortunately, we've got plenty of mountain onions in the yurt. Wild onions and wild eggs, a true, and absolutely delicious, wildwood meal. Yang Ke, you go peel the onions; Chen Zhen, you break open the eggs; Zhang Jiyuan, you get a basket of dried dung. I'll do the cooking."

About half of the eggs were broken, giving each of the friends eight or nine. It was a party atmosphere, and in no time the fragrant, oily smell of onion-fried duck-egg pancakes filtered out of the yurt and was spread by the wind. Dogs picked up the scent and crowded up to the yurt entrance, salivating and wagging their tails; the wolf cub strained noisily against his chain, jumping up and down and growling viciously. Chen decided to save a little for the cub to see if he'd eat something fried in sheep fat.

While the men were gobbling up pancakes, they were interrupted by a shout from Gasmai outside. "Aha, all that good food and you didn't invite me over!" She opened the door, walked in with Bayar, and pushed the dogs out of the way. Chen and Yang made room for them in the seat of honor.

Chen handed them both some pancakes and said, "I didn't think herdsmen ate stuff like this. Here, try it."

"I smelled this all the way over at my place, a good thousand feet away, and it made me drool. So here I am, my little mutt and all. Not eat these? I sure do." She picked up a pair of chopsticks and dug in. "They're delicious," she said. Bayar wolfed his down, never taking his eyes off the stove, worried there wouldn't be more. Herdsmen eat a morning meal of curds, meat, and tea, then don't eat again until the main meal in the evening. So mother and son were hungry.

"This is really good," Gasmai said, "like eating 'restaurant food,' without having to go into town. Today I'm going to stuff myself."

"I've got a bucketful here," Gao said with a little laugh. "If we run out of broken eggs, we'll cook the whole ones. You won't leave hungry, I guarantee it." Putting the broken eggs to one side, he cracked open half a dozen whole ones and made pancakes just for Gasmai and Bayar.

"But Papa won't eat these," Gasmai said. "He says that eggs belong to Tengger and should be left alone. What that means is, I'll have to come over here to eat."

Chen said, "Last year I was there when Papa asked the family of someone at headquarters for a dozen chicken eggs. What was that for?"

"One of the horses was sick," Gasmai said. "Too much internal heat. He pinched the animal's nose closed so it would raise its head, then broke a couple of eggs against its teeth and poured the contents down its throat. After he did that a few times, the horse was cured."

Yang Ke leaned over and whispered to Zhang Jiyuan, "Now we've done it. Thanks to us, the herdsmen will start eating things they never used to eat. In a few years, not only swans but even wild ducks will disappear from the grassland."

Bayar's spirits rose with each bite. With grease running down his chin, he said, "I know where there are more of these. Make us one more serving, and tomorrow I'll take you there. You'll find plenty in abandoned marmot holes on hillsides. I saw some by a stream when I was looking for stray lambs this morning."

"Great!" Gao Jianzhong exclaimed. "There's a hillock near the stream with lots of holes in the sand, which means the horses will stay clear of the place." While he was frying the pancakes, he told Chen to break open a few more eggs. In no time, a new thick, oily egg pancake came out of the pan. Gao cut it in two and gave half to Gasmai and half to her son. Sweat beaded their heads as they ate. Oily smoke rose from the pan, into which the next bowlful of eggs was dumped with a sizzle.

After Chen took out the spatula, he said, "Now I'm going to treat you to something different." First he put in some sheep fat, then broke a couple of eggs, frying them until they were lightly cooked. Gasmai and her son got up on their knees to look into the pan. They stared wide-eyed at what they saw. Chen gave each of them one of the fried eggs, over which he sprinkled a bit of soy paste.

"This is even better than the pancakes," Gasmai said. "Two more, please."

"In a minute," Yang said with a laugh, "I'll fry you some eggs with leeks, and when you say you're full, we'll have old Zhang make a bowl of egg-drop soup. We all have our special dishes."

Fragrant, oily smoke filled the yurt as the six people ate until they could eat no more and laid down their chopsticks. The wildwood feasters had gone through more than half of the eggs in the bucket.

Gasmai said she had to leave; there was much to do in the wake of the recent move. She belched contentedly and said with a laugh, "Don't breathe a word about this to Papa. Come over to my place in a few days, and I'll treat you all to a meal of curds mixed with fried rice."

Gao reminded Bayar, "Don't forget to take me looking for more eggs tomorrow."

Chen ran out and stuffed a big piece of egg pancake into Bar's mouth. Bar spat it onto the ground; but after inspecting it, sniffing it, and licking it, he decided it was edible. Beaming happily, he picked it up and ate it slowly, wagging his tail in thanks to Chen.

Once their guests had left, Chen ran over to see how his cub was doing.

It was gone! Chen broke out in a cold sweat. Panicked, he ran up close, where he discovered that his cub was hiding in the tall grass. He figured that the two strangers and all those unfamiliar dogs had frightened him. Obviously, he knew instinctively how to hide from danger. Chen breathed a sigh of relief. The cub looked around and, seeing that the strangers were gone, jumped to his feet and began sniffing Chen's body, heavy with the aroma of fried eggs. He licked Chen's oily hands.

So Chen went back inside, asked Gao for half a dozen eggs, which he threw into the pan with plenty of oil, and made egg pancakes for the cub and the dogs. That wasn't nearly enough to fill them, but he felt a need to at least let them have a taste. Grassland dogs seemed to prefer snacks over regular meals, and giving them snacks was one of the best ways to bond with them. When he was finished, Chen divided the pancakes into four large pieces and three smaller ones. The large pieces were for the three dogs and the cub, the three smaller ones for the puppies. The dogs were still hanging around the doorway, refusing to leave, so Chen held back the piece for the cub, crouched down, and tapped each dog on the head with his spatula to have it wait its turn and not take food from one of the other dogs. He gave the biggest piece to Erlang, who took it in his mouth and wagged his tail spiritedly.

After the dogs had left to frolic in the grass, and the pancakes had all cooled down, he put the last big piece in the cub's bowl and walked over with it. Yang Ke, Zhang Jiyuan, and Gao Jianzhong followed, all wanting to see if the cub would eat the egg pancake, something no grassland wolf had ever seen or eaten. "Little Wolf," Chen called out, "Little Wolf, time to eat." He'd no sooner placed the bowl into the pen than the cub came running as if it were chasing down a newborn lamb, grabbed the oily pancake in its mouth, and gobbled it down; it took no more than a second.

The men looking on were disappointed. "I feel sorry for the thing," Zhang said. "He's content just to have food in his belly. Look up *wolf* in the dictionary, and you won't find the word *savor.*"

Looking pained, Gao said, "All those good duck eggs gone to waste."

"Who knows," Chen explained to ease their disappointment, "maybe wolves' taste buds are in their stomach."

That got a laugh out of them.

Chen went back into the yurt to straighten things up after the move. His friends decided to go tend to their animals, but before they left, Chen said to Zhang, "Want me to grab your horse by the ears to help you climb into the saddle?"

"No need," Zhang replied.

He picked up some clean clothes, borrowed a copy of Jack London's *The Sea Wolf,* and went outside.

He mounted up and led the horses in the direction of the mountains to the southwest.

21

Chen Zhen saw that several clusters of sheep had left the lakeshore ahead, so he rounded up his flock and led them to the lake. Once they were on the move, he rode over ahead of them. A small herd of horses, having drunk their fill, was standing in the water, resting with their eyes closed, unwilling to return to dry land. Wild ducks and a variety of waterbirds were swimming on the lake, a few of them actually sporting around the horses, flitting beneath their bellies and between their legs. Swans cruised on the surface in the center of the lake away from the horses and on the opposite shore, where reeds still grew.

Suddenly, the silence was shattered by loud bleating on a sandy ridge on the northwestern shore, as Chen's sheep smelled the water. In the summer, sheep were watered every other day, and the animals were voicing their thirst. They ran to the lake, raising a cloud of dust. The herdsmen and their livestock had been on the new land slightly more than a week, but the grass near the lake had already been trampled into the sandy soil by all the cattle, sheep, and horses that had drunk there. The sheep rushed into the lake, crowding the horses as they greedily lapped up the water.

Chen's sheep had barely climbed to the top of the ridge after drinking their fill when another flock of thirsty animals ran noisily to the lake's edge, raising another cloud of dust.

Laborers had set up four or five tents on a gentle slope a few hundred feet from the lake, where dozens of men were hard at work digging trenches. Under Bao Shungui's direction, they were building a dipping pool for sheep, a wool storage shed, and a provisional headquarters building. Chen saw some of the laborers and members of their family dig trenches and plow plots of land for vegetable gardens. Another group of laborers had dug a stone quarry on a distant hill and were loading bright yellow rocks and flagstone onto large wagons, which were driven back to the work sites. Chen hated to see scars opened on the virgin land, so he turned back to his sheep and herded them off to the northwest.

The flock crossed a mountain ridge into a grassy basin. Bilgee had asked that the livestock not graze exclusively in the basin; since the summer days were so long, he said, the animals should be taken as far away as possible. That way there would be no need to move again as summer turned to fall. He planned to have the animals make several large sweeps of the basin and its outlying areas to keep the grass from growing out of control and patting down the loose soil as a means of mosquito control. Chen's flock, forming a crescent, moved slowly toward mountains to the west.

In the glare of sunlight, the thousand or so sheep and their lambs sparkled like a field of white chrysanthemums, in stark contrast to their green surroundings. The lambs, whose coats were getting fluffy, alternately suckled and grazed the field. Their round tails were filling out and were nearly as big as those of their still-nursing mothers. Chen felt his eyes fill with the golden luster of yellow daylilies, which had just bloomed on the mountainside. Tens of thousands of bushes, two feet tall, offered up large, trumpet-shaped yellow flowers, with long, thin new buds dotting the branches below, ready to open soon.

Chen got up, mounted his horse, and rode over to an even denser field to pick the flowers, which had been introduced into the Beijing students' diets: lilies and lamb dumplings, lilies and mountain onion salad, lilies and shredded lamb soup, and more. After going without vegetables all winter, they took to the wild greens and flowers like sheep to grazing land. The local herdsmen were amazed, since wildflowers were not something they ate. Before Chen left the yurt in the morning, Zhang Jiyuan had emptied out a pair of schoolbags, denying him the pleasure of reading while he tended the flock, so he and Yang could bring back a load of wildflowers before they withered and died. He blanched them in boiled water and dried them for the coming winter. In a few days they had already filled a sack half full of dried flowers.

The sheep grazed on the field behind Chen as he quickly filled a bag with flowers. While he continued to pick, he spotted some wolf droppings by his foot. He bent down and picked up a piece to examine it closely. It was gray, about the length of a banana, and already dry, though he could tell that it was still relatively fresh. He had just sat down to study it when it dawned on him that this must have been a resting spot for a wolf only a few days before. What was it doing there? He checked but found no bones or animal fur, so it wasn't where it had eaten a kill. Small clusters of sheep often passed through the area, with its tall flowers and dense grass, so maybe this was the wolf's hiding place, an ideal spot for an ambush. Suddenly quite nervous, he stood up and looked around, happy to spot some shepherds surveying the surroundings while they rested. Since his flock was several hundred feet behind him, he relaxed and sat down again.

Chen was familiar with wolf droppings, but this was his first opportunity to study them up close. He broke off a piece; inside he found gazelle fur and sheep's wool, but not a shard of bone. There were a couple of field-mouse teeth and a few calcified chunks of wool. He crumbled the piece in his hand, but that was all it contained. The meat, skin, bones, and tendons of the sheep and mice the wolf had eaten had been completely digested, leaving behind only the fur and teeth. When he looked even closer, he saw that only the coarsest hair had passed through the wolf's body. No dog had as effective a digestive system as that, he knew, since you can normally find undigested items like bone and kernels of corn in their droppings.

The efficiency with which wolves, the grassland's sanitation workers, disposed of everything—cows, sheep, horses, marmots and gazelles, wild rabbits and field mice, even humans—was astonishing. As the animals passed through the wolf's mouth, stomach, and intestines, the nutrients were removed, leaving behind only bits of hair and teeth, not even enough to feed germs. The grassland remained clean down through the ages thanks largely to its wolves.

The wildflowers swayed in a breeze. Chen crumbled the last of the wolf dung, which was carried off by the wind, settling to the ground to become one with the grassland, leaving no waste at all. With wolf dung it was truly a case of ashes to ashes and dust to dust.

Chen was by then deep in thought. Over the centuries, the herdsmen and hunters of the grassland returned to Tengger with no burial and no markers, and definitely no mausoleums. Men and wolves were born on the grassland, lived there, fought there, and died there. They left the grassland exactly as they found it.

Every month, or at least once every season, a grasslander was given a sky burial to send his soul to Tengger. Chen lifted his hands to the blue sky and said a silent wish that all those souls were at peace.

Summer days are dreadfully long on the Mongolian grassland. The sky is light from three in the morning till nine at night. The sheep are not taken out until eight or nine o'clock, after the sun has burned off the frost. At night they are not returned to their pens until after dark, since the period between sunset and darkness is when they eat the most ravenously and fatten up. Tending sheep in the summer takes nearly twice the time as it does in the winter. Summer is the shepherds' least favorite season of the year. After breakfast, they go hungry until nine o'clock at night; all day long they bake under the sun, fight off the urge to sleep, go thirsty and hungry, and are bored stiff. At the height of summer, the mosquitoes turn the grassland into a torture chamber. Compared to the draining days of summer, the long cold winters are happy times.

Before being exposed to the hordes of mosquitoes, Chen had believed that hunger and thirst took the greatest toll on people. Herdsmen, on the other hand, tolerated hunger and thirst well, even though most of them were bothered by stomach ailments. During their first summer, the students took dry food along when they let the sheep out to graze, but eventually they followed the local custom of going without a midday meal.

While Chen was standing there in the tall grass, Dorji rode up and asked how he'd like some roast marmot. Chen salivated over the prospect. "They're all over the place," Dorji said. "That mountain ridge to the west is pockmarked with marmot holes. Let's survey the place today, then lay out a dozen traps tomorrow. We'll catch some by noon, and we can have roast marmot for lunch. That'll take care of our hunger and keep us from napping in the middle of the day." Dorji looked out at the two flocks of sheep, his and Chen's, and saw that none of the animals were up and grazing. So the two men rode over to the mountain ridge, where they hid behind some limestone boulders, in sight of the sheep behind them and the marmot holes in front. They took out their telescopes. The ridge was still, the dozens of marmot holes seemingly empty; sunlight glistened on the bits of mineral ore in the limestone.

Before long, they heard the chirps and squeaks of marmots, exploratory noises made by animals before emerging from their holes. If they detected no responses, they'd pop up in large numbers. There were no responses, so out they came, dozens of them, big and small, filling the air with chirps. From every hole, it seemed, a female emerged to survey the area, and when they saw there were no predators nearby, they chirped a slow, rhythmic all-clear signal, following which hordes of young animals shot out of the holes and began eating clumps of grass as far as thirty or forty feet from the safety of their holes. With vultures circling high above in the deep blue sky, the females kept a careful watch. If their winged natural enemies descended, the marmot mothers chirped a frantic warning, which sent the young animals scurrying back to the safety of their holes, where they waited for the danger to pass.

When Chen moved slightly, Dorji laid his hand on his back to have him stay still. "Look at that hole over there," he whispered. "There's a wolf. He's looking forward to a meal of marmot, just like us." Chen immediately grew alert and turned his head to look. A large male marmot was standing in front of its hole, front legs folded in front of its chest as it scanned the area, obviously reluctant to leave the hole to graze on the grass. Male and female marmots live separately. The females live in one hole with their offspring; the males live alone in another. A large clump of tall grass lay not far below this particular male's hole, and as it swayed in gentle breezes, the tops of brown rocks peeked through. The shifting shadows made it difficult to discern anything farther below.

"I don't see a wolf," Chen said. "Nothing but a few rocks."

"There's a wolf hidden beside one of those rocks, and I'll bet it's been there for a long time."

Straining to look closer, Chen thought he could make out the partial figure of a wolf. "You've got better eyes than me," he said. "I didn't spot it."

"If you don't know how wolves hunt marmots," Dorji explained, "you'd never spot one like this. They have to stay downwind of their prey, hidden in a clump of grass below a marmot hole. Catching one of those things is hard, even for a wolf, so they concentrate on big males. See that big one standing there? Damn near as big as a newborn lamb. It's enough for one wolf meal. If it's a wolf you're looking for, head for the nearest male marmot hole, then scan the tall grass downwind from it."

"Well, I learned another trick today," Chen declared happily. "But when will the marmot decide to go down and eat? I want to see how the wolf catches it. There are holes everywhere, and the minute the wolf shows itself, the marmots will scramble down the nearest one."

Dorji said, "It takes a smart wolf to catch a marmot. They have a trick to keep marmots from getting into a hole. Let's see how this one does."

They looked downhill, where their sheep were still lying in the grass, so they decided to be patient and see what happened. "Too bad we didn't bring a dog," Dorji said. "If we had, we could wait till the wolf got this one, then turn the dog loose and follow it on horseback. The marmot would become a meal—but ours, not the wolf's."

"Why don't we chase it anyway?" Chen said. "We might catch it."

"No way," Dorji said. "Just look. The wolf is on the mountain ridge, so it would be heading downhill, and we'd be riding uphill. And once the wolf made it over the ridge, you'd never see it again. Besides, with all those marmot holes, our horses can't run fast." Chen gave up on the idea.

"No, we'll lay some traps tomorrow," Dorji said. "I just brought you here today to look around. Wolves will only be catching marmots for another couple of weeks. Once the rains come and the mosquitoes emerge, they no longer go after them. Why? Because they're afraid of the mosquitoes, who attack their noses, eyes, and ears, making them jump into the air and give themselves away, which sends the marmots scurrying back into their holes. That's when the wolves give up on marmots and turn their attention to our sheep and horses. That's bad news for us and our livestock."

The big male watched the other marmots gorging themselves on the grass until it couldn't stand it any longer and left the safety of its hole for the tempting grass several feet away. After a few tentative bites, it ran back to its hole and chirped loudly. "See how it won't eat the grass around its hole? They save that as a sort of barrier. Things out here are never easy," Dorji said. "One careless moment is all it takes to lose your life."

Chen watched the wolf with growing anxiety. It didn't seem to have a clear view of the marmot from its hiding place, and would have to rely on sound to determine the location and movements of its prey. It pressed itself down so flat that it had nearly burrowed into the ground.

After four or five lightning trips to the grass and back, the marmot relaxed, sensing there was no danger, and ran over to a spot where the grass was at its most lush. Five or six minutes passed; then, all of a sudden, the wolf stood up. What surprised Chen was that instead of rushing over to pounce on the marmot, the wolf pawed at some loose rocks, sending several of them rolling downhill, making noise as they built up speed and grew in number. Chen watched as the marmot, now twenty feet or more from its hole, looked up in fright, turned, and raced back toward safety. But the wolf streaked toward the marmot hole, reaching it at about the same time as its inhabitant. Before the marmot could scurry down the hole, the wolf had it by the scruff of its neck. It was quickly flung to the ground, where the wolf sank its teeth into its neck. Then the wolf picked it up and ran off, quickly crossing the ridge. The whole maneuver had taken less than thirty seconds.

All the other marmots had vanished. The two men sat up. Images of the wolf catching its prey replayed in Chen's head. He was speechless. The wisdom of the wolf was unfathomable. An almost magical beast.

* * *

The sunlight had turned from white to yellow, and the sheep were once again grazing, having moved several hundred feet to the west. Chen and Dorji talked for a few minutes before deciding to return to their flocks, turn them around, and head back to camp. But just as they were about to climb into the saddle, Chen noticed some stirring among his sheep. Quickly taking out his telescope, he trained it on the left edge of the flock, where he spotted a large wolf slipping out of the bed of flowers and pouncing on one of his sheep, pinning it to the ground. Chen's face turned white from fright, and he was about to scream when Dorji stopped him. He swallowed the scream and watched as the wolf tore flesh from one of the live sheep's rear legs. As one of the lower animals, sheep won't make a sound when they see blood. This one struggled, pawing the ground with its front legs, but, unlike a goat, made no sound, no plea for help.

"We're too far away to save the sheep," Dorji said. "Let the wolf eat. When it's gorged itself till it can't run, we'll get it. All right, you damned wolf," he continued calmly, "you think you can take one of our sheep right under our eyes. Well, we'll see about that!" They moved over behind a big rock so as not to give themselves away too early.

Obviously, they'd encountered a bold and very hungry wolf. Seeing that the flock had been unattended for a long time, it had moved through the tall grass and wildflowers up next to it, then pounced and immediately started eating the fat sheep. It saw the men and horses up on the ridge, but didn't run away. Keeping one eye on the men and calculating how far away they were, it ate as fast and as much as it could. No wonder the cub back at camp turns mealtime into a battle, Chen was thinking. Out on the grassland, time is food, and a wolf given to leisurely eating will starve to death.

Chen had heard shepherds tell stories about trading sheep for wolves, and this encounter appeared to be shaping up as one of those strategic battles. Trading a sheep for a mature wolf was a bargain. A single adult wolf will eat ten or more sheep every year, not to mention the occasional horse or colt. A shepherd who trades a single sheep for a wolf will be neither criticized nor punished by the brigade; he will be commended. What worried Chen was the possibility of losing a sheep without bringing in a wolf. That would be considered a serious loss. He stared at the wolf through his glass, watching as an entire leg—wool, skin, and all—wound up in the wolf's stomach in half a minute or less. That sheep was doomed, and Chen was hoping the wolf would eat the whole animal. He and Dorji moved slowly toward their horses. They removed the fetters, clutched the reins tightly, and waited with their hearts in their throats.

Sheep are truly stupid animals. When the wolf knocked the unfortunate sheep to the ground, the other sheep scattered in fright. But the entire flock soon calmed down, and there were even a few animals that timidly drew closer to watch the wolf eat a member of their flock. As they looked on, more joined them, until at least a hundred sheep had virtually penned the wolf and its bloody victim in; they pushed and shoved and craned their necks to get a better look. Their expressions seemed to say, "Well, the wolf is eating you and not me!" Either that or, "You're dying so I can live." Their fear was measured by a sense of gloating. None made a move to stop the wolf.

Startled by the scene, Chen was reminded of the writer Lu Xun, who had written about a crowd of dull-witted Chinese looking on as a Japanese swordsman was about to lop off the head of a Chinese prisoner. What was the difference between that and this? No wonder the nomads see the Han Chinese as sheep. A wolf eating a sheep may be abhorrent, but far more loathsome were cowardly people who acted like sheep.

Dorji was in a quandary. Known throughout the brigade as a first-rate hunter, he was now in the unenviable position of having abandoned his flock to take a Beijing student marmot hunting, in the process losing a nice fat sheep to a lone wolf in broad daylight. With the female sheep gone, her lamb would not be able to suckle and grow big and fat, dooming it for the coming winter. In a brigade devoted to raising livestock, this counts as negligence, for which Chen was sure to be criticized and Dorji implicated. Worst of all, why had this happened to the two individuals who were raising wolf cubs back at camp? Someone who doesn't care about sheep should not be a shepherd, and wolves will seek revenge against anyone who raises one of their own. Every member of the brigade who opposed the idea of taking a wolf out of the wild would jump on the incident as proof that they were right. Chen's fears mounted.

Dorji kept his glass trained on the wolf, gradually gaining confidence in what they were to do. "I'll take responsibility for the loss of the sheep," he said. "But the pelt will be mine. Once I hand that over to Bao Shungui, you and I will come off looking good."

The wolf sped up the pace of its eating, never taking its eyes off of the men watching it. Tearing off hunks of flesh and swallowing them whole, it seemed almost crazed. "Even the smartest wolf will do stupid things when it's hungry," Dorji said. "Doesn't it realize that pretty soon it won't be able to run away? This is definitely not one of the smart wolves, and one that's no good at catching marmots. It probably hasn't eaten for days."

Chen saw that the wolf had already consumed half a sheep; its belly was round and taut. "What are we waiting for?" he asked.

"Take it easy," Dorji replied. "Let's wait a little longer. But then we have to move fast. We'll come in from the south and drive the wolf in the opposite direction, since that's where the other shepherds are. They can help us run it down."

Dorji watched a while longer, then cried, "Mount up!" Leaping into their saddles, they rode down the slope south of the flock. The wolf had already planned its escape route, and the instant it saw the men riding toward him, it bit off and swallowed a couple more bites, abandoned what was left of the now dead sheep, turned, and headed north. But it hadn't gone far when it staggered, realizing it had miscalculated badly. It skidded to a halt, lowered its head, and hunkered down.

"Uh-oh, that's bad!" Dorji shouted. "It's bringing up what it just ate."

Chen watched as the wolf arched its back and vomited great heaps of sheep flesh. This was their chance. They spurred their horses on, frantically shortening the distance between them and the regurgitating wolf.

Chen was aware that wolves will bring up food for their young, but this surprised him: a wolf vomiting food that would slow it down. It may have been a starving wolf, but it was not a stupid one, and if it succeeded in emptying its stomach, the men's potential problem would become a real one. Chen whipped his horse on, but Dorji was outdistancing him, all the while shouting to scare the wolf and alert the shepherds on the mountain ahead. When he was dangerously close, the animal stopped vomiting and ran for its life, gaining top speed in no time. When Chen rode up to where the wolf had stopped, he saw a large pile of bloody meat, and the sight momentarily unnerved him; but then he whipped his horse mercilessly and rejoined the chase.

The wolf must have stopped vomiting before its stomach was empty, and what remained had not had time to turn to energy. It was fast, but slower than usual, and Dorji had no trouble keeping up with it. Seeing that it could not shake its pursuer, the wolf veered off in the direction of a steep hill, a trick all grassland wolves resorted to when their lives were in imminent danger. Then, out of nowhere, the shepherd Sanjai appeared at the crest of the hill; raising his lasso pole, he cut off the wolf's escape route, making it shudder in fear. That lasted only an instant before it abruptly changed course and headed straight for a flock of sheep that was grazing nearby. The wolf, Chen was surprised to realize, was going to create havoc in the flock, putting the sheep between it and the riders, who would have to rein in their horses. It would then break out on the other side and get away.

But the animal's momentary hesitation had given Dorji a chance to gallop up next to it and Sanjai enough time to block its way. As it turned to change course a second time, Dorji leaned forward in the saddle, thrust out his lasso pole, shook the rope to form a noose, and neatly looped it around the wolf's neck, immediately pulling it tight before the wolf had a chance to pull its neck back into its shoulders. With his rope looped tightly around the animal's throat, behind its ears, Dorji spun his horse around and began dragging it behind him.

The fight went out of the wolf as its weight further tightened the noose. Its tongue lolled from its open mouth as it struggled to breathe, but bloody froth was already seeping out. Dorji began dragging it uphill, increasing the stranglehold. Chen rode up and watched as the death spasms began. He breathed a sigh of relief. Their screwup wasn't going to get them in hot water after all. He was relieved, yes, but not excited, for he was witness to the violent death of a wolf that had been alive and active only moments before. The grassland is a cruel place, exacting terrible costs from all who struggle to survive in its core. The slow, the clumsy, and the dull are ruthlessly eliminated. A heavy sorrow filled Chen's heart. The dying wolf had been possessed with intelligence and strength. In the world of humans, would anyone that smart and that courageous have been eliminated?

The wolf had gone limp by the time Dorji was halfway up the hill, but it was still breathing and still losing blood. Dorji jumped to the ground, jerking the pole with both hands so the wolf could not get to its feet. When he'd pulled it up to where he stood, he grasped his herding club and crushed the wolf's head with it. Then he took out his Mongol dagger and buried it in the animal's chest. The wolf was dead by the time Chen got down off his horse. After kicking the animal a couple of times and seeing no reaction, Dorji mopped his sweaty forehead, sat down, and smoked a cigarette.

Sanjai rode up and looked down at the dead wolf. "Good job," he said, and then went out to round up Dorji's sheep. Chen rode over to his flock to do the same and get them headed back to camp. He then went back up the hill to watch Dorji skin the wolf. In the heat of summer, there is always a concern that a pelt will begin to stink, so instead of skinning the animal with the legs intact, the grasslanders skin the wolf like they do a sheep, producing a flat pelt. By the time Chen reached him, Dorji had already laid the pelt out on the ground to dry in the sun.

"That's the first time I've seen a wolf killed with a lasso pole," Chen remarked. "How were you so confident?"

With a bit of a gloating laugh, Dorji said, "I saw right away that this wasn't a very smart wolf. A really clever one would have shaken off the noose as soon as it landed by drawing its neck in."

"You've got sharp eyes," Chen complimented him. "I'm no match for you, and couldn't be if I spent the next five years trying. Then there's my horse. Next year I'm going to get some good stud horses. You can't get by out here without a good horse."

"Have Batu give you one of his," Dorji said. "He's your big brother; he'll do it."

Suddenly, Chen was reminded of the wolf cub he'd given Dorji. "There's been so much going on lately," he said, "I haven't had a chance to ask about your cub."

"Didn't they tell you?" Dorji shook his head. "What a shame. I killed it a couple of days ago."

"What?" Chen blurted out, suddenly heartsick. "You killed it? Why? What happened?"

"I should have chained it up, like you did," he said. "My cub was smaller than yours, and not as wild, so I kept it in a pen with some puppies. After a month or so, it had gotten used to being around dogs, and everybody treated it like just another dog. But it soon outgrew the puppies, and got more and more like a wolfhound. Everyone favored him, especially my four-year-old son. But a couple of days ago, while they were playing, out of the blue he attacked my son, taking a bloody bite out of his belly. It scared the hell out of the boy, who screamed and bawled. Unlike a dog's, a wolf's fangs are lethal, and I was so startled I clubbed it to death. Then I rushed my son over to see the brigade's barefoot doctor, Peng, who gave him a couple of shots. Fortunately, that was the end of it, except that my son's belly is still swollen."

Chen felt a sense of panic coming over him. "Don't let it go at that," he said anxiously. "You need to give him another shot, and soon. If it's rabies, a series of injections will take care of it."

"The herdsmen all know you need to get injections if you're bitten by a dog," Dorji said. "With a wolf, it's even more important. Dogs and wolves are different, and the locals have been saying I shouldn't try to raise a wolf. Well, it looks like they were right. You can't take the wildness out of them, and sooner or later there'll be trouble. I advise you to give it up. That cub of yours is bigger and wilder, and has an even more lethal bite. It could kill you with its teeth alone, and chaining it doesn't guarantee safety."

Chen, bothered by a nagging fear, thought for a moment, then said, "I'll be careful. I've raised it this far. It hasn't been easy, but I can't give up now. Even Gao Jianzhong, who hated it at first, has taken to it. He plays with it every day."

The sheep had wandered off, so Dorji rolled up the wolf pelt and tied it to his saddle. Then he mounted up and began driving his flock back to camp.

Chen was thinking about his cub as he walked up to the half-eaten sheep. He took out his knife to slice off a piece where the wolf had been eating and then fished out the intestines; he left the heart and lungs. After tying the sheep by its head to the saddle to take home to feed the dogs and the cub, he climbed onto his horse and headed slowly home, weighed down with anxiety.

The next day, the story of how Dorji had traded a sheep for a wolf spread through the brigade. After Bao Shungui received the wolf pelt, he couldn't praise Dorji enough; he circulated a commendation throughout the brigade and rewarded him with thirty bullets. A few days later, a young shepherd from Group Three who had decided to use his sheep as bait, left his flock alone, hoping to swap a sheep for a wolf. But he encountered a wily old wolf that ate only one and a half legs of the sheep, enough to be reasonably full, but not enough to influence its ability to run; in fact, the wolf ran faster than usual and was quickly out of sight. Bilgee gave the shepherd a tongue-lashing in front of the brigade and punished him by not letting his family kill a sheep for food for a month.

22

Once again, Chen Zhen was assigned the night shift for tending the sheep. With Erlang along to keep guard, he was free to stay in the yurt to read and to write in his journal. He moved his squat table up next to the door, then set two books on edge between the lamp and his sleeping comrades so as not to waken them. The grassland was perfectly still; no wolves were baying that night, and none of the three watchdogs was barking, though they were awake and alert. He left the yurt only once, to take a turn around the flock with his flashlight, and the sight of Erlang lying awake and alert on the northwestern edge put him at ease. He rubbed the big dog's head to express his appreciation. Back in the yurt, he read some more to keep from dozing off. Finally, in the early-morning hours, he fell asleep. When he woke the next morning, he went out to feed the wolf cub.

After coming to the new grazing land, the cub awoke every day at the crack of dawn and crouched down, as if ready to pounce on unsuspecting prey, staring at the door of the yurt and glaring at his food bowl. To him, the bowl was his prey, and, like an adult wolf, he waited patiently for the right moment to attack it. The moment it came close enough, he pounced, and the meat he ate from it was the flesh of his prey, not something supplied by humans. That was how the young wolf preserved his wolfish independence. Chen helped by feigning fear of the cub and backing off; still, he was seldom able to mask his delight.

Before the summer rains come, the Mongolian plateau is visited by dry hot air for a time, but the heat this year seemed worse than usual. As far as Chen was concerned, the Mongolian sun not only rose earlier than it did in China proper but seemed lower in the sky. It was as hot at ten in the morning as it was at noon down south; the sun baked the grass around their yurt until each blade was nothing but a hollow green needle. The mosquito scourge hadn't yet begun, but maggot-born bigheaded flies swarmed across the land and launched assaults on men and their livestock. They focused on the eyes or the nose, on chapped corners of mouths, or on bloody strips of raw lamb hanging inside yurts. Men, dogs, and wolves waved arms and swished tails in an unending and futile attempt to bear up under the assault. Yellow was expert at lightning-quick grabs of flies in his mouth, which he chewed up and spat out, and it never took long for the floor around him to be littered with the bodies of flies, like the empty husks of melon seeds.

The temperature continued its inexorable rise above the steaming ground, so hot that the basin was like a gargantuan iron cook pot and the grass took on the appearance of dry tea leaves. The dogs lay sprawled in the narrow crescent-shaped shadow north of the yurt, mouths open and tongues lolling as they panted to cool down, their bellies rising and falling rapidly. Chen noticed that Erlang wasn't among them, so he called his name. He didn't come, and Chen wondered where he'd gotten off to. Maybe to the river, where it was cooler.

Erlang was a reliable watchdog when Chen had the night shift, and members of the brigade no longer called him a wild dog. But come sunrise, when the dog was off duty, Chen's control over him ended, and he wandered away. Yellow and Yir, on the other hand, stayed close to home during the day, still watchful, still loyal.

The weather was particularly hard on the cub, since its chain was too hot to touch and there were no shady spots where he could get out of the sun for a while. He just sweltered. The grass in his pen had succumbed to his trampling; the ground was now more like desert than grassland, or like a platter on a lit stove, filled with hot water and sand. The cub himself was like a chestnut that had been roasted until it was burned to a crisp and about to pop. The pathetic creature was a captive in an overheated prison.

The instant the gate swung open, the cub rose up on his hind legs, nearly choking on the chain collar. He kicked the air with his front paws, and anyone watching would have known that what he wanted was neither shade nor water but food. Food is the core of a wolf's existence, and Chen could see that his appetite was not affected by the extreme heat. He kept kicking the air as a sign for Chen to put his food bowl down in the pen. Once he had his "prey" in his grasp, he snarled and drove Chen out of the pen.

Chen was growing anxious; the herdsmen had told him that, once the summer months arrived, their customary fare was milk products, seldom supplemented by meat. Tea in the morning and dinner in the evening, but without the handfuls of meat he'd gotten used to. There were noodles, millet, fried rice, and a variety of milk dishes: sour curds, yogurt, butter, and whey. The herdsmen preferred to eat fresh dairy products in the summer, something the Beijing students did not enjoy. To begin with, they weren't used to substituting dairy products for meat, but, more important, none of them liked the idea of getting up at three or four in the morning to milk cows for four or five hours, followed by churning until the milk curdled. Even less inviting was waiting till the cows came back at five or six in the evening, then milking them for three or four hours, followed by all the cooking, pressing, chopping, and drying that was required. They'd rather eat boiled and steamed millet, vegetarian noodles, buns, or dumplings than curds. So while the local herdsmen ate their curds in the summer, the students picked wild vegetables—onions, garlic, leeks, daylilies, ash greens, and dandelions, plus something the northeastern Mongols called *halagai,* a wild plant whose thin, broad, lip-numbing leaves had a spicy taste. The change of diet during the summer months profoundly affected Chen and his cub.

Few sheep were slaughtered in the summer, since there was no way to keep the meat from spoiling. Thanks to the heat and the flies, it turned maggoty in less than two days, so the locals cut it into strips and coated it with flour to keep the flies from laying eggs in it. The strips were hung in the coolest corner of a yurt to dry. A few were then added to noodles to give them a meaty taste. Sometimes, when the sky was overcast for several days, the meat would turn moldy and go bad. So summer was the season when the sheep fattened up. It was important for them to add muscle in the summer and fat in the fall. If they didn't, the meat was thin, with little grease and no taste; the herdsmen wouldn't eat it. Summertime was also when the sheep were sheared; their skins are worth little and can only be made into thin jackets worn in the spring or the fall.

Slaughtering a sheep in the summer is wasteful, Bilgee once told Chen.

Government policy those days, when cooking oil was scarce and meat was rationed, dictated that the Olonbulag herdsmen were to treat every sheep among their vast flocks as precious and not kill and eat them in large numbers. People, even the meat-loving students, could survive the meat ban. But for the wolf cub, it was a different matter altogether.

One morning, Chen filled the cub's bowl with half a strip of spoiled meat to take the edge off his hunger. Then he carried the empty bowl back to the yurt to figure out what to do next. As he ate his breakfast of pickled leeks and soupy lamb noodles, he picked out the few pieces of dried lamb and put them into the cub's bowl. Unlike the dogs, the cub would not eat porridge or rice if it had no meaty flavor; if he was given a bowl of food with no meat or bones, he'd anxiously and angrily gnaw on his chain.

So after finishing his breakfast, Chen dumped the remainder into the wolf's bowl and stirred it to bring bits of meat from the bottom to the top, where the cub could see it. He sniffed the mixture; he could barely smell meat, so he decided to pour in some of the sheep oil from the lamp. The congealed oil in the ceramic jug was turning soft and starting to go bad in the heat; but since wolves prefer rotting meat, the cub was sure to appreciate the sheep oil.

Chen scooped out a big ladleful of oil and added it to the bowl. It stirred up into a nice oily mixture. This time he was satisfied with the smell; the cub was in for a tasty meal. He added some more millet but could not give up more of his oil.

The dogs, forced to go without meat all summer and

hungry most of the time, were waiting for him when he opened the door. So he fed them first, pausing until they'd licked their bowls clean before going out to the shaded area behind the yurt with the cub's food. "Little Wolf, Little Wolf," he called out as he always did. "Time to eat." By the time Chen reached the pen, the cub's eyes were red with anticipation; he was jumping around so excitedly he nearly choked himself. Chen laid down the bowl and stepped back to watch him eat. The cub appeared to be satisfied.

Every day at mealtime he called out to the cub, hoping that would spark a bit of gratitude. He often found himself thinking that when the day came that he married and started a family, he'd probably not be as fond of his own children as he was of the young wolf. Since he had taken it upon himself to raise the cub, his mind was often tormented by mythlike dreams and fantasies. He'd read a Soviet story in elementary school about a hunter who rescued an injured wolf and returned it to the forest after nursing it back to health. One day later, the hunter opened the door of his shack and found seven dead rabbits in the snow, and several sets of wolf tracks... It was the first story he'd read about friendships forged between wolves and humans, and the first to show a different side of wolves from all the books he'd read and movies he'd seen. The books were mostly of the "Little Red Riding Hood" variety or of wolves eating little lambs, or cruel and scary stories of wolves eating the hearts and livers of small children. The Soviet story was one he had never forgotten. He often dreamed that he was the hunter tramping through the forest to enjoy life with his wolf friends, wrestling and riding them across the snow...

Finally, the cub had licked the bowl clean. He had

grown to three feet in length, and now that he had finished eating, he looked bigger and more intimidating than ever. He was already half again as big as the puppies he'd grown up with. After leaving the bowl outside the gate, Chen walked back and sat down to spend some time with the cub. He held him in his arms awhile, then turned him over and laid him on his lap so he could rub his belly. When dogs and wolves fight, the adversary's belly is a prime target. If one of them can get its fangs or claws into the other's belly, the wounded animal is doomed. That is why neither dogs nor wolves will expose their bellies to anyone they do not trust absolutely, animal or human. Though Dorji's little wolf died because it had bitten Dorji's son, Chen offered up his fingers for his cub to lick and nibble on while he was holding it. He was confident the cub would not bite him, and gnawing on one of Chen's fingers was much the same as biting one of its littermates, always stopping short of breaking the skin. Since the cub was willing to lie on his back and let Chen rub his belly, why shouldn't he put his fingers in the cub's mouth? They trusted each other.

It was nearly noon, and the sun had wilted the hollow green needles. Time for the cub to suffer again. His mouth hung slack and he panted nonstop, drops of liquid falling to the ground from his lolling tongue. Chen had opened the felt covering the yurt all the way to the top. Mongol yurts are open to the air on eight sides, like a pavilion or an oversized birdcage. That way he could keep an eye on the cub from inside the yurt, where he'd gone to read.

Unable to think of anything that might help the cub cool off a bit, Chen settled for observing the young animal to determine his level of tolerance for heat. The breezes entering his yurt were getting hotter; cows out in the basin had stopped grazing and were lying in the mud of the riverbank, while most of the sheep were sleeping in a mountain pass to catch the relatively cool winds. Three-sided white tents were going up on the mountaintop, as shepherds fended off the unbearable heat by sticking their lasso poles into marmot holes, then draping their thin white deels over them and anchoring the edges with rocks. These makeshift tents kept them out of the harsh sunlight. Chen had tried that, and had found it effective in keeping cool. Two occupants shared the tents, one sleeping while the other kept watch over the flock.

But as he baked in the merciless heat, the cub suffered whether he lay down or remained standing. Waves of heat rose from the sandy ground, scalding his paws and making it impossible to keep all four paws on the ground at one time. He kept looking around for his puppy playmates, and when he saw one of them lying in the shade under a wagon, he strained at his chain in exasperation. Chen ran out of the yurt, convinced that if he didn't do something soon, the cub would be roasted like a chestnut. If the animal suffered heatstroke, the pasture vet would not lift a finger to save him.

So Chen scooped out a panful of water from the water wagon and laid it out for the cub, then watched as he thrust his head in and didn't stop drinking until there was none left. He then ran up and hid from the sun in Chen's shadow. Like a little orphan child, he stepped on Chen's feet to keep him from leaving. So Chen stood there until he felt the back of his neck prickle, and he knew that his skin would begin to crack if he didn't move. After walking out of the pen, he dumped half a bucketful of water onto the sandy ground, sending clouds of steam into the air. The cub, seeing that the ground temperature had fallen at that spot, ran over and lay down to rest. But the ground soon heated up, and the torment returned. Chen was out of options. He couldn't keep watering the ground, and even if he could, what would happen when it was time to go out and tend the flock?

Back inside the yurt, Chen didn't feel like reading; he could not shake the fear that the cub would get sick, or lose too much weight, maybe even die in the cruel summer heat. By chaining him, he realized, he was preserving the safety of people and their livestock, but not the life of the cub. If there were only an enclosure in which the cub could run free, he could at least find shelter at the base of a wall.

All Chen could do was keep an eye on his wolf and try to figure out something; nothing came to mind.

The wolf walked around and around, his brain apparently doing the same. The cub seemed to realize that the grassy ground outside the pen was cooler than the sandy ground inside. He turned and stepped on the grass with his hind legs; finding that it was, in fact, cooler, he lay down on the grass, leaving only his head and neck on the scalding sand inside the pen. With the chain pulled taut, he could finally stretch out and get some rest, part of his body no longer baked by the sun. Chen was so happy he could have kissed the young wolf; this manifestation of the cub's intelligence gave him a thread of hope. Now he knew what to do. As the temperature continued to climb, he'd make a new pen for the wolf, this time with grass, and each time the cub trampled it down and exposed the sand, he'd move him again. A wolf's power to survive was greater than that of humans. Even without a mother's guidance, a young wolf solves the problems it faces, in a pack or alone. With a sigh, Chen lay back against his bedroll and began to read.

A flurry of hoofbeats resounded on the road some sixty or seventy feet outside the yurt; assuming it was horse herders galloping by, Chen wasn't particularly curious. So he was caught by surprise when two horses left the road and headed for his yurt, then veered off toward the wolf pen, where the startled cub stood up on his hind legs and straightened out the chain. The rider in front looped his lasso pole noose over the cub's neck and jerked it back, lifting him off the ground. The force of the man's movement left no doubt that he wanted the wolf dead, expecting the pull of the chain to decapitate him. The cub had no sooner fallen back to the ground than the second man used his lasso pole as a whip, hitting him with such force that he rolled over. Meanwhile, the first man halted his horse, grabbed his herding club, and was about to dismount and kill the cub with his club when Chen let out a shriek, picked up his rolling pin, and ran out like a madman. Seeing the defiant look in Chen's eyes, the two men spun their horses around and rode off in a cloud of dust. Chen heard one of them shout, "Wolves killed our fine horses, and you think you can raise one of them! Well, sooner or later, I'm going to kill that wolf!"

Yellow and Yir ran after the men, barking ferociously, and both were struck by lasso poles as the men headed off to where the horse herds were grazing.

Chen could not see who the attackers were, but he assumed that one of them might have been the shepherd whom Bilgee had rebuked and the other a member of the horse herders' Unit Four. They clearly had come with murderous intentions, and Chen was witness to the fearful blitzkrieg tactics of Mongol horsemen.

He ran over to where the wolf lay, his tail between his legs, nearly frightened to death. His legs were so wobbly he couldn't stand, and when he spotted Chen, he tumbled into his arms like a chick running for the mother hen after escaping the clutches of a cat. Chen, who was also trembling, held him tight, man and wolf a chorus of shaking. He anxiously felt the cub's neck and was relieved to see that it was still intact, though some of the fur had been pulled off by the hemp noose and a bloody gouge circled his neck. The cub's heart was racing. Chen did what he could to calm the young wolf down; it took some time, but eventually they both stopped quaking. Chen then went back to the yurt, where he took down another strip of dried lamb. That had a soothing effect on the cub. Picking him up again, Chen held him in his lap and pressed his face up against the cub's face while he rubbed his chest until his heartbeat was back to normal. But the cub's fears lingered, and he wouldn't take his eyes off Chen. Suddenly he licked Chen on the chin; it was the second time the wolf had done so but the first time that the gesture was an expression of gratitude. As Chen saw it, the story of a rescued wolf showing its gratitude with the gift of seven rabbits had not necessarily stemmed from someone's imagination.

The thing Chen had feared the most had finally occurred, rekindling his concern. His decision to raise a wolf had offended most of the herdsmen, and the coolness of their attitude toward him was palpable. Even Bilgee had nearly stopped coming to visit. In the eyes of the herdsmen, it seemed, there was little difference between him and Bao Shungui and his laborers, all outsiders who had no respect for grassland customs. The wolf is their spiritual totem, but a physical enemy. Raising one like a pet is something a herdsman could not condone; it was a blasphemy in the spiritual sense and consorting with the enemy in the physical realm. He had broken one of the grassland's prohibitions, violated a cultural taboo—of that there was no doubt. He was no longer sure if he could continue to protect the cub or even if he ought to keep raising it. Sincere in his desire to record and investigate the secrets and value of the "wolf totem" as the "soul of the grassland," he saw this as a once-in-a-lifetime opportunity; he needed to be unyielding, to grit his teeth and carry on. So he went looking for Erlang. When that dog was watching over things, no one but herdsmen in Chen's unit would dare to come near without being invited. Erlang was capable of driving away an unfamiliar rider by nipping at the man's horse and sending it off in a panic. The two attackers must have seen that Erlang was not around before making their move.

The sun still had not reached the peak of its daily onslaught, but it seemed that all the heat of the basin had gathered in the wolf pen. The cub's torso was no longer being baked unbearably, but his head and neck remained atop the sand; the injuries from the foiled attack made it impossible for him to lie down for any length of time, so he was forced to walk around inside the pen until, after several revolutions, he lay back down on the grass.

No longer in the mood to read, Chen busied himself with household chores. He picked some leeks, broke open several duck eggs, rolled out some dough, added filling, and then fried flat bread, all of which kept him occupied for half an hour. When he looked out at the pen, he was shocked to see the cub digging a hole in the sand, his tail and hindquarters sticking up in the air. Sand flew up from the ground like a fireworks display. Chen wiped his hands and ran outside, where he crouched down to see what the cub was doing.

The cub was digging frenetically on the southern edge of the pen, and by the time Chen arrived, half of his body was in the ground. Sand kept coming up through his legs, dispersed by a briskly wagging tail. He backed out of the hole, covered with dirt, and when he spotted Chen, there was a wild, intense look in his eyes, as if he'd been digging for buried treasure.

What was he up to? He wasn't trying to uproot the post, was he? No, that couldn't be it; the hole wasn't lined up with the post, which was, after all, buried too deeply for the cub to dig under. No, he was digging with his back to the post and toward, not away from, the direction of the sun's movement. Then it hit him! Chen knew exactly what the wolf was doing.

The cub went back to work, digging out more and more dirt, his mouth hanging open as he dug and dug for a while, then moved out the dirt. Lights flashed in his eyes, bright as the sun, and he had no time to take note of Chen, who watched as long as he could before calling out, "Slow down, Little Wolf, you might break off your claws." The cub looked over at Chen and squinted to form a smile, seemingly pleased with himself and what he was doing.

The sand dug out of the hole was moist and much cooler than the surface sand. It takes a resourceful wolf, Chen was thinking, to dig its way to safety, away from the sun, the heat, the people, and a variety of dangers. This has to be what the cub is thinking: a hole will be cool and dark, and as for direction, the opening faces north, the tunnel faces south, so the sunlight cannot bake its way into the hole. As the cub dug deeper, Chen noted, most of his body was protected against the lethal sun's rays.

The deeper he dug, the weaker the light; beginning to taste the pleasures of darkness, he was nearing his target depth. Wolves love darkness, for it contains coolness, safety, and contentment. From now on, he would no longer be vulnerable to intimidation and attacks from the much larger cows, horses, and humans. His digging grew more frantic and brought him such pleasure he couldn't close his mouth. Another twenty minutes passed, until nothing showed above the surface except the tip of his bushy tail; he had all but buried himself in the cool earth.

Amazed once again at the cub's extraordinary talent for survival and his native intelligence, Chen was reminded of the ditty "A dragon sires a dragon, a phoenix breeds a phoenix, but a rat's baby knows how to dig a hole." But a rat knows how to dig a hole because it has observed adult rats at work. This wolf was taken from his mother before his eyes were fully open; he had never seen an adult wolf dig a hole. Surely none of the dogs would have taught him this skill, since they're not by nature hole diggers. So who taught him? In particular, how had he learned the precision of location and direction? If he'd dug farther from the post, the chain would have kept him from digging as deeply as he needed. No, the hole was midway between the post and the edge of the pen, which allowed him to take half of the chain into the hole with him. Where had he learned that? It was not the sort of skill an adult wolf would have prepared him for, yet he'd worked it out perfectly.

Chen's hair stood on end. A three-month-old wolf cub had solved a problem that threatened his survival without having been taught how by anyone. Chen got down on his hands and knees to watch more closely, feeling not so much that he was raising a pet as facilitating the growth of a young teacher who commanded his respect and admiration. He was convinced that there would be more lessons from the wolf in the days to come.

The cub's tail was wagging excitedly. The deeper he dug, the cooler and happier he was, almost as if he could smell the mud of the dark place where he'd been born. Chen believed that the cub was not just digging a hole to be cool and safe but also trying to excavate pleasant memories of his earliest days and find his mother and his brothers and sisters. He tried to imagine the wolf's expression as he dug. It was probably a complex mixture of excitement, hope, luck, and a bit of sorrow . . .

Chen's eyes grew moist as he experienced powerful qualms of conscience. His feelings for the young wolf were growing stronger by the day, yet he could not deny that he was the one who had destroyed the cub's free and happy family. If not for him, all those young wolves would now be off fighting wars with their father and mother. While it was only a guess, Chen had a feeling that the current king of the wolves had sired this splendid cub. Maybe, under the tutelage of the wolf pack, with its vast battlefield experience, the cub would one day be the leader of that pack. Lamentably, his and their brilliant future had been forfeited by a Han Chinese from a faraway place.

The wolf had dug as far as the chain would allow, and Chen was not interested in making the chain any longer. The ground around the hole was loose sand with a thin layer of grassy roots, and in the off chance that a horse or cow stepped too close to the hole, the cub could easily be buried alive. The cub's enthusiasm for digging was brought to a sudden stop; he howled his displeasure and backed out of the hole to tug on the chain. The collar rubbed painfully against his injured neck, drawing a gasp. But he kept at it until he had exhausted his strength; he then sprawled on the excavated earth and panted. After a brief rest, he stuck his head down into the hole, and Chen wondered what he might be up to now.

As soon as the wolf cub had caught his breath, he scampered down into the hole, and in no time, more dirt came flying out, which Chen found almost stupefying. He bent down and looked into the hole, which the cub was now making wider, another sign of his intelligence.

Once construction on the cool, protective hole was completed, the wolf lay comfortably inside and ignored Chen's calls to come out. When Chen looked inside, the cub's eyes, open wide, a bloodcurdling green, gave him the appearance of a wolf in the wild. Obviously, he was enjoying the dark, the coolness, and the smell of earth, as if he'd returned to his first home alongside his mother and his littermates. He was at peace, having finally left the surface, where he was in a constant state of anxiety, surrounded by humans and their livestock; he had taken shelter in his own den and reentered his natural realm. Finally, he could sleep in safety to dream the dreams of wolves. Chen smoothed out the earth around the opening. With his cub in a safe place, he was once again confident of the young wolf's ability to survive.

Gao Jianzhong and Yang Ke returned at sunset, and when they spotted the wolf hole in front of their yurt, they were amazed. "After a day out there tending sheep,"

Yang said, "we were baked dry and dying of thirst, and I figured the wolf cub wouldn't make it through the summer. He's smarter than I thought."

"We're going to have to be more careful around him," Gao said, "be on our guard. We need to check out the chain, the post, and his collar every day. Who knows, he could make big trouble for us at a critical juncture. The herdsmen and the other students are just waiting to have the last laugh."

All three men saved a portion of their oily duck-egg-filled fried flat bread for the cub, and the moment Yang announced mealtime, the cub scrambled to the surface, picked up the food, and took it back down with him. It was a space that belonged to him and only him, off-limits to everyone else.

Erlang, out on his own all day, returned home, his belly taut, his mouth coated with grease. Obviously, he'd hunted down something out there. Yellow, Yir, and all the puppies, half crazed from not having tasted meat in a long time, ran up to Erlang to lick at the grease on his snout.

The cub came out of his cave as soon as he heard that Erlang was back. When the dog walked up to him, he too licked his greasy snout. Then Erlang noticed the hole in the ground and, apparently surprised and pleased, made several turns around it. With what sounded like a laugh, he squatted down at the opening and stuck his nose inside to sniff around. The cub leaped onto his surrogate father's back, where he jumped and rolled and somersaulted happily, the wound on his neck completely forgotten as his wild vitality burst forth.

At sunset, the hot air dissipated and cool breezes blew. Yang Ke put on a jacket and went out to see to his flock. Chen went along to help drive them home.

It was not a good idea to make the sheep move too fast after they'd eaten their fill; for the men, herding the flock into a circle at camp, where there were no fences, was like a casual stroll. During the summer, the sheep spent the nights in the vicinity of the yurts, not in pens, which made the summertime night watch especially hard and dangerous. Vigilance was essential, now more than ever, for a pack of wolves might detect the presence of the cub in camp and take that opportunity to wreak vengeance.

The cub's day began late at night. He'd run around in his pen, rattling the chain, frequently stopping to admire the fruits of his labor. Chen and Yang sat at the edge of the pen quietly enjoying the spectacle of the cub running around, his emerald eyes shining through the darkness.

Chen filled Yang in on that day's activities. "We've got to get our hands on some meat," he said. "The cub won't grow big and strong without it. Erlang hasn't been hanging around recently, which makes for a dangerous situation."

Yang said, "I had a meal of roasted marmot up in the mountains today, thanks to Dorji. If he manages to trap a lot of them, we can ask for one for the cub. The problem is, the shepherds and their flocks have raised hell out there, scaring the marmots and keeping them out of the traps."

Weighed down with anxieties, Chen said, "I'm worried that the wolf pack will come at night and create a bloodbath with our sheep. You can't find a more vicious female anywhere than a mother wolf. And the craving for revenge after the loss of her offspring has probably driven this one nearly insane. If she brought the pack for a nighttime raid on our flock and slaughtered a bunch of them, we'd be screwed."

Yang Ke sighed. "The herdsmen all say that the females will come sooner or later. This year on the Olonbulag we raided dozens of dens, and all those females are looking for a chance to avenge the loss of their young. The herdsmen are united in their desire to kill this cub, and the students in all the other units are against keeping it. I almost got into a fight with one of them today. They say that if anything happens, it'll make things hard for all the students. We're getting hammered from all sides. What do you say we quietly let it go and say it broke the chain and ran off? That would solve our problems." Yang picked up the young wolf and rubbed his head. "But I'd hate to give him up. I'm not this close to my own kid brother."

Chen clenched his teeth and said, "We Chinese are afraid of the wolf in front and the tiger behind. Since we went into the den and got this cub, we can't give up halfway. If we're going to raise him, let's do a good job of it."

"It's not the responsibility that bothers me," Yang quickly replied. "It's just that seeing him chained up all day like a prisoner is heartbreaking. Wolves demand freedom, but we keep him shackled the whole time. Doesn't that bother you? Me, I'm totally in the wolf totem camp, and I can see why Papa doesn't want you to raise the cub. He considers it blasphemy."

Chen was conflicted but could not show it, so he got in Yang's face and said, "Do you think I've never thought of setting him free? But not yet—there are still lots of things I need to know. If the cub is freed, that makes for one free wolf, but if one day there are no wolves on the grassland at all, what sort of freedom is that? You'd feel more remorse than anyone."

Yang thought about that for a moment, and decided to compromise, though with a bit of hesitation. "Okay, we'll keep at it, and I'll find a way to get my hands on some firecrackers. Wolves are like men on horseback: they hate firecrackers; the sound freaks them out. If we hear Erlang tangle with a wolf, I'll light off a string of crackers and you throw them into the middle of the pack."

"If you want to know the truth," Chen said, softening his tone, "you've got more wolf in you than I do. You're not afraid of taking a chance. Do you really plan to marry a Mongol girl? I hear they're tougher than wolves."

Yang Ke waved him off. "Don't tell anybody," he pleaded. "If you do and some Mongol girl gets the wild idea to come after me like a wolf, I won't be able to fight her off. First I have to get my own yurt."

23

With his back to the noisy, chaotic work site, Yang Ke gazed quietly at the swan lake. He didn't have the heart to look at the work going on behind him. Ever since Bao Shungui had killed and eaten the swan, he'd been troubled by dreams in which only blood came out of the lake, in which the surface of the water had turned from blue to red.

The three dozen or so laborers from the farming areas of Inner Mongolia had put down roots in the new grazing site, and with lightning speed had built sturdy adobe houses. These men had spent years engaged in full-time or seasonal work in pasturelands, but their grandparents had been herders and their parents had spent half their time farming and the other half herding in areas where Mongols lived alongside Han Chinese. Most of that grassland had turned into poor, sandy farmland in their time, and it could no longer provide for them. So, like migratory birds, they came out here. Fluent in Mongolian and Chinese, they were also conversant in both husbandry and farming. Compared to the Han Chinese in agrarian areas down south, they had considerably more intimate knowledge of the grassland; they knew how to utilize local materials and possessed the unique talent of building agricultural facilities. Every time Chen Zhen and Yang Ke led their sheep to drink at the lake, they stopped by the work site to chat. There was so much to do in a very short time that Bao Shungui had ordered that the temporary warehouse and medicinal dipping pool had to be completed before the rainy season. Apparently, they hadn't had time for the swans—not yet.

Yang had to admire the laborers' construction skills. Outer walls for a row of adobe houses appeared on what had been a vacant lot only the day before. And as he rode around for a closer look, he saw how they had transported bricks they'd made from clay dug out of the grassy alkali lakeshore. The bricks, with grass mixed in, were double the width and thickness of those used to build the Great Wall. The soil was grayish blue and very sticky, and when completely dry, the brick walls would be sturdier and stronger than rammed-earth walls. And the supply of bricks was virtually inexhaustible. When he kicked a finished adobe wall with his riding boot, it felt like reinforced concrete.

The bricks were laid with the grassy side down, showing the roots. After they were smoothed over, they were further flattened with a spade before the next layer was added. Divided into three shifts, the builders were able to complete the walls in only two days. Roofs and beams would be added once the walls were completely dry. The grassy marshland from which the bricks were taken was transformed into a muddy pool looking like a rice paddy before planting, forcing the livestock to skirt the area on their way to the lake.

The hillside stone quarry was also shaping up. On the Mongolian grassland hills, all one has to do to get weathered stone slabs and rocks is to clear away the thin layer of grass-covered sandy soil and pebbles. Stone and rocks can be pried off with a carrying pole. No need for a hammer, pickax, or explosives. Seven or eight laborers were moving stones from the pit, creating huge piles on the green hillside, like grave mounds.

Within days, two dozen more laborers were driven up on trucks, and construction work was at full speed. Gaudy, colorful bundles and luggage filled the trucks; the workers had brought their wives and children, even domestic geese from northeastern China, as if they were putting down roots on the grassland. Nearly heartbroken, Yang complained to Chen, "This pristine pasture will soon become a dirty little farming village, and the swan lake will become a pond for domestic geese."

With a frown, Chen replied, "The most important thing for an overpopulated race is to stay alive. There can't be any nutrients left over to feed aesthetic cells."

Yang learned that the laborers mostly came from Bao Shungui's hometown, and that he hoped to move half the village out to the grassland.

A few days later, Yang saw several laborers plowing the land near their houses. Four deep furrows formed a large vegetable garden, and within a few days, vegetables began to sprout: cabbages, radishes, turnips, cilantro, yellow melons, green onions, and garlic. Beijing students were already lining up to place orders for Chinese vegetables that were unavailable on the grassland.

Winding oxcart paths were straightened out by tractors used for carting lamb's wool. The tractors brought more family members to gather wool and apricot pits, to dig up medicinal roots, and to cut wild leeks. It was like opening a treasure box that attracted migrants from the farming areas; their northeastern-accented, Mongolian-influenced Chinese was heard deep in the grassland.

"The agrarian Han civilization assimilated the Manchus of the Qing dynasty," Chen said to Yang, "because the three northeastern provinces, the Manchus' ancestral land, had vast stretches of fertile black soil, which made it easy to adopt an agrarian lifestyle. That sort of assimilation isn't such a big problem. But if they attempt that here, we'll be looking at a true 'yellow peril.' "

Bao Shungui spent nearly all his time at the construction site. Already aware of the new grassland's potential for reclamation, he planned to move all four brigades over the following year, turning the place into the sole summer pasture and leaving the black soil in the original pasture for farming. That way they would have both grain and meat whenever they wanted, and he would be able to move all his friends and family to this treasure land, with its perfect feng shui, and set up a Bao Family Agri-pasture Land. Not surprisingly, the laborers readily accepted Bao's tough demands on the construction progress.

Bilgee and other old-time herders fought with the workers almost daily, asking them to fill up the furrows around their vegetable garden, since their horses often fell into them at night. The furrows were filled in, but a waist-high rammed-earth wall appeared before long. Uljii walked around with a clouded look, beginning to wish he'd never opened up the new grazing land.

Yang Ke turned his back to the clamorous, chaotic work site and concentrated on the scenery in front of him. He stood there for a long time admiring the swan lake, wanting to burn the sight into his memory. In recent days, his infatuation with the lake had grown stronger even than Chen Zhen's infatuation with wolves. He was worried that before the year was out, the opposite shore and grassy slopes would be crowded with livestock belonging to the other three brigades and, even worse, big ugly work sites created by the laborers.

If the reeds along the shore were cut down, the surviving swans would lose their green curtain of protection.

Yang rode toward the lake to see if there were any cygnets swimming there. It was the season for the females to have their young. Luckily, except for the few oxen, there was no livestock near the lake; the clean flowing water from the stream washed away the filth they deposited there while bringing spring water from a distant forest to turn the lake crystal clear. He hoped the birds would enjoy a spell of peace and quiet.

But a flock of waterbirds suddenly took flight, followed by startled cries and calls. Wild ducks and geese skimmed the surface heading southeast; the swans quickly rose into the air and headed for the marshland to the north. Yang took out his binoculars to search the area in the reed, worried that someone was out there hunting for swans.

The lake surface remained still for many minutes. Then into his lenses sailed a camouflaged raft of the type used during the war with Japan. The raft quietly glided out with its two occupants, both wearing camouflage caps made of green reeds, and capes of the same material draped over their shoulders. Stalks of cut reed were strewn across the raft, making it look like a floating cluster of reeds; without careful scrutiny it was hard to tell the reeds from the raft. It appeared that the men on the raft had made a kill. One man was removing his cap and cape while the other, using a spade as an oar, was rowing slowly toward the shore.

As the raft drew closer, Yang saw that it was actually constructed of six inner tubes and several door planks. He knew who the men were: Old Wang and his nephew, Ershun, who was moving the green reeds away to reveal a metal basin filled with bird eggs of various sizes, including two the size of small melons, their shells smooth and shiny, as if carved from fine jade. His heart fell. Swan eggs! He felt like crying out. What he feared but could not help seeing was the partially exposed swan under the reed cape, red stains on the bright white feathers. Yang's blood rushed to his head, and he could barely stop himself from running up and overturning the raft. But he knew he must control his anger. The swan was dead. He could do nothing about that, but he had to try to save the eggs.

As soon as the raft reached the shore, he ran up to it. "Who said you could kill swans and take their eggs? Come with me; you can explain yourself at brigade headquarters."

Short and stocky, with a black beard that was neither Mongolian nor Han, Old Wang was actually quite shrewd. He glared at Yang. "Director Bao told us to. What's your problem? With game like this to eat, the construction team can save you lots of cows and sheep."

"All Chinese know that ugly toads love to eat swans. Are you Chinese or aren't you?"

Old Wang sneered. "No Chinese would let a swan fly over to the Russians. How about you? Do you want to deliver the swans to them?"

Yang had learned that the migrants could argue with the best of them, and he didn't know what to say.

When the swan was dragged ashore, Yang saw an arrow in its chest. A large bow made of thick bamboo and a quiver of arrows lay in the raft. No wonder he hadn't heard gunfire. He realized that a bow and arrow could be a more lethal weapon than a firearm, since it would not startle other swans or waterbirds, making it easy to kill more of them. Reminding himself to take these people seriously, he decided that strategy rather than firmness was the only way to stop them.

Forcing himself to keep his anger in check, Yang changed his expression as he picked up the bow. "What a great bow. Really great, good and stiff. Is this what you used?"

Seeing that Yang had decided to be more reasonable, Old Wang boasted, "What else? I made it out of a bamboo wool-teasing bow I found in the brigade yurt. It's so powerful it could easily kill a man."

Yang took out an arrow. "Can I try it?"

Old Wang was sitting on a grassy knoll at the water's edge watching Ershun unload the dead swan. As he puffed on his pipe, he said, "Arrows take a lot of time to make, and I need to hold on to what I've got to hunt with. You can shoot one, but that's all."

So Yang Ke took a moment to get the feel of the bow, which was made of thick bamboo and was three fingers in width. The string, constructed of thin strips of cowhide twisted together, was the thickness of a pencil. The arrow had been carved out of willow branches, with wild-goose feathers on one end. Yang was surprised to see that the tip was made from a tin can; he could even make out the word *braised* on it. A triangle had been cut out of a can and wrapped around the willow branch, the tip of which had been whittled to a point; then the ends had been nailed together. Yang tested the tip with his finger; it was firm and very sharp. He checked the heft of the arrow; the shaft was light, but the tip was heavy, so it wouldn't sail when fired.

The bow was so stiff he had to strain to pull the string halfway. After fitting the arrow on the string, he took aim at a grassy knoll thirty or forty feet away and let go. The tip of the arrow was buried in the knoll.

Yang ran over and carefully extracted it from the dirt, then cleaned it off and saw that the tip was sharp as ever. At that moment he fantasized that he had been transported back in time to when the Mongol hordes were armed with bows and arrows.

Yang walked back to Old Wang. "How far away were you when you shot the swan?"

"No more than seven or eight paces."

"And the swan never saw you?"

Old Wang knocked the ashes out of his pipe and said, "Yesterday I went into the reeds and found the nest. This morning we got up very early, camouflaged ourselves with reeds, and rowed our way in. Fortunately, it was so misty the swan couldn't see us. The nest was as tall as us. The swan was inside sitting on her eggs, while the male was swimming around nearby for protection."

"Which one did you shoot, the male or the female?"

"We had to stay low in the raft, so we couldn't get a shot at the female inside the nest. We waited for the male, and when it glided up near us, I fired. Got it right in the heart. It flapped around weakly and died. When the female heard the racket outside the nest, she flew off, and that's when we got the eggs."

The ability of these migrants to survive and to wreak havoc is considerable, Yang was thinking. They have no guns, so they make a bow and arrow; they have no boat, so they make a raft. To top it off, they're good at concealing themselves; they hit their target on the first try. Supply them with guns and ammunition and a tractor, and there's no telling what they'd turn the grassland into. Their ancestors were herders, but after they were conquered and assimilated, they became enemies of the Mongolian grassland. For over a thousand years the Chinese have taken pride in their ability to assimilate other races. But they've only been able to assimilate people with a lower level of civilization, and they've never been willing to discuss the often catastrophic consequences of the assimilation. As Yang Ke was now witnessing those consequences, his heart bled.

After Ershun had cleaned off the raft, he sat down to rest. Yang couldn't get those two swan eggs out of his mind. Since the female was still alive, he felt compelled to take the eggs back to her nest, hoping that once the young birds were born, they'd fly off with their mother, all the way to Siberia.

With a broad if not natural smile, Yang said to Old Wang, "You're good at that. I hope someday you'll teach me some of your skills."

Old Wang smiled proudly. "I'm not good at much, but you won't find many better than me at hunting birds and marmots and wolves, or at setting traps, finding herbs, and digging up mushrooms. We used to have all those back home, but too many Chinese moved into the area. You students from Beijing have been given local household registration. How about speaking up for us outsiders when you get a chance? That way the local Mongols won't drive us away. They'll listen to you. If you'll do that, I'll teach you a thing or two. I guarantee you can earn a thousand a year with what I teach you."

"Well, then, I'll just call you my teacher from now on."

Old Wang edged close to Yang and said, "I hear that you and the herdsmen have lots of sheep oil. Think you could get some for us? There are forty or fifty of us involved in backbreaking labor, and we have to pay black-market prices for the grain to go along with the wild vegetables we pick, all without a drop of oil. But you use it in your lanterns. What a waste! How about selling us some at a good price."

Yang laughed. "No problem," he said. "We've got two vats of the stuff. Tell you what. I like the looks of those two swan eggs, so how about trading them for half a vat of oil?"

"They're yours!" Old Wang replied. "I'd just take them home and fry them, which is the same as eating five or six duck eggs. Go ahead, take them."

Yang quickly took off his coat and wrapped the eggs in it. "I'll bring the oil over tomorrow."

"I trust you," Old Wang said. "You Beijing students are as good as your word."

Yang exhaled loudly and said, "It's still early. Can I borrow your raft? I'd like to go see that nest. I find it hard to believe it could be as tall as you."

Old Wang glanced over at Yang's horse. "How's this?" he said. "I'll trade you my raft for your horse. I have to get this swan over to the kitchen, and it's almost as heavy as a sheep."

Yang stood up. "It's a deal... But hold on—tell me where you found the nest."

Wang stood up and pointed to the reeds. "Go east," he said, "and when you reach the end, head north. You'll find a path through the reeds where the raft went. Just keep going, and you're bound to find it.

"When you get back," Old Wang instructed him, "be sure to tie the raft the way you found it." He picked up the dead swan and laid it across the saddle. Then he climbed on, sat behind the bird, and headed slowly toward the work site, Ershun following behind, lugging the heavy basin.

Yang waited until the men were far enough away for him to go back to the shore, pick up the coat with the eggs inside, and put it in the raft. Then he rowed as fast as he could, heading east.

* * *

Yang was breathing fast and his hands were shaking as he rowed unsteadily toward the nest, pushing floating reeds out of his way with the spade, wanting to approach it as slowly as possible.

Yang stood before the nest almost in a state of shock. It was the biggest, the tallest, and the most unusual bird's nest he'd ever seen. After assuring himself that the female was away, he began examining the nest closely. He pushed against it with both hands; like a three-foot-thick tree trunk, it didn't budge. Though it was built on the water, its roots were as deep as a banyan tree's.

As the wind over the lake cooled, the green color of the reeds deepened. Yang held the two eggs close to his chest, trying to give them a bit of warmth from his body. He carefully climbed up and held on to the edge with one hand, while gently putting one of the eggs back into the nest. He took the second egg out from under his coat and put it back with equal care. Then, as he stepped back onto the raft, he breathed a sigh of relief, believing that the eggs, resting on the totem pole of a nest post, would, like two giant gemstones, shine brightly among the reeds and send their brilliance into the sky to call back the swan queen soaring through the air.

Finally a white dot appeared and circled in the sky. Yang quickly untied the rope and quietly rowed the raft into the waterway. He straightened the reeds flattened by the raft and pushed away the floating stalks and leaves with his spade, hoping that new reeds would grow in the area to shield the exposed nest.

He saw a swan's hurried descent before he left the reedy path; when he came ashore, the swan was no longer in the sky.

* * *

Yang Ke walked back to the construction site kitchen, where Ershun told him that his uncle had ridden over to Section Three to buy sick oxen. Outside the kitchen was a makeshift stove, on which sat a giant pot. On the ground was a pile of wet feathers. Steam rose from the pot, where pieces of swan meat the size of a fist were cooking. He saw the bird's head bobbing in the boiling water. A young woman dressed like a Han was sprinkling a handful of Sichuan peppers, cut green onions, and chopped ginger into the pot. She poured half a bottle of cheap soy sauce over the swan's head. Overcome by dizziness, Yang Ke collapsed against an oxcart.

"Quick," the woman said to Ershun, "take him inside. We'll give him a bowl of the broth to bring him around."

With a wave of his hand, Yang pushed Ershun away; he was so angry he felt like knocking over the pot. He couldn't stand the smell coming from it, but he didn't dare kick it over or otherwise let them see how angry he was. Ershun, after all, was a peasant, while he was one of the "mongrel bastards" sent "up to the mountains and down to the countryside" for reeducation.

When he returned to camp, Yang Ke told Chen Zhen and Gao Jianzhong what he'd seen and felt that day.

Chen was too upset to say anything. It took him a while to calm down. "What you've told us is a microcosm of what has happened between nomads and farmers in East Asia over thousands of years. The nomads become farmers, then turn around and destroy the grassland, inflicting damage on both nomads and farmers in the process."

"Why does it have to be like that?" Yang asked. "They're born of the same roots, so why are they so quick to fight? Why can't both the nomads and the farmers stick to their own lifestyle?"

Chen said coldly, "It's a small world, and everyone wants the good life. Human history is essentially a chronicle of fighting over and safeguarding living space. The small farmers of China have devoted their lives to taking care of the tiny piece of land they farm, making them narrow-minded individuals with tunnel vision. If we hadn't come here, wouldn't we be looking at the world through the beady eyes of a mouse, believing we're always right?"

Early the next morning, Yang, Chen, and Gao were awakened by gunfire at the lake. They stamped their feet in anger and regret. As if crazed, Yang leaped onto his horse and stormed toward the lake. Chen asked Gombo to watch his sheep before following with Gao on horseback.

They waited anxiously for the raft to come ashore, and what they saw made them feel as if a member of the family had died. On the raft lay another swan, along with several wild geese and ducks, plus two blood-splattered eggs. Obviously, it was the female swan who, to protect her precious eggs, had not flown away from the lake of terror in time and had ended up like her mate. Her head shattered by bullets, she was a worse sight than the male. She had died on top of her unborn cygnets, giving them the last bit of warmth from her own blood.

Yang's face was bathed in tears. If he hadn't returned the eggs to the nest, the female swan might have been spared.

As he was thinking, Little Peng, the barefoot doctor, jumped breathlessly off his horse, snatched up the two bloody eggs, put them in a bag stuffed with lamb's wool, remounted, and galloped off.

In a holiday mood, the workers carried their loot back to the kitchen, under the bewildered and angry glare of the herders, who could not understand why these Mongols, who dressed like Chinese, could be so cruel to sacred grassland birds. How did they have the nerve to kill and eat creatures that could fly up to Tengger? Bilgee, who had never witnessed anything like this before, was so angry his goatee quivered. He cursed Wang for the slaughter, for being disrespectful to a shaman, the sacred bird, and for forgetting his Mongolian roots.

Yang later heard that Peng, who had swapped oil for the swan eggs, turned out to be a collector of rare and precious objects, someone who knew a technique for keeping the eggshells intact. After punching a little hole in the bottom of the egg with a syringe, he sucked out the contents and then sealed the hole to prevent the shell from rotting or exploding. The two beautiful eggs, though the lives inside were lost, could now be preserved forever. He also went to the pastureland carpenter shop, where he made two cases out of wood and glass. He then added yellow silk padding to cradle the eggs, creating rare and exotic works of art. He stashed his two precious cases in his trunk, never showing them to anyone. Years later, he gave them to an official who had come to recruit students for the Workers, Peasants, and Soldiers College. And that was how Little Peng, on wings borrowed from the swans, was able to fly back to the city and enter college.

24

Summer nights on the Mongolian grassland can be as cold as late autumn. Hordes of fearsome mosquitoes will soon be on the offensive, leaving but a few peaceful days.

The sheep, newly sheared, lay huddled together as they chewed their cud; a low grinding sound hovered above the flock. Erlang and Yellow looked up from time to time, sniffing the air alertly as they made their rounds with Yir and the three puppies. Chen Zhen, carrying a flashlight and dragging a piece of felt about the size of a blanket, walked over to where the dogs were patrolling, picked a good spot, and spread the felt on the ground. He sat cross-legged, a tattered, thin coat over his shoulders, not daring to lie down. After coming to the new grazing land, a good night's sleep had become a rarity, the long days given over to tending the sheep, shearing wool, and caring for the wolf cub, while the short nights were a time for reading, writing in his journal, and of course keeping watch. All he had to do was lie down to almost immediately fall asleep so deeply that not even a barking dog could rouse him. He wanted to catch up on his sleep before the mosquito onslaught, but he knew the grassland wolves would take advantage of his slackness.

Having attacked a sick cow at the work site, the

wolves showed that their appetites had shifted to domestic livestock. The young gazelles could already run, the marmots were jittery, and field mice could not sate the appetite of the hungry wolves; only livestock could do that, and since the herds were not completely settled in the new grazing land, Bilgee called a series of meetings to caution the herdsmen and students to be like the wolves themselves, sleeping with their eyes shut but their ears alert to all sounds. The Olonbulag was poised for another man-wolf war.

Chen cleaned the cub's area every day, covering the ground with a layer of fresh sand after removing the waste not only for hygienic reasons but also to conceal the cub's presence and location. He had been reliving the days since finding the cub in the temporary den, fearing the wolf pack would initiate a murderous attack to reclaim it. He had taken every precaution to prevent the cub from leaving its scent on the way to the new grazing land so that even if the mother ran down the cub's scent in the former camp, she would have no way of knowing where the cub had been moved to.

It did not seem to Chen as if the smell of wolves was in the air. The three half-grown puppies ran up to him. He petted each one. Yellow and Yir followed the pups over to get their share of attention. Erlang alone, loyal as ever, kept watch on the flock. He, more than other dogs, understood wolves and was always as alert as any wolf could be.

The night winds grew colder, drawing the sheep closer and closer to keep warm, shrinking the space they occupied by at least a fourth. The three pups crawled under Chen's tattered deel as they settled down in the dark, intensely cold night.

After a couple of turns around the flock with his flashlight, he had barely sat down on his felt mat when, from somewhere not far off, he heard the mournful baying of a wolf—*Ow... ow... ow...*—trailing off slowly, with only the briefest of pauses between each pure, resonant trill, a sound mellow yet sharp-edged, simultaneously seeping into and boring through the consciousness. Before the sound had died out, low echoes rebounded from the mountains on three sides—north, south, and east—and swirled in the valleys and in the basin, as well as along the lakeshore, where they merged with the rustling of reeds in the gentle breezes to create a chorus of wolf, reed, and wind. The melody turned cold, carrying Chen Zhen's thoughts off to the Siberian wilderness.

It had been a long time since he'd listened to the call of a wolf late on a calm and clear night, and it made him shudder. He drew his deel even more tightly around him, but that could not keep out the fearful chill of the howls, which penetrated his deel and his skin, then moved down his spine to his tailbone. He reached out and pulled Yellow to him, wrapping his deel around the dog, and that brought him a bit of warmth.

This was just the overture, somber and drawn out. Next came the high-pitched bays of several powerful male wolves, which set all the dogs in the brigade camps barking. The dogs around Chen, big and small, ran to the northwest perimeter around the flock and raised a din of ferocious barking. Erlang rushed noisily toward the howls but stopped and headed back, fearing an attack from the rear. Taking up his place before the flock, he continued barking. Flashlights shone at all the brigade camps that snaked past the foothills on the edge of the basin; the hundred or more dogs belonging to the brigade barked for half an hour before gradually quieting down.

The night was, if anything, darker still, and colder. The wolf leader began baying again; the answering calls of more wolves, like three walls of sound bearing down on the camps, were so loud that they drowned out the dogs, whose barks had a flustered, surging quality. All the night-watch women flicked on their flashlights and frantically swept the area where the sound was coming from as they cried out: *Ah-he... wu-he... yi-he...*, wave after wave of shrill cries pressing down on the wolf pack.

Taking a cue from their human masters, the dogs set up a ferocious storm of noise: a mixture of barks, howls, roars, provocations, intimidations, and jeers produced a cacophonous drumbeat. Chen added his uncontrolled shouts to the mix, but his weak shouts were immediately swallowed up by the night.

On the new grazing land, the proximity of the yurts had the effect of concentrating and invigorating the herdsmen's vocal and light-beam counterattack, producing a warlike tension.

The wolves' cries were quickly overwhelmed. The close concentration of yurts, devised by Uljii and Bilgee, had worked as a strategy. The unified camp would hold, making an attack from the wolves unlikely.

Suddenly, Chen heard the sound of a rattling chain and ran immediately to the young wolf, who was jumping up and down outside the hole, snarling and baring his claws, wildly excited by the sound-and-light war between humans, wolves, and dogs.

Darkness is kind to wolves: they are liveliest at night and at their most warlike. It is a time of plunder, of gorging themselves on flesh and blood, of dividing up the spoils of a kill. But a metal chain kept the young wolf imprisoned, turning him into a crazed animal. As he struggled in vain against the chain, roaring his anger over being denied the fight he sought, he curled into a ball, then burst out and raced to the path he had worn in the pen. He leaped into the air, snapping at imaginary targets as he ran, stopping abruptly before the next charge and rolling on the ground. Then he closed his mouth, ground his teeth, and shook his head, just as if he had taken down a large animal and was waiting for it to die from his death grip.

Moments later, the cub was standing on the northern edge of the pen, staring straight ahead, his ears pricked straight up, and not moving a muscle, poised to launch another charge. His fighting instincts had been stimulated by the prebattle tension and palpable sense of fear in the air, and he seemed incapable of distinguishing between friend and foe, so long as he could enter the fray on any side. It seemed as if killing a puppy or killing another cub would have made him equally happy.

The cub rushed up to Chen Zhen as soon as he saw him coming, but he then backed up so Chen would come into the pen. Chen took one step into the pen and was about to crouch down when the cub attacked like a hungry tiger, wrapping his legs around Chen's knee and opening his mouth, ready to bite. Chen was prepared for the attack; he jammed his flashlight up against the cub's nose and turned it on. The blinding light stopped the attack.

The cub cocked his head and listened enviously to the warlike howls of the big dogs, then lowered his head thoughtfully, as if just discovering that he could not bark like they could. He opened his mouth, determined to learn from them. Chen was surprised; he crouched down to see what the cub would do next. The young wolf opened his mouth and managed, with considerable difficulty, a strange guttural sound; but it sounded nothing like a dog's bark, and that made him furious. So he tried again: he took a breath and held it, then constricted his belly over and over, copying the movements of the dogs; but the raspy sound that emerged belonged to neither dog nor wolf, tormenting the cub, who spun in circles of exasperation.

As he watched the cub's bizarre movements, Chen nearly laughed out loud. The cub could not yet make wolf sounds, so he'd tried to imitate the barking of a dog, but that was simply too hard. Most dogs are able to imitate the sounds of wolves, but wolves have never tried to bark like dogs, possibly finding that demeaning. But at that moment, a young wolf maturing among dogs wanted only to sound like them. The poor thing was having an identity crisis.

Yet even as the cub fretted over his inability to bark like a dog, he refused to stop trying. Chen walked up, bent down until his mouth was next to the cub's ear, and barked. The cub, appearing to understand that his "master" was trying to teach him something, briefly had the embarrassed look of a slow student but quickly followed that with the defiant glare of a shamed classroom bully. Erlang came running over, stood beside the cub, and began to bark, slowly, like a patient teacher. A moment later, Chen heard the cub cry out in the cadence of a dog's bark, but without the sound a dog makes—*orf orf.* The cub was so excited he leaped into the air and began licking Erlang's mouth. From then on, the cub made the same un-doglike sound. It made Chen laugh.

The strange sound brought the three puppies running, while the other dogs made deriding sounds as if mocking the cub. Every time he went *orf orf,* Chen answered with an *arf arf,* and before long the camp was awash in a battle of strange, unharmonious sounds: *orf orf—arf arf.* The cub may well have been aware that the man and the dogs were making fun of him, but that only increased the intensity of the *orf orf—arf arf.* The puppies were so happily caught up in the atmosphere that they were rolling on the ground. Before long, all the brigade dogs stopped barking, and with no models to follow, the cub turned mute.

The people's voices had stilled when the wolf cries came from the surrounding mountains, and the flashlights had been turned off; by then even the dogs were just going through the motions. When the wolves responded by howling even louder, Chen Zhen was convinced that they were plotting something. Maybe the pack had discovered how tight the man-and-dog line of defense was, and had settled on a strategy of wearing the enemy down; once the herdsmen and their dogs were worn out from the battle of sounds, they would launch a sneak attack. The state of paralysis could last several nights. Grassland wolves had perfected tactics for wearing down an enemy.

Chen lay back on the felt mat, his head pillowed by the dog Yellow. In China the baying of wolves enjoyed a fearsome reputation. It was a sound the inhabitants of China's Central Plain equated with "wails of the Devil." Chen had grown accustomed to hearing wolves over the years, though he'd never understood why the baying was so sad, so desolate-sounding, like a mournful lament, a long drawn-out torment. The sound did indeed call to mind the incessant wailing of widows at a grave site, and the first time he heard it, he wondered how the hearts of the savage, arrogant wolves could be so full of anguish. Was it an expression of the difficulty of life on the grassland? Were they complaining about their wretched fate at a place where death from starvation, the freezing elements, and mortal combat was so common? Chen had long felt that the wolves, so fierce and tenacious, were burdened with weak, fragile hearts.

But in the wake of two years of contact with them, especially over the past six months or so, he'd come to disavow that view. To him, the grassland wolves, with their hard bones, hard hearts, and survival skills, were tough as steel, consumed by a bloodlust, and unflinching even in the face of death. The agony over the loss of a female wolf's young or the grave injury to a male wolf, even the loss of a leg, was only temporary and immediately led to thoughts of vengeance that grew more intense with each passing day. The several months he'd spent with the cub had convinced him of that. He had yet to discover a single moment of weakness in the young wolf; except for those times when he was overcome with exhaustion, his eyes were always aglow, his energy never flagged, he was full of life. Even after the time his neck had nearly been broken by the herdsman, he'd sprung back to life almost immediately.

As he continued listening to the wolves, Chen began to detect an arrogant, menacing quality to their baying, but he wondered why the threat to men and their livestock had to sound like mourning. What was the reason their baying adopted the sound of wailing? His reflections went deeper into the heart of the matter. The mighty wolf may have its moments of sadness, but at no time, at no place, and under the sway of no emotion does it cry. Crying is alien to a wolf's character.

Clarity of mind settled in after Chen had been listening for much of the night. Dogs and wolves just sounded different. Dog barks are short and rapid; the baying of a wolf is a drawn-out sound. The effect of these diverse sounds on the listener is radically different. The baying of a wolf travels greater distances than the bark of a dog. The barks of dogs from the northernmost yurts in the brigade aren't nearly as crisp as the baying of wolves in the same vicinity. Chen was also able to make out the baying of wolves in the mountains to the east, but no dog barks could ever travel that distance.

Perhaps that was the reason the wolves chose to wail—over thousands of years of evolution, they had discovered it was the sound that hung in the air longest and was able to travel the greatest distances. The grassland wolves are known for long-range raids, for splitting up to scout a situation and then joining for an attack. As pack animals, they range far and wide while hunting, and this highly advanced system of communication is how they make contact across great distances. In the most ruthless battles, results are all that count; how they sound is immaterial.

The baying thinned out gradually; but then, quite suddenly, a juvenile howl emerged from somewhere behind the yurt and the flock of sheep, momentarily paralyzing Chen. Had the wolves managed to sneak up from behind? Erlang charged, barking ferociously, the other dogs right behind him. Chen scrambled to his feet, grabbed his herding club and flashlight, and ran after the dogs. When he reached the yurt, he saw Erlang and the other dogs growling as they stood around the cub's pen in puzzled fashion.

With the aid of his flashlight, Chen spotted the cub, crouching next to the wooden post, his snout pointing into the sky as he howled. So that's where the sound was coming from! It was the first time Chen had heard the cub actually bay like a wolf, something he thought the cub wouldn't do until he was fully grown. But here he was, only four months old, and already sounding and acting like a mature wild animal. Chen was as thrilled as a father hearing his son say "Daddy" for the first time. He bent down and stroked the cub's back; the cub turned and licked the back of his hand, then went back to baying.

The dogs were so bewildered they couldn't tell if they should kill the cub or just get him to stop howling. The arrival of a mortal enemy in their midst had thrown the sheepherding dogs into total confusion. A dog belonging to their neighbor, Gombu, stopped barking; some of the other dogs ran up to see what was happening and offer their support. Erlang happily walked into the pen and licked the top of the cub's head, and then sprawled alongside him and listened to him howl. Yellow and Yir glared hatefully at the cub—in those few minutes, the cub had given himself away to the dogs he'd lived with for months, exposing his true identity. He was a wolf, not a dog, a wolf no different from a wild wolf in a battle of howls and barks. But when Yellow and Yir saw their master smiling and stroking the cub's head, they could only fume silently.

Chen crouched down beside the cub to listen to him howl and watch his movements. He saw how the young wolf raised his snout into the air before making a soft, drawn-out, even sound that Chen found so pleasant; it was like the sound a dolphin makes as it gently noses out of the water, sending ripples in all directions. It occurred to Chen that pointing the snout into the air was how wolves were able to communicate with their distant kin. Their long, mournful baying and their snout-in-the-air attitude were characteristics that had helped make it possible for them to survive on the grassland. The perfection of the wolves' evolution was nothing less than Tengger's masterpiece.

Blood surged through Chen's veins. Most likely, no herdsman deep in the Inner Mongolian grassland had ever before stroked the back of a living wolf and listened to it bay into the night. No one heard the round, gentle, pure sound of the cub's howls more clearly than he; while they were typically wolf, there was no sorrowful quality to them. On the contrary, the cub was bursting with excitement, stirred to his soul that he was finally able to sing out like a wolf, each howl longer, higher, and more intense than the one before. He was like a novice singer getting rave reviews for a debut performance, glued to the stage as he soaked up the applause.

Over several months, the cub had done many things to surprise Chen, but this amazed him. Since he hadn't been able to imitate the barking of dogs, the young wolf had turned instinctively to the sounds a wolf makes, and mastered it at once. But how had the posture come to him? That was something he could not have seen, certainly not in the dark of night.

Each howl the cub made was more natural, louder, and more resonant than the one before; and each one pierced Chen's heart. A stolen gong will never ring out, they say, but this stolen and human-nurtured wolf rang out with no help from the thief, in triumphant self-assertion. Then Chen realized that the cub was howling to be found: he was calling for the wild to which he belonged. Chen broke out in a cold sweat, feeling suddenly hemmed in between man and wolf.

Then the cub loosed a howl that dwarfed all those before it.

At first, there had been no response to the young wolf's calls, not by humans, by dogs, or by distant wolves, since all had been caught unprepared. The wolves, however, were the first to react. After the cub's third and fourth immature attempts, the wolves in the surrounding mountains stopped in midhowl and fell silent.

Chen surmised that the wolves out there—pack leaders, old warriors, alpha wolves, or females—had never before heard a wolf howl emerge from a camp of humans, and he tried to imagine their unbelieving shock. The pack had to be completely mystified, and Chen imagined that they were staring at each other, momentarily silenced by what they heard. He knew that, sooner or later, the wolves would realize this was one of their own and that a prairie fire of hope would be kindled in the hearts of the mothers whose young had been taken from them; they would want their offspring back. Thanks to the cub's sudden self-revelation, Chen's worst fears were about to become reality.

The dogs were next to react to the wolfish howls. A round of ferocious barking erupted, filling the night with a canine din of unmatched savagery, turning the grassland virtually upside down. Prepared for a deadly battle, they alerted their human masters that the wolf pack had launched a surprise attack and warned them to pick up their rifles and engage the enemy.

The last to react were the people. Most women on the night watch had fallen asleep from fatigue and hadn't heard the cub's baying; it was the extraordinary ferocity of the dogs' barking that woke them. But now that they were awake, their shrill cries cut through the night, their flashlights penetrated the darkness. A wolf attack just before the mosquito onslaught was the last thing any of them had imagined.

The waves of ferocious barking unnerved Chen Zhen. It was an uproar he had caused, and he wondered how he was going to face the wrath of the brigade members when the sun rose in the morning. He worried that a group of herdsmen would arrive and fling his cub to Tengger, especially since the cub showed no interest in bringing an end to the noisemaking; he howled as if celebrating a rite of passage, stopping only long enough to wet his throat with a bit of water. The darkness was beginning to lose ground to early-morning sunlight; women not on watch were getting up to milk the cows. Starting to panic, Chen wrapped one arm around the young wolf and held his snout closed with his left hand to get him to stop howling. But it was not in the cub's nature to be bullied, and he fought with all his might to loosen Chen's grip. By then he was a fully half-grown animal, and much stronger than Chen could have believed. He easily broke free from the arm around him, and Chen knew he had to hold on to the snout or he would surely be bitten.

The cub resisted furiously, his blazing, awl-like eyes all the proof Chen needed to know that he had now become the enemy. With Chen still holding his snout, the cub struck out with his claws, ripping Chen's deel and gouging the back of his right hand. Shocked by the pain, Chen screamed, "Yang Ke! Yang Ke!" The yurt door flew open and Yang ran outside, barefoot; a moment later, the two men succeeded in pinning the cub to the ground, where he panted and puffed as he dug furrows in the sandy ground with his claws.

With Chen's hand bleeding noticeably, the men counted—one-two-three—before letting go and quickly backing out of the pen. With plenty of fight left in him, the cub charged his retreating captors but was held back by the chain. Yang ran into the yurt to get some antiseptic powder and a bandage from the first-aid kit to treat Chen's wound.

All this activity awoke Gao Jianzhong, who stumbled out of the yurt, cursing. "You treat this damned wolf like royalty, day in and day out, and it bites you anyway. If you won't do away with him, let me have him!"

"No," Chen said anxiously, "don't do anything. It's not his fault. I clamped his mouth shut. That set him off, and for good reason."

It was getting light by then, but the cub's passion hadn't cooled. Jumping and leaping, he panted noisily until finally crouching at the edge of the pen and looking up into the northwestern sky to howl yet again. Strangely, however, in the wake of the exhausting struggle he had just experienced, he couldn't howl—the newly mastered sound was forgotten. He tried and he tried, but all that emerged was a series of doglike barks that set Erlang's tail wagging happily and eliciting whoops of joy from the three men looking on. Angered and embarrassed by his failure and the reaction to it, the cub snarled at Erlang, his adoptive father.

"The cub now knows how to howl," Chen said unhappily, "like an adult wolf. Everyone in the brigade must have heard him, and that means trouble for us. What do we do?"

Gao Jianzhong was unmoved. "I say kill it. If we don't, the pack will take up positions around our flock night after night, howling nonstop, which will get all the dogs barking, and no one will get any sleep. And if they take any of our sheep, you'll have more trouble than you can handle."

"We can't kill him," Yang said. "Let's just quietly set him free and say he escaped."

"We can't kill him," Chen echoed, grinding his teeth, "and we can't let him go! We'll hold on, take it one day at a time. If we're going to set him free, it can't be now. There are dogs in every camp, and they'll pounce on the cub almost as soon as we let him go. For now, you tend the sheep when the sun's out, and I'll take the night shift. That way I can keep my eye on him during the day."

"I guess that's all we can do," Yang said. "If an order to kill him comes down from brigade headquarters, we'll turn him loose someplace where there aren't any dogs."

"You're a couple of dreamers," Gao said with a derisive snort. "You just wait. The herdsmen will be here before you know it. The damned thing kept me awake all night, and I've got a splitting headache. I tell you, I'm ready to kill it."

The sound of horse hooves arrived before they'd finished their morning tea. With a deep sense of foreboding, Chen Zhen and Yang Ke ran to the door, where they saw Uljii and Bilgee circling the yurt on their horses, looking for the cub. The second time around, they spotted the chain leading into a hole in the ground. They dismounted for a closer look. "No wonder we couldn't find him," Bilgee said, "he's hiding down here."

Chen and Yang ran up to grab the reins and tie the horses to the axle of an oxcart. They stood without speaking, like men awaiting sentencing.

Uljii and Bilgee crouched just outside the pen and gazed into the hole where the cub was lying, unhappy that strangers had come to disturb his rest. He snarled as he poked his head out and glared at the crouching men.

"He's grown since the last time I saw him," Bilgee commented. "He's bigger than young wolves I've seen in the wild." He turned to Chen Zhen. "You've spoiled him," he said. "Even digging a hole so he can cool off. I was thinking that by leaving him out in the heat every day, you'd have made it easy for us: we wouldn't have to kill him, the sun would do that."

"Papa," Chen replied cautiously, "I didn't dig that hole, he did. He was dying out in the sun, and after a while he hit on the idea of digging the hole."

With a look of astonishment, the old man stared at the cub. "He knew how to do that without a mother teaching him?" he said. "Maybe Tengger doesn't want this one to die, after all."

"Wolves have agile brains," Uljii said. "They're smarter than dogs, and in some ways smarter than humans."

Chen Zhen's heart was racing. "I . . . ," he said breathlessly. "I was puzzled too over how a wolf this young could figure that out. His eyes hadn't even opened when I took him out of that hole. He'd never so much as seen his mother."

"Wolves have amazing native intelligence," Bilgee said. "Their mothers might not be around, but there's always Tengger to teach them. You must have watched how he bayed last night. Wolves are the only grassland animals that howl up into the sky; you'll never see a cow, a sheep, a horse, a dog, a fox, a gazelle, or a marmot do anything like that. Do you know why? I've told you that wolves are Tengger's pride and joy. Well, when they're in trouble, they look up and howl so that Tengger will come to their aid. They get most of their abilities directly from Tengger. They know how to 'ask for instructions in the morning and submit a report in the evening.' When people run into trouble out here, they look up into the sky and ask for Tengger's help, just like the wolves. We're the only two species that pay homage to Tengger."

The old man's gaze softened as he looked at the cub. "In fact," he continued, "we learned that from the wolves. Before we Mongols came to the grassland, the wolves were already raising their voices to Tengger. It's a hard life out here, especially for them. Old-timers often shed tears of sadness when they hear wolves bay at night."

Chen knew that what Bilgee said was the truth, for he had observed that only wolves and humans revered Tengger, with their howls or with their prayers. Life on this beautiful yet barren spot of land was burdensome for humans and for wolves, and in frustration they unburdened themselves by their daily cries to Tengger. From a scientific perspective, it was true that wolves bayed at the moon so that their voices could be heard far and wide. But Chen preferred Bilgee's explanation. Without spiritual support, life would be unendurable. Chen felt tears filling his eyes.

The old man turned to him. "You don't have to hide that hand from me. The cub clawed you, I bet. I heard everything last night. You thought I came to kill him, didn't you? Well, you should know that some horse and sheep herders came to see me early this morning to demand that the brigade have the wolf killed. Uljii and I talked it over, and we've decided you can keep him for now, but only if you're more careful. I tell you, I've never seen a Chinese so smitten by wolves."

Chen was momentarily speechless. "Are you really going to let me keep him?" he finally managed to say. "Why? I don't want to be someone who brings harm to the brigade, and I'd hate to add to your troubles. I was thinking about making a leather muzzle to keep him from baying."

"It's too late for that," Uljii said. "All the mother wolves out there know we've got a cub, and I predict they'll be here tonight. But Bilgee and I organized the camps so they'd be close together. Given our numbers—people, dogs, and rifles—the wolves won't actually attack. What worries me is that when we decamp to move to the autumn grazing land, you'll be in grave danger."

"By then," Chen said to reassure him, "our puppies will be fully grown, so we'll have five dogs, including Erlang, our wolf killer. We'll go out to check more often, and we can always light off firecrackers. The wolves won't bother us."

"We'll see," Bilgee said.

Still worried, Chen said, "Papa, what did you say to all those people demanding to have the cub killed?"

"The wolves have gone after our horses lately, and we've suffered considerable losses. If the cub can bring the wolf pack over here to us, horses will be saved, to the great relief of the herders," Bilgee said.

"So raising that wolf cub has had at least one positive effect," Uljii said. "But don't let it sink its teeth in you. That would be a disaster. A few nights ago, a migrant laborer tried to steal some dried dung from a herdsman's house and was bitten by one of the family's dogs. He damn near died."

Bilgee and Uljii mounted up and rode off toward where the horses were grazing, which must have meant there had been more trouble with the herd. As Chen gazed at the dust in their wake, he couldn't have said if he felt relieved or even more nervous.

25

Chen Zhen took out the last two pieces of meat, added some sheep fat, and made a pot of thick, meaty porridge for the cub, whose appetite was growing so fast that a full pot was no longer enough for him. With a sigh, Chen went back inside the yurt to get some sleep so that he'd be well rested for the dangerous night battle. Sometime after one in the afternoon, he was awakened by shouts; he ran outside.

Zhang Jiyuan had ridden up on a big horse that was carrying something on its back. Blood covered the front half of the horse, who was acting skittish and afraid, reluctant to get close to the oxcarts. Dogs rushed up and surrounded the horse and rider, wagging their tails. Rubbing his sleepy eyes, Chen was startled to find an injured foal lying across Zhang's saddle. He rushed up to grab the bridle to calm the big horse. In obvious pain, the foal struggled to raise its head as blood continued to drip from the wounds on its neck and chest, staining the saddle and the big horse, whose eyes bulged with fear; it snorted and pawed the ground. Seated bareback behind the saddle, Zhang had a hard time dismounting, afraid that the bloody foal would fall off and frighten the big horse. Chen held one of the foal's front legs while Zhang, after removing his foot from the stirrup with difficulty, dismounted and nearly fell to the ground.

Standing on either side of the horse, they picked up the foal and gently laid it on the ground. The big horse turned and sadly looked down at the foal. No longer able to raise its head, the foal could only look at them with its lovely big eyes. Crying out in pain, it pushed against the ground with its front hooves, but it was no use.

"Can we save it?" Chen asked.

Zhang said, "Batu checked the wound and said it was beyond help. We haven't had meat in a long time. Let's kill it. Laasurung sent another injured foal over to Bilgee."

Chen's heart skipped a beat. He got a basin of water so that Zhang could wash up. "Has there been another attack on the herd? How bad was it?"

Zhang replied glumly, "Don't ask. Wolves killed and ate two horses last night and injured another. Laasurung fared even worse; the wolves got five or six of his. I don't know about the other herds, but I'm sure they didn't do well either. The brigade leaders all went down to check on them."

Chen said, "I know the wolf pack surrounded the camp and howled all night long. But if they were here, how did they end up attacking the horses?"

"That was their plan: an all-out attack from four sides, hitting the east to divert attention from the west, covering for each other, feigning an attack on one side while mounting a major assault on the other; they advanced when they could, and when they couldn't, they tied us up so that we couldn't cover both the head and the tail, or both east and west. Their strategy was more lethal than combining forces to launch assault waves." He finished washing his hands and added, "Let's kill the foal quickly. We won't be able to let out any blood once it dies, and blood-clogged meat doesn't taste good."

"They're right when they say that horse herders are more like wolves than anyone. You look like a real herder now, and you sound like one, with some of the cruel savagery of an ancient grassland warrior." Handing his brass-handled Mongolian knife to Zhang, he said, "You do it. I can't bring myself to kill such a beautiful foal."

"Wolves killed this foal," Zhang said, "not humans. This has nothing to do with human nature. I'll do it. But that's all I'll do. You have to do the rest—skin it, gut it, and cut up the meat. Agreed?"

"Agreed."

Taking the knife, Zhang put his feet on one side of the foal's chest while holding down its head. Following grassland tradition, he let the foal's eyes face Tengger as he plunged the knife into its neck and severed an artery. There wasn't enough blood to spew, barely enough to drip slowly. As if looking at a butchered sheep, Zhang watched the foal struggle and finally die.

"I killed one the other day," Zhang said, "but it wasn't as big and meaty as this one. We horse herders had two meals of horsemeat buns. Foal meat is tender and fragrant, but the herders eat it in the summer only when that's all there is. After thousands of years, foal has become a grassland delicacy." After washing his hands again, Zhang sat down on the shaft of a water wagon to watch Chen skin the horse.

Chen was happy to see all the tender meat under the foal's skin. It was a good-sized animal, nearly as big as an adult sheep. "After a month, I've almost forgotten what meat tastes like," he said. "Actually, I'm doing fine without it. It's the cub that concerns me. Without meat, it's more like a sheep, and I'm afraid one day he'll bleat like a lamb."

"This was the first foal born this year, and both its parents are big. If you like the meat, I'll bring you another one in a few days. Summer is the season of death for horses. The mares are foaling, and the wolves love to go after the babies. Every few days, a herd will lose one or two foals to the wolves, and there's nothing we can do to stop them. Mares add a hundred and fifty foals to each herd. The grass is good and the mares have plenty of milk, so the foals grow fast. They run around a lot, so the stud horses and mares can't look after them all the time."

Using an axe, Chen removed the wolf-bitten areas on the foal's head, chest, and neck, and chopped them into small pieces. The six dogs had surrounded Chen and the foal, five tails wagging like reeds in an autumn wind. Erlang was the only exception—his tail stood out straight as a bayonet as he watched Chen, waiting to see how he'd divide up the meat. The cub, which hadn't tasted fresh meat in many days, was running around anxiously, making doglike noises.

The meat and bones were divided into the usual three big portions and three little ones. Chen gave half of the head and half of the neck to Erlang, who wagged his tail and took his share over to enjoy in the shade under an oxcart. Yellow, Yir, and the three puppies all got their portions and ran into shady areas or over next to the yurt. Chen waited for the dogs to leave before cutting the select chest meat and bones into small pieces and filling the cub's bowl half full. Then he poured the remaining blood from the foal's chest over the bones, before walking up to the cub and shouting, "Little Wolf, Little Wolf, time to eat."

The skin on the cub's neck had grown thick and tough. When he saw the fresh bloody meat, he strained so much against the chain he looked like an ox pulling a wagon up a hill; he was drooling. Chen rushed the bowl over and placed it in front of the cub, who pounced on the meat as if tearing the flesh of a live horse; he snarled at Chen to chase him away. Chen went back to work on the foal's hide, continuing to scrape the bones and slice up the flesh meat as he watched the cub out of the corner of his eye. The young wolf was gobbling up the meat frantically, but he kept a wary eye on the humans and the dogs. His body bent like a bow, he was prepared to drag the fresh meat over to his dugout if necessary.

"Can't you horse herders do anything about the wolves?"

"I've been a herdsman for nearly two years, and I think the weakest link in herding on the grassland is the horses. Each herd has four or five hundred horses, but only two herders. That's just not enough, even with the addition of a student for each herd. Two or three people take turns and work in shifts, meaning there's only one watching the herd at any given time. It's an impossible situation."

"Why don't they assign more to each herd?"

"Horse herders are the aviators of the grassland. It takes a long time to train one. No one would let an unqualified herder out there with the horses; a guy could lose half his herd in a year. It's a tough, exhausting, high-risk job. When a white-hair blizzard strikes, the temperature can be thirty or forty degrees below zero and it can take all night to round up the horses. You can lose your toes to frostbite if you're not careful. In the summer, the mosquitoes can suck your and your horses' blood dry. Lots of horse herders quit after eight or ten years; they either do some other kind of work or stop working altogether because of injury. Of the four student herders who started out two years ago, I'm the only one still at it. There just aren't enough to go around."

"Why would a herd of horses run off, as if asking to be killed?"

"Many reasons. First of all, it's so cold in the winter that they run to keep warm. Then in the spring, they need to sweat in order to molt, so they run. They run against the wind in the summer to escape the mosquitoes, then they fight the cows and sheep over good grazing land in the autumn, so they need to sneak away. But mainly they run to get away from wolves. All year round they're running for their lives. Dogs won't stay with a horse herd because it moves too much and too often. So a herder has to watch over a bunch of cowardly horses without the help of dogs. How's he supposed to do that? On moonless nights, wolves often come out to prey on horses. If there aren't too many of them, the herder and his stud horses can keep them at bay. But if it's a big pack, the herd is startled into flight, like a defeated army on the run. At times like that there's nothing the herder or stud horses can do.

"Now I know why Genghis Khan's cavalry could travel so fast," he continued. "His horses were forced by wolves to run night after night, building up speed and stamina for long distances. I often witness the relentless, tragic struggle for survival between horses and wolves. The wolves attack at night, ruthlessly, and they never let up, not giving the horses a chance to rest. Once they lag behind, the old, sick, slow, and small horses, as well as the foals and the pregnant mares are surrounded and eaten alive. You've never seen the sad sight of horses running for their lives. They run and run, foaming at the mouth, drenched in sweat. Some use up all their strength to escape; they die as soon as they stop and lie down. They're literally run to death. The fastest ones can take a break and gobble up some grass when they get a chance. They're so hungry they'd eat anything, even dry reeds, and so thirsty they'd drink anything, whether it's foul water or water mixed with cow or sheep urine. The Mongol horses rank number one in strength, stamina, digestion, immune system, and the ability to withstand cold and heat. But only the horse herders know that all these qualities were forcefully developed by the wolves' speed and fangs."

Captivated by Zhang's description, Chen took the foal meat and the bones inside and then came back out and spread the skin over the top of the yurt. "After more than a year as a horse herder," he said, "you're an expert. I want to hear more. It's hot out here. Let's go inside. You talk while I make the fillings and wrappings."

Back inside the yurt, Chen chopped green onions, made the dough, minced the meat, and heated pepper oil for the meaty buns that were so popular among the herders.

Zhang drank some cool tea and continued: "I think about horses all the time. In my view, it was wolves that nurtured the endurance and toughness of Mongol horses, which in turn created a cavalry for the Huns, Turks, and Mongols."

"According to history books," Chen said, "there were more horses than people on the ancient Mongolian grassland. When the Mongols went to war, riders would take five or six horses to ride in turns, which was how they could travel a thousand *li* a day. They were a primitive motorized army, specializing in blitzkriegs.

They had so many horses that they could turn injured ones into food for the soldiers. They ate horsemeat and drank horse blood, saving the trouble of having to supply troops."

Zhang laughed. "That's right. I remember you said that all the grassland tribes that waged war here, from the Quanrong, the Huns, the Tungus, and the Turks, down to the present-day Mongols, understood the secrets and value of wolves. That's making more and more sense to me. The wolves have given the Mongols their ferocious combat nature, the wisdom of sophisticated warfare, and the best warhorses. These three military advantages led to their stunning conquests."

As he kneaded the dough, Chen continued, "You've made an important discovery, figuring out how wolves have trained the battle-savvy Mongol horses. I used to think that the wolf totem was the sole reason why the Mongols were so brave and fierce, as well as wise in military strategy. I didn't realize that wolves were their unwitting trainers, drilling world-class army horses for the Mongol hordes. Such formidable horses were like wings for people who already possessed exceptional character and wisdom. I'm impressed! You haven't wasted your time out there."

Zhang smiled. "I owe it all to the influence of a true wolf fan. Over the past couple of years, you've shared what you learned from history books, so I'm obligated to repay you with some living knowledge."

Chen laughed. "That's a fair trade. But one thing I'm still not clear on. Exactly how do the wolves kill the foals?"

"They have many ways. I'm always on edge when we take the horses to a spot where the grass is high or the layout of the land is complex. Wolves can crawl like lizards. Without looking up, they can locate their prey by smell and sound. The mares often call out to their foals, softly, which helps a wolf determine the location of the foals as they inch closer. If a stud horse isn't around, the wolf will pounce on a foal and bite through its neck before dragging it away to finish it off in a secluded spot. But it will quickly run away if discovered by the mare or the stud horse, then come back to finish the foal off after the herd leaves, since the herd cannot take the dead foal with it.

"The most cunning wolves are especially good at tricking the foals. When a wolf finds a mare by a foal's side, it'll crawl over to where the grass is tall and lie on its back, hiding in the grass and sticking out its paws, waving them back and forth. From a distance, they look like the ears of a wild rabbit or some other animal looking around, but nothing like a dog or a wolf. The newborn foals are naturally curious, and they'll run over to check out anything smaller than they are. The wolf will snap the foal's neck before the mare can stop it from leaving her side."

"Sometimes I feel that wolves are demons, not animals," Chen said.

Zhang agreed. "You're right, they are. Just think, the horses are spread out during the day, making it hard for us to be sure that everything is okay, even though we stay with the horses. Come nighttime, the wolves run wild; they steal and snatch at will. If they can't do either, then they attack as a pack. The stud horses will keep the mares and foals safe inside the herd while fending off the wolves with their hooves and teeth. It's hard for an average-sized pack of wolves to break through the united line of defense of a dozen big stud horses. But when the weather is bad and the wolves are driven by hunger, the stud horses are powerless. That's when we're expected to protect the herd with lights and rifles. If we fail, the wolves will get into the herd and kill the foals. By this time the wolf cubs are grown and the demand for food increases dramatically. If they can't catch gazelles or marmots, they turn their attention to the foals."

"How many are lost each year?"

Zhang paused for a thoughtful moment. "Last year the herd Batu and I watch had over a hundred and ten foals, but we only have about forty left this summer. Seventy were killed or eaten by wolves. That's a sixty percent loss, but it was actually the best record in the brigade. Section Four only has about a dozen left from last year, an eighty percent loss. I asked Uljii once about the average loss in the whole pasture each year, and he said it's usually about seventy percent."

"That's a high mortality rate. No wonder horse herders hate the wolves with such passion."

Chen fell silent as he started to make wrappings.

Zhang washed his hands to help Chen make the buns. "But we can't do without them," he continued, "no matter how tired we are or how hard the work is. Batu says that the quality of the horses would drop without the wolves, that they'd get fat and lazy, unable to run. Mongol horses are short to begin with, and they wouldn't command a good price without speed and stamina, since the military wouldn't use them as warhorses. Also, the herd would grow too fast without wolves. Just think, a herd can have over a hundred foals each year, a twenty or thirty percent growth if most of them survived. Each year there would be new mares ready to give birth, which means the growth rate would be even higher. The number of horses in a herd would double after three or four years. Under normal circumstances, we only sell four- or five-year-old horses and keep the younger ones. Uljii says that except for rodents and rabbits, horses do more damage to the pasture than any other animal. A Mongol horse can consume enough grass to feed several cows, even a hundred sheep. The herdsmen complain that horses are taking the grass away from the sheep. If we didn't control the growth of the horse herd, in a few years the cows and sheep would have no grass and the Olonbulag would become a desert."

Chen hit the chopping board with his rolling pin and said, "So the herders use the wolves to conduct birth control for the horses, while raising or maintaining their quality, is that it?"

"Yes. The grasslanders are the best practitioners of dialectic materialism and are good at 'the middle way,' unlike the Han Chinese, who prefer extremes. We promote the east wind overpowering the west wind, or vice versa. But here they're experts in making use of contradictions to strike a balance while achieving two goals with one action."

"But this kind of controlled balance is cruel," Chen replied. "In the spring the horse herders raid wolf dens, taking and killing a hundred, even two hundred cubs, without completely killing them off. In the summer, the tables are turned; the wolves start killing foals, taking seventy or eighty percent of them, since you herders won't allow them to take all the babies. The price of this controlled balance is blood flowing like a river. It requires the herders to be forever vigilant, always ready for combat. This sort of 'middle way' is more combative and more real than the Han Chinese 'middle ground.' "

Zhang said, "These days, all the officials are from farming areas. They know nothing about life on the grassland. All they care about is quantity, quantity, quantity. In the end, they'll lose everything by being single-minded. No more wolves, no more demand for the Mongol horses, nothing but yellow sand rolling over the Inner Mongolian grassland; the cows and sheep will die of starvation, and we'll all go back to Beijing."

"You wish. Historically, Beijing has been taken more than once by Mongol armies, who then made it their capital. The city can't even hold back the horses, so how can it stand up against the sand, a new yellow peril that is thousands of times more powerful?"

"We can't do anything about that," Zhang replied. "Millions of peasants keep having babies and reclaiming the land. The population equal to an entire province is born every year. Who can stop all those people from coming to the grassland?"

Chen sighed. "No one, which is why I worry."

Zhang added, "I have a soft spot in my heart for the Quanrong and the Huns, both outstanding races. They were the ones who created the wolf totem, a tradition that has existed ever since."

"The wolf totem has a much longer history than Han Confucianism," said Chen, "with greater natural continuity and vitality. In the Confucian thought system, the main ideas, such as the three cardinal guides and the five constant virtues, are outdated and decayed, but the central spirit of the wolf totem remains vibrant and young, since it's been passed down by the most advanced races in the world. It should be considered one of the truly valuable spiritual heritages of all humanity. There'd be hope for China if our national character could be rebuilt by cutting away the decaying parts of Confucianism and grafting a wolf totem sapling onto it. It could be combined with such Confucian traditions as pacifism, an emphasis on education, and devotion to study. It's a shame the wolf totem is a spiritual system with a scant written record. The fatal weakness of the grassland race is its backwardness in written culture. Chinese Confucian scholars and historians were not interested in recording the culture of the wolf totem, even though they were in contact with grassland races for thousands of years. I wonder if Confucian scholars, who hated wolves with a passion, intentionally deleted everything related to wolves from the history books. It's like finding a needle in a haystack to read anything about wolf totems in Chinese history books. The books we brought don't help, so we'll have to try to find more when we're back home."

Zhang added some dried dung to the fire. "One of my relatives is a minor leader in a paper mill, where confiscated books are piled high. The workers roll their cigarettes with pages from traditional thread-bound books that are to be pulped. Anyone who loves books could trade cigarettes for printed classics. I make over seventy yuan a month as a horse herder, a fairly high wage, so I'd be happy to buy cigarettes to trade for books. But since the founding of the country, our government has encouraged people to kill wolves. Those who do so are the new grassland heroes. It won't take long for the Mongol youths, especially the shepherds and horse herders who have only had an elementary or junior high school education, to be completely ignorant of the wolf totem. So what's the point of it all?"

Chen took the lid off the pot. "True scientific research has to do with curiosity and interest," he said, "not whether something is useful or not. Besides, you can't really say that something is useless if you manage to figure out what it is you didn't understand at first." The meaty buns were taken out amid hot steam. Chen tossed one of them from hand to hand to cool it off before taking a bite. "Delicious," he said. "The next time a foal is injured, make sure you bring it home."

"The other three yurts want them too, so we take turns."

"At least bring back the parts bitten by the wolf for me to feed to the cub." The two friends finished off the buns in one steamer and Chen stood up, utterly sated. "I can't recall how many times we've enjoyed wolf food," he said. "Let's go play 'throwing a meat bun at the wolf.'"

They waited for the buns to cool before they each grabbed one and happily walked out of the yurt to visit the young wolf.

"Little Wolf, Little Wolf, time to eat," Chen shouted. Two meat buns gently landed on the wolf's head and body, sending him scurrying into the cave with his tail between his legs. Yellow and Yir immediately picked up the meat buns. Chen laughed and said, "We're idiots. He's never seen a meat bun, so how would he know if it's good or not? Wolves are naturally distrusting; hell, he doesn't even trust me. He probably thought they were stones, since the Mongol kids passing by never miss a chance to throw stones at him."

Zhang walked up to the dugout. "He's a cute little thing," he said with a smile. "I can't wait to pick him up and play with him."

"He only plays with Yang Ke and me," said Chen. "We're the only ones who can pick him up. Gao Jianzhong won't even touch him, afraid he'll bite. I don't think you should try."

Zhang bent down to get closer to the dugout. "Little Wolf, don't forget I'm the one who brought you the horsemeat. You're not the type to forget a friend after he's fed you, are you?" He called out a few more times, but the cub bared his fangs and refused to come out. Zhang was about to pull on the chain when the cub shot out of his hole, mouth open, ready to bite. Zhang backed off so fast he fell down. Chen wrapped his arm around the cub's neck to stop him, and then rubbed his head to calm him down.

Brushing the dirt off and standing up, Zhang said, "Not bad. He's still as ferocious as those in the wild. It'd be no fun if he turned into a dog. I'll bring him some more horsemeat when I come next time."

Chen told Zhang about the dangers the little wolf's howls could bring down on their heads. Zhang returned *The Sea Wolf* and picked up *A History of the World.* "Experience tells me that the wolf pack could be here tonight, so be careful, and don't let them take our cub away. They're afraid of explosives, so toss a double-kick firecracker if they break into the sheep flock. Make sure those I got you last time are still dry."

"Yang Ke wrapped them in wax paper and put them in a wooden box, so they should be dry. A few days ago, he got into a fight with the migrants and lit three of them. Scared the hell out of them."

Zhang Jiyuan mounted up and rode back to his herd.

26

After dinner, Bao Shungui came to Chen's yurt from Bilgee's place and gave Chen and Yang a large flashlight that required six batteries; it was a weapon and a tool that normally only horse herders were qualified to use. The gift was accompanied by a special task: "Flash this light if wolves get close to the sheep; instead of using firecrackers, let your dogs take them on. I've already told the others around here to rush over with their dogs as soon as they see your light.

"I didn't realize that raising this little wolf might work out so well," Bao said with a smile. "If the mother and the rest of the pack come tonight, we can kill seven or eight of them. Where are you going to find a better opportunity to lure wolves than with one of their own cubs? This time we'll turn the tables on them. Be careful, you two. One of these lights can blind a person for several minutes, and even longer for wolves. You still have to have your spades and clubs ready, just in case."

After Chen and Yang gave him their promise, Bao left to pass out instructions to other yurts, forbidding them from firing their weapons, since that would scare away the wolves and could injure people or their animals. Then he rushed off.

The excitement of luring wolves by using one of their own energized the grasslanders, even though the consequences, since this had never been tried before, could not be predicted. A few young herdsmen, whose hatred of wolves ran so deep they had stopped visiting Chen and Yang, now came by to gauge the lay of the land. They seemed unduly interested in this new hunting strategy. "Female wolves are so protective of their cubs," one of the shepherds said, "they're sure to come if they know one of them is here. I'd love to see them every night, so we could kill wolves every day."

"Wolves never fall for the same trick twice," said a horse herder.

"What if a whole pack attacks?" one of the shepherds asked.

"Our dogs'll outnumber them," the herder replied. "And if that's not enough, we'll join in with our lights and shouts. We can open fire or set off firecrackers."

After they'd left, Chen and Yang sat on a felt rug near the cub with heavy hearts, feeling profoundly guilty. "This is so ruthless," said Yang. "If we succeed in luring the mother wolf, that'll mean that after raiding her den, we now exploit a mother's love to kill her. We'll rue this day for the rest of our lives."

"I'm beginning to wonder again whether raising this cub was such a good idea," Chen said, his head bowed low. "Six cubs paid with their lives for this one, and who knows how many more will die. But I can't stop now. Scientific experimentation is like butchery sometimes. It's hard on Bilgee, trying to lead the people, too much pressure. He has to endure the sadness of wolves slaughtering the livestock, while feeling the pangs of having to kill wolves. But for the sake of the grassland and the people, he has to do whatever's necessary to preserve the balance of interdependent relationships. I wish I could ask Tengger to tell the mother wolves not to come tonight, not tonight or tomorrow night. They'd run right into a trap. Give me a little more time and I'll return the cub to his mother when he's a bit older."

Later that night, Bilgee came to check on their battle readiness. He sat with them and silently smoked a pipe. "The horses are going to suffer again when the mosquitoes come in a few days," he said softly, as if to console them. "If we spare the wolves, we won't have many ponies left this year, and that won't please Tengger either."

"Do you think the mother wolf will come tonight, Papa?" Yang Ke asked.

"Hard to say. I've never seen anything as ruthless as luring a mother wolf with a cub raised by humans. Never heard of it either. But Director Bao has ordered us to use him as bait. So many foals died that we're forced to let him and the horse herders kill a few wolves to vent their anger."

The old man left and the pasture was quiet, except for the sheep chewing their cud and the occasional flicking sounds of their ears as they tried to drive away the mosquitoes. The first swarms had come quietly, without fanfare, but only a small squadron of recon aircraft; the heavy bombers hadn't yet appeared.

The men chatted softly some more before turning in. Chen went to bed first, while Yang, staring at his night-glow wristwatch and gripping the large flashlight, kept a watchful eye on the area, his firecracker-stuffed book bag hanging from his neck.

After finishing the horsemeat, the cub sat at the edge of his pen waiting expectantly, stretching the chain taut and pricking up his ears, focused on sounds he longed to hear. His shiny eyes seemed to pierce the mountain ridge; he looked as sad as an orphan yearning for his kin.

The howls came soon after midnight, as the wolves launched a bombardment of noise: a relentless howling from three sides, intended to wear the enemy down. The dogs immediately counterattacked, responding with loud barks. The howling stopped, but it started up again as soon as the dogs went quiet, this time more ferocious than ever. After several rounds, the dogs barked only intermittently, as if there were no immediate danger and also to conserve their voices for a real war.

Chen Zhen and Yang Ke quickly walked up to observe the cub in the faint starlight. The clanging of the chain sounded in the pen as he circled anxiously. When he tried to imitate the howl, he was drowned out by the barking dogs, so he started to bark like a dog, since Erlang, Yellow, and Yir were nearby. Part bark, part howl, his voice was having trouble finding its own way. Erlang led the other dogs, nervously running back and forth on the northwestern edge of the sheep flock, barking constantly, as if they'd discovered the enemy's whereabouts. Soon wolf howls were heard from that direction, seeming much closer to Chen's flock. Dogs from other teams gradually stopped barking, as the wolf pack seemed to be gathering in the hills behind Chen's yurt. His lips quivering, Chen said softly, "The main force is directed here, where the cub is. Wolves truly never forget."

Beginning to grow frightened, Yang gripped his flashlight tightly and felt for the firecrackers in his book bag to reassure himself. "If they concentrate their attack on us, I won't hold back. I'll throw these at the pack, and you signal with the flashlight."

The dogs finally stopped barking. Chen whispered to Yang, "Crouch down and watch the cub. He's going to howl."

With no interference from the dogs, the cub listened to the howls from the wild. He stuck out his chest, pricked up his ears, and closed his eyes. He'd learned to listen carefully before trying to imitate the sound. The howls were aimed at him, and he was anxiously trying to identify the source, turning his head toward the sound. He began running around, since the howls came from three sides.

By listening carefully, Chen detected a difference in that night's howls. The night before, they had been more unified, as if to harass the humans, but now there were variations, some high, others low, like questioning, testing, even perhaps a mother wolf calling out to her cub. Chills ran through his body as he listened.

There were many stories about the love of a mother wolf for her cubs. In order to teach them to hunt, she'd take great risks to catch a live lamb under daunting circumstances; in order to protect her cubs in the den, she'd fight hunters to the death; for the cubs' safety, she'd carry them to a different place each night; and to feed them, she'd gorge herself to the point of bursting, and then empty the contents for them. And, in the interest of the pack, females who had lost their cubs nursed others' cubs.

Bilgee had told them that hunters and horse herders never took every cub in a den after a kill. The remaining cubs would have plenty of wet nurses and would grow strong with all that milk, which is why Mongolian wolves were the biggest, the strongest, and the smartest of all the wolves on earth. Chen had felt like adding, "And that's not all. A mother wolf's love can extend to human orphans even though humans are their chief enemies."

At that instant, he felt the urge to untie the leather collar and let the cub be reunited with his mother, along with all the other mothers. But he didn't dare. He was worried that, once the cub left the area under the camp's control, his own and the neighbors' dogs would tear it to pieces. And he didn't dare take him into the darkness to set him free, for that would place him in the midst of the frenzied mother wolves.

The cub seemed to detect the differences in the howls but did not know what to do about the sounds coming from all directions. Obviously, he did not comprehend the nuanced differences in the varying howls, nor did he know how to respond. The howls slowly died down, after failing to receive any response. They were probably puzzled by the cub's silence.

At that moment, the cub steadied himself, faced northwest, and lowered his head as he made the first tentative noise. Then he breathed in, raised his head, and sent out the second tone. Eventually he managed a howl, though it was slightly off. The distant howls stopped abruptly. What was that sound? The wolf pack waited.

A moment later, a sound echoing the cub's emerged from the pack, perhaps from a young wolf. Chen could tell that the cub was puzzled; he didn't understand the question being asked. Like a deaf mute who has regained his hearing and voice, he couldn't tell what was being said and was therefore unable to express himself.

After getting no further response, the cub lowered his head and breathed in deeply, then raised his head and released a long sound. This time he reached the heights of the night before. Obviously happy with his effort, he released one long howl after another without waiting for a response from the pack.

Led by Erlang, the dogs directed their ferocious barking to the northwest, and when they stopped, the cub began to howl again. Little by little, he learned to ignore the dogs' interference and skillfully and accurately produce wolf howls. After five or six in a row, he stopped and ran over to the water bowl, where he drank before running back to the same spot to howl again. He stopped after a moment and pricked up his ears to listen.

There was a long silence, and then a deep, somber howl arose on the western slope. Short and with distinct intonation, it was a sound with authority, probably an alpha male. From it, Chen could envision the animal's powerful body, broad chest, wide back, and full throat.

Surprised at first, the cub then leaped joyfully into the air. After lowering his head to breathe in, he stopped, not knowing how to respond. So he tried imitating the howl he'd just heard. His voice was obviously young, but it was a good imitation. He repeated it several times but drew no response.

Chen Zhen racked his brain to guess the meaning of this dialogue and its effect. Maybe the alpha male was asking the cub, "Who are you? Whose child are you? Answer me!" But the cub simply repeated the questions, even attempting to imitate the alpha male's commanding tone, which must have angered the adult and increased his suspicions.

By daring to imitate the alpha male's questions, the cub was revealing his ignorance of the hierarchy and protocol within a wolf pack. The other wolves must have been thinking that the cub was brazenly ignoring authority and was disrespectful of his elders, for a short noise then erupted from the pack, maybe indignation or maybe a heated discussion.

The pack soon quieted down again. The cub, on the other hand, was just getting started. Though he didn't understand the alpha male's questions or the pack's anger, he sensed that the shadows in the darkness had noticed his existence and wanted to communicate with him. He was eager to continue the dialogue but didn't know how to express himself, so he kept repeating what he'd just learned, howling at the darkness. "Whose child are you? Answer me! Answer me! Answer me!"

The wolves must have been growing anxious, not knowing what was happening, for they were probably the first pack in thousands of years to encounter such a cub, one living with humans, dogs, and sheep, a careless youngster who was full of nonsense. Was he really a wolf? If so, then what was his relationship to a wolf's natural enemies—humans and dogs? He sounded eager to communicate with the pack, but also seemed to get along well with dogs and humans. His voice was full, which meant he must eat well. Since people and dogs were good to him, what was he up to?

Chen tried to imagine what the wolves were thinking as they stared into each other's green eyes, increasingly suspicious of the cub.

The cub stopped howling, perhaps wanting to hear responses from the dark shadows; restless, he pawed the ground and waited anxiously.

Chen was disappointed and worried about how this was turning out. The alpha male could be the cub's father, but the cub did not know how to communicate with him. Chen was worried that the cub might lose the opportunity to gain his father's love, and if he did, would the lonely cub truly belong to humans now, to him and Yang Ke?

Suddenly, a long howl cut through the darkness. It was a gentle, tender, and mournful sound filled with the pain, sorrow, and longing of a mother wolf. The end note quivered for a long time, apparently a howl invested with deep meaning and emotion. Chen guessed it might mean: "Little Cub, do you still remember me? I'm your mother. I miss you; I've been looking all over for you, and now I finally hear your voice. My dear child, hurry and return to your mother. We all miss you-u-u."

A mother's song to her child, echoing through the ancient, desolate grassland. Chen was unable to hold back his tears; Yang Ke's eyes were also glistening.

The cub was apparently deeply touched by the intermittent sad sound. Instinct told him that it was a call from his own family, and that sent him into a frenzied struggle against the chain. Nearly strangled by the collar, he stuck out his tongue and panted loudly. The mother wolf began to howl again, and was soon joined by more mother wolves with the same sad voices, plunging the grassland into deep sorrow.

Their dirgelike howls rose and fell repeatedly on the grassland that night. It was as if the mother wolves wanted to vent their accumulated bitterness of losing cubs year after year over the millennia, submerging the vast, dark grassland into thousands of years of sadness.

Chen stood up silently, feeling the bone-chilling cold, while teary-eyed Yang walked slowly up to the cub, where he held the collar around the cub's neck and patted him on the head and back to comfort him.

As the mournful howls from the mother wolves gradually faded, the cub broke free of Yang and jumped away, as if afraid the sound would disappear altogether. He leaped toward the northwest and steadfastly raised his head to send out long howls from his limited memory.

Chen's heart sank. "It's all over," he whispered to Yang. "They can tell that his howl is different from the mother wolf's." He seemed to have focused on imitating the sad, plaintive voice. But his voice lacked power, and since he couldn't sustain a long howl, the pack went silent.

Staring at the slope that had suddenly gone quiet, Chen speculated on the anger in the hearts of the mother wolves that were anxiously looking for their cubs. How dare he make fun of their suffering? Experts in setting traps to lure their prey, the alpha male and lead wolves, who had often seen their kind snared by humans, must have concluded that the cub was bait, a seductive and lethal wolf in disguise.

Possibly the pack concluded that it was a dog, not a wolf. On the Olonbulag, the wolves often spotted men in green carrying rifles on the road up north. They were always accompanied by five or six big dogs whose ears stood straight up, just like the ears of wolves; some of them could howl like a wolf as well. They were far more menacing than any local dogs, and every year there were wolves who fell victim to them. More than likely, this little bastard would grow up to be one of those wolf-eared dogs.

Then again, maybe the pack believed it was a real wolf, Chen speculated, because the cub urinated on the slope when Chen took him out on his evening walks. Maybe some of the mothers could detect the smell of their cubs. In any case, while the grassland wolves were certainly clever, they could not easily overcome the cub's ineptitude with their language.

Silence still reigned in the wolf pack.

On the quiet grassland, there was only the howl of a chained cub whose throat was swollen and hoarse. But the long howls he made were so confusing, so unintelligible, that the wolves stopped their probing, ignoring the young wolf's pleas for help. The poor cub had now missed his chance to learn how to howl from the wolves.

Chen sensed that the pack was withdrawing.

The dark, gloomy slope was deadly quiet, like the sky-burial ground on Chaganuul Mountain.

Feeling no desire to sleep, Chen and Yang engaged in a whispered discussion; neither could explain to the other why things had turned out as they had.

At dawn the cub finally stopped howling; sad and despairing, he slumped to the ground and stared wide-eyed at the misty slope in an attempt to see the dark shadows. The morning mist slowly dissipated, revealing a familiar grassy slope devoid of shadows. The cub closed his eyes as if falling into a deathlike despair. Chen rubbed him gently, his guilt mounting as he thought of the cub's missed opportunity to rejoin his family.

The production teams and the rest of the brigade had made it through another scary night; no camp was attacked and the livestock had gone unharmed. The surprised herders were talking about it, unable to understand why the mother wolves, who would protect their cubs with their own lives, had retreated without a fight. Even the old men shook their heads. It would be the most mystifying incident Chen witnessed in his years on the grassland.

Bao Shungui and some of the herders who had expected to lure and kill the wolves were disappointed. But Bao came to Chen and Yang's yurt at dawn to praise them for their innovation and courage, helping to pull off an unprecedented victory of defeating the enemy without a fight. He said that they could keep the flashlight as a reward and that he'd publicize their experience. Chen and Yang breathed a sigh of relief, knowing they at least could continue to raise the cub.

Around the time for morning tea, Uljii and Bilgee came over for some tea and horsemeat buns.

Uljii seemed to be in good spirits for someone who hadn't slept well the night before. "That was a scary night," he said. "I really worried when the pack began to howl, since dozens of them had surrounded you on three sides and at times were only a hundred yards or so away. We were afraid they'd tear down your yurt. That was close."

"If I hadn't known you had all those 'crackling cannons,' I'd have ordered everyone and all the dogs to come to your rescue," Bilgee said.

"Why didn't they attack the sheep or try to snatch the cub away?" Chen asked.

The old man took a drink of tea and puffed on his pipe. "I think it could be that your little cub wasn't speaking real wolf language, and the dogs were barking, which confused the wolves."

"You're always telling me that wolves have a spiritual connection. So why didn't Tengger tell them the truth?"

"Of course the three of you and a few dogs would have been no match for them," the old man said. "But all the people and dogs here were geared up for a real battle, and if the wolves had decided to mount a frontal attack, they'd have been in serious trouble. Director Bao may be able to trick others, but not Tengger. Tengger didn't want the wolves to be trapped, so he ordered them to withdraw."

Chen and Yang laughed. Yang said, "Tengger is very wise."

"Scientifically speaking," Chen said to Uljii, "why didn't the wolves attack?"

Uljii thought for a moment. "I haven't seen or heard anything like what happened last night before. I think the pack might have considered the cub to be an outsider. The grassland wolves have their own territory, and those without territory leave sooner or later. Territory is more important than their lives. The local wolves often engage in mortal combat with wolves from other areas. Maybe your cub speaks a language unintelligible to the pack, and they didn't think it was worth their while to fight over an alien cub. The alpha male was here last night, and he's not easy to trick. He must have seen through the trap, since he understands that deception is the battlefield norm. He grew suspicious when he saw how close the cub was to humans and dogs. He won't take a risk unless there's a seventy percent chance of success, and he never touches anything he doesn't understand. He treats the females well and doesn't want them to be tricked either, which is why he came to check things out for them. He led them away when something didn't look right to him."

Chen and Yang nodded in agreement.

They saw their guests out. Still despondent and visibly thinner, the cub was sprawled on the ground, resting his chin on the back of his paws, staring straight ahead. He looked as if he'd had both good and bad dreams the night before and was still unable to return to reality.

The old man stopped when he saw the cub. "Poor little wolf. The pack didn't want him and his parents couldn't recognize him. Will he live the rest of his life attached to a chain? When you Chinese came to the grassland, you broke down our established rules. My heart aches when I see you shackle a clever little wolf like a slave. Wolves are very patient. Just you wait and see. He'll escape one of these days; you'll never win him over, not even if you feed him a fat little lamb every day."

No wolf howls sounded around the camp on the third night, or on the fourth, except for the lonely and forlorn howls of the cub rising above the quiet grassland and echoing in the valley. There was no response. After a week, he all but stopped.

For some time after that, no wolves came to attack the sheep or cattle in Yang and Chen's care, or any livestock belonging to the two nearby production teams. The women on night shift all smiled and said to them, "Now we can get a good night's sleep, all the way through to milking time."

During those days, when they talked about raising wolves, the herdsmen went easier on Chen. But none of them expressed any interest in raising a cub themselves, not even to scare away a wolf pack. Some old herdsmen in Section Four said, "Why not let them do it? We'll see what happens when the cub grows bigger and turns wild."

27

During this period, the cub had plenty to eat, thanks to Zhang Jiyuan's supply of horsemeat. Whenever he was reminded of how the mother wolves took care of their young in the pack, Chen felt he should give the cub better and even more food, and walk him more often. But even though he reserved all the meat for the cub, the supply eventually ran out and the entrails were barely enough for one more meal. Chen was concerned.

One evening Gao Jianzhong told him that an ox grazing on a slope had been struck by lightning, so early the next morning Chen went up the hill with his knife and a gunnysack, but he was too late. Nothing but the skull and some of the hardest bones remained; the wolves hadn't left a shred of meat behind. He sat down to check out the bones and saw tiny tooth marks left by cubs in the cracks. Working together, the adults had gobbled up great chunks of meat while the cubs had eaten the shreds, finishing off the ox completely. Even the flies buzzed in anger and flew away after a nibble or two. An old cow herder in Section Three came up while Chen sat there; the pile of bones appeared to have belonged to an animal in his herd. He said to Chen, "The wolf pack didn't dare come for the sheep, so Tengger killed an ox for them. See, Tengger even picked the right moment, at night, when the workers couldn't be here to haul it back for its meat. Young man, Tengger sets the grassland rules and punishes people who break them." With a dark face, he closed his knees around his horse's sides and rode slowly down the hill toward his herd.

The rules the old herdsmen talk about are the natural laws of the grassland, Chen was thinking, set by heaven, that is, the universe. Raising a wolf under nomadic, pastoral conditions clearly disrupts the mode of production. The cub has already caused the grassland trouble, and who knows what new troubles it might cause in the days to come. He returned empty-handed, his head a jumble of thoughts. Gazing up at Tengger, he thought of lines of poetry: "The sky covers the earth like a terrestrial roof," and "The sky is dark, the wilderness vast / The grass bends when the wind blows / No wolf can be seen." Out there, a wolf pack is like a will-o'-the-wisp, coming and going in a flash; people often hear the wolves and are witness to the damage they do, but they seldom see them in the flesh, which is why, in the minds of the people, they are so mysterious, so cunning, so magical. That was also why Chen could not control his own curiosity, his desire to learn and to study. With the cub, he knew he had a living wolf that was surrounded by a belief in a wolf totem. He'd gone through so much trouble, had endured so much pressure, and had risked so much that he felt he couldn't stop even if he wanted to.

He went over to the laborers' camp, where he paid a steep price for some millet. Without meat, all he could do was add more grain to the cub's food, hoping the diet would sustain it until the next time a sheep was slaughtered. Then he'd be able to give the dogs some meat too.

Back in the yurt he was about to take a nap when the three puppies yelped happily and ran off. Chen went out and looked to the west; it was Erlang, Yellow, and Yir returning from the mountains. Both Erlang and Yellow held their heads high, holding large prey in their mouths. Constant gnawing hunger had driven Yir and Yellow to follow Erlang up into the mountains to hunt. Obviously, they'd had a pretty good day; not only had they taken care of their own bellies, but they were able to bring some home for the puppies.

Chen rushed up to greet the dogs, as the puppies fought for the food in their mouths. Erlang laid down his catch to chase the puppies away, then picked it up again and ran toward home. Chen's eyes lit up, for Erlang and Yellow each carried a marmot and Yir had a foot-long prairie dog, its head the size of a turnip. It was the first time Chen had seen his dogs bring prey back, and he happily ran up to take it.

Eager for Chen's praise, Yellow and Yir quickly laid their catch at his feet and jumped up and down, yelping and wagging their tails and running in circles around him. Yellow even did a split with his front legs, with his chest and neck nearly touching the dead marmot, something completely new to Chen. He appeared to be telling him that it was he who'd caught it. A row of pink, swollen nipples on the marmot's belly showed that it was a nursing female. Chen patted both dogs on the head. "Good dogs," he said. "Good dogs."

Erlang, on the other hand, refused to lay down his catch; he walked around Chen and then ran toward the cub. Seeing it was a big, fat marmot, Chen ran up and grabbed Erlang's bushy tail, then snatched the marmot from him. Erlang wagged his tail to show he didn't mind. Holding one of the animal's hind legs, Chen figured it weighed over ten pounds, a male with shiny fur that had accumulated a thick layer of meat, though it wouldn't have any fatty flesh until the fall. Chen planned to save it for himself and his yurt mates; it was a delicacy they hadn't enjoyed for a very long time.

Holding all three catches, Chen walked happily toward the yurt, followed by the three dogs, who were snarling playfully at each other. Chen put the big marmot inside the yurt and closed the door. The puppies sniffed at the other catches curiously; Chen decided to give the skinny female to them and the prairie dog to the cub so that he could taste wolves' favorite food and learn to eat an animal on his own.

In the summer, marmot fur is virtually worthless; the purchasing station wouldn't buy one, so Chen quartered the animal and gave three portions, skin and flesh, bones and entrails, to the puppies, and saved the last quarter for the cub. The puppies knew exactly what to do when they saw the bloody meat. They sprawled on the ground to eat their share, no fighting or yelping. The three big dogs were wagging their tails, showing their appreciation of how Chen divided up the food, something he'd learned from Jack London's *The Call of the Wild,* a book he knew he'd never get back after lending it out, now that it was in circulation among students in two brigades.

The bellies of the big dogs bulged; they'd eaten their fill in the mountains. But their accomplishment still had to be rewarded, an established rule on the grassland. So Chen walked out of the yurt with four pieces of candy and gave two to Erlang, who held them in his mouth and looked at Chen out of the corner of his eye to see how he'd reward Yellow and Yir. When Erlang saw the other two dogs get one piece each, he happily tore open the wrappers with his paws and teeth, then made a crackling noise as he chewed the candy. Yellow and Yir did the same, not at all upset over getting less than Erlang. Chen suspected that Erlang might have caught all the prey himself, and the other two dogs had merely helped him bring it back.

The smell of blood had the cub so frenzied that he stood up on his hind legs and clawed at the air. Chen tried not to look in his direction, for that would have gotten him excited enough to pull the chain too tightly around his neck. He didn't attend to the prairie dog until he'd finished taking care of the dogs. There is a wide range of rodents on the grassland, the most common of which are ground squirrels, prairie dogs, and field mice. Prairie dogs are everywhere, always within a fifteen- or twenty-foot radius of any given yurt, where they stand outside their holes and squeak loudly. Sometimes, when a yurt is set up right over their holes, they abandon their grass diet and switch to eating grain. They steal grain, dairy products, and meat, leave their droppings in food bags, and sometimes even gnaw on books. When people move, they often find rodents' young in boots and shoes they haven't worn for a while. Infant prairie dogs squirming like meaty worms is a disgusting sight. The herders and the students also hated the mice; Chen and Yang took a special dislike to them, for these rodents had destroyed two of the literary classics in their collection.

According to Bilgee, in ancient times, live prairie dogs were used as targets by Mongol children to practice archery.

Chosen for their speed and keen eyes, the prairie dogs were good targets for Mongol children, whose parents told them not to come back home until they'd shot a certain number. It was the children's favorite game, the grassland their amusement park, and they were often so caught up in it that they forgot to go home to eat. When they grew older, they exchanged their small bows for bigger ones and practiced shooting from horseback. Jebe, Genghis Khan's general who conquered Russia, was a famous archer who had learned to shoot like that. He could shoot a prairie dog in the head on a galloping horse from a hundred yards. Bilgee said the Mongols' riding and shooting skills both protected the grassland and helped them conquer the world. Shooting the smallest, cleverest, and most difficult target, the prairie dog, was how they honed their archery skill.

Chen picked up the prairie dog by its tail and examined it. He'd seen large ones when he was out with the sheep, but a foot-long specimen that was thicker than a baby bottle could grow only in the fertile grassland of the mountains. He assumed that its meat would be fatty and tender, for it was a favorite food of the wolves. He imagined how the cub, once he smelled the blood, would pounce on it and nearly swallow it whole.

Chen held it upside down; blood from its wounds dripped onto the sandy ground. Standing outside the pen, he shouted, "Little Wolf, Little Wolf, time to eat."

The cub stared until his eyes turned red; he'd never seen food like that, but the smell of blood told him it was something good. He leaped up over and over, but Chen kept raising it higher; the exasperated cub kept his eyes fixed on the fat prairie dog, not on Chen, who insisted that the cub look at him before he'd give him the food, but after seeing the dead animal, the cub had changed; he was now more like a fierce wild wolf, fangs bared, claws pawing the air. His mouth was opened wide, exposing all four canines, all the way back to the gum line. The cub's demonic look terrified Chen. He waved the prey a few more times but was still unable to divert the cub's gaze. Finally he gave up and tossed it over. Then he crouched by the pen, expecting the cub to tear the animal to pieces and gobble it down. So he was surprised by what the cub did after catching the prairie dog in midair; it was something he could neither explain nor forget.

As if he'd caught a piece of hot steel, the cub immediately dropped it and backed away. Then, standing a few feet back, he stretched his neck and body and stared at the dead rodent with apparent fright; that continued for three minutes, until fear no longer showed in his eyes. Then he arched his body and leaped seven or eight times before running up and pouncing on the prairie dog. He took a bite, jumped back and stared at it again for some time. Seeing that the rodent wasn't moving, he pounced, took another bite, then stopped and glared at it. He repeated this three or four times before finally calming down.

Reverence replaced the ferocity in the cub's eyes. He walked up to the prairie dog and stopped beside it. He respectfully bent his right front leg, then the left; he touched the prairie dog with the right side of his back before rolling over. Then he got up, shook off the sand, straightened out the chain, and ran to the other side of the rodent, where he repeated the action, but in reverse order.

Chen watched with nervous curiosity, unsure of what the cub was doing, where he had learned those movements, or why he'd touched the rodent's side and rolled over. The cub was like a little boy who's been given a whole roasted chicken to himself for the first time: he's eager to eat but cannot bring himself to begin, so he turns it over and over in his hand. The cub repeated the actions three times.

Chen could hardly believe his eyes. He'd given the cub plenty of tasty meat, sometimes fresh from a kill, but the little wolf had never done anything like that before. What was so different about this prairie dog? Was it a way for the cub to congratulate himself on getting an animal? Or was it a ritual before eating? His respectful, reverent manner resembled that of a Catholic taking communion.

After thinking until his head ached, Chen realized that what he'd given the cub this time was different. No matter how good the food, he'd always given the cub broken pieces of bone and chopped meat, food processed by humans. But this was natural, wild, intact food, a "live" animal that, like he himself, had a head and a tail, a body and paws, skin and fur, just like oxen, sheep, horses, and dogs. Maybe for wolves this "live" food, with its distinct shape, was a meal only noble wolves were entitled to enjoy.

The cub took a breath but did not start right in. He shook his body to smooth out his coat before trotting slowly around the dead animal. Then his eyes narrowed; his tongue lolled out of the side of his mouth; he picked up his feet and put them down slowly, like one of those white horses in a Russian circus, carrying out well-rehearsed movements in a clearly defined performance. After several rounds of this, the cub quickened his pace but did not change the size of the circle made by his footprints on the sandy ground.

Feeling a tingling in his scalp, Chen was reminded

of the mysterious, frightening wolf circle by the pile of dead army horses in the early spring. Created by dozens of wolves running around a dense pile of horse carcasses, it had seemed like a sort of demonic writing or spirit painting. The elders believed that it was a letter of inquiry and thanks from the wolves to Tengger. That circle was nearly perfect, and so was the one made by the cub; and in the middle of both circles was prey.

Was it that the cub had to first thank Tengger before enjoying the fresh food?

The cub was still running in circles. He hadn't had fresh meat all day and was ravenously hungry. Normally the sight of bloody meat turned a hungry wolf into a frenzied one. So why would the cub act against nature and instead perform something befitting a religious devotee, managing to control his hunger to carry out a set of complicated "religious rites"? Did a primitive religion exist among wolves, one that could control their behavior via a strong spiritual power, even for a cub who had been separated from the pack before he opened his eyes?

Finally, the cub stopped. Crouching by the prairie dog and panting, he waited until his breathing became normal before licking his lips twice. A savage flame of greed and a hungry glare shone brightly in his eyes; he quickly changed from a primitive religious accolyte into a wild and hungry wolf. He pounced on his prey and bit into it, then tossed his head and tore off half the rodent's skin and fur, exposing the bloody mass of flesh underneath. Shaking violently all over, he tore and he ate. After swallowing the meat and bones from one side of the prairie dog, he emptied out the entrails and wolfed down everything without clearing out the acrid grass in the stomach or the excrement in the intestines.

As he ate, his manner grew increasingly wild and excited; he made happy, rhythmic snorts that sent shivers down Chen's spine. He was getting increasingly wild and savage in the way he devoured the rodent, treating everything equally; the flesh, the bones, the skin, the fur, the bladder, and even the bitter gallbladder were all delicacies to him. In no time, there was nothing left but the head and the short tail. But that didn't stop him; he held the head up with his paws and bit off half of it, including the teeth. Then he finished off the other half. He didn't even spare the hairy yet bony tail; he bit it in two, and down it went. In the end there was only a bit of blood and some urine stains left on the sandy ground. But he still was not sated, for he stared awhile at Chen before finally confirming that the young man's hands were empty; reluctantly, he walked part way toward Chen, then lay down on the ground looking disappointed.

Chen now knew that the cub had a fondness for grassland rodents, for they awakened his instincts and his potential, which was perhaps why the Olonbulag had had no serious damage from rodents over thousands of years.

Love and affection for the little wolf surged in Chen's heart. He could enjoy a good drama nearly every day; it was always lively and profound, full of instructional significance, turning him into the cub's most loyal fan.

While the cub stared longingly at the puppies gnawing on bones, Chen went into the yurt to skin the marmot. He cut out the head and neck area that had been bitten through by the dogs, and put the pieces in a basin to serve as the cub's dinner. He then chopped up the meat. It half filled the pot and would make a fine meal for three.

In the evening the cub sat sedately in his sandy pan, facing west to watch anxiously as half of the setting sun slowly disappeared. As soon as the dying sun left only a few specks of light on the grassy hilltop, he whipped around to face the yurt door and made a series of odd movements, like beating a drum or pouncing on food or executing somersaults and backflips. Then he clanged his chain to remind Chen or Yang that it was time for his walk.

Chen ate some of the meat before the others returned so that he could take the cub for a walk, followed by Erlang and Yellow. This semifree time at dusk was the happiest moment of the cub's day, even more eagerly anticipated than mealtime. But walking a wolf was not the same as walking a wolfhound. It was the most enjoyable yet the most exhausting and difficult labor of the day for Chen.

With his ferocious appetite, the cub had grown much larger and a head longer than a dog of the same age and he weighed half again as much as a puppy. He had shed his fetal hair, which had been replaced by shiny gray-yellow fur. The row of dark mane on his back stood long and straight, nearly the same as on a big wild wolf. His once round head had flattened out, and white spots appeared amid the fur. His face had also elongated, with a moist tip on a nose that looked like a rubber bottle cap, hard and tough. Chen liked to pinch that nose, which made the cub sneeze; it was the cub's least favorite sign of affection. His ears had grown hard and long, like pointed spoons. From a distance, he looked like a wild wolf.

His eyes were the most fearsome and yet the most fascinating part of his face. They were round, but slanted upward and outward, and were more striking than the eyes painted on the face of a Beijing Opera performer. The inner corners of his eyes slanted downward to form a dark tear-duct line, giving them an especially eerie appearance.

The cub's eyebrows were a light gray-yellow mass of fur, not particularly effective in showing anger. For that, the eyes held the key. Most terrifying were the furrows that formed alongside his nose when he was angry.

The cub's eyes differed fundamentally from those of humans or other animals. The "whites" were more an amber yellow, which, Chen felt, had a penetrating power over human and animal psychology. The cub had small irises, dark and forbidding, like the tiny opening in the blowpipe used by the black man in one of Sherlock Holmes's stories. When the cub was angry, Chen dared not look him in the eye.

After the cub had gotten used to him, Chen could take advantage of his happy moments by grabbing his ears and holding his face. He'd been reading that face for more than a hundred days, and he knew it well. He often saw a fetching smile, but there were other times when what he saw scared him. The eyes alone could send chills down his spine, and he was scared witless when the cub exposed the four sharp fangs that were more lethal than those of a cobra. He frequently opened the cub's mouth and rapped his fingers against the fangs. They were strong and tough, the tips sharper than an awl. The enamel was much harder than that on the teeth of humans. Tengger had favored the wolves by giving them such a powerful yet handsome face, with all its terrifying weapons.

Over a period of weeks, the cub's strength had increased much faster than his body weight. Chen was no longer walking the wolf; he himself was being dragged along. The moment he left the pen, the cub pulled Chen toward the grassy slope like an ox pulling a cart. Chen and Yang would run to help the cub build up strength in his legs and hone his skill at running. The cub would use all his might to drag them along when they were too tired to run any longer, sometimes for an hour or more.

Chen Zhen's hand hurt, his arm ached, and he sweated profusely. The air was noticeably thinner here than in Beijing, and the cub often made him run so much that Chen's face paled and his legs cramped. In the beginning, he'd planned to run with the cub to toughen himself up. But he lost his confidence once the cub's potential for long-distance running exploded; even the fastest Mongol horses cannot keep up with running wolves. Chen and Yang began to worry about how they'd manage to "walk" the cub once he grew to adulthood. If they weren't careful, he might drag them into the middle of a wolf pack one day.

Sometimes the cub flipped Chen or Yang onto the ground, to the sheer delight of women and children in their yurts. Though they disapproved of raising the wolf, they enjoyed watching the Beijing students walk the cub, waiting for Tengger to punish them for their "scientific experiment."

A middle-aged herdsman who knew a bit of Russian once said to Chen, "Humans cannot tame wolves, nor can science."

Chen defended himself by saying he just wanted to observe and study the cub and had no intention of taming him. But no one would listen to him. His idea of mating the wolf with a hound had spread across the pasture and, like the story of the cub flipping the young men to the ground, was a joke shared by herdsmen. They said they'd wait to hear about the wolf devouring a bitch.

The cub ran happily, dragging Chen, who was panting hard, trying to keep up. At first the cub had run aimlessly, but in recent days he'd begun dragging Chen to the northwest, where the nocturnal wolf howls had been concentrated. His curiosity aroused, Chen let the cub lead him where he wanted to go. They passed through a ravine and arrived at a gentle slope; it was the farthest they'd ever gone.

Chen saw that they were three or four *li* away from the yurt, which worried him a bit. But, with the protection of the two dogs and his club, he decided not to force the cub to turn back. They ran for another half *li* or so before the cub slowed down to sniff at everything around him: a pile of cow dung, a small mound, a piece of white bone, a clump of grass, a rock, anything that lay on the ground. He sniffed his way to a clump of cogon grass and, all of a sudden, the hair on his back stood up like quills. His eyes lit up in surprise and joy, while he continued to sniff at the clump of grass as if wanting to bury his head in it. Then he looked up and howled at the setting sun. It was a sad, dreary moan, not the excited, happy howl of the past. Maybe he was complaining to his kin about his life in prison, Chen thought.

Erlang and Yellow sniffed at the grass, and the hair on their backs also stood up. As they pawed at the soil and barked frantically, it dawned on Chen that the cub and the dogs had detected the smell of wolf urine. He parted the grass with his shoe. Several stalks of grass were yellowed at the bottom. A pungent odor assaulted his nose, making him nervous; this was fresh urine, which meant that the wolves were still hanging around the camp.

The setting sun shrouded the slope in a dark green shadow. A gentle wind blew over the undulating grass, making it seem like the backs of a pack of wolves. Chen shuddered, fearing an ambush. Just then, the cub raised his leg to urinate.

The mother wolf clearly missed her cub, and now he had learned how to send her a message. If he made contact with her, the consequences would be unimaginable. Without a second thought, Chen flipped the cub backward. Having his desire and his plan to find his mother interrupted, the cub glared and crouched down before exploding forward and leaping at Chen like a true wild animal.

Chen backed away instinctively, but he tripped and fell by the clump of grass. The cub bit him savagely on his calf. Chen cried out as a searing pain and a sense of terror coursed through his body. The fangs had bitten through his pants and sunk into the flesh. He quickly sat up and pushed his club against the tip of the cub's nose. But the cub had gone wild; he would not let go, as if the only thing that would please him would be to take a chunk out of Chen's leg.

The dogs were stunned, but they sprang into action. Yellow grabbed the cub by the nape of his neck and tried to drag him away, while Erlang barked menacingly at him. The thunderous bark finally shocked the cub into letting go.

Chen nearly collapsed from fright. He saw his blood on the cub's teeth. Erlang and Yellow were still restraining the young wolf, so Chen grabbed him by the neck and held him tightly in his arms, where the cub continued to struggle and growl, eyes glaring, fangs bared.

Chen yelled at the dogs until they stopped barking. The cub stopped struggling. As Chen loosened his grip, the cub shook himself and backed away, glaring at Chen, the hair on his back still standing straight up. Chen was both angry and scared. "Little Wolf," he said breathlessly, "have you gone blind? How dare you bite me?" The familiar voice finally brought the cub back from his bestial madness. He cocked his head to study the man before him, as if slowly recognizing who Chen was. There wasn't a hint of apology in his eyes.

Chen's wound was bleeding, the blood seeping into his shoe. Scrambling to his feet, he plunged his club into a rodent hole and looped the iron ring on the chain through this temporary post. Afraid that the sight of blood would give the cub the wrong idea, he took a few steps and turned around before sitting down to take off his shoe and roll up his pant leg. There were four tiny punctures in his calf. Luckily, the pant fabric, which was like canvas, had taken most of the force of the bite, so the wounds weren't deep. Chen pressed the skin around the wounds to release clean blood and clear out the toxins, a trick he'd learned from the herdsmen. After squeezing out about half a syringe of blood, he tore off a strip of his shirt to wrap around the wound.

Chen stood up again, took the chain, and pointed the cub's head in the direction of the yurt. Signaling the cooking smoke rising out of the yurt, he shouted, "Little Wolf, Little Wolf, time to eat. Drink some water." He and Yang had figured out that that was the only way to get the cub to return after each walk. When he heard food and water, he drooled and, forgetting what had just happened, dragged Chen toward home.

The cub ran to his bowl, eagerly awaiting his food and water, so Chen looped the iron ring over the post and buttoned the cap, then gave the marmot's neck and half a basin of clean water to the cub, who ignored the neck and instead buried his face in the basin of water and gulped it down. In order to ensure that he'd return willingly each time after the walk, they'd stopped giving him water all day before walking him. After running until he was famished and parched, he'd drag them back at the mere mention of water.

Chen went into the yurt to tend to his injury. The sight of the wounds so alarmed Gao Jianzhong that he made Chen promise to go get a shot. Not wanting to risk infection, Chen rode over to the students' yurt in Section Three, where he asked the barefoot doctor, Little Peng, to give him a rabies shot, apply some salve, and bandage the wounds, while begging him not to tell anyone about the bite, for which he'd let Peng keep a book he'd borrowed and lend him two more, a biography of Napoleon and Balzac's *Père Goriot*.

Peng agreed, though not without some grumbling. "The Brigade office clinic only gives me three or four vials of antirabies serum at a time," he said. "I've already used up two on laborers who were bitten by herders' dogs, so now I have to go back there on a hot day."

Chen appeased the man, though he was barely aware of what he was saying; all he could think about now was how he was going to keep the cub. It had finally bitten him and, according to the laws of the grassland, even a dog was killed if it bit a sheep and was beaten to death on the spot if it bit a person. With a wolf cub that had bitten a human, there'd be no way out. Raising a wolf was already "violating the laws of nature," and now its survival was threatened. Oblivious of his injury, Chen got back on the horse, slapping his own head on the way home, wishing he could dream up a way to save the cub.

Back at the yurt, he heard Yang and Gao arguing about how to deal with a cub that had begun biting people. "What an animal!" Gao shouted. "If he'll go after Chen Zhen, who won't he attack? We have to kill him. What if he bites someone else? In the fall, when we move to a new pasture, the sections will be so far apart I don't know how anyone could manage to get a rabies shot. A wolf bite is worse than a dog bite. You can die from it."

Yang Ke said softly, "I'm afraid the brigade won't give us any more vaccine. It's so precious they keep it for people who are bitten by a wolf or a dog on the job. What I'm thinking is, we set the cub free as soon as possible. Otherwise, they'll send someone to kill him."

"You're talking about setting free a wolf that's already bitten someone? How dense can you be? It won't work, not now."

Chen knew what he had to do. He clenched his teeth and said, "I've made up my mind. We won't kill him and we won't set him free. If we kill him, my wounds would all be for nothing and our efforts over these months would be wasted. And setting him free would be a death sentence. Even if he returned to the pack, the wolves would treat him as an outsider or a 'traitor wolf.' How would he survive then?"

"Then what do we do?" Yang said with a dark look.

"All we can do now is perform tooth surgery. We snip off the tips of his teeth, a wolf's most lethal weapon. He'll still be able to bite, but he won't draw blood and there'll be no need for rabies shots. We can cut the meat into small pieces to feed him."

Yang shook his head. "It's doable, but that's a death sentence too. A wolf without fangs can't survive out here."

"It's the only thing I can think of. In any case, I say we don't stop just because I got bitten. Maybe the tips will grow back. For now they're a threat to us."

The following morning, Chen and Yang performed the surgery on the cub before taking their sheep out to graze. After giving him plenty of food to make him happy, Yang grabbed him by the back of his head and forced open his mouth with his thumbs. The cub was used to such antics, and didn't mind them a bit. Facing the sun, they took a close look into the cub's mouth. The fangs were slightly transparent and the root visible. They could see they wouldn't damage the roots if they just clipped off the tips. He could keep his canines, which might be sharp again before long.

Chen let the cub sniff and play with the clippers for a while so as not to fear them. Then Yang forced open his mouth, and Chen quickly and carefully snipped off the tips of the fangs, about a quarter length of each tooth. Thinking that clipping off the cub's canines would be as hard as pulling a tiger's teeth, they'd been prepared to tie the cub up and battle him over the forced surgery. The whole process took less than a minute, with no injury to anyone. The cub licked at the broken surfaces, seemingly unaware of what he had lost. They set him down gently. They wanted to give him something good to eat but decided not to for fear of hurting him.

Now they breathed a sigh of relief, no longer having to worry that the cub might bite someone. But for several days they were saddened by what they'd done. "Trimming a wolf's fangs is crueler than castrating a man," Yang Ke commented.

Chen had to ask himself, "Have we moved too far from our original purpose in raising a cub?"

They also felt bad about the books lent to Little Peng. Among the hundred or so students in the brigade, only they had brought along cases of classics condemned as "feudal, capitalist, and revisionist." After the first two stormy years, tedium and boredom had spurred the students to begin devouring the banned books in secret. Once a book was lent out, there was little hope of ever getting it back. But Chen had had no choice. Bao Shungui would certainly have killed the cub when the leaders heard about what had happened. As it turned out, the classics did their job; for a long time no one in the brigade learned that Chen Zhen had been bitten by his wolf cub.

28

East-central Inner Mongolia probably has more mosquitoes than anywhere in the world. They find welcoming habitation in the many rivers and lakes, the tall, dense grass, and the dens of hibernating marmots; they live on an endless supply of blood, cold and hot: the blood of humans, cattle, and sheep, plus that of field mice, hares, snakes, marmots, and Mongolian gazelles. Swarms of them, crazed from feasting on wolf blood, had recently all but destroyed the nerves of a sixteen-year-old student, who was sent back to Beijing.

That summer was a particularly bad year for mosquitoes.

One afternoon, Chen Zhen sat inside the protection of his mosquito net reading. He got up, put on a beekeeper's mask, picked up a fly whisk made of horsehair, and walked out of the tightly sealed yurt to see how the wolf cub was doing. It was the time of day when the fiercest mosquito attacks occurred. Chen walked into a clamor more terrifying than an air-raid siren.

The big yellow Olonbulag mosquitoes lack the intelligence of wolves, and attack with greater disregard for their own survival. They will go after any creature as soon as they smell out its existence and have no concern over how many of them will die from a lethal tail swish by horse or cow; in fact, the crushed bodies of their splattered comrades are likely to send them into a blood lust.

The window of Chen's protective mask was virtually closed by the swarming mosquitoes. He was terrified to see that they not only swarmed in great numbers but appeared larger than normal. Their wings never stopped moving, so fast that only their bodies, the size of tiny shrimp, were visible to the naked eye, and he suddenly felt like a man who had sunk into a lake and was looking up at vast schools of plankton.

Chen's fettered white horse had no interest in grazing as it stood in the middle of a fertilizer trough. Filled with sheep dung, and devoid of even a blade of grass, it offered some respite from the mosquitoes. Some, but not enough, since the insects had blanketed the horse's hide like a layer of rice husks. The horse spotted Chen approaching, preceded by the fanlike motions of a whisk, and inched toward him. Chen quickly removed the fetters and led the horse over to the oxcart, where there were fewer mosquitoes, then replaced the fetters. The horse's head never stopped bobbing, the tail angrily fanning the air around its belly, rear legs, and flanks, while its mouth was its only weapon against attacks from the front. Tens of thousands of the insects parted the hair on the horse's hide and buried their sucking needles in its flesh. When their bellies were full, they looked like little wolfberries, red and shiny. The horse swished its tail with all its might, producing bloodred splotches where it landed, until its tail was wet with blood, the hairs sticking together like a rug. Its tail produced a blood-soaked killing field; the once white animal now looked like a horse that had run a gauntlet of bloodthirsty wolves.

Chen used his whisk to help drive mosquitoes away

from his horse's back and front legs. The animal displayed its gratitude by bowing its head. But more mosquitoes gathered around them, wave after wave, and Chen's horse could not free itself from them.

Chen's thoughts were on the wolf cub, so he left the horse and ran over to the pen, where the hole was half filled with water, making it impossible for the cub to hide from the mosquitoes. His thin summer coat was little protection against the attacking needles, and the exposed skin on his nose, ears, eyelids, face, head, and belly were under such an assault that the poor animal was on the verge of madness. For grassland mosquitoes, wolf blood may be a tonic, which is why the cub was attracting a yellow cloud of flying attackers. Rolling around on the ground had no effect, and he was driven to running madly around his pen, unwilling to expose his tongue as he reached a stage of exhaustion; had he opened his mouth to breathe, he'd have sucked insects into his throat. After a moment, he stopped running, folded himself into a ball, with his hind legs under him and his front legs covering his nose. Chen was amazed to discover that the young wolf, a tyrant of the grassland, could be brought to such an ignominious state by mosquitoes. And yet the cub's eyes were full of life, his gaze as penetratingly arrogant and unyielding as ever.

Bilgee had said to Chen, "Mosquito plagues are always followed by wolf plagues, because the killer insects leave starved, crazed wolves in their wake, for which humans and their livestock pay a price. The greatest terror on the grassland is linked plagues, especially mosquitoes and wolves." A climate of fear had settled over the entire brigade.

The cub was obviously being worn out, but didn't appear to have lost weight. The onslaught of mosquitoes continued day and night, yet he ran around the pen even more than usual. Faced with the fury of the mosquito plague, his obstinate nature held fast; his appetite did not diminish even a little. The young wolf actually fleshed out in the midst of the plague-filled season. Chen was like a doting father. As long as there was meat to eat and water to drink, the cub could withstand anything.

But now, with no warning, the cub began leaping around as if demented. A mosquito had managed to squirm under his belly and stick its needle into his little pecker. The excruciating pain left him no choice but to stop trying to evade the attacking mosquitoes and raise his rear leg to attend to his cherished appendage with its teeth; the moment he did that, hundreds of mosquitoes swarmed over his belly, causing such unbearable pain that he writhed in agony.

Leaving the cub to his afflictions, Chen grabbed his scythe, threw the willow basket over his back, and ran toward a culvert on the western hill where mugwort grew. The year before, when there were far fewer mosquitoes, he'd gone there with Gasmai to cut down mugwort. Soon after moving to the new grazing land, the rains came and Chen had gone out to determine where the mugwort grew most plentifully. Although the rains brought the mosquito plague, they also fed vast areas of mugwort, and as the plague of blood-sucking insects reached its peak, the medicinal odor of the plant filled the air. Chen looked up at Tengger and said, "This plant is what makes human survival on the grassland possible."

There wasn't a breath of wind down in the grassy culvert, and Chen's denim shirt was soaked with sweat. Swarms of mosquitoes buried their needles halfway into the thick fabric, and Chen could not pull them out;

the shirt was transformed into a pincushion of flying insects. He had no time to worry about that; he'd let them die there, impaled in his shirt. But then he felt a stabbing pain on his shoulder; he swatted the spot and drew back a bloody imprint.

Chen entered the patch of mugwort, where the number of mosquitoes dropped off dramatically. The plants, with gray-blue-white stalks, grew at least three feet high; the leaves had a succulent, downy surface. A bitter medicinal plant, mugwort went untouched by cows, sheep, and horses, which is why it grew in such profusion. As soon as he saw the tall plants, he slowed down, gripped his scythe tightly, and bent over cautiously into a battle stance. He and the other Beijing students had been warned by older shepherds that they should be especially careful around mugwort when they were out tending their flocks; since there were few mosquitoes, wolves often hid within these patches, rolling around and crushing the plant to coat their fur with the acrid smell, a natural mosquito repellent.

Not daring to venture too far into the patch without his dogs, Chen stopped and shouted twice. He detected no movement. He waited a few moments, then walked slowly in among the plants, where he felt surrounded by the miracle of salvation. He took aim at the densest patch he could see and began chopping like a madman, staining his scythe green and saturating the air with the strong medicinal odor. He breathed in deeply, as if to fill his innards with the smell.

After packing his basket with cut mugwort, Chen headed back, almost running, picking up a handful of the stuff along the way, squeezing out its juices, and rubbing it on the back of his hand. As expected, the exposed skin attracted few mosquitoes.

As soon as he was back in his yurt, he stoked the fire in the stove with dried cow dung, then ran outside to bring in seven or eight chipped water basins from the willow basket. Choosing the biggest of the lot, he dumped in some smoldering dung and covered it with mugwort. Dense white smoke reeking of mugwort rose immediately.

Chen carried the basin to the edge of the cub's pen, upwind, and watched as a breeze spread the smoke out over the pen. Mugwort is the mosquito's deadliest enemy; they retreat at the first whiff even if they're drawing blood from a victim at the time. It took only a moment for the greater half of the pen to be clear of mosquitoes.

The mugwort had come to the cub's rescue, but the sparks from the burning dung and the smoke made him tremble with fear. With a terrified look in his eyes, he leaped and ran as far away from the basin as the chain would allow, where he continued to struggle. Like all animals in the wild, he was deathly afraid of fire and smoke. Chen knew that this fear had been passed down generation after generation by the cub's ancestors. He added more mugwort to the fire and shook the basin to surround the young wolf with the smoke. He'd have to train the cub to adapt to the smoke treatment, since that was the only way he'd survive the terrible mosquito plague. Out in the wild, his mother would have led him up the mountain or over to a patch of mugwort in order to escape from the mosquitoes. But here at the camp, Chen was obliged to be a surrogate parent and smoke the mosquitoes away.

The smoke billowed and the wolf cub struggled, nearly strangling himself. But Chen refused to be moved; he kept adding more plants to the fire. Eventually, the cub stopped struggling, exhausted, and was forced to stand amid the smoke and shiver. Fearful of the smoke though he was, he seemed more relaxed now that the mosquitoes were gone. Finding that strange, he looked all around, then lowered his head to examine his belly. The little marauders that had poked around down there, making him leap into the air, were gone too. The look in his eyes was a mixture of confusion and joy as his spirits soared.

The smoke kept rolling toward the cub, who cringed when he saw it; and when a couple of sparks flew out of the basin, he nearly flew over to a spot as far away from the smoke as he could get. But all that earned him was an encirclement by waiting mosquitoes, which attacked him mercilessly. When covering his face did nothing to help the situation, he started running around madly once again. As his speed slowed after a dozen or so revolutions, he suddenly seemed to grasp the reality that there were fewer mosquitoes in some places than in others, and that those places were under the clouds of smoke. He stared wide-eyed and disbelieving at the white smoke, but soon spent more time in it than out of it. The cub, a smart youngster, sped up his thought processes to analyze what was happening around him. Still, the fear of smoke would not leave, and he floundered between smoke and no smoke.

The dogs lying beneath the oxcart quickly discovered the smoke. Grassland dogs all know the virtues of the white smoke. Their eyes lit up as they excitedly led the younger dogs over to the smoky refuge; now that the mosquitoes had left their bodies, they staked out positions where the smoke was thick enough, but not too thick, and stretched out comfortably, fully enjoying the chance to sleep. This was the young dogs' first encounters with the benefits of mugwort smoke. They followed the adults into the smoky air and rejoiced; they too found spots to lie down and rest. The restricted area that comprised the cub's pen was quickly occupied by half a dozen dogs that lay there, a sight that seemed to surprise the cub.

His happiness manifested in his squints, his open mouth, and his upturned tail. He often tried to get the dogs to come play with him, but they invariably ignored him. But on this day they came without being invited, all of them, including Yir, the bitch who hated the cub, and the cub was more excited than if he'd been given half a dozen fat mice. His fear was immediately forgotten as he rushed into the cloud of smoke and jumped onto Erlang's back, then rolled around with one of the female puppies. Now the lonely wolf was part of a happy family. He smelled them, kissed them, and licked them all over and over. A happier wolf, Chen Zhen thought, would be hard to find.

With all the dogs and one wolf cub, the limited amount of smoke began to lose some of its potency, and the pen's generous "master" was nudged out of the stream by the canine visitors to his territory. He tried to move back in, but the two male puppies blocked his way. He was obviously puzzled, and endured the attacks by mosquitoes as he tried to figure out the dogs' behavior. A few moments later, the light of understanding shone in his eyes. The questioning look was gone. He knew that the dogs had come not for his company, but for the white smoke, smoke that he had feared but that was a comfort zone where none of the wretched mosquitoes dared to enter. But it was his place. For the first time in his young life, he had gotten the worst of a situation, and that made him angry. He charged into the cloud of smoke, claws poised and fangs bared, to drive the puppies out of his territory. One defiantly refused to budge and was dragged away from the smoke by his ear, crying out in pain. The cub recaptured his spot, where the smoke was thick enough to keep mosquitoes away but not thick enough to choke him, and lay down to enjoy in comfort the freedom from mosquitoes. The cub, whose inquisitiveness and need to get to the bottom of things were so well developed, kept his eye on the basin, fascinated by the way smoke spewed from it.

Chen heard the sound of approaching horse hooves. His horse too was seeking refuge in the white smoke. He ran up, removed the fetters, led the horse over to the far edge of the wolf pen, and then replaced the fetters. The thick layer of "rice husks" flew up into the sky, and the white horse snorted heavily, lowered its head, and fell asleep, its eyes still half open.

In the midst of the great mosquito plague, the mugwort basin, like a delivery of coal in a snowstorm, brought salvation to a wolf cub, an adult horse, and half a dozen dogs. The eight creatures were all Chen's beloved animals, and he was comforted by the thought that he'd been able to come to their aid when they most needed it.

Mugwort fires were lit in all the brigade camps that night, hundreds of them releasing dense smoke in the moonlight and creating an image of giant dragons rolling and dancing in the air. It was as if the primitive grassland had suddenly entered the industrial age, with factory chimneys spewing white smoke to create a magnificent panorama. The smoke not only held off the crazed mosquitoes but also had an awesome effect on the wolves, who had been starving under the plague.

Sometime before dawn, Chen saw that a few of the distant camps were no longer burning mugwort. He then heard shouts from women on the night watch and the sounds of Beijing students driving their sheep home. Either they had used up all their mugwort or someone was hoarding his precious dried cow patties.

The mosquito swarms grew denser, the movement among them more intense, the buzzing louder. Peace no longer reigned at half the brigade's camps, where human shouts and dog barks rose in the night, in which more and more beams from flashlights were visible.

Suddenly the night quiet was shattered by two rapid gunshots, and Chen Zhen's heart sank. The wolf pack had struck again. After enduring unimaginable suffering from mosquito bites, they had spotted an opening. Chen sighed as he wondered whose head this calamity had fallen onto. At the same time, he was comforted by the thought of how his fascination with wolves had worked to his advantage. The more one understood the wolves, the less vulnerable one was to disaster.

The grassland returned to stillness after a while. Shortly before sunrise, dew began to settle, wetting the wings of the mosquitoes to keep them grounded. The fires died out gradually, but the dogs remained alert as always, making their rounds to see that all was well. It must be about time for the women to come out and milk the cows, Chen estimated, which meant that the wolf pack had retreated. He covered his head with a pair of thin fur jackets and fell fast asleep, the first real sleep he'd enjoyed over the last twenty-four hours. He slept for four solid hours.

The following day was sheer agony for Chen as he tended his sheep up on the mountain. Shortly before sunset, when he drove the flock back to camp, he felt as if the welcome mat had been laid out for him: There, stretched out on top of the yurt were two large sheepskins; the cub and all the dogs were joyfully feasting on lamb and large bones. He stepped inside to find strips of meat hanging from the rack where the bowls and utensils were kept and all along the sides of the yurt. A pot filled with meat was cooking on the stove.

"The flock at Olondun's place up north was hit last night," Yang told him. "Like Dorji, Olondun is a Mongol from northeastern China who came to the grassland years ago. A new bride from an area that's half agrarian, half nomad had just come into the family, and she was still used to sleeping through the night. So after setting a few fires, she lay down and slept alongside the flock. Well, the fires went out and the sheep ran off into the wind. They met up with some wolves that killed a hundred and eighty of them and injured a few more. Fortunately, the dogs' barks were loud enough to awaken the people in the yurts. The men grabbed their rifles and rode out, driving the wolves away with gunfire. If they'd been a little later, the whole pack would have been involved, and there wouldn't have been many sheep left alive."

"Bao Shungui and Bilgee were busy all day," said Gao Jianzhong, "mobilizing all the manpower they could to skin and gut the dead animals. Half of them were trucked into town to sell cheaply to the cadres and the laborers; the rest were kept for us in the brigade, two per yurt, free, but the skins have to be returned. We brought back two big ones, one dead, one still alive. I don't know how we're going to finish off all this meat in such hot weather."

Chen Zhen was speechless, and very happy. "Have you ever heard anyone who's raising a wolf cub complain about too much meat?" Then he asked, "How is Bao Shungui going to punish that family?"

"They have to pay up. Half their pay will be deducted every month till Bao says they've paid enough. Gasmai and all the other brigade women tore into the stupid husband and his mother for letting a new bride from outside the area take the night watch during a mosquito plague. When we first came out here, Gasmai and the others went out at night with us for two months before they'd let us take the watch on our own. Bao also gave the couple a tongue-lashing, telling them that they'd brought shame to all Mongols from Manchuria. But he made sure the laborers from his hometown benefited from the disaster by handing a third of the dead sheep over to Old Wang, which pleased the hell out of his people."

"That bunch really benefited from the wolf attack," Chen said.

Gao Jianzhong opened a bottle of grassland liquor. "Eating the wolves' meat," he sang out, "will make this stuff taste especially good! Come on, you guys, drink up while we feast."

That appealed to Yang Ke, who said with a laugh, "I think I'll get potted! Everyone's been waiting to see what will happen to us for raising a wolf cub. So what happens? We get to laugh at somebody else. They don't know it, but a wolf can teach people not only how to steal a chicken but also how to keep the rice you used to lure it."

That made them all laugh.

The cub lay sprawled beside his food basin, so stuffed he couldn't move. But Chen noted how he guarded the meat remaining inside the basin—like a wild animal guarding its prey. It was, in a way, a meal provided by his wolf kin as disaster relief, Chen thought wryly.

29

It took Batu and Zhang Jiyuan two whole days, during which they each switched horses four times, to drive their herd of horses to a mountaintop northwest of the new grazing land. Given the strong winds, there was no need to worry that the horses would turn back and gallop into the wind. The men were so tired that their legs felt fused to their saddles, and they weren't sure if they could even dismount. But after taking several deep breaths, they managed to roll out of their saddles and lay immobile on the ground. They opened their deels at the neck to let the cool mountain air rush in and dry their sweat-soaked tops.

The wind blew from the northwest; the lake lay in the center of the southeastern plains, where the herd was spread across the gently rounded mountaintop. The horses, choosing water over running into the wind to rid their bodies of blood-sucking mosquitoes, took off running toward the wild-duck lake, thousands of pounding horse hooves driving hordes of mosquitoes up out of the tall grass; these new, and very hungry, insects fell upon the sweaty hides of the running horses, biting so savagely that the terrified animals, trying to drive the assailants away with their hooves and their teeth, stumbled crazily.

Seeing their herd running down the mountain, Batu

and Zhang fell asleep, not even buttoning up the collars of their deels. Mosquitoes spotted the openings and attacked the men's necks, but even their stinging bites did not waken them.

In their mad dash for the wild-duck lake, the herd carried the mosquitoes with them like a coat of dust. Their blood nearly sucked dry, they were so thirsty that hardly any sweat oozed from their pores. They leaped into the water, more desperate to wash the mosquitoes from their hides than to quench their thirst, and fought to make it to deep water. The cool water killed the insects and stopped the itching; the horses whinnied their excitement and shook off the dead bugs, which covered the surface of the lake like a layer of chaff.

Men and horses all awoke at about the same time. None had eaten for several days, so Batu and Zhang rode over to the nearest yurt, where they drank as much tea and soupy yogurt and ate as much meat as they could. Then they slept again. The hungry horses climbed onto the bank to graze. The high sun baked their hides, opening up cracks in the protective mud, which attracted new swarms of mosquitoes. Grass alongside the lake had already been heavily grazed by cattle and sheep, so in order to keep from starving and to regain their strength in case of a wolf attack, the horses returned to their original slope, where they suffered anew the agony of mosquito assaults as they grazed the tall grass.

An all-cadre meeting was under way at Bilgee's home. "The clouds are neither thick nor especially thin," said the old man, "so don't expect any rain. In this muggy weather, the mosquitoes will probably eat our horses alive. We don't have enough people to watch our livestock properly, and since the disaster that hit the flock of sheep, we can't spare anyone to go out and relieve the horse herders." Bao Shungui and Bilgee decided to assign the brigade cadres to tend the sheep.

Zhang Jiyuan, though weakened by unrelieved exhaustion, knew that once he made it past the current calamity, he'd be permitted to herd horses alone on the grassland. Chen and Yang gave him a great deal of encouragement, out of the hope that one of the students from the yurt where the wolf cub was being raised would produce a first-rate horse herder.

The afternoon turned muggier still; with no prospect of a heavy rain in sight, even the hope for a drizzle was dashed. Grasslanders look forward to rain but fear it as well. Heavy rains keep the mosquitoes from flying, but afterward more insects are born, and when increasing numbers are sated with wolf blood, they produce offspring that are more wolfish and more prone to attack. The Olonbulag was transformed into hell on earth, and Zhang Jiyuan was prepared to go down into that hell, joining the other horse herders in riding out to the marshy grassland.

But Bilgee, in company with Batu and Zhang, drove the herd out to a desert region some sixty or seventy *li* to the southwest, where there was a scarcity of both grass and water, resulting in fewer mosquitoes. The spot was a buffer zone about a hundred *li* from the border. The other three brigade herds followed Bilgee's example, driving their horses as rapidly as possible to the arid land.

"This desert was once fine Olonbulag grazing land," Bilgee said to Zhang, "with streams and lakes and some of the best grass anywhere. Cattle and sheep could fatten up slowly without having to stuff themselves with diminishing amounts of grass." He looked up into the sky and sighed. "And this is what it's become in only a few short years. Sand has even filled in the dry riverbeds."

"How did it happen?" Zhang asked.

The old man pointed to the herd. "They grazed it into ruin, them and the migrants from down south. The country had only recently been liberated, and there weren't many motor vehicles. The army needed horses; so did farmers and the people who transport material, including loggers in the northeast. The whole country, it seemed, needed horses. Where were all these fine horses to come from? Inner Mongolia, of course. We were ordered to set aside the best grassland for horses. People from down south came here to try out, select, and buy horses, and before we knew it, the place had been turned into a racetrack of sorts. Over the centuries no ruler would have had the heart to turn this land into an area for raising horses. It didn't take many years to create a wasteland. Now, as a desert, it has one virtue; there are relatively few mosquitoes, so we can bring the horses out here during a mosquito plague. Uljii has given the order that this sandy spot is only to be used when it's the sole means of keeping the herds alive. He wants to see how long it will take for the grassland to reassert itself in the sandy soil. But he has to give in this year."

"Papa," Zhang said, "now that trucks and tractors are so common, and tanks have taken the place of cavalry during wartime, there won't be as great a need for horses. Will the grassland be able to make a comeback?"

The old man shook his head. "Men and tractors are even worse, and with the increased preparations for war, the authorities decided to establish a production and construction corps on the grassland. People and tractors are on their way."

Zhang was speechless. He hadn't expected the establishment of the corps to occur so soon.

"In the old days," the old man continued, "the farmers' hoes and fires were our greatest fear. Now it's tractors. A few days ago, Uljii and some old-time herdsmen wrote a letter to the Inner Mongolia Autonomous Region authorities asking them not to turn the Olonbulag into a farming region. Who knows if it will do any good? Bao Shungui has been in a terrific mood lately. He says it's a terrible waste for all this land to go unused, when it could support farms, and sooner or later, it's going to be used to . . . expand . . . expand the production of grain."

A silent moan arose in Zhang's heart. Now that the age of tractors had arrived, a conflict between those who lived off the grassland and those who lived by leveling it was nearing its end game.

As night began to fall, four herds of horses entered the Bayan Gobi, an area of several dozen square *li,* where the moist sandy ground occasionally gave way to a variety of desert plants that had grown astonishingly tall in the rainy season. There were no longer any signs that this had once been grazing land; rather, it looked like an abandoned construction site. "The grassland has but a single life," Bilgee said. "The roots of the edible grass have to overwhelm the weedy growth, but once those roots are eradicated, the weeds and sand take over."

The herds moved to the center of the desert. Though there was precious little edible grass for them out there, the relative absence of mosquitoes allowed Bilgee to rest the horses and give them a brief respite from the ravaging insects.

Bao Shungui rode up with Uljii. "This is all we could do," Bilgee said to them. "We'll have to let them go hungry at night. In the morning, when there's dew on the ground, we can herd them over to the marshland to eat, then drive them back when the mosquitoes are out again. They won't put on much weight, but we can at least keep them alive."

Bao heaved a sigh of relief. "Thanks to the wisdom of you two, these horses can live on. I've been sick with worry the past couple of days."

But Uljii's forehead was creased with anxiety. "I can't stop worrying that the wolf pack has been waiting for the herds to show up. Anything we can dream up, the wolves can too."

"I distributed an extra supply of ammunition to the herders. My worry has been that we won't find the wolves. I'm hoping they do come," said Bao.

On the first night, spared the harassment of mosquitoes and wolves, the herds were fully rested by morning, when the dew kept the mosquitoes from flying. The herders immediately led their horses to the marshland, where they gobbled up the tasty grass. As the sun burned off the dew, the mosquitoes rose into the air, and the horses headed back to the desert on their own. The second night was a repeat of the first. On the third night, Bao Shungui sent over a pair of large sheep on a light wagon; the herders, having caught up on their sleep, sat around the fire after dark, happily eating and drinking. They sang and shouted as they feasted on the food and spirits, scaring away any wolves in the area. Zhang's capacity for liquor had grown noticeably over the preceding year; now drunk, he entertained the others with a rendition of "The Wine Song" at the top of his lungs; his voice, it seemed, had taken on the quality of a wolf's drawn-out howls.

On the morning of the fourth day, a messenger galloped up to tell them that two officials from the production and construction corps had shown up at the brigade headquarters and wanted Uljii and Bilgee to brief them. The two men had no choice but to head back, but before they left, Bilgee stressed the importance of staying alert.

Once the two authority figures were gone, some of the young herders began thinking and talking about the women they'd left behind. As night was falling, two of them rode off to find young women who were heading out for the night watch. The term *night watch* had two meanings on the Olonbulag, and if anyone joked about it, the young women would stay up all night waiting.

The herds had grazed the land until only dry stalks remained. The endurance of the horses, deprived of their nightly consumption, was waning. But the stud horses were like unyielding prison guards, keeping a close watch on members of their families, stopping any that took even a few steps in the direction of the marshland. They were all being punished by hunger, but the stud horses maintained their tight patrols.

Where they waited patiently, concealed in the tall weeds, the wolves too were starving, and had been drawn to the smell of the meat cooking in the camp. The paucity of mosquitoes had given them a chance to build up their strength, and they were prepared for a fight. Batu predicted that half the Olonbulag wolf packs were in hiding somewhere in the desert region, though they hadn't yet found the courage to attack. The herders were armed and ready for anything; powerful stud horses had taken up positions on the periphery of the herd. A few that were looking for a release for their wildness stamped their hooves and roared threateningly at wolf shadows in the darkness, as if what they needed was to sink their teeth into a wolf's spine, fling it into the air, and, when it crashed to the ground, crush its skull with their powerful hooves. And yet, there were soft spots in the herds—no dogs accompanied them. The grasslanders simply had no interest in training their family watchdogs to guard horse herds.

After dinner, Batu took Zhang to the far perimeter to look for traces of wolves amid the weeds. They kept looking, enlarging the circle as they searched, but found no new tracks. That did little to lessen Batu's worries, for when, a few days earlier, he'd been out scouting in the distance, he'd spotted a couple of wolves, although he hadn't seen any at times when security around the herds was relatively lax. He was well aware that before the wolves launched an attack, they often separated themselves from their target in order to confuse the livestock with a feigned retreat.

For some strange reason, Zhang Jiyuan was on edge—it was too peaceful for him. Both he and Batu simultaneously thought about the weather and looked up into the sky. No stars, and dark clouds were pressing down on the desert. They turned their horses around and raced back to camp.

The shouting began sometime before midnight, as flashlights lit up the sandy ground. Fearless herders and powerful stud horses ringed the herds, some of the larger animals seeming to sense the presence of wolves; they moved to the perimeters to form walls of flesh and blood to protect the mares, the young horses, and the foals, who did not budge from their mothers' sides. Zhang imagined that he could hear the rapid beating of all those hundreds of equine hearts, a pace that equaled his own.

Sometime after midnight, strong gusts of wind were followed by the explosive crackles of thunder. The ground shook and the mountains swayed, sending all the horses into the start of a panicky stampede. The stud horses turned, reared up, and beat back their terrified charges with their lethal hooves. The herders shouted at the top of their lungs and used their whips to help the stud horses maintain the last line of defense. But another series of thunderclaps followed the lightning that streaked across the heavens like spastic nerve endings snaking down toward the herds, which split like ruptured dikes, the horses breaking through the perimeter defense created by the stud horses and horse herders. They ran as if possessed.

The thunderclaps drowned out the shouts, the whinnies, even the gunfire; lightning bolts blotted out the flashlights beams, and in the brief instance of nearly blinding light, the gray figures of wolves were visible as they stole into the herds. The herders' faces paled from the sight.

"Wolves!" shouted Zhang Jiyuan in a voice even he barely recognized. "The wolves are here!" For the first time in his life, he was witnessing a massive concerted attack by packs of wolves, aided by the deafening peals of thunder and electrifying bolts of lightning sent down by an angry Tengger. Like a heavenly army sent down to exact vengeance for the grassland, the wolves were intent on their murderous mission—to annihilate Mongol horses, the scourge of the grassland.

The terrified horses came under attack from all sides by the prideful wolves. They began to run for their lives. Under the protection of darkness, and aided by the heart-stopping thunder and lightning, the wolves penetrated the defenses like arrows and met in the center, where they turned and launched their assault, creating mass confusion among the panic-stricken horses, which was precisely what they needed to attack individual animals.

Foals were the first victims. Having been subjected to the terrifying sight and sound of thunder and lightning for the first time, the young horses, paralyzed by fear, were taken down one after another by the big wolves. Within minutes, a dozen or more lay dead or dying on the sandy ground. The more courageous foals stayed close to their mothers as they ran like the wind; if they could not find their mothers, they avoided being slaughtered by seeking out their more powerful fathers.

Zhang Jiyuan anxiously looked for his favorite, the one he called Snow White, fearing that a white horse would be especially visible, and therefore more vulnerable, in the enshrouding darkness. As two more bolts of lightning lit up the sky, Zhang saw a pair of stud horses fighting with teeth and hooves to protect a white foal from an attack by three wolves. The foal stuck to its father like glue, and even dredged up the courage to kick out at its attackers. The pack's greatest asset was speed; the instant they saw that it had failed them, they retreated into the black night to seek out another hapless foal. The stud horses called out to the mothers in the herd, for they were the only other animals who had the courage and the composure to protect their offspring, which they did with all the weapons available to them as they made their way toward their mates, their foals alongside. The fiercest stud horses and the most courageous females and foals warded off the first assault by the lightning above and the wolves below, forming mutually protective clusters of families.

The greater part of herd unity, however, had collapsed. The battle-tested wolves threw themselves into the fight, like lethal bombs, sending waves outward like ripples on a lake. No vestige of protection remained for the herders, and within half an hour, they had nearly lost contact with each other.

Batu, on the verge of being completely unnerved, signaled with his flashlight and shouted, "Forget the southeast! Concentrate on driving the horses to the northwest! Don't let them head to the border!" This snapped the herders out of their confusion and, to a man, they galloped toward the northwest.

The first taste of victory had increased the wolves' wills and their appetites. Not content with killing the slow-moving foals that had been separated from their mothers, they went for the panic-stricken two- and three-year-olds. After starting one-on-one, the wolves began to attack in groups of two and three, bringing down several young horses in succession, their tendons and arteries bitten through, sending blood flying and throwing such a fright into the rest of the herd that the surviving members cared about nothing but running for their lives.

With the thunder and lightning gone from the skies, the herders' shouts and flashlights had regained their effectiveness; the fleeing horses began to return to their families following the whinnying of the stud horses. The herd was heading south, picking up equine soldiers along the way. Thirty or forty powerful stud horses formed a line in front of the herd and bore down on the wolves, who turned and ran. That was the sign for weak, young, and injured horses to rejoin the herd, the source of their salvation, while many of the stud horses brought their reduced families back into the fold, where there were calls for family members to come together.

The wolf pack retreated in orderly fashion, apparently in no hurry to return to the downed animals and begin the feast, choosing instead to go after stragglers before the herders and stud horses brought them back into the herds. Batu and some of the senior herders rode up to the front to count the number of stud horses, and discovered that a third were unaccounted for. This chilling development sent Batu to the rear of the herd, where he told four herders to split up into pairs and expand the roundup area to the east and to the west. The other herders were told to drive their animals ahead. Finally he sent Zhang Jiyuan to the southeast to drive the wolves out of the area.

Wolves in the northwest raced to link up with those in the southeast, who were in a killing frenzy; some of the horse families had lost all their foals. After joining forces, the wolves went after the sick and crippled adult horses. Shouts and whinnies from the northwest drew nearer, but the wolves concentrated on the killing, leaving the eating for later. Seeing that one man was powerless to drive the wolves away, Zhang decided to go back and help with the herds. The wolves, with their intimate knowledge of grassland weather, seemed to be waiting for the right moment to make their big move.

The herders had driven the horses to within three or four *li* of the sandy hill when hordes of mosquitoes from the marshland rose like a dense cloud to envelop the herd. The most vicious mosquitoes of the year immediately buried their needles in horseflesh. After surviving the dual attacks from lightning and wolves, the horses erupted into uncontrolled madness.

The punishment almost immediately fell on the hide of the protectors of the herd, the stud horses. The powerful animals, with their smooth, almost hairless hides and taut muscles, had suffered for days, their tails sticky with blood, until their ability to sweep away the mosquitoes had fallen to zero. The greatest concentration of insects focused their attention on the stud horses' eyelids and genitals, which drove them crazy, robbing them of their reason and their sense of responsibility. At that moment, the mosquitoes' enemy, the wind, died down and pointed out the direction the herd needed to take to create some wind. The stud horses, bitten nearly blind and half mad, abandoned their mates and offspring and ran like the wind into the wind.

The herders had come out from the sandy hill, where there were few mosquitoes, and were not wearing masks. Their faces, necks, and hands were immediately bitten mercilessly by the blood-sucking insects. Their eyelids were swollen, their eyes mere slits; their faces were "fat," as if burned. Their lips were so puffy that they twitched painfully, their fingers thickened until they could barely hold their lasso poles. Mounts ignored their riders' commands, rearing and prancing crazily. One minute they'd lower their heads and stretch their necks to relieve the itching; the next they'd take off running again, barely able to keep from rolling on the ground, with no thoughts for their riders.

The fight had been taken out of men and horses as they sank into a sea of mosquitoes. Most of the herd animals were running pell-mell into the wind; the stragglers took their lead, racing to the northwest.

Crazed stinging, crazed running, crazed killing—mosquitoes, horses, and wolves. A convergence of plagues—thunder and lightning, winds, mosquitoes, and wolves—fell onto the Olonbulag horse herds, and Zhang Jiyuan once again sensed with his entire being the difficulty of life on the grassland; he doubted that any other race of people could possibly survive in such a cruel environment. Ashen-faced Batu whipped his horse frantically, even on the animal's head to make it forget the stings of mosquitoes. Zhang Jiyuan, impressed by this bold display, confidently and courageously turned and charged.

"Force the herd west!" Batu shouted. "There's sand there! Move! Move! Make sure they don't head for the border."

"Hey! Hey!" the herders shouted in response.

A scream caught Zhang Jiyuan's attention; he saw a horse stumble and throw its rider to the ground. No one came to help; they were too focused on charging ahead.

But how could horses burdened with riders be expected to catch up with riderless horses being harassed by mosquitoes and wolves? The herders' inability to drive the horses westward shattered their last hope. And still, Batu and the other men shouted at the top of their lungs and kept the chase going.

Suddenly, beams of light split the darkness from a distant mountain. "The brigade has sent a rescue team!" Batu shouted. The herders shouted excitedly as they flicked on their flashlights to show the newcomers where the herd was. Robust shouts emerged from the riders behind the mountain as they stormed up a ridge and swept the area ahead with their flashlights, as if setting up a blockade to keep the horses from running off. All this resulted in getting the herd rounded up and turned around. As the horses were forced to huddle together, they crushed mosquitoes between their bodies.

At this critical juncture, Bilgee, like a tribal leader, arrived on the scene to take charge; the herders, reinvigorated by the sight of their old wolf king riding up, launched an assault on the wolf pack, which had been caught unawares by the shouts and bright lights. They did, however, recognize Bilgee's voice, it seemed, for the alpha wolf turned and beat a hasty retreat, all the others right behind him. Their objective was clear: they were heading back to the first killing field, where they would eat as much as they could before disappearing into the mountains.

Along with Bao Shungui and Uljii, Bilgee led a dozen or more sheep and cattle herders, as well as Beijing students, in bringing the horse herd together and racing off to the sandy refuge. He sent one of the herdsmen to tend to the injured herder. Chen Zhen rode up to Zhang Jiyuan to find out what had happened during the night and to tell him that Bilgee and Uljii, having anticipated an attack on the horses, had organized a rescue squad even before the weather had turned bad. "That was close!" Zhang said. "We could have lost the whole herd this time."

Once they were safely on the sandy hill, the sky lightened. Herders rounded up some of the strays, but the losses to the herd had been substantial. Four or five of the old, sick, and disabled horses had been killed, as had twelve or thirteen of the two-year-olds. Foals had suffered the most, with fifty or sixty taken down by the wolves, making a total loss of over seventy members of the herd. Lightning strikes, wind, and mosquitoes had abetted the massacre this time, but the actual killer had, as always, been the wolves!

Bao Shungui surveyed the scene on the sandy hill and the marshland. "Didn't I tell you that eliminating the wolves was our highest priority in setting up the new pasture?" he said angrily. "But you people wouldn't listen. Well, look around—this is your punishment for not heeding my warning! From now on, anyone who speaks up for the wolves will lose his job and be sent to attend a study session. And make restitution for our losses!"

With one hand cupped over the other, Bilgee looked up into the sky; his lips were moving, and both Chen and Zhang had a good idea what he was saying.

"Mastering the grassland is too hard on a man," Chen whispered, "and anyone who tries will likely wind up as a scapegoat for failures."

Zhang went up to Bao Shungui. "No one could have held off a natural disaster of this magnitude," he said. "I think we got off lightly, and we're fortunate that Bilgee and Uljii had the foresight to send the herd over to this sandy area five days ago. We'd have lost the whole herd if they hadn't."

"I don't care what you say," Bao argued. "Those wolves killed a lot of our horses last night. Mosquitoes don't kill horses, no matter how many there are of them. Would this have happened if we'd wiped out the wolves when I wanted to? The corps commanders have spent the last few days at brigade headquarters. If they saw all these dead horses, they'd demote me in a heartbeat. These packs are scourges, and we're going to keep killing wolves until there are none left. That's the only way to protect our livestock. The corps is getting ready to move into our pasture, and if you won't kill off the wolves, I'll ask them to do it. It'll be easy, with their trucks, jeeps, and machine guns."

The herdsmen went out in groups to clear the scene of slaughter, which kept them busy and depressed all morning.

The surviving foals trembled when they saw the bodies of those that had died. This lesson in blood would make them more vigilant and courageous the next time they were caught in the middle of a calamity of this nature. But a disturbing thought occurred to Chen Zhen: Will there even be a next time?

30

A cold autumn rain abruptly ended the short summer on the Inner Mongolian grassland and froze the mosquitoes.

Staring intently at the quiet grassland, Chen Zhen thought he understood why the mosquitoes and the wolves would be in such a frenzied state. Summers are short out there, but the fall is even shorter, followed by a six-month-long winter, the season of death for animals that do not hibernate, including the mosquitoes, half of which would die out even if they managed to hide in the marmots' caves. Without fat and thick fur, the wolves cannot survive the winter, when most of the scrawny, old, sick, and wounded are killed off. That is also why mosquitoes must take advantage of the short growing season to suck as much blood as possible; the crazed attacks are their way of saving their own lives. The wolves too must engage in bloody battles to prepare for the winter and possible famine in the following spring.

Two stinking front legs and the entrails remained from the foal allocated to Chen Zhen's yurt. The cub had been able to enjoy a period of full stomachs, and even now the rotting meat was enough to last him a few more days. His nose told him there was still food left, so he was in a good mood. He liked his meat fresh and bloody but did not mind when it was rotten and crawling with maggots, which he swallowed along with the meat. "He's fast becoming our trash can," Gao commented.

What surprised Chen more was that the cub never got sick, no matter how foul, rotten, or dirty the food was. Chen and Yang admired the cub's ability to endure cold, heat, hunger, thirst, foul odors, filth, and germs. One had to be impressed by a species that had survived millions of years of selection in an unimaginably inhospitable environment.

The bigger the cub grew, the handsomer and more magnificent he looked. Now he was a grassland wolf in every respect. Chen gave him a longer chain and tried calling him Big Wolf. But the cub preferred to stick to his old name. Whenever Chen called out "Little Wolf," the cub ran over to play with him, licked his hands, rubbed up against his knees, jumped onto his stomach, even lay down on the ground and exposed his belly for Chen to scratch him. But he ignored Chen if he called him Big Wolf. He'd look around to see who Chen was calling.

Chen laughed at him. "You're a foolish wolf. Will I still have to call you Little Wolf when you're old?" The cub stuck his tongue out, as if teasing Chen.

Chen admired every part of the wolf's body. For a while, he enjoyed playing with his ears. Being the first part of him to grow to adult size, they stood straight up, sturdy, clean, unmarred, and alert. And the cub had a growing sense of self-awareness that was instinctual of grassland wolves.

Inside the pen, Chen would sit cross-legged and play with the cub's ears. But the cub would only let him do that after Chen had scratched the base of his ears and his neck, which made him tremble contentedly. Chen liked to fold the ears backward and then watch them spring to their upright position again. If he bent both at the same time, they sprang back one after another, never together, making popping sounds that startled the cub as if he'd heard enemy movements.

For some time, Chen had noticed an increased number of military vehicles on the grassland, raising trails of dust, a sight that distressed him. He realized that he belonged to the first, and perhaps the last, group of Han Chinese to actually live and observe the lives of nomadic herdsmen in the farthest reaches of Inner Mongolia. He was not a journalist or tourist; he enjoyed the proud status of a nomadic shepherd. He also had an observation site that he could be happy with—the Olonbulag, hidden away in a spot where large numbers of wolves still roamed. And he was raising a wolf cub he had personally taken from a den.

He vowed to memorize his observations and contemplations, not leaving out the tiniest detail. In the future he'd tell his story to friends and family over and over, until the day he departed this world. It was a pity so much time had passed since the Yellow Emperor's descendants had left their grassland origins. A nomadic lifestyle would soon come to an end, and the Chinese would never have a chance to return to the pristine place of their origin to pay tribute to their ancestral matriarch.

Should he secretly set the cub free, returning him to the cruel but open grassland and giving him back the life of a wolf? He didn't dare. The cub had lost the weapon he needed to survive on the grassland when

Chen snipped off the tips of his fangs. They were no longer sharp like awls, but round and blunt, worse than dogs' teeth.

What pained Chen most was the crack the pincer had caused in one of the teeth. He'd been careful not to damage the roots, but the crack, though tiny, went all the way down. A short while later, he realized that the tooth was infected; it had turned black, like the diseased tooth of an old wolf. Whenever he saw that black tooth, his heart ached. It might fall out within a year. Teeth are the source of life for grassland wolves. If the cub only had three blunt teeth left, he couldn't even tear at meat, let alone hunt and kill.

As time went on, Chen's despair deepened when he saw the consequences of his reckless decision. He could never return the cub to the grassland, nor could he ever travel deep into the grassland to visit his wolf friend. He regretted not freeing the cub weeks earlier, when the mother wolf had come for it. Scientific research was not for him, for he had neither the temperament nor the qualifications to conduct it. The cub was not a lab rat raised for medical dissection, but his friend and teacher.

The grassland inhabitants were waiting anxiously for the arrival of the Inner Mongolian Production and Construction Corps. The letter signed by Bilgee, Uljii, and other elders had achieved its purpose; the corps decided that the Olonbulag would be used for herding, but that the Olonbaolige Pasture would be converted to a herding regiment, with a portion of the land given over to farming. The remaining pastures and all the other communes would be turned over to agricultural production. The Majuzi River area, where the famous

Ujimchin warhorses were raised, would be a large-scale farmland, leaving a small area for both farming and herding.

The corps' grand design had already incorporated the ancient Olonbulag. The main idea was to quickly end the primitive nomadic herding style of production that had dominated the area for thousands of years, and create settlements. The corps would supply money and equipment, along with engineering teams, to build brick houses with tiled roofs and sturdy animal pens made of cement and stone; it would also dig wells, pave highways, and build schools, hospitals, post offices, auditoriums, shops, and movie theaters. The teams would also reclaim the fertile land to plant grass and grain for animal feed, and vegetable crops. They would set up mechanized harvesting and transport teams, and tractor stations. They would eradicate the damage caused by wolves, disease, insects, and rodents. They would strengthen the grassland's ability to fight commonly occurring natural disasters. They wanted to ensure that herders, who had lived for thousands of years under the most inhospitable and difficult conditions, could gradually settle down and lead stable, happy lives.

The students and young herders, as well as most of the women and children, looked forward to the arrival of the corps, anticipating the beautiful future described by Bao Shungui and the corps cadres. Most of the older and middle-aged herdsmen, on the other hand, were quiet. Chen Zhen went to talk to the old man. Bilgee sighed and said, "We've always wanted a school for our children, and hoped we no longer had to take our sick to the banner hospital by oxcart or horse-drawn wagon. We don't have a hospital, and many people have died who needn't have. But what will happen to the grassland? It's already too fragile to support the heavy load of livestock. It's like an oxcart that can carry only a limited number of people and animals. More people and their machines will tip the cart over, and when that happens, you Han Chinese will just go home. But what about us?"

What worried Chen the most was the future of the wolves. Once the farmers came, the swans, ducks, and wild geese would either be eaten or fly away. But wolves aren't birds. Would they, after generations on the grassland, be exterminated or chased out of China, their home?

After downing two bowls of cool tea, Yang said to Chen, "Who'd have thought that the corps would be here so soon? I hated the military life during peacetime, and I barely managed to avoid being sent to the Heilongjiang Production and Construction Corps. Who'd have thought I'd one day be under the control of its Inner Mongolian counterpart? I don't know what's going to happen to the Olonbulag, but we have to figure out something for the wolves, and soon."

As they talked, a fast horse sped toward them along the oxcart path, trailing a long cloud of yellow dust. One look told them that Zhang Jiyuan was back to get some rest.

They sat down to eat some steamed and boiled millet, mutton stewed with mushrooms, and pickled wild leek flowers.

"You have a fast horse, and you're up to speed on news," Yang said to Zhang, "so tell us about the corps."

"Well, the brigade office is now the corps office, with the arrival of the first group of cadres, half Mongols, the other half Han. Their first task may be to exterminate the wolves. They were outraged when they learned how many young horses they killed. They said the first thing the army traditionally did when they arrived on the grassland was to wipe out the bandits. This time they'll kill the wolves first. They've sent their best men. They say they're doing it for our good, but it's put the old Mongols in a tight spot. Trying to explain the benefits of wolves to farm boys in uniform would be like playing music to an ox. The wolves' coats are full now, so their pelts will fetch a good price. The corps cadres aren't well paid; even the staff officers and clerks get only about sixty or seventy yuan a month. A wolf pelt can bring in twenty yuan, plus an award. That's why they're so eager to get started."

Yang Ke sighed. "Mongolian wolves," he said, "the end is near for you. The situation has changed; the age of heroes is over. Hurry up and flee to Outer Mongolia."

31

Early one morning, two open-topped military vehicles stopped by Chen Zhen's yurt. Seeing the giant objects and smelling gasoline for the first time, the cub shot into his hole. The dogs, on the other hand, surrounded the vehicles, barking madly. Chen and Yang ran out to stop the dogs and chase them away.

The doors opened to reveal Bao Shungui and four soldiers, who headed straight for the cub's hole. Not knowing what was happening, Chen, Yang, and Gao rushed over to them. Chen tried to remain calm. "Director Bao, you've brought someone to see the cub."

Bao smiled. "Let me make the introductions." He pointed to two officers in their thirties. "These men are with the corps advance party, Staff Officer Xu and Staff Officer Batel." Then he pointed to the two drivers, "This is Old Liu and this is Little Wang. They're going to put down roots out here and bring their families over when the houses are finished on the corps office site. They've been sent to help us kill the wolves."

Chen shook hands, his heart beating wildly. He invited them inside for tea.

"No need," said Bao. "We'll see the cub first. Bring it out; these staff officers made a special trip to see it."

Chen forced a smile. "So you're interested in wolves, are you?"

In a thick Shaanxi accent, Xu said cordially, "Wolves are bloodthirsty killers, so the division and corps leaders have sent us out to exterminate them. We've never seen grassland wolves, which is why Old Bao brought us here."

Batel, who spoke with a Shandong accent, added, "Old Bao says you and the others know a lot about wolves, that you're good at killing them and taking their cubs, one of which you're raising so you can study the wolf's nature. A smart, bold move. We'll need your help when we go after them."

The men were cordial and personable, and Chen felt better after learning that they hadn't come to kill the cub. "Wolf...wolves are complex animals," he stammered. "It would take days to tell you all about them. Let's go see the cub. Stay back; don't step inside the pen. He bites strangers. He almost bit a league cadre once."

Chen took two pieces of meat out of a bag and picked up an old chopping board before walking quietly toward the cave opening. He laid the board down on the ground and shouted, "Little Wolf, Little Wolf, time to eat." The cub flew out the cave and pounced on the meat. Chen quickly pushed the board over to block the entrance before jumping out of the pen. The cub was usually fed in the morning and afternoon. This was the first time he'd been fed so soon after noon, which made him very happy; he tore at the meat. Bao and the others backed away.

The observers crouched in a semicircle. With the arrival of these men and their unfamiliar scents, the cub behaved strangely. Instead of charging them threateningly, as he normally did, he tucked his tail between his legs and made himself small as he carried a piece of meat to the far end of the pen, where he laid it down and then went back to get the second piece. With his hackles standing up, he went ahead and ate, but he was unhappy about being surrounded by so many people. After a couple of bites, he changed his demeanor, wrinkling his nose and baring his fangs as he rushed the soldiers. His savage look and his speed caught them by surprise, and all five frightened men fell backward. Even with the chain, the cub came within three feet.

Staff Officer Batel sat up and dusted off his hands. "That's some wild animal, a lot meaner than our wolfhounds. That chain saved us."

"Not even a year old, and it's already as big as a full-grown dog," Xu said. "Thanks for bringing us here, Old Bao. Now I really feel like I'm on a battlefield." He turned to Batel. "Wolves are faster and a lot sneakier than dogs. And their attacks are lightning quick."

Batel nodded as the cub turned and leaped at the meat, gobbling it down while making hoarse, threatening growls.

The two men measured the cub's size with their eyes and took a good look at his fur and skin. They concluded it would be best to aim at the head or the chest from the side. That would kill a wolf without damaging the pelt.

"These youngsters know their business," Bao said, his face glowing, "All the herdsmen and most of the students were against raising this cub, but I told them to go ahead. If you know your enemy as well as you know yourself, you can't lose. I've brought lots of people over to see the cub. The Chinese, who are afraid of wolves, are the most eager to see them. They all say it's a better animal than the ones they see in the zoo. It's a rare opportunity to see a live wolf at close range. This is the only one out here. When the corps leadership comes to inspect, I'll make this their first stop."

"I'm sure they'll come when they hear about the famous Mongolian wolf cub." Then Xu turned to Chen. "Make sure the chain and post are secure."

Bao looked at his watch. "Now back to business. We're here not only to see the cub but also to get one of you to come with us. These marksmen were sent to help us eliminate the wolf scourge. Staff Officer Xu shot a high-flying hawk yesterday. From the ground it looked like a pea. One shot was all it took. So which one of you will it be?"

Chen's heart sank. The Olonbulag wolf's mortal enemy had arrived. Following the rapid growth of the farming population, military vehicles and cavalry troops had finally pushed all the way to the border. "The horse herders know where to find the wolves," he said glumly. "Get one of them to be your guide."

"The old ones won't come," Bao said, "and the young ones are useless. All the experienced ones have gone into the mountains to tend the horses. Since these two officers have taken the trouble to come all this way, one of you has to go, just this one time."

"Why not ask Dorji, the brigade's most famous wolf killer?"

"The deputy commander already took him. Commander *Li* loves to hunt, especially from a moving vehicle." He took another look at his watch. "Stop wasting time."

Seeing they had no choice, Chen said to Yang, "Why don't you go?"

"I don't know the wolves as well as you. It's... it's better that you go."

"I'll decide," Bao said impatiently. "Chen, you come with us. But if you're like Bilgee, always letting the wolves go, and we come back empty-handed, I'll kill your cub. No more nonsense. Now let's go."

Chen's face paled; he instinctively took a step to block the cub. "Okay, I'll go. I'm ready."

The two vehicles sped west, trailed by a pair of yellow dust dragons.

Chen had not ridden in a motor vehicle for more than two years. The rare opportunity to hunt this way would have made him feel privileged if he hadn't become so fascinated by wolves, if he'd just arrived at the grassland, if he hadn't been learning from the wolves. How exciting, how pleasurable to speed across the grassland like the wind in pursuit of wolves! It should have been more satisfying than fox hunting with British aristocrats, or hunting bears in a snowy forest with Russian tsars, or joining encirclement hunts with thousands of horses, like the Manchu imperial family.

But at the moment, Chen's only wish was that the vehicle would break down. He felt like a traitor, leading an army to arrest friends. Bao knew how he felt toward wolves, and he wondered how he'd manage to protect his cub and spare the other wolves.

The corps' wolf-extermination campaign had already begun throughout the grassland. This time, the wolves would be chased out of China and off the stage of history, condemned with a terrible reputation, while their invaluable influence and achievements would be obliterated. No one but Bilgee, the grassland devotees of the wolf totem, and his two friends back in the yurt would understand how sad he was. Chen's sorrow was that he was simultaneously too advanced and too ancient.

On the Olonbulag, one encountered a different wind every five miles and another rain every ten. Now Chen was riding down on a wet, sandy road. The howling autumn wind helped clear his head. He concluded that they had to go to a place where they could find wolves, but one from which the wolves could easily escape.

He turned to Bao in the backseat. "I know where there are wolves, but the vehicle will be useless. It's too hilly and too reedy."

Bao glared at him. "Don't play games with me. Mosquitoes are concentrated in reedy areas at this time of year, and you won't find wolves there. Don't you think I'd know that after hunting wolves these past six months?"

Chen corrected himself. "What I meant was, we can't enter the mountains or the reedy area, so we'll have to go to the sandy hills and big gentle slopes where there aren't so many mosquitoes."

Bao wouldn't let him off the hook that easily. "The horse herders chased the wolves away after that incident with the young horses on the sandy hills. We didn't see any wolves yesterday when we drove around there. I can tell we won't be able to use your talents today. So listen carefully. I don't go back on my word. We didn't kill any wolves yesterday, and that has made us very unhappy." Bao took a drag from his cigarette and blew the smoke into the back of Chen's head.

Chen realized how difficult it would be to put anything over on someone shrewd enough to climb all the way up from the bottom of the bureaucracy. "I know another patch of sandy land," he said, "northwest of the

Chaganuul Mountains. It's a sandy area with little grass because of the wind, but there are lots of mice and prairie dogs, quite a few marmots too. Now that the wolves have no horses to eat, they have to move to places with lots of small animals."

Chen decided he'd take them to the northwesternmost corner of the pasture, where there was poor sandy soil and little grass. It was also a good place to avoid the mosquitoes and graze the horses, but it was near the border and the herders never took their horses there. Chen hoped that the soldiers would be able to see wolves that could then easily cross the border and escape.

Bao considered the suggestion. He smiled and said, "You may be right. Why didn't I think of that? Old Liu, head north. That's where we'll go today, so step on it."

Chen added, "It'll be better to walk if we want to kill wolves. These vehicles make too much noise, and the wolves will run into the grass when they hear us. We've had lots of rain this year, and the grass is tall, which makes it easy for them to hide."

Staff Officer Xu said, "You just find the wolves, and leave the rest to me."

Chen felt he'd made a serious mistake.

They sped northwest, following an ancient dirt path created by herders making seasonable moves from pasture to pasture. Autumn grass had grown back on the lamb-birthing pasture, which had been grazed barren by livestock in the spring; the dense grass, roiling like waves, was dotted with swaying daisies. A strong fragrance typical of fine grass filled their noses. A few purple swallows followed to eat moths and other insects stirred up by the vehicles, but they quickly fell behind, only to be replaced by new ones, creating one purple arc after another.

Chen breathed in the intoxicating aroma of autumn grass and flowers. This was where they would come back for lamb birthing. Seventy percent of the pasture's income came from the sale of wool and sheep, so the birthing pasture was a precious place, the source of life. He paid close attention along the way and saw there was excellent grass, almost like a carefully tended wheat field. Not a single yurt had been put down here since the production team moved to the summer pasture. He felt a sense of gratitude toward the wolves and the horse herders. An enticing, fragrant pasture would have been ruined by gazelles, wild rabbits, and mice but for the wolves.

Everything Chen saw in the lush panorama contributed to the hardships endured by the horse herders, who, in spite of the heat and mosquitoes, had worked day and night to check the appetites of their gluttonous charges by taking them to a hilly pasture to graze on second-rate, goatee-like grass, or grass left behind by the cattle and sheep. They'd never let their horses near the birthing pasture. While they loved their horses as much as their own lives, when it came to grazing, they treated them like thieves or locusts. If not for them, this pasture, the source of life, would have been left with nothing but horse droppings from poorly digested grass and clumps of dead grass burned by animal urine. How could soldiers from agricultural areas understand all that?

These thoughts made it impossible for Chen to hold back. "See how well protected the pasture is?" he said to Staff Officer Xu. "When the brigade came here for the spring birthing of lambs, tens of thousands of gazelles had stormed over from Outer Mongolia. We couldn't chase them away, even with rifles. If they ran off during the day, they returned at night to fight over grass with the birthing ewes. Luckily the wolves came and, in a matter of days, the gazelles were gone. If not for the wolves, there'd have been no grass for the ewes and no milk for the newborn lambs; we'd have lost tens of thousands of lambs. Husbandry is different from agriculture. When there's a disaster, the most a farmer will suffer is a year's crops, but a disaster out here can mean the loss of eight or ten years, even as much as a herder's lifetime income."

Xu nodded, though his hawklike eyes continued searching the grassland. After a while, he said, "How could you have relied on wolves to kill the gazelles? That's so backward. The herdsmen have inferior rifles and marksmanship, and no trucks. Watch us next spring. We'll use motor vehicles, assault rifles, and machine guns. No gazelles will be our match, no matter how many there are. I've hunted them out west. The best way is to turn on the headlights at night; they're afraid of the dark, so they crowd around the light. Then keep driving and fire as you go. You can kill hundreds of them in a single night. So you have gazelle here. That's great. The more the better. The people at division headquarters and the agricultural corps will have meat now."

"Look!" Bao Shungui called out softly, pointing to his left.

Chen looked through his telescope and said, "A fox. Let's get it."

Bao observed it carefully. "Yes," he said, disappointed. "It's only a fox. Forget it." Then he turned to Xu, who had his rifle up. "Don't shoot. Wolves have keen ears. We'll go home empty-handed if you startle them."

"This is our lucky day," Xu said happily. "Where there are foxes, there are wolves."

The closer they got to the sandy pasture, the more wildlife they saw: sand swallows, sand grouses, desert foxes, and sand mice. Rusty red sand grouses were the most common; they flew in large flocks, their feathers making the sound of pigeon whistles. Pointing at the gentle ridge in the distance, Chen said, "The sandy area is just over that ridge. The older herders say there used to be a big pasture with a spring here. But many years ago, the Olonbulag suffered a terrible drought, which dried up the lakes, the rivers, and the wells, all but that spring. So the livestock was driven here for water. From dawn to dusk, large numbers of animals were lined up, stomping and grazing the grass. It took less than two years for the pasture to turn to sand. Luckily, the spring didn't dry up, and the grass slowly returned. But we'll have to wait decades before it returns to its original condition. The grassland is so fragile that it turns to desert whenever it exceeds its capacity."

Squeaking mice scampered away from the wheels. "The capacity includes those mice," Chen said. "The destruction they cause is worse than livestock. Wolves are the main reason the grassland isn't overburdened. If you kill a wolf, I'll open its belly and show you its contents. During this season, you'll find mainly mice and field mice."

"I didn't know that wolves eat mice," Xu said.

"The cub I'm raising loves them. He swallows them tails and all. The grassland never experiences a scourge of mice because the herdsmen don't kill all the wolves. If you do that now, the mice will run wild, and that will spell disaster for the grassland—"

Bao cut him off. "Pay attention and keep your eye out for wolves."

As they neared the ridge, Staff Officer Xu tensed. He checked the lay of the land and told the driver to head west. "If there are wolves here, we can't go right in. We'll have to take the sentry wolves first."

They entered a gentle ravine that ran east to west. The narrow oxcart path was flanked by mountains on the left and sandy hills on the right. Looking through his high-powered binoculars, Xu searched the grassy land on both sides and whispered, "Two wolves on the hill to the right." He spun around to signal the vehicle behind. Chen saw the wolves too, big ones, trotting westward, three or four *li* away.

"Don't go over there," Xu said to Old Liu. "We'll follow the dirt path and maintain speed. See if you can drive parallel with the wolves so I can get a side shot."

"Got it." Old Liu turned in the direction of the wolf at a slightly faster speed.

The man obviously had combat experience. Going at the wolf like that not only shortened the distance but also gave the wolves the illusion that they were just passing by, not going for them. The border station patrol cars followed strict rules that prohibited the soldiers from firing except under extraordinary circumstances, which helped keep their presence secret and gave them the element of surprise. As a result, the wolves had grown accustomed to the presence of motor vehicles in the area.

Seeing that the wolves did not speed up, Chen felt a pang in his heart, sensing that they were in trouble this time. These were not ordinary border patrol cars; these men were here to kill wolves. They were crack shots the likes of which the wolves had not encountered before. Their range was far greater than the herdsmen.

The vehicles were nearly parallel to the wolves, and the distance had shortened from fifteen hundred yards to seven or eight hundred; the wolves grew tense and sped up a bit. But the vehicles driving down the dirt path confused them; they had not been wary enough of the people. Chen wondered if the wolves were trying to lure or detract their pursuers. The two marksmen took aim, and Chen felt his heart leap into his throat; he fixed his gaze on Staff Officer Xu's movements, hoping that the vehicle would stop when he fired, which might give the wolves a chance.

They were about to catch up with the wolves; the distance had shortened four or five hundred yards. The wolves paused and looked over at the vehicles; then, apparently seeing the rifles, they raced toward the ridge. Bang bang. Chen heard the shots and saw the two wolves drop almost simultaneously. "Good shooting!" Bao yelled.

Chen broke out in a cold sweat. Neither he nor the wolves could have imagined that the two men in moving vehicles could hit their targets on their first try. But to the two sharpshooters, this was only an aperitif. Staff Officer Xu gave Old Liu an order. "Hurry over to the sandy area. Step on it." Then he signaled to the other vehicle. They both shot off the path at full speed and headed to the sandy hill on the right.

Old Liu drove over the hill onto a sandy grassland, where he headed for the nearest, highest point. Xu stood up with his hand on the handrail to survey the area. Two distant groups of young wolves were running separately to the northwest and due north. Chen saw through his telescope that there were four or five large animals in the northbound pack, while most of the eight or nine wolves in the other pack were midsize cubs born that year.

"Let's go after the northbound pack," Xu said. Then he turned to the vehicle behind him and pointed to the northwestern group. The vehicles separated and gave chase.

The sandy grassland, with its gentle hills, was an ideal battlefield for the vehicles. "Hold on tight and watch me," Old Liu shouted. "I can run one down without firing a shot!"

They were traveling so fast it felt like they were flying. *Deadly speed* flashed through Chen's mind. On the grassland, only gazelles are able to compete at this speed; not even the fastest lasso horses or wolves can run that fast, even if they run themselves to death. The two vehicles went after the packs like Death itself. After twenty minutes, the wolves that had been the size of sesame seeds were now the size of green peas, and slowly becoming as large as soybeans. But Xu held his fire, which puzzled Chen. If he can bring down a hawk the size of a green pea, why not shoot now?

"Now?" Bao asked.

"Still too far," Xu said. "If we fire now, the pack will disperse. But if we wait till we're closer, we can get two more and not damage the pelts."

Old Liu said excitedly, "Maybe today we can each get one."

"Just worry about driving," Xu said. "We'll be wolf food if we flip over."

They passed a dune and all of a sudden a giant ox carcass materialized on a small sandy hill directly in front. Its broken horns looked like spears or rifles, or like an antler barrier on an ancient battlefield. The wolves could jump over it, but it was an impossible obstacle for Old Liu, who spun the steering wheel, sending the vehicle lurching to the side, its right tires leaving the ground. The occupants left their seats and nearly flew out of the vehicle; they were screaming in terror.

They brushed past the pile of bones; Chen was still dazed, even after the vehicle had righted itself. He knew the wolves had begun to use the topography in their retreat, and their trick had nearly destroyed the vehicle and killed everyone in it. Bao Shungui, his face an ashen gray, yelled, "Slow down! Slow down!"

Old Liu wiped the cold sweat from his forehead and slowed down, widening the gap between them and the wolves.

"No, step on it!" Xu yelled as dry weeds came into view on the sandy ground. Chen had grazed sheep here and knew the area. He shouted, "The ground ahead is lower and filled with weeds. We could easily flip over. Slow down."

But his words had no effect on Xu, who gripped the handrail and stared straight ahead. "Faster! Faster!" he shouted.

Old Liu floored the gas pedal, and the vehicle shot out, from time to time leaving the ground altogether or careening on two wheels. Chen had a death grip on the handrail, feeling his insides toss and churn.

He knew the wolves were using the land to their advantage as they ran for their lives, and that their pursuers would not be able to follow once they entered the lowland.

Old Liu screamed, "Those are damned smart wolves. Why did they have to run to a place like this?"

Staff Officer Xu said coldly, "Get a grip on yourself. This isn't a drill, this is war!"

The mad chase went on for seven or eight more *li*, closing the distance to the lowland, which was strewn with stumplike weeds. But they had drawn to within range. "Swing around!" Xu shouted. Liu swung the vehicle around like a battleship, its big guns trained to the side. Xu had the wolves where he wanted them. Bang! The biggest wolf fell, shot in the head. The pack scattered, but another shot brought down a second wolf.

Almost at the same time, the remaining wolves reached the dry weeds, out of range. They ran toward the border and disappeared in the grass. Guns to the northwest fell silent as their vehicle came to a stop at the place where the slope met the lowland.

Mopping his sweaty brow, Xu said, "Those wolves are too smart. I should have been able to take down a few more."

Bao gave him two thumbs up. "That was fantastic! Four wolves in less than thirty minutes. I've been doing this for six months and have yet to kill a single one."

Xu, still on a high, said, "The topography is too complex here, a good place for the wolves' guerrilla warfare. No wonder they can't be eliminated."

The vehicle moved slowly toward the dead wolves. The second had been shot in the chest, its blood soaking the grass around it. Bao and Liu carried the heavy carcass around behind the vehicle. Old Liu kicked the wolf. "There's enough meat on this one for ten people." He opened the trunk, took out a canvas bag, and laid it on the backseat. Then he took out two large burlap sacks and stuffed a wolf into each before loading the sacks into the trunk. He left the tailgate down, intending to use it to carry the other two carcasses.

Chen wanted to open up one of the wolves' bellies to show what it held, but the soldiers had no interest in skinning them there. "Do you really plan to eat wolf meat?" he asked. "It's sour. The herdsmen never eat it."

"Nonsense," said Old Liu. "Wolf meat isn't sour; it's like dog meat. I've eaten it back home. It's better than dog meat if you know how to cook it. See how fat this one is? Cooking wolf isn't much different from cooking dog. You put it in cold water for a day to get rid of the gamey smell, then add garlic and chili pepper and stew it for several hours. It smells wonderful. Back home, the whole village would show up to ask for some if you stewed a pot of it. Everyone says wolf meat gives you courage."

"The herdsmen out here practice a form of sky burial," Chen said, somewhat maliciously. "When someone dies, the family carries the body to a burial ground to feed the wolves. Are you really prepared to eat wolves that have eaten human flesh?"

Liu didn't care. "I know all about that. It's okay as long as you don't eat the stomach or intestines. Dogs eat human excrement, but have you heard anyone say dog meat is dirty? We use night soil to fertilize vegetables. Do you consider them filthy? We Chinese love to eat dog meat and vegetables. The corps sent down so many people that lamb has been rationed. Everyone's going crazy just thinking about meat. These wolves won't be enough to feed them all. But there are more sheep in the world than wolves." Liu thought he was being funny.

Staff Officer Xu laughed. "The division bosses placed an order for wolf meat with me before I came out here. I'll have to take these to them tonight. Some say wolf can cure bronchitis, and a few sufferers have signed up. I'm like a doctor. Killing wolves is wonderful work; first, you get rid of the scourge for the people; second, you get yourself a pelt; third, you help the sick; and fourth, you cure people who hunger for meat. You see, four birds with one stone. Four in one!"

Chen realized he'd never be able to dampen their wolf-killing spirit even if he managed to show them a belly full of dead mice.

Liu drove back to where the first wolf had fallen. The head was shattered, for the bullet had entered from the back, sending gray matter and blood oozing to the ground. He was relieved to see there was no white stripe on the neck and chest. This was not the White Wolf King. He was sure it was an alpha male that had led a few fast wolves to lure the enemy away from the pack. But it had been unprepared for something like the vehicle and for sharpshooters and their weapons.

After wiping off the blood and gray matter with clumps of grass, Liu and Bao happily bagged the wolf, carried it over to the tailgate, and tied it down. "This wolf's head is almost the size of a two-year-old bull," Liu commented. They got into the jeep to drive over to Staff Officer Batel.

The two vehicles met up. Batel pointed to the bulging hemp sack in the backseat and shouted, "We encountered nothing but willow-tree stumps and could hardly move. I had to fire three times to bring down a cub. This pack was all females and cubs, one big family."

Xu said emotionally, "The wolves here are demonic. The males left the best retreat route for the females and their cubs."

Bao shouted, "Another one! A victory. A great victory! This is the happiest day I've had since coming to the pasture. Finally, a chance to vent my anger. Let's go pick up the other two dead ones. I brought food and drink, so we can celebrate."

Chen jumped out to check out the cub. He untied the sack and saw that it looked like his cub but was bigger. He was surprised that his cub was smaller than the wild one even though he'd given him the best food he could manage. The wild cub was fully grown in less than a year and had learned to hunt and to feed itself. But it died at man's hand just as its life had begun. Chen rubbed the dead cub's head as if touching his own cub; this one died because he wanted to keep his.

They drove south. Chen felt miserable as he turned back to look at the border grassland. In less than an hour, the alpha male and lead wolf had been killed in a sort of attack they'd never encountered before. The rest had escaped across the border and might never return. But how could they survive without a strong leader? Bilgee once said, "A pack without its territory is worse than a dog that has lost its owner."

They returned to where the first shot had been fired. The powerful wolves lay in their own blood, encircled by swarms of flies. Unable to bear the sight, Chen walked off by himself to sit on the grass and gaze at the distant sky across the border. What would Bilgee think if he knew that Chen had led men on a wolf hunt? He'd taught him so much about wolves, and now he'd used that knowledge to kill them. He didn't know how he was going to face the old man. By nighttime, the wolves would come looking for their dead, and they'd find only bloodstains. The grassland would be filled with sad howls that night.

The two drivers carried the burlap sacks over to the second vehicle and laid them under the backseat.

On some large gunnysacks spread out on the grass they placed several bottles of grassland liquor, a large bag of spiced peanuts, a dozen cucumbers, two cans of braised beef, three jars of canned pork, and a basin of meat. Bao Shungui, liquor bottle in hand, and Staff Officer Xu went over to Chen and dragged him back to the picnic site. Bao patted him on the shoulder. "Little Chen," he said, "you did well today, and did me a great favor. Without you, our hunters wouldn't have had a chance to show off their skill."

The four soldiers raised their cups to toast Chen Zhen. "Drink up," said Xu. "This one's for you. Thanks to your research on wolves, you took us right to where we needed to be. Director Bao took us around over a hundred *li,* and we never saw a single wolf. Come on, drink up. We owe you our thanks."

Chen's face was a ghostly white; he wanted to say something but held his tongue. Instead, he accepted the cup and emptied it, wishing he could find a place to have a good cry. Instinctively, he picked up a raw cucumber and began eating. The laborers' private gardens were already producing cucumbers, which he hadn't tasted in more than two years. Maybe all Han Chinese were born to be farmers. Otherwise, why had he picked out a cucumber, of all things? Its light succulence turned to bitter juice in his mouth.

Xu patted him on the back. "Don't feel bad about the wolves we killed, Little Chen. I can tell you have emotional ties to them after raising one yourself, and you've been influenced by the old herdsmen. Granted, wolves make a contribution to the grassland by killing rabbits, mice, gazelles, and marmots. But that's a primitive way to go about it. We live in an age when man-made satellites soar into space. We can protect the grassland with scientific methods. The corps will be sending crop dusters to eradicate the mice."

That caught Chen off guard, but he immediately understood what Xu meant. "No, you can't do that," he said. "If the wolves, foxes, desert foxes, and hawks eat the dead mice, they'll all die off."

"What's the use of having wolves if all the mice are dead?" Bao said.

"Wolves have lots of uses," Chen argued. "I'm trying to make you understand that wolves can reduce the number of gazelles, rabbits, and marmots."

Old Liu, his face red from the liquor, burst out laughing. "Gazelles, wild rabbits, and marmots are all famous game. There won't be enough for our people when they come, and there definitely won't be any left for the wolves."

32

After they finished eating, Bao Shungui had a brief conversation with Staff Officer Xu, and then the two vehicles sped toward the northeast.

"We're heading the wrong way," Chen Zhen said. "We're better off retracing our steps."

Bao said, "We're a hundred and forty *li* from the brigade, and we have to make it worth our while for the long trip back."

Staff Officer Xu said, "If we avoid the areas where the shots were fired, we might run into more wolves. If not wolves, maybe foxes, and that wouldn't be too bad either. We must continue the glorious military tradition of keeping the fight going and accumulating victories."

Soon they entered a vast winter pastureland where acres and acres of needle grass spread before Chen's eyes. This was high-quality winter grass, with two-foot-long blades and tassels a yard long. The winter snows seldom if ever covered it completely; both the stalks and the tassels were fine livestock feed. The sheep could also get to leaves buried beneath the snow. During the seven months of winter, this pasture kept the livestock alive and thriving.

An autumn wind sent the grass rippling like waves spreading from the border all the way to the vehicles and submerging their wheels; they knifed through the grassy waves like fast ships. Chen breathed a sigh of relief. Even a telescope would be useless in finding wolves on a pasture with such tall, dense foliage. He felt renewed gratitude toward the grassland wolves and the horse herders. The seemingly pristine grassland was actually maintained through their efforts. Both labored hard at their tasks. Whenever Chen heard the herdsmen singing folk songs that echoed wolf sounds, he was happy, knowing that through their songs the herdsmen were acknowledging their debt to the wolves for their part in preserving the winter pasture.

The vehicles sped along, carrying the slightly drunken hunters, who scanned the landscape with binoculars in search of wolves. Chen was lost in his own thoughts, for this was the first time he'd had a chance to contemplate the primitive beauty of the winter pasture before the people and livestock arrived.

Not a single column of smoke, no horses, cows, or sheep. After six months of rest, the pasture looked bleaker than the spring-season birthing pasture, where there were many animal pens, storage sheds, well terraces, and other traces of human effort. In the winter pasture, people and livestock took water from the snow, eliminating the need for wells and terraces. The lambs and calves were fully grown, so instead of sheds and pens, the herders formed semicircle windbreaks for the sheep using wagons, mobile railings, and large pieces of felt.

The vehicles were now speeding along an ancient path. The soil was sandy and hard, but the grass was short and lush. Chen spotted three black dots in the grass not far to his right. He knew it was a large fox standing on its hind legs to keep an eye on the humans traveling through the pasture. The orange afternoon sun turned the fox's white fur a soft yellow, making it indistinguishable from the grass tassels. The three black spots above its neck were its ears and nose.

When they went fox hunting, Bilgee always pointed out the three black spots to Chen, especially on snow-covered ground. Experienced hunters would aim at those spots. The cunning grassland fox could not deceive grassland hunters, but could turn the sharp-eyed hunters seated next to Chen into blind men. Chen kept quiet, wanting to see no more bloodshed. The beautiful, sly foxes were expert mice catchers. As the vehicles drew closer, the black spots slowly disappeared in the dense grass.

As they continued, a wild rabbit stood up in the grass to stare at them. Its color was close to that of the tassels, but its camouflage was ruined by its big ears. Chen whispered, "There's a fat rabbit up ahead. They're enemies of the grassland. Want to take it down?"

"Not now," said Bao Shungui. "We'll get the rabbits after we kill all the wolves."

Unafraid of the vehicles, the rabbit did not crouch down and disappear until they were only ten or fifteen yards away. The fragrance of the needle grass grew stronger. With the realization that they would not find any prey here, the hunters turned and headed for the hilly autumn pasture.

Here the grass was shorter, but the herdsmen made it their autumn pastureland because of the abundant grass seeds. In the fall, seeds of wild wheat, clover, and peas were rich in fat and protein. The sheep would fatten up by eating the seeds right off the plants. Outsiders, who did not understand this primitive technique, could not manage to fatten their sheep enough to survive the winter, and large numbers of lambs would die in the spring when the ewes could not produce enough milk.

Chen had learned almost everything about the grassland from Bilgee in the two years he'd stayed with him. He reached down and pulled up a handful of grass seed, which he rubbed between his palms. The seeds were ripening; it was almost time for the brigade to move to the autumn pasture.

The shorter grass widened their view and allowed the vehicles to speed up. Bao Shungui spotted some fresh wolf droppings in the dirt. The hunters reacted excitedly; Chen began to worry once again. They were now sixty or seventy *li* from where they'd used their guns, and wolves around here wouldn't be on guard against motor vehicles quietly approaching from the north, where there were no traces of human beings.

"Wolf! Wolf!" Three of the passengers cried with soft urgency after they crossed a gentle slope. Chen rubbed his eyes and saw a giant wolf, as big as a leopard, some three hundred yards ahead. On the Olonbulag, large, powerful, fast-moving wolves often went out on their own, and while they appeared to be loners, they were actually scouting for the pack.

The giant wolf looked as if it had been startled out of a nap by the sound of the vehicles; it raced into the dense grass of a gulley. Old Liu stepped on the gas and shouted excitedly, "Don't even think about getting away!" By blocking its escape route, he forced the wolf to spin around and run toward the hilltop, nearly at gazelle speed, but Staff Officer Batel's vehicle caught up with it. Coming at the wolf from opposite directions, they had yet to reach top speed, while the wolf was running as fast as it could.

The hunters deferred to one another. Xu shouted, "Go ahead, you have the best shot."

"No," Batel replied. "You're a better shot, you take it."

Bao waved and yelled, "Don't shoot. Don't anyone shoot. I want a pelt with no bullet holes. I want to skin it alive. A live pelt, with its bright, shiny fur, fetches the best price."

"Great idea!" the hunters and their drivers shouted in unison. Old Liu even raised his thumb at Bao. "Watch me. I'll chase that son of a bitch down."

Little Wang joined in: "I'll chase it till it coughs up blood."

The gentle slope made for easy maneuvering, and this wolf was not going to escape the two-pronged motorized attack. It was already foaming at the mouth. What should have been a tense battle between man and wolf now became nothing more than entertainment for humans. It was the first time since his arrival on the grassland that Chen saw the tremendous edge humans had over the wolves. The Mongolian wolves, having dominated the grassland for thousands of years, were now more pathetic than the rabbits.

The skilled drivers followed at a leisurely pace, speeding up when the wolf ran faster and slowing down when the wolf's pace slackened, all the while forcing it to keep running by blowing on their horns and keeping a distance of fifty to sixty yards between them. The wolf was fast, but the chase was taking its toll; after twenty *li,* it was panting hard, its mouth opened as wide as possible, but still it was having trouble catching its breath.

The wolf ran for its life, exhausting its will and strength; seemingly, it could run forever, so long as the enemy did not catch up with it. Chen wished that a giant hole or dip in the ground, or a pile of ox bones would rise up before them; he wouldn't have minded being tossed out of the vehicle.

The faces of the hunters, exhilarated by the chase, were red and shiny, as if they were drunk. Bao yelled, "This wolf is bigger than any we've gotten before. Its pelt is big enough for a blanket without having to sew pieces together."

"Let's not sell the pelt," Xu said. "Let's give it to the corps commander."

"Good idea," Batel said. "That way the corps leaders will know how big the wolves around here are and what a danger they are to the grassland."

Old Liu banged on the steering wheel. "The Inner Mongolian grassland is so rich that within a year or so we'll all have better houses than we could ever get in the city."

Chen's fists were clenched until they were sweating. It was all he could do to stop from pounding Liu in the back of the head. The image of the cub flashed before his eyes, and a warm current coursed through his heart, as if a nursing baby were waiting for him at home. His arms fell weakly to his sides; he felt empty from head to toe.

They'd finally chased the wolf onto a long, wide-open slope, with no gulley, no hilltop, no holes, and no lowlands, nothing the wolf could use to defend itself. Under the blaring of the vehicles' horns, it began to slow down, its legs twitching from exhaustion.

Bao grabbed Xu's rifle and fired two shots less than a yard from the wolf, grazing its fur. It was the sound that the wolves feared most, and it squeezed out the last of its strength; after managing another half *li* or so, it stopped, turned, and sat down for its final gesture.

The vehicles screeched to a stop about three or four yards away. Bao leaped off with his rifle; seeing that the wolf wasn't moving, he fixed his bayonet and walked up to it. It was quaking, its eyes unfocused. It remained motionless as Bao walked up, so he stabbed at its mouth, still getting no reaction. He laughed. "We've chased it stupid." Then he reached out to rub the wolf's head, like petting a dog.

Bao may well have been the first man in thousands of years who dared to touch the head of a living wolf sitting in the wild. The wolf crumpled to the ground as Bao's hand moved toward its ears.

Chen Zhen returned home feeling like a sinner, finding it difficult to enter the yurt. He hesitated before finally walking inside, where he found Zhang Jiyuan talking angrily to Yang Ke and Gao Jianzhong about the brigade's wolf extermination campaign. "Everyone's gone mad about killing. The hunters and workers use trucks and cars, given all the gasoline and ammunition they need. Even the doctors have joined in. They inject an odorless and colorless poison into the bone marrow of dead sheep that they then tossed into the wild. I have no idea how many wolves they've poisoned. The worst are the corps' road repair crews. They use any weapon they can find. They even found a way to insert explosives into sheep bones, smear them with sheep fat, and then leave them at places frequented by wolves. The rigged bones blow wolves' heads off when they bite down. The workers have put the sheep-bone bombs everywhere. They've already killed several of the herdsmen's dogs. The wolves have fallen into the abyss of the people's battle. Everywhere people are singing, 'Kill the wolves! Generation after generation, we won't stop fighting until all the jackals are dead.' I hear that the herdsmen have lodged a complaint with the military district."

"The workers in our team have also joined the fray," Gao said. "They killed five or six big wolves. These herdsmen-turned-farmers are even better at killing wolves; it cost me two bottles of liquor to find out how they do it. They use wolf traps, but they're much sneakier than the herders. The herders leave traps near dead sheep, and after a while the wolves figure it out. They're cautious with dead sheep in the wild; they won't touch them until the alpha male, with its sharp nose, sniffs and digs out the trap. But the workers do it differently. They set traps at places where there are lots of wolves, with no dead sheep or bones, on level ground. Guess what they use for bait? You couldn't guess in a million years. They soak horse dung in melted sheep fat and dry it. Then they break it into small pieces and spread it around the traps. That's their bait. When a wolf passes by, it'll smell the sheep fat, but it won't be on guard since there are no dead sheep or bones. It sniffs around, and sooner or later it's caught. How cruel is that! Old Wang said that's how they killed all the wolves in his hometown."

Unable to bear any more, Chen went out and walked to the wolf pen, where he called softly to the cub, who had obviously missed him that day. He was waiting for Chen at the edge of the pen, his tail standing straight. Chen crouched down and held the cub for a long time, his face touching the cub's head. The moon seemed cold on this frosty autumn night; the wolves' tremulous howls were distant memories on the new pasture. Chen no longer worried about the mother wolves coming for the cub; now he wished they'd come and take him north across the border.

He heard footsteps behind him; it was Yang Ke, who said, "Lamjav said he saw the White Wolf King leading a pack of wolves across the border before the corps could react. I don't think he'll ever return to the Olonbulag."

Chen couldn't sleep that night.

33

You can tame a bear, a tiger, a lion, or an elephant, but you cannot tame a Mongolian wolf.

The cub would rather be strangled than move to a new place.

The brigade's cows and sheep left soon after dawn and the caravan of transport wagons, separated into sections, crossed a western mountain ridge on their way to the autumn pastureland. Those from the Section Two students' yurt, with their six heavy oxcarts, had not yet started out, even though Bilgee and Gasmai had sent people twice to tell them to get on the road.

Zhang Jiyuan took time off to help them move, but he and Chen Zhen were helpless in dealing with the fiercely stubborn cub. Chen never dreamed that they would fail in the move after weathering so many storms with the cub over the past six months.

The little wolf had been a recently weaned cub no more than a foot long when they'd put him in a wooden box used for dry cow patties to move from the spring pasture. After a summer of voracious eating, he'd grown into a midsized wolf. They didn't have a cage big enough for him now, and, even if they had, Chen would not have been able to put him in it; besides, there wouldn't have been space. There weren't enough carts to begin with. All six carts were seriously overloaded (the students' books alone filled one cart) and ran the risk of overturning or breaking down on the long trek. Weather was the determining factor in choosing a date for the move; the brigade wanted to avoid the coming rains. Chen was in a tough spot.

Sweat beaded Zhang Jiyuan's forehead. "What have you been doing all this time?" he grumbled. "You should have trained the wolf to walk with you."

"How do you know I didn't try?" Chen fired back. "I could drag him along when he was small, but that couldn't last forever. All summer long he pulled me where he wanted to go, and if I tried to assert myself, he threatened to bite me. Wolves aren't dogs; they'd rather die than change. Have you ever seen a wolf perform in a circus like a tiger or a lion? No animal trainer could manage that. You've been around more wolves than I have, you ought to know that."

Zhang clenched his teeth and said, "I'll try again. If it doesn't work this time, we're going to have to do something drastic." He walked up to the cub, herding club in hand, and took the iron ring from Chen. As soon as began to pull on the chain, the cub bared his fangs and growled, staying glued to the spot by leaning backward and digging in with all four paws. Zhang pulled with all his might but couldn't budge the little wolf. So he turned around and draped the chain over his shoulder to pull like a coolie dragging a boat on the Yangtze River.

He barely managed to move the cub, whose paws gouged tracks in the sandy soil, leaving two small mounds at the end. Unhappy about being dragged along, the cub shifted his weight forward and prepared to pounce, sending Zhang flying headfirst to the ground and covering his face with dirt. That dragged the cub even farther, and now man and wolf were a tangled mess, the cub's mouth no more than a foot from Zhang's throat. Terrified, Chen rushed up, grabbed the cub around the neck, and held tight. The cub was still snarling at Zhang.

Both men were gasping for breath, their faces ashen. "We're in big trouble," Zhang said. "The move will take two or three days, which means a round trip of at least five. If it was only a day, we could leave him here and come back with an empty cart. But the guard at the wool shed and the workers haven't moved yet, and if we leave him here longer than that, either they'll kill him or the corps wolf hunters will. We have to get him to move with us. How's this? We'll tow him along behind a cart."

"I tried that a few days ago. It didn't work. I just about strangled him in the process. Now I understand the meaning behind 'unbridled wildness' and 'death before surrender.' The wolf would rather be strangled to death than follow our orders. I think we're stuck."

"I can't accept that," Zhang said. "Why don't you do it first with one of the puppies to show him?"

Chen shook his head. "I tried that too. Didn't work."

"Let's try it again." Zhang brought over a loaded oxcart, slipped a rope around the neck of one of the puppies, and tied the rope to the rear axle. Then he circled the wolf, the obedient puppy tagging along behind.

"We're going to a nice place," Zhang said as he walked, trying to win over the cub. "See, like this, follow the cart. It's easy. You're smarter than a dog; you know how to do this, don't you? Here, take a good look."

The cub stared at the puppy, his head held high out of disdain. Chen coaxed and cajoled, dragging the wolf behind the puppy a few steps, though it was actually he who was being pulled along by the cub, who followed because he liked the puppy, not because he wanted to do their bidding. After completing one revolution, Chen looped the iron ring over the shaft, hoping the cub would follow the cart. But the moment the chain was attached to the cart, the cub pulled against it with all his might, straining harder than when he was tethered to the wooden post and making the heavy cart creak.

Chen looked at the scene in front of him: not a single yurt or sheep left. Panic began to set in. If they didn't get on the road soon, they wouldn't reach the temporary campsite before dark. With so many sections and so many twists and turns along the way, what would happen to Yang Ke's sheep and Gao Jianzhong's cows if they were lost? How would the two men find a place to stop for food and tea? More dangerous yet was the night shift, when everyone was tired and they didn't have the dogs around. If something happened to the sheep because of the cub, Chen would be criticized again and the cub would probably be shot.

Anxiety finally hardened Chen's heart. "He might die if we drag him along, but he'll surely die if we let him go, so let's seek life in death and drag him along with us. You get the carts moving and let me have your horse. I'll bring up the rear with the cub."

Zhang sighed. "Obviously, raising a wolf under nomadic conditions is just about impossible."

Chen moved the cart tethered with the puppy and the cub to the rear of the caravan. Then he tied the rope from the last ox to the shaft of the cart ahead of them. "Let's go," he shouted.

Since Zhang couldn't bring himself to sit on the cart, he walked along holding the rope tied to the first ox. One after another, the carts started moving. The puppy followed as the last cart began moving, but the cub stayed put even when the three-yard-long chain was stretched taut. Gao Jianzhong had picked the best and fastest six oxen for the move. They had followed grassland customs by feeding the oxen nothing but water for three days. When their stomachs were empty was the best time to put them to work. So when they got under way, the cub was no match; he was jerked forward and fell head over heels before managing to dig his paws into the ground.

Startled and angry, he struggled, clawing wildly as he rolled around and got to his feet time and again. He'd run a few steps, then stop and dig in. But then, once they were on the path, the carts picked up speed. The cub stumbled and bounced around for a dozen yards or so before he was dragged backward, pulled along like a dead dog, the hard grass stubble scraping off a layer of his fur.

The puppy cocked her head to look at the cub sympathetically; she whimpered and raised her paws as if telling him to walk like her or he'd be dragged to his death. But, too haughty to act like a dog, the cub ignored her and continued to resist...

Chen could see that the cub would rather endure the pain and struggle against the chain than be led along like a dog. His resistance marked the fundamental distinction between wolves and dogs; between wolves and lions, tigers, bears, and elephants; and between wolves and most humans. No grassland wolf would surrender to humans. Refusing to follow or to be led was a core belief for a Mongolian wolf, and that was true even for a cub who had never been taught by members of a pack.

As the cub struggled, the road grit rubbed his paws

bloody, a sight that stabbed at Chen's heart. The wolf, a totem for the stubborn grassland people over the millennia, possessed spiritual power that would shame and inspire awe in humans. Few people could live according to that code without bending and compromising; fewer still would pit their lives against a nearly invincible external force.

These thoughts made Chen aware that his understanding of wolves was still incredibly shallow. For a long time he had thought that food, and hence killing, was the most important thing for wolves; obviously, that was not the case. He had based that assumption on his understanding of human behavior. Neither food nor killing was the purpose of the wolves' existence; rather, it was their sacred, inviolable freedom, their independence, and their dignity. It was this principle that made it possible for all true believers among the herdsmen to willingly be delivered to the mystical sky-burial ground, in hopes that their souls would soar freely along with those of the wolves.

After four or five *li,* the stubborn cub had lost about half of the fur around his neck, which was now bleeding. The thick pads on his paws were rubbed raw, exposing the flesh underneath. Finally the exhausted cub could no longer roll over; now, like a dying wolf dragged along by a fast horse and a lasso pole, he no longer struggled. When drops of blood began to fall from his throat, Chen realized that the collar had opened a wound there. He shouted for the carts to stop and jumped off his horse, picked up the quaking cub, and walked with him in his arms for a yard or so to loosen the chain. His arms were quickly smeared by blood from the cub's neck. Seemingly close to death, the cub continued to bleed; he scratched Chen's hands with paws whose claws had been blunted from his ordeal and were now a bloody mess. Chen's tears merged with the wolf's blood.

Zhang Jiyuan was shocked to see the state the cub was in. Walking around and around, but not knowing what to do, he said, "How could he be so stubborn? Doesn't he want to live? What do we do now?"

Chen had no idea what to do except hold the cub; the tremors nearly broke his heart.

"He won't let us pull him along now, and he's not yet fully grown," Zhang said, wiping off the sweat on his forehead. "Even if we manage to get him to the autumn pastureland, we'll have to move every month. How will we take him with us? I think... I think we ought to... set him free, here... and let him live on his own."

Chen's face was steely gray. "You didn't raise him!" he shouted. "You don't understand. Live on his own? That's the same as killing him. I'm going to see that he grows to adulthood. I'm going to let him live."

Fired by his determination, Chen jumped to his feet and ran over to the cart carrying cow dung and other odds and ends, where, puffing with anger, he untied the rope and moved the cart to the end of the caravan. Then he picked up a willow basket and dumped out half a load of the dry cow dung. He'd decided to convert the basket into a prisoner transport, a temporary jail cell in which to move the cub.

"Are you crazy? This load of fuel is how we'll eat and drink tea on the journey. If it rains, we won't be able to eat. And we'll need dry dung for days after we get there. How dare you dump that just so you can transport the wolf! The herders won't forgive you, nor will Gao Jianzhong."

Chen quickly reloaded the cart. "I'll borrow some from Gasmai when we get to camp tonight. Then when we get to the new pasture, I'll go collect cow dung. Rest assured, you'll have your meals and your tea."

Having barely escaped death, the cub stood stubbornly on the ground despite the pain in his paws; his legs were still shaking, and blood continued to drip from his mouth, but he stiffened his neck and dug in his heels in case the cart started off again. He stared at it with a defiance that said he was prepared to fight to the death, even if his paws were rubbed raw, down to the bones. Chen crouched and laid the cub on the ground with his paws up in the air. Then he went for some medicated powder to treat his paws and neck. Seeing the blood dripping from his mouth, Chen took out two pieces of meat, spread the powder over them, and held them out to the cub, who swallowed them whole. Chen hoped the medicine would help stop the bleeding. He then retied the basket and rearranged the odds and ends to clear a space on the cart. After laying down a piece of untanned sheepskin, he tore off half of a felt blanket to use as a cover; the space was barely big enough to contain the wolf. But how was he going to get him into it?

Undoing the chain, Chen rolled up his sleeves and picked up the cub. But as soon as he took a step toward the cart, the cub began to growl and struggle. So Chen ran, hoping to toss the cub into the basket. Before he got there, however, the cub chomped down on his arm and wouldn't let go. Chen screamed in pain and fear. He broke out into a cold sweat.

The cub did not let go until he was back on the ground. Chen shook his arm to relieve the pain. He looked down and saw that, while he wasn't bleeding, there were four purple welts on the skin.

Zhang's face was a ghostly white. "You're lucky you snipped off the tips of his fangs, or he'd have bitten through your arm. I don't think we can keep him anymore. When he grows up, even blunted fangs could break your arm."

"Don't talk about his teeth, okay? If not for that, I might have been able to return him to the grassland. Now he's handicapped. How could he survive with fangs that can't even break the skin? I maimed him, so I'll have to feed him. Now that the corps is here, and they're talking about settling down, I'll build a stone pen for him after we settle, and there'll be no need for the chain."

"All right," Zhang said, "I won't try to stop you. But we have to find a way to put him on the cart and get on the road. Let me try, since you're hurt."

"I'll carry him," Chen said. "He doesn't know you, and he could bite your nose off. Tell you what. You stand there with the felt blanket and cover the basket as soon as I toss him in."

"Are you crazy? He'll bite you, and hard, if you pick him up again. Wolves are ruthless when they're that angry. He'll go for your throat if you're not careful."

Chen paused for a moment. "I'm going to have to pick him up, even if he bites me. I guess I'll have to sacrifice a raincoat." He ran over to one of the carts and took out his army raincoat, with green canvas on one side and black rubber on the other. Then he took out two more pieces of meat to keep the cub busy while he forced himself to stop shaking, opened up the raincoat, and flung it over the young wolf. He quickly tightened his grip and carried the frantically struggling cub, disoriented and unable to see where to bite, over to the cart, where he tossed him in, raincoat and all. Zhang ran up and dropped the felt blanket over the basket. By the time the cub struggled out of an opening he'd made in the raincoat, he'd become a prisoner. After the two men secured the felt cover with a horse-mane rope, Chen collapsed on the ground, gasping for breath and drenched in sweat. The cub made a turn in his new prison, prompting Chen to jump up to be ready if the cub tore at the felt blanket or rammed his head against the basket.

The carts were now ready to set out, but Chen was worried that the flimsy willow basket would not be strong enough to hold an angry, powerful animal. He coaxed and cajoled, and even tossed several pieces of meat into the cage. After bringing the dogs back to the rear of the caravan to keep the cub company, he signaled to get Zhang moving. On one of the carts, Chen found a club, which he was prepared to bang against the basket to stop the cub from struggling if necessary, while he rode alongside to keep an eye on him. He fully expected that the cub would try to chew a hole in the basket to get loose from a prison far worse than any chain.

He needn't have worried, for when they began moving, the cub stopped struggling; rather, fear showed in his eyes, something Chen had never witnessed before. Not daring to lie down, he lowered his head, arched his back, and, with his tail between his legs, stood staring at Chen, who watched as he grew increasingly frightened, to the point where he shrank into a ball. He wouldn't eat, drink, growl, or bite; like a seasick prisoner, he'd lost the capacity to resist.

Shocked by this turn of events, Chen stuck close to the cart as they crossed a mountain ridge. The cub's eyes seemed to show that his head remained clear, though he was clearly exhausted, his paws were injured, and his mouth was still bleeding. But he didn't dare lie down to rest, as if out of an instinctual fear of the cart's motion and of being lifted off the ground. After six months with the cub, Chen was still flabbergasted by his repeated, unfathomable behavior.

The caravan traveled fast but at a smooth pace. As Chen rode along, he was quickly lost in thought. How had the often violent cub suddenly become so fearful and weak? That was so unlike a grassland wolf. Do all heroic figures have a fatal flaw? Was it possible that the grassland wolf, which Chen believed to have evolved to the point of perfection, had a character defect? He turned his attention to the difficulties facing him in the frequent moves they would be making throughout the winter. The cub would be fully grown by then, and there simply wouldn't be enough resources to transport him from place to place. No solution presented itself.

The oxen smelled the cows after they crossed over the hill and picked up the pace in order to catch up with earlier caravans some distance away.

As they were moving through a mountain pass on the edge of the summer pastureland, a light truck came from the opposite direction, trailing clouds of dust; instead of waiting for the carts to yield, it drove off the road and continued past them.

Chen saw two rifle-toting soldiers, some laborers from the brigade, and a herdsman in a thin deel. The herdsman waved; it was Dorji. Chen's heart was in his throat again at the sight of the skilled wolf killer in a truck that had become infamous for killing wolves. He rode up to the front. "Is Dorji taking people to hunt wolves again?" Chen asked.

"There's nothing around here but mountains, lakes,

and streams," Zhang said. "The truck would be useless in places like that, so how could they be going to hunt wolves? They must be going back to help move the storage shed."

When they reached the grassland, a horse came galloping toward them from the caravan up front. They saw it was Bilgee, looking grim. "Was Dorji on that truck?" he asked breathlessly.

They confirmed that he was. "Come with me to the old campsite," Bilgee said to Chen. Then he turned to Zhang Jiyuan. "You go on ahead with the carts; we'll be right back."

"Check on the cub when you can," Chen whispered to Zhang. "If he gives you any trouble, don't do anything till I get back." He then galloped off with the old man.

"Dorji must be taking those people to hunt wolves," Bilgee said. "These days, his skills have been in great demand. Since he speaks Mandarin, he's become the wolf-killing adviser to the corps, leaving the cows to his younger brother. He takes people out hunting every day. He's on great terms with the officials. A few days ago, he even helped one of the division big shots shoot several wolves. He's their hero now."

"How do they hunt when there's nothing but mountains and rivers? I don't get it."

"When a horse herder told me he was taking them back to the old campsite, I knew what he was up to."

"What?"

"He's putting out poisoned bait and setting traps on the old campsite. The old, sick, and injured wolves are in such bad shape that they have to survive on leftover bones from the pack, or food left behind by people and their dogs. They go hungry half the time. So whenever the herders move to a new place, they look for food in the ashes and garbage at the old sites. They'll eat anything, rotting sheep pelts, stinking bones, sheep skulls, leftover food, and stuff like that. They even dig up dead dogs, sheep, and cows. All the old herdsmen know this. Sometimes, when they've left something behind during a move, they go back to get it and see traces of wolves. As good-hearted believers in Lamaism, they know those wolves are in bad shape, so they'd never set traps or leave poisoned bait behind. Some even leave food for the old wolves when they move."

The old man sighed. "It didn't take the outsiders long to learn all about the old wolves. Dorji has followed in his father's footsteps, by leaving dead sheep stuffed with poison and setting traps when they move. They go back a few days later to skin the dead or trapped wolves. Why do you think his family sells more pelts than anyone else? They don't believe in Lamaism, and they don't respect the wolves. They don't mind using the cruelest means possible to kill them all, including the old and injured ones. See what I mean? Wolves could never be as evil as humans."

With sadness brimming in his eyes, the old man continued, his beard quivering, "Do you know how many wolves they've killed lately? The wolves are so spooked that they don't dare go out to look for food. I figure that even the healthy ones will go to the old site to look for food, now that the brigade has moved on. Dorji's far more devious than wolves. If they keep killing them, no one here will ever again go up to Tengger, and the grassland will be doomed."

Chen knew there was nothing he could say to heal the wounds of this last hunter of the nomadic herdsmen. No one could stop the explosion of the farming population or the farmers' plundering of the grassland. Unable to ease the old man's feeling, all he could say was, "Watch me. I'm going to remove every one of those traps."

They crossed the ridge and headed toward the nearest campsite, seeing tire tracks left by the truck, which had already driven to the other side of the slope. They approached the site cautiously, not wanting their horses to get caught in a trap.

The old man checked the area and pointed to the cooking pit. "Dorji's good at setting traps. See those ashes? They look as if the wind blew them over there, but in fact he sprinkled them over the traps. And he left two meatless sheep hooves near them. If those had any meat on them, the wolves would be suspicious. But meatless hooves are trash, just waiting to trick the wolves. He smeared his hand with ashes to mask the human odor before he set the traps. Only wolves with the keenest sense of smell could detect his odor. The old ones' sense of smell has been dulled with age."

Shocked and angered, Chen could say nothing.

Pointing to half of the carcass of a sick sheep, the old man said, "I guarantee you that sheep has been poisoned. I hear they got some powerful poison from Beijing. The wolves can't smell it, but once they ingest it, they'll be dead before you can smoke a pipe."

"Then I'll toss that carcass down an abandoned well."

"There are too many campsites. You can't do that in all of them."

They got back on their horses and checked four or five sites. Dorji hadn't left anything at some of the sites, but he'd set traps or left poison at others. He'd planned it out well, employing plenty of deception. He would alternate methods, leaving small hills between the camps, so that if a trap caught a wolf in one place, that wouldn't affect the ones set in the next spot.

They also saw there were more sites with poison than with traps. He'd made use of the cooking pits and the ashes inside, which was why he could finish so quickly; he hadn't had to dig fresh holes for the traps.

They had to stop there, or Dorji would have seen them. The old man turned his horse around as he muttered, "These are all we'll be able to save." When they reached a site where Dorji had worked, the old man got off his horse and walked toward a rotten sheep leg. He took out a small sheepskin pouch, opened it, and spread some grayish white powder over it. Chen knew exactly what he was doing. The stuff was low-grade animal poison sold at the local co-op; not very powerful, it had a strong odor that was effective only on the stupidest wolves and foxes. Dorji's work would be in vain now that the poison could be detected by most wolves.

The old man is, after all, smarter than Dorji, Chen was thinking. But a question occurred to him. "What if the smell dissipates in the wind?" he asked.

The old man said, "Not to worry. The wolves can smell it even if we can't."

At places where there were traps, Bilgee told Chen to pick up some sheep bones and throw them at the traps to snap them shut. That was one of the ways cunning old wolves dealt with traps.

Then they moved to the next site and did not turn back until the old man had used up all his low-grade poison.

"Papa, what if on their way back they see that the traps have snapped shut?"

"They're probably off to hunt wolves, so they won't worry about these," the old man said.

"But what if they come back to check the traps and see they've been touched? You could be in serious trouble for sabotaging the wolf extermination campaign."

"Not as serious as the trouble the wolves will be in. Without them, the mice and rabbits will rule the grassland. Then, when the grassland is gone, they'll be in trouble too. No one can escape it. I've managed to save a few wolves. We'll just have to be happy with that. Olonbulag wolves, run for your lives, run over there. To be honest, I hope Dorji and the others do come back and see what I've done. I've got a score to settle with them."

They reached the top of the ridge, where they saw several wild geese crying sadly and circling in the air, looking for their own kind. The old man reined in his horse, looked up, and sighed. "Even the wild geese can't form a flock. They've eaten nearly all of them." He turned back to look at the new pastureland that he had opened. Tears filled his murky eyes.

Chen was reminded of the beautiful paradise they'd found when he'd first arrived at the new pastureland with the old man. It had taken only one summer for the people to turn the lovely swan lake area into a graveyard for swans, wild geese, wild ducks, and wolves. "Papa," he said, "we're doing a good deed, so why do I feel we have to sneak around? I feel like crying."

"Go ahead and cry. I feel that way myself. The wolves have taken away generations of old Mongol men, so why am I going to be left behind?" He looked up at Tengger with a tear-streaked face and wailed like an old wolf.

Tears streamed down Chen's face, joining the old man's tears as they fell onto the ancient Olonbulag.

* * *

The cub endured his pain, standing in the cage for two whole days. Chen Zhen and Zhang Jiyuan's carts finally arrived at a gentle slope dense with autumn grass on the evening of the second day. Their neighbor, Gombu, was putting up his yurt. Gao Jianzhong had already released the cows onto the new pasture and was waiting for Chen and Zhang at a yurt site Bilgee had chosen for them. Yang Ke's sheep were also approaching the new site.

Chen and his friends quickly put up their yurt. Gasmai sent Bayar over with two baskets of dry cow dung. After the two-day trek, the three friends could finally make a fire to cook and to boil water for tea. Yang Ke made it back before dinner, with a surprise for everyone—a rotten cart shaft he had dragged back with him, enough fuel to cook a couple of meals, which finally appeased Gao Jianzhong, who had been sulking over the dung that Chen had thrown away.

The three men walked up to the prison cart. When they removed the felt blanket, they were shocked to see a hole the size of a soccer ball in one side of the willow basket, made by the cub with his blunted claws and dulled fangs.

Chen looked closer and saw bloodstains on the chewed-up willow branches. He and Zhang quickly unloaded the basket, and the cub scrambled onto the grass-covered ground. Chen untied the other end of the chain and carried the cub up next to the yurt, where he sank the post, looped the chain, and placed the cap over it. The cub, after all the torture and shock, seemed to still be feeling the effects of the moving cart, for he quickly lay down in the grass. That way, his injured paws weren't touching anything hard; he was so tired he could barely lift his head.

Chen grabbed hold of the cub and forced open his mouth with his thumbs. There wasn't much blood from his throat wound, but one of his teeth was bleeding. Gripping the cub's head tightly, Chen told Yang Ke to feel the tooth. Yang moved it back and forth. "The root's loose, so the tooth is probably useless." To Chen, it felt worse than losing his own tooth.

For two days the cub had struggled, causing a number of serious injuries to his body and ruining a tooth. Chen let go of the cub, who kept touching the bad tooth with his tongue, a clear sign that it hurt. Yang carefully applied some medicine to the cub's paws.

After dinner, Chen prepared a basin of semisolid food, using leftover noodles, small pieces of meat, and soup. After it cooled off, he gave it to the young wolf, who gobbled it down. Chen could tell, though, that the animal was having trouble swallowing; it was as if something was stuck in his throat. Then he went back to touching the bad tooth with his tongue, soon began coughing, and spit out some bloody, undigested food. Chen's heart sank; the cub not only had a bad tooth but something was wrong with his throat as well. But where would he find a vet who would examine a wolf cub?

"Now I understand something," Yang Ke said to Chen. "The wolves are unyielding, not because the pack has no 'traitors' or wimps, but because the merciless environment weeds out the unfit."

"This cub has paid too high a price for his wild, untamed nature," Chen said sadly. "You can see what a person will be like as an adult when he's only three, and what he'll be like as an old man when he's seven, but with wolves, it only takes three months to foresee an adult wolf and seven months to see into his old age."

The following morning, when Chen was cleaning the wolf pen, he saw that the usual grayish droppings had been replaced by black ones. Startled, he quickly opened the cub's mouth and saw that his throat was still bleeding. He got Yang Ke to hold the cub's mouth open while he tried smearing some medicine on the wound with a chopstick and a piece of felt . But it was too deep for the chopstick to reach. They tried everything, all the home remedies, until they were both exhausted, regretting that neither of them had studied veterinary science.

On the fourth day, the color of the droppings started to lighten, and the cub regained his vitality. The two men breathed sighs of relief.

34

Bilgee was never again invited to attend the corps or division production meetings. Chen often saw him at home, silently doing leatherwork in his yurt.

The leather bridles, reins, bits, and hobbles belonging to the horse, cow, and sheep and horse herders' horses had all been softened in the summer and autumn rains; after drying in the sun, the leather had stiffened and cracked, making it less durable. It was not uncommon for a horse to snap its reins or break its hobbles and run back to the herd.

With time on his hands, Bilgee was able to make new leather fittings for his family, the section's horse herders, and the Beijing students. Chen Zhen, Yang Ke, and Gao Jianzhong often took time out to learn leatherwork from the old man. After a couple of weeks, they were able to produce passable bridles and whips. Yang even managed to make a hobble, which was hardest of all to make.

The old man's spacious yurt was transformed into a leather workshop. Finished work was piled high; the smell of leather salt permeated the air. All they needed to do now was to apply marmot oil.

Marmots produced the best oil on the grassland. During severe winters, oil from sheep and other animals solidified; marmot oil, the sole exception, could be poured even at thirty degrees below zero. It was a grassland specialty found in the homes of all herdsmen. When the white-hair blizzards blew in the depths of winter, all the people had to do to keep their faces free from frostbite was to smear on a layer of marmot oil. Mongolian flour cakes fried in marmot oil were golden brown and delicious; they usually only appeared at wedding banquets or for special guests. And on burns the oil was as effective as badger fat.

Marmot oil and pelts were two important sources of income for herdsmen. In the fall, when the marmot skins were at their thickest, herdsmen went into the mountains to hunt them, keeping the meat for themselves and sending the skins and oil to the purchasing station to swap for bricks of tea, silk, batteries, boots, candy, and daily necessities. A large skin sold for four yuan, and a catty of oil fetched at least one. Ideal for women's coats, the skins were exported for foreign exchange.

But income from hunting was not steady. Wildlife on the grassland is no different from fruit trees in other parts of China; there are good years and bad years, determined by weather, growth of grass, and natural disasters. But the herders on the Olonbulag knew how to control the scale of their hunting and never set a growth rate for each year. They would hunt often if there were many animals, less often if there were fewer, and stop altogether when there were none. It had gone on like that for thousands of years, which was why there were always animals for them to hunt. Most of the time they sold the marmot skins but not the oil, for it was used widely, mostly on leatherwork, turning it a rich brown color, soft yet resilient. The leather would retain its salt if marmot oil was regularly applied during the rainy season, thus prolonging its life and reducing the frequency of accidents. They often ran out before hunting season arrived.

With an eye on his leatherworking tools, one day Bilgee said to Chen, "I only have half a bottle of oil left, and I have a craving for marmot meat. It tastes best at this time of year. In the old days, aristocrats wouldn't eat mutton around this time. Tomorrow I'll take you out hunting for marmot."

"When he brings them home," Gasmai said, "I'll treat you to some tea and cakes fried in marmot oil."

"That's great news," Chen said, "but I can't keep coming here for food."

Gasmai laughed. "Once you started raising the cub, you pretty much forgot about me. How often have you come for tea over the past few months?"

"You're the section leader, and I've already caused you trouble over that cub. I haven't dared come to see you."

"If not for me," Gasmai said, "your cub would have been killed by herdsmen long ago."

"What did you say to them?"

Gasmai smiled. "I said that the Chinese hate wolves and they eat them, all but Chen Zhen and Yang Ke, that is. The cub is like their adopted child. They'll be just like us Mongols once they learn everything about wolves."

Filled with gratitude, Chen thanked her effusively.

Gasmai laughed out loud. "You can thank me by making some dumplings for me. I also like your mutton-stuffed flat bread." That made Chen happy. She then signaled with her eyes and pointed to the dejected old man. "Papa likes those Chinese mutton cakes too."

Chen laughed. "We still have half a bundle of the

green onions Zhang Jiyuan bought at the brigade office. I'll bring it over tonight, and you and Papa can eat all you want."

A faint smile appeared on the old man's face. "No need to bring any mutton; we just killed a sheep. Gao Jianzhong's mutton cakes are much better than those sold in the restaurants. Make sure you ask Yang Ke and Gao Jianzhong to come drink with us."

That night, Gao taught Gasmai how to make the fillings, roll the wrappings, and fry the cakes. Then they sang, ate, and drank until the old man abruptly put down his bowl and said, "The corps wants the herdsmen to settle in one place, saying that way we wouldn't get sick so often and our workload would be reduced. What do you think? You Chinese like to settle in one place, right?"

"We're not sure the herdsmen can change their nomadic lifestyle after all these years," Yang Ke said. "I personally don't think so. The shallow grass here can't stand trampling, so the people and their livestock have to move to a different site after a month or two. If we settled in one place, it wouldn't take a year for the surrounding area to turn to sandy land, and the place would be nothing but a desert. Besides, how and where is each family supposed to choose a place to settle down?"

The old man nodded. "It's crazy to promote settlements on the grassland. People from farming areas know nothing about it. They like to settle down, and that's fine. Why force others to do the same? Everyone knows that life would be easier if we didn't keep moving. But we've been doing that for generations. It's what Tengger wants us to do.

"Take the pastureland, for example. Every seasonal pasture has its separate function. The spring birthing pasture has good grass, but it's short. The livestock would die if a winter snowstorm covered the grass. We can't settle there. There's tall grass on the winter pastureland, but it wouldn't last long if the livestock grazed there through the first three seasons. The summer pasture has to be close to water, or the animals would die of thirst. But those are all in the mountains and the animals would freeze to death in the winter. We move to an autumn pasture for the grass seeds, but would there still be seeds left if the livestock stayed to graze in the spring and summer? Every pasture has many downsides and one advantage. The whole point of nomadic herding is to avoid the downsides and make good use of the advantage. If we settle in one spot, we'll face all the downsides, with no more advantage. Then how do we keep herding?"

The three Chinese students nodded in agreement. Chen, of course, could find one advantage in settling down—it would make raising his cub easier—but he kept silent.

The old man drank a lot and ate four big cakes stuffed with green onions and mutton, but his mood seemed to worsen.

Chen exchanged shifts with Yang Ke the following morning so that he could go hunting with Bilgee. A gunnysack with dozens of traps was tied behind the old man's saddle. Marmot traps are very simple: a two-foot wooden pole and a steel noose made of eight thin wires twisted together. A hunter sets the trap by planting the wooden pole near a marmot's den and places the noose about two inches above the ground at the entrance. When a marmot leaves the den, it is caught by the neck or hind leg.

"The last time I used your traps," Chen said, "I didn't catch any big ones. Why's that?"

Bilgee chuckled. "I didn't teach you the secret of trapping marmots, that's why. Olonbulag hunters never reveal their secrets to outsiders, afraid they'll kill off all the animals. But I'm getting old, so I'll teach you my secret. The outsiders use fixed traps, but the marmots are smart—they scrunch up their bodies to slip out of the noose. My traps are flexible and will tighten at the slightest touch. Once a marmot is caught, by either the neck or the hind leg, it'll never get away. So before you set a trap, you need to make the noose smaller, then enlarge it. When you let go, watch the noose spring back."

"How do you make it stay open?"

"You have to make a tiny hook with the wire, then loop the opening of the noose through the hook and bend the hook gently, but not too gently. If the hook isn't bent enough, the wind will blow the noose close. But if the hook is bent too much, the noose won't close by itself and you won't catch a marmot. It has to be just right, and flexible. When a marmot goes through the trap, it touches the wire at some point and the noose snaps shut. Do it that way, and you'll get seven big marmots with ten traps."

Chen slapped his forehead. "Ingenious!" he said. "No wonder my traps never worked. The marmots could come and go as they wished."

"I'll show you later. It isn't easy, because you also have to take into consideration the size of the den and the animal's tracks. There's one additional trick. You can watch me; then you'll know how to do it. But don't reveal this to anyone else."

"I won't," Chen promised.

"One more thing. You hunt only males, or females with no young. If you catch a mother and her babies, you have to let them go. No grassland Mongol would break the rules of our ancestors, which is why, after hunting marmots for hundreds of years, we still have marmot meat to eat, marmot skin to sell, and marmot oil to use. The marmots damage the grassland, but they benefit us. In the past, poor herdsmen survived the cruel winters by hunting marmots. You Chinese will never know how many poor Mongols the marmots have saved."

The horses sped through the dense autumn grass, their hooves kicking up moths in various colors: pinks, oranges, whites, blues. There were also green, yellow, and multicolored grasshoppers and other autumn insects. A few purple swallows circled overhead, singing in their shrill voices; sometimes they darted right past the horses, and sometimes they shot up into the sky, enjoying the insect feast provided by the horses and humans. When they'd gorged themselves, a new batch appeared to eat its fill. The old man pointed at the hills ahead with his club and said, "That's the Olonbulag marmot mountain. The animals there are fat and furry; to us it's a treasure mountain. You'll also find plenty of them on a small marmot hill on the south and another to the north. In a few days, the herdsmen's families will come, since marmots will be easy to catch this year."

"Why is that?"

The old man's eyes darkened as he heaved a long sigh. "With fewer wolves, the marmots are easily trapped. The wolves fatten themselves up with marmots in the fall; without the fat, they wouldn't survive the winter. They only kill the big ones, so they'll have marmots to eat every year. Out here, only the herdsmen and the wolves understand the rules set by Tengger."

* * *

As they neared the marmot mountain, they spotted some tents in one of the gulleys. Cooking smoke was rising by the tents, where a large cart and a water wagon gave the impression of a temporary work site.

"Oh, no! They're one step ahead of us again." The old man's face darkened as he rushed toward the tents, his eyes burning bright with anger.

They could detect the aroma of marmot meat and marmot oil even before they reached the tents. They quickly dismounted to see a giant pot on the stove. It was half filled with boiling marmot oil in which the carcasses of large marmots were stewing after having been fried and their fat removed. The meat was golden brown and crispy. After scooping out a fried marmot, a young worker was adding another skinned and gutted animal to the pot. Old Wang and another worker were sitting on a rickety wooden box, beside which lay a bowl of yellow sauce, a dish of salt and pepper, and a plate of green onions. They were happily drinking from a bottle and chewing on meat.

A large wash basin nearby was filled with skinned marmots, mostly young foot-long animals. Set up on the grass were several door planks and a dozen willow baskets. Marmot skins of various sizes, as many as two hundred of them, had been laid out to dry. Chen walked into one of the tents with the old man and saw more than a hundred dried skins piled waist-high. In the middle of the tent was a three-foot gas can half filled with marmot oil; there were also a couple of smaller cans.

The old man ran out of the tent and walked up to the basin, where he brushed aside the smaller marmots on top with his club. Below them were a few thin female marmots with little fat, the sight of which so angered the old man that he banged on the basin with his club and shouted at Old Wang, "Who said you could kill the females and their babies? This is brigade property; these marmots have survived thanks to the efforts of generations of herdsmen. How dare you! Look how many you've killed without permission!"

Old Wang, who was half drunk, continued eating. "I wouldn't dare kill marmots on *your* territory," he said casually. "But this is not your territory anymore, is it? Your brigade is now part of the corps, right? We were sent here by Chief of Staff Sun, who said that marmots not only destroy the grassland but also serve as the main source of food for the wolves before winter sets in. If we kill all the marmots, the wolves won't survive the winter. So marmots are included in our wolf-extermination campaign. The doctors at the division hospital also say that marmots carry the plague. With so many people coming here, will you take the responsibility if someone dies from one's bite?"

Bilgee was quiet for a while, but soon he was no longer able to contain his anger. "That should not be done, even if the order came from the corps!" he shouted. "What will the herdsmen use to make leather goods if you kill all the marmots? Who will be responsible if someone's reins break, startling the horse and injuring the rider? You are sabotaging production."

Old Wang belched. "We have orders from our superiors, so naturally someone will take the responsibility. Go talk to them if you want. Why yell at those of us who do the hard work?" He glanced at the gunnysack on the old man's saddle. "You came to hunt marmots, didn't you? So you can, but we can't, is that it? You don't raise these animals, so whoever kills them gets to keep them."

His beard quivering in anger, the old man said, "Just you wait. I'll go get the horse herders. These pelts and this oil have to be delivered to the brigade."

"The corps mess hall asked for the meat and oil, so that's who's getting it. You can have people come and take them by force if you want, but someone will take care of you afterward. As for the pelts, well, the officials want them and Director Bao is going to deliver them himself."

With his hands hanging limply at his sides, the old man choked on his anger and was speechless.

Chen Zhen said coldly, "You're really proud of yourself, aren't you? All those dead marmots, big and small. What will you kill next year?"

"Didn't you people call us migrants? Migrants, migrants, mindless immigrants. What do we care about next year? We go where there's food and never worry about the year after that. You have plenty of concern for marmots, but who cares about us migrants?"

Chen knew it was pointless to reason with these ruffians. Now he just wanted to know how they'd managed to kill so many—had they learned to set traps?—so he changed his tone. "How did you catch so many?" he asked.

"So you want to learn from us," Wang said smugly. "Well, you're too late. There aren't many dens left. We sent back a cartload of meat and oil two days ago. But, if you really want to know, then go up that hill and take a look. Hurry or you'll miss everything."

Chen helped the old man back onto his horse, and then they rode up to the hilltop. Down on the northeastern slope four or five men were bent over, busy at work. Chen and Bilgee galloped toward them. "Stop!" the old man shouted. "Stop!" The workers stood up and looked around.

Chen was shaking at the sight. There were six marmot dens on the hillside, which, Chen knew, were connected. Four holes were blocked with rocks.

What terrified Chen most was that the leading worker was holding a young two-foot-long marmot in his hand. A string of firecrackers was tied to the struggling marmot's tail, which was attached to a rope that was in turn wrapped around a piece of old felt the size of a fist. Red specks of chili peppers were sprinkled all over the felt, which reeked of diesel fuel. Beside that worker, another worker held a box of matches. If Chen and the old man had come a moment later, the workers would have already put the young marmot down the hole and lit the firecrackers to smoke out the den.

The old man ran up and stuck his foot in the hole. Then he sat down and screamed at the two workers, telling them to put down what they had in their hands. Since they had been under Bilgee's supervision over the summer, they didn't dare argue.

Never before had Chen witnessed such a greedy, malicious extermination scheme. Young marmots carrying into the dens lit firecrackers, along with chili peppers and diesel fuel, would wipe them out.

Marmots boasted the deepest, steepest animal dens on the grassland, with a highly intricate internal structure, including built-in smoke prevention mechanisms. If men tried to smoke them out, they'd quickly block off the narrow passage in the main hole. But they were caught off guard by the ruthless method adopted by these worker-hunters from the semiherding areas. The frightened young marmot would run straight to the animals at the bottom of the cave, and before they had a chance to block off the passage, the firecrackers would go off and the pungent smoke would force an entire den of marmots to flee. With only one opening left, they would be met with clubs and gunnysacks. Simple but unimaginably cruel; all the workers needed was a young marmot for bait. Within a few days, the men had virtually wiped out a marmot mountain that had been in existence for thousands of years; the marmots were now near extinction.

Bilgee banged his club on the ground, sending broken shards of rock flying all over. His eyes nearly popping out of his head, he shouted, "Cut off those firecrackers! Cut the rope, and put the young marmot back into the den!"

The workers took their time untying the rope and refused to let go of the marmot. Old Wang rode over on a light wagon. He no longer appeared drunk. With a broad grin, he gave the old man a cigarette and then turned to scold the workers. He walked up to the man holding the marmot, snatched the animal away, and cut off the rope. Then he went back to the old man and said, "Don't worry; I'll let this one go."

Bilgee got slowly to his feet and brushed the dirt off. "Let it go this minute. And don't interfere with our work ever again."

Old Wang smiled ingratiatingly. "I wouldn't dare," he said. "I'm just following orders. We won't stop the wolves if we don't kill off the marmots, so this is considered eliminating a scourge for the people. But you're right, of course. Without the marmot oil, the reins won't be durable, and accidents could happen. We need to leave some marmots for the herdsmen."

He put the marmot down on the flat surface outside

the hole, where the animal swiftly disappeared from sight.

Old Wang sighed. "In all fairness, it's hard getting a whole den of these things. We went to a lot of trouble to catch that young marmot today. Since we've been using firecrackers, they've been too scared to come out."

Not giving an inch, the old man said, "We're not done yet. You send the stuff to the brigade office immediately. If Lamjav and the other horse herders got wind of this, they'd come and knock over your tent and your carts."

"We'll get our stuff together and be on our way. I'll report to Director Bao myself."

The old man looked at his watch. Clearly worried about the marmot mountain to the north, he said, "I'm going to see someone. I'll be right back." Then he and Chen mounted up and rode toward the border highway.

Firecrackers went off behind them after they had crossed a pair of hills, and then everything turned quiet. The old man said, "We've been tricked." They turned back and rode up to the top of the hill, where they saw Old Wang, a damp cloth covering his mouth and nose, directing the workers to catch and kill the marmots. Dead animals were already strewn on the ground outside the marmots' den, while thick, acrid smoke continued to pour from it. The last few marmots were clubbed to death the moment they came out. The old man was coughing violently, so Chen helped him over to a place upwind as he thumped him on the back.

With damp cloths over their faces, the workers looked like bandits; they quickly dumped the marmots into a gunnysack, which they then tossed onto the cart before riding down the mountain.

"How could they trap another baby marmot so quickly?" Chen asked Bilgee.

"They'd probably trapped two, and had one in the hemp sack that we couldn't see. Or they might have tied firecrackers to a long pole. They're nothing less than bandits, worse than horse thieves in the old days!"

Bilgee stood up with the aid of his club and surveyed the marmot dens, now completely emptied. He was shaking; tears streaked his face. "What cruelty! I know these dens," he said. "I set traps here with my father when I was a boy. Generations of my family caught marmots here, and now there are no more. Year after year, they'd be chirping happily. It was a fertile den for well over a hundred years, and those bandits wiped it out in the time it takes to smoke a couple of pipes of tobacco."

Chen was as upset as Bilgee, but he tried to console the old man. "Don't be angry anymore, Papa. Let's go see if there's anything we can do."

As they traveled along, their horses slowed down to graze from time to time. Chen saw that the grass was much greener there than back at the pastureland. It had thicker stalks and was bursting with seeds. He spotted little piles on the ground, each the size of a magpie nest, and knew that field mice had been gathering grass and leaving it outside their dens to dry before they carried it in.

The old man reined in his horse where the grass was densest. "Let's stop and rest a bit," he said. "The horses can get some of the good grass from the mice. See how they thrive, now that the wolves are gone? These piles are several times thicker this year than last."

They dismounted and removed the horses' bits so they could graze. They happily nosed away the dry yellow surface grass to get at the fresh green grass underneath. With green juice streaming from their mouths, they snorted as they ate, one pile after another, permeating the air with a grassy fragrance. The old man kicked a pile away to reveal a hole the size of a teacup; a large mouse stuck its head out to check around. When it saw someone touching its winter stockpile, it ran out, bit the old man's boot, and scurried noisily back into the hole. A moment later, they heard the sound of a bridle shaking. They turned around in time to see a foot-long field mouse biting one of their horses on the nose, which was already bleeding. Loud squeaks erupted all around them.

"What has the world come to," the angry old man shouted, "when a mouse is bold enough to bite a horse? If they keep killing wolves, the mice will start eating people." Chen ran over, grabbed the reins, and tied them to the horse's front leg so that the horse would be sure to cover the opening with its hoof before starting to eat.

The old man kicked at some more piles. "See how close they are to each other? They've picked out the best grass; not even Xinjiang mating sheep get grass this good. The mice, which pick only the good stuff, are worse than grass cutters, which cut down the bad along with the good. If they store up enough this winter, not many of them will die of hunger or cold, which means the females will have plenty of milk in the spring and give birth to even more mice. They'll steal our grass and make more holes. Next year they'll overrun the place. See, when there are fewer wolves on the grassland, the mice turn from thieves to bandits, no longer having to sneak around."

As he looked down at the piles of grass, Chen's sadness was mixed with fear. A battle between humans and mice was waged on the grassland every autumn. The mice were a sneaky enemy, but they had a weakness. By digging holes deep enough to store food for the winter, they needed to pile the grass to dry, or it would rot inside their dens. That made them an obvious target, providing the opportunity for people to initiate their mouse extermination campaigns.

When a herdsman spotted a pile of grass on a pastureland, he sounded an alarm for the production teams to bring back the sheep, cows, even the horses to forage the piles of grass. The pastureland grass would be turning yellow, while the piles made by the mice would still be green and fragrant, with oily seeds. The livestock would fight over the grass, and it would take them only a few days to finish it off before it dried. It was a natural form of mouse population control.

But humans and their livestock needed the cooperation of wolves when they launched their autumn battles. This was when the mice were at their fattest, perfect for the wolves to feast on. Mice that were cutting and moving grass were easy to catch, and the piles showed the wolves where to find the biggest rodents. But most important, the wolves made the mice wary during their critical grass-collecting season, which indirectly led to starvation in the winter. Humans had their livestock finish off the grass while the wolves were a deterrent to the mice from cutting down grass at will.

For thousands of years, wolves and humans, along with their livestock, worked together to effectively control the population of mice. The grass they gathered delayed the process of yellowing, which in turn supplied the livestock with green grass for about ten days, extra time to store up fat. And so, the battle waged jointly by men and wolves achieved many purposes. Meanwhile, on the distant winter pastureland, beyond the reach of man and their livestock, wolves disrupted grass-collecting activities by the mice, which they then ate. How could farmers understand the strategies of grassland combat, which in the end preserved them all?

The horses' bellies bulged as they gorged themselves for nearly half an hour. The brigade's livestock would be outmatched by the vast supply of grass piles. In the face of an unprecedented battle scene, the old man was lost in thought. "Can we bring the horses here? No, that won't work. This pasture belongs to the sheep and the cows. Bringing the horses would disrupt the established order. But there are so many piles that even baling machines would be unable to complete the job. This is a disaster in the making."

"A man-made disaster," Chen said angrily.

They remounted and continued on, heading north, utterly dispirited. Along the way, they saw more piles of grass, some denser than others, all the way to the border.

As they neared the small northern marmot mountain, they heard some loud cracks that sounded like neither gunfire nor firecrackers. Then it was quiet again. Bilgee sighed. "The corps leaders sure found the right person to be their extermination adviser," he said, despair in his voice. "Wherever you find wolves, you'll find Dorji, even at the wolves' last outpost."

They spurred their horses on, only to encounter an army vehicle coming out of the valley. They reined in their horses as the vehicle came to a halt. In it were the two sharpshooters and Dorji. Staff Officer Xu was driving, and Dorji was in the backseat, with a bloody gunnysack by his feet. The trunk was filled. The old man's gaze was drawn to the long-barreled rife in Staff Officer

Batel's hand. Chen could see that it was a small-caliber hunting rifle, something the old man had never seen before; he couldn't take his eyes off it.

"Out hunting marmots?" Batel asked. "No need, I'll give you two of ours."

"Any reason we shouldn't go up there?" Bilgee asked, glaring at the man.

"We killed all the ones outside their dens, and those inside don't dare come out."

"What's that in your hand?" Bilgee asked. "Why does it have such a long barrel?"

"It's used for duck hunting," Batel said. "Small-caliber ammunition is perfect for killing marmots. They keep the fur virtually undamaged. Here, take a look."

The old man took the rifle and examined it and the bullets very carefully.

Wanting to show the old man the advantage of his rifle, Batel got out of the vehicle and took it from Bilgee. He spotted a squeaking mouse on the grass pile outside its cave about twenty yards away. He took aim and fired, blowing the mouse's head off. The old man shook all over.

Staff Officer Xu laughed. "The wolves all left for Outer Mongolia," he said. "Dorji took us everywhere, but we didn't see a single one. Luckily I brought the rifle with me for killing marmots. They're so stupid they didn't even run back to their dens when we got closer, as if they were waiting for our bullets to hit them."

"These two can hit a marmot's head from fifty yards," Dorji gloated. "We killed every one we spotted along the way. It was a lot faster than setting traps."

"Why don't you turn back and go home?" Batel said. "I'll drop two large marmots off at your yurt on my way back."

The vehicle took off before the old man had regained his composure from the shock of witnessing the power of this new weapon. As the smoke and dust from the army vehicle cleared, Bilgee turned his horse around and draped the reins over its neck to let it find its way home. Everyone talks about how China's Last Emperor suffered, Chen was thinking as he rode beside the old man. But the last nomadic herdsman is suffering a great deal more. How much more difficult it must be to accept the destruction of a ten-thousand-year-old grassland than the overthrow of a thousand-year-old dynasty. The once energetic old man was deflated, his body suddenly shrunk to half of its original size. Tears coursed through the wrinkles on his face, spilling onto patches of wild blue-white daisies.

Not knowing how to lessen the old man's sorrow, Chen held his tongue, before finally stammering, "Papa, the autumn grass is really good this year... The Olonbulag is truly beautiful... Maybe next year..."

"Next year?" the old man replied woodenly. "Who knows what bizarre things will happen next year? In the past, even a blind old man could see the grassland's beauty. It's no longer beautiful. I wish I were blind so that I wouldn't have to see how it's being destroyed."

He swayed in the saddle as his horse plodded ahead. He closed his eyes. Old, guttural sounds emerged from his throat, infused with the aroma of green grass and fading daisies. To Chen, the lyrics sounded like simple nursery rhymes:

Larks are singing, spring is here;
marmots are chirping, orchids bloom;
Gray cranes are calling, the rain is here;
wolf cubs are baying, the moon is rising.

He sang the same thing over and over, as the melody turned ever lower and the lyrics became indistinguishable, like a stream flowing from some faraway place, crisscrossing the vast grassland before disappearing in the undulating grass. Chen Zhen wondered if the nursery rhyme had been sung by the children of the Quanrong, the Huns, the Tungus, the Turks, and the Khitans, as well as the offspring of Genghis Khan. Would the future children of the grassland be singing the song or even understand it? Or would they be full of questions: What are larks? What's a marmot? Gray cranes? Wolves? Wild geese? What are orchids? What's a daisy?

A few larks rose up above the vast, yellowing grassland; they flapped their wings and hovered in midair, singing clear and happy songs.

35

The first winter snow melted, moistening the air, while chilling and freshening the fields. The dense winter grass on the wild field was yellow and sere, so bleak it resembled a desert plateau where no grass would grow.

Only the sky was the same blue as in late autumn. The sky was high and clouds were sparse, like a clear lake. The vultures flying high in the sky were smaller than rust spots on a mirror. Unable to catch marmots and mice, which were hibernating inside their dens, the vultures had to fly high into the clouds to broaden their search for rabbits, but the wild Mongolian rabbits, which could camouflage themselves by changing color, hid in the tall grass, hard for even foxes to find. Bilgee had once said that many vultures starved to death each winter.

When the snow covered the bottom half of the grass, the livestock had much less grass for winter grazing, which was why the herders had to move once a month. Once the pastureland turned white from all that grazing, they'd herd the cows and sheep to another yellowish snow field, leaving the remaining grass beneath the snow to the horses, who could dig up the grass with their hooves.

None of the moves took them very far, just far

enough to be away from where the livestock had been grazing. It usually took half a day, too little time for the cub to bite through the cage no matter how hard he tried. Chen breathed a sigh of relief, having finally, after two weeks of racking his brain, found a solution to the problem of the cub's survival during their constant moves.

Chen and Yang had also figured out how to make the cub enter the cage: they would trap him under a covered basket on the ground, then lift the shaft of the oxcart and slide the cart under it with the cub inside. All they had to do after that was lower the cart and secure the basket, and the cub would be safely on the cart. They reversed the procedure when they reached a new site. They were hoping to move the cub the same way each time until they settled in one place, where they would build a stone pen; that would be the end of their troubles and enable them to live side by side with the cub. They'd raised him with puppies, and since they had basically grown up together, they'd surely produce results—a few litters of wolfhounds, true descendents of the grassland wolves.

Chen and Yang spent a great deal of time sitting with the cub, rubbing his head as they chatted. At moments like this, he would rest his head on one of their legs, prick up his ears, and listen curiously to their conversation. When he was tired, he'd shake his head and rub his neck against their legs or raise his head for them to scratch his ears or cheeks. The scene would draw the two men deeper into their fantasy about their lives with the cub.

Holding the cub to brush his coat, Yang said, "Our little wolf wouldn't try to run away if he had his own litter. Wolves care about their families, and male wolves are model mates. So long as no wild wolf came along, we wouldn't have to chain him; he could play on the grassland and return to the pen on his own."

Chen shook his head. "He wouldn't be a wolf if he did that. I don't plan to keep him here. My initial dream was to have a real wolf friend. If I rode into the hills by the border and yelled out, 'Little Wolf, Little Wolf, time to eat,' he'd bring his whole family, a group of true grassland wolves, and run happily toward me. There'd be no chains around their necks, their teeth would be sharp, and they'd be strong. They'd roll in the grass with me, lick my chin, and bite my arms, but not hard. But now that the cub's sharp teeth are gone, my dream has become just that, a dream."

Chen sighed softly. "But I don't want to give up. I have a new fantasy now: I've become a dentist and have given the cub four sharp steel teeth. Next spring, when he's fully grown, I'll secretly take him to the border and free him in the mountains of Outer Mongolia, where there are still wolf packs. Maybe his father, the White Wolf King, has fought his way to freedom and opened a base for them. This cub is smart enough to find his father, and when they're together, the White Wolf King will sniff out the bloodline in the cub and welcome him back. Armed with his sharp steel teeth, the cub will be invincible and may even take over as king in a few years.

"Little Wolf clearly has the best genes of all the Olonbulag wolves. He's stubborn and extremely smart; by rights, he should have been the next king of the wolves. But only if he could return to the real Mongolia, where few people inhabit a vast territory. There are only twenty million people in the real Mongolia, which is a spiritual paradise that venerates the wolf totem; it is free of a farming population that hates wolves and wants only to kill them. The vast, lush grassland is where our little wolf ought to display his prowess. I committed a crime when I destroyed the future of such an outstanding little wolf cub."

Yang fixed his gaze on the distant mountains, the light darkening in his eyes. He sighed and said, "If you'd come here ten years earlier, maybe your dream could have come true, but your latest fantasy is a pipe dream. Where are you going to find a set of dental tools? Not even the banner hospital has those. The old herdsmen have to travel eight hundred *li* to the league hospital to have their teeth fixed. What are the chances of taking a wolf there? Stop dreaming. We need to face reality."

That reality was the cub's injuries. His paws had healed, but the blackened tooth was getting looser by the day and the gums were swelling up. He no longer tore at his meat, and sometimes, when his hunger made him forget about the bad tooth, he took a big bite, but the pain caused him to drop it and open his mouth wide to suck in cold air. He licked the bad tooth until the pain was gone before he started eating again, this time chewing on one side, and very slowly.

What worried Chen most was the injury to the cub's throat, which had yet to heal. He continued to smear medicated powder on the food, but the cub still had trouble swallowing, even though the bleeding had stopped. He coughed constantly. Since he didn't have the nerve to ask for help from the vet, all Chen could do was borrow books to study on his own.

The cows and sheep that would feed the people through the winter had been slaughtered and frozen. The four people in Chen's yurt were allocated six sheep each for the winter, twenty-four in all. They also were given one cow. Their grain allotment remained the same, thirty *jin* each a month, while the herdsmen, though given the same amount of meat, received only nineteen *jin* of grain. As a result, the meat in Chen's yurt was enough for all: people, dogs, and the cub. In addition, there were sheep that had died from the cold or illness, and since the herdsmen didn't eat them, they could be fed to the dogs and the cub. Chen no longer had to worry about finding enough meat for the cub.

Chen and Gao Jianzhong took most of the frozen meat to their section's storage shed, three rammed-earth rooms on the spring pasture. They kept only a basket of meat in the yurt and went to the shed to restock their supply.

Winter days are short on the grassland, with only six or seven hours for the sheep to graze, barely more than half of the summer grazing time. But, except for the white-hair blizzards, winter is a time of rest for the herders. Chen planned to spend more time with the cub and do some reading and take notes. He was waiting to see what sort of show the cub would put on for him during snowy days. Grassland dramas centered on the wolves' wild nature, wisdom, and mysteriousness, and Chen was confident the cub wouldn't disappoint his biggest fan.

During the long, severe winter, wolves that had fled across the border faced conditions ten times harsher than on this side of the border, while his cub would be living in a herders' camp, where there was an abundant supply of meat. His fur was now fully grown, and he looked bigger, every bit like a mature wolf. When Chen buried his fingers in the thick coat, he could feel the cub's body warmth, like a burning brazier, better than gloves. The cub still would not respond to his new name, Big Wolf. He feigned deafness if they called him that, but would run over happily to jump onto their legs and knees if they called him Little Wolf. His puppy companion often went into the pen to play with the cub, who no longer bit down hard. Sometimes he'd even mount the puppy, as if mating. Watching the intimate yet violent behavior, Yang Ke would smile and say, "Looks like we can expect something next year..."

There were things about the cub's wolf nature that never changed: one, no one could be near him when he ate, not even Chen or Yang; two, he would not let anyone pull him along when out walking, and anyone who tried would be in for the fight of his life. Chen always tried his best to honor his rules. The cub's craving for and enjoyment of food was much stronger during the freezing winter months than in the other seasons. Each time Chen fed him, he would snarl and bare his fangs until Chen was nearly out of the pen before he felt safe enough to return to eat. Even then he'd growl menacingly at Chen. Though still not completely recovered from his injuries, he was gaining strength and seemed to be making up for the lost blood with his voracious appetite.

Nonetheless, the bad tooth and the injury in his throat affected his wolf nature; it now took him seven or eight bites to swallow a meal that he'd once been able to gobble down in two or three mouthfuls. Chen wondered if he would ever completely recover.

A leaden bleakness heavier than in the depths of autumn permeated the winter pastureland at the border region rarely visited by humans. The quiet, dreary, monotonous grassland looked even more lifeless than ever. A sense of unending, boundless sorrow rose up repeatedly in Chen Zhen; he thought he'd lose his mind or go numb from the boredom if not for the cub and the books he'd brought from Beijing. Yang Ke once told him that when his father was a student in England he learned that the suicide rate was much higher among Europeans who lived close to the North Pole. The Slavic Depression that had been common for centuries on the Russian grassland and Siberian wasteland was closely tied to the long, dark winters on vast snowy fields. But how did the Mongols manage to spend several thousand years in a similar environment with healthy bodies and high spirits? They must have developed those as a result of their tense, violent, and cruel battles with the wolves, Chen concluded.

Physically, the grassland wolves were half of the grassland residents' enemies, but they were the inhabitants' spiritual masters. Once the wolves were exterminated, the bright red sun would no longer light up the grassland, and the stagnant stability would bring dejection, a withering decadence and boredom, and other more terrifying foes of the spirit, obliterating the masculine passion that had characterized them for thousands of years.

After the disappearance of the wolves, the sale of liquor on the Olonbulag nearly doubled.

Wolf totem, the soul of the grassland, the symbol of the grassland people's free and indomitable spirit.

The young wolf grew bigger; the chain grew shorter. The sensitive cub, never an animal to be cheated, protested like an abused prisoner when he realized that the length of the chain was disproportionate to his size. He pulled at it with all his might, tugging and ramming the wooden post as a way to get Chen to lengthen the chain; he wouldn't stop until he was satisfied, even if that meant being strangled to death.

Chen added a few inches to the chain, as the wound on the cub's throat had yet to heal. But even he had to admit that it was still too short for the grown-up cub. The only reason he didn't lengthen it more was that extending the cub's running distance would give him more power when he tugged at the chain. Chen was worried that one day he'd wear the chain out, or break it.

The cub, seemingly engaged in a prison battle, cherished every inch added to the chain. As soon as it was lengthened, he'd run madly in circles, rejoicing over the new inches of freedom he'd gained. The desolation vanished from Chen's heart each time he sat down by the cub, as if he'd received a transfusion of roiling wolf blood.

As he watched him, he realized that the cub wasn't only celebrating the added length of his chain, for after the excitement abated, he kept running, and Chen felt that his instincts were telling him to train for speed, for the skill to escape. He struggled against his chain with more power than during the summer and fall. As he grew stronger and more mature by the day, he stared out at the grassland with a longing in his eyes; he could almost reach out and touch the freedom, and that made him hate the chain even more. Chen realized how cruel his imprisonment was yet felt the cub would surely die if he ran away to roam the snowy land in the depths of winter, when even adult wolves are barely able to survive.

The cub continued to fight the chain, which delayed the healing of his throat. Chen felt his own throat tighten whenever he looked at the cub. All he could do was check the chain, the collar, and the post more often to prevent the cub from running away into the land of freedom and death before his own eyes.

Pangs of guilt struck Chen's heart. In this barren, uninhabited land, he enjoyed the company of a young wolf whose life generator created the power to help him through the seemingly endless winter. He'd learned so much from the clash in nature and destiny of two species on a fertile yet bramble-covered wasteland. He worshipped and admired the wolves. Had it really been necessary to imprison the cub and deprive him of his freedom and happiness so he could overcome Han ignorance and prejudice and succeed in his study of the wolves?

Chen sank deep into doubts and worry regarding the series of actions he'd taken.

It was time to do some reading, but he couldn't seem to lift his feet. He felt he'd developed a spiritual and emotional dependence on the cub. He finally dragged himself away, though not without constantly looking back and wondering what else he could do for the imprisoned animal.

The cub's temperament eventually sealed his fate.

Chen Zhen always felt that losing the cub in the harsh winter climate was an inevitable plan by Tengger, who also launched a lifelong assault on Chen's conscience, so that he'd never be forgiven.

The cub's injury took a turn for the worse on a windless, moonless dark night when the dogs did not bark and the stars did not shine. The ancient Olonbulag was quiet and lifeless, like vegetation trapped in a fossil rock.

In the second half of the night, Chen was awakened by a violent shaking of the chain. A heightened sense of fright made his head unusually clear and his hearing uncharacteristically keen. He detected, amid the sounds of the chain, indistinct wolf howls from the mountains across the border. The intermittent howls sounded old and sad, anxious and angry. Defeated wolf packs that had been driven out of their homeland may have been under attack by stronger wolves from the other side of the border; maybe only the White Wolf King and a few wounded and lone wolves were left, and they had run south to the no-man's-land between the border marker and the highway. They could not return to the old blood-soaked place. The White Wolf King's anxious howl seemed to be an urgent search to gather together the defeated and dispersed wolves for one final battle.

It had been over a month since Chen had last heard the howls of free Olonbulag wolves, and the tremulous, feeble, anxious howls transmitted a message that had been worrying him. He wondered if Bilgee was crying at that moment, for hearing the howls of desperation was worse than hearing nothing at all. Most of the strongest, most ferocious, and smartest males had already been eliminated by the hunters. After snow blanketed the grassland, the army vehicles were of no use, so the hunters exchanged them for fast horses and continued to hunt wolves, who seemed to have lost the power to find their way out and create a new territory for themselves.

This was Chen's greatest fear. The return of the long-absent wolf howls rekindled hope, longing, resistance, and a fighting spirit in the cub. Like an imprisoned grassland prince, he heard his aging father's call, a call for help, and he grew anxious, agitated, and violent, so much so that he wanted to respond with a howl as loud as a cannon shot.

But his injured throat would not allow him to answer his father and his own kind. Crazed by anxiety, he grew reckless, jumping and running, jerking the chain and the wooden post, oblivious to the possibility of mortal injury. Chen felt the frozen ground move; given the clanging and clamoring from the pen, he could imagine the wolf cub running, crashing, coughing up blood.

Frightened, he jerked away his felt blanket and quickly put on his fur-lined pants and deel before running out of the yurt. Blood was visible in the beam of his flashlight. The cub was bleeding openly, but he kept running and crashing, his tongue lolling involuntarily from the pressure of the tightening collar. The chain was stretched taut, like a bow at the breaking point. Bloody icicles hung from his chest, while beads of blood splattered the ground.

Chen ran up, without regard for anything, in an attempt to hold the cub by his neck, but the cub took a large patch of sheepskin from Chen's sleeve the moment he reached out. Yang Ke ran over anxiously, but even with two of them they couldn't get close. The madness that had been building up inside the cub turned him into a demon with eyes reddened from killing, or a cruel, enraged, suicidal wolf. They hurriedly dragged over a large thick, filthy felt used to cover the cow dung, and lunged at the cub to press him to the ground.

Seemingly engaged in a bloody life-and-death struggle, the cub went completely wild; he gnawed at the ground, bit the felt and anything else he came into contact with, and continued shaking his head to free himself from the chain. Chen felt as if he himself were losing his mind, but he forced himself to calm down and call out in a tender voice, "Little Wolf, Little Wolf." Finally, the cub exhausted his energy and slowly gave in. Chen and Yang sat wearily on the ground, gasping for breath as if they'd been engaged in hand-to-hand combat with a wild wolf.

In the light of dawn, they pulled the felt away to see the consequence of the cub's crazed struggle for freedom and longing for his father's love: The infected tooth was now protruding from his mouth; the root had broken when he tore at the felt. He was bleeding, his wounds possibly made worse by the dirty felt. His throat was still bleeding as well, worse now than when they'd first moved here. The old wound had clearly been reopened.

His eyes bloodshot, the cub kept swallowing the blood, but it was everywhere: on their deels, on the felt, inside the pen, a worse sight than when a foal was killed. The blood quickly turned to ice. Chen's knees buckled from the fright and he stammered in a shaky voice, "It's all over. He'll die for sure."

"He's probably lost half his blood," Yang Ke said. "He'll bleed to death if we don't do something fast."

They didn't know how to stop the bleeding. Eventually, Chen got on his horse to go ask for Bilgee's help.

The old man, shocked by the sight of blood on Chen, went back with him. "Do you have anything to stem the bleeding?" the old man asked.

Chen brought out four bottles of Yunnan White Powder. Bilgee entered the yurt, where he found a cooked sheep lung, which he soaked and softened in warm water from a vacuum bottle. He cut off the hard windpipes and separated the two halves before smearing powder on the surface of the softened lungs. He took it out to the pen for Chen to feed the cub, who caught and swallowed one of the halves as soon as Chen pushed the food basin in. He nearly choked, for the lung had swelled up after soaking up the blood in his esophagus. The soft organ remained in the throat for a while, like blood-stemming cotton, before slowly going down. The expanded lung put pressure on the blood vessels while helping to medicate the esophagus, slowly reducing the bleeding after the cub had swallowed both lung halves.

The old man shook his head and said, "It's useless. He's bled too much, and he's injured his throat, a mortal wound. Even if you could stop the bleeding this time, could you stop it the next time he heard wolf howls? This is terrible for the cub. I told you not to, but you insisted on raising him. Seeing him like this is worse than having a knife in my throat. It's no life for a wolf; not even dogs have it this bad. It's worse than the ancient Mongolian slaves. Mongolian wolves would rather die than live like this."

Chen pleaded with the old man. "Papa, I want to raise him to old age. Please, is there any way to save him? Please, teach me all your cures."

The old man glared at him. "You still want to raise him? You need to kill him now, while he still looks like a wolf and has a true wolf spirit. That way he'll die as if in battle, like a wild wolf. Don't let him die an ignoble death, like a sick dog! Let his soul complete its cycle."

Chen couldn't stop his hands from shaking. He never imagined that one day he would have to kill the cub with his own hands, a cub he'd raised in the face of incredible hardships. Holding back his tears, he made one last attempt to plead with the old man: "Papa, please. How could I bring myself to kill him? I have to save him, even if there's only a tiny shred of hope."

The old man's face darkened. He began to cough out of anger. He spat out a gob of phlegm and shouted, "You Chinese will never understand the Mongolian wolves."

Incensed, he climbed onto his horse and, with a vicious whip on the animal's flank, rode off in the direction of his yurt without looking back.

Chen's heart felt the blow of that whip.

The two friends, Chen and Yang, stood on the snowy ground like wooden posts, completely lost.

Yang looked down. "This is the first time Papa ever got that angry with us. The cub really isn't a cub anymore. He's a grown wolf, and he'd fight us for his freedom. They really are the 'freedom or death' species. Look at him; he's not going to live. I think we should follow Papa's advice and give the cub the dignity he deserves."

Tears had by then formed a string of icy beads on Chen's face. He sighed and said, "It's not that I don't understand what Papa said. But how can I bring myself to do it? If I have a son someday, I don't think I'll dote on him the way I did the cub. Just give me some time to think."

The cub, having lost most of his blood, got to his feet shakily and walked to the side of the pen, where he pawed at the snow piled on the edge. He opened his mouth and Chen quickly grabbed him. "He must be trying to numb the pain with the snow," he said to Yang. "Should I let him do it?"

"I think he's thirsty. How could he not be after losing so much blood? I say let him do whatever he wants; let him be the master of his own fate from now on."

Chen let go and the cub gulped down mouthfuls of snow. Weakened and assaulted by the cold and pain, he shook violently, like an ancient grassland slave stripped of his fur deel as punishment. Finally, no longer able to stand, he fell to the ground, where he struggled to curl up, covering his face with his tail.

The cub convulsed violently each time he sucked in a lungful of cold air, and the convulsions stopped only when he breathed out. That went on for a long time, sending tremors through Chen's heart. He had never seen the cub in such a frail, helpless state. He went and got a thick felt blanket, and when he placed it over the cub, he seemed to feel that the animal's soul was leaving his body little by little, as if he were no longer the cub he had raised.

At noon, Chen cooked a pot of porridge with diced sheep rump. After cooling it with some snow, he took it over to the cub. Although still displaying his usual ferocious appetite and greedy look, the cub could no longer eat like a real wolf. Instead, he took many breaks to cough and to bleed. Obviously, the wound in his throat still had not healed. A pot of meat porridge that the cub would normally finish in one meal lasted two days for three meals.

Over those two days, Chen and Yang took turns watching the cub, their hearts in their throats. But he was eating less and less, and could barely swallow anything except his own blood from the previous meal. Chen Zhen got on his horse with three bottles of grassland liquor to get help from the brigade's veterinarian. The vet took a look at the blood on the ground, and said, "Don't bother. Lucky it's a wolf; if it were a dog, it'd be long dead."

Not leaving a single pill, the vet leaped back onto his horse to visit another yurt.

On the third morning, Chen walked out of the yurt and saw that the cub had pushed the felt aside and lay on his back, stretching his neck to take in short, rapid breaths. He and Yang ran over to check on him and were thrown into a panic. His neck had swollen so much it was almost bursting through the collar, which was why he tilted his head back to breathe. Chen quickly loosened the collar by two holes; the cub kept gulping in air, while struggling to his feet. They forced open his mouth, only to see that the throat was swollen, as if from a tumor, and the skin had turned cankerous.

Chen fell to the ground, in total despair. The cub strained to push himself up and drag himself over to sit in front of Chen, his mouth hanging open, the tongue lolling to one side. Bloody saliva oozed from the corner of his mouth as he sat there looking at Chen, like watching an old wolf, as if he wanted to tell him something. He was breathing so hard he couldn't make a single noise. Tears rained down Chen's face; he held the cub by his neck and touched his head and nose against the cub's for one last time. The cub's strength vanished and his front legs began to tremble violently.

Chen jumped to his feet and ran to the side of the yurt, where he found a spade with a broken handle. He turned, holding the spade behind him, and ran toward the cub, who was still sitting there panting hard, but on the verge of toppling over again. Chen stepped behind him, raised the spade, and, with all the strength he possessed, brought it hard down on the cub's head. The cub didn't make a sound as he slumped to the ground, a true Mongolian grassland wolf till the very end.

At that instant, Chen felt that his own soul had been crushed out of him; he seemed to hear again the sound of his soul leaving through the top of his head, but this time it appeared to be for good. Like a ghostly white icicle, he stood frozen in the wolf pen.

Not knowing what had happened, all the dogs came over and sniffed at the dead wolf; they then ran off in fright, all but Erlang, who barked angrily at Chen Zhen and Yang Ke.

Yang said tearfully, "We have to follow Papa's example and take care of the rest. I'll remove the pelt. Why don't you go inside and rest."

"We raided the den and took the cub together," Chen said woodenly, "so we have to take the pelt together."

They struggled to control their shaky hands and carefully removed the pelt from the cub's body. The fur was still dense and shiny, but the cub's body had only a thin layer of fat left. Yang placed the pelt on top of the yurt while Chen found a clean gunnysack for the body and tied it behind his saddle. They rode up into the hills, where they found a rocky surface covered with hawk droppings. They brushed the snow away and gently laid the cub's body down.

On that cold, solemn sky-burial ground, the peltless cub no longer looked like his old self. To Chen, he was like any other adult wolf that had been skinned after dying in battle. Facing the ghastly white carcass of their precious cub, Chen Zhen and Yang Ke didn't shed a single tear.

On the Mongolian grassland, nearly every wolf arrived in a fuzzy coat and then left skinned, leaving their courage, strength, wisdom, and the pretty grassland behind for the humans. At this moment, the cub had been stripped of his battle garb and relieved of the chain; he could finally roam the vast grassland freely, just like members of the pack and all other grassland wolves that had died during the extermination. He would return to the pack and rejoin the ranks of grassland warriors, for Tengger would never reject his soul.

They looked up at the sky at the same time, where two hawks were already circling above their heads. They looked down and saw that the carcass was freezing, so they quickly got on their horses and rode down the hill. On flat ground, they looked back to see the hawks spiral near the rocky surface. The carcass hadn't completely frozen, so the cub would be given a quick sky burial and taken to lofty Tengger by the hawks.

By the time Chen and Yang returned to the yurt, Gao Jianzhong had already found a long birch pole and placed it by the door. He stuffed the pelt with dry yellow grass, while Chen Zhen threaded a thin leather rope through the cub's nostrils and tied one end to the tip of the pole. Together, the three of them raised the pole and planted it in the snowbank by their door.

A fierce northwestern wind sent the cub's pelt soaring, combing through his battle garb and making him appear to be dressed formally for a banquet in heaven. Pale smoke rising from the yurt's chimney wafted under the pelt, making it seem as if the cub were riding the clouds, roiling and dancing freely and happily in the misty smoke. At that moment, there was no chain around his neck and no narrow, confining prison under his feet.

Chen's vacant gaze followed the impish, lifelike figure of the cub's pelt as it danced in the wind; it was the undying outer shell the cub had left behind, but the beautiful and commanding figure seemed to still contain his free and unyielding spirit. Suddenly, the long, tubular body and bushy tail rolled a few times like a flying dragon, soaring in the swirling snow and drifting clouds. The wind howled and the white hair flew. The cub, like a golden flying dragon, rode the clouds and mist, traveling on snow and wind, soaring happily toward Tengger, to the star Sirius, to the free universe in space, to the place where all the souls of Mongolian wolves that had died in battles over the millennia congregated.

At that instant, Chen Zhen believed he saw his very own wolf totem.

Epilogue

Early in the second spring after the wolves disappeared from the Olonbulag, the Inner Mongolian Production and Construction Corps sent down an order to reduce the number of dogs so that they could save the precious sheep and cows to supply the agricultural units in need of meat. The first unfortunate victims were the puppies. Nearly all the newborn puppies were tossed and sent to Tengger, and sad wails from the bitches could be heard everywhere on the grassland. Sometimes the mother dogs were seen digging up puppies their owners had buried behind their backs; they would often run around in circles holding the puppies in their mouths. The women wailed; the men shed silent tears. The big dogs were getting thinner by the day.

About six months later, someone in a corps truck shot and killed Erlang after he'd left the yurt and was wrapped in his own thoughts out in the grass. The killer took his body. Outraged, Chen and the other three students ran to the corps headquarters, but no culprit was found. The newly arrived Chinese, united behind the issue of eating dogs, hid the killer as if shielding a hero who was being pursued by an alien race.

Four years later, one early morning during a white-hair blizzard, an old man and a middle-aged man rode alongside an oxcart heading to the border highway; on the cart lay Bilgee's body. Two of the three sky-burial grounds had already been abandoned, as some of the herdsmen had adopted the Han custom of underground burial. The old man insisted on being sent to a place where wolves might still roam, so two of his cousins took his body to the no-man's-land north of the border highway.

The younger cousin said, "The wolves up north howled all night, and didn't stop till daybreak."

Chen Zhen, Yang Ke, and Zhang Jiyuan believed that Bilgee had suffered more than most but that he was also the luckiest, the last Mongol to have a sky burial and return to Tengger.

Not long after that, Chen, Yang, and Gao were assigned to company headquarters, where Yang became a grammar school teacher, Gao was sent to drive tractors, and Chen worked as a storehouse guard. Zhang Jiyuan was the only one left, kept on as a horse herder.

They left Yir and her puppies with Batu, while the loyal Yellow followed Chen. But every time Gasmai came with her oxcart and dogs, Yellow had a great time with his family and followed the carts back to the herding team. No one could stop him, and he would return to Chen only after spending a few days back home. He'd return no matter how far the herding section moved, even from a hundred *li* away; but he always looked unhappy on his arrival. Chen was worried that something might happen to Yellow on the way, but his worries vanished when the dog showed up again. He wouldn't deprive Yellow of the pleasure and freedom of being with his grassland family. A year later, however, Yellow was "lost." The grassland people knew that their dogs would never get lost or be eaten by wolves, since there were no more wolves; even if there had been, a wolf pack would never kill a lone dog. Yellow could only have been killed by people, people who did not belong to the grassland.

Chen and Yang were back in a place inhabited mostly by Chinese, living a settled life. Most of the people around them were professional soldiers and their families from all parts of China, as well as soldiers from the Student Army Corps from Tianjing and Tangshan. But emotionally, they knew they could never live a purely Han-style life. After work and study sessions, they often climbed a small hill nearby, where they could gaze into the distance at Tengger in the northwest, searching for traces of the cub and Bilgee in the blindingly bright, towering clouds.

In 1975, the Inner Mongolian Production and Construction Corps was formally disbanded, but the Majuzi River area, with its lush grass and abundant water, had already been turned into a desert by farming. Most of the workers—along with their concepts and lifestyle, as well as their houses, machines, vehicles, and tractors—remained. The Olonbulag regressed by the year, and a sheep killed by a wolf would be a topic of discussion for days, whereas more and more horses were stepping in mouse holes, injuring themselves and their riders.

A few years later, before Chen Zhen returned to Beijing to take the graduate school entrance exam, he borrowed a horse to say good-bye to Batu and his family. Then he made a special trip to visit the ancient den where the cub had been born. The den was still dark, deep, and solid, but spiderwebs covered the entrance and a pair of slender green grasshoppers were struggling to free themselves. Chen pushed the grass aside to look in and detected an earthy smell, not the pungent, acrid odor of wolves. Tall grass grew on the land outside the cave where the seven cubs had played and sunned themselves. Chen sat by the cave for a long time, but there was no wolf cub, no hunting dogs, not even a puppy with him.

In the thirtieth summer after the Beijing students had been sent down to the Olonbulag, Chen Zhen and Yang Ke left the capital in a blue Jeep Cherokee on their way to the grassland.

Upon graduating from the Academy of Social Sciences, Chen had joined a national affairs institute at a university where he conducted research on system reform. After receiving a bachelor's degree in law, Yang went on to get a master's degree and was given a license to practice law. By this time he was the founder of a highly regarded Beijing law firm.

The two old friends, now in their fifties, had never stopped thinking about the grassland but had been afraid to return. At the thirty-year mark, an important anniversary in the life of a Chinese, they decided to go back to see their friends, to the Great Ujimchin Steppe they'd been afraid to visit, and the old wolf cave at the foot of Black Rock Mountain.

The sky was still a clear blue when the Jeep entered Inner Mongolia, but anyone who had spent a long time there knew that Tengger was not the same. The sky was dry and cloudless; the Tengger of the grassland was now the Tengger of the desert. Under the dry hot sky, no dense green grass was visible; large patches of hard sandy soil filled the spaces between sparse, dry yellow grassland, as if giant sheets of sandpaper had been spread out across the ground.

On a highway, half covered with dry sand, caravans

of trucks equipped with iron cages to transport sheep and cows rumbled toward them, trailing thick columns of yellow dust as they made their way to China proper. They hardly saw a yurt or a herd of horses or cows along the way; every once in a while they spotted a flock of sheep, but they were small and thin, with dirty, tangled black wool. Even the "processed" sheep looked better than those. The two friends nearly gave up on the trip, not wanting the moist, lush grassland in their hearts to be replaced by dry dust.

Yang pulled over and stopped, and, as he brushed the dust off of his body, said to Chen, "I've been so busy over the past decade I haven't had time to come back. Now that the people in my firm can work independently, I've finally found some time, but to be honest, I'm scared about seeing the grassland. Zhang Jiyuan came for a visit this past spring and told me about the desertification. So I've had plenty of time to prepare myself emotionally. But I'm afraid it will be worse than I imagined."

Chen patted the steering wheel. "Why don't I take over? It's barely been twenty years since Papa died, and we're already seeing the bad end he predicted. We really should pay our respects to him, and, besides, Little Wolf's cave will be filled up by sand if we wait a few more years. That cave is the only remaining relic left by wolves that dominated the grassland for thousands of years."

"I miss Uljii too," Chen added. "I'd really like to see him again so I could ask about the wolves and the grassland. But unfortunately he felt so bad about the grassland that he left after retirement and now lives in the city with his daughter, where he's recovering from some illness. Since China doesn't have a competitive, scientific, and democratic system for selecting top talent, honest and frank people are denied a chance to rise up. Uljii, a rare expert on wolves and grassland, was buried under the yellow sand of our current system, which is far worse than the yellow sand of the grassland, because the system was the true origin of the dust storm there."

The Jeep continued in the dry, dusty wind for over five hundred miles, and by the time they were close to the Olonbulag their arms were tanned and prickly from the sun. They entered the Olonbulag the next day, and finally saw connected patches of sparse pastureland, since this was, after all, a border area corner of the Great Ujimchin Steppe. But they could not bear to look down at their feet, for just beneath the grass, sand and surface, rocks met their eyes. Sometimes there were long, thin gray mushrooms that looked like bean sprouts. In the past, decomposing fertilizer from livestock droppings would be at the base of the dense grass.

Chen and Yang were worried. They knew that farther on there was a thousand-year-old river, with water that came up to the horses' knees or even their bellies. Big trucks had been the only vehicles that could cross it, and Jeeps like theirs had to speed up if they had any chance of crossing. During the rainy season, the flood river would cause the suspension of mail delivery and create shortages of food and other necessities for two weeks, even a month. As Chen and Yang talked about how they were going to cross the river, they reached the near riverbank. One look ended the discussion. The fast-flowing water of the old days had receded until the rocky riverbed was exposed; nothing but wet sand and a few wormlike streams crisscrossed the dry rocks. The Jeep crossed the river easily, but their hearts grew heavier.

Shortly after crossing the river they felt as if they'd entered a battlefield; cement posts and wire fences were all over the once vast and lush Olonbulag, and the Jeep had to travel down passages created by chain-link fences. Chen studied the fences, which enclosed areas of several hundred acres each. The grass inside the enclosure was much taller than that outside, but the overall appearance was still of a sparse pastureland, for sandy soil was visible under the grass.

Yang Ke said, "Those are what they call grass *kulun*. After receiving a parcel of pastureland and some livestock, herdsmen build fences around them for lamb birthing and don't live here during the other three seasons."

"How could so little grass be enough?" Chen asked.

Yang replied, "I've heard that the herdsmen have been reducing the number of livestock, some cutting the total in half."

They passed a few more of the grass *kulun* areas, where they saw three or four redbrick houses with tiled roofs and birthing pens. But obviously, no one lived there at the moment, for no smoke rose from the chimneys, nor were there any dogs or calves by the front doors. The people might have herded their livestock deep into the mountains, where the animals were free to roam.

As he looked at the chain-link fences, Chen said emotionally, "In the past, who would dare build a fence on a grassland famous for its Ujimchin warhorses? At night, a horse could get tangled up in it and, in the worst cases, die struggling. But the horses whose hooves once shook the world have been driven off the Mongolian grassland. I've heard that sheepherders now use motorcycles, a sign of prosperity they show on television. Actually, that was because the grassland could no longer feed the horses, which disappeared after the wolves. The cows and sheep will soon follow, I'm sure. Horseback races have turned into motorcycle races, and may one day evolve into a race of ecological refugees. We've witnessed the 'impressive victory' of an agrarian society over a nomadic herding society. Current government policy has developed to the stage of 'one country, two systems,' but deeply rooted in the Han consciousness is still 'many areas, one system.' It doesn't matter if it's farmland or pastureland, forest or river, city or countryside; all they want to do is mix them all up to create a 'unified' flavor. With the 'impressive victory' has come a tremendous amount of subsidies, but the grassland could not return even if the subsidies continued for the next century."

They rode along a dirt path leading to the site of their previous company headquarters, eager to see the herdsmen or, for that matter, anyone. But they crossed the familiar mountain ridge, only to see the old site replaced by a dying yellow sandy grassland overrun by mice whose tracks snaked across the ground amid piles of dry sand. The row of brick and rammed-earth houses was gone. As Chen drove around the once bustling company headquarters, he didn't have to worry about running into any walls, but he got stuck several times in collapsed mouse dens. It had only been two decades, but the remains of the past were completely covered by yellow sand, as if wiped off the face of the earth.

Chen sighed. "Mice are kings on a wolfless grassland. They dig deep holes and store up large quantities of food, giving them hegemony over the grassland. We like to say that everyone shouts 'Kill it!' when a mouse crosses the street, but deep down we worship the mouse and place it at the head of our zodiac."

Yang took the wheel and sped off to a nearby hill. They looked to the north, where they spotted some cows and a few houses with chimney smoke, but still no yurts. Yang headed toward the nearest chimney smoke.

They had been driving for a dozen *li* when a column of yellow dust rose up on a dirt path in the distance. Chen hoped it would be a herder on a fast horse, but when it drew close enough, they saw it was a shiny Yamaha motorcycle. The rider was a Mongol teenager wearing a jacket-like shirt and a baseball cap. The motorcycle screeched to a stop by the Jeep. Chen was shocked to see a small-caliber rifle slung over the youth's shoulder and a medium-sized hawk tied to the seat, dripping blood. Chen was reminded of the startled and fearful look in Bilgee's eyes when he first saw one of those weapons, and was surprised to see a young Mongol boy in possession of one, not to mention that he was riding an advanced, imported two-wheel vehicle.

Yang greeted the boy in Mongolian and identified himself. A distant look of indifference appeared on the fair-skinned boy's face. Staring at the Cherokee, he told him in Chinese with a Shandong accent that he was Chulu's youngest son and was spending his summer break from a high school in the league capital. It took Chen a moment to recall that Chulu had been an outsider, a minor cadre in charge of basic construction at the old pasture headquarters. Zhang Jiyuan and other old classmates had told him that the pasture employees and retired soldiers from the corps who stayed behind were all given land and livestock after the grassland system was changed. They became Han-style herders, adding an additional 30 percent of Han settlement pastureland to the Olonbulag.

Chen asked the youngster, "Why'd you shoot the hawk?"

"For fun."

"You're a high school student. Don't you know you're supposed to protect wild animals?"

"The hawks take the lambs, so why can't I shoot them? There are so many mice here that hawks fly over from Outer Mongolia. So what if I kill a few of them!"

Yang asked about Batu and Gasmai's house. The boy pointed to the north and said, "On the other side of the border highway, the last and biggest stone pen in the north." Then he spun around and sped off to the hills with his hawk, not looking back.

Chen and Yang suddenly felt like outsiders; they sensed they were not welcome there. Yang said, "Let's go to Batu's. Only with him and Gasmai will we feel like we belong."

The Jeep sped up and headed toward the border highway on the ancient path they'd taken when moving to a new pasture. Chen scanned the hills for marmots but didn't see a single one, even after driving dozens of *li*. "Do you really think you'll find marmots now that teenagers have hunting rifles?" Yang asked. Chen stopped searching.

They passed some occupied houses, but few dogs ran out, and those that did were small. No more scary scenes of being surrounded, chased, and nipped at by a dozen or so big furry dogs when they passed a yurt. Even the barking was devoid of the ferocity that had been so effective in repelling wolves.

Yang said, "Now that the wolves are gone, the dogs will disappear, and when they're gone, there'll be no more battles. Without battles, only sloth and inertia remain. Grassland dogs may become pampered pets even before the dogs in Beijing."

The Jeep entered Section Two's golden treasure land—the spring birthing pasture. But what greeted them was a monochrome of barren land and sandy grass, with yellow dust and grainy salt in the air. Chen's eyes reddened as he stared at far-off Black Rock Mountain to the northeast of the grass fields, wishing he could ask Yang Ke to head straight for the foothills.

Yang said, "I've watched *Animal Kingdom* on TV for twenty years, and the more I watch, the angrier I get at you and at myself. If not for you, I wouldn't owe the grassland so much. Those seven cubs were the finest, each a precious, rare specimen of its kind, and they all died at our hands. I was your number one accomplice. Even my son, whenever he mentions it, calls me stupid and ignorant. Peasants! Cruel! From the legal perspective, I have to shoulder substantial responsibility, because I supported you when you wanted to raid the wolf den. If I hadn't gone with you that night, you wouldn't have had the courage to do it alone. We committed a crime, and that will never change."

Chen was silent.

Yang went on, "You've spent twenty years studying systems models, economic politics, and urban and rural issues in China and abroad. Why, in the end, did you return to the topic of national character?"

"Do you think other problems can be solved if that one can't be?"

Yang gave the question some thought before answering. "I guess you're right. We haven't found a solution to this problem since Lu Xun brought it up more than half a century ago. We Chinese seem incapable of ridding ourselves of that flaw. It's been twenty years since the launching of the reforms, and we've made quite a bit of progress, but we're still on shaky legs."

The Jeep reached a high point on the highway from which they could look down on the seemingly unending border, a sight that made them stare wide-eyed. The twenty-*li*-wide military zone and no-man's-land had been breached by growing human and livestock populations and had become a lively pasture. It was the first place deserving of being called a pasture they'd seen, after driving five hundred miles.

The grass was about half the height of what they'd been used to seeing, but it maintained the dark green color. Protected by the military restricted zone for decades, this part of the grassland showed no obvious signs of desertification. The moisture from the primitive grassland across the border might also have helped lend the land a dewy, moist, tender shade of green, replacing the dry, withered scenery that had greeted them along the way.

There were redbrick houses with tiled roofs on land that was dotted with stone pens and sheds, like fortresses spread across the border. The houses were all built on higher ground, clearly the center of the pasture settled by each family. Dozens of flocks of sheep and herds of cows were grazing. What amazed the two men was the size of the sheep flocks, likely three thousand in each, some reaching four thousand. Nomadic herding had clearly been replaced by settlement grazing to have flocks that big.

Yang took out a pair of binoculars and scanned the area carefully. "These flocks are way too big," he said. "You and I never herded any this size. There are twice as many sheep than we herded. Won't the shepherds die of exhaustion?"

Chen said, "The flocks we used to herd belonged to the collective. With a privately owned flock, size isn't a problem. If an individual can't handle it, he can hire people to tend to the flock and create jobs. Profits always increase the incentive to work harder."

Facing such a vibrant settlement pasture, Chen's knees went wobbly. He felt that what they were seeing was actually a false prosperity, just before the Inner Mongolian grassland died off.

Two motorcycles and a fast horse rushed toward the Cherokee; Chen Zhen finally saw a horse rider, something he hadn't seen in a long time. The motorcycles reached them before the horse, and a brawny man in a blue deel was on one of them. Chen and Yang shouted at the same time, "Bayar! Bayar!"

When they jumped off the Jeep, Bayar gave Chen a bear hug. "Chen Zhen!" he shouted. "Chen Zhen! Aniang—Mother—knew it was you when she saw the vehicle, so she told me to come show you the way." He gave Chen another hug before moving on to hug Yang Ke. "Aniang knew you'd be with Chen Zhen. Come, you can both stay with us."

With Bayar were two teenagers, one sixteen or seventeen, the other fourteen or fifteen. Bayar said, "Say hello to Grandpa Chen and Grandpa Yang." The boys greeted them and circled the Cherokee to check it out. "They're on summer break," Bayar said, "back from school in the league capital. I'd like them to go to college in Beijing so that you two can keep an eye on them. Get in your Jeep. Aniang is almost sick from waiting for you to arrive, has been ever since she heard from Zhang Jiyuan that you were coming back."

The Jeep followed the motorcycles and the horse as they raced toward the farthest chimney smoke. Batu and Gasmai, now both gray-haired, had walked two *li* to welcome them. Chen leaped off the Jeep. "Aniang! Aniang! Batu!" They hugged each other as hot tears streamed down their faces. Gasmai's tears fell on Chen's shoulder, as she pummeled him with both fists and said indignantly, "It took you twenty years to return! Other students have been back more than once. I thought I'd die before you came."

"You can't die," Chen said. "I'm the one who deserves to die, so let me go first."

Gasmai wiped off his tears with her calloused hands and said, "I knew you'd forget everything, even Papa and Eeji, once you buried your nose in a book, so how could you remember your grassland home?"

"I've thought about the grassland every day over the past twenty years," Chen said. "I'm writing a book about this place and your family. I could never forget my home on the grassland. I've been living here, with you, all along."

Chen helped the two of them into the Jeep and drove them back to their house. They had a gigantic stone pen, twice the size of the one back at the herding team. As they passed the pen he saw, to the west of the fence, a row of spacious new houses, equipped with TV antennae and wind-powered generators. Beneath a window was an old Beijing Jeep with a faded canvas top. Sandy soil covered the area; nothing grew there except for sparse, waist-high wild vegetation. Chen parked by one of the houses, feeling intense disappointment that now, twenty years later, he could not step into the yurt where the old man had lived.

Chen and Yang unloaded cigarettes and liquor, canned drinks, jellies and milk candy, shawls, knee patches, leather belts, lighters, and other gifts, like pesticides. They took everything into the Mongolian-style living room, which was over a hundred square feet, furnished with sofas, tea tables, a TV and VCR, a liquor cabinet, and drinking paraphernalia. In the middle of the wall hung a large yellow tapestry showing Genghis Khan from the waist up. The Great Khan's slanting eyes seemed to be observing his Mongol descendents and their guests with a tender look. Chen spent a few respectful moments before the picture.

Gasmai said, "A relative of Papa's brought that over from Outer Mongolia when he visited the Olonbulag. He said we were doing well over here and our roads were nice, but our education and pasture weren't as good as theirs."

They all sat down to some milk tea and fresh dairy products. Gasmai had outgrown her love for the milk candy, but she appreciated their thinking of her. She said with a smile, "You remembered! Back then you gave the candy to the dogs, not to me."

Gasmai quickly found a new favorite in the fruit gelatin, which she tried for the first time. Mimicking Chen Zhen, she squeezed the gelatin squares into her mouth, one after the other, and laughed. "How did you know I lost all my teeth? These are perfect for a toothless old woman."

Chen touched the side of his head and said, "I'm getting old too. See the gray hair here? I've lost a few teeth too. But how could I have forgotten you? I've told lots of people in Beijing about how you grabbed a wolf's tail and even broke its tailbone, all by yourself. Many of them want to come to the grassland to meet you."

Waving her hands, she said, "No, no. Our Outer Mongolian relative said that they have a special preserve for the wolves and have banned wolf hunting. On TV here they're also talking about banning wolf hunting. So why do you keep telling people about the bad thing I did?"

It was getting dark, and from outside came the familiar sounds of sheep hooves. Chen and Yang went outside, where they were surrounded by sheep that rushed toward them like a flood. A shepherd dressed in Chinese clothes was herding the flock on horseback. Chen thought that the man must be a new employee on the grassland. They went up to help him herd the flock into the pen. Batu smiled. "I see you two haven't forgotten your old profession. Even after twenty years you remember not to herd sheep too fast when they're full."

Chen laughed. "I'll never forget anything about the grassland. This is a huge flock. How many are there?"

Batu said, "Nearly four thousand."

Yang whistled and said, "If they bring in an average of a hundred and fifty yuan or more, you're talking about nearly seven hundred thousand yuan for the sheep alone. Add in the cows, the houses, the cars, and the motorcycles, and you're a millionaire."

"Assets on sandy land aren't reliable," Batu replied. "If this pasture turns into a desert, like those of the outsiders, then we'll be poor herders again."

"How many sheep can your pasture support?" Yang asked.

As he closed the gate of the pen, Batu said, "With enough rainwater, the pasture can support over two thousand sheep, but only a thousand if there's a drought, which we've had regularly in recent years. We haven't had enough rainwater for four or five years. Keeping even a thousand is very hard."

Chen was shocked. "Then why are you still raising so many?"

"You're probably going to talk about capacity, right? The herders here are from Gasmai's herding section and were trained by Papa. They understand the importance of capacity and take good care of the grassland. I'll raise half of the flock for only six months and will sell two thousand before the snows come. That means selling fourteen hundred or more big lambs born this year, plus a few hundred brown sheep, and the old ewes. Then we'll have enough grass to feed the remaining flock for most of the winter, and make up the difference by buying a big pile of dry green grass with some of the money from the sale of the sheep. In late summer or early fall, I'll take the sheep into the mountains. Because of the droughts, most of the mosquitoes died out, so the sheep can survive and put on some fat in the mountains."

They went back into the living room. "The families in our section still follow the old Mongolian ways," Batu continued. "We raise more sheep when the grass is good, and fewer when the grass is bad. When raising our sheep, we follow Tengger and the grass, and avoid greedy people. But, of course, the outsiders know nothing about the old rules, so they often sneak their sheep over to eat our grass when they finish theirs. It's very upsetting. Then there are the local Mongolian drunks. They trade all the sheep they were allocated by the government for liquor. Then when their wives run away and their children go astray, they live off the rent they collect from leasing the pasture, about ten or twenty thousand yuan a year."

"Who leases their pastures?"

"Outsiders from farming-herding areas," Batu said indignantly. "These people don't give a damn about capacity, so they raise two or three thousand sheep on land that can only support five hundred. Their sheep graze the land for a few years and turn it into sand; then they get out of their lease, sell their sheep, and go back home to do business with the money they got here."

"I never imagined that the outsiders could actually get worse," Yang said to Chen. "Sooner or later they'll ruin the grassland completely."

Feeling more confident about Batu and Gasmai's pasture and family enterprise, Chen said, "I'm so happy to see you're doing well."

Gasmai shook her head. "The big grassland is gone, and our small one won't last forever. The land is dry, and Tengger refuses to give us rain. Our pasture is getting worse by the year. I have to put four kids through school, then save some money so they can get married and build houses. There are also the medical expenses and the savings we need for hard times. Kids these days only care about today and want to buy whatever they lay their eyes on. They saw your fancy Jeep just now, and they're already trying to get Bayar to buy one like yours. I'm afraid that once the old folks are gone, the youngsters will ignore the old rules and raise as many sheep as possible so they can own new cars, big houses, and nice clothes."

"Now I see why they pestered me about the price of the Jeep as soon as I got out," Yang said.

"Mongols should also practice birth control," Gasmai continued. "The grassland can't support too many children. The two boys will have to return to herd sheep if they can't get into a college; then we'll have to divide up the household and the sheep after they get married. Each flock will be smaller, which will likely make them want to raise more. But the size of the pasture doesn't grow. The grass will be crushed if a few more houses are built on this tiny piece of land."

Bayar was slaughtering a sheep outside; after a while,

his wife, an equally robust Mongol woman, came in with a basin brimming with meat. Chen and Yang brought out the cans and other vacuum-packed food. Even though it wasn't completely dark yet, the lights were turned on in the living room.

Chen said to Batu, "Hey, that's bright. Now you herders no longer have to use sheep-oil lamps. Back then I often burned my hair when I tried to read by an oil lamp."

"How long does the electricity from the wind-powered generator last?" Yang asked.

Batu laughed. "When it's windy, the generator will churn all day and store the electricity in batteries that will last two hours. If that's not enough, I also have a small diesel generator."

Soon car horns sounded outside; nearly everyone in Gasmai's "tribe" arrived in cars and motorcycles, turning the spacious living room into a sardine can. The old grassland friends were particularly affectionate; friendly thumps from fists kept falling on Chen and Yang, who were then made to drink so much they began to sway and spew nonsense.

Lamjav, Laasurung, Sanjai, and other old friends followed suit and asked to borrow the car from Yang, who, in a drunken stupor, said yes to them all. "No problem. No problem at all. And come to me when you need to file a lawsuit." Then he tossed the keys to Lamjav.

The others all burst out laughing, before breaking into song. The last song was one made popular by Mongolia's most famous male singer, Tenggeer. The voices were high, old, and sad, with the resonance of wolf howls.

The drinking and singing went on all night; the tears never stopped flowing.

During the drinking feast, "orders" were placed for Chen Zhen and Yang Ke as if they were divorcés sent back from Beijing. There would be two feasts a day, each hosted by a different family with drinking, eating, and singing. The blue Cherokee was turned into a vehicle for the old herders for test drives and entertainment, and for transporting the liquor they bought. It was also used to bring over friends from other sections, turning Batu's yard into a parking lot.

By the following afternoon, nearly half the cars and motorcycles from the brigade were parked outside Batu's house, but there were few horses. One of the herders said, "People would probably give up raising Mongolian horses if not for the difficulty of herding sheep on motorcycles during snowy winters. Only one of the Second Brigade's four horse herds is left, and it's only half its previous size."

"The wolves are gone and grass is getting sparse," Batu said. "The horses are lazy and can't run very fast. They're smaller than before. No one wants our horses anymore."

Chen noticed that all the old men of Bilgee's generation were gone. The grammar school students that Yang Ke had taught were now the main workforce.

In three days, the two men drank so much that their blood pressure shot up and they suffered accelerated heartbeats. Luckily, the Han vegetable garden was well stocked, so they enjoyed a large salad at every meal; otherwise, even their cholesterol levels would have suffered. Half of the herding in the section was halted by the series of drinking parties, and the families had to rely on outside help. Chen was told by one of the hired hands that they were paid two hundred a month plus two adult sheep, room and board included. They also got year-end bonuses for a good job.

Both friends spent that day and slept the night in the homes of their former hosts.

On the fourth day of their visit, Chen chatted with Gasmai and her family well into the night.

On the early morning of the fifth day, Chen Zhen and Yang Ke got into the Jeep Cherokee and headed toward Black Rock Mountain.

The mountain gradually came into view as the Jeep crossed the border highway. Yang Ke slowed down on the grassland dirt path.

Chen sighed and said, "The presence of wolves is the ecological index to the existence of the grassland. When the wolves are gone, the grassland loses its soul; life here has completely changed. I miss the lush green, primitive grassland."

Rubbing his temple with one finger, Yang said, "I'm nostalgic too. As soon as I got here, my head was filled with herding scenes. It may be thirty years, but it seems like yesterday."

The Jeep was now entering the pasture south of the highway, where the grass was so short it looked if it were hugging the topsoil, like a driver training ground. Yang drove off the dirt path and headed toward Black Rock Mountain.

The reedy grove in the foothills was long gone, leaving behind dry, yellowing land of short, sparse grass through which the Jeep traveled up the gentle slope.

Yang asked, "Do you think you can find Little Wolf's den?"

"How could a student forget the location of his teacher's house?" Chen said forcefully. "I'll stop at the foothills nearest to the old den, and we can walk the remaining distance. We have to walk."

As the Jeep neared the birthplace of the cub, Chen felt a sudden anxiety, like an old war criminal asking for forgiveness at a memorial, which, in this case, was the burial ground of the seven Mongolian wolf cubs he'd killed. Five hadn't opened their eyes or been weaned, and the sixth had just learned to run. He had snipped off the canines of the seventh cub, stripping him of his freedom with a chain during his short life, and in the end crushing his head. Someone who loved freedom and was increasingly respectful of freedom had committed a vicious act of the kind perpetrated only by the most tyrannical, totalitarian people. He had trouble facing the bloody crimes he'd committed in his youth. Sometimes he even loathed the result of his own research, for it was precisely his curiosity and research interests that had taken away the happiness and freedom of seven wolf cubs. The manuscript he'd completed was written with their blood, animals in which the noble blood of the White Wolf King may have flowed. For over two decades, he'd been tormented by this blood debt. But he also understood why grasslanders who killed wolves would willingly give their own bodies to the wolves at the end of their lives. It was not simply so that their souls would rise up to Tengger, or as a consequence of their belief in "returning flesh after eating flesh." They probably also felt a heavy burden of guilt and wanted to repay a debt to the grassland wolves they revered. There were no more sky-burial grounds on the grassland.

Over the past two decades, the admirable, lovely, and pitiable Little Wolf had often appeared in Chen's dreams and thoughts, but not once did the cub bite him or seek revenge. Little Wolf always ran to him joyfully, wrapping his legs around Chen's, rubbing up against his knees, and licking his hands and chin. In his dreams, Chen would wake up on the grassland to see Little Wolf lying by his head, and he would instinctively cover his throat with his hand. But the cub saw him waking up and would simply roll on the grass to expose his belly for him to scratch. In the countless dreams over the past two decades, Little Wolf never showed resentment; instead, he was as affectionate as a loving child. What puzzled Chen was that not only did the cub not hate or snarl at him, but he always displayed the friendship and affection of a wolf. This sort of ancient, bleak, tender, and innocent affection could never be found in the human world.

At the sight of the loose rocks and wild grass on the barren slope, Yang seemed to recall the cruel extermination of nearly thirty years ago; guilt feelings and self-reproach showed in his eyes.

The Jeep stopped, and Chen pointed to a level area and said, "That was the cubs' temporary hiding place. I was the one who dug them out; I was the culprit. The cave had collapsed when I left the Olonbulag and not a trace of it remains now. Let's walk from here to the old den." With Chen leading the way, with a backpack, they meandered their way toward the small hill.

When they reached it, they saw that the dark spot originally hidden by tall brambles and grass stalks had turned into a barren slope. The green tent of reeds the wolves had used as a cover was also gone. Several yards ahead, the hundred-year-old cave came into view. Now completely exposed, it looked bigger than before, almost like an abandoned cave dwelling on a loess hill in northern Shaanxi. Holding his breath, Chen rushed up and, as he got closer, realized that the cave was the same size. It only looked bigger because it no longer had tall grass as a screen. The shape hadn't changed much, owing to years of drought, but the ground was littered with pebbles and dirt. After walking up to kneel by the cave, Chen took a few seconds to calm himself before looking inside, which was half filled with tumbleweeds and bramble stalks. He took a flashlight from his backpack to shine into the opening and saw that the bend in the tunnel was nearly blocked by rocks, yellow sand, and weeds. Despondent, he sat down on the ground and stared blankly at the ancient cave.

Yang shone his flashlight at the tunnel. "This is it," he said. "This is the cave. You crawled inside from here. At the time, I was scared witless, afraid you'd run into the mother wolf and fearful that the wolves outside would attack me. I don't know where we got our nerve back then."

Bending down, Yang yelled into the cave, "Little Wolf, Little Wolf, time to eat. Chen Zhen and I are here to see you." He acted as if he were once again calling out to the cub at the new pastureland, where the young wolf had dug a cave of his own. But this time the cub would not leap out.

Chen rose and brushed the dirt off, then squatted down to pull up the grass in front of the cave. Then he took out seven Beijing sausages. The biggest one was intended for the cub he had raised. After respectfully placing them on the ground, he took out seven sticks of incense, stuck them in the ground, and lit them. Finally, he took out the first page of his completed manuscript and burned it as an offering. With the flame licking at Chen's name and the title, *Wolf Totem,* Chen hoped that the souls of the cub and the old man, Bilgee, would receive his promise and his deep sense of remorse. The fire did not die out until it reached his finger. Then he took out a bottle of the old man's favorite liquor and sprinkled it on the sandy ground around the cave. He knew the old man had left his footprints by every old wolf den on the Olonbulag pastureland. He'd upset the old man by ignoring his objections to raising a cub, and that was something for which he'd never be able to atone.

Chen and Yang stretched out their arms, palms up, and looked at Tengger, following the rising green smoke to search for the souls of the cub and the old man.

Chen wanted to yell out, "Little Wolf, Little Wolf... Papa, Papa... I'm here to see you." But he couldn't bring himself to do it, for he didn't deserve it. He didn't dare disturb their souls, afraid that they'd open their eyes to see the yellow, dying "grassland" below.

Facing the quiet wolf mountain, Chen Zhen did not know when he'd be back again.

In the spring of 2002, Batu and Gasmai phoned Chen Zhen to say, "Eighty percent of the Olonbulag pastureland is now desert. In another year the whole area will change from settlement herding to raising cows and sheep, more or less like the animal pens in your farming villages. Every family will build rows of big houses."

Chen Zhen didn't know what to say.

A few days later, a yellow-dragon sandstorm rose up outside his window, blocking the sky and the sun. All of Beijing was shrouded in the fine, suffocating dust. China's imperial city was turned into a hazy city of yellow sand.

Standing alone by his window, Chen looked off to the north with a sense of desolation. The wolves had receded into legend, and the grassland was a distant memory. A nomadic herding society was now extinct; even the last trace left by the wolves on the Inner Mongolian grassland—the ancient cave of the wolf cub—would be buried in yellow sand.

Glossary

Banner: An administrative unit roughly equivalent to a county in China proper.

Capitalist-Roaders: Party officials who implemented pragmatic economic policies in the countryside in response to the disastrous Great Leap Forward. The president, Liu Shaoqi was labeled the "Number one capitalist-roader in the party." The term became the catchword for witch hunts during the Cultural Revolution.

Deel: A long belted robe, often made of animal skins.

Four Olds: Old ideas, old culture, old customs and old habits. "Destroy the four olds" was a campaign, launched in 1966, during which the Red Guards terrorized the countryside.

Heilong River (jiang): The river (Black Dragon) after which China's largest northeastern province is named.

League: An administrative unit roughly equivalent to a prefecture.

Li: About one third of a U.S. mile.

Production Brigade: The largest labor unit in a commune.

Study Sessions (groups): Meetings, usually scheduled as punishment for political errors, for which reform was the goal, the works of Mao Zedong the tool.

Three Difficult Years: Three years between 1959 and 1962, following the so-called "Great Leap Forward" (1958), during which upwards of twenty million people died of starvation.

Work Points: Computations of labor rewards in the countryside.

Yellow Emperor: The mythical founder of the Chinese race.

Yuan: Chinese currency, valued at the time (the 1970s) at roughly four to the dollar.

Yurt: A round felt building. The preferred Mongol term is "ger."